KU-048-792

OF LOVE AND LIFE

Three novels selected and condensed
by Reader's Digest

CONDENSED BOOKS DIVISION

The Reader's Digest Association Limited, London

With the exception of actual personages identified as such, the
characters and incidents in the fictional selections in this volume
are entirely the product of the authors' imaginations and have no
relation to any person or event in real life.

The Reader's Digest Association Limited
11 Westferry Circus, Canary Wharf, London E14 4HE

www.readersdigest.co.uk

ISBN 0-276-42732-7

For information as to ownership of copyright in the material of
this book, and acknowledgments, see last page.

CONTENTS

The
Marrying Game

Kate Saunders

The four Hasty sisters—beautiful, thrifty Rufa, irresistibly sexy Nancy, fey, passionate Lydia and clever, rebellious Selena—are down on their luck after the tragic death of their father means that Melismate, the home of the Hastys for generations, will have to be sold.

In a different century, the girls might have used the only assets at their disposal—their breeding and beauty—to catch rich husbands. But these days nobody marries for money any more.

Or do they?

PART ONE

Chapter One

'THIS ONE IS THE SET of Narnia books, from Roger,' Nancy said. 'This one is Barbie and her strangely enormous pony, which looks more like a dray horse—that's from Mum.' She held the gaudy parcels up before her sister's dazed, melancholy face. 'And mine's coming later. That's at least three more presents than we thought.'

'Four,' Selena said, from the depths of her book. Her obsessive reading never stopped her joining in the conversation. 'I made her some chocolate fudge, and I thought I'd put it in my painted box—she's always fancied it. Has anyone got any spare wrapping paper?'

'I have,' Rufa murmured. 'I'll wrap yours when I do mine.'

Lydia was smiling mistily, like sun breaking through cloud. 'It's going to be all right, isn't it? I can stand anything, as long as Linnet has enough presents. You're all wonderful—I don't know how to thank you.'

'You can stop her getting up at dawn,' Nancy suggested. 'It's so cold, I need at least an hour's notice before I leave my virgin couch.'

Rufa laughed softly. 'You'll be lucky. She's set her alarm clock for five.' She was stretched out on the sofa, exhausted after weeks of Christmas cooking. Her long auburn hair, the colour of garnets, poured over the hideous orange cushions. Her three younger sisters sprawled on the floor, their long ropes of hair brushing the ashy carpet. Each had a slice of herself wedged against the fender, exposed to the tiny fire.

'Liddy,' Nancy said, 'get that monstrous bum of yours out of the way.'

'Monstrous bum—look who's talking.' Lydia's soft voice was gently steeped in complaint as she wrestled the cork from a bottle of cheap red wine.

Selena finally raised her head from the pages of *Paradise Lost*. 'Biscuit, anyone?' From the darned folds of her huge jersey, she produced a packet of chocolate digestives.

'My God!' Nancy exclaimed. 'Where did you get those?'

'Brian gave them to me. I think he's sorry for us.'

Brian was the man from the auctioneers, currently estimating the value of the ancient house and its dilapidated contents. Melismate, home of the Hasty family for nearly 1,000 years, was about to go under the hammer.

Selena tore the packet open and her sisters shot out begging hands. The appalling lack of money made chocolate biscuits seem as exotic as caviar. They had been living on their mother's leek soup for several weeks, hoarding every penny for the last Christmas at Melismate.

'That was nice of him,' Rufa said, with her mouth full.

'He's rather odious at times, but it's not his fault we're ruined.'

'Don't say "ruined" like that,' Lydia murmured, handing cups of wine round. 'Every time I think about the future, I feel sick.'

It was Christmas Eve. The Man was enjoying his first Christmas in heaven. The house he had left was freezing. Under the hammer, his family were being beaten to smithereens. Next day's lunch, a supermarket chicken the size of a canary, sat in the echoing fridge downstairs in the kitchen, where their mother played with Lydia's little daughter. The Hasty girls had gathered, as they often did, in the nursery, on the top floor of the old manor house.

The Man was their late father. He had flown out of the world six months before, leaving the rest of them to drop to earth like so many spent rockets. The Man had been divinely handsome, dazzlingly autocratic, royally eccentric and utterly charming. He had loved parties. He liked his house teeming with people and ringing with laughter. He had loved to lose his heart, and his wife and daughters had nursed him tenderly through his many infidelities, when that susceptible organ was sent back in pieces—somehow, even his adultery was different, did not count as betrayal. Nobody could remember when they had started calling him the Man. Rufus Hasty had simply been the ultimate male, the Man to crown all Men. When he died, all the colour had bled out of the world.

Rufa struggled into a sitting position to sip her wine. She had adored her father, but had to admit that the Man's highly individual morals had had a blighting effect on the romantic lives of his daughters. He had given them a fatal preference for the ornamental over the practical.

Rufa's first romantic disappointment had been a major one; so heartbreaking and humiliating that, even three years later, she wanted nothing more to do with love.

And it's not just me, she thought. Look at the others.

Lydia had come home, with her little girl, after the failure of her ludicrous marriage. Nancy was currently in love with the doctor's son, who lived in a caravan in his parents' garden. Selena was still at school, but she already had an instinctive taste for a good-looking loser.

Lydia said, 'If only there was something we could do!'

Nancy helped herself to another biscuit. 'Well, there isn't. Unless we all marry money.'

'We might,' Selena pointed out. 'It's a possibility.'

'What, before the auction?' Rufa laughed. 'We don't even know anybody rich. Let alone anybody rich enough to pay the Man's debts and save the house.'

'I got the only available man for miles around,' Lydia said wistfully, 'and just look at him. We never meet anyone.'

'You can say that again,' Nancy agreed. 'This place is like Brigadoon. God knows what century it is out there.'

'Actually . . .' Rufa began. Her eyes were fixed thoughtfully on a snake's tongue of flame that had shot out of the red embers. 'Actually, Selena's right. You're all lovely-looking girls, you know. And I'm not bad. It's almost a shame Brian can't put us up for auction along with the furniture.'

There was a silence. It had never occurred to them that their beauty might do more than give them first pick of the local talent.

Rufa, at twenty-seven, was a Burne-Jones nymph in jeans and Timberlands. Her skin was transparently soft and white against the royal burgundy of her splendid hair. Her eyes were of a rare dark blue that could blacken in shadow and suddenly blaze sapphire. She was as tall as the Man had been, and very thin.

Nancy, at twenty-six, was a Renoir in everything but flesh. Her curves were slender, her voluptuousness spiritual rather than physical. She was a kind of alternative, X-rated version of Rufa—less gaspingly beautiful, more absolutely sexy. Her large, firm breasts were the envy of her skinny sisters. She was an orchid among lilies of the valley.

Twenty-four-year-old Lydia was smaller than Rufa and Nancy. Her eyes were of a lighter, brighter blue, and her billows of curly hair were golden brown. At her best she was a Hilliard miniature, exquisite in every detail.

Selena, the Man's afterthought, was seventeen. She was very tall and lanky, but it was difficult to tell exactly what she looked like. Her hair was worn in matted dreadlocks and she was further disguised by small round glasses and studs in her nose, lower lip and tongue.

Regretfully, Selena said, 'Nobody marries for money any more.'

'People have always married for money,' Rufa returned, 'and they always will. Most of our ancestors did. Nobody bothered about romance in those days.'

'Marriage without love is totally pointless.' Lydia spoke with unaccustomed authority. She was the only one of them who had ever been married. 'It's total agony anyway. I could only leave Ran when I stopped being in love with him.'

'There would have been a point, if he had money,' Selena said.

Rufa tipped more wine into her teacup. 'In this family, we've always made love far too important. Maybe we should think about marrying money now. A hundred years ago, it would have been the only sensible thing to do.'

Unwillingly, the others drew the real, outside world into focus. 'I suppose I could just about marry a man I don't love,' Nancy said thoughtfully. 'But I draw the line at someone I don't fancy.'

'I'm sure you could make the effort,' Rufa said, 'since you seem to fancy just about anything with a backbone.'

Nancy smiled. 'If I was as fussy as you are, I'd never have any fun at all.'

Rufa sighed. 'Being fussy didn't do me much good, did it?'

She did not often talk about this episode in her life—the one time she had been at odds with the Man. He had teased her relentlessly about the affair with Jonathan, the man who had broken her heart.

'It was like a tasteful film on Channel Four,' he used to say, smiling down the dinner table, over Rufa's bowed auburn head. 'Tonight, after the news, poncey London novelist rents country cottage, falls for local redhead—then rushes home to his wife, to write it all down.'

That had been more or less it, in a nutshell. Rufa had never found out why Jonathan took fright so suddenly. She suspected the Man—of what, she did not know; but it was the one canker in her memories of him.

'If you ask me,' Nancy said, snatching the wine bottle, 'love is the only thing that makes life on earth worth living. But I'm not sure about marriage. I mean, look at Liddy.'

'God, yes,' Lydia sighed, 'look at me.'

Ten years ago, the teenaged Lydia had fallen wildly in love with Randolph Verrall, who raised goats on Semple Farm, a neighbouring smallholding. Ran's mother lived in a ruined Scottish castle, which she had turned into a commune. His father, long dead, had left him a Georgian farmhouse that squatted on a few scrubby acres. It was here that Ran tended his goats and meditated naked.

Ran's extraordinary dark beauty had blinded Lydia to his absurdity. Like the Man, he was an Old Etonian of the purely ornamental kind. Lydia had married him in a meadow, wearing Indian cotton and a wreath of buttercups.

As the Man had cheerfully predicted from Day One, the marriage ended in a mire of droppings and disillusion. Ran's incompetence was spectacular. After the goats caught something and died, he had tried various methods of making money without success. But it was the adultery Lydia could not bear. Also like the Man, Ran was prodigiously unfaithful. Lydia had finally despaired of him and had crept home to Melismate. The family had been overjoyed to have her back—it meant that they had Linnet, and they all adored Lydia's little girl.

Because Ran was the father of the blessed Linnet, and because he was an amiable soul, the sisters were fond of him. But you could not call him an advertisement for marriage. Or, for that matter, love.

'Falling in love,' Rufa announced, 'is overrated. Looking for a rich husband has got to be better than shagging Tim Dent in a caravan.'

Nancy groaned softly. 'So what? I might be grateful for that caravan soon. When this place is sold, we won't have time to chase rich men. We'll be too busy earning a crust and finding somewhere to live.'

'I won't,' Selena put in sulkily. 'I have to live in that shitty cottage in Bangham, with Mum and Roger, until I leave St Hildegard's.'

Lydia was frowning anxiously. 'Mummy said she'd always find space for Linnet, but there won't be room for me. And I could never live apart from her, anyway. So it looks as if I'll end up camping in Ran's barn—with that horrible girlfriend of his over in the farmhouse.'

'That leaves you and me, Ru,' Nancy said. 'And I'm not as lacking in ambition as you seem to think. I have made plans for the future, you know. When the time comes, I shall do extra shifts at the pub.'

Rufa laughed. 'That's ambition, is it?'

Nancy, who had achieved neither A levels nor university, did her bit for the family finances by working as a barmaid in the village pub, the Hasty Arms. When the Man heard that she had got herself a job there, he had not known whether to laugh or cry. His own coat of arms decorated the creaking pub sign, with its family motto, *Evite La Pesne*. The Man said this meant 'Avoid Fatigue', and it was not appropriate for a genuine, Norman-blooded Hasty to pull pints and call time. Nancy had won him round, however, by giving him free drinks. The Man had said oh well, he always hoped to have a daughter called to the bar.

Nancy enjoyed her work and she was good at it, but Rufa, who suspected that her favourite sister was the cleverest of all of them, wished she had done something a little more elevated with her life.

Rufa had the family's only A levels (English, Latin, History of Art), and would have gone to university, if the Man had not been so vehemently against it. With tears dripping from his eyes, he had begged Rufa never to leave him. He needed all his people around him at all times.

Staying at Melismate, however, had not dimmed Rufa's natural capacity for earning money. In the fruit season, Rufa made tons of excellent jam, and drove in her old blue Volvo round the Cotswolds selling it to tourist shops. For the past six weeks she had been making mincemeat, and little crocks of brandy butter, decorated with pretty labels she had drawn herself. She also cooked for local dinner parties. The sums of money were small, and won with backbreaking toil, but they helped 'keep the wolf from the door' the Man had admitted once.

The Man's teasing about work had been relentless and very funny, yet he truly hated Rufa taking orders from the neighbouring gentry. The Man had not considered himself a snob. He had defined snobs as people unreasonably obsessed with keeping their houses and families clean, and felt he did not need to prove his gentility with any outward show. The Man had followed a long line of handsome, russet-headed forebears to Eton, and inherited a house that was listed Grade One. It had taken him years to realise this did not entitle him to any special protection.

Rufa was under no such illusion. Firmly slotted into the real world, she was the Little Dorrit of the family, slaving to finance a fantasy she could not share. Sometimes she envied Lydia and Selena for their ability to float through the world without truly seeing it.

Nancy was another matter. It was to Nancy that Rufa addressed herself now. 'All right, look at the available choices,' she said. 'You could go on working as a barmaid, and living in Tim's caravan—knowing that Mum, Roger and Selena are crammed into a nasty cottage next to a garden centre. Knowing also that Liddy and Linnet have to doss down in Ran's barn. Or you could take a mad stab at marrying money.'

'God, she's serious!' Nancy exclaimed.

'I am, actually. There must be rich men ready to fall in love with looks and breeding. Both of which we have in abundance.'

Selena suddenly resurfaced. 'You could always divorce them, once you'd got your hands on the cash.'

Nancy could not help showing she was interested. 'Well, find me a rich man, and I'll be happy to consider it,' she said, reaching out, bracelets jangling, to pull Rufa's watch towards her. 'Bags I the bath. I'm going out to dinner at the Dents'.'

She stood up on the ragged hearth-rug, and stretched luxuriously.

Her tight black jersey strained across her chest and rode up to reveal her navel. 'It'll be incredibly dull, but I have some important business. Thanks to my tireless efforts, there's a fab present waiting for me under the Dents' tree.'

'Lucky cow,' muttered Selena. 'What is it?'

'Ma Dent asked if there was any special treat I'd like. I said there certainly was.' She smiled down at her sisters, enjoying their suspense. 'It's a fairy outfit, in rainbow tulle—'

'Oh, Nancy!' Lydia cried, in ecstasy.

'—comprising sticky-out skirt, wings, wand and tiara.'

'You darling.' Lydia was almost in tears. 'She'll be in seventh heaven.'

Rufa beamed. 'It'll make Linnet's day. You are a love, Nance.'

'I just wish they made them in a size twelve,' Nancy said. 'Then I could wave my magic wand, and make the Dents interesting. In the name of humanity, don't drink all the wine while I'm out—the doctor's house is as dry as a bone.'

'"And it was always said of him, that he knew how to keep Christmas well, if any man alive possessed the knowledge . . ."'

Rufa heard the low, tearful voice of her mother as she went into the cavernous kitchen. Rose Hasty sat beside the range, with a battered paperback in her hand and Linnet on her knee.

'"May that be truly said of us, and all of us! And so, as Tiny Tim observed . . ."'

Her voice wobbled, and failed.

Linnet finished for her. '"God bless Us, Every One!"' She squirmed off Rose's knee. '"The End."'

Rose closed the book and leaned back in her chair with a loud sniff. 'My God, the emotional drainage!'

'Well, if you will read Dickens,' Rufa said.

'I know. I must be mad.'

Rose was fifty: an ex-beauty not so much running as dashing to seed. It was still possible, however, to trace the outlines of the exquisite flower child who had captivated the Man thirty years before, at a muddy rock festival down in the West Country.

'Kettle's on,' she said. 'Get us some tea, there's a love.'

Rufa stuffed two tea bags into two mugs, and filled them from the heavy kettle on the range.

'Twenty minutes to bedtime, plum,' she said.

Linnet growled irritably from beneath the huge kitchen table. 'Can't you see? I'm busy in my house.'

15

She was five, and as beautiful as a child could be. Her mother's porcelain features and blue eyes had gone into the genetic mixer with Ran's glossy, dead-straight black hair, and the result was a pale, grave little Rapunzel. She wore a bright green jersey, with a yellow jersey showing underneath through the holes, and somehow radiated dignity.

Sipping her tea, Rufa knelt on the stone floor beside the table. Linnet had furnished her house with a very dirty cushion, and a bald twig supposed to represent a Christmas tree. Her two brown bears, the Ressany Brothers, lay at drunken angles upon a towel. Two of Linnet's socks were tacked to the table leg, at bear height.

'This is their fireplace,' she explained. 'They've just hung up their stockings.' She wrapped two wrinkled conkers and a tarnished brass doorknob in tinfoil. 'Bless them,' she said indulgently, nodding towards her bears. 'They're so excited. Calm down, boys.'

'It's nearly time to hang up your own stocking,' Rufa said. 'And we mustn't forget to leave a little something for Father Christmas.'

Linnet emerged from her house on all fours. 'We gave him gin and tonic last time.'

'No gin,' Rose sighed.

'A cup of tea and a biscuit,' Rufa suggested. 'It's what I'd fancy myself, on a night like this.'

Linnet nodded, satisfied. 'And some sugar lumps for the reindeer.'

'OK.'

Rufa kissed the top of Linnet's head and went to find sugar lumps. They were elderly, and stained a rather sinister brown colour.

Linnet giggled. 'They look like little poos.'

The door flew open, and Nancy blew in on the draught. 'Miss Linnet, your mother wants you upstairs.'

She was fresh from the bath, in a cloud of glorious hair and unidentifiable perfume. She had changed into a black knitted dress that showed the outlines of her nipples and hugged her braless breasts.

'Oh, not yet!' Linnet protested.

Nancy said, in a pert, squeaky voice, 'Come on, Linnet, I'm sleepy.' In a deep, gruff voice, she added, 'It'll make Christmas come quicker!' Nancy was a Mel Blanc of vocal characterisation. She had invented voices for all Linnet's principal toys, and could 'do' the Ressany Brothers for hours at a time.

'Come up with me,' Linnet ordered.

'All right.' Nancy picked up Rufa's cup of tea, and dropped in three of the discoloured sugar lumps.

Linnet gave her good-night kisses, and the two of them departed.

Rufa moved to the range, to make herself another cup of tea. While she waited for the kettle to come back to the boil, she looked round the room. This enormous kitchen, and the vaulted Great Hall that adjoined it, were the oldest parts of Melismate. They had been built in the fourteenth century, and their massive walls had sunk deep, immovable roots into the Gloucestershire earth. Now that she was about to lose her home, Rufa ached for all the lost opportunities. What a house it might have been, if there had been enough money to restore it properly.

She said, 'Mum, what do you think about marrying for money?'

Rose stretched out her legs in their faded blue corduroys. 'Seriously? Oh, of course you're serious—you're never anything else. Have you met someone rich?'

'No. I'm theorising. What would you think if I married a very rich man, without necessarily being in love with him?'

Rose narrowed her eyes thoughtfully. 'I'd think,' she said slowly, 'that you were either very cynical, or very naive. Cynical to marry without love. Naive to imagine you can live without it.'

'I can,' Rufa said dismissively.

'You can't marry without love, Ru. You'd have a nervous breakdown.' She leaned forward. 'Darling, we will make out, you know. It won't be such a tragedy. We'll only be living like millions of others.'

Rufa's gaze did not waver. 'It means too much to let go. I can't do it.'

'You're young,' Rose said. 'Don't set out to bugger up your life.' She stood up, and took a bottle of red wine off the dresser. Deftly, she plucked out the cork and found two bleary glasses. 'Apart from anything else, you'd have to meet some rich men first.'

'We'd need to be in London,' Rufa murmured. 'And buy some decent clothes.'

'Wake up, lovey. With what? Not one of us has a bean.'

'We'd think of it as one of the Man's games,' Rufa went on. 'The Marrying Game.'

'Marriage is not a game.'

'And we could stay with Wendy. I'm sure she'd have us.'

Wendy Withers had been their nanny. She had put up with the state of the house, and the irregularity of her wages, because she had been hopelessly in love with the Man. They had enjoyed one of his brief, intense affairs, and she had followed him home on the strength of it. The girls had loved her, and Rose had become very fond of her. When, after five years, Wendy had left to make room for some Balinese dancers, both women had wept. Rose was impressed that Rufa had carried her idea this far.

'You're right, she'd be thrilled to have you.'

Rufa was planning. 'I can get a few thousand for the car, and we might squeak by.'

The fire, sunk into sullen red embers, turned her auburn hair the colour of the wine. Its light fell golden against her cheek. She was so beautiful, Rose thought. And she was wasting her life here. 'Take a risk,' she said impulsively. 'For once in your life, do something silly. Your Marrying Game is the soundest bloody idea I've heard in ages.'

Rufa was startled. They stared at each other, intrigued.

The moment of intimacy was broken by the sound of the front door opening ponderously, with a creak like Dracula's coffin lid.

The massive, veined door that joined the Great Hall to the kitchen opened, and frigid air whipped into the smoky warmth. Roger came in, unzipping the Man's old Barbour. He was a pale, weedy man of thirty-five. His hairline was in fluffy retreat on the dome of his forehead, and a thin brown ponytail hung between his shoulder blades. The main fact of Roger's life—all you needed to know about him—was that he loved Rose, and would love her devotedly until he died. He had arrived at Melismate, by accident, ten years before, and had shared Rose's bed ever since. The Man, glad to have his wife's bed decently occupied, had grown fond of him. And they had all benefited from his minuscule private income and quiet normality.

'Sorry I'm late,' he said affably. 'Ran's girlfriend has left him and he wouldn't let me leave him on his own, so I brought him with me.'

'Another mouth to feed,' Rose said, 'but I can't find it in my heart to protest. That boy's love life is as good as the telly.'

Ran sprang into the room, jostling Roger aside. 'Merry Christmas, girls.' He dropped a damp sack on the table and darted forward to kiss Rose and Rufa. 'God, it's cold. Give me a drink.'

'You'll be lucky,' Rose said. 'There's a long waiting list for this wine.'

Ran was another one, she thought, who was allowing outrageous good looks to rust away in this rural backwater. Linnet's young father was wearing a tie-dyed waistcoat and silly embroidered hat, but his beauty shone through them. His eyes and his thick, shoulder-length hair were dark and lustrous and he had the face of a Renaissance angel.

'It's really nice of you to have me,' he said, fixing Rose and Rufa with his poignant gaze. 'I know how tight things are, so I brought a carload of logs, plus the onions I couldn't shift at the farmers' market.'

Rufa examined the sack on the table. 'Brilliant. I can throw some into the soup.'

Ran was looking around hopefully. 'Where's Linnet?'

'Upstairs. Liddy's putting her to bed.'

'Couldn't she stay up for supper?' he asked.

'No, we're too knackered. Roger, make yourself useful. Roll us a joint.'

'Hmmm. Better not,' Roger said. He lowered his voice. 'We've got Edward with us.'

Rose groaned softly. 'Can't he find someone else to lecture?'

Rufa glanced up from the onions she was slicing. 'Don't, Mum. He's only trying to be kind.'

Edward Reculver, whose farm abutted Ran's doomed acres, was Rufa's godfather, and the family's most persevering friend. The Reculvers had farmed this corner of Gloucestershire for centuries, and had fallen out with the Hastys at the time of the Civil War. The Hastys had been Royalists, while the Reculvers were for Parliament. The ancient quarrel was only a historical curiosity but Edward Reculver still looked like a grizzled Leveller beside the Man's curled Cavalier. Curiously, this Roundhead had been the Man's closest male friend.

He had criticised the Man without mercy, but the Man had respected him as a kind of offshore conscience, and listened to his strait-laced views with detached interest. Reculver inhabited a solitary, misanthropic world of speckless neatness and austerity. He grew herbs, recycled every scrap, and was the last being on earth to darn without irony.

He had not always been like this. Until six years ago, he had been an officer in the army. His farm had been let, and he had made occasional, dramatic drops into the lives of the Hasty children, to treat them to a circus or pantomime. Rufa vividly remembered, throughout her childhood, Edward's returns, tanned and inscrutable, from various exotic hot spots. He had been decorated after the Falklands War, and had a small scar on his upper arm where a sniper's bullet had nicked him in Bosnia. She admired Edward, and had always been slightly in awe of him. It had felt strange at first, when he left the army, and she often wondered, as they all did, what made him leave. The Man would sigh, and say, 'Poor old Edward, he left the army because his heart was broken. He still can't live without her.'

In the fifteen years since the death of his wife, Edward had been in gradual retreat from the world. Rufa vaguely remembered Alice: a quiet, fair woman who had looked slightly away in photographs, so that she could never be recalled completely. They had been childless, and Edward had made no move to marry again.

After the death of the Man, Edward had taken a dim view of the continued chaos and squalor at Melismate, but nevertheless he showered the Hastys with kindness. The Man had died owing him large sums of money, which he never mentioned. He had done the clearing up after the Man's death, when no one else could bear to.

Rose stood up crossly. 'I know he's only trying to be kind,' she muttered, refilling her wineglass. 'That's the awful part—why is it so easy to resent someone who's trying to be kind?'

She stopped abruptly. Reculver was in the doorway. He looked gravely at Rufa and Rose, then gazed around the room. His gaze seemed to throw a lurid, pitiless light upon saucers brimming with dog-ends, poo-coloured sugar lumps, and the anaemic pan of soup on the range.

'Hello,' he said.

He never kissed anyone, but Rufa made a point of crossing the room to kiss his cheek. He was her godfather, after all; and she minded more than the others about not being grateful enough. Reculver was a tall, lean man aged somewhere in the forties. He had a close-cropped beard of iron grey. His thick hair was also iron grey; he had it mowed short at the barber's every market day. He was very handsome, though this was never what people noticed first.

'Edward,' Rose said wearily, 'what a nice surprise.'

Reculver did not waste words. 'Find some dry clothes, or that man will die of pneumonia.'

'Man?' Rose echoed. 'What man?'

Reculver looked over his shoulder. 'Come in—it's marginally warmer.'

He stood aside, to admit a stranger. The stranger wore a suit and tie, and city shoes. He was soaking wet.

'Oh yes, this is Berry,' Ran said carelessly. 'He was at school with me.'

Berry was a round, rosy young man, with startled deer's eyes behind designer glasses.

'Hector Berowne,' he said. And, as an afterthought, 'Hello.'

Chapter Two

HECTOR BEROWNE HAD NO IDEA, as he drove his new BMW through the frost-bound lanes, that he was about to slip into another dimension. He had assumed that he was heading for a mellow farmhouse which he and his fiancée, Polly, had rented for the holiday.

'Good King Whatsit pom-pom-pom,' he sang to himself.

Berry had a gift for contentment. The vexations of work fell away from him as he dwelt on the delights to come. He still loved the anticipation of Christmas Eve. Log fires and claret—the whole world holding its breath at midnight—he knew for a fact it would be perfect.

Polly had spent the past six weeks ordering hams, ironing sheets and breaking in new corduroys. Polly, whom Berry had loved comfortably since their final year at Oxford, was very big on the Correct Thing: drawing rooms and napkins, circling port and no yellow flowers in the garden. She tended to be a little neurotic about the social face she presented to the world, marinading herself in graciousness to obscure the regrettable fact that her parents were Australian.

Some people, for instance his sister Annabel, had accused Berry of being scared of Polly. What nonsense. He was only rather in awe of his own good luck, that he had landed such a pretty, charming woman.

'Sire, the night is darker now,' sang Berry.

Actually, the night did seem to be getting darker. Berry slowed the BMW to a crawl, then halted. The only light showing for miles blazed from a deserted Volvo, entirely blocking the narrow lane. Its two front doors stood open. Berry waited for a long moment, and when nobody came he switched off the engine, pulled out the key, and got out of the car. The shock of the cold took his breath away. Shivering in his navy suit and thin city shoes, Berry advanced towards a tangle of spiked bare boughs, five yards or so from the side of the road. Through the fog of his own breath Berry made out two figures at the edge of a small pond.

A lifeless pheasant lay upon the frozen turf. One of the figures knelt beside it. In a wretched voice, he said, 'I'll never stop blaming myself. I made you take the short cut, and I destroyed this life.'

Another voice said, 'I'm freezing my bollocks off here. Bury it, or give it mouth-to-mouth, then we can go home.'

Sobs broke from the kneeling man. He turned his head towards Berry. The light made diamonds of the tears in his beautiful dark eyes.

They stared at each other. The meeting was so unexpected, it was beyond surprising.

'Ran?' Berry hazarded. 'It is Ran Verrall, isn't it? From school?'

Ran sprang up, dragging a sleeve across his face. 'Shit, I don't believe it—Hector Berowne.'

'Well, hello,' Berry said. 'I was just wondering whose car—'

'My leading man from *The Mikado*,' Ran said, grinning suddenly. He gestured at the shadow-striped figure of the other man. 'This is Roger.'

Berry and Roger exchanged uncertain smiles.

'This is incredible,' Ran said happily. 'Berry and I were at school together, Rodge. I was Yum-Yum to his Nanki-Poo. I had to kiss him on the lips, and that's not something you forget easily.'

Berry had made himself forget. At the time, knowing he was the envy of half the school had almost disabled him with embarrassment.

'He had a gorgeous voice,' Ran went on. 'I was only chosen because I looked sweet in a kimono. Well, well. How are you?'

'Oh, absolutely fine,' Berry said. 'Er—could you possibly move your car? It's blocking the lane rather.'

'It must be ten years, at least,' Ran said.

'Yes.' Berry had a general feeling of losing his grip on the conversation. 'If you could let me through—'

'I've got a daughter,' Ran announced, seemingly oblivious to the bitter cold. 'Her name's Linnet. She's five. Have you reproduced yet?'

'Not yet. I'm getting married next summer.' How absurd, Berry thought, to be having a cocktail-party conversation out here.

'Have lots of children,' Ran said. 'They're the only things that make any sense in this life.' He looked down at the lifeless pheasant, and a sob escaped. 'My Linnet would have loved this bird. We knocked it over. I made Roger stop, but there was nothing I could do.'

Berry watched helplessly. Polly would be waiting, and her dinners were the sort that spoiled.

'His girlfriend left him,' Roger explained.

'Oh.'

'Come on, St Francis. Let's get back to Assisi.'

'I have to follow his spirit,' Ran said. 'It's still hovering.'

With horrible suddenness, the pheasant twitched back to life. In a great flap of wings, it rose up and fluttered drunkenly into Berry's face. His hand-stitched leather soles slithered on clods of frozen earth.

The next few seconds unfolded as if in slow motion. Berry had one moment of still, isolated despair, before he toppled forward and crashed through a layer of ice into two feet of freezing water. Knife-blades of iciness sent his testicles into the Retreat from Moscow.

The embarrassment added to the horror. Berry struggled upright, trailing strands of weed. He managed to grab Roger's outstretched hand and staggered back to the bank, his glasses speckled with mud.

'You all right?' asked Roger.

'Think so—'

'I didn't kill him,' Ran said jubilantly. He pointed to the pheasant, scuttling away into the bushes.

It was at this moment Berry realised, with the bottom falling out of his stomach, that he was no longer holding his car keys.

'I dropped my keys!' he croaked. 'Oh, God in heaven!'

Not that he was scared of Polly, but she would kill him for this.

He stood groaning on the bank, in an ecstasy of shivers. Roger rolled up his sleeves, lay down on the ground and began feeling about in the congealing water. Ran shrugged off his donkey jacket, draped it round Berry's shoulders, and lay down beside Roger. The two of them splashed and swore while Berry wondered how on earth he had got himself into this ghastly situation.

Another car was coming along the lane. It braked sharply behind the Volvo. There was an irritable blast of horn.

'Great,' muttered Roger.

A car door slammed. A tall, bearded man stepped into the silver glare of the headlights. He saw Ran and snapped, 'I might have known. What's going on?'

He listened in silence to the garbled explanations. Ran introduced him as Edward Reculver. He frowned when he took Berry's hand. 'You're perished,' he said. 'Where's your house?'

'I don't know—about twenty miles—'

'We'd better take you to Melismate.'

'I c-can't leave m—'

'Don't worry about the car. I'll drive you to Melismate, then come back with a net and drag the pond properly. It's not deep.'

Through his St Vitus's dance of shivers, Berry was aware of Reculver introducing some good sense into this nightmare. The door of the BMW was unlocked. Reculver got in, released the handbrake, and ordered Ran and Roger to push it off the road.

Berry had lost all power of movement. Reculver had to almost lift him into the passenger seat of his Land Rover, before they roared off down the lane, behind the Volvo Roger was driving.

Berry glanced at Edward. 'This is really good of you.'

'Not at all,' Reculver said.

'Wh-where did you say you were taking me?'

'Melismate. The old manor, a couple of miles away.'

Berry began to feel a little less ghastly. Polly would not be too angry, if he eventually rang her from a real manor house. He could borrow some clothes, and the rational Mr Reculver would reunite him with his stranded BMW. Then he could escape from bonkers Ran Verrall, and not see him again for another ten years.

'God knows what they'll think of me,' he said. 'I can't believe I've got myself into this ludicrous mess.'

'Yes,' Reculver said. 'Randolph often has that effect. He used to be married to one of the girls at Melismate. I ought to warn you about the house. It's a dreadful mess. They're about to sell up. They haven't a penny.' He frowned. 'This will be their first Christmas without their father. He died last June.'

'Oh,' Berry said, 'how awful.'

'It was. None of us have come to terms with it yet. He made a terrific thing of Christmas. They must miss him cruelly.' He slid a speculative glance at Berry. 'I know I do. I grew up with him. And I've known the girls since they were babies. He would have expected me to look out for them.'

'You're fond of them,' Berry observed.

'Yes,' Reculver said. 'Are you thawing?'

'A bit.'

'We'll get some tea down you, and a slug of brandy.'

Berry fastened his imagination to the proposed tea and alcohol and found that he was comforted.

He did not realise he had dozed off, until he woke. The car had stopped and Reculver was gently shaking his shoulder. 'We're here.'

Impressions loomed at Berry out of the darkness, like fragments of some crazed dream. There was a great doorway, with a weatherworn coat of arms carved in stone above it.

'Be nice to them,' Reculver said. 'They're all more or less dotty. But they have an excuse. They'll do anything to avoid the truth about their father.' He helped Berry out of the car. 'The fact is, he blew his brains out—sprayed them all over the sitting room. Do bear that in mind, if they start spouting nonsense at you.'

Rufa showed the shivering stranger into the only working bathroom: a dank tunnel on the first floor containing a huge cast-iron tub and a geyser that clung to the wall like a malevolent insect. Berry said nothing, but behaved as if he had arrived in a shantytown and was too riven with compassion to dream of criticising.

Edward met Rufa at the bottom of the stairs, carrying a ragged fishing net. 'Look what I've found. Just the thing.'

'You're not going straight out again?'

He laughed. 'Roger and I have to trawl for that poor chap's car keys. And like Captain Oates, we may be some time.'

'It's awfully good of you.' Rufa felt this was not said to Edward often enough. He was shamefully taken for granted.

'I don't mind,' Edward said dismissively. 'He seems like a nice boy.'

'Well, don't die of exposure.' She turned back towards the kitchen.

'Wait a minute . . .' He put a hand on her arm. 'I never get a chance to talk to you alone. Are you . . . all right?'

'Me? Of course I am. I'm fine.'

'You look exhausted. Everywhere I go these days, I'm confronted by your jars of mincemeat.'

'I hope you've bought some.'

He was serious, and would not let her lighten the tone. 'You shouldn't be spending your days flogging mincemeat, Rufa.'

Rufa sighed. 'The hardest part wasn't the work,' she said. 'It was persuading them all to pay the electricity bill, instead of buying gin.'

He let out a grim bark of laughter. 'Lazy bastards!'

'Oh, they're not that bad. Nancy's done loads of overtime. She came home with a fortune in tips last night.'

'Nancy's a career barmaid,' Edward said. 'But you're a clever girl, and I wish to God you'd make something of your life. I always told your father he was disgustingly selfish, talking you out of university.'

'Should I have ignored him?' Rufa asked, without rancour.

Edward sighed. 'I couldn't refuse him anything either.'

'If you're pushing university, I wish you'd work on Selena. A girl who reads Milton and Spenser for fun should be doing Eng. lit. at university.'

'I'm talking about you,' Edward said, looking into her face. 'I'd be a rotten sort of godfather, if I let you throw yourself away.'

Rufa knew, absolutely, that Edward would be dead against the Marrying Game. She wanted to get him off the subject of the future.

'I don't think the Man meant godfathering to be such hard work,' she said, smiling. Edward had been only seventeen when the Man selected him for the honour, but he had always taken his duty seriously.

He gave her one of his rarer smiles, grave and tender. 'I don't think of it as work. And I think I'd worry about you, whether you were my godchild or not.'

Rufa was touched. She forgot, for long periods, that Edward was such a handsome man. It struck her again now, and made her feel suddenly awkward. 'You really mustn't.'

Edward said, 'You know, losing Melismate could be the best thing that's ever happened to you.'

She drew in her breath sharply. This was heresy.

'No, listen to me. I don't mean the Man dying, of course not. But at least this way, I won't have to stand by and watch you falling into the same trap—the fantasy that inheriting a pile of old bricks somehow cuts you off from ordinary life. That's what killed your father.'

He would not allow her to protest.

'Once this house is sold, I want you to join the real world. I don't care what you do, as long as it's more constructive than skivvying for your hopeless relations. You're worth the lot of them put together.'

He pulled something out of his jacket pocket. 'I want you to have this. It belonged to my mother.'

He put a small box of worn leather into Rufa's hand. Inside, on a faded velvet bed, was a Victorian brooch of thick gold, set with diamonds and sapphires.

'It's lovely—but I couldn't—' Rufa stammered.

'She would have wanted you to have it. You always were her favourite.' He chuckled softly. 'And she would have expected you to sell it. I'm told it's worth a few bob.'

'Oh, Edward . . .' Rufa's mind had flown straight back to the Marrying Game. The brooch might bankroll her assault on London, without her having to sell the car. Edward need never know. She sidestepped her guilt by telling herself that his mother would have supported her. She had liked old Mrs Reculver—a brisk, horsy lady, who had died five years before. Edward's mother would have considered marrying money a positive duty for a well-born but impoverished gel.

She smiled at him. 'Thank you.'

Edward kissed her forehead. 'Merry Christmas.' He tweaked her nose, as he used to do when she was a small child. 'And don't you dare tell the others.'

Before he left, with Roger, to drag the pond for Berry's keys, Edward carried in his official Christmas gift to the family—a large box of assorted bottles. Rose yodelled with joy and gave him a stifling hug. After he had gone, she poured a handsome shot of Gordon's into the nearest glass.

Lydia and Selena had come down to the kitchen, lured by the sound of company and the smell of onions. Lydia was radiant, because Linnet was asleep and Ran's latest girlfriend had left him.

The door opened. Very slowly and cautiously, Berry crept in. He was tall, with an ample stomach. His borrowed brown corduroys did not do up at the waist, and the gaping flies were only partly covered by a billowing pink jersey. His brown hair had dried into a hearth brush and the seam of the trousers went right up his crack.

They all collapsed in howls and screams of laughter. Suddenly, miraculously, it felt like a real Christmas. The kitchen was crowded with laughing people, as it had not been since the death of the Man. Berry had stopped being startled by this peculiar family. Now, he remembered only that they had lost their father—in horrible circumstances—and were about to lose their home. The girls were eye-poppingly gorgeous, but there was no self-interest in Berry's longing to comfort them.

The soup, plentifully peppered and onioned by Rufa, made the room dim with its savoury steamings. Berry helped to lay the table, and his high spirits had quite a loaves-and-fishes effect on the quantities.

Warmed by the alcohol, which they were hoovering up at an incredible rate, they began to sing carols. At some point, a piece of paper appeared under the door to the stairs.

'Oh God, it's Linnet,' Rose said. 'We've woken her up, and now she's dropping leaflets.'

The note said: WAT IS THAT OPORLING RAKET?

Lydia, dreamily sozzled, sighed. 'Mummy, couldn't she?'

'Go on, then.' Rose was full of gin-flavoured indulgence. 'Go and let her in. It is Christmas Eve, after all.'

Ran leapt up to open the door, and returned to the table with his daughter in his arms. She wore her blue duffle coat over Barbie pyjamas, and carried a dark brown teddy bear under each arm. She settled on Ran's knee. 'Who's that man in Granny's jersey?' she demanded.

Berry got on famously with Linnet, because he did not make the fatal mistake of altering his manner when he talked to her. He related the story of his lost car keys, and she listened enraptured.

Rufa was arguing with Rose about opening the brandy, which she wanted for tomorrow's pudding, when Nancy returned from the Dents'.

'It's bloody freezing out there,' she said. 'Look at my nipples—standing out like a couple of bottle-tops.'

Rufa said, 'You're back early.'

'Yes, thank God. The Dents are driving to some posh Midnight Mass, miles away. I escaped before they could make me go with them.'

She noticed Berry. Her lips curved into a lush smile. 'Hello. I'm Nancy. You must be my Christmas present—oh, girls, you shouldn't have.'

'Shut up, don't tease him,' Rufa said, laughing. 'His name's Berry. He was at school with Ran.'

'And he's really nice,' Linnet said.

Berry flushed puce.

In a slow, puzzled voice, Nancy asked, 'Why can't we deliver presents at Melismate, Father Christmas?'

And in a deep, plummy voice, she said, 'Sorry, Reindeer—there's a naughty little girl who won't go to sleep.'

Linnet commanded, 'Make the Ressanys say it's all their fault.'

Deep voice: 'How dare you cast aspersions on those innocent bears? Off to bed with you!'

Ran stood up, squeezing Lydia's shoulder with one hand. 'I'll take her up, darling.'

'Well, I'm not going,' Linnet said testily. 'I'm not tired.'

'Come on, madam. You've had a good innings.' Ran gathered her into his arms. 'Kiss your hand to everyone and say Happy Christmas.'

'Happy Christmas.' Linnet kissed her starfish hand, and Ran sweetly bore the child out of the room.

Nancy said, 'Ma Dent saw the bookshop woman crying in a wine bar. Do I take it she's left Ran?'

'You missed his suicidal grief,' said Rose.

'What a shame. I always enjoy that.'

'Bitches.' Lydia was plaintive. 'He's trying to be cheerful for Linnet's sake. You shouldn't be so mean.'

At eleven, Edward and Roger returned, in triumph. 'I've driven a new BMW, I can die happy,' Edward said, holding up Berry's keys.'

Rufa touched Berry's arm. 'Look—you're free.'

Berry tore his eyes off Nancy with such an effort, you could almost hear it. 'Sorry?'

'Your keys.' Edward forced them into his hand. 'You can go.'

'Oh, don't!' Selena cried.

Berry said, 'I've no intention of going. I just need to fetch something from the boot.'

The cold cleared his head, but did not bring him back to his senses. He had lost those the moment he saw Nancy. He was elated, terrified, new-born. She was a red-headed goddess, with breasts he wanted to lick. One glimpse of her hard nipples, under that clinging black dress, and he was burbling like a Flowerpot Man.

He opened the boot of his car. His address book, containing the number of Polly's rented farmhouse, lay on top of a wicker hamper. Berry thrust the book aside impatiently. The hamper was filled with luxurious jars and tins, and an enormous turkey. A client had sent it to him that morning, and Polly need never know. He hefted it out on the cobbles, grinning to himself. This had been sent by heaven, he decided, to lay at the feet of the foodless, fatherless Hastys.

Berry departed, in a sudden, guilty flurry, an hour after midnight. Thanks to Berry's hamper, Christmas at Melismate was celebrated in a style that had not been seen since the Man's last store card bit the dust, and the Hastys managed to take a few days' holiday from grieving.

Rufa performed miracles of stretching with the food. She made turkey pie, turkey curry and turkey risotto—not one atom of that Sumo wrestler of a beast was to be wasted. Finally, on New Year's Eve, she boiled up the picked bones to make a rich turkey broth. She stood patiently over the simmering pan, her spirits having dwindled along with the bird. The wolf was still lounging at the door. The Man was still dead.

This, she could not help thinking, is the last day of the worst year of our lives.

Roger ambled into the kitchen. 'Still at it?'

'Not long now.'

'You've been standing there for hours. Here. Let me do it.' Roger took the spoon out of her hand, and gently nudged her away from the range. 'You can trust me. I'm famed for my patience.'

This was true, and Rufa felt a surge of fondness for Roger. His patience and unstinting devotion had kept Rose from losing her head in the days after it happened.

'Thanks, Rodge. It needs to reduce about another half-inch.'

'Righto.'

Rufa made herself a mug of tea, then climbed the rickety stairs up to the old nursery. Nancy lay on the sofa, nursing a tiny fire and reading a ragged *Woman's Weekly*, while heavy rain hammered against the leads and water dripped through the holes in the ceiling, pinging discordantly into an enamel bucket and two chamber pots.

'Hello,' she said. 'Is the soup ready?'

'Nearly.'

'Can I have some before I go to the pub? I'm on at six.'

Rufa said, 'It seems a shame, working on New Year's Eve.'

Nancy, without raising her eyes, said, 'The money's good, and heaven knows, we need it.' She looked up. 'I didn't want to stay here. The memories would choke me.'

'I know. I'll miss you, though.'

'Don't, Ru. I'm sorry.' Nancy frowned. 'What a ghastly day.'

'I just wish we knew why,' Rufa sighed out. 'What made him do it, Nance?'

'We'll never know,' Nancy said sadly. 'So we might as well stop asking, and try to let him go.'

Rufa was shaking her head. 'There should have been a note. You know he never could do anything without a fanfare.'

'It could never have said enough for us. We would always have wanted more.'

'Just "Goodbye" would have been enough,' Rufa said. 'Goodbye and I love you.'

'Stop beating yourself up.' Nancy's face was gentle, but she made her voice bracing. 'This is a new year, and we should be doing something about the future. Edward's right about that.'

'I won't give in, Nance. I'm not going down without a fight.' Pale and determined, Rufa told Nancy about Edward's brooch. 'He says he'll help me to get a good price for it, if I promise to do something constructive with the money, like paying for a course. Don't let on you know about the brooch. I promised I wouldn't tell any of you about it.'

'Miserable old sod, he obviously thought we'd fleece you. Why *are* you telling me, by the way?'

'I wanted to ask you something.'

Nancy threw down her magazine and leaned closer to Rufa. 'Darling, tell me you're not still thinking about that cock-eyed Marrying Game!'

'I can't get it out of my mind,' Rufa said earnestly. 'And theoretically it's possible, now we have some money. We can invest in the right clothes, go to the right places. Will you do it, Nance?'

Nancy sighed, pensively gazing into the fire. 'Yes, I suppose I will. Actually, it's come at rather a good time. Things with Tim—well, he isn't the man I took him for. I need to broaden my horizons.'

The Marrying Game had rooted stubbornly in Rufa's mind. 'The men—our potential husbands—would have to be very, very rich,' she said. 'We're faced with a ruined house and an absolute mountain of debts. It would take a tycoon to help us without feeling any pain.'

'All right,' Nancy said, 'as long as we can find a couple who aren't fat old trolls.'

Rufa was stern. 'Fat trolls, if necessary. We're not doing this for fun. Our mission is simply to find some very rich men and make them fall in love with us. I couldn't bear it if you were treating this as a joke.'

Nancy smiled, and nudged her favourite sister affectionately with her foot. 'Don't worry, I'll be incredibly serious. And I bet I score first.'

'Oh, I don't doubt it,' Rufa said. 'But I bet I get the first proposal that isn't indecent.'

Wendy Withers had just retreated from a vigorous argument with her fastidious gay lodger (as opposed to her uncouth straight lodger) when Rufa's phone call came. It irradiated the January morning like a bolt of lightning. Afterwards, Wendy cracked open a packet of Mr Kipling's Almond Slices. To hell with the calories. Rufa and Nancy were coming to London and a celebration was called for.

Wendy was a large woman in her early fifties. Since her exile from Melismate, her life had been a tedious struggle against penury and encroaching middle age. She dressed in the flimsy Indian cottons that had been fashionable in the 1970s, she wore her hennaed hair long, and her tallow cheeks were always slathered with blusher, even when she was stuck in the basement all day with her reflexology clients. Alternative therapies had been a great boon, she often thought, to women like her, without family, qualifications or talent.

'We insist on paying you,' Rufa had said. 'Or we won't come. I've just sold something, so we're not as skint as usual.'

'Just a token, then,' Wendy had agreed. Privately, she congratulated Rufa for having found a piece of portable property. During her time at Melismate, there had been a constant exodus of silver, china, furniture, and everything else that was not nailed down.

'Just stick us in the attic, or something.'

Wendy would not have dreamt of it. God knew, there was enough room in this dingy old house. Besides herself, there were only her two lodgers, Max and Roshan, who lived on the top floor. Her beloved girls could have the large room at the front of the first floor, next to hers.

A great-aunt had left Wendy the house in Tufnell Park. It was full of swirly pub carpets and sad Formica things from the sixties, with legs like a sputnik. Wendy was grateful to have a roof over her head, but there was never enough money to do more than put down a few Indian rugs, and the place made her feel defeated and helpless. The narrow, four-storey semi cried out for the youth and energy of the Hasty girls.

Rufa and Nancy arrived the following afternoon. Wendy met them on the front steps, with a shriek of joy and a damp explosion of tears. She had not seen the girls since the Man's funeral, and could not help weeping over them again.

Kind, patient Rufa patted her and soothed her, then made them all mugs of tea in the cramped kitchen. Two mugs of tea and one packet of Maryland cookies later, Wendy blew her red nose and led them upstairs. The two girls were thrilled with their room.

'Isn't it clean,' Rufa sighed.

'Isn't it divinely warm!' exclaimed Nancy. She dropped her rucksack on one of the beds and nodded towards a poster of Gandalf on the wall. 'Some elderly relation of yours?'

Wendy giggled delightedly. The Man had teased her like this. 'I'm afraid you'll have to share the bathroom with my lodgers.'

Nancy asked, 'How many lodgers?'

'Just the two.'

'Sex?'

'Not on the premises,' Wendy said solemnly. 'It creates too much upheaval.'

Nancy snorted with laughter. 'I meant, male or female?'

'Both male.' Wendy's lodgers were her great subject, and she did not register the gleam of interest in Nancy's eyes. 'Roshan has my top-floor front. He's an Indian from Leicester, and he's a journalist. And he's gay.'

'Oh.' Nancy's interest faded. 'I suppose the other one's his boyfriend.'

'Quite the opposite,' Wendy said primly. 'I had to make my No Sex rule when I kept meeting different girls in the kitchen. His name is Max and he works at the BBC. He claims to be writing a novel.'

Nancy raised her eyebrows at Rufa. 'More your type, possibly.'

'He can be quite nice,' Wendy rattled on innocently, 'except that he leaves the sink full of little black dots when he shaves. And Max is the one to watch if you've left anything in the fridge—don't imagine labelling it will put him off. Roshan, on the other hand, wouldn't touch anything in my kitchen with a bargepole. Oh, no. He has his own fridge.'

Rufa was not attending to this barrage of pent-up grievances. She faced Nancy sternly. 'You're not to fall in love with either of them. I forbid it.'

Nancy sighed. 'You're a hard woman. First you make me wear knickers and now you say I can't fall in love.'

Rufa opened her mouth to argue further, but caught sight of Wendy's baffled face. 'I'm starving,' she said quickly. 'Shall we order a pizza for supper?'

She was not starving, but hoped the pizza would take Nancy's mind off non-profit-making romance. It did—next to love, food was Nancy's favourite thing. She devoured slices of ham and pineapple pizza with groans of joy, while Rufa told Wendy all about the Marrying Game.

'Identifying our targets will be the hardest part,' she said. 'But once we have, we'll get ourselves into the places where they hang out. It can't be impossible. We'll need new clothes, of course. The Man said you could crash in anywhere by simply looking as if you belonged.'

'Won't that be terribly pricey?' Wendy asked.

Mention of money made Rufa uncomfortable. She spoke irritably. 'We haven't got much—we'll have to stick to the essentials.'

'Underwear,' announced Nancy, 'is not an essential.'

'Yes, it is. Try to grasp this difficult concept—you have to look like a lady. And behave like one.'

'Listen to her,' Nancy said, through drooping strings of mozzarella.

'She's sure I'll use the wrong fork at dinner. Lighten up, old girl.'

Rufa, however, was determined to make Nancy play by strict rules. 'I meant it about falling for the lodger.'

'Keep your hair on. I swear I won't even look at him, OK?'

Rufa snorted with laughter. 'Bitch. You've got your fingers crossed.'

Roshan Lal was a slight and delicate young man, with skin the colour of strong tea. Wendy found him waspish and complaining, but he was a reliable tenant and she hoped he would not be annoyed by the invasion of Hastys.

She need not have worried. When Roshan entered the unlocked bathroom next morning, he found Nancy lying in the bath, smoking and reading *Private Eye*. 'Hello,' she said. 'You must be the gay one. Could you pass me a flannel?'

Within minutes he was perched on the lavatory seat, shrieking with laughter, and promising to take Nancy round all the gay pubs in Camden Town. When he met Rufa, slender and aloof as a lily, he fell into absolute worship.

Before Rufa could stop her, Nancy told Roshan about the Marrying Game. He immediately voted himself onto the committee. 'I'm exactly the person you need. I read every magazine in the world, and I can tell you who's really gay. You'd be amazed.'

Looking reverently at Rufa, he invited the sisters to breakfast in his top-floor bedroom. It was exquisitely tidy, as crammed with comforts and luxuries as a Pharaoh's tomb. He had a microwave, a steam iron and a hissing coffee machine. Nancy, wrapped in a shocking-pink bathrobe, lay down on the double bed while Roshan poured coffee and put chocolate croissants into his microwave.

'It's heaven to meet you two in the flesh,' he said. 'Wendy never stops talking about you. Her bedroom's plastered with pictures of your father.'

'She's frozen in the time she fell in love with the Man,' Nancy said. 'Like a sort of seventies Miss Havisham.'

'He was very fond of her,' Rufa felt she should say.

'Oh, yes,' Nancy agreed. 'The Man could only sleep with someone if he loved them. Though as a general rule, it wasn't a particularly good idea to fall in love with him.'

'Nance!' Rufa was shocked. This was blasphemy.

'He was the greatest darling in the world,' Nancy said calmly. 'But to the naked eye, he could seem like a bit of a bastard.'

Rufa would never allow herself to consider the Man in this unflattering light. She finished her coffee in silence.

Roshan and Nancy were attacking a pile of glossy magazines, hooting with laughter. They were searching for suitable husbands, but, according to Roshan, everyone except the Archbishop of Canterbury was a closet gay. Rufa left them to it, and went downstairs to take their washing out of Wendy's machine.

While she was folding Nancy's collection of very small T-shirts and her own seemly knickers, Max Zangwill, the other lodger, dived into the kitchen and wrenched open the fridge.

Rufa introduced herself, with sinking spirits. She would never keep Nancy away from this man. He was gorgeous—tall and brawny, with wicked, almond-shaped black eyes and thick black hair. His ripped jeans and faded plaid shirt marked him out as another impoverished beauty, of the type Rufa knew only too well.

Max made Rufa a cup of tea and put four of Wendy's crumpets under the grill. 'I'm ravenous,' he said. 'I've driven all the way from Sevenoaks this morning.'

From the top of the house, they heard a loud scream from Nancy, and a burst of laughter. Max glanced up curiously.

'Ru!' There was a sound of bare feet pounding downstairs. Nancy flew into the kitchen in her dressing gown, clutching a glossy magazine. 'Ru—oh, sorry—' Her white, redhead's skin flushed becomingly.

'This is Max,' Rufa said resignedly. There were enough plain men in the world, God knew. Why couldn't Wendy have chosen one of them as her lodger?

'Hi.' Nancy smiled. 'I'm Nancy. Ru's sister.'

'Yes, I can see the resemblance. I'm Max—the straight lodger, horribly affected by the sight of beautiful, scantily clad young ladies. I don't hold out much hope for my blood pressure with you two around.'

Roshan entered the crowded kitchen in time to hear this. 'Morning, Max. Ignore him, girls,' he said. 'Max has a PhD in corny pick-up lines.'

Max laughed. 'I was at Cambridge with this dear little brown man. He loves me really—it's sweet, and rather sad. We're like A. E. Housman and Moses Jackson.'

Nancy asked, 'Who?'

'A. E. Housman was a poet,' Rufa said, willing Nancy to look at her, so she could signal a warning not to flirt.

Max tore his gaze off Nancy and turned to Rufa. 'So you're the brainy one?'

'Not necessarily,' Nancy cut in. 'People just think she's brainier, because she has smaller bosoms.'

Rufa could not help laughing. 'Just in case you hadn't noticed.'

34

Nancy, remembering why she had come down, pushed the magazine at Rufa. 'Look at this, Ru—it's too hilarious.'

It was folded open at a page of society photographs, taken at a charity ball. Rufa looked at it blankly, until Nancy pointed out a picture of two people in evening dress, standing on either side of the Duchess of Gloucester. One was a slender, fair-haired woman, and the other . . .

'Oh my God,' Rufa gasped. 'It's Edward!'

'The secret life of Major Edward Reculver,' Nancy said. 'By day, he wears wellies and cleans the nuts on his tractor. By night, he rubs shoulders with royalty.'

'He does look handsome, though,' Rufa said. 'Don't you think?'

'Oh, everyone looks tasty in a dinner jacket,' Nancy said.

'I don't remember Edward saying anything about this,' Rufa remarked, studying the page curiously. 'It says here that he's a patron of the Fox Trust, whatever that is. Oh, hang on—its something to do with leukaemia, and that's what Alice died of, poor thing. I think the woman must be Alice's half-sister Prudence. The one he doesn't approve of.'

'She keeps getting married,' Nancy explained to Max and Roshan with a brilliant smile. 'She ought to be our role model. We're just starting careers in marriage ourselves.'

They held their first committee meeting the following evening in Wendy's sitting room. Max insisted on joining them. He could not decide whether the Marrying Game was hilariously funny or a monstrous insult to his socialist principles, but was too fascinated by the Hasty girls to keep away. Roshan provided Thai takeaway and a towering pile of glossy magazines: *Harpers*, *Tatler*, *Vogue*, *Hello!*, *OK!*.

'Right,' Rufa said, aware that everyone was looking at her expectantly. 'First of all, we have to find our targets.'

'Targets!' Max protested. 'Is that what you call these hapless fools?'

'Our future husbands, I mean,' Rufa said quickly. 'I propose we make a list of suitable candidates, which we can then narrow down to two— one each.' She divided the tower of magazines into five smaller piles, and pushed one to each person across the rug.

Max asked, 'Are we looking for rich and sexy, or just rich?'

'Just rich,' Rufa said. 'Once we've got our first list of rich men, we can decide who's sexy.'

'What if none of them are?'

'You're missing the point,' Nancy said. 'A big bank balance is like a big willy—if a man's got one, you can always find something sweet to say about him.'

Max snatched a copy of *OK!* from the top of his pile of magazines and began to flick through its gaudy pages. 'All right, find something sweet to say about this one.'

He slapped down a photograph of a particularly silly old rock star, and they all—even Rufa—exploded into laughter.

'His teeth are in quite good shape,' Wendy said.

'It's a serious test,' Max said, looking at Nancy. 'Could you marry a guy like this?'

'He's simply not rich enough,' Nancy told him. 'Personally, I think he's an absolute Adonis, but we're not playing this Game for fun.'

'I just don't get it,' Max said. 'You talk about this as though it were a sacrifice. As if you were doing something virtuous. You're so addicted to being posh, you'll sell yourselves to men you don't even fancy!'

Rufa's lips were pale. Max had accused them of the worst kind of hypocrisy. He couldn't see that they were playing the Marrying Game for a reward that was worth a real sacrifice.

Nancy, glancing at her, said quickly, 'It's not because we want to be posh. It's about saving a family home that means a lot to all of us—and meant everything to our father. We have to do this. We owe it to him.'

Max softened. 'I'm sorry. But there's something so bloody sad about it. You're both denying yourselves the chance to fall in love properly.'

There was another silence. Nancy could see that Rufa was shrinking away from a wave of desolation. It had all got far too heavy. 'How do you know we won't fall in love?' she demanded. 'If you don't want to help us, go and make a round of tea.'

Roshan jumped gracefully to his feet. 'I'm miles ahead of you all, so I'll make the tea. Max—are you with us, or against us?'

Max, glancing at Nancy, pulled his pile of magazines towards him. 'With you. I think it's crazy, but you need me.'

After hours of wading giddily through parties, film premieres and race meetings, they had pencilled in their first two targets. They had argued fiercely, scribbling names and crossing them out. Max, who did not seem to be able to do anything less than passionately, had been very useful, isolating the men who would be easiest to approach.

'Well, I think we can declare the meeting over,' he announced at half past one in the morning. 'Roshan and I can ransack the cuttings libraries at work, to compile proper dossiers.' Max was a trainee arts producer at BBC Radio Four, and Roshan was the assistant deputy style editor of a Sunday newspaper.

Max yawned noisily, stretching and showing perfect white teeth.

'Though I must say, I'm disappointed you girls don't have more contacts of your own. I thought you upper-class types all knew each other.'

'The Man didn't like upper-class society,' Rufa said. 'He dropped out when he fell in love with our mother. She's from a different sort of world.'

Max was intrigued. 'He married out, did he? That explains a lot. I have an uncle who married out, and nobody's spoken to him for years. English gentry types and posh Jewish types evidently have bags in common.'

'It wasn't that people didn't approve of our mother,' Rufa added quickly. 'He didn't introduce her to anyone, that's all, because nobody was good enough. And her parents weren't remotely posh. They ran a shop.'

'The fact is, we're hybrids—half landed gentry, with a bloodline stretching back to William the Conqueror,' said Nancy. 'And half corner shop, closed Wednesday afternoons. That's why we don't know anybody. The Man was rejected by most of his friends and he annoyed most of the neighbours.'

Max asked, 'Do people really care that much about class these days?'

Roshan sighed. 'God, how romantic—love across the social divide!'

'The Man was the most romantic man in the world,' Wendy said solemnly. 'The normal barriers were simply invisible to him. For instance, I remember a West County Show, back in the late eighties, when he made Lady Garber give up her seat for me because a pig had trodden on my foot—'

Nancy and Max and Roshan snorted with laughter. Rufa's lips twitched, but she managed to sound sober. 'Max, didn't you say you had an interview tomorrow morning? I think we'd all better go to bed.'

Wendy beamed round at them all—she had had an entirely wonderful evening. 'All right. But do let's have one last reading out of the notes. I keep getting them mixed up.'

Max had written down basic details of the two targets. He read out the notes he had made, in an insolent, challenging drawl.

'*1. George Hyssop, Earl Sheringham of Sheringham.*
Age: 32.
Marital Status: Single.
Financial Status: Seriously rich. Owns several London districts and a large slice of Canada.
Address: Lynn Castle, Sheringham, Norfolk.
Remarks: Linked with several women, nothing long-lasting. Seldom photographed or written about. Classically stuck-up and operatically refined.

*May be a tad hard to approach at first, but committee feels he would be so
ideal for Rufa that this does not matter.*
2.Timothy 'Tiger' Durward.
Age: 29.
Marital status: Divorced. No children.
*Financial Status: Vast fortune from great-grandpa's chain of supermarkets.
His mother is an earl's daughter.*
Address: Hooper Park, Wooton, Wilts.
·· *Remarks: Tiger is regularly all over the tabloids like a rash. His hobbies are
fighting, getting drunk and chasing totty. Married a Page Three model
when he was 21. Divorced and paid her off two years later. The committee
regards this big lummox as beneath contempt, but Nancy is stubborn and
insists she can handle him.'*

The others had been laughing and catcalling all the way through, and
'big lummox' made them howl.

'Of course I can handle him,' Nancy declared. 'I regularly chuck out
two or three like him from the Hasty Arms every Friday.'

Rufa looked down at the photographs Max had fastened to each page.
Chasing a man like Earl Sheringham would certainly be a challenge. He
was tall and thin, of a white-blondness that seemed to give him a silvery
aura. Every line of him was bred to its ultimate refinement. She could
cast him as the Handsome Prince destined to save her father's kingdom.

It was a shame they had to chase a man like Tiger Durward at the
same time. His beefy body and ruddy, guffawing face were a familiar
sight in the tabloids attached to headlines like 'My Jacuzzi Love-Romps
With Tiger'. Still, perhaps he was not as bad as he was painted.

Rufa knelt to gather up mugs and plates. 'I'm off to bed. Tomorrow,
we'll plan the first moves.'

'I beg your pardon,' Roshan said. 'Tomorrow we're buying you some
decent clothes.'

Ignoring Rufa's pained expression, Roshan interrogated her about the
exact amount of money in her bank account, and dismayed her by ear-
marking the whole lot for shopping.

'I refuse to let you do this in a halfhearted manner. If you girls really
want to marry serious money, clothes are going to be your biggest
investment. I'm afraid you look like two little girls from the country.'

Fashion was his religion and his livelihood. He escorted Rufa and
Nancy along Bond Street with the reverence of a verger showing visitors
round a cathedral.

'Surely it doesn't have to be this expensive?' Rufa pleaded. 'I can't believe how much I've just spent on four pairs of shoes and two handbags.' They had already made a huge crater in Edward's brooch money.

'*Prada* shoes and handbags,' Roshan said, with exaggerated patience. 'If you're not prepared to deal in thousands, you're wasting your time.'

'He's right, and you know it,' Nancy said. She halted suddenly, in front of a shop window. It displayed a single mannequin, dressed in a scrap of lime velvet. 'Isn't that divine?'

'Moschino? Forget it.' Roshan tugged at her sleeve, to pull her away. 'It is lovely, and you'd probably stop the traffic in it. But it's completely off-message.'

'Well, what do you suggest, then? Twin-set and pearls?'

'Yes,' Rufa said. 'We need to look posh.'

'You need to look *stylish*,' Roshan corrected her. 'You need Armani, Miu Miu and God knows what else. For the last time, leave it to me.'

Roshan had vowed to himself that the sisters should be launched into society dressed like princesses. He dragged them from shop to shop, until they were laden with gilded bags and boxes. The short January day was darkening by the time he hailed a taxi to take them back to Tufnell Park.

'Not that we've finished—we need at least a week to sort out some evening dresses. But I have an idea about that. Trust me.'

Chapter Three

BARELY ONE WEEK after the selection of the targets, Roshan swept straight into the kitchen to tell them that he had found their opening event.

The pianist Radu Lupu was giving a recital at Sheringham House, in aid of the Rheumatoid Arthritis Fellowship. Sheringham House, in Kensington, was the London residence of the Earls Sheringham. The tickets were prohibitively expensive, and had been sold out for months. Roshan had managed to wangle himself a rare press pass.

'I knew the PR from college,' he said gleefully. To Max, he added, 'It was Hermione Porter, of all the useful people.'

Max nodded. 'Rich and thick. It figures.'

'She's thick, all right. She believed me when I said I was a music critic.

I pray to heaven she doesn't find out I'm a hack from the Style pages—just the type of riffraff she's employed to keep out.'

Max and Rufa were sitting at the table, watching Nancy trying to cook spaghetti bolognese. Max was grinning, entranced by the way Nancy's hips moved as she hacked an onion on the counter.

'Brilliant!' Rufa said. 'It's exactly the sort of thing we need.'

'You'll be able to size up your future home,' Nancy said, shaking dried oregano into the pan, 'and decide where to put the new conservatory.'

'Radu Lupu's terrific,' Rufa said. 'The Man took me to Cheltenham to hear him once. Do you know what he's playing?'

Nancy said, 'I don't care if he plays chopsticks. What do we wear, and how do you get us in?'

Roshan, his movements neat and unhurried, uncorked a bottle of wine and took four glasses from the cupboard. 'It's black tie, so you absolutely must have really *profound* evening dresses.'

The whole question of evening dresses had been troubling Rufa. On the one hand, she yearned for a beautiful dress as ardently as Cinderella. On the other hand, there was the ever-present problem of money.

'Couldn't we hire them?' she asked wistfully.

'No,' Roshan snapped. 'I'm not taking you to Sheringham House covered with someone else's soup stains.'

He plucked a cup of peppermint tea from Rufa's hand, and replaced it with a glass of red wine.

'What would you say if I could get you a couple of frocks for nothing?'

'Where from?' Nancy demanded. 'Oxfam? Why should anyone give us evening dresses out of charity?'

'They wouldn't. I was thinking of using one of my professional contacts.' Roshan was suddenly very excited. 'My editor is obsessed with class, but he's as common as muck. And so is his paper, whatever he thinks. We can never get ourselves invited to any decent society event. If we do manage to blag our way into something, we can never find anyone posh enough—or pretty enough—to let us photograph them. Frankly, he'd commit murder to have pictures of a couple of high-bred doxies like you two spread all over his Style pages. Especially if we could snap you whooping it up at Sheringham House.'

'I see,' Max said. 'The little brown man wants to put your Marrying Game in his newspaper. Why don't you go the whole hog and advertise?'

'Shut up!' snapped Roshan. 'If I were writing the piece, it would be in my interest to play up the Norman blood like mad and make you look as if you'd been properly invited—nobody's going to check.'

'Maybe not,' Max said, 'but how will you get your photographer in?'

'There's a reception before the concert. Hermione mentioned that they're letting in a few snappers then. I'm sure I can sneak one past her.'

Nancy and Rufa looked at each other. 'You're saying someone would give us free dresses, just to get them in the paper?' Rufa said.

'Certainly—once they see how gorgeous you make them look,' Roshan said, utterly confident. 'One tiny mention in the copy and they'll be inundated with rich old bags begging to look the same.'

Rufa said, 'I don't know.'

'You're thinking of Edward,' Nancy said. She leaned closer to her sister. 'Relax. He's too mean to buy a newspaper—he gets all his news from Radio Four. We could be spread all over Page Three, jumping naked out of a pie, and he'd never know.'

This was perfectly true. Rufa joined in the hoots of laughter. 'Well, if you really think we could carry it off—but won't your editor mind that we're not genuine society girls?'

Roshan smiled. 'Not unless he knows about it. All he cares about is the end result. If in doubt, remember the first rule of journalism—'

Together, he and Max chanted: 'Make it up!'

Sheringham House took up one side of a three-sided square facing Kensington Gardens. It was a flat Georgian building of yellowed stucco, with immense windows that were lighted theatres of opulence. A long line of cars inched slowly towards the handsome, pillared front door. Two policemen stood beside the pillars, watching men in dinner jackets and women in furs climb out onto the chilly pavement.

Rufa stared out of the taxi window at the line snaking round the square. She was magnificently calm, but her eyes were feverish with excitement. 'How amazing,' she murmured, 'to think of all this just going on. I mean, in the same city as Tufnell Park. It's another world, isn't it?'

'Another dimension,' Roshan said, fingering his bow tie nervously.

'Rather scandalous really,' Nancy commented amiably. 'I've counted three Rollers and four Bentleys, and any amount of endangered species. We ought to string them all up from the nearest lamppost.'

Rufa laughed. 'What a time to turn socialist.'

'Well, I'm beginning to think there's a lot to be said for socialism,' Nancy said. 'At least it's cheap and easy to join. Aren't you scared, Ru?'

'Certainly not,' Rufa said briskly. The richness of this world intoxicated her. It was so ultimately safe; all danger and ugliness filtered out by a great mesh of old money. 'This is everything we've been working for since Christmas, and we both look terrific. If we get scared now, we might as well go straight home to Melismate.'

Roshan checked his watch, for the hundredth time. 'Why is this taking so long? And what the hell are those policemen for? I don't like the look of them at all.'

'Oh, I don't know,' Nancy said, 'the black one's not bad.'

'I'm serious,' he snapped. 'Hermione didn't tell me it would be like breaking into the Kremlin. Let's go through it one more time—' Both sisters sighed and rolled their eyes, but he persisted. 'I'll have my invitation ready, and I'll just flash it at them quickly as I'm rushing in. You two must stick to me—acting as if you owned the place.' The anxiety melted from his face as he surveyed them. 'It shouldn't be too hard, when you both look like angels. Clare should be paying you to wear those dresses.'

From his packed Rolodex of contacts, Roshan had unearthed a pearl: an ambitious young designer named Clare Seal. Clare earned her bread designing the 'Larger Than Life' range of a well-known chain store, but she saw herself as the Madame Grès of the twenty-first century. Roshan had written an article about her graduation show at St Martin's. That had been helpful, but her sumptuous silk and velvet dresses needed to be seen on the backs of the beautiful and privileged.

Roshan had taken Rufa and Nancy to Clare's dusty loft, at the Hoxton end of the City Road. When she saw Nancy and Rufa, and realised Roshan had not been exaggerating about their looks, she offered to lend them as many gowns as they needed, in return for photographs on Roshan's Style pages and a credit in the copy. It had been that easy.

Rufa was not sure that she would have chosen a dress like this for herself. Clare and Roshan had insisted on a long, plain sheath of heavy bronze silk velvet. It had a peculiar cut, a little like a medieval robe. She had to admit, however, that the colour was wonderful with her hair, which Roshan had made her wear loose and unadorned.

He had brushed Nancy's long, wild red curls into a smooth knot at the nape of her neck. Her dress was deep yellow silk crepe, with a low neck and 1930s fishtail skirt. Rufa thought she looked sensational; perhaps the stuck-up earl would prefer to make a countess of her sister. She hoped this did not mean she would be lumbered with Tiger Durward.

Clare had thrown in two taffeta evening coats, lined with velvet, and Roshan had contributed two pairs of satin pumps, dyed to match at Anello and Davide.

Rufa smiled at him affectionately. 'You've been so nice to us, Roshan. We couldn't have done any of this without you.'

Roshan beamed. 'You don't have to thank me—you two fulfil all the doll-dressing fantasies I suppressed as a child.'

The taxi drew up at the front door. Roshan paid the driver, gallantly helped out the two girls, then trotted ahead to spy out the land. He ran back in a state of agitation. 'This is ghastly—oh God—let's not panic—'

Nancy patted his shoulder. 'Calm down. What's the problem?'

'They're checking invitations, just inside the building.'

A large group of people, all middle-aged or elderly, were drifting towards the gates of paradise with enviable ease. Rufa and Nancy strolled as near to the front door as they dared, doing their best to imitate the ease.

Rufa tried to assess the situation. Beyond the two policemen, the heavy front door stood open. Inside, a young woman in a black dress, flanked by two men in dinner jackets, sat at a small table, scrutinising each invitation and checking names on a typed list. She guessed this was Hermione. 'We'll never get past them.'

'You're not bottling out, are you?'

'Certainly not,' Rufa said briskly. 'We'll have to resort to Plan B, that's all.' She took Nancy's arm. 'Keep looking casual.'

'In this outfit? You must be joking.' Nancy stifled a nervous giggle. 'Let's just pretend we belong.'

'I do belong,' Rufa said. 'I'm as good as anyone here. This is exactly the sort of world I want. And you should want it, too. Think of the Man, and remember you're a Hasty.'

'I'm a Hasty. A Norman-blooded Hasty, with no seaside sweetshop in my coat of arms.' She wrestled down another burst of giggling.

Roshan ran to them, and pulled them away from the legitimate guests. 'This is a nightmare. Apparently they've laid on extra security because Princess Michael of Kent is coming. It looks hopeless.'

'Oh, for God's sake.' Nancy took a firm hold of Rufa's hand. 'Don't you two know anything about gate-crashing? Roshan—you go in and find that photographer of yours. We'll meet you in there. Go on!'

Roshan passed through the pillars, giving the girls a miserable look over his shoulder, as if they had pushed him into the last lifeboat on the *Titanic*.

Rufa asked, 'What are you up to?'

'Shh, don't spoil it.' Clutching Rufa's hand, Nancy fell into step behind a party of ten or so people. Behind the table where the invitations were being checked, the hall was crowded. In the far wall, a pair of double doors stood open, giving a tantalising glimpse of rows of gilt chairs, set out for the recital.

Nancy waited until the large party in front of them were swamping the table. Then she fixed her gaze somewhere in the middle distance, waved enthusiastically, and shouted, 'Daddy! Daddy!'

There were a couple of indulgent smiles, but nobody took much notice of the two girls finding their father. They had passed the table. They were inside.

Rufa was breathless with surprise. 'Nancy, you're brilliant—I've never seen such utterly barefaced cheek.'

Nancy felt the knot of hair at her neck. 'That's as brilliant as I get, darling. You'll have to work out what the hell we do next.'

Rufa glanced around. New arrivals were making their way to a door on the left of the hall, shrugging off coats and wraps. They followed three middle-aged women to a small sitting room that had been turned into a cloakroom. Two smiling Filipino women in black dresses helped them out of their coats.

A wrinkled lady with white hair, wearing dark blue chiffon, smiled at them kindly. 'What lovely frocks!' she said.

'Thank you,' Rufa replied, with a plummeting heart. This was the moment she knew their glamorous theatrical dresses were all wrong. Everybody else here seemed to be old and rather dowdy. Still, it was too late to turn back now. She held her head a little higher.

They sauntered into the room where everyone was gathering. Just inside the door, a small table held a heap of glossy programmes. They each took one and Nancy took a glass of champagne from the tray.

Rufa murmured, 'Didn't we agree not to drink?'

'You and Roshie did. I agreed to no such thing. I'm not turning down free champagne.'

'All right. Just don't get plastered.' She looked round the room, searching for Roshan and the photographer sent by his newspaper.

'There he is,' Nancy said. 'Come on.'

She had spotted Roshan making faces at them from the shadow of an icy-white marble fireplace. A large, red-faced man with a camera stood beside him, staring round with a mixture of resentment and contempt.

'You got in!' Roshan whispered gleefully. 'Isn't this fabulous?'

'This? It's a collection of dull old farts,' Nancy said. 'I feel like organising a game of musical bumps to get the party going.'

'You're in, and you're being seen. That, surely, is the point.'

Rufa glanced round the room again. A slender man, with grey hair, was gazing at them thoughtfully. She turned her back on him. 'Where's the earl?'

'Not here yet,' Roshan said. 'He's probably hobnobbing with the princess behind closed doors. This is Pete, by the way.'

The photographer ran a finger round the inside of his collar. 'Hi, gels. Where d'you want 'em, Rosh?'

Roshan nodded towards the door. 'Here's the earl, with Radu Lupu—see if you can get a couple of them with the princess.'

Pete let out a slow chuckle. 'Princess Pushy. I like her.' Unhurried, he ambled off through the crowd.

Rufa was looking at Earl Sheringham. Her heart jumped nervously, but she felt nothing—except awe—at the huge gulf between breaking into this man's house, and persuading him to marry her. He was paler and smaller than his pictures. When he turned towards the princess, his smile was gentle and charming, but when he turned away to survey everyone else, his face became blank and cold.

Pete was changing his roll of film. 'Let's get the gels by the mantelpiece, then I can bugger off.'

'Good idea,' Roshan said. 'Chat to each other, you two. Try to look as if you're having a whale of a time.'

Pete danced and ducked round them, firing the camera rapidly. 'That's nice—put your hair back, love—yeah, that's great. Rosh, d'you want one with Pushy and Lord Snooty in the background?'

'Yes,' Roshan said. 'Then get me a couple of Radu Lupu and you can call it a night.'

Rufa was covertly watching the earl, wondering how on earth to begin the mysterious process of making him fall in love with her. Should she faint at his feet? Find some slim pretext to engage him in conversation? If she could only get past that frigid air of superiority—

The earl moved away from the princess and the pianist. His eyes made one more chilly circuit of the room until his gaze snagged against Rufa's. Her spine turned cold. There was a definite hint of opprobrium in his bad-smell expression. The earl turned his back on Rufa and went to speak to Roshan's pretty friend Hermione at the desk.

The relief did not last long. The man from the hall table looked over the earl's shoulder, directly at Rufa. His expression changed to one of unmistakable annoyance.

Oh God, she thought, remove me from this place. She had imagined she could handle something like this, but the mortification was absolutely piercing. She nudged Nancy.

'What? What is it?'

Wordlessly, Rufa nodded in the direction of the forbidding-looking man now walking purposefully towards them.

Nancy said, 'Whoops.'

The man came close to them and addressed Roshan. The quietness of his voice gave it a disagreeable intimacy. 'I don't believe these ladies, or you, are on our guest list.'

Feebly, Roshan said, 'I have a press pass—'

'We've only invited selected music critics,' the man said. 'We certainly did not give you permission to do a photoshoot. I think you and your—your *models* had better leave immediately. Don't you?'

'Drat,' murmured Nancy, 'we haven't done the topless shots yet.'

Rufa, severely weakened by embarrassment, gave a snort of laughter. She caught Roshan's eye and they both began shaking helplessly.

The man's annoyance deepened. He put a hand on Nancy's bare elbow, as if arresting her, and marched her towards the door. Rufa and Roshan stumbled after them, yelping with suppressed giggles. The horror of it was so huge, it was funny.

And then, near the door, one of Rufa's shoes came off. She stumbled, and halted to pick it up. The arresting man looked balefully over his shoulder. Heads turned all over the room. Rufa froze, not knowing whether he wanted her to follow with her satin shoe, or leave it marooned on Earl Sheringham's carpet.

A cool hand touched her sleeve. The elegant man with thick grey hair, who had been watching her earlier, was holding out her shoe. 'There you are, Cinderella,' he said quietly, smiling.

'Thank you.' Rufa took it, and limped over to the door, with burning cheeks and eyes wet with laughing.

The arresting man shooed them down the narrow passage leading to the cloakroom. After hurriedly collecting their coats, the man led them through the kitchen. 'I hardly need to add,' he said, 'that you will not be permitted to use any of those photographs.'

Then it was over. The three of them were shivering on the other side of the back door, in the mews behind Sheringham House.

'That,' Rufa said, 'was the most utterly wince-making experience of my entire life.'

Wendy was bristling with indignation. 'Honestly, they might have let you stay. You weren't doing any harm.'

An hour and a half after being bounced, they were all crowded round Wendy's kitchen table, sharing greasy packets of fish and chips. Roshan had removed his dinner jacket and was sitting in his shirtsleeves and red braces, delicately dipping chips into a plate of mayonnaise. Nancy and Rufa were in their dressing gowns.

Max's hand accidentally brushed against Nancy's as they both reached for the last piece of battered haddock. 'I don't think we should write the evening off as a complete waste of time,' he said. 'We should think of it as a learning experience. A dress rehearsal.'

'It was our bad luck to choose a party where they were so strict about gate-crashers,' Nancy said, with her mouth full. 'Should we carry on chasing the earl, or cross him off the list?'

Rufa frowned. 'Well, I'm having nothing more to do with him. Nobody has ever dared to look at me like that.' She was pale with outrage. 'I'll choose myself another target from our list. In the meantime, Max is quite right—we must at least have learned something.'

Roshan became businesslike. 'I'm afraid we went over the top with those frocks. We have to strike the perfect balance between being nicely noticeable and positively sticking out.'

Rufa stood up to make them second cups of tea. 'And next time, we need legitimate entry to an event where class doesn't matter so much. A place where photographers are welcome, and simple faith means more than Norman blood.'

'Simple faith, or bosoms,' Nancy said.

Roshan beamed, delighted that the Game was still up and running. 'Leave it to me.'

The official invitation to the Cumbernauld Foundation Ball said 'White Tie'. Rufa was alarmed by this, but Roshan said not to worry. 'All it really means is permission to wear more glitter—half the women will use it as an excuse to give their big puffy wedding dresses another outing.'

Rufa, after last time, was anxious to know as much as possible in advance. 'What if someone recognises us from Sheringham House?'

He snorted. 'Highly unlikely. None of those toffee-noses would be seen dead at this do. They'll sell the tickets to anyone who has the money and they adore the press. It's perfect for a spot of Tiger-hunting.'

Lady Helen Durward, Tiger's mother, was a patroness of the charity. Tiger (who had recently split up with his soap-star girlfriend) was to be at her table, along with Anthea Turner, who had agreed to draw the raffle, and Alan Titchmarsh, who was to conduct the auction.

'So it's not quite top-drawer?' Nancy asked.

Roshan said, 'It's not even in the bureau. This time, we are entering at the highest level—I have an acquaintance on the organising committee.' This was Anita Lupovnik, wife of the well-known Bond Street jeweller. Lupovnik's had donated a pair of earrings for the auction.

'Fear not, we won't be getting the bum's rush again,' Roshan said complacently.

Egged on by Nancy, he hired himself white tie and tails. On the evening of the ball, he strutted down Wendy's staircase, singing.

Nancy, Rufa and Max, assembled in the hall, burst into a round of applause. Roshan was ravishing. The tailcoat, and the expanse of boiled shirt-front, set off the grace of his slight figure.

Rufa kissed him. 'You look like Fred Astaire. I wish Wendy could see you.' Wendy was staying with a friend for a couple of days.

Nancy gave Roshan a friendly slap on the bottom. 'You look prettier than we do—where did you get it all?'

Max tweaked one of his tails. 'Must have set you back a bit.'

'I'm putting it on expenses, you poor fool. Now—' Roshan turned briskly to the girls. 'Let's have a look at you.'

That afternoon he had called Rufa from work, to tell her that he had been struck by a lightning bolt of inspiration—they must swap dresses. Rufa and Nancy had been thrilled by this idea. Though Nancy was two inches shorter than Rufa, and differently distributed, they were the same dress size. It was intriguing to see how the characters of the two gowns were transformed. The yellow crepe fishtail hung loosely upon Rufa's elongated frame, giving her the brittle elegance of a 1930s film star. Her thick auburn hair was wound into a ballet dancer's chignon, exposing her back and shoulder blades. Nancy's curves gave a tactile sexiness to the sober bronze velvet, and her loose red hair was a magnificent riot.

'I'm a genius,' Roshan announced. 'And you two are simply divine.'

The ballroom was a gigantic, flower-decked hangar on Park Lane, thronged with people. Instead of a genteel hum, the conversation was a roar, seasoned with brays and shrieks. From the top of the stairs that swept down to the dance floor, Rufa and Nancy gazed across a seething mass of black tailcoats and pastel tulle.

Nancy murmured, 'This is more like it. We might even have a good time.' She raised her glass to Pete the photographer who had been snapping them sipping champagne.

'Come on,' Rufa said, starting down the staircase. 'Let's have a look at the seating plan, so we know where to find Tiger.'

Nancy put a hand on her arm. 'Wait a minute, I need another drink.'

'Let me do the honours,' Roshan said. He went to join the other tailcoats at the bar, leaving Nancy and Rufa to mop up admiring glances at the top of the stairs. Rufa was glad to note that Nancy was getting plenty of these—how could Tiger Durward resist her?

Roshan returned with more champagne. Rufa sipped hers and found it delicious. Her spirits lifted. This time, everything seemed to be going beautifully. She went down the great staircase, feeling festive and elegant. This was exactly the sort of scene she had imagined when she first dreamed of the Marrying Game.

At the foot of the stairs was a large board, displaying a list of the people at each table. Rufa found their quarry among the Ds. 'Here he is—Mr Timothy Durward, Table Twelve.'

'And here we are, right next door at Table Eleven,' Roshan said. 'I told you dear old Anita would do us proud.'

Nancy pressed against him, to read over his shoulder. 'Oh God—I don't believe it!' She began to laugh softly. 'Ru, who's the last person you want to see tonight?'

'Edward,' Rufa said promptly. 'Don't tell me he's here.'

'Not quite as bad, but nearly. It's the Abominable Dr Phibes.'

'You're joking!'

Roshan asked, 'Who on earth are you talking about?'

'He's the master of our local hunt,' Rufa said coldly. 'He didn't exactly see eye to eye with the Man. Especially as he and Edward used to join the protesters at the Boxing Day meet every year.'

'Could that be awkward?'

'I don't see why. He's at Table Forty-two; he ought to be easy enough to avoid. And I can't think why you're fretting about Dr Phibes, Nance, when you're about to display yourself all over a national newspaper. Let's find our table.' She swept away through the numbered tables.

Roshan whispered to Nancy, 'God, I love her when she's like this!'

'She means it, darling—it's not put on,' Nancy said, shaking her head. 'Somehow, our parents managed to raise a perfect, high-born lady. That's why I'm determined to bag Tiger. I can handle the vulgarity of marrying for money, but she can't. It would kill her. Deep down, she's an utter romantic still hoping to fall madly in love.'

'She might,' he said, following in Rufa's wake.

'Yes, but we can't afford to wait for it. I'll win this game because I'm more of a realist.'

Roshan laughed. 'You? Rubbish. You're addicted to falling in love—I've heard your history in some detail, don't forget. Rufa will make a great match, and you'll elope with the window-cleaner.'

Nancy tried to be indignant, but could not help laughing.

The band stopped playing. There was scattered applause, and a general surge towards the tables. Suddenly Roshan was still and alert, staring at the next table. He quietly said, 'There.'

A tall, broad man, in black tie and a loud brocade waistcoat, was taking his place. Nancy and Rufa beheld Tiger Durward, in the considerable flesh. He had the physique of a rugger player and ruddy, blunt features permanently hovered on or around an inane, face-splitting grin. His laugh honked, his voice made the glassware rattle.

Uncertainly, Nancy murmured, 'Is he good-looking?'

'No,' Rufa said.

Roshan said, 'Yes, in a way. That sort of energy can be very compelling. And you must admit, his body's excellent.'

'Nance—' Rufa leaned across Roshan. 'You don't have to go through with it.' Rufa could not imagine many things more ghastly than being yoked to Tiger Durward.

'You know me,' Nancy replied. 'I prefer the simple ones. They're usually kind-hearted.'

Roshan filled their glasses with white wine from one of the bottles on the table. 'Yes, like a big dog that slobbers all over your shoes.'

Dinner passed pleasantly, though it was impossible to forget they were here on business, with Tiger's loud laugh honking out every few minutes. By the time the raspberry mousses arrived, he was barking drunk behind a forest of bottles.

Coffee (tepid and sour) appeared, and the band started up again.

Roshan signalled to Pete, who was looking bored on the other side of the table. 'We'll want some pictures of the girls dancing—with Tiger, if he can still stand up.'

The younger, noisier guests were running onto the dance floor. At the next table, Tiger stood, and gaped around him, swaying slightly.

Nancy rose. 'I think this is my cue to introduce the notion of dancing into that solitary brain cell, before it shuts down.'

Pete grinned, taking the cover off his camera. 'If he gropes you, I'll deck him for you.' Upper-class women were a mystery to him, but he had decided he liked Nancy.

'Thanks,' she said. 'I'm glad there's someone to defend my honour.'

Rufa watched, fascinated and fearful, as Nancy shimmered across the few yards of carpet to Tiger's side. All she had to do was brush against him, and murmur, 'Sorry—'

Tiger made a series of dazed, effortful faces, drawing her into focus. Nancy walked in slow motion, waiting for the thought to form.

He put out his hand. 'Hi. Want to dance, or something?'

And it really was as simple as that. Nancy introduced herself. Tiger took her elbow, and steered her out onto the floor. Pete sprang up, to bag the star shots of the evening. The band was playing 'Red Red Wine'. Tiger, as if someone had pressed a button inside him saying 'Dance', instantly began thrashing and leaping. Nancy caught Rufa's eye. She was laughing, ducking Tiger's windmill arms. Rufa was glad she found it amusing. It had been easy, back at home, to theorise about putting up with unattractive men. The reality was another matter entirely.

A little anxious about Nancy, but generally satisfied that the evening was going according to plan, Rufa rose, and made her way back up the staircase towards the ladies' cloakroom.

The cloakroom was large, and as brightly lit as was consistent with flattery. Rufa emerged from her cubicle and faced one of the mirrors. Her hair was still fine, but her lipstick needed attention. Frowning slightly, she leaned forward to apply the overpriced stick to her lips.

A cubicle door banged, and a lanky, middle-aged lady with neat grey hair took the sink beside Rufa. In the mirror, their eyes met. Rufa froze.

Lady Bute, wife of the Abominable Dr Phibes, gaped at her for a moment. Her expression of shock hardened into one of righteous outrage. She hissed, 'You!'

'Hello.' Rufa did not know what else to say.

'Well, I must say I'm surprised to see you here.' Lady Bute unscrewed a lipstick, in a vicious shade of pink. 'It's not where I'd expect to see the daughter of someone apparently too poor to pay a debt.'

Rufa stiffened. How dare she bring this up? The Man had always maintained that the Butes were essentially vulgar. 'We are poor, Lady Bute. Thank you for reminding me.'

'Your father owed us the cost of an expensive saddle, not to mention a pair of jodhpurs, after that disgraceful incident at the Boxing Day meet.'

'My father is dead,' Rufa said.

'Yes, and that's the only reason my husband didn't pursue the matter. He heard you were selling up and decided there was no point. But if you have enough money to swan around at a ball, in an expensive dress— well, that puts a different complexion on the matter, doesn't it?'

Rufa's voice was tight with anger. She needed the anger, to boil away the threat of tears. 'I didn't realise there had been a demand for money. Tell Sir Gerald to put it in writing. We'll add him to the list of creditors.'

'Will there be enough to pay the creditors?'

'No.'

'You're as rude as he was,' Lady Bute snapped. 'I don't see why we should all pretend he wasn't, simply because he's dead.'

The door of a cubicle opened behind them. Their hostess, Anita Lupovnik, whom they had met at the reception earlier, emerged, rummaging in her bag for a lipstick. Rufa and Lady Bute fell into silence.

Anita was plump, with vivid, humorous dark eyes. 'I couldn't help hearing, and now I have to know—what was the disgraceful incident?'

Lady Bute bridled, and pointedly said nothing.

Rufa said, 'My father put Superglue on her husband's saddle.'

Anita stared for a moment, then let out a shriek of delighted laughter.

White with rage, Lady Bute swept out of the cloakroom.

Rufa found that her back and shoulders were knotted with tension. When Lady Bute had gone, she relaxed, and some of her fury fizzled away. If it hadn't been for Anita, she might have melted into tears—she felt like kissing the woman. Instead, she smiled. 'Her husband's the master of our local hunt. My father didn't approve of hunting. He said glueing up Sir Gerald's arse might stop him talking through it.'

Anita subsided into giggles again. She began dabbing carefully at her make-up. 'You look so bloody refined. I didn't imagine you knew words like arse. It's made my evening.'

Rufa laughed. 'I'm glad, since you paid for our dinner. I was going to thank you later, but I might as well do it now—it's awfully nice of you. We're having a wonderful time.'

'Don't mention it. You'll find more coffee back at the table. I'll join you when I've repaired the damage.'

At the top of the grand staircase, Rufa met Roshan. He was breathless and agitated. 'I've lost them.'

'What?'

'Nancy and Tiger—they went off together and now I can't find them anywhere.'

'Oh.' Rufa considered this. 'Well, that's good, isn't it? I mean, they must be getting on well.'

Roshan did not stop glancing round anxiously. 'To tell the truth, Nancy didn't look all that keen—she was making faces at me—'

'She wanted to be rescued!' Rufa gathered up her skirts determinedly. 'Oh, Roshan! Show me where you last saw them.'

He led her down the stairs. Rufa, eyes narrowed, searched the writhing figures on the dance floor. 'What's behind the stairs?' she asked.

'Just one of the service entrances—oh, Rufa, don't be silly—' Roshan sprang to follow Rufa into the obscure shadowland under the stairs. 'He's hardly going to take her here!'

There was a pair of swing doors, covered with dark red vinyl. Taking no notice of Roshan, Rufa swept through them. They opened into a carpeted passage, meanly lit, with three doors on one side.

'No, for the last bloody time, I won't—I will not give you "a snog", you great slavering—let me go!'

It was Nancy's voice, rising in anger. Rufa pushed open the nearest door. Nancy, pressed uncomfortably against a bare desk, was furiously dodging Tiger Durward's fleshy mouth.

'Look, I don't want to knee you in the nuts, but if you don't—'

Rufa's simmering anger flashed out like white lightning. Yelling 'You bastard, you take your hands off my sister!', she flew at Tiger's back and dug her fingers hard into his eyes. He roared. Both his hands flew to his face, and Nancy wriggled free.

She hugged Rufa. 'I never was so pleased to see you in my life—where the hell did you learn that?'

'Edward, of course,' Rufa said crisply. 'He taught me basic self-defence after one of my dinner party men got fresh.'

Tiger groaned. He shouted, 'Bitch. That really fucking hurts!'

Roshan had been standing in the doorway, gaping. This insult snapped him into his senses. 'It was meant to hurt!' he hissed. 'Girls, go upstairs and tell security—I'll stay here with him.'

Nancy took his arm affectionately. 'Darling, you're far too weedy to subdue this monster. I'm fine, and he's incapable. Let's just go home.'

Tiger pulled his hands from his face. His eyes rolled back into his head, and he passed out.

Once again, the four of them were gathered round Wendy's kitchen table for a post-mortem. This time, however, Max was not laughing. He looked at Rufa with a new respect.

'If you hadn't come in at that moment—well, you're not going out to anything else without an armed escort, that's all. I'd have killed him.'

'I didn't need an armed escort, I had Ru,' Nancy pointed out, leaning over to squeeze her hand.

The Sunday after the ball, Roshan's Style section had printed the hedonistic photographs of Nancy and Rufa. Spread across the page in glorious colour, the two of them looked—as Max said—good enough to eat. Rose had been absolutely dazzled, to the extent of ringing them on the off chance that they had some spare cash.

The sober truth, however, was that their funds were dwindling horribly fast. Rufa was wondering how she could find people to cook for to boost their finances. Nancy was, once again, threatening to get herself a job behind a bar. The weather was cold and wet. Tufnell Park was dark and perpetually dripping.

'This Game is like snakes and ladders,' Nancy observed, gazing dully out of the bedroom window. 'The minute we get our feet on a ladder, we slide down a huge snake, straight back to square one.'

Rufa, feeling horribly poor and unconnected, was dutifully poring over *Harpers & Queen* on her bed.

'Oh God! Look at this!' Rufa leapt off her bed and slapped Jennifer's Diary down in front of Nancy.

Nancy stared at the page. 'It's Berry!'

'Yes, it's Berry. His father's a lord, and just look at his house!' She laughed. 'If Ran had mentioned it, he could have saved us a lot of trouble.' She was reading the captions of the photographs over Nancy's shoulder. 'Shit, he's engaged—I forgot about that. Just our luck.'

Lord and Lady Bridgmore were pictured in their splendid drawing room, before a large painting by Gainsborough, which looked sumptuous enough to buy up the whole of Melismate, debts and all. The occasion was a ball to celebrate their thirty-fifth wedding anniversary and the engagement of their son, the Honourable Hector Berowne. His fiancée worked at a famous Bond Street gallery, Soames and Pellew.

'Well, well, well,' Nancy said softly. 'I vote we move Berry straight to the top of our list. This is a chance from heaven.'

'But, Nance, he's engaged!'

'Tell me he didn't fancy me.'

'He fancied you like mad,' Rufa admitted, 'but obviously not enough to change his mind about that girl.'

'Just watch me, Ru. You're looking at the future Lady Bridgmore.'

Chapter Four

THE FUTURE LADY BRIDGMORE, known for the time being as Polly Muir, sat at her desk in her Bond Street gallery. She was a pretty, neat young woman, whose long, straight blonde hair was tied back in a black velvet clip. This morning she wore an understated short black skirt—her legs were admirable—and a plain white silk shirt.

The pursuit of understated excellence was her life's mission. Soames and Pellew mainly paid her to be pretty and posh, but she could easily combine this with her real work, which was going through her immense databank of mental lists.

Firstly, the list of those to be invited to her wedding. Polly had combed and manipulated her family history so that it could pass muster anywhere—but the fact remained that she was horribly short of suitable relations. Apart from her great-aunt, widow of a Scottish baronet, they were hopeless—all twanging Australian accents and perma-tans. She must somehow fill her side of the church with well-born friends.

In Polly's life, everything had to be checked and double-checked for rightness. Was it absolutely right, for instance, to have one's wedding list at Peter Jones? Come to that, was it absolutely right to have a wedding list at all? Polly did not mind appearing to be grasping. People born into the English upper class were the most grasping she had ever met. It was simply that one had to be careful to grasp in the right way.

When the two russet-haired goddesses walked into the gallery, Polly was resting her mind warmly upon the cosy figure of Berry. Darling old Berry, she could not wait to be married to him, and living in the sweet Chelsea house his parents were bestowing as a wedding gift. They were darlings too. The only non-darling in the glorious picture was Berry's ghastly sister, Annabel; and who cared about her? In the aristocracy, sisters did not count for much.

The redheads were examining the watercolours on the panelled walls. Polly rose behind her desk, and trained her radar on them. They wore excellent clothes—Polly owned the pale blue version of the taupe jacket. Their shoes and handbags were unmistakable Prada.

'Hello,' she said, walking towards them. She did not, of course, say, 'May I help you?', which smacked of the shopkeeper.

The girl with the redder hair (taupe jacket) smiled. 'Hello, I hope you don't mind us having a look. We just love smudgy pictures of flowers—and you never know when I might be making my wedding list.'

Her tall, pale sister (black suit) looked alarmed. 'Nancy!'

'And anyway,' Nancy went on, 'we couldn't walk past when we saw the name in the window. Berry told us you worked here, and we've both been longing to meet you.'

'I'm sorry—I don't believe we've—'

Nancy held out her hand. 'Nancy Hasty. This is my sister, Rufa.'

Polly's mental computer processed the name. These were the well-born but impoverished people who had taken care of Berry when he had that idiotic adventure on Christmas Eve. Dear old Berry—how like him to miss the glaring fact that the Hasty girls were stunning.

She smiled and shook their hands. 'Of course. How lovely to meet you. Now I can thank you properly for being so sweet to Berry.'

'I hope your Christmas improved after that.'

'It was heavenly, thanks. Your part of the country is so peaceful. Are you in London for long?'

'Well—' Rufa seemed confused.

'Just for a week or two,' Nancy put in smoothly. 'Until our money runs out. I expect Berry told you how poor we are.'

Berry had mentioned their poverty, in a way that Polly had found rather worrying. Now she could see that theirs was a Prada-shod poverty, her last doubt died.

'I know he'd love to see you again,' she said. 'Look, this is wretchedly short notice—but why don't you pop along to our opening, tomorrow night? Six thirty onwards.'

Polly's mind was working rapidly. Her employer, Jimmy Pellew, was always on at her to cheer up openings with ornamental people. Rufa and Nancy, would lend the party glamour.

'What fun,' Nancy said. 'We'd love to.'

Berry had not been looking forward to the evening. Left to himself, he would have gone home to the Fulham flat he shared with Polly, and eaten something comfortable in front of mindless television. Instead, he was doomed to hours of holding in his stomach, smiling until his face hurt, and trying not to guzzle too many tiny sausages.

'Victorian watercolours,' Adrian mused. 'They always make me think of tablemats. But Naomi took her divorce settlement in paintings, and my decorator insists I need something uncontroversial for my walls.'

'This is really good of you, Adrian,' Berry said.

He had been amazed when the director of his merchant bank had agreed to come to the opening. Adrian Mecklenberg was ludicrously rich, and a famous collector of beautiful objects. Polly said that if Mecklenberg bought significantly tonight, Jimmy Pellew would give her the Edward Lear parrot she had coveted for ages, as a wedding present.

The Daimler slowed outside the gallery, and Berry stole a quick glance at his boss. Adrian sucked all available elegance from the atmosphere. His clothes sat upon him without creasing, and his thick grey hair lay as sleek as a sheet of steel. Berry's own hair was standing up like the crest of a cockatoo, despite being plastered down with a ton of fragrant gunk from Jermyn Street.

Polly was waiting, fresh and dustless in her green cocktail dress. She swept aside a girl holding a pile of glossy catalogues and kissed Berry. She kissed Adrian. She provided them both with drinks, and whisked Adrian away towards Jimmy Pellew, who was standing casually beside the most expensive paintings.

Berry's stomach leapt with a terrible pleasure that was almost pain. Silhouetted against a faded pastoral landscape, he saw Nancy Hasty. Instantly, the whole world took on a new intensity.

Oh God. Nancy.

What on earth was she doing here? Since Christmas Eve he had flogged himself guiltily into never thinking of Nancy (except when masturbating, which he absolutely could not help). Now, two months later, he had almost trained himself not to dream about her. And all that hard work was undone in a second.

'Berry—hello.'

A soft voice cut across the upheaval. He turned, and was glad to see Rufa, whose beauty was of the distant, untouchable sort.

She kissed his flushed cheek. 'Didn't Polly tell you we were coming?'

'No—she must have—she gets into the most tremendous state before an opening.' Rufa was blessedly easy to talk to, and Berry found himself relaxing a little. 'How are you all? How's my little friend Linnet?'

Rufa smiled. 'In fighting form, when I spoke to her last night. Nancy and I have to phone her every evening. Nance has to do a voice for Trotsky.'

'Trotsky?'

'The guinea pig Ran gave her for Christmas. He's rather witless and obese, but she hasn't noticed yet. How are you?'

'Oh—witless and obese as ever, thanks,' Berry said cheerfully. 'Do give them all my love, won't you? I take it things are—I mean, you both look—' Berry was struggling to be delicate.

Rufa helped him. 'We've come into a little bit of money since then. So we've moved to London for a while. We're staying with an old friend.'

In Berry's world there were always bits of money, and useful old friends. He was sincerely delighted to hear that the Hastys were, apparently, still hovering above the vortex. 'Business or pleasure?'

'Mainly pleasure,' Rufa said, 'but I wouldn't mind finding some work. I do cooking for dinner parties—I don't suppose you know anyone who needs an occasional caterer?'

'Polly certainly does. Give me your number and I'll ask her.'

'Well, look who it is,' Nancy said, stepping between them.

Berry squeaked, 'Hello.'

'Do excuse me—' Polly appeared from nowhere. She took Berry's elbow and pulled him away. He experienced one split second of pure terror (had she noticed?) then saw that her mind was firmly on business.

He managed to say, 'What's up?'

'It's Adrian. He's ignoring the paintings. All he wants to do is stare at Rufa Hasty. You have to introduce them. Do it now!'

'Of course.'

Polly glided away, to direct her determined sparkle at a gaggle of jewelled dowagers, and Berry returned to the Hastys. His guilty conscience made him brisk. 'Rufa, do come and meet the big cheese from my bank.' He steered Rufa through the press of people. 'His name's Adrian

Mecklenberg,' he whispered into her ear. 'And he's the richest person here. Think of my home life—beg him to buy something.'

Rufa asked lightly, 'How rich is he?'

'Rolling in it. He usually buys Picassos. And when his ex-wives make off with them, he buys more Picassos.'

'Is he married at the moment?'

'No,' Berry said. 'He's just got shot of Number Three.'

Adrian's pale grey eyes were studying Rufa with the avidity of the expert collector. During Berry's introduction he held her hand a little longer than necessary. He said, 'Hello, Cinderella.'

Her polite smile disappeared. Her ears burned red. 'You . . . you're the man who rescued my shoe. Oh God.' Would that mortifying experience at Sheringham House never cease to haunt her?

'I thought it was you,' he said. Her confusion and embarrassment appeared to please him. 'I thought I recognised you, at that tiresome concert. You could only be the daughter of poor old Rufus Hasty.'

Forgetting her embarrassment, Rufa broke into a smile like the sun rising. 'Oh, did you know him?'

'I certainly did. I was his fag, at school.'

She laughed. 'You're the boy who refused to make toast?'

'The same. Though, actually, I admired Rufus enormously. I think I rebelled purely to impress him—not that it worked.'

Berry had never seen Adrian so animated. The man had a reputation for charm. For the first time he was watching the charm at work.

Berry glanced round furtively at Polly, to check that this was part of the plan. Across the room, she smiled at him. Good. Adrian was placing his red dot. As far as he was concerned, Rufa was sold.

Adrian saw Rufa and Nancy into the taxi. The moment it had swung round the corner, Rufa murmured, 'My God, I've scored a lunch!'

'Not with him?' Nancy looked alarmed. 'Oh, Ru, you've got to be kidding. He's ancient.'

'You're just jealous because I've got the first real date. With a properly available man.'

'Jealous? He gives me the creeps.'

'I think he's rather nice. And he's a much better bet than Berry.'

'Rubbish. Berry's worth ten of him. He doesn't sleep in a coffin or avoid mirrors, for a start.'

'Oh, ha, ha. Adrian's charming,' Rufa said crossly. 'Yards better than the sort of man we imagined when we started.'

Nancy groaned. 'You can't marry a man like that. Being miserable wasn't part of the deal. You know your trouble, Ru? You don't know anything about love.'

'The Marrying Game isn't about love,' Rufa said stubbornly.

'Oh, I know it's not about romance,' Nancy said. 'But I always assumed we'd be looking for men we could be—I don't know—fond of.'

'I was always afraid you wouldn't have the stamina,' Rufa said. 'You'd better leave it to me.'

Nancy frowned. 'Listen, if I bag Berry I'll be the winner of this game. And my prize will be you ditching Adrian.'

Rufa was silent for a long moment. 'If you bag him,' she said. 'If.'

Chapter Five

THE FIRST LUNCH TOOK PLACE three days later, at the Connaught. Rufa wore the taupe jacket over an ivory silk shirt.

Adrian gently suggested that he should order for her, which was a neat way of getting round the tense ritual of studying the menu.

They ate English oysters and Dover sole. With each course, a delicate white wine appeared. He was watching her intently.

'I thought the Connaught would be a good backdrop for you,' he said. 'It's a timeless classic, and so are you. You're absolutely clear—like a piece of crystal. You should wear more yellows and greens. Leave the autumnal tints to your sister. The jacket looked better on her.'

Rufa smiled. 'I wondered if you'd notice.'

'When I notice a woman,' Adrian said, 'I always notice her clothes. You make me think of spring—you're Botticelli's *Primavera* made flesh, as I'm sure you've been told before.'

He seemed to want a reply. The thing not to do, Rufa guessed, was protest. Adrian Mecklenberg would not care for a woman who flinched at heavy compliments. 'Yes,' she said. 'The Man used to say it.'

'I own a Botticelli,' he said, in a curiously passionless tone. 'It's my favourite possession. No wife has managed to chisel it out of me.'

Rufa said, 'Berry told me you're a famous collector.'

'Rather denuded, at present. The last Mrs Mecklenberg wouldn't budge without half my paintings.'

'You must miss them,' she said, wondering where this was leading.

'All my wives adore art,' Adrian said. 'I'm obviously drawn to women who are profoundly affected by art. As I think you are.'

Rufa changed her smile slightly, to accommodate the sudden intimacy. This, she thought, was like being interviewed for a job. Her qualifications—breeding and beauty—had got her past the first stage. Now he was checking that she would fit the corporate image.

'In any case—' Adrian began again abruptly, after a short silence. 'I'm looking forward to beginning again. A new collection for a new era. Perhaps I'll only collect paintings of redheads.'

It was difficult to smile graciously while eating fish. Adrian's compliments were cool and casual: statements of observation. It was a very deliberate form of wooing, and also a kind of test, to see if she could take admiration without squirming.

'I can't understand,' he said, 'how Berry managed to keep you a secret.'

'My brother-in-law was at school with him, but we only met last Christmas.' Rufa told the story of the pond and the lost keys, and felt she was making progress when Adrian chuckled. She liked him more because he evidently liked Berry.

'A thoroughly decent sort,' he pronounced.

Rufa said, 'Polly seems nice, too.'

'Ah, Polly. Radiant with love for the title and the house, and the peerless collection of eighteenth-century paintings. She's not in love with Berry himself, of course. That sort of woman doesn't fall in love in the ordinary way. She's programmed to hold out for the whole package.'

This was uncomfortable territory. 'Surely Berry wouldn't want to marry her, if she's like that!' protested Rufa.

Adrian was watching her narrowly. 'You're missing the point. A marriage is a contract. It exists because each party has something the other needs. What Polly provides for Berry, in return for the title, is probably entirely satisfactory. Sex, companionship. Effective management.'

Rufa did not like the way the conversation was going. Was Adrian telling her she had been rumbled as a gold-digger? Or was it a veiled assurance that her emotions were irrelevant to the final deal? It was humbling, and she was hardly in a position to blame him for it.

Something in the defensive set of her shoulders pleased Adrian. He smiled, and, for the first time, it reached his eyes.

'I've shocked you,' he said softly. 'What a delightful experience. I forgot I was talking to a romantic Hasty. If ever I wanted you to marry me, I'd have to make you fall in love with me first.'

Afterwards, he saw her into a taxi and put twenty pounds into the hand of the driver. He spoke of their next meeting. It was to be another lunch, but it would involve a drive out to a little place he knew in the country. Without a single kiss or caress, Adrian was assuming a courtship.

Staring sightlessly out of the rain-spattered window, Rufa assessed the situation. She had done amazingly well, with almost no effort. Adrian was beginning a process, at the end of which Rufa would be in love with him. Over coffee, she had told him something about the affair with Jonathan, leaving out the subsequent death of her libido.

Adrian guessed, however, and appeared to like the idea of waking the Sleeping Beauty. She wondered if he had the power to make her fall in love with him. She wished (hoped) it would happen. He was charming, and very good-looking, if rather ancient. As far as she could be, she was attracted, and intrigued. Perhaps this was a man who could lead her back to love, stage by stage?

Rufa felt a little careworn when she let herself into Wendy's house, but she congratulated herself on a job well done. The others would be dying to know how it went, but Rufa felt oddly defensive and slightly ashamed. Fortunately, Wendy was busy in the basement, prodding the feet of a client, and Nancy was still out, having declared, before lunch, that she intended to make another move on Berry.

Rufa made herself a mug of tea, then went upstairs with the Anita Brookner she had found in Wendy's airing cupboard. She had earned a rest.

An hour later, the doorbell rang. Rufa ignored it, thinking it must be someone for Wendy. She was still deep in the novel when Wendy's head appeared round the door.

'It's Edward Reculver. He's waiting downstairs to see you.'

Rufa shut the book, and leapt off the bed. Her heart galloped. She had a ghastly feeling she'd been found out. 'I'll go down and see him.'

Edward Reculver waited rigidly in the narrow hall. His iron-grey hair was black from the rain. Rivulets ran off his waxed coat.

'Edward, what a surprise!' Rufa ran down the stairs and kissed his bristled cheek. 'Why didn't you tell me you were coming?' She could not say it was a pleasure to see him. He was plainly furious.

'I need to talk to you.'

'Of course,' Rufa said. 'We'll go up to my room.'

She led him into the bedroom, and closed the door. She knew she was about to get the dressing-down of all time.

He asked, 'Where's Nancy?'

'She's gone out.' Rufa was glad about this. Nancy, in full campaigning rig—Wonderbra and searing new lipstick—would annoy him mightily. 'Won't you take your coat off and sit down?'

'No,' he said. 'Thank you.' Edward folded his arms. 'I dare say you know why I'm here.'

'Just tell me, Edward. Please don't make a song and dance about it.'

'All right. I ran into Mike Bosworth in Cirencester this morning.'

'Oh.' Bosworth's were the auctioneers who had valued Melismate.

'I asked him what was happening about the sale,' Edward said. 'And I was absolutely staggered to discover that it had been postponed.'

Rufa looked down at her knees. 'We wanted a little more time.'

'The time ran out long ago.' Edward shrugged off his wet coat and draped it over a chair. 'The debts are piling up, the house is ready to collapse—I expected craziness from Rose. But not from you.'

'Did you speak to Mum?'

'I drove straight round to Melismate to find out what was going on. And out it all came. How halting the sale was all your idea. How you had gone to London with the avowed intention of marrying a man rich enough to sort out the whole bloody mess.'

Rufa hung her head. Put like this, it sounded crude and stupid.

'I didn't bother to ask what you and Nancy were doing for money,' Edward went on. 'I naturally worked that one out for myself. It appears that I have bankrolled the entire operation.'

'Edward, I'm sorry,' Rufa said. She made herself raise her head, to look at him. She was sorry. 'I had to tell you all those lies. If you'd known the truth, you would have taken back the brooch.'

'The brooch was a bloody present,' Edward snapped.

'With definite strings attached.'

'You sound exactly like your father—which you will, doubtless, take as a compliment. And I really thought you were the one person in your family with some sense. To sell yourself for money—Well, we needn't go into it any further. Get your things together—if you want to argue, you can do it in the car.'

Rufa's guilt boiled over into anger. 'You have no right to storm in here giving me orders. If that brooch was a gift, I can do what the hell I like with the money. And I'm using it to save my home.'

'You think that will make you happy?'

'Yes!' she shouted—she had never shouted at Edward. 'I'll be incredibly, deliriously happy with any man who gives me back my house! You have no right to charge down here and spoil everything.'

'I'm trying to help,' he said. 'I—I do it because I care for you.'

She could not accept this. 'No, you don't—part of you was jealous of the Man, and now you're thrilled to see his show-offy family being forced to be ordinary! You think it serves us right! Oh God—'

Rufa was appalled by this piece of horror that had bubbled out of her subconscious like pond scum. She knew at once that she had dealt him a serious blow. He was astonished that she had such weapons.

'I didn't understand,' he said. 'You're as much a fantasist as he was, clinging to this ludicrous notion that the world owes you a living— merely because you've loafed around on the same bit of land for a few centuries. Does this make you a special case? There's nothing clever or admirable about getting yourself born into an old family!'

Rufa was trying not to cry. 'You know it's more than that. Melismate is part of us, and what we are. Without it, we're nothings and nobodies.'

'Rubbish. You're a beautiful, intelligent woman. You could do any-thing. Listen. I'm only trying to stop you ruining your entire life for the sake of a heap of stones. What would it take, for God's sake?'

'You'd have to find a few million quid,' Rufa said, 'and give it to me— without telling me how to spend it.'

'I see.'

'You don't!' She found his obstinacy infuriating. 'You never will! I know you mean to be kind, Edward, but please don't interfere. Please. I want this more than I've ever wanted anything!'

They both stared down at the swirly carpet, casting round for some way to part as friends. There was a long, hardening silence.

'Well, I tried,' Edward said abruptly. 'I offered to help clear up this mess, and you turned me down. I won't interfere again.'

Rufa moved to the bedroom door, making a wide circle round him, and jerked it open. 'Goodbye, then.'

Chapter Six

AFTER BREAKFAST, on the morning of Rufa's first lunch with Adrian, Nancy had made a secret phone call to Rose. 'She can't marry this man, Mum. Please take my word for it—he makes my blood run cold.'

Miles across the rain-spattered country, Rose had chuckled. 'Don't get into one of your states, darling. Rufa won't do anything silly.'

Nancy was not so sure. The Marrying Game had seemed terrifically amusing when the rich men only existed in theory. The cold actuality of a man like Adrian Mecklenberg, and Rufa's willingness to sacrifice herself to him, had come as a severe shock. Unless Nancy did something about it, the Marrying Game could turn rather nasty. If she wanted to beat her sister to the altar, she would have to ignore her advice about delicacy and refinement, and tackle things in her own style.

Wearing her Wonderbra and a tight black sweater beneath a creamy, classic Margaret Howell raincoat, she set off later that afternoon for the Square Mile to do a little research.

The offices of Berry's bank were in Cheapside, near Threadneedle Street. Nancy stood on the opposite side of the road, watching the building with open curiosity. Its sheer glass walls towered above a sea of moving corporate golf umbrellas, like huge mushrooms with logos. Berry emerged, struggling with his own umbrella. He was deep in conversation with another man, and did not see Nancy when she slipped into the crowd, a few umbrellas behind him.

They turned into a narrow side street. Nancy's interest quickened. Berry and his companion were furling their umbrellas at the low doorway of a place called Forbes & Gunning—which, though it claimed to be a wine merchant to the gentry, was essentially a wine bar.

Nancy, folding herself into the tide of charcoal suits, went down a cramped wooden staircase and found herself in an enormous vaulted cellar, reverberating with male noise. Berry and his friend fought through to the bar, emerged with a bottle of red wine, and sat down at a round table in a relatively quiet corner.

Nancy was just deciding she was too conspicuous here, and had better leave, when a beautiful opportunity presented itself—like the hand of destiny, as she said afterwards. A young man, in a long apron like a Toulouse-Lautrec waiter, touched her arm.

'Hi—sorry to keep you waiting. You've come about the job, right?'

She did not get back to Wendy's until past midnight. Two bottles of Forbes & Gunning's house champagne distended the pockets of her raincoat. The young man, whose name was Simon, had hired her on the spot, offering her an hourly rate which seemed like an absolute fortune. She went straight onto the evening shift and was further dazzled by the amount she made in tips. The men had been surprisingly unbothersome. She could not believe how easy this was. She had forgotten how much she relished the raucous bustle of a busy bar.

She put her bottles on Wendy's kitchen table and switched the kettle on. Wendy's voice quavered from the next room, 'Is that you, Nancy?'

'Yes,' Nancy called back. 'I'm making tea.'

Wendy appeared at the door and her eyes widened when she saw the champagne. 'What have you been up to?'

'I've landed myself the most divine job—the job of my dreams. Where's Ru? How was her lunch with Count Mecklenberg?'

Wendy was solemn. 'She's upstairs.' Briefly and breathlessly, she outlined the visitation from Edward.

'Oh God,' Nancy groaned. 'The miserable old git. How could he? He knows perfectly well what Ru's like—she acts all cool and collected, but she's about as tough as a marshmallow. And she's the only one of us who gives a damn about his good opinion.'

Nancy pulled down two mugs from the shelf and made some tea. 'We'll be down in a minute. Put the champagne in the freezer, there's a love.'

She carried the tea upstairs. As soon as she turned the handle to their room, a muffled voice cried, 'Go away!'

'Darling, it's only me. I sleep here too—unless you'd like to exile me to Max's room.'

Rufa lay sprawled across her single bed, her face raw and bloated with tears. Nancy felt a spasm of pure rage against Edward, but managed to pin on a cheerful smile.

'I've brought you a cup of tea.'

Nancy very rarely made tea for anyone. Rufa sobbed, 'Th-thanks—' and struggled blearily into a sitting position.

'I'm sorry I wasn't here to give him a handsome piece of my mind.'

'He's found out about the Marrying Game. He thinks we're disgusting.' Rufa shakily sipped her tea. 'I said the most awful things to him— he'll never speak to me again, probably.'

'Good,' Nancy said. 'I'm always telling you, don't listen to him. The Man loved him dearly but never took a blind bit of notice.'

Rufa's lips quivered. 'What'll happen to us without Edward?'

'We'll survive, that's what,' Nancy declared. 'Don't go nuts, but I've got myself a bar job.' She reached into her Wonderbra and pulled out a crumpled bunch of banknotes.

The corners of Rufa's mouth twitched into the beginnings of a smile. 'Don't tell me you made all that pulling pints,' Rufa said.

'Pints of champagne, my dear. I'm working at Berry's local—down a city alley with one of those tactless historical names, like Great Cripple Street, or Leper's Yard. Admit it,' Nancy coaxed, 'you're impressed.'

Rufa smiled now—a watery sketch of a smile that went to Nancy's heart. 'God, yes. It was stupid of me to be snotty about you being a barmaid. I wish I could find some work myself.'

'Didn't Berry say he'd ask around about your dinner parties? I'll remind him.'

'Of course,' Rufa murmured. 'You'll be seeing him.'

'Seeing him? I'll be having a wild affair with him, and then I'll be marrying him. So stop crying, honey. Come down and have a glass of my champagne. Forget about Edward. Honestly, darling, it's not worth getting this worked up over a man unless you're in love with him.'

Nancy was Berry's introduction to the phenomenon of stress. In the usual way of things, he bobbed serenely between work, fiancée and family, never much disturbed by anything. Nancy's astonishing, overbalancing appearance behind the bar at Forbes & Gunning rapidly turned him into a restless, coffee-guzzling nervous wreck.

The worst of it was that other men noticed her—how could they help it? She was a red-headed Hebe, dispensing nectar with unhurried ease. In a matter of weeks, she had a cult following, coming from as far as Canary Wharf to get a look at her wicked blue eyes and gorgeous breasts.

The enigmatic Adrian was, as far as Berry could tell, very serious about his pursuit of Rufa. And the more serious he became, the greater Polly's determination to cultivate the future Mrs Mecklenberg.

Adrian moved methodically. In a matter of weeks, the lunchtime assignations progressed to concerts and dinners. And as the courtship developed, Polly grew more friendly with Rufa and more willing to tolerate Nancy. The culmination came one evening when Berry returned from the office and found a red-haired Hasty in each corner of his Knole sofa. Polly had invited them both to supper.

'I hope you don't mind,' Polly said to him, privately, in the kitchen, as she arranged asparagus spears in balsamic puddles. 'I couldn't very well invite Rufa on her own. It's not that I don't like Nancy, but let's face it, she'll never have Rufa's sheer quality. I'm afraid there's something rather provincial about her. If not borderline vulgar.'

To Berry's dismay, he was seized by a pang of active dislike for Polly. It had never happened before, and it shocked him into facing the truth.

This had turned into more than infatuation. This was the real deal, the whole nine yards. He had fallen in love with Nancy. She brought the sun into a room with her, and it sank into chilly gloom when she left. Her charm, her laughter and her high spirits charged the atmosphere with magic. He was madly in love with Nancy. And he was unavoidably engaged to marry Polly. He could jilt her, and despise himself for ever. Or he could ignore Nancy and die of a broken heart. Either way, he was condemned to a lifetime of misery.

He lost interest in food. As the spring days lengthened, his paunch melted. All his suits were taken in three times, then discarded. His jaw was lean, and there were poignant hollows underneath his cheekbones.

Polly was delighted. Why, Berry wondered, didn't she notice? How could she want to marry a man who was burning with love for someone else? He allowed himself the small treat of being annoyed with Polly for her complacency, but that was as far as it went. He was still determined to marry her. He was a man of his word.

By the middle of March, Adrian and Rufa had reached a significant stage in their courtship. He was taking her to dinner with his sister, at her house in Holland Park. The revelation that he had a sister at all had been, in itself, shockingly intimate. Her name was Clarissa Watts-Wainwright, and, as far as Rufa could gather, she was at the centre of Adrian's private circle. She suspected this was the final inspection, the final test, before the runways were cleared for sexual contact. So far, Adrian had kissed her cheek on meeting and parting—with almost imperceptibly increasing warmth. Rufa liked him. She was attracted by his cool cleanliness, but she was very anxious to know if her urge-free body would submit happily to sex with him.

The affair was black-tie. Rufa had cooked her first two professional dinners (for a charming acquaintance of Polly's) and had invested her earnings in a long sheath of midnight-blue chiffon. This way, she did not feel so guilty about Edward's diminishing money. Thinking about him at all made her sore all over. She bitterly regretted their quarrel.

Adrian's sister was a female version of Adrian: formidably immaculate, and with the same very clean shade of grey hair. Rufa noticed, as she was introduced round the room, that she was the youngest here by at least twenty years. It was plain that she was being presented, officially, as Adrian's next consort. Clarissa reinforced this, by continually scooping her into the conversation during dinner.

At the coffee stage, there was a movement back to the drawing room. Adrian appeared, with the pashmina Roshan had made her buy. He draped it round Rufa's shoulders and led her outside, on the pretext of admiring the communal gardens.

Holding his arm, shivering slightly in the raw spring evening, Rufa looked out across rolling lawns and shrubberies, ringed by banks of glowing, golden windows.

'You're cold,' Adrian observed. He uncurled her passive hand and put his arm round her. 'I shouldn't expose a creature like you to the elements. You belong behind glass.'

She was not going to argue with this, but couldn't help thinking how Nancy would have laughed to hear it.

'Do you have any plans for the weekend after next?' he asked.

A weekend meant sex. Rufa was suddenly frightened. If she could not handle it, she would be trapped. 'You know I never have plans.'

In the darkness, she heard the smile in his voice. 'Then will you come with me to Paris?'

'I . . . I'd love to.'

'Good. Though there's nothing in Paris—or out of it—to compare to you. You are beautiful. I haven't said it often enough'

His face was moving towards hers. Time slowed. She was aware of the sharp definition of his features. His lips were cool. Rufa was very still, willing herself to relax. After the initial shock of contact, she found that she could bear this easily. It was even pleasant.

For one mad second, she wanted to giggle. Beyond the act of sex, which she now knew she was unlikely to fail, lay the wild relief of saving Melismate.

Nancy slammed the door of the washing machine and stood up. 'If I don't do something fast, Ru's going to make a dreadful marriage.'

Max was leaning against the counter in Wendy's kitchen, staring at Nancy with naked admiration. 'Let her make her own mistakes,' he said. 'She can always divorce him, when she's spent all his money.'

'I don't think getting divorced is exactly a barrel of laughs, darling. And just imagine how badly Rufa would handle it.'

'True. Heaven save us all from serious types.' Max's bright, pagan dark eyes raked over her slowly. 'How come the two of you are so different?'

He could say anything to her, and, these days, it all meant the same thing. Every remark, however innocuous, was a gate standing open. Nancy felt the sex blasting off him in waves, and was amazed by her own strength of mind in resisting him. She fancied him desperately. Damn Rufa and her blasted Marrying Game!

She smiled, dropping her gaze. 'We're more alike than we seem.'

This was meant to mean: I'm more of a prude than I look, and less easy to get into the sack than appearances suggest.

Such a waste, Nancy thought regretfully, watching Max covertly as he weighed up the likelihood of seducing her, and decided to go back to his work upstairs.

The doorbell rang. Nancy went to answer it. There was a man waiting on the doorstep: tall and lean, probably in his early forties. His hair was thick and dark grey, his face unlined and clean-shaven. His navy suit was several degrees too elegant for Tufnell Park Road on a weekday afternoon. And he was blindingly handsome.

He said, 'Hello, Nancy.'

The shock woke her like a hard slap. She met the cool eyes of the handsome stranger, and gasped, 'Oh my God!'

It was Edward Reculver.

Edward, without the beard and the darned clothes from Millets. Edward, with a proper haircut, instead of the usual convict's trim. It was staggering. Nancy was both amused and impressed that she had been tricked into finding him sexy—old Edward, of all people.

'Yes, it's really me,' he said. He smiled his usual, lopsided smile, unshadowed by the beard that he had worn since leaving the army.

She gasped, 'What's happened to you?'

'I've learned humility, seen sense and shaved,' he said. 'In that order. Do you approve?'

'Definitely,' Nancy said, laughing softly as she stared at him. 'You look about a million years younger. And expensively redesigned.'

Edward laughed outright at this. 'Ghastly child—that's exactly what your father would have said. Is Rufa here?'

Nancy remembered that she was supposed to be angry with him— the novelty of the transformation had blown everything else from her mind. 'No. So if you're here to have another go at her, bad luck.'

He winced touchily, but his voice was mild. 'Before you say anything else, I'm really sorry about last time. What I said to her was—bloody unforgivable. That's why I'm here.'

'You're kidding,' Nancy said. 'You never apologise.'

'Well, perhaps I've changed,' he said, sighing heavily.

There was something very nice about Edward when he spoke in this quiet, direct way, thought Nancy. Since the Man's death, she realised, he had only shown them his lecturing, hectoring side. But this might have been as much a sign of grieving as Rufa's obsession with saving Melismate—or her own hunger for romance. 'I'd be lying if I said Ru wasn't upset. But that's only because you hit a few bull's-eyes.'

He was touched. 'Am I crazy, to be worried sick about her?'

'No. I am too, rather.' Nancy opened the door wider. She could not let him go yet. 'Come on in. Have some tea.'

'Thanks, I'd love to.' He seemed relieved. Nancy wondered what sort of reception he had expected as she led him down the passage to the kitchen. 'Sit down. Do you fancy something to eat?'

'No, thanks.' Watching her curiously, as if he did not know what to make of her away from Melismate, he sat down.

'In that case, you'll have to excuse me while I stuff myself with toasted cheese,' Nancy said. 'I'm off to work in a minute.'

'You've got a job?'

'Well, as I said to Rufa, there's always gainful employment for an experienced barmaid.' Seeing Edward was genuinely interested and prepared to be amused, Nancy told him about Forbes & Gunning, embellishing the story, as the Man would have done.

Once Nancy was settled at the table, with a cup of tea and a plate of toasted cheese, Edward said, with an effort, 'I really upset Ru, didn't I?'

'She was devastated. I found her crying her eyes out.'

'Hmm. Do you think she'd let me see her, so I can show her how sorry I am?'

'Of course she'll see you,' Nancy said. 'But she's over at Berry's all day. His fiancée's having a dinner party, and Ru's doing the cooking. The address is 8b Pemberton Villas, off the Fulham Road.'

'Will she mind my just turning up there?'

Rufa would mind, Nancy realised. Adrian was to be present at the dinner party, and the momentous trip to Paris was scheduled for the following weekend. Rufa would not care to have Edward turning up at this critical stage. But sod that, Nancy thought suddenly—it might be the saving of her earnest, hurtable sister.

'I don't care if she minds. See if you can stop her marrying Adrian.'

This was the first time Edward had heard the name of Rufa's target. His eyes narrowed warily. 'Who?'

The time had come, Nancy decided, to let him have the truth. 'He's called Adrian Mecklenberg. He's filthy rich, and cold as an icicle. She can't marry him, Edward. She's not remotely in love with him—though she's trying to kid herself that she is.'

He nodded thoughtfully. 'You're sure she doesn't care for this man?'

'Positive. She's only doing this because she assumes she'll never be happy again, and staying at Melismate is the best she has to hope for.'

'You're worried about her too, aren't you?'

She nodded. 'I can't watch her marrying that man, and killing herself by inches.' She was pouring this out like a confession, and it was a huge relief. 'Someone's got to stop her throwing her life away, and she might just listen to you.'

Edward said, 'I'll do my best.'

Rufa thought it appropriate that Polly had a 'galley' kitchen—she certainly worked her employees like galley slaves. All we need, she thought, is a surly man in a vest banging a drum, to keep us all in rhythm. The Colombian cleaning lady and a stout Spanish waitress had been lashed round the flat all day by Polly's high-pitched commands. Mindful that Rufa was the next Mrs Mecklenberg, Polly was more gracious to her, and disguised her orders as sweet requests. Could she slice the smoked goose more thinly? Could she wash the rocket leaves in Evian, not tap water? She wanted to like Polly, because she liked Berry, but it was an uphill struggle.

At half past five Polly burst into the kitchen, just as Rufa had perched on a stool with a cup of tea.

'There's a man begging to see you—and frankly, I wish it was me he was begging for, because he's quite a dish. Says he's your godfather.'

'Edward?' Rufa jumped down from her stool. She had not registered the part about Edward being a 'dish'. All she could think was that he had buried the hatchet because of some particularly dreadful disaster at Melismate. She pushed past Polly into the drawing room.

'Hello,' Edward said. He came over to her and solemnly planted a light kiss on her forehead. 'Oh God—you've gone as pale as a ghost. I'm not bringing bad news, all right?'

The transformation was extraordinary. Rufa was suddenly shy. For a fraction of a second she had not recognised him.

Edward put his hand on Rufa's shoulder. 'Polly, can I take her away for half an hour? We need to talk.'

'Oh, I'm afraid I still have to—' Rufa began.

Polly smiled. 'Don't be silly, there's ages yet.'

The coffee shop opposite the flat was crowded, but Edward managed to find a small, marble-topped table in a corner. They sat down and stared at each other gravely.

Edward suddenly laughed. 'Go on, say it.'

'You look terrific without your beard,' Rufa said, smiling. 'I almost didn't know you.'

'Hmm. Is that a good or a bad thing?'

'I said "almost". You're not that easy to disguise.' She could not stop staring at him, trying to work out his age. He could not be a day over forty-five, she realised. The eternally youthful Man had been quite a few years older than his friend. 'Does your face feel naked without it?'

'It feels a little cold,' he said.

A waitress came to the table. Edward ordered them both large cups of tea and blueberry muffins.

'Sorry,' he said. 'I should have asked you first. But I know you're hungry, even if you don't know it yourself. You look bloody exhausted. What on earth have you been doing?'

He was right, Rufa was exhausted. 'This is my third dinner party in four days,' she said. 'Polly's been so kind about recommending me to all her friends. And they all seem to live at a perpetual dinner party.'

The muffins arrived, smelling deliciously of vanilla. Rufa tried to work up the energy to eat hers. Edward said, 'Rufa, I have to apologise for the way I stormed out last time.'

'Please—' Rufa felt she could not bear any replay of that argument, even in the form of an apology.

'It's all right, I'm not here to bully you.' His grey eyes were very serious. Rufa could feel the weight of the matter, whatever it was. 'I just want you to know what an effect it had on me.' He smiled grimly. 'I drove home in a fury. I didn't sleep that night. But by the time I switched on the *Today* programme at six, I'd more or less worked it out.'

'What?'

'Eat your muffin. You'll have to be patient with me. There's a lot of ground to cover. I think I'll start with Alice.' He looked down at the table. 'I think you'll remember how devastated I was when she died.'

'Of course I do,' Rufa said. It had been an accepted thing that Edward was a man with a broken heart.

He said, 'Alice and I were first cousins. She was the child of my father's older brother. We grew up together. We fell in love and got married.' He glanced up at her. 'Does that strike you as odd?'

It did, slightly. 'No,' Rufa said.

'There wasn't any particular moment of falling in love. We used to say we fell in love the day we met, when her mother brought her to the farm.' He laughed briefly. 'She was three, by the way, and I was four. We were different in lots of ways, but somehow locking together, in a way that made each of us both complete. Do you see?'

'Of course. You were soul mates,' Rufa suggested gently.

'There was a tremendous fuss about us getting married. My mother loved Alice like a daughter—but she thought we'd have defective babies. In the event, we didn't have any babies at all.'

His face was a mask. The pain could not be expressed, only distantly described. 'She wanted a child,' he said, 'more than anything else in the world.' He studied the surface of the table, as if reading the past, then raised his head. 'Anyway. That's not what I . . . the only thing you have to know about is the money.'

'Sorry?' Rufa was lost. He had taken an unexpected turning.

'A brief sketch of my dysfunctional family,' Edward said. 'Alice's father—my uncle—had two children. Besides Alice, there was Prudence, her half-sister. My uncle never married her mother. Alice and

72

my Aunt Katherine took refuge with us, essentially because they couldn't live with my uncle. I won't go into details now. All you have to know is that he was a wicked man'—he brought the word out forcefully—'and they couldn't stay with him. He was also very rich.'

He looked briefly up at Rufa.

She said, 'Oh.'

'He disinherited Alice. But she was married to me. So I, as his nephew, got most of the money.'

'What . . . you?' Rufa was fascinated. Edward's parsimony was as much a part of him as the facial hair had been. 'What happened to it?'

Edward said, 'Nothing.' He was rigid with embarrassment. 'Put simply, I was only to get that bloody money on condition that I divorced Alice and married someone else. It was all so Victorian.'

Rufa was amazed. She had never suspected the prosaic Edward of having such a piece of Gothic romance in his background.

Edward gazed down into the palms of his hands. 'Then, of course, Alice died. We were still living in Germany when it all started. She went to the doctor, because she thought she might be pregnant, and we found out what was wrong with her when he gave her a blood test.'

'How awful. I didn't know.'

He glanced up, trying to smile. 'Don't let me go off into a blow-by-blow account. That's not the point. The point is, I wanted to die too. And the business with the money seemed like a perfect excuse not to even think about marrying again. I felt I owed it to her.'

He was silent and motionless for several minutes, head bowed over the table. Then he straightened and said briskly, 'I've told you about Alice, and the money. Now I have to say something about you.'

'Me?' Rufa was puzzled.

He frowned, choosing his words cautiously. 'I was insensitive last time. I didn't understand how deeply you felt about Melismate. I was tarring you with the same brush as your father. But I can see now, in your case, the purely romantic isn't necessarily bad. It took that obscene Marrying Game of yours to show me what Melismate really means to you. And . . . and . . .' He drew a deep breath. 'And what you mean to me.'

Heat surged into Rufa's face. His contrition made her ashamed.

Very gently, slightly formally, Edward held her hand. 'I can't let you do it, Ru. It would break my heart. I've had a special love for you, ever since I left the army and came home to find you'd grown up. I can't tell you how I've admired the way you tried to hold your family together after you lost your father. But there's no way on earth I'm going to stand by and watch you marrying a man you don't remotely love.'

'How do you—?' Rufa began, with a show of indignation.

'Please.' Edward squeezed her fingers. 'I haven't finished. I now realise what I was meant to do with all that money. You must marry me.'

The shock drove the breath from Rufa's body. She cast round for some sign that she had slipped into a crazy dream.

Edward's wary eyes left her face again. 'I don't, of course, mean you *must* marry me—I put that extremely badly. I mean that I would be . . . I would love it if you did. You're not in love with me, in the usual sense. But I think you're fond of me. I think you'd be an awful lot happier with me than with your Mr Mecklenberg.' He risked looking up at her again. 'For one thing, you'd be sure of getting Melismate sorted out.'

After the astonishment, Rufa braced herself for a declaration of passion. When it did not come she was relieved; though the relief was curiously tinged with disappointment.

He released her hand and looked directly into her eyes. 'Before you say anything, I don't want you to think I'm doing this to . . . the purpose of the offer is not to take advantage of you. This can't be about sex, Rufa. Not because you're not beautiful—which I think is obvious—but because I refuse to play your Marrying Game. I want to help you to save Melismate, but I can't do it as part of a sordid exchange for sex. Before your father died, he asked me to take care of you all. Now I see this is the way it has to be done.'

He spoke with the quiet, immovable assurance Rufa had missed so much. He was always absolutely certain, and never wrong. They were silent. Rufa was dazed, trying to work out the turmoil of her feelings. She tried to imagine being married to Edward. This was totally different from imagining being married to Adrian.

Adrian was unknown, and she had known and trusted Edward most of her life. She liked him. She liked the ordered sobriety of his life. And, in a way, she loved him, too. Gradually, Edward's staggering proposal began to dawn on her as a godsend. For the first time in years—most certainly, for the first time since the death of the Man—she would be able to drift off to sleep without worrying about her family.

Edward said, very quietly, 'Say yes, and you can stop all this nonsense about the Marrying Game, once and for all. You're very tired, Ru, and you're obviously miserable. I can't bear it any more. Tell Polly she'll have to cope with her dinner party, and let me take you straight home.'

She closed her eyes. It was as if the iron band round her heart, which had chilled her and trapped her since the day of the Man's death, had suddenly melted into air. If she drew a deep, unconstrained breath, she would soar away into the sky.

She felt weak and giddy with the relief of it. 'Yes,' she whispered. 'Yes, please.' She started to sob. The sobs had been battling to get out for months and would not be pushed back.

Edward, in the unhurried and deliberate way he did everything, stood up and came round to Rufa's side of the table. She felt him pulling her out of her chair, and firmly propelling her out of the café.

'Sorry . . . sorry . . .'

Edward wrapped his arms round her and drew her head down on his shoulder. 'It's all right,' he murmured. 'It's all over now.'

Eventually, she was able to take her wet face off his shoulder. He put a clean handkerchief into her hand.

She blew her nose. 'I think I should go back to help Polly.'

He smiled. 'I think you'd better have some more tea first.'

They returned to their table, and Edward ordered the tea. Rufa felt hollowed out and scraped clean. She had sensed the strength and depth of his love for her, and for her family. Melismate was saved.

It was nearly seven when she dashed back to Polly's flat. She had stepped through the looking glass, and the world was now entirely, enchantingly different.

Nancy morosely spooned the last bit of froth from her cappuccino. How handy, she thought, that Berry lived directly opposite a trendy coffee shop. It meant that she could watch his front door and recover from the row with Rufa at the same time. She had flounced out of Wendy's in a screaming fury, and sobbed her way through a whole packet of tissues on the tube. God, she would never have opened out to Edward, told him about her sister's aching vulnerability, if she had dreamt that he would stop the Marrying Game by marrying Rufa himself.

It was sick. It was disgusting. At the height of the row, Nancy had screamed that it was practically incest.

Her eyes smarted again. She sniffed angrily, sorry that she had spoiled her own argument by overreacting. All right, incest had been a bit strong. But Rufa only wanted to marry him, as far as Nancy could see, because he was not Adrian, and better the devil you knew. Her favourite sister, who was worth all the rest of them put together, was about to fling herself into a marriage that could only be grotesque.

There was just one way to save her. Nancy had come here for the express purpose of screwing a proposal out of Berry. Before their row, she remembered Rufa had mentioned that Polly was due at the hairdresser's this morning. That had carried her straight here, determined to seize the day. Rufa would have tried to stop her, but she knew nothing about her plan; she was driving to Melismate with Edward, supposedly in triumph.

Nancy sighed impatiently. Forty-five minutes she had been sitting here, waiting for Polly to emerge from her flat.

At last the door opened. The brisk, assisted-blonde figure of Polly appeared on the front steps, dug in her Fendi handbag for her car keys, climbed into her dainty silver Jeep, and neatly removed herself.

Action stations. Nancy left the coffee shop, walked across the road, and pressed Berry's buzzer. Her heart was beating hard.

His voice crackled out of the entryphone. 'Hello?'

'Hi, it's Nancy Hasty. Can I come up?'

'Nancy?' Berry's voice leapt up to a quavering falsetto. He cleared his throat. 'Er . . . Polly's not here, I'm afraid.'

'Oh, drat,' Nancy said. 'What a disappointment. Still, you're here. I'll pop in anyway.'

There was a short but significant silence. The door buzzed and Nancy pushed it open.

Berry was waiting for her upstairs, at the door of his first-floor flat. He was barefoot, in black jeans and an old blue sweater. She realised that apart from Christmas Eve, she had only ever seen him in his City work clothes . . . dark suit, tie, cuff links, hard collar. Without these, and with his tousled hair falling over startled deer's eyes, he looked absurdly young and extraordinarily sexy. Nancy's spirits rose.

'Hi.' He was tense and anxious. 'Polly's at the hairdresser's.'

She firmly kissed his cheek and pushed past him into the flat. 'Highlights, is it? Poor thing, she'll be gone for ages. How very tiring, to have roots that need so much attention.'

He hovered, visibly trying to control a rising agitation. 'Would you . . . er . . . like some coffee?'

'Not yet.' Nancy sank into the sofa and slipped off her shoes. 'It's actually you I came to see. It's a delicate matter. Not the kind of business I can settle with Polly around. Now, sit down. You're making me nervous.'

'Sorry.' Berry lowered himself cautiously onto the sofa. 'Business?'

'You'll never guess,' Nancy said. 'So let's cut to the chase. I popped round to fuck the daylights out of you.'

Berry whispered, 'Oh God—'

She leaned across the sofa, unhooked his glasses and kissed him on the mouth. He submitted as if in a trance. His arms went round her. He sighed tremulously into her lips and pulled her against him. They kissed rapturously.

Gently, he pushed her away. Nancy began to unbutton her cardigan.

'No,' Berry said breathlessly.

'Mmm—want me to keep it on?'

'Yes. I mean, yes. I do.' His voice gathered force. Painfully, he scrambled for his glasses and stood up. 'We mustn't—I can't.' He sounded as if he were trying to convince himself. 'Nancy, I can't do this.'

'What?' Nancy was astounded. 'Are you saying you don't want sex with me?' Nobody had ever not wanted sex with Nancy. 'Don't be silly.' She sat upright, her voice sharpening. 'Of course you do.'

Distractedly, he raked his hair into Stan Laurel peaks. 'Nancy, for God's sake, please don't make it harder for me.'

'What's the problem?'

'Stop it. You know perfectly well. I'm not saying that if I'd met you sooner, or in another life . . . God, I'm babbling.' He was gathering dignity with every word. He stood straighter, and squared his shoulders. 'Because I'm going to marry Polly.'

Nancy stared at him. 'But you don't love her nearly as much as me!'

'I do love her.' Berry said fiercely. 'I love her far too much to cheat on her. I can't even think of it. I couldn't live with myself afterwards.'

He meant it. The world darkened around Nancy, as the truth sank in.

Rufa had been right. Here was a rare man who valued other things besides sex. He could not be seduced, and would never be persuaded to marry Nancy, which meant that Rufa would certainly ruin her life by marrying Edward. She drew in a breath and exhaled it in a loud sob.

'Nancy . . . oh my God . . .' She felt Berry's tentative hand on her arm.

'It's not you,' she gasped. 'It's everything . . . everything bad that's happened to us . . . if he hadn't done it, things would all be the same—'

'Hadn't done it? Oh God, you mean your father.'

The cushions beside her sagged under his weight. He put his arm round her and she found herself sobbing into his shoulder. She wept for what seemed ages. He did not speak, but stroked her back gently, in a way that was deeply comforting. Eventually, she pulled herself away from him. 'Sorry. I'm a stupid cow. Don't worry, I'll go now.'

'Don't go yet,' he said kindly, walking towards the kitchen. 'I'll make some coffee. How do you like it?'

'Black, three sugars, please. Strong enough to blow a safe.'

'Righto.' He dug in his pocket for a handkerchief. 'Have this.'

He went to the kitchen. Nancy curled on the sofa, feeling an utter fool. When he came back with the coffee, she had rallied a little.

'Berry, you are nice. I'm so sorry for ruining your Saturday morning.'

'You haven't. Honestly.'

'I'm having one of those days when everything looks bloody, that's all.

Usually, I have an incredible capacity to ignore it.' She sipped her coffee. 'Did Ru tell you about her engagement?'

'Yes, and it was rather a shock. We assumed that she and Adrian—'

'This is far worse,' Nancy said. 'This is a catastrophe.'

Berry offered her a plate of croissants. 'Have one of these. Why is it a catastrophe?'

'Oh, come on. Edward Reculver, of all people. Don't you think it's disgusting?' Nancy bit angrily into a croissant.

'No,' Berry said. 'I like Edward. Rather more than Adrian, actually. And to see Rufa's face, when she came back with him—well, it was too obvious for words. She was radiantly happy.'

'She's not happy,' Nancy said, through a mouthful of croissant. 'She only thinks she is.'

Berry smiled. 'Well, isn't that enough?'

'You don't understand her. Nobody does, because she looks so capable. She's been totally bonkers since the Man died. In fact, we all have.'

Berry said, 'You love Rufa a lot, don't you?'

'Ru's my right arm. I can't bear that he's taking her away.' Nancy willed herself not to start crying again. 'I can't believe I've blabbed all this out to you. The ghastly truth is that I came here with the dotty idea of making you marry me, so Ru wouldn't have to go through with it.'

Alarm flashed across Berry's face for a moment, then he smiled. 'And you were going to stick me with the bills for mending your house?'

'I'm afraid so, darling. And the debts. You've had a lucky escape.'

'So have you,' he said, laughing softly. 'I couldn't have afforded you.'

Nancy was startled. 'Don't be daft. I've seen pictures of your house!'

'I thought you, of all people, would know what big, posh houses cost to run. Most of my father's money goes straight back into the estate. It won't be my problem until I inherit—and, thank God, my father is exceptionally hale and hearty. He's giving me a house, when I get married. Otherwise, I have to work, like everyone else. And I don't earn enough to save Melismate.'

'But . . .' Nancy was bewildered. 'The way you live? This flat?'

'This? It's Polly's.'

'Oh.' Nancy started laughing. He laughed too. They laughed until they almost wept.

Berry went to the kitchen to make another pot of coffee.

'You've been an angel,' she said, when he returned.

He grinned shyly. 'Rubbish.'

'You have—I can practically see your wings. Old Waltzing Matilda is a lucky girl, and I hope she knows it.' She sighed gustily and reached for another croissant. 'I'm glad you're not as filthy rich as we thought—it makes you less likely to end up with a gold-digging bitch like me.'

'You're not a bitch, Nancy,' Berry said, reddening. 'You were doing it to help Rufa—but I still don't see why you're so against Edward,' he said, in a firmer voice. 'I think he's terrific. That night he rescued my car keys, he told me how much he loved you all.'

'Did he?' Nancy's sore eyes filled with yet more tears. 'So you think I'm too hard on him?'

'Yes. I think he loves your sister very much.'

Silence fell.

Nancy blew her nose again with finality, like a full stop. 'I'd better start mending a few fences.'

Chapter Seven

SPRING HAD COME to the soft countryside around Melismate, scattering bluebells and pale primroses in pockets of woodland, and tufts of green across the raw brown fields. The broom was out, and there were banks of waxen yellow daffodils. The air that rushed through the open window of Edward's Land Rover smelt of damp soil and young grass.

Rufa, now officially his fiancée, was in the passenger seat beside him. The change in the weather was appropriate, she thought, for the first day in this new era of her life. She wanted the world to look different, as proof that a happy ending was in sight.

She still felt angry with Nancy. Her sister had been out until the small hours, working at her bar and then carousing at a Soho club with Roshan. Rufa had broken the news of the engagement this morning. She had been unprepared for Nancy's outrage, taking it for granted that her sister would be pleased. Nancy's disgusting accusations had made Rufa furious. Apart from anything else, the sheer ingratitude took her breath away. Didn't she realise what Edward was doing for them?

But she would not sustain her indignation. The truth was that she was desperate for Nancy's approval. Nancy was her favourite sister, and as necessary to her as salt. Her absence took the gloss off Rufa's triumphant homecoming.

Edward glanced aside at her, trying to puzzle out her mood.

Somehow, before reaching Melismate, the two of them had to step into their new roles as lovers. Edward could not see how they were to do this. Rufa had not guessed—he had been unable to tell her—how passionately she was loved. It was still surprising to Edward; it was only after their quarrel, when he had stayed up all night wrestling with his anger, that he made this great discovery. For the past six years, since his return to the farm, he had been living out the private drama of being in love with Rufa, who in the time he had been living abroad had grown up to be a tall, grave and disturbingly beautiful young woman. It had fed all his relations with the family, like an underground stream.

Their situation was ridiculous, he thought. They were engaged, but if they were ever to be real lovers, he now had to begin the process of courting and winning her. And God alone knew how he was to do that, when he had such a terror of seeming to force her, though he wanted her desperately.

He had, he realised, lost the language of sexual courtship. I'm calcified by loneliness, he thought; it's turned me into a statue. I don't know how to set about showing this girl I'd die for her.

He cleared his throat. 'Are you all right?'

Rufa, turned to him, smiling. 'Fine.' When they spoke, normality reasserted itself.

'You're not fine,' he said. 'Is it me?'

'No, of course not.'

'Is it Nancy?'

Her silence told him he was right.

'I was under the impression,' he said, 'that I would be driving Miss Nancy today. Am I to take her absence personally?'

Rufa had her meditative, inward look, which he recognised as anger. 'She's in one of her tempers. We had a massive row.'

'About me, I suppose. About you marrying a superannuated old fart.'

'Well, yes. But she'll calm down.' Rufa said this forcefully, willing it to be true. 'She usually does in the end.'

Edward gripped the steering wheel aggressively, swallowing his intense annoyance. Nancy had all the Man's faults, he decided, and precious little of his charm. Rufa's feelings, however, were his chief consideration. He had been alarmed by the chasm of pain that had opened up in her yesterday, when he proposed. She was not as self-possessed as people thought. Thinking of this reassured him. He was doing the right thing; he was not taking advantage. She needed him.

'I don't suppose your Mr Mecklenberg was thrilled, either.'

She sighed. She hadn't told him yet about Adrian's reaction. 'No, he wasn't, though he wouldn't let me explain. He just gave me an icy look and said that you were a lucky man.'

'Well, you've done it now.'

'Yes.' She was drifting back into silence.

Edward asked, 'Do you mind if we stop off at the farm on the way?'

'I'd love to.'

He kept his stern eyes on the road. 'You might think about what needs to be done there. The outside's in good nick, but the inside hasn't been touched in twenty years.'

'Don't let me change anything,' Rufa said. 'I couldn't stand the responsibility.'

'It's not a shrine.' Edward was firm. 'It's got to be your home. Our home.' He dropped this in carefully. They had not mentioned it before—that Rufa, in order to save the house she loved, must live in exile. He felt brutal for pointing it out, and half expected her to protest.

She smiled. 'OK, but nothing fancy. I like the farm as it is. It reminds me of your mother.'

'She'd be terrifically pleased about this,' Edward said.

'Only if I make you happy.'

'You will.'

'I hope so—I mean, I hope there's something in it for you. I'd hate it if marrying me was just another example of your doing something kind.'

Here was his cue to assure her that there was everything in it for him, because he adored her. And all he could manage was, 'I don't go and marry people in the way that I fix drains.'

He turned the car off the road, down the narrow track that led to the farm. They halted in front of the plain, square, trim Georgian house that had not changed since Rufa's childhood.

She got out of the car and stood gazing at her new home. Edward was surprised to see how happy she seemed: eager and determined to be pleased. He unlocked his front door. There was a pile of mail on the mat. He stooped to pick it up, then went across the broad, tiled hall to the drawing room. Rufa followed obediently, like a visitor.

In his army days the house had been let to tenants, while he and Alice had mostly lived abroad. It still had an impersonal feel. There were no traces of Alice except for two photographs in silver frames on the chimneypiece. One was of Alice outside their house in Germany. In the other, she was holding her baby nephew Tristan, son of her half-sister. Rufa looked at these, then looked away. Light-headed with the longing to touch her, Edward wrapped his arms round her.

For the smallest fraction of a second, Rufa tensed defensively. A quarter-second later, she smiled again, and relaxed against him in the old friendly way, but it was enough. He released her gently. She was not ready. It horrified him that she might think of sex with him as a duty. Too many ghosts. He saw Alice, faded to sepia, quietly leaving and closing the door behind her. It was too soon. They both needed more time.

He said, 'Do you want some tea?'

She was grateful, which was awful. 'I'll make it.'

'Thanks. There's a carton of long-life milk in the larder.'

Rufa went to the kitchen. Edward heard her opening doors, humming to herself. He sat down on the sofa to open his letters.

She brought the tea things in on a dented tin tray, decorated with a worn picture of a Scottie dog, which she had coveted as a small child. She handed him his tea, and settled contentedly against his leg—the unthinking physical contact moved him deeply, and increased the distance between them.

'Isn't this lovely?' she said. 'It feels like we've been married for ages.'

'Well, here's to the latest Russian play,' Rose said, holding her fourth glass of champagne up to the bleary light. 'The one where Rufa Rufusova marries the elderly neighbour to save the orchard.'

'He's not elderly, but you can say anything you like now,' Rufa said calmly. She was moving between the range and the kitchen table, assembling a lavish supper. She had made Edward take a detour to the supermarket in Cirencester on the way, knowing there would be nothing at Melismate. 'I don't care—as long as you're civil to him when he's here.'

'Come on—wasn't I the very pink of politeness? Weren't we all?'

Rufa said, 'You know what I mean.' There was steel beneath her serenity. She was alone with her mother for the first time since her triumphal return. Edward had wisely lubricated the homecoming with a dozen bottles of champagne. Even so, Rufa had sensed that her mother and sisters did not protest only because they were too limp with amazement. It had been a relief when Edward went home, leaving her here. Now they could talk openly, and have a screaming row if necessary.

Rose, slouched in her drinking chair beside the range, watched Rufa narrowly. 'Daughters are the most puzzling creatures,' she said gloomily. 'How can you possibly be happy?'

'Mum, for the last time, please believe me.' Rufa turned to face her, so that Rose could see she meant it. 'I'm happier than I've been in ages. I feel as if a great weight has been lifted off my shoulders.'

'Darling, that weight wasn't for you to carry.'

'Look, I love Edward very much, and I'm radiantly happy,' she said. This absolutely had to be true, and therefore was. Rufa did love Edward, in the sense of being deeply fond of him, dependent on him, anxious to have his good opinion. She was sorry she had not been prepared when he put his arm round her at the farm. He had backed off too quickly, she thought. It was difficult, when both of you felt you were play-acting at being in love.

'Why can't you just accept it, and start looking forward to the future?'

'I've lost the art,' Rose said. 'The future always looks shitty to me.'

'It's going to be heavenly. I'm so excited.' Rufa squeezed lemon over plates of smoked salmon. 'Edward says he'll bring over a friend of his who's a structural engineer, to decide what major work needs to be done—the foundations, the roof, the west wall—'

Rose groaned. 'Spare me.'

'I'm sorry if it bores you,' Rufa said, with a hint of sharpness.

'It's not the plans for the house I mind,' Rose said. 'The Man would have been thrilled.'

Rufa ground black pepper over the salmon. 'I wish we'd been able to save the house when he was alive. It might have changed everything.' She had tried to make her voice sound casual, but it cracked.

Rose said, 'It wasn't really because of the house.'

'Because of everything it stood for, then.'

'No, there was more.' Rose was finding it easier to talk about the Man with resignation, if not detachment. 'Lost looks, lost years. Hitting fifty was dreadful for him. He couldn't roll back time.'

'All the same, I wish time did roll back.' Rufa's voice cracked again.

Rose swallowed a twinge of anger with the Man. Though she had barely admitted it to herself, she read selfishness and aggression into his suicide, and despised him for it. Couldn't he have seen what it would do to his girls? Especially Rufa, his best beloved. He must have known there was a good chance that Rufa would be the one to find his body. She had been a basket case ever since. In the end, it had been very hard to believe he gave a damn about any of them.

She levered herself out of her chair, filled the kettle at the sink and banged it down on the hot plate. 'It's you I'm worried about, darling. If Edward truly is the man you want, I'll welcome the tiresome old fart with open arms.'

Rufa's face brightened. 'He is. Don't you think he's handsome, without the beard?'

'God, yes, there's no dispute about that. I must say, the pair of you look fabulous together—you'll be the best-looking couple this parish has seen in years.' Rose poured water and made tea. She took her cup back to the drinking chair. 'Well, if you're honestly happy, I suppose I am too. I can even start enjoying the un-pain. No more agonising over the debts. A mended roof over my Linnet's little head. Unlimited gin.'

At last, at last, Rufa thought. This was the reward she had been working for all along: to see the strain lifting off her mother's face.

'I wish Nancy felt the same,' she said. 'She refuses to believe I can possibly be happy. Couldn't you talk to her?'

'I could try. She won't listen, though. Leave her to come down in her own time—she's mostly hot air. God, she's like the Man sometimes.'

The door to the stairs opened. The small, airy figure of Linnet ran in, strangely bulky because the Ressany Brothers were stuffed into the front of her yellow jersey. 'Granny, are you too drunk to give me a bath?'

'Drunk? Me?' Rose stood up, gulping her tea. Rufa had noticed before that however much she had put away, Rose was always brisk and collected with Linnet. 'Certainly not. But don't you want Ru to bath you?'

'No,' Linnet said imperially. 'She's going to tell me a story afterwards.'

'Am I?' Rufa laughed. 'OK.'

'It has to be about the Ressanys. I wish Nancy was here to do the voices,' she said wistfully. 'Is she coming soon?'

'Very soon,' Rose said firmly, with a smile at Rufa. 'As soon as she's got all the hot air out of her system.'

Linnet said, 'I didn't know Nancy had hot air. Is it in her bosoms?'

Rose and Rufa, weakened by champagne, howled with laughter. The laughter had scarcely died away when the front door slammed. Out in the empty, echoing Great Hall, a high voice shrilled, 'Trotsky! Put on your saddle, we're going for a ride!'

A guttural, accented voice replied, 'Yes, Mr Ressany—'

'Nancy!' Linnet shrieked, the light flooding her face. The door between the Hall and the kitchen opened, and there was Nancy.

She knelt to embrace Linnet, and to cover her face with smacking kisses. 'Oh, my peach blossom! I've missed you so much, and I've such naughty stories to tell about the Ressanys!' She kissed the bears, through Linnet's jersey. 'What are they doing here?'

'They're not born yet,' Linnet said. 'They're going to come out as tiny new babies, and I'll have to feed them in the middle of the night.'

Rose crossed the room to kiss Nancy. 'Darling, how lovely to see you.'

Over her mother's shoulder, Nancy looked imploringly at Rufa, and mouthed, 'Sorry.'

Rufa smiled at her delightedly. 'I'm so glad you changed your mind.'

'You're just in time for my story,' Linnet said.

Nancy turned back to the little girl. 'All right. Give me a few minutes to have a cup of tea, then I'll tell you about the Ressanys' school trip to London. Ask Mummy to do your bath. I want to talk to Granny and Ru.'

Linnet considered this suspiciously, then nodded. 'All right. If you come up straight afterwards. And if Ru sings me a song.'

'Yes, yes—God, you drive a hard bargain,' Nancy said.

The moment Linnet had scampered upstairs, Nancy blurted out, 'Ru, I'm so sorry. I was an utter bitch, and I didn't mean a word of it.'

Rufa put the kettle back on the range. She was radiant. Nothing felt right when she was at odds with Nancy. 'I'm sorry too. Let's just forget it."

'Is Edward here?'

'No, he had to go back to the farm. He's coming back for supper, though—you'd better get used to it.'

'Ru, darling—I actively want to see him. I want to apologise.'

'That'll be worth watching,' Rufa said, laughing. Nancy being home made this seem like a happy ending.

Rose was wrestling with the foil of a champagne bottle. 'This is just like the bit in *Little Women* where Jo and Amy bury the hatchet, after Amy nearly drowns—'

'Shut up, you doting old crone,' Nancy said. 'Get me a drink. And a large cup of strong tea. I've had a very stressful day.'

The champagne was opened, with a festive pop. Rose handed Nancy a glassful. The three of them settled at the kitchen table.

'So,' Rose said, 'you've decided to give your sister your blessing.'

'I was crazy this morning,' Nancy said, pensively sipping champagne. 'I was so bonkers, in fact, I went straight round to Berry's and asked him to marry me.'

'You didn't! What on earth did he say?'

Nancy's smile wavered a fraction. 'I had a go at seducing him. It didn't work. You were right, Ru—he's determined to marry the Digger.' She sighed, and made a visible effort to brace her smiling muscles. 'And this is the really good bit—he's not rich enough for us, anyway. I was aiming myself at the wrong target all along.' Her smile finally gave up, and faded away. 'He was lovely. He made me coffee, and let me rant at him, and pointed out what a good egg Edward is. And then he drove me back to Wendy's. So I bunked off work, got on the train and took the world's most expensive taxi from Stroud. And here I am.'

Rufa rose to meet her future in a state of joy that was almost dreamlike. Everyone else, however, found living happily ever after rather hard work. Edward quickly made it clear that Melismate was under new management, and the days of mouldy damp blotches and howling pipes were officially over.

On the Monday after his engagement, Edward sat Rose down at her own kitchen table and bombarded her with details of builders and scaffolders, foundations and drains.

Rose did her best to keep up, but it was too much to take in all at once. Bewildered, she sipped her coffee and nibbled at the posh chocolate biscuits Rufa had laid out on a plate (on a plate!). Rufa looked as serenely radiant as the mild spring weather, but there was a formality about Edward's courtship (there was no other word for it) that puzzled Rose. At this stage of her own courtship, she and the Man had spent entire days in bed, beyond the reach of the world. Edward and Rufa were strangely visible, Rose thought. He had given her a fabulous ring, an old-fashioned hoop of whopping great diamonds, that had belonged to his mother, but otherwise you might assume nothing had changed between them. They seemed to think only about restoring Melismate.

Edward said that he would oversee the building work, while Rufa dealt with the interior. They had obviously spent hours discussing this, when normal couples would have been thrashing about under a duvet with the phone off the hook. Her attention strayed to one of the posh biscuits, which had a little picture of something engraved in the chocolate. She examined it more closely.

'Mummy—' Rufa was plucking gently at her sleeve.

'Oh, it's an elephant.' Rose laughed. 'I thought its hat was an udder.'

'Wake up, old thing,' Roger said, with his mouth full. 'He's asked you three times now.'

'Asked me what?'

The muscles of Edward's jaw were tense. 'I want to know if you can be ready to move out in ten days.'

Rose shrieked, 'What? You promised we wouldn't have to leave!'

'Just for a few weeks,' Rufa assured her, 'while the work's being done. It's going to be a huge upheaval.'

Rose was outraged. 'Where the hell are we supposed to go?'

'My mother's old cottage is empty at the moment,' Edward said. 'And pretty well ready to move into. The furniture's a bit shabby, but I'm assuming you won't mind that.'

'Well, you can assume again, because I'm not going,' Rose said hotly. 'Why does it have to be such a hassle? All we need is a spot of paint, and a bit of cement. Roger's friend Spike could do it.'

'Is Spike that unscrupulous character who covered your main fuse box with Sellotape?'

'That's right.'

Edward slammed down his pencil. 'Rose, have you listened to a single word? This house is going to fall down—quite literally—unless we take it apart brick by brick, and reassemble it from scratch.'

'This is the Man's home,' Rose said stubbornly. 'I'm letting you change it because you're marrying my daughter. But I refuse to move out.'

Roger laid a hand on Edward's rigid forearm. 'Count to ten, Ed,' he advised softly.

'No, I will not count to bloody ten!' Edward barked. 'You can camp on the lawn if you like, but you're having this house repaired properly—not by some local half-wit with a roll of Sellotape!'

The back door opened, and Linnet walked in. Ran had picked her up from school and dropped her at the gate. She was wearing a multi-coloured jersey Rufa had made, and a furry Pikachu rucksack Nancy had bought her in London. She looked round at their frozen faces. 'I heard shouting,' she said.

'Sorry, darling,' Rufa said, looking reproachfully at her mother. 'We've finished now.'

Linnet dug a dirty hand into the pocket of her jeans. Very solemn, she walked round to Edward. 'Daddy gave me fifty pence to stop being cross. I think you'd better have it.'

For a long moment, Edward stared down at the coin she had put in the palm of his hand. Then, as suddenly as he had lost his temper, he started laughing. Rufa remembered that the Man had always managed Edward by making him laugh. Satisfied with the transaction, Linnet reached for the plate of biscuits.

Edward, still chuckling, handed back the fifty pence. 'Thanks very much, Linnet, but just this once, I'll stop being cross for nothing. Sorry, Rose. I was being highhanded, wasn't I?'

'I can't get over you apologising all the time,' Rose said irritably. 'Why bother, if it's not going to change your mind about throwing me out.'

Rufa sighed. 'Mum, he's not throwing you out!'

'If you want to stop Rose being cross, it'll cost more than fifty pence,' Roger said.

This made Edward laugh again. He pushed the plate of biscuits closer to Linnet. 'We were talking about all the repairs this house needs,' he told her. 'A lot of workmen have to come, and it's going to be a terrible mess for a while—though it'll be lovely when it's finished. In the meantime, I thought everyone here could come to stay at my cottage. But Granny doesn't want to.'

'I don't either,' Linnet said promptly. 'This is where we live.'

'You could think of it as a holiday,' he suggested. 'It's a very nice house, right next to Chloe's field.' Chloe was Edward's rather elderly horse.

'And you wouldn't have such a long drive to school,' Rufa put in.

Linnet went straight over to the enemy. 'Can I ride Chloe? Will she let me comb her mane and tail?'

'She'll be only too happy,' Edward said, with a teasing glance at Rose.

It was settled, though Rose was still chafing rebelliously, and muttering under her breath. While Rufa cooked pasta shells for Linnet's tea, they began to discuss arrangements for the move.

'I wish I knew why Mummy's being so troublesome,' Rufa said later, while she and Edward were walking in the meadow.

Edward said, 'She'll come round. They all will.'

'I hate the way they treat you—as if you're the one who ought to be grateful.'

'Well, so I ought,' Edward said quietly. 'I have you.'

She turned quickly, hoping to see the tenderness of his voice reflected in his face. But he strode on steadily, eyes fixed to the horizon.

'I'm glad I got you on your own,' he said. 'I wanted to speak to you. I have to go away for a few days. To Paris.'

He made the announcement sound momentous. Rufa—surprised that he felt in any way accountable to her—murmured, 'Oh.'

'I'm seeing Prudence. Alice's half-sister. I have to tell her about us getting married. It's something that has to be done in person.' He turned to face her. 'The money aspect makes it a bit of an issue for her.'

Rufa was, distantly, alarmed. 'Why?'

In the brief silence that followed, she understood two things—first, that she had asked a difficult question, and second, that he had prepared an answer to it.

'If I died unmarried, her son would have inherited everything I've been planning to spend on your house.'

'But that's totally unreasonable,' Rufa said, 'surely.'

'Not totally.' He paused. 'It's not just the money. Pru's loaded with money. The fact is, she and I have a bit of a history.'

'You mean you had an affair with her.' There was no reason why this fact should chill her blood. Rufa fought down her paranoia. There were a million things she wanted to ask—starting with 'Did you love her?'—but she did not feel she had the right.

'It happened the year after Alice died,' Edward said sternly. 'We both missed her. And since Prudence had just got divorced, it seemed natural. Maybe it was all too easy. I began to think I might be falling in love with her—but then it finished.'

'Oh,' Rufa said. Her voice was pregnant with unspoken questions.

'She fell in love with someone else. It wouldn't have worked out, in the long term. But it does mean I have to tell her properly about you. I owe her that much. Do you understand?'

'Of course I do.'

'I knew you would. While I'm in Paris you can go back to London for a few days, start choosing wallpaper, and so forth. I think,' Edward said carefully, 'that we could both do with a few weeks' grace.' He did not want to talk about Prudence. Rufa sensed his annoyance when she asked questions. He made her feel that her curiosity was indecent. She tried not to worry that the unknown woman had already taken the best of him.

Selena took her head out of her book long enough to announce that she refused to live in Edward's cottage. 'What am I supposed to do there? Why can't I go to London and stay with Wendy?'

'I thought you'd be going back to school,' Rufa said. 'Mrs Cutting said you were her star pupil.'

'Bum to school. If you make me go back, I'll burn the place down,' she said, stubbornly shooting out her studded lower lip.

Rose said she was not letting Selena loose in London. 'You're seventeen years old, and you've never seen a town bigger than Stroud—you must think I'm crazy.'

'Ru and Nancy could keep an eye on me,' Selena said. 'They'd make sure I don't get knocked up, or start selling heroin.'

Rose had expected Edward to support her, but he was on Selena's side. 'Why shouldn't she see something of London? Ru will be there, and you know what a fusspot she is.'

'I am not!'

Rose laughed. 'You're right. With Ru around, it'll be just like a convent. And I must say, it'll be nice to have a holiday from Selena. She only raises her head from that bloody book long enough to sneer at us.'

Rufa was the soul of familial duty, and agreed to return to London with both Nancy and Selena. In her heart of hearts, she did not relish the prospect. She felt she had lost the plot with Selena when the girl had changed from an amusing child to a sullen adolescent.

Edward had a way of being right about things, Rufa reflected. Perhaps Selena did need the experience of London, to blast her back into the land of the living. She was ashamed of her reluctance. It was not fair to blame Selena for making her feel uneasy, when she knew the real cause of her unease was Edward himself. During her week at Melismate, he had taken her out to dinner at charming old manor houses. He had taken her on very grown-up dates, to concerts and plays in Cheltenham and Bath, as if they had been a couple for twenty years. Yet still he demanded no kisses or embraces. He was, she decided, too punctilious to let her feel that sex was an obligation.

She returned to London, her victory a little tainted by the doubts. Shameful as it was, sex with Edward would have made her triumph more secure. Jonathan had been her only lover. Somewhere at the core of herself, she was still paralysed, or frozen.

On her second morning at Wendy's, a special messenger arrived with a large cardboard box. It was lined with damp cotton wool, and densely packed with bluebells from the little wood behind Edward's house. They filled the kitchen with the sappy oozings from their pale stems.

There was a soggy card with them. 'I Love You. E.'

Rufa saved this carefully, wishing she could wring the love out of it to warm away the fear.

Wendy was delighted to clear her remaining bedroom for Selena. As far as she was concerned, the youngest Hasty was the family baby for all time. Selena, wrapped in the eternal book, silently chomped her way through packets of Jammy Dodgers. Occasionally she stowed the current book in her rucksack, and disappeared for hours.

She never said where she was going, and Rufa worried endlessly.

Nancy said, 'Stop fussing, Ru. She's probably met someone—and I say good luck to her.'

Rufa said, 'Anything might happen to her. She acts tough and street-wise, but she's only seventeen.'

In fact, Selena was leading a blameless life. Between bouts of reading and eating, she was steadily indulging her passionate and un-Hastyish craving for culture. Shuttling round the city in the warm, sooty tube, Selena worked down her list of essential places to see.

She went to Dr Johnson's house, Keats's house and the British Museum. She wandered round the Inns of Court and the alleys of Clerkenwell. She examined the Wallace Collection and the V & A. She attended a series of baroque concerts at St John's Smith Square. It was more than blissful. Everything mattered so intensely, she felt she needed three more lifetimes to absorb it all.

Selena had always been addicted to books. After the death of the Man, the magical, bodyless realm of the mind had been her only refuge. The physical world was dark, and horribly fragile. Literature was eternity. Selena could not make Rufa see that schoolwork was a monstrous intrusion. She wished they would all get off her case.

To Rufa's surprise, however, Selena was markedly less surly with Roshan. He had read English at Cambridge, and dared to interrogate her about her reading, coaxing her out of her spiky shell. For the first time Selena had the intoxicating experience of trying out her opinions. Rufa prayed he would sell her the idea of university. He managed, before Selena had been in London a week, to remove the studs and dreadlocks, which he despised on the grounds that they were 'provincial'.

Without the facial armour, and with her dark blonde hair shorn close to her skull, Selena was suddenly as graceful as a swan, and looked ridiculously young. Rufa heaped her with new clothes, taking her transformation as a sign that her shattered family was finally pulling itself together. Roshan assured her that Selena was 'seriously clever', and she allowed herself to dream of her little sister at Cambridge.

Unfortunately for Rufa's dreams, however, Selena found herself a career. On one of her wanderings round the National Gallery, she was caught by a 'spotter' from a model agency. Her long, skinny body proved to be a perfect hanger for clothes; her brittle, thin-boned face photographed like a dream. In a shockingly short space of time, she was pulled into a vortex of studios and magazine offices, photographed for the cover of *Vogue*, and dazzled by the promise of future riches.

'God, the irony of it all,' said Nancy. 'There we were, working round the clock to marry money—and there it was all along, right in our own back yard. We could have sent Selena out to work and stayed at home.'

Rufa murmured, 'I'm so glad I didn't have to marry for money, in the end.' Yet only after she had said it did Rufa realise how true this was. If Edward suddenly lost all his money she would be devastated, but she would never be able to let him go. In some way she did not quite understand, she was bound to him.

They were suddenly face to face, on the narrow strip of pavement outside the Coffee Stores in Old Compton Street.

'My God, Rufa,' he said. 'Rufa Hasty.'

He seemed smaller and shabbier, and altogether diminished. Rufa, breathless with the shock of finding herself in the middle of a fantasy she had outgrown, stared at his untidy brown hair, slightly downturned brown eyes and thin, intense features.

'Jonathan,' she said. 'How are you?'

There had never been a moment of falling out of love with Jonathan. When he left so suddenly, Rufa had frozen right at the summit of besottedness. It had never occurred to her then that there would be a day when she could look at him like this, and know that she was cured.

Jonathan was far more shaken. 'My God,' he said again. He cleared his throat. 'What on earth are you doing in London?'

Rufa wanted to laugh. What had she ever seen in those ludicrous, quivering nostrils? 'I've just been to a fitting, for my wedding dress.'

He winced. 'You're getting married? That's great. Congratulations.'

'Thanks.'

'When's the Big Day, in inverted commas?'

'June, of course,' Rufa said. 'We're doing it all in a tearing hurry, so I can be a traditional June Bride—without the inverted commas.'

He relaxed into a laugh. 'What's his name?'

'You know him,' Rufa said. 'It's Edward Reculver.'

She thought his reaction strange—first, a flicker of alarm at Edward's name, then half-amused resignation. 'Of course. I should have guessed.'

Rufa wanted to know why he should have guessed. Jonathan was the first person who had not been surprised by her engagement.

He was smiling. In a way, he seemed relieved. 'My darling. You're as fearfully beautiful as ever. And I made such a mess of it.'

'I forgave you ages ago,' Rufa said.

'You've had other things to think about.' He laid his hand on her arm. 'I heard about your father. I'm so sorry.'

They stood in silence, paying their respects to the drama of the past.

His hand still rested on her arm. 'We're blocking the pavement. Come and have lunch with me. Then we can treat ourselves to explanations and recriminations, and tie all the ends up neatly.'

Rufa smiled. 'Like a novel.'

'I beg your pardon, not like one of mine. I'd sell far better, if I didn't have this uncommercial itch to reflect real life.'

Jonathan's novels, she thought, were quite a lot like real life, in that they were repetitive and often dull. It had taken her ages to realise that he was not a genius.

Because she was so curious about her own feelings, she agreed to lunch, and they walked round the corner to L'Escargot. They were shown to a discreet and intimate corner table upstairs. Jonathan ordered a bottle of white wine.

'Do you realise, we've never been in a restaurant together?' He rested his elbows on the table, and folded his hands under his chin. 'I couldn't have done it when we were . . . when I was in love with you. I was afraid you'd perish in the outside world, like the Lady of Shalott.'

'And you were paranoid about being spotted by your wife,' Rufa said.

'That as well, obviously.' He had the grace to look slightly ashamed. 'I really was in love with you, Rufa. Madly in love.'

'I know. I read the novel.' She could not resist gently rubbing it in. 'The end was a bit of a downer, though—why did I have to die?'

'Sorry about that,' Jonathan said. 'It was a touch of what your father would have called "Symbollocks". Seriously, were you furious?'

'Of course not. I was flattered.'

He frowned down at the tablecloth. 'I'm sorry. I know you must think of me as a complete bastard, and you're right. I'm not cut out for adultery—you were the only one.'

'Did you ever tell Harriet about me?'

'Well, yes,' he said. He looked pained. 'She would have worked it out when she read the book—so I had to do the full confession well before I'd finished it.'

'Was she angry?' Rufa asked.

'She certainly was.'

'But you made it up, didn't you?'

'Yes, in the usual way.' Jonathan reached into his breast pocket for his wallet, and flipped it open to show a snapshot of smiling children.

He had never shown her his children. Once, not long ago, the picture would have caused her agonies of shame and sorrow. Now, it meant nothing. She said, 'You've had another one.'

'That's right. The big ones are Crispin and Clio, and the baby's Oliver, the olive branch—the price of Harriet's forgiveness.'

'I think you got off lightly,' Rufa said. 'He's gorgeous.'

Their first courses, two buttery moulds of potted shrimps, arrived at the table. Jonathan stowed his wallet away protectively. They had done the foothills. It was now time to scale the main peak.

Rufa fortified herself with a sip of wine. 'Jonathan, do you mind if I ask you something? I'd really like to know what made you leave so suddenly. It was the Man, wasn't it? Something he said or did?'

'Your father?' Jonathan was taken aback. 'No. He extracted a high price for his daughter, in the shape of free drinks at the Hasty Arms. But he didn't run me out of town. That was Edward.'

'What?' She frowned.

'Didn't you know? He was fine when I first moved into his cottage,' Jonathan said. 'But when I started seeing you, he took to appearing in the cottage doorway, with a shotgun broken over one arm. One day, he came to tell me that I was a shit, that I was using you, ruining your life. He said I had twenty-four hours to fuck off out of his house, after which time he would personally tell Harriet and break both my legs.'

'*Edward* said all that?' This was fantastic, unbelievable.

'And plenty more, though he's not a man of many words. He said he refused to stand by and watch while I broke your heart.'

She stared down at her plate, trying to adjust her internal picture of her great, doomed love. 'I was blissfully happy. How did Edward know you were going to break my heart?'

Jonathan sighed. 'Do we have to go over all this?'

'Yes,' she snapped. 'You promised to tie up all the ends.'

'All right, all right.' He laid down his fork, which had a pathetic shrimp impaled upon one prong. 'Well, first of all Edward asked me if I intended to leave Harriet and the kids, and marry you.'

There was a silence. 'And you said no.'

'Rufa, please try to understand—quite apart from the children, I couldn't bear to turn my back on Harriet. I just couldn't do it.'

'So you always meant to leave me,' Rufa said coldly.

'Look, I'm sorry. I suffered too.'

Rufa took another sip of wine. Recriminations were ridiculous. 'I'm sorry too. I didn't mean to start accusing you—it's all ancient history now. And I suppose I'm relieved, in a way. I didn't enjoy blaming the Man.' Her eyes smarted. She willed them not to fill with tears.

Jonathan took a few deep breaths. His voice, when it emerged, was deliberately friendly and bracing. 'I hope I haven't made you blame Edward instead. I don't. It was obvious where he was coming from. And if I'd had my wits about me, I'd have noticed sooner.'

'Sorry—noticed what?'

'Well, that he had the major hots for you.'

Rufa whispered, 'What? No—you're quite wrong—' And as soon as she said it, she knew he was not wrong. Suddenly she saw why the Marrying Game had made him so furious.

Her face was hot. She was shocked to hear about this unfamiliar version of Edward. He did desire her, and that underground desire had escaped in a flash of searing sexual jealousy.

Jonathan lit a cigarette. 'I'm glad we got all that out,' he said. His shoulders relaxed, and he smiled at her.

'So am I. Now we can just enjoy our lunch.'

They talked about his work, his children, his house in Dulwich. Rufa smiled and prompted, encouraging Jonathan to take over the conversation. She ought to have been angry, because he had made her doubt the Man. But her main emotion was a restless, fearful excitement.

Sunlight shifted and gleamed on the surface of the moat, newly cleaned in honour of Rufa's wedding.

It was nine o'clock. Gnats and dragonflies were assembling above the glassy water, like the first guests. Rufa wandered out onto the terrace in her dressing gown. Smiling, she breathed the golden, hay-scented air. A perfect June morning. This was her last chance to savour its loveliness before the bustle indoors escalated into pandemonium.

Lydia was leaning against the lichened stone balustrade, gazing out across the gardens. She smiled as Rufa joined her. They stood in companionable silence, listening to the peckings and splashings of the two swans in the moat. These graceful creatures were a wedding gift from the Bickerstaff twins, the builders who had contracted to do the work at Melismate. One wing of the house was still swathed in scaffolding and tarpaulin. Rose had insisted on moving back the moment the water and electricity had been restored. The Great Hall, drawing room and kitchen were finished. One room upstairs had been cleaned for the putting on of bridal finery. The family were camping in the attics.

Lydia softly asked, 'Well, are you nervous, then?'

'Yes. Is that normal?'

'I was incredibly nervous,' Lydia said.

'You were incredibly young.'

'It all seemed so momentous and emotional. Magical.' She turned mournful blue eyes towards her sister. 'I hate it when people say marriage is just a worthless bit of paper. It's so much more.'

On her own wedding day, Rufa found Lydia's failed marriage wrenchingly sad. She wondered if all failed marriages carried this air of unfinished business. 'Oh, Liddy,' Rufa said gently, 'I'm so sorry, but I think walking away from Ran was the best thing you ever did.'

'I didn't want to.'

'You were miserable!' Rufa watched as one of the swans began to patrol the moat in a menacing manner. 'I wish you'd get over Ran.'

'So does he, but it's no good. I can't. He's the only man I've ever loved.'

The historic coming together of Lydia and Ran was part of family legend. Lydia had lost her heart and her virginity to Ran at the age of fourteen, when he returned from India to live at Semple Farm. Rufa had a clear memory of Lydia's wedding day. Her sheer loveliness as a bride had transcended the silliness of the event. They had all trooped off to the registry office first, and the Man had kept them in agonies of giggles. He had always mocked everything to do with officialdom.

At the main part of the ceremony, however, when Ran and Lydia had exchanged their vows in the meadow, the Man had been inconsolable. Lydia had stood barefoot in the long grass, wild flowers winding through her hair, as ethereally beautiful as an Edwardian dream-child, and promised to love Ran until the stars turned cold.

Lydia had certainly kept her side of the bargain, and still clung to the belief that Ran would come back to her. Nothing her mother or sisters said made any difference.

Very secretly, Rufa envied Lydia for embarking on marriage in such a state of certainty. She longed for a sign that Edward truly loved her. Since his return from Paris, all those weeks ago, he had been distant and preoccupied, preparing for the wedding with a kind of grim resignation that did not fit Jonathan's intriguing description of a man in the grip of wild passion. All he would say about Prudence was that their meeting had been 'difficult'. Rufa did not dare to press him for the details she longed for. The headline was that Prudence and her son—Edward's only family—were not coming to the wedding.

It might have been a sign of disapproval. Or it might have been because Prudence could not bear to see a stranger in her dead sister's place. Whatever it was, upon his return from Paris, Edward frequently disappeared into black-browed silences.

He explained that he was anxious about some business connected with his time in the army, and Rufa wished he trusted her enough to confide in her. He had saved her home, but this was not enough. She sensed something heavy on his mind, and worried that it was the prospect of marrying her.

Rufa, feeling it was only proper, had asked Clare Seal to design and make her wedding dress. Left to herself, she would have chosen something more conventional, but she had to admit that Clare had been inspired. Seeing the elegance Rufa had given to the bronze silk velvet, she had made another slender column, cut on the bias with a nod to the 1930s, in heavy white silk. It left Rufa's arms and shoulders bare, and was of a ruthless simplicity. The veil was of stiff, filmy white silk, which lay round her in crests and billows. It was held in place by old Mrs Reculver's diamond tiara, which Edward had unexpectedly disinterred from a bank vault.

Rufa stood rigidly in the gleaming Melismate kitchen, displaying her bridal finery. Her mothers and sisters stared at her, almost afraid of her white perfection. Rose was trying not to cry.

Linnet said, 'You look just like a princess.'

Rose gasped. 'What's that round your mouth?' She made a dive at Linnet and grabbed her chin. 'You've been at the chocolate! For the love of heaven, don't eat anything else till it's over, do you hear?'

Until twenty minutes ago, Linnet had been wearing pyjamas crusted with Weetabix. She was now as exquisite as a china fairy in a Kate

Greenaway dress of pale yellow silk and white kid slippers.

Rufa touched the chaplet of yellow rosebuds on the small dark head. 'You look like a princess yourself. Doesn't she?'

'Better,' Nancy said. 'Real princesses would be jealous.'

Nancy wore a clinging but essentially sober dress of dark gold silk, and a black cartwheel of a hat. Selena—down for two days between photoshoots—had appeared in a short skirt and skimpy silk cardigan of pale blue. Her cropped hair was now silver-white, and Rose could not get over her elegant otherness. Selena revealed very little about her mysterious new life, but it appeared to suit her. She had a new coolness and detachment, and regarded them all with distant amiability, as if through the wrong end of a telescope.

Lydia was a hedge-creature who cared not what raiment she put on. Rufa had bought her a trailing purple dress from Ghost. She refused a hat, and wore her long curls loose. Rose was unrecognisable, and surprisingly pretty, in a dress and broad-brimmed hat of spotted navy silk. For the first time in years, she had put on make-up.

'OK, girls. Time to scramble.' Roger, in a hired grey morning suit, appeared at the door. 'The cars are here, and I swore to Edward we wouldn't be late.' He was to give Rufa away. To honour the occasion, he had cut off his ponytail.

'Rose, Nancy, Liddy and Selena in the first car,' Roger said. 'Ru, Linnet and I will follow exactly ten minutes later. Get a move on—Edward's timing me with a stopwatch.'

Rose stared again at Rufa, then leaned forward to give her a delicate kiss. 'You look stunning. The Man would have been so proud of you.'

Rufa asked, 'Would this have pleased him?'

'Yes, when he'd had time to think about it,' Rose said. 'He loved Edward. He wouldn't have let anyone else catch you.'

'Come down, O love divine,' Berry sang. 'Seek thou this soul of mine—'

People often had this one at weddings. In just under three weeks, everyone would be singing it at his own wedding. The reality had not hit him, until he saw the transformation of Rufa. What power a wedding dress gave to a woman, he thought. It was the oddest mixture of the sacrificial and the triumphant. He hoped he would look as splendid as Edward, but did not think he would cut such a commanding figure in morning dress. Edward stood ramrod straight, his eyes burning into Rufa's. But he was controlled enough to flash a grin at Linnet.

Berry thought Linnet looked scrumptious. He surprised himself by thinking how extraordinary and wonderful it would be, if he ever had a little girl of his own. No wonder Ran drivelled on about fatherhood—it was the only thing he had ever done properly.

Polly turned to smile at him. Berry felt fond of her, and very proud that he had had the strength of mind to resist Nancy. He squeezed Polly's hand in an affectionate and husbandly manner.

Yes, he was looking forward to the peace and certainty of being married to Polly. They would have a magnificent wedding, then Polly would set the rest of his life running on oiled casters to the grave. Certainty was a blessing. Everything else was an illusion.

For Rufa, the rest of the day was a series of snapshots from a dream. She spoke her vows, and signed the book in the vestry. Edward was her husband. She posed for photographs outside the church, clinging to his arm. Hundreds of people, including the vicar, kissed her.

Wendy, incoherent with happiness, threw biodegradable confetti. She wore a purple velvet hat, like a squashed pancake, and darted about taking photographs, getting in everyone's way. The new gravel on the Melismate drive was scrunched by the wheels of dozens of cars.

There was champagne, of course, chosen and paid for by Edward. There was a wedding breakfast which was a proper lunch (poached salmon and strawberries). There were speeches, to which Rufa listened carefully and instantly forgot. Edward's best man, an old friend from Sandhurst, told lumbering anecdotes about the army, and proposed a rousing toast to Linnet. Edward himself spoke very briefly, mainly to thank everyone for coming.

Everyone round the four long, flower-decked tables in the Great Hall took the depth of his feelings for granted. The locals studied the improvements to Melismate, and measured them against the beauty of the bride. Nobody was at all surprised that Rufa had married so well. And after the food and the speeches, there was a general spillage onto the sunny terrace for more champagne.The guests fell back into their cliques, to tell each other that the Hastys had an inborn talent for landing on their feet.

Nancy had taken off her hat and let down her hair. She and Berry had greeted each other with strained jollity, and a brief kiss that left them both blushing. They had seen each other in the wine bar since Nancy crashed into his flat, but she had avoided serving him if she could.

Polly the Perfect had not registered the blushes. She's counting the hours till her own wedding, Nancy thought dully. She had never seen the Digger looking so pretty. Polly wore a linen suit and her hat was just plain stupid; but, somehow, she shone.

Nancy supposed she wished the woman joy. Berry, of all people, deserved joy. She dared to glance at him, and caught him at the exact moment when he was sneaking a glance at her. They both reddened again, and turned their backs. The aura of failed sex around their last encounter was a permanent embarrassment. Nancy ran down the terrace steps, across the moat and out over the sweep of turf.

'Nancy—'

Max was hurrying to catch her up. She slowed down, thinking how sexy some men could look in morning dress.

'This place is fabulous,' Max said. 'I think I begin to understand your Marrying Game now. I never imagined you came from a place like this.'

Nancy laughed. 'The point is, I didn't come from a place like this. Before Ru liberated Edward's money, it was a dump.'

'I'm sure it was always beautiful,' Max said. 'As beautiful as you are.'

'Oh, get along with you.'

'I mean it. Why did you take off the hat?'

'It was in the way,' Nancy said. 'I couldn't kiss anyone.'

Max followed her into the ragged circle of shadow under the huge acacia. 'Talking of which, why haven't I kissed you yet?'

'Because you haven't been asked.' Nancy fancied Max but her insides no longer turned somersaults when his wicked eyes raked her body.

'Why haven't I been asked?' He was laughing, but the question was serious. 'We had something brewing at one time, you and I.'

'Yes, but other things kept getting in the way.'

'You were chasing your Lord Whatsit. But you don't have to do that any more.' Max leaned against the tree. 'Now that your sister has effectively won the Marrying Game, you can go back to playing for love.'

'I wish it was that simple,' Nancy said.

His voice softened. 'So, what are you going to do with yourself now? Come home to the ancestral pile?'

'Don't be silly. I have to be back behind the bar on Monday.'

Max was thoughtful. 'Is it such a great job?'

'Best I ever had.'

'And the only place you get to see him.'

Nancy groaned. 'God, am I that obvious?'

'Glaring. It seems that Cupid's little arrow has at last found a chink in your tough hide. You've gone and fallen in love with your target.'

'Yes,' Nancy said, 'I think that's what this must be. I think this is what being really in love is like. It's the difference between *Romeo and Juliet* and a musical comedy.' She sighed. 'And it feels rather shitty, darling. Especially when he's about to marry someone else.'

He smiled at her. 'I wouldn't totally bet on it. He hasn't taken his eyes off you for a second. Send him a rope ladder as a wedding present.'

'Not a hope,' Nancy said sadly. 'You haven't met Polly. She's had him electronically tagged. No power on earth will loosen her grip.'

Polly now knew what she had sometimes suspected. She had never been properly in love before. At some point during the service, she had slipped into another dimension.

His name was Randolph Verrall. He wore a foolish suit and his hair was far too long. He was being shadowed by a droopy ex-wife and her beady child. None of this was relevant. Polly had been swimming in Ran's black velvet eyes since Berry had introduced them.

'Careful,' Ran said.

They were walking round the moat, away from the noise of the reception, and the haunting presence of the ex-wife. Ran took her hand, to steady her. She felt the contact hit her, like a rush of electricity. She murmured, 'This is the most disturbingly beautiful place I've ever seen.'

'Ridiculously romantic,' Ran said. 'There ought to be a law against it.'

They halted, still hand in hand. The two swans paddled past majestically, their long necks arching and twining.

'The moat was two inches deep and choked with weeds a month ago,' Ran said. 'It stank so much they had to keep the windows shut.'

'Of course,' she said, 'you know them all terribly well. You were married to one of them.'

Ran said, 'How could I help it? I was the boy next door.'

Polly shivered a little, because Ran's warm fingers still held her hand. 'Did you fall in love with them all?' she teased.

Ran, however, considered the question seriously. 'I fancied the older ones, but that all stopped when I got it together with Liddy. Women change when you marry their sisters. They turn into harpies.' His great eyes were tragic. 'Nancy chucked a dustbin at me once.'

Polly asked, 'Why? What had you done?'

'I fell in love. That's the only crime I ever commit.'

Breathlessly, Polly stated, 'Falling in love is never a crime.'

'Do you think so? I wish Liddy would see it.' Ran heaved a sigh. 'We turned into a habit. The bond is eternal, but there's no more music.'

'Music?' Polly was mesmerised.

'The music two people hear when they fall in love. Listen!'

They were silent for a long moment.

'Violins,' whispered Polly.

'A fanfare,' Ran said, his mouth moving towards hers. Their lips met.

Polly caught the bouquet, and Lydia began to leak tears. Berry might not have noticed anything, but she had seen the hormonal storm clouds gathering round the angelic form of her ex-husband. He was falling in love again. She knew the signs.

Rose knew them too. With a sigh of resignation, she collapsed into the chair beside the range and eased off her new shoes.

'Have a cup of tea,' Roger suggested tenderly. 'You're knackered.'

They were alone, in the chaos of bleary glasses and empty bottles. The caterers were clearing away in the Great Hall. Nancy and Selena had dragged Lydia up to the old nursery, for red wine, consolation and bracing advice. Linnet was asleep on the new sofa in the drawing room.

'It went all right, didn't it?' Rose asked.

'Brilliantly. Edward even thanked me. Nothing to worry about.'

'And Ru's OK, isn't she?'

'I'd say so.' He handed Rose a mug of tea. 'Wouldn't you?'

'I don't know,' Rose said wearily. 'She swears she's happy. I have to take her word for it.'

'**Y**ou'd better change,' he said, hearing the dryness of his own voice and cursing himself for it. 'The traffic won't be too bad, but we ought to leave plenty of time.' Owing to what Edward described as 'a slight balls-up on the booking front', they were driving straight to the airport, to catch their flight to Italy. He thought it was probably just as well. His blood raged to make love to Rufa, but while they were in his house there was too much awkwardness to work through first.

He had chosen the villa in Tuscany because it was the most obviously romantic backdrop he could imagine. Somehow, in the space of a few hours, he had to shake off the image of faithful family friend, and transform himself into a lover. He was alarmed by the distance that must be travelled before they could reach the right level of intimacy.

He took an envelope from his breast pocket. 'I nearly forgot. Nancy told me to give you this.'

Rufa took it from him. The envelope said: 'Mrs Rufa Reculver. Don't open this until you are at home.'

Inside was a Polaroid photograph of a row of bare bums. Nancy, Lydia and Selena—their best wedding clothes bundled untidily round their waists—were doing low Japanese bows away from the camera. Underneath was written: 'Full moon tonight!'

Rufa laughed till she cried. Then she did cry. Tears spilled from her eyes. She buried her face in Edward's shoulder, suddenly shaking with sobs. He put his arms round her, and felt the love she had for him, trying to beat its way through the barrier of the bargain they had made. He felt strong, and strangely peaceful.

'It's all right,' he whispered.

'I'm so sorry. I'm sorry about everything.' She pulled away from him. 'The thing is, I do love you. I haven't told you properly.'

'You don't have to.' He pulled out a handkerchief and put it into her hand.

She laughed dismally. 'You're always having to find me hankies.'

'Well, I'll find you as many as you want.'

She mopped her eyes. 'It wasn't just about the money, you know.'

'Are we talking, by any chance, about your infamous Marrying Game?' Edward was smiling, a little grimly.

'Yes.'

'Hmm. The general consensus seems to be that you played an absolute blinder.'

'Please don't joke about it. Until you asked me, I hadn't really admitted how wrong it was, though I sort of knew deep down.' Rufa was struggling for words. 'I probably would have married Adrian, and been miserable. But then you came along, and saved me.'

Edward did not like the avuncular, Father Christmas image of himself as family Saviour, but he could not help being touched by her faith in him. He circled her waist with his arm, manfully ordering his erection to subdue itself until they were several hundred miles outside Gloucestershire, and led her to the window. The night was clear, hung with stars. There were bars of moonlight across the lawn.

'Perhaps you saved me, too,' he said gently. 'If you hadn't dreamt up your Marrying Game, I'd have been trapped in my old life, rapidly turning into a grey-bearded, barmy old git.'

'You might have married someone else.'

'I didn't, though, did I? Because I happened to be in love with you.'

She whispered, 'Did you . . . did you love me before we had that row?'

He could tell this question was crucially important to her. Mentally he shuffled the pack of truth cards, to find a configuration that would not alarm her. 'It's not as simple as that. My life came to a standstill when I left the army. Without that to hold me together, I found I was still grieving for Alice. I wasn't in a position to fall in love with anyone. Your Marrying Game forced me to take action, when I thought nothing on earth could. I'd never have married you—or anyone—without it.'

She had stopped crying. 'Honestly?'

'Honestly. Whether I admitted it to myself or not, I realised I've loved you for years.'

'Did you?'

'Oh God.' Edward was laughing softly to himself. 'I don't believe it. I've never actually spelt it out to you.' He held her face between his palms. 'Rufa, you're the most beautiful woman I've ever seen. Even with make-up running down your face.' Smiling, he wiped the smudges under her eyes with his thumbs. 'All the times I've watched you—whether you've been happy, or sad, or angry—I've never seen one mood of yours that made you anything but beautiful. Your soul shows in your face. And that's beautiful too.'

He was deeply moved to see how eagerly Rufa drank in his tribute.

'Then I don't need to worry that you're sorry you married me.'

Sorry? He wished to God he had the words to tell her that his happiness was almost too great to comprehend. 'I wish I knew how to stop you being so anxious, Ru. What are you afraid of?'

'I don't really know.' She searched for an answer. 'Of not being good enough for you, perhaps. I still think you deserve something better.'

He smiled down at her. 'Then it's up to us to build something better. The real Marrying Game is only just beginning.'

PART TWO

Chapter One

'HER NAME'S POLLY,' Linnet said. 'I call her Smelly.'

Rufa tipped fat beads of rice into her new kitchen scales, doing her best to swallow an unholy snort of laughter. 'She's not that bad.'

'Yes she is. She's as smelly as a fart. She keeps whispering with Daddy.'

Linnet was dismissive. Though she never approved of Ran's girl-friends, she seldom lost much sleep over them—they came and went too frequently. Rufa was glad she had not yet noticed that this affair seemed to be far more serious. 'Look on the bright side,' she said, 'Polly might persuade Daddy to buy a television.'

Ran thought television was the new opium of the people, used by the government for mass brainwashing; but Rufa could not see Polly surviving a child in the house without one.

'Might she?' Linnet's face was inscrutable as she considered this. Then she became brisk. 'Can I watch some now?'

'All right. As long as you don't make a fuss when it's time to go home.'

'I won't.' Linnet jumped from her chair and scampered along the stone passage to the drawing room of Edward's house.

Ran had dropped his daughter off at the farm. He had stuck his head out of the car window long enough to shout, 'Hi, Ru—hope you had a nice honeymoon—can't stop—I expect you've heard about Polly.'

Rufa had heard. She and Edward had returned from Italy at eleven the previous night. This morning, Rufa had found the whole country-side seething with the news: Ran had a new girlfriend, a posh blonde who had made rather a fool of herself at the village store asking for bal-samic vinegar. This blonde had left a fiancé standing at the altar, chucked in her job, and moved stacks of luggage into Semple Farm.

If Rufa had not heard it from Rose first, she would not have believed it. She had seen Ran and Polly together at her wedding, but had no idea their heated glances could have boiled over into this, in just three and a half weeks. Even Polly valued passion above good sense. She had won herself a splendid prize in the Marrying Game, and thrown it all away. What cared she for her goose-feather bed?

Rufa wished she could relearn the mysteries of passion. It must be something I'm doing wrong, she decided. With Jonathan, her only other lover, passion had been instinctive—but she now saw that she had only responded to him, without first having to win him. The Tuscan honey-moon had been paradise seen through a sheet of glass.

She had been enchanted by the hard blue skies, the hot nights ringing with crickets, the beauty that dripped from every medieval gable. They had arrived, euphoric with the sense of escape, in the afternoon of the day after the wedding. Edward seemed more relaxed than he had been for weeks. When they sat on the terrace of the villa, he had been tender with her; gentle and loving. It had seemed natural to Rufa to go ahead of him up to their shuttered bedroom. Her throat dry with anticipation, she had slipped off her dress and stretched naked under the lavender-scented linen sheet.

But Edward had not come. She had fallen asleep, and by the time she woke up, everything had changed. She had found Edward tightlipped and abstracted. His manner to her had been as considerate and courte-ous as ever, but something had upset him.

Later—in no detail at all—he had told her. Prudence, Alice's sister, had called him, and although the conversation had not been easy, they were, essentially, reconciled. What did this mean? If the news was good, why did Edward seem so anguished? Rufa did not want to consider why the woman thought she had a right to intrude on their honeymoon.

The official wedding night had been a washout. Rufa had once again gone upstairs first, and once again lain in naked anticipation under the single sheet. Edward had bewildered her by reacting with anger. He had told her no performance was necessary; he could not make love to her until he had lost the sense that he was collecting a purchase.

Rufa, numb with humiliation, had spent the night clinging to the extreme edge of the bed, muffling her sobs in the hard pillow, while Edward—forbiddingly clad in pyjamas—had slept beside her.

The following morning he had apologised very sweetly. They had spent a magical day together, strolling round a local market and eating lunch under a vine. Edward had honoured her by confiding in her. He explained that he had more than Prudence on his mind—he was engaged in a long and painful correspondence with the War Crimes Commission in The Hague, concerning his experiences in Bosnia. For the first time, he talked to her about the disillusion with soldiering that had made him leave the army. He had been fascinating, charming. Rufa had wrapped herself in his undivided attention, always so difficult to win at home. And at the end of this golden day, they had gone up to bed together, and still not made love. The tone of their honeymoon was set.

Not making love had become a routine. Night after night, Rufa had lain awake beside her husband, listening to his steady breathing. She would have worried that there was something wrong with him, or with her, if not for that one time.

The memory made her breathless. She returned to it obsessively and a little shamefully, as if clinging to the memory of a dream.

'It's a sort of local version of brandy, I'm told,' Edward said. He poured two measures of pale golden liquid, and handed one to Rufa. The scent, like the concentrated essence of a million grapes, mingled giddily with the scents of lavender and pine. They were both languid with heat and repletion after a long lazy lunch at the villa.

They sat in the shade of a big green umbrella. 'This is heaven,' Rufa said. 'Total heaven. I never want to leave.'

Edward said, 'Have some more,' and refilled their glasses.

They had been talking, as they often did, about the work still going on at Melismate. Edward was making Rufa laugh with some of Rose's dottier suggestions for improvements. The brandy flooded her senses with sweetness. She held out her glass again.

Edward, relaxed and affectionate, was laughing at her. 'Don't be silly, you're completely pickled already.'

'Why not? I never get pickled. I didn't realise it felt so lovely.'

'It makes you wonderfully mellow,' Edward said. 'At last you've stopped looking round for the next thing to do.'

Rufa sipped more brandy. She lay back against the fat calico cushions, gazing out across the patchwork of ochre and umber fields. Profound peace swirled round her—though when she moved her head, the world rocked alarmingly. It was better if she shut her heavy eyes, but she did not feel she wanted to sleep. Her body ached with tenderness. Every cell felt alive. She was dreamily conscious of her nipples brushing the inside of her silk dress, and the swollen warmth between her legs.

Edward's arms were round her. His voice was soft and teasing. 'Look at you—drunk and incapable. You'd better lie down.'

She sighed. 'I can't move.'

'You don't have to.' The world rocked again as he lifted her out of her chair and carried her across the terrace. They were both laughing. The soft mattress of the big double bed was underneath her. Distantly, she heard Edward murmur, 'Do you want me to take your dress off?'

'Mmmmm. Yes.' She could not have done it herself, if her life depended on it.

She felt his fingers, warm and firm, unfastening the buttons down her front. She felt him peel away the silk, exposing her flesh. She felt his lips on her breasts, and heard—as if from a great distance—her own shuddering sigh of longing.

And suddenly, jumping ahead several frames, he was on top of her, still fully clothed, moving inside her. Another jump ahead, and her legs were round his waist, gripping him against her. Nothing existed, beyond the delicious urgency of being fucked by him. She came, tightening round him, and he came too, rocking the bed beneath them.

Afterwards, Rufa lay watching Edward in the shadows of the shuttered room, swiftly and silently tearing off his clothes. She marvelled at the old Rufa, who had considered poor Jonathan a good lover. Edward was in another league entirely. Mesmerised, she stared at his erection, wondering how he had got such a thing inside her; faint with the desire to have him inside her again.

He made love to her slowly this time, gazing down into her face, keeping iron control until he came with a long groan of release. The room dissolved around Rufa. She lay against his chest, and slipped into a sleep of dizzy, mindless happiness.

Sighing, she pushed the memory away—but too late to avoid recalling the next day. She had woken in the early morning with a ferocious headache, and spent the entire day throwing up. Edward had been marvellously considerate. That evening, when she had recovered enough to drink camomile tea under the moon, he had quietly apologised. When she begged him to believe that no apology was necessary, he had ignored her. They had not made love again.

Rufa longed for Edward to make love to her, and had several times humiliated herself by dropping delicate hints—which he had ignored. She did not dare risk rejection by asking him outright. His spells of depression, when he would raise a black wall round himself, intimidated her too much. Though the moods had never been directed at her, they had turned him into a stranger.

He was more like himself now that they had come home, and Rufa's spirits had risen to something like their premarriage level. She had overcome her last shreds of reserve about spending Edward's money, and begun to indulge her passion for excellence. At the delicatessen in Cirencester she had bought a big lump of Parmesan, hard and chalky. She had bought a great bag of fresh, fat, purple figs, and slices of Parma ham and air-cured beef, thin as whispers. From Edward's garden she had gathered a large basin of scarlet tomatoes, and aromatic handfuls of oregano and rosemary. She was in a quiet, sunny kitchen, creating a beautiful dinner. If this was not happiness, it was surely very like it.

A door clicked across the passage. Edward came in, massaging his eyes. He had found a large pile of letters waiting for him, including one about Bosnia, which had taken most of the afternoon to answer. Rufa assumed this was the reason he looked so tired.

'Darling,' he said. He was not a great man for endearments, and when he used them, they had a special resonance.

Rufa was wary. 'What's the matter?'

'My darling, I'm so sorry. I wish to heaven I didn't have to throw this at you, but it's too late to do anything about it now. I'm afraid Prudence is about to land on us.'

'What?' Rufa could not help sounding dismayed.

He sighed. 'I know it's short notice. She didn't tell me until she was on the motorway. There's been a fire at her London flat, apparently.'

'What's wrong with her Paris flat?' Rufa snapped.

'She lent it to someone. But she won't be staying for more than a couple of days—I promise.' The look of vexation melted from his face. He smiled wryly and wrapped his arms round her, kissing her neck. 'Tristan will be impressed with my pulling power,' he said. 'He thinks I couldn't pull a muscle.'

Rufa started to laugh. 'So we're expecting the boy as well. I'd better make up the beds.'

Edward released her, with another affectionate kiss. 'It's nice of you not to be furious,' he said.

Warm from his embrace, Rufa smiled and said, 'I know.'

Polly tipped the contents of the cutlery drawer out on the scarred kitchen table. It was nasty stuff, stained and bent. She would add it all to the teetering pile of rubbish outside the back door. There was a terrifying amount of throwing away to be done before she could unpack her own immaculate kitchenware. Now that Ran had gone out to take his daughter to Rufa's, she was free to tear through his cupboards.

It would all have to go. One expected a certain amount of dilapidation in a farmhouse kitchen, but it only suited things that had been good in the first place. Everything here was shoddy, dented, buckled and grimed. If necessary, they could stay in a hotel while Semple Farm was being gutted.

And a temporary relocation might have the welcome side effect of keeping the child out of the way, until Polly had worked out how to treat her. What *did* one do with them all day, if one did not have a nanny? Linnet had spent the whole time clinging to Ran like a limpet, and looking daggers at Polly. They had not had a second to themselves.

Polly had not discussed this state of affairs with Ran. There was never time. They could not be alone together without falling ravenously on each other's bodies. Polly sighed, and stretched luxuriously. The heat made their passion more intense. Night after night they lay naked under a single sheet, moist and musky with sweat. Polly loved to lick the salty sheen on Ran's smooth skin. Ran parted her legs in the moonlit darkness. The springs in his lumpy, world-weary mattress creaked when he rolled on top of her. They became one flesh, rocking urgently towards climaxes that seemed to last for hours. Polly felt drunk with the wonder of Ran's beauty, and knew that she would never leave him.

The jilting of Berry had been ghastly, but she had made up her mind to manage it as efficiently as she managed everything else. She had made sure it was a Friday, so Berry did not have to go to work the next day with a broken heart. Before he came home, Polly had resigned from her job then booked a firm of packers for Monday morning.

By the time she heard Berry whistling outside the door, Polly had called an estate agent about putting the flat on the market. Berry did not realise it, but his home had gone before he turned his key.

Remembering the scene gave Polly pain. She had sat poor Berry down on the sofa and given him a glass of brandy. She had explained—looking bravely into his shocked, vulnerable brown eyes—that her sudden rebirth was no reflection on him. She was dreadfully sorry, but this passion was bigger than both of them.

Berry had, of course, been severely upset, but (this was something Polly refused to dwell on) in a way that was somehow not quite satisfactory. He had not cried, or begged her to stay. Mostly, he had tried hard—too hard?—to be helpful. Anyway, that unpleasantness was now history. Polly had spent all her time since then at Semple Farm, falling deeper and deeper into fathomless love.

Love had not affected her capability. Ran had to see his child, and pootle about at what he described as 'work'—for instance, taking the late plums to the farmers' market, and digging sporadically in his onion patch. Love certainly did not blind Polly to the fact that he was a useless farmer, but his renovation would come later.

The house was Georgian, and rather a gem. It could be made gorgeous—once Polly had provided Ran with more children, and the two smelly dogs were dead. She sang quietly to herself as she made plans for the future. This was a long-term project. Polly loved a challenge.

Rufa closed the kitchen door behind her, and punched Wendy's number into the phone. It was answered almost immediately by Nancy.

'Nance, hi. It's me.'

'Darling, I was hoping you'd ring. How's it going?'

'Fine. More or less. I'm making her some coffee.' Rufa, the receiver tucked into her shoulder, opened a box of posh chocolate biscuits—mostly for the look of the thing, since Prudence seldom ate anything except steamed spinach—and arranged them neatly on a china plate.

Nancy asked, 'When's she going?'

Rufa lowered her voice, though a corridor and two closed doors separated her from the drawing room. 'Not till Tuesday.'

'Why do you have to put up with her? She's Edward's responsibility.'

'He's doing his best, but he's so busy.' Rufa did not add that Edward had also become short-tempered and secretive. 'She's not all that bad, and Tristan's lovely. But she makes me realise how much I miss Wendy's. Do give them all my love.'

Nancy asked, 'Are you really OK?'

'I told you, I'm fine. How about you? Have you seen Berry lately? Is he visibly heartbroken?'

A heavy sigh gusted down the phone. 'He's gone to Frankfurt. He's taken a posting there and he won't be back for months.'

'You should follow him.' Rufa was firmer, now that she had managed to nudge Nancy onto her favourite subject. 'Get a job in a Bierkeller.'

'Don't encourage to me to make an idiot of myself,' Nancy said disconsolately. 'I have to face the fact that he was the first decent man to cross my path and I blew it.'

'Rubbish,' Rufa said bracingly. 'You wait, he'll be back. Oh God, the kettle—I must go. Speak tomorrow?'

'Ru, wait! What's up? I know something's the matter.'

All sorts of things were the matter. Glances, hints, veiled anger. But these things Rufa could not explain to Nancy.

'I'm fine,' she said. 'Bye.' She hung up.

She carried the tray of coffee to the drawing room, and was annoyed when she caught herself wondering if she should knock. This was her own house—why was she behaving like an upper servant?

Probably, she thought suddenly, because I'm being treated like one.

Prudence, in a white linen shirt and grey linen trousers, was on the sofa, leafing through a copy of *Vogue*. Her beautiful face was discreetly but perfectly made up, and she looked completely at ease. She had recently divorced her fourth very rich husband. Edward had explained that Pru's upbringing had been very different from Alice's. Their father had seduced his housekeeper, and though he never married the woman, he had lavished money and attention on their child, Prudence. If his intention was to divide the half-sisters, however, he failed. The two households, both miserable, had huddled together for warmth.

The two sisters were very different. Alice had been quiet and retiring, devoted to Edward. Prudence, who had no scruples about her father's money—or anyone else's—had chosen the exotic international lifestyle of the very wealthy.

'How lovely,' Prudence exclaimed. 'You're so sweet. I'm afraid I'm being the most frightful nuisance.'

'Not at all.' Rufa set down the tray on the low table, and knelt on the floor to pour the coffee.

'Sylvia's coffee set. I haven't seen this for years. Is that cream? Yes, I will have a little, please.'

Sylvia was old Mrs Reculver. Rufa gave Prudence a cup of coffee.

Prudence said, 'Mmm, you do everything so exquisitely. You're a paragon. No wonder Edward fell madly in love with you. The way to a man's heart, and all that.'

Rufa smiled. 'He just eats what's put in front of him. I don't think he particularly cares.'

'Oh, all men care. And life with you seems to suit him, although he does seem distracted at the moment,' Prudence mused. 'Not like my idea of a man newly returned from his honeymoon. I do hope he's all right.'

'He's fine,' Rufa said lamely.

'You know,' Prudence went on, with one of her pretty, catlike smiles, 'I might get him to talk to me when we're alone. I was always rather good at getting him to open out.'

Rufa struggled for a polite and casual way to assure her that Edward told her absolutely everything. 'He tends to clam up when there are other people in the house.'

Prudence was having none of it. 'Yes, the poor man hates expressing his feelings. It all reminds me . . . you probably don't remember what he was like after Alice died.'

'Not really.'

She scrutinised Rufa, narrowing her eyes. 'It must be odd for you, living in the shadow of your predecessor. Especially when it was such a famously happy marriage.'

'Edward doesn't talk about her much.'

'I think Alice took the best of him with her. He lost the ability to fall in love. Don't you find him a little unresponsive sometimes?'

She seemed to expect an answer. Rufa fiddled with the tray.

Prudence took her silence as affirmation. 'I suppose he's told you about his thing with me? Yes, of course—he's such a stickler for being truthful, and all that jazz. It didn't work out because I needed more warmth. More passion, if you like. I assume he *was* passionate with Alice. Although she never confided in me—she was like him, the buttoned-up type.' With a smile, she crossed her long legs and changed gear. 'Mind you, both of them were much less buttoned with Tristan. He still worships Edward. I always used to send Edward to his school sports day—frankly, I couldn't stand that kind of thing.'

She paused, to let the message sink in: Edward was a father to her son; the centre of her family. Rufa thought what a cow Prudence was, getting someone else to visit her child at boarding school.

'It's so funny seeing Tristan's sudden passion for the countryside. I sent him to school in the middle of nowhere, and he never stopped complaining about it. And now he's begging to stay here until term starts. Do you think Edward would mind?'

'No, of course not. He'll be really pleased.' Rufa could say this with confidence. Edward was very fond of Tristan, now twenty and at Oxford.

'Edward's been a rock to me, an absolute rock. Through all my ghastly life, all my stupid marriages. I took him rather for granted. I should have bagged him while I had the chance.'

Rufa's cheeks burned. Panic gripped her. 'When did he ask you?'

'He didn't,' Prudence said. 'I should have asked him. But I didn't think it was necessary.' She continued to smile, but Rufa could sense her anger. 'Did he say anything about what happened in Paris?'

'Yes, he said you'd had a row. About me.'

'Not about you personally,' Prudence said. 'I suppose about the fact that Edward thought he was single, free to marry anyone else at all.'

This changed the world too much to be understood all at once. Did Prudence think she was his rightful wife? Surely not.

Something in her reaction softened Prudence. The aggressive sweetness left her face. She looked tired. 'It's one of the basic differences between men and women,' she said. 'When a woman says she's single, she means just that. But when a man says he's single, he only means the woman he's screwing isn't good enough.'

'Edward's not like that,' Rufa stated. She was not going to take Prudence's word for this.

'Oh, I know he's the soul of honour and chivalry—and God, he never lets you forget it.' Prudence was bitter now. 'This was why he had to ride in like the cavalry, to mend your roof and save your family. It was all tied up in his ridiculous loyalty to your father.'

Rufa bowed her head. Her own silliness, coupled with the family poverty, had virtually forced Edward to do the decent thing and marry the Man's eldest daughter without considering the feelings of the woman who loved him.

Edward came into the room. 'Oh, here you both are.'

Prudence smiled at him. 'Hello. Where have you been hiding all morning?'

'Sorry, I had work to do.'

'Rufa's been taking wonderful care of me.'

Edward frowned. He often did when with Prudence. 'Good. We ought to leave, if we're having this lunch. Please don't make me wear a tie.'

'In this heat? I'm not such a sadist.' Prudence jumped up to kiss Edward's cheek. Her fingers brushed an imaginary speck off his shoulder. 'And in any case, you look gorgeous in that shirt.'

He frowned again, but Rufa saw, for the first time, exactly why it made her so uncomfortable to observe Edward and Prudence together. There was no physical reserve between them. In the private language of women, as inaudible to men as a dog-whistle, Prudence was telling her what had happened in Paris. She and Edward had still been lovers, and as far as Prudence was concerned, the affair was not yet over.

For a moment, standing in the empty drawing room gripping the tray, Rufa was giddy with fear. The old terror of the surrounding blackness, which had tormented her since the death of the Man, came rushing back. If Prudence wanted to destroy the tender shell Rufa had just begun to build against the blackness, she could.

The fear receded as soon as Rufa thought of Edward, and took him properly into account. He was the world's most honourable man. He loved her. The least she could do for him, when he had done everything for her, was trust him.

Sunlight lay upon the clean kitchen surfaces in pools of silver. She picked up old Mrs Reculver's white and gold coffeepot from the tray. It slipped through her fingers, smashing explosively on the stone floor. Rufa leapt with shock and burst into tears. She was sick of performing and pretending. She was sick of skivvying for Prudence. She wanted to be at home, where you could have an ordinary, unambiguous row.

'Rufa?'

She leapt again. Tristan stood in the doorway—she had forgotten she was not alone in the house. Mortified to be caught sobbing, Rufa brushed away the tears and gasped, 'Hello, you made me jump—' with a ridiculous stab at sounding breezy.

Rufa and Tristan had been careful to maintain a distance. Prudence and Edward spoke of him as a boy, when he was actually a young man, just seven years younger than Rufa. He was tall and beautiful, with golden brown hair that curled to his shoulders and eyes of a warm blue.

'Sorry,' Rufa said. 'This is silly of me. Don't take any notice.'

He was distressed to see her crying. He looked down at the shards and slivers of porcelain strewn across the floor. 'Was it valuable?'

Rufa did her best to smile. 'God, no—it was just the last straw.'

Tristan stood in the kitchen doorway, absurdly Rupert Brookeish and Bridesheadish, gazing at the kitchen floor. 'I know what this is about,' he said gravely. 'My mother's been having a go at you.'

'Oh, no—' This was exactly the matter, and she could not make the denial sound anything but feeble.

'And you're exhausted, because you've been letting her treat you like a slave.' He was indignant, which was comforting.

Rufa sighed wearily. 'I can't not do things when she asks.'

'Yes, you can,' Tristan said. 'She should wear a sign round her neck: "Don't obey me". Like the diabetic dog at the pub you mustn't feed.'

Rufa laughed properly for the first time since the arrival of Prudence.

'I've begged her to stop being a bitch to you, but she pretends not to know what I mean. I think I'm supposed to be too young to understand what you've done.'

'Done? Me?'

Tristan was matter-of-fact. 'Well, you married Edward, didn't you? He wasn't meant to marry anyone. She only came here to get a good look at you. To get a handle on you, so she can make snide remarks about you to Edward.'

The relief of calling things by their right names was immense. Rufa started to relax. 'Do you think that's what she's doing now?'

'Probably.' Tristan grinned. 'Think of it as a backhanded compliment.'

'I'll try.'

He knelt down and helped her clear away the remains of the coffee-pot. 'Thanks, that's terrific. Did you come in search of lunch just now?'

'Well, yes. I'm sorry, but I'm ravenous.'

'I'll make something.'

'No, please—how can I let you cook for me now?'

They both laughed and stared at each other curiously, as if they had only just been introduced.

He asked, 'The pub does lunches, doesn't it? Let me take you there.'

Rufa smiled. 'You're very kind, but my sister used to work at that pub, and she told me what they put in the steak and kidney pies. The food's much better here.'

'OK, let's stay here. Only I'll make the lunch, and you can sit and watch.' He looked into her eyes again. 'On the understanding that comments are forbidden.'

His attempt to be masterful was unexpectedly endearing. Rufa said, 'Well, if you insist, there's some ham in the fridge, and I picked—'

'Shut up, I'm in charge now. All you have to do is sit down and make polite conversation. Or better still, rude conversation. I don't know about you, but I'm sick to death of politeness.'

Rufa, beginning to enjoy herself, sat down at the kitchen table and surrendered herself to the lazy pleasure of watching him. 'It's not polite-ness,' she said. 'I'm sick of hiding what I really feel.'

He looked over his shoulder. 'What's that? You can tell me.'

It was easy to talk to him. But he was the son of Prudence, and it was wise to be tactful. 'I suppose I'm tired of pretending to be part of an old married couple, when I haven't even been married two months. I still feel rather like a visitor here. I get rather tense.'

Tristan grabbed a bottle of champagne. 'This should help.'

'Oh, not for me, thanks.'

'Why not? It's high summer, it's boiling hot and neither of us has a thing to do.' He opened the bottle and poured two glasses.

'I suppose it wouldn't do any harm, would it?' She sipped her cham-pagne. Its delicious coldness spiked her bloodstream. Tristan was making sandwiches with huge slabs of crusty white bread, thick slices of farm-cured ham and lumps of fresh tomato. 'Let's eat outside,' he said, putting the sandwiches on a large pottery plate Rufa had found in Sienna.

Suddenly enchanted by the idea of a picnic, Rufa took the champagne, their glasses and a rug, and led him to a large oak tree on the sloping ground behind the house. Rufa handed him his glass, and spread the rug beneath the tree. She settled against the trunk and tilted her face upwards. They were in a tent of leaves. Daubs of sunlight shifted round them. One lay upon Tristan's forehead, heating his hair to gold. They ate his huge sandwiches in a haze of contentment, laughing softly when pieces of tomato dropped out into their laps.

Tristan lay sprawled on his side, propped on one elbow, gazing at Rufa. A bee droned clumsily between them.

Rufa sighed luxuriously. 'This is bliss.'

'You should do this more often,' Tristan said.

'I'm bad at doing nothing. I get twitchy if I'm not doing something that has a tangible result. I have to see that I've made a difference.'

'That's only the outside. It's just as important to pay attention to the inside of yourself.' He reddened, forcing the words out. 'And don't tell me you don't like poetry, because I won't believe you. You couldn't look like that and—and not have a soul to match.'

Rufa opened her drowsy eyes properly. Tristan stared, wary of her response. He was so lovely, she thought her heart would break. Tentatively, he reached across to touch her hand. As his warm flesh met hers, Rufa felt a tautening at the pit of her stomach.

She moved her hand away smartly, wondering why she was not angry, or afraid.

Two days after the departure of Prudence, Edward abruptly told Rufa he was leaving. For a splinter of a second she was gripped by terror. Then she realised he was not talking about running off with his Camilla Parker-Bowles. He was only explaining that he had been summoned to The Hague, to give evidence at the War Crimes Tribunal. This was the business that had been grating at him for most of the year, and Rufa felt vaguely guilty for not treating it more seriously.

'Sorry,' he said. 'But I can't even try to get out of it.'

'No, of course not.'

They were driving over to Melismate. Edward liked to discuss difficult subjects in the car, where he could avoid eye contact. 'Basically, I'm to be a witness at the trial of a Serbian gangster, who has finally been fingered for God knows how many murders. It would give me deep satisfaction to see the little shit behind bars.'

Rufa asked, 'How well did you know him?'

'I've never laid eyes on the man,' Edward said, with a harsh laugh. 'I've only seen his handiwork. Do you remember when I told you about serving with the UN force?' He did not expect an answer here. 'Someone took me and five Dutch officers to a mass grave. They'd excavated the grave by the time we got there,' he said, 'like an archaeological find. The bodies lay at the bottom in a pathetic tangle.'

She said, 'Oh God,' hoping he would not tell her too much, and uncover the things she could not bear to face. Lately she was finding it hard to ignore them. Edward knew she had been having nightmares, though she had fiercely resisted all attempts to talk about them. Faintly, she asked, 'How many?'

'Forty-nine. We counted, of course. Forty-nine Croatian Muslims— so we were told—rounded up and shot in the name of ethnic cleansing. We met two women who claimed to have witnessed the massacre.'

He slowed the car briefly, to let a tractor turn into a gate. 'Unfortunately, the grave was destroyed by NATO bombing, and nobody seems to know the whereabouts of the women who spoke to us—the chaos there is beyond belief. So that leaves the report we filed.'

'Did you . . . aren't there any photos?'

'One mass grave looks a lot like another,' Edward said. 'I think they're trying to make out that we photographed another one, somewhere else. There's no shortage of them in that bloody country.' He kept his eyes sternly on the road ahead. 'The whole experience was one more reason why I couldn't take the army any more. When you see what an army can do, in the name of God knows what—the men in that grave had their hands tied behind their backs. They'd all been shot in the head, at close range. The skulls all had great gaping holes in them.'

'Edward . . .'

'These people are atrocious. They don't deserve democracy.'

'Edward—please—could you stop?'

'What?' He looked round at her sharply. Rufa's face was bloodless, with a sheen of sweat on her white forehead. Immediately he swerved off the road, braking the car on the narrow grass verge.

Rufa wrenched the door open, almost fell out of the car, and vomited over the grass. Her body was possessed and consumed with throwing up. Distantly, through the miasma of sickness, she was aware of Edward getting out of the car, putting his arm round her shoulders, and gently pulling her upright when the horror had been expelled.

'Ru, darling, I'm so sorry.' He wrapped his arms round her. 'I'm a complete insensitive idiot—I should have remembered.'

Rufa was determined not to remember. With her accustomed briskness, she straightened her picture of the world. 'Sorry about that. I don't know what got into me. Could it have been the smoked haddock?'

'Smoked haddock my arse.' She felt his breath warm in her hair. 'Tell me when you're feeling better, sweetheart, and I'll take you home.'

Rufa ducked irritably away from his arm. 'Rubbish, I'm fine now. Let's go. I don't want to miss Linnet's bedtime.' She was ordering him to forget it, but he went on staring at her with that terrible compassion— couldn't he see that going on about it would bring it back?

'Wait—' He put his hand on her arm. 'Don't rush away from it.'

'From what?' she snapped. 'I'm not rushing away from anything. I'm totally fine. Please let's go.'

He sighed, resigned. 'All right. Just get a breath of air first, eh?'

They stood in silence for a few minutes, both overwhelmingly aware of what could not be said.

In the most normal, conversational voice she could summon, Rufa asked, 'When do you go to The Hague?'

'End of next week.' There was another silence. 'Terry Poulter says he can manage the farm. And Tristan's coming back tomorrow, so you won't be alone.'

'There's no need for Tristan to stay. I'm fine on my own.'

He smiled, with a warmth and kindness that was, for some reason, almost unbearable. 'I'd still rather know you have Tristan around, even if it's just to scare the burglars.'

'I do wish you'd stop treating me like the walking wounded.' She was challenging him, knowing that if he wanted to disagree, he would have to open the closed book. Knowing also that he could not bear to put her through that pain.

He did dare to say, 'You're not as tough as you think. You've got to get rid of this idea that you have to be responsible for everyone and everything, and allow me to take care of you.'

'Sorry,' Rufa said. 'It's lovely that you want to. I'm just not used to it.'

Edward stepped forward and kissed her forehead, then got back into the car. Over his shoulder, he said, 'I feel I've almost worked you to death since we got back. At least you won't be waiting on Pru.'

'I absolutely hated her,' Rufa announced suddenly.

He laughed. 'I gathered.'

Rufa got into the car, and they were back on the road. On impulse, Rufa asked, 'Did you sleep with her in Paris?'

He was startled—more startled than she had ever seen him—then wrathful. 'No,' he said shortly. 'I did not.'

'But you did sleep with her recently, didn't you?' The weeks of pining for his sexual attention had made her reckless. 'Not just after Alice died.'

Edward scowled at the road. 'It's over, Rufa. That's all you need to know.'

He was silent for a long time. The car slowed at the new gates of Melismate, and turned into the drive. 'The past doesn't matter,' he said calmly. 'I won't say you're the only woman I've ever loved, but you're the woman I love now.' He pulled the handbrake sharply. 'Pru may have kicked up a bit of a fuss, but you won. All right?'

They were at the door, and Linnet bounced out of it before he could say any more.

Rufa kept reminding herself that being loved by a man like Edward was a privilege. She waved him off to The Hague with as much serenity as she could muster. Only at the very last minute, when Edward was on the point of going through to his gate at the airport, did Rufa understand how desperately she would miss him. Her world, without his reassuring presence, looked unfamiliar and frightening. He put his arms round her and with an air of doing something illicit, he kissed her on the mouth with real and startling heat. Then he was gone, and Rufa was left to feel lonely and useless.

Tristan came back, and Rufa had to admit that Edward had been right; she was glad not to be alone. The presence of Tristan did not exactly add to her security, but it infused the place with quickness and youth. He had arrived for what he described as his 'one-man reading party' with a box of books, a box of CDs and a small rucksack of clothes.

Tristan spent his days reading, and in the evenings he ate supper in the kitchen with Rufa. These evenings quickly became the focus of her day. She cooked for him tenderly, and he entertained her with the stories of his life. Words gushed from him. He could not tell her enough.

He told her about his moneyed, unsettled childhood with Prudence and a succession of stepfathers. He told her about his boarding school, and about losing his virginity on the tennis court with his housemaster's daughter.

Rufa said—as she had said to nobody else—'I lost mine in the bedroom of old Mrs Reculver's cottage. It was enormously romantic.'

Tristan's eyes were deep blue in his tanned face, and full of devotion. He said, 'I felt stupid with my bare bum in the air. I wish I'd saved myself for someone more like you.'

All their conversations tended to turn to love. Rufa knew perfectly well that Tristan was in love with her. He was in a constant state of wonderment at the strength and poetry of his own emotions. If her hand brushed his accidentally, a blush surged up to the roots of his hair. He stammered if she stood too close to him. Rufa did not feel there was any harm in this, as long as nothing was said. She was sure she could handle it. All that blushful worship only made her more conscious of the difference in their ages.

Edward seemed impossibly far away. When he telephoned, Rufa took great pains to sound interested in his accounts of wrestling with Eurocracy and waiting in windowless, air-conditioned corridors. But their nightly conversations were deeply unsatisfactory. He was as remote as Australia. She wanted him, and he apparently wanted her. So why, why, was the marriage going so badly? Whatever the reason, she was determined to make it work when he came home.

An outsider might not understand the oddity of the whole situation. Rufa was careful not to let her mother and sisters come sniffing round. They would see Tristan's infatuation in a moment; particularly Rose, who had a bloodhound's nose for romance. Fortunately, most of Rose's attention was taken up by a new episode in the drama of Lydia. As if Rufa's marriage really had solved all the family's problems, Lydia was undergoing an awakening. In the face of the upheaval at Semple Farm, she was rediscovering her purpose and energy. She sent Linnet to her father with ironed and mended clothes. She cooked, without being asked—rather well. And one morning when Rufa had driven over to Melismate, she announced that she had joined a choir, the Cotswold Chorus, a highly regarded choir, of which Edward was a patron.

'You remember how much I loved the choir at school. It was practically the only thing I was good at,' Lydia said. 'So I plucked up my courage and wrote in for an audition.'

'An audition?' Rufa could not imagine Lydia daring to do such a thing.

Lydia giggled. 'I was incredibly nervous. But Phil Harding—he's the conductor—was really patient. I'm going to the rehearsal this Friday. They're just starting the Mozart *Requiem*.'

'Hooray for you,' Rufa said warmly. She took a piece of shortbread from a plate in front of her on the table. 'This shortbread is fab.'

'I made it with Linnet this morning.'

Rufa was amazed to hear of Lydia doing something as organised as making biscuits with her child.

'We made a tray each,' Lydia said, laughing. 'She took her grimy efforts over to Ran's.'

'This isn't for Ran's benefit, is it?' Rufa said. 'Please don't tell me you're trying to win him back by turning yourself into Nigella Lawson.'

Lydia's Gioconda smile did not waver, but there was a steeliness in her soft, pale eyes. 'Don't be silly, I'm not doing anything for him. I've decided I have to start doing things for myself.' She was hesitant, and very serious. 'To find myself, if you like. I can't hang about waiting for him. I owe it to Linnet to move myself on.'

'I don't believe it—that I should live to see this day.' Rufa was laughing softly. 'Wait till I tell Nancy.'

Lydia looked puzzled. 'Tell her what? That I've joined a choir?'

'That you've finally given up on Ran, of course.'

'Oh, no,' Lydia said. 'I'm never doing that—I'm as married to him as I ever was. But he's got to come to me. He's got to win me back.'

Rufa was gentle. 'Polly's a very determined person. She's bound to make him marry her.'

'He'll never marry her,' Lydia snapped. 'I know he thinks he's madly in love with her. But I know—I absolutely know—that in the end he'll see where he truly belongs, and come back to Linnet and me.'

Rufa was silent. There was no point in arguing with Lydia about anything to do with her ex-husband. But the signs of waking up to the rest of the world were distinctly promising.

'We should go shopping,' she said impulsively.

'What?' Lydia was bewildered. Her mind did not change gear quickly.

'You're the only one of us who hasn't been made over—the only bit of Melismate that hasn't been restored. Let's go down to London and be ridiculously extravagant. Come on, Liddy. It'll be brilliant.'

'Are you sure? I mean, I haven't any money.'

Rufa took Lydia's hand. 'You don't need any. This is all on me. You're going to be waxed and dressed and groomed, and then Ran had better watch out, because you'll be the most gorgeous woman for miles.'

Chapter Two

THEY HAD TO GET UP horribly early, to miss the traffic and give themselves plenty of time to raid the shops. Tristan had insisted on coming with them on the shopping excursion, and took the wheel of Edward's Land Rover Discovery after they stopped at a service station.

They arrived at Wendy's just before nine o'clock—to leave the car, and eat breakfast. Roshan (an effortless early riser, like Rufa) had prepared a plate of croissants and a jug of fresh orange juice. Nancy, dressed for the heat in a kind of elongated orange vest with apparently nothing underneath, took Tristan on board with her usual easy warmth, but the raised eyebrow she cocked at Rufa behind his back was a little disturbing. Selena had left a rather grumpy note explaining that she was on a shoot.

Rufa was looking affectionately round Wendy's cramped, crowded kitchen, which now seemed more agreeably raffish and bohemian. 'I've missed this house,' she said.

'It's funny how quickly things change,' Wendy remarked happily. 'Max sent his love, but he's staying with his new girlfriend.'

Lydia asked, 'Isn't he the one who fancied Nancy?' She had not kept pace with the plot. Her own plot was too absorbing.

Tristan, his mouth full of toast and jam, said, 'Excuse me, must have a pee,' and left the room. His energy had a nervous edge today, and he needed to pee constantly. Rufa found this almost painfully endearing.

The second he had gone, Roshan turned on Rufa. 'Mrs Reculver, who on earth is that divine boy?'

'I told you, he's Edward's first wife's—'

'Yes, we've had the family tree, thank you.' Roshan sat down at the table. 'But I take it you've noticed he's a burnished young sex god?'

'Of course she hasn't,' Nancy said. 'Ru never notices a man's attributes without written permission.'

Rufa was relieved that Nancy had not read the signs. For the moment, she was off the hook. She attempted a laugh. 'He refused to be left behind at the farm, and he's sharing the driving. He's—awfully nice, actually.' She lowered her voice. 'I didn't really want him to stay, but Edward seems to think I need someone male to look after me.'

'Well,' Roshan said, 'if it was any other woman but Rufa, we'd be deep in the third act of *Desire Under the Elms*. Because that young man is so gorgeous, it's a joke.'

Rufa quickly tried to deflect Roshan's beady gaze by asking for advice. It seemed to work. He fetched paper and pen, furnished them with a neatly written list of shops, and personally telephoned a hairstylist who owed him a favour. Then he called a minicab to take them down to the West End. Rufa began to think she had hauled the general attention away from anything awkward.

Nancy, however, managed to corner her in the hall before they left. She grabbed Rufa's wrist. 'Are you all right? You're awfully thin, Ru.'

Rufa laughed. 'I thought one couldn't be too rich or too thin. And look who's talking—if you lose any more, there'll be nothing left to snare Berry.'

'Are you sure everything's OK?'

'Nance, what is this? Why shouldn't it be?'

'I don't know.' Nancy was searching her sister's face. 'It's so long since I've seen you—not since your all-star wedding. You look different.'

'Of course I do,' Rufa said, more forcefully. 'Think of me this time last year—making jam like a woman possessed to pay the undertaker's bill. If I've changed, it's because things are so much better.'

'Are they?' Nancy was doubtful. 'I suppose so.' She hugged Rufa. 'Promise you'll ring me. It doesn't feel right that you're so far away.'

Rufa glanced outside to where Tristan stood beside the minicab. 'Come home occasionally. Then you'll see for yourself that we're all absolutely fine.'

By eleven o'clock Lydia was sitting in front of a mirror at John Frieda's salon in New Cavendish Street, while the stylist sifted her masses of light brown hair through his fastidious fingers. Rufa and Tristan left her, to buy presents for Linnet at Hamleys. They bought her a Spacehopper (Tristan's idea) and two dolls' jerseys for the Ressany Brothers.

Back at John Frieda's, they found Lydia quivering with excitement and deliciously transformed. The stylist had reduced her hair to a short bob, which curled as sweetly and naturally as a lamb's back. It exactly suited the fragile prettiness of her heart-shaped face. She looked youthful and vibrant, and unexpectedly chic—every stitch she owned suddenly seemed wrong. Lydia had now woken up to the urgency of the situation and was impatient to remake herself.

Tristan gently hinted that he was hungry. Rufa bought them all a hurried lunch at Dickins and Jones, then she and Lydia plunged into an orgy of shopping. Edward had said they were to push the boat out for Lydia, so they bought linen trousers at Margaret Howell, jerseys from Joseph, a suit, jeans and a handbag from Emporio Armani. They bought stilettos with lethal pointed toes from Russell and Bromley, and silver Donna Karan trainers. By late afternoon the three of them were sitting round a table in a coffee shop. Slippery cairns of carrier bags were heaped around them.

Lydia attacked a chocolate pretzel with gusto. 'Ru, I've had the most terrific day. Thanks so much—and please thank Edward.' She smiled at Tristan. 'Thank you, too. I know men don't like being dragged round shops. When it happens to my husband, he starts to cry.'

He laughed. 'I managed to fight back the tears. It wasn't too bad.'

'No need to thank me,' Rufa said. 'I've had a sublime day.'

Lydia wrapped a second chocolate pretzel in a napkin, for Linnet. 'Will the traffic be dreadful if we go home now?'

'Don't worry.' Rufa squeezed her hand. 'It won't take long.'

Tristan leaned forward, smiling persuasively. 'Lydia, why don't you take the train? We could take you to the station, someone could meet you at the other end, then Rufa and I could drive down when it's quieter.'

Rufa's heart lurched. The prospect of being alone with him in London was dazzling, but also terrifying. The delight and the sense of impending disaster were impossible to separate.

He stared into her eyes, as if they were the only two people in the world. 'I had this mad idea that we might catch the *Dream* at Regent's Park. This is the perfect weather for it.'

Rufa cried, 'Oh, how lovely! But we'll never get in—'

'Prudence uses this up-market ticket agency that gets her into everything. Let me phone them.'

'I really don't mind going on the train,' Lydia assured Rufa, perking up hopefully. She liked trains. Cars always made her feel hemmed in. 'Honestly. Then you wouldn't have to hurry.'

It was settled seamlessly. Tristan arranged the tickets for the Open Air Theatre with his mother's breathtakingly pricey agency. They bundled Lydia and her shopping into a taxi, escorted her to Paddington Station and put her on a train. Rufa then rang Melismate, and told the affable Roger when to meet Lydia at Stroud.

Lydia kissed them both gratefully. 'This has been wonderful. When I wake up tomorrow, I'll think I dreamed it.'

The train pulled out and Rufa and Tristan were alone. Tristan tucked Rufa's hand firmly into his arm, and dragged her through the streams of hurrying people to the taxi rank.

Nothing could be said aloud, but the guilty, dreadful, intoxicating fact shouted in both their minds. Tristan was more desperately in love than ever, and his love was chafing inside him, fighting to express itself.

Rufa had never been to the Open Air Theatre at Regent's Park. The place enchanted her. In the centre of London, on this still and tropic night, they sat, leaning against each other's shoulders, inside a magic circle of trees. On the stage below them, Shakespeare's lovers suffered and sighed while the fairies played football with their hearts. Above them, the sky slowly faded from blue to pearl to black, and points of light appeared in the trees. It was beautiful. They could not have found a more purely beautiful spectacle in the whole city.

Like a child at the pantomime, Rufa could not bear the enchantment to end. Her head was filled with poetry and romance as they made their way to the park gates, unwilling to return to reality.

'Shall we walk to the main road?' Tristan asked softly. 'We need to get back to the car.'

'Yes.' Rufa let him take her hand and they walked until they met a lighted taxi. Tristan hailed it and they sat in silence, holding hands, until the taxi dropped them in Tufnell Park Road.

A light was visible behind the skimpy curtains of Wendy's sitting room. 'Let's not go in,' Rufa murmured. 'Let's go home.'

'OK. Give me the keys. I'll drive—you're too tired.'

'Would you mind?' She was deathly tired; too tired to think.

Tristan took the keys from her and opened the passenger door. In the car, he tilted her seat back a few inches. She clipped in her seat belt. Her eyes slid shut. Inside her head, she saw lighted trees, fairies in glinting spangles, bewildered lovers falling thankfully into each other's arms. The warm dream of a midsummer night.

Back at the farmhouse she quickly forced herself to snap out of her light-headed state. It seemed years since they had left, but the solid sameness of the house helped her to wrestle back some self-control.

Outside, the car door slammed, the electric lock cheeped. Rufa hurried along the passage to the kitchen, switching on all the lights. She filled the kettle, frantic to look casual and ordinary when Tristan came in.

He stood in the doorway, staring. She stared back, mesmerised. It was too late. He could not be stopped. Slowly, never taking his eyes from hers, he went across to her and took her in his arms.

A great pang of longing shuddered through her. His warm lips gently met hers, and when their mouths locked together the delight was so intense, she almost came. Alarmed, she pulled away from him.

'I can't,' she said.

His arms tightened round her waist. 'My darling.' He bent his head to kiss her again.

Rufa broke free, with some force. 'No,' she said, trembling. 'I can't.'

'Why not? What have I done?'

'For God's sake.' Rufa was bewildered. 'I was talking about Edward. I'm married. There's no question of my—'

Tristan's own bewilderment was hardening into anger. He looked younger than ever. 'But you've been sending out the signals all day. That was the whole point of getting shot of Lydia and going to the theatre. You were telling me it was going to happen.'

'I didn't tell you anything of the kind,' Rufa said. Being angry with Tristan made it easier to resist him. 'Don't you think I love my husband? This is his house, Tristan. Do you really think I'd cheat on him the minute his back's turned?' Her outrage was genuine.

'No, of course not.' Once more Tristan was bewildered, wondering if he could possibly have imagined the surprising strength of Rufa's kiss a moment ago. 'Rufa, I'm sorry—I'm really sorry if I was wrong. But this isn't just about sex.' He bounded across the room to seize her hand. 'Don't be angry with me. God, Rufa, I'm so in love with you it hurts.'

It was no use. She was powerless. The pain in his eyes melted her.

'Hundreds of times I've wanted to fling myself on the ground and beg you to love me.' His clear eyes were swimming with tears. 'I'll go mad if you say you don't feel anything for me.'

Two hot tears scalded Rufa's cheeks. 'Of course I feel something for you. But it's totally against my will, and I have to fight it.'

'You're going to say it's your duty, or something,' he said sadly.

'You think duty has nothing to do with love. But it's actually all about love—that's the whole point. And when I say I love Edward, it's not just a matter of liking him a lot. He's everything that holds me together.'

'But he's not here,' Tristan murmured urgently. 'If we made love, how would he ever know? Please, Rufa—' He pressed her hand into his groin, against his erection. 'Please—please, or I'll die of wanting you—'

Rufa whipped her hand away. He was begging her for illicit sex, in the house of her husband. The picture veered round to another angle, and the romantic idyll suddenly appeared shameful and sordid. 'Tristan, I'm sorry. You picked the wrong woman to fall in love with.'

He frowned. 'You just don't want to admit what's happened. You refuse to see how important it is, because you're so scared of screwing up your nice, comfy house, and all those sacks of money—'

'How dare you?' Rufa raged. 'Oh, you bloody well worship me when you think everything's going your way—but the minute you don't get what you want, you accuse me of only wanting Edward's money!'

'Well, are you telling me you didn't? Come on. Stop playing games.'

'This isn't a game. Why won't you believe me when I say I love him?'

Tristan shook with anger. The tears jumped and sizzled on his lashes like sparks. 'If you really loved him, you'd sleep with him.'

Rufa whispered, 'Who . . . what the hell are you talking about?'

They were both very still. Tristan was almost afraid to look into her white, anguished face, but he was still angry enough to blurt out, 'Prudence told me. She said she asked Edward what was wrong, because she knew something was on his mind, and he told her you don't have sex. Frankly, it's the only thing that's been keeping me sane—if I'd had to think of you having sex with him, I'd have killed myself.'

Rufa leaned against the kitchen table. She felt as if a great fist had punched into all the assumptions of her life, shattering it to fragments. Edward had betrayed her. He had discussed their deepest, darkest secret with—of all people—Prudence.

'She was lying. It's not true.'

'No—you're the one who's telling lies. You're living one. Your entire life is one, enormous lie.' Tristan was crying and burning; battering her with his fury. 'And you know what the irony of this is?' he demanded. 'I might have been able to protect myself from you, if I'd paid more attention to Edward. Why do you think he asked me to stay here with you? Why do you think he insured me to drive the car, and all that shit? He doesn't think you're fit to take care of yourself. Until I came along, you were one step away from falling apart.'

'Get out!' Rufa shrieked. She did not recognise her own demonic voice, dredged up from the soles of her feet. 'Get out! Get out!'

'And why do you think they had that row in Paris? Did he tell you he's been Prudence's lover for fucking years and years? If he'd married anyone, it should have been her!'

'Get out!'

Tristan dragged the sleeve of his shirt across his face. 'Oh, I'm going. You've destroyed my life. I hope you're satisfied, you frigid bitch.' He pushed past her roughly. The front door slammed and then Rufa heard Edward's car hurtling away down the track.

Rufa stood listening, absolutely still. Tristan had gone. She had lost him, and she loved him more than she loved anyone on earth. He loved her, and she had thrown his love away.

She had resisted for Edward's sake, and Edward thought she was a basket case, a liability, a mistake. Tristan was right, the two of them were living out a huge, outrageous lie.

Reality dimmed, as the pictures took over her mind—visions of Edward, of the Man, of Tristan, always rushing away from her, leaving a world utterly bereft of love.

She sat down, buried her head in her arms, and cried until she lost consciousness.

Rufa woke, with a racing heart, to the shrilling of the phone. Snapping back to consciousness, she found herself lying with one cheek pillowed on the kitchen table. Sunlight poured in at the window over the sink. She jumped up, staggering slightly because one leg had gone to sleep. If this was Edward, she must do her best to sound normal.

'Hello?' It came out as a croak.

'Ru, it's Tristan. And before you say a word, I'm sorry. I was a shit to you last night, and I'll never be able to make it up.' His voice was rapid, pleading. 'You have every right to slam the phone down and never speak another word to me ever again. It would utterly break my heart, but I'd deserve it. Hello? You are there, aren't you?'

Rufa felt she had been reborn in Technicolor, after months in miserable monochrome. Suddenly she was aware of the morning's shimmering beauty. 'Yes, I'm here—where are you?'

'Cirencester. I've had a bit of a problem with Edward's car. I need my credit card—it's in my wallet. Could you bring it?'

'Why do you need a credit card?'

'Come and fetch me, and I'll explain everything,' Tristan said. 'To know all is to forgive all. Are you really not cross?'

'How cross should I be?'

'Well, very cross indeed, if I'm honest.'

Laughter bubbled up inside Rufa; she felt ridiculously happy. It was like a veil lifting. 'You'd better tell me where you are,' she said.

He was waiting on the forecourt of the garage that the car had been towed to. The moment she saw him, Rufa's heart contracted with longing. His white jeans and shirt were streaked with grime, and one side of his long hair was matted and blackened. There was a square of lint taped to his forehead. He looked beautiful. She saw all this as she braked her Renault beside the carwash.

Tristan ran over as she leapt out. They did not know how to greet each other, and stood awkwardly looking at the ground.

A young man in overalls ambled over to them. Tristan looked up. 'Ken, this is Mrs Reculver. It's actually her husband's car.'

'Oh, right.' Ken grinned at them significantly. 'You'll have some explaining to do.'

'Ken very kindly towed me here and took my credit card on trust— did you bring it?'

'Tristan, what happened to your head? Are you all right?'

'Just a few stitches, that's all,' he said.

'I had to pick him up from Casualty. You'll do your nut when you see the car,' Ken said, still grinning.

He led them round the side of the main building into an oily, echoing shed. Directly in front of them was a wrecked car, lacking a windscreen and one door. The bonnet had buckled like a concertina, and the air bag drooped limply off the steering wheel. Rufa suddenly realised she was looking at Edward's Land Rover Discovery. The world reeled.

Tristan quickly took her hand. 'Sorry, I should have warned you.'

'God almighty,' she said. 'You—you could have been killed.'

'He's the lucky sort, this one,' Ken said, staring at Rufa. 'He walked away from this mess with just a couple of stitches.'

'Rufa, I'm so sorry,' Tristan said. 'But you should be able to collect on the insurance, because I wasn't pissed or anything.'

'It's not the car I care about, you idiot.' She was recovering. 'It's you. I nearly lost you.' The dreadful nearness of death terrified her.

'Would you have minded?'

'Don't be stupid. It would have destroyed me.'

'Oh, my darling—' He was radiant. It was settled, and there was no need to say any more. Gently, Tristan took Rufa in his arms.

Ken coughed elaborately. 'Where's that credit card, then?'

Rufa and Tristan disengaged, and climbed down from the realm of the angels. They went into a small office and Tristan paid the bill.

Then they were free. Tristan glanced at his watch. 'Half past ten. Can we have a coffee somewhere?' He smiled into her face. 'I always seem to be saying this to you, but I'm absolutely starving.'

They found a café and ordered tea, croissants, English muffins and a toasted bacon sandwich. Tristan fell upon this savagely—he had not eaten, Rufa remembered, since yesterday.

'I was mad,' Tristan said. 'I hardly even knew I was driving. I hated myself for what I said to you—which I didn't mean.'

Rufa looked into her tea. 'Some of it was quite accurate.'

'No, it was all totally childish. I had no right to assume anything.'

'Where did you crash?'

'I went into a stone wall near Hardy Cross. It was on a bend, and I didn't see it in time.' The colour rose in Tristan's face. He took her hand across the table. 'Actually, I didn't see it because I was crying.'

She looked up quickly. 'So was I. How ludicrous, to think of us both crying, when all I had to do was admit the truth.'

'The truth that you love me?'

'Yes. I don't know why I got so scared.' This was not true. She was scared of losing the person whose good opinion mattered most in the world.

'Because of Edward,' he said, as if Edward were a tiresome obligation. She added quickly, 'I'm not saying I'm scared of *him*.'

'God, I am,' Tristan said. 'Particularly now that I've fallen in love with his wife and trashed his car. He'll probably garrotte me.'

'Don't be silly.' Rufa was sharp; annoyed to be put in the position of defending Edward, and slightly annoyed by Tristan's youthful levity.

She was silent for a moment. 'You have to understand how it hurts me to betray Edward. But I've gone too far now. And if I can't love you, it'll kill me.'

Tristan withdrew his hand. 'You're always talking about dying, and being killed. Feelings are like knives to you. I knew that the first evening we spent together—when you cooked that fabulous Italian meal. You were impossibly beautiful, but I had a tremendous sense that you were unhappy. Sort of lost inside yourself. That's how you got to me.' He reached for the other half of his sandwich, took a wolfish bite, and hurried on with his mouth full. 'When I drove off last night, I thought the world had ended. The second before I crashed, I think I felt rather noble, because I was dying for you.' He smiled radiantly—as far as he was concerned, everything was happily settled now. 'Then I wasn't dead, and I just felt like a prat. The door was bent, and I couldn't get out.'

'Were you there for long?'

'Well, it seemed like ages. Apparently some old biddy in a bungalow heard the smash and called out every service short of Mountain Rescue.'

'Did the police charge you with anything?'

Tristan, gulping tea, shook his head. 'I wasn't drunk, and you can't book a guy for driving while sobbing uncontrollably, can you?'

Rufa could not help laughing. 'No, I suppose not.'

Under the table, his knee brushed Rufa's, and she ached to kiss him again. When they returned to the farm, they would make love. Her stomach lurched with anticipation.

The barber's was a deeply unprepossessing shop. Black and white photographs of common-looking men, sporting various antiquated hairstyles, leered around the yellowed walls. Heaven only knew why Ran had insisted upon coming to this place, when there was a perfectly adequate hairdresser's round the corner.

The barber was not pleased to see Ran. He gave the head of the balding pensioner whose hair he was clipping a final polish, and whipped the nylon bib from his shoulders. 'Yes?'

Polly firmly pulled Ran into the shop. 'I'm sorry, but there seems to have been a slight misunderstanding. We wanted a haircut.'

'But I just cut his hair!'

'I'm afraid you didn't do it properly.'

The barber looked belligerent. 'Look, I only did what he asked for, right? He said to just tidy the ends. Tell her, mate.'

He turned to Ran, who shrugged helplessly.

'There must have been a mistake,' Polly snapped. 'I thought I made it quite clear that he wants it short at the back and sides, with a long bit on top—well, I don't suppose the name Hugh Grant means much to you.' She glanced contemptuously at the gallery of photographs, then singled one out. 'Rather like that one, but without the gel.'

'I don't want it that short,' Ran muttered. 'I'll look like a dick.'

'No you won't. For the last time, your hair looks perfectly absurd like that. Only motorcycle messengers have ghastly long hair.'

The barber looked doubtfully at Ran. 'Well?'

Ran stood, his hands balled in the pockets of his new black linen trousers, miserable and defeated. 'Yes, all right.' He sat down in a vacant barber's chair while the pensioner paid his bill and left.

Satisfied that the matter was settled, Polly sat down on a small and wobbly plastic chair in one corner, flicking open her new copy of *Vogue*.

The barber picked up the scissors, and took up his station behind Ran. 'Shut your eyes, mate. We'll do it quicker,' the barber said. 'And next time, you'd better bring a note from her.'

Ran scrunched his eyes shut. Deftly and neatly, but with no very good grace, the barber attacked his hair. He snipped close to the back of Ran's skull, and reached across for the electric clipper. When he switched it on, Ran bleated pitifully. The barber hesitated.

'Oh, for heaven's sake,' Polly said.

The clipper whirred. Ran's hair was shorn round the back and sides. One thick lock fell romantically across his forehead. Polly closed her magazine, to watch intently.

'All done,' the barber said. 'You can open them now.'

Ran opened his eyes, met his new self in the mirror, and groaned.

'Yes, that's excellent—and it didn't hurt a bit, did it?' Polly was on her feet, digging in her handbag. 'Exactly what we wanted.' She paid, adding a handsome tip, and led Ran out of the shop.

He said, 'I look like an arsehole.'

'Darling, don't be silly. You look stupendous.' Polly was jubilant. She could hardly believe how beautiful he was now: sensitive, with just a seductive hint of tousling. This was just how she wanted to appear before Justine and Hugo that evening. Justine had been at school with Polly, and she had telephoned to say they would be coming into darkest Gloucestershire to stay with Hugo's mother. Naturally, though she had fed Polly all the formalities about missing her, Justine was desperately curious to get a good look at Ran. She would rush back to London to report to the rest of Polly's circle, so proper presentation was essential. Semple Farm was not yet fit to show off. Polly had arranged to meet

Justine and Hugo at a concert, and take them to dinner at a country house hotel afterwards.

If only Ran would cheer up. He shook Polly's hand off his arm and mooched gloomily along beside her. Deliberately ignoring this, she took the latest list from her bag. 'I saw a rather fascinating little shop, with some adorable tapestry cushions, which might take the newness off the sofa covers. I want a sort of organic, antiquated look.'

He did not reply. Polly, however, was used to this. Bless him, he did not like changes, and tended to react by sulking.

Delicious as he was, Ran was becoming increasingly stroppy. He kept taking back things she had thrown away. The attic at Semple Farm, which Polly had privately earmarked for a future nanny, was crammed with rubbish. Did the idiot not realise she was doing him a favour? More to the point, did he not realise how much money her plans were going to cost her?

She reached up to caress his shorn head. 'Please don't be cross, darling. I'm trying to make the whole world see how divine you are.'

Their eyes met. The current of mutual desire crackled between them. Polly slowly ran the tip of her tongue round her pink lips. This was their private code for oral sex. Ran smiled, his blood heated as predictably as a pan of milk on a stove. All resistance was at an end, for the time being. Polly slipped her hand into his, and the two of them sauntered into the main street.

'Look,' Ran said, 'it's Rufa.'

She was on the other side of the road, almost running. Her car keys were in one hand. She carried a wicker basket full of cut flowers.

'She looks wonderful,' Polly said critically. She had not seen Rufa since the fateful day of her wedding. 'Marriage suits her, obviously.' This was a small hint for Ran, who was curiously reluctant to set a date.

'She's happy, that's all,' Ran said, his dark eyes following her sadly. 'You don't have to get married to be happy.'

Tristan rolled onto his back, with a long sigh. 'Sorry, that was quicker than I intended. You shouldn't be so bloody beautiful.'

'You're utterly depraved,' Rufa said. 'You'll get us both arrested.'

They were lying in a patch of cowslips, at the edge of a field full of stubble. He propped himself on one elbow, leaning over to kiss her nipples. 'I can't help it. I want to fuck you all day and all night. I want to make you come till you cry. I want to worship you with my body.'

Rufa's purple silk dress was bunched round her waist, and unbuttoned down to her navel, exposing her breasts to the warm sky. Her dishevelment was more wanton than nakedness. She felt replete and tender, unwilling to cover herself.

Since the day of the car crash, they had been making love continually. They had shut themselves away at the farm, resisting all callers, ignoring time. She had scarcely even gone to Melismate. Tristan was a sublime lover, young enough to come again and again, and sleep like the dead in her arms afterwards. He did not know that she watched him while he slept, dripping tears into his hair. The happiness was painful, because it was bought with the pain of others and could not last. It was hard to convey this to Tristan. His emotional vocabulary simply did not contain the concept of betrayal.

'We ought to go,' she murmured, not moving.

Tristan asked, 'Did you catch Edward?'

Rufa tensed. Yes, she had caught Edward. For the first time, she had not been available for his daily call—she had allowed Tristan to lure her into making love standing up, in the shower. She had felt terrible when she found Edward's message on the machine. He had sounded particularly distant and disapproving when she called him back—though he might simply have been in a hurry. She said, 'Yes, just briefly.'

Aware that the subject upset her, Tristan made his voice mild and neutral. 'Did he say anything?'

'He doesn't know when he's coming back, if that's what you mean.'

'Good.'

'Don't, Tristan—it makes me feel so evil.'

'You're not evil. You're an angel.' He sat up, fastening his trousers. 'I can't feel as guilty about Edward as you do. He's across the sea. That means I have more time in paradise.'

Rufa sighed. 'I wish we could live like this for ever. I can't bear to think of you going back to Oxford.'

'Stop talking about it,' Tristan said. 'It hasn't happened yet.' He bent down to kiss her forehead. 'You're having one of your dreaded attacks of postcoital heaviness.'

'Sorry. I'll lighten up, or the concert will be too turgid for words.' She sat up, to button her dress. They brushed crumbs of earth from each other, laughing as they checked for grass stains. He was right not to fret about the future. Being together was all that mattered.

Rufa no longer cared about appearances. Lydia was singing the Mozart *Requiem* with the Cotswold Chorus tonight. She could not miss it, and she could not leave Tristan behind. She had brazenly ordered two tickets in Edward's name, at the special rate for CC life patrons. Fortunately, they would be in a group—there was safety in numbers.

In the large church where the concert was being held, Rufa quickly found Rose, Roger and Linnet among the milling crowd of people. Rufa introduced Tristan. Rose beamed at him. 'I'm awfully glad to meet you. I can't think why Ru hasn't brought you over to Melismate.'

'He's meant to be too busy studying,' Rufa said.

'In this heat? Nonsense.'

Linnet wrapped her arms round Rufa's legs. 'I'm not letting go of you—you'll have to come home with me.'

'I've stayed away for far too long, haven't I? But I'll come to see you tomorrow.' Rufa stroked the dark head, despising herself for neglecting the little girl. 'It's the last day before you go back to school, isn't it?'

'Yes, and I'm in a new class, and the two girls I hate are in Miss Shaw's.'

'Oh, good.'

Linnet's attention had darted to the main door of the church. 'Daddy! It's Daddy! HI, DADDY!'

Ran had come in, with Polly and two strangers. His rather careworn face lit up. He rushed towards Linnet and swept her into his arms.

'Ye gods,' Rose muttered, 'what has she done to his hair? Eaten it?'

Oblivious to Polly's expression of dismay, Ran swung Linnet back down to the floor, and danced with her through the crowd. People stood back to make way for them, smiling indulgently at the exuberant young father and his gleeful little girl.

Rose kissed him warmly. 'Fancy seeing you. I wouldn't have put you down as a friend of the Cotswold Chorus.'

His face clouded. 'I respond at a very deep level to all types of music, Rose. I thought you knew that. What are you lot doing here?'

'Mummy's singing in the choir,' Linnet said, swinging on his hand.

'What? What?' Ran was startled. 'You're joking.'

'You've got short hair,' Linnet noticed, at last. 'You match Mummy now. She's cut all her hair off too.'

'*What?*' he exclaimed. 'It's her best feature.'

Polly approached, with her friends, and a blazing social smile. She moved forward to embrace Rufa. 'You look simply marvellous, I do hope you had a wonderful time in Italy.' She giggled softly. 'Oh God, people are staring at the Scarlet Woman.'

Rufa flinched, then realised Polly meant herself. 'You certainly surprised us all.'

'We must have lunch, so I can tell you the whole, incredible story. This is Justine D'Alambert, and her husband, Hugo.'

'How do you do.' Rufa shook hands with Justine and Hugo.

'This is Rufa Reculver, indirectly responsible for my fit of madness.

What a shame Edward can't be here.' Polly took hold of Ran's sleeve. 'Come along, darling, or all the good pews will be gone.' With one more conspiratorial smile at Rufa, she marched her party away up the aisle.

'We ought to bag a place near the front,' Rose said. 'Liddy's so nervous, I don't want her to have to search for us.'

Rufa hung back, so that she could take Tristan's hand without her mother seeing. He turned, and smiled at her with special intimacy. Rufa smiled back, and they both reconnected with the memory of making love less than an hour before. She sat down close to him, feeling the warmth striking off his body, smelling her own scent mingled with his. She didn't care that Rose was now turning curiously to look at them.

The members of the orchestra took their places. There was applause as the choir filed into the chancel. Clutching her score, Lydia looked round anxiously, saw Linnet, and shot her an enchanting smile.

On the other side of the aisle, Polly felt a frisson of alarm. If she had known that Lydia was singing, she would never have come to this blasted concert. It was a considerable shock to notice that droopy Lydia was transformed into what she could only count as a rival. Proprietorially, she hooked her arm through Ran's.

The applause rose in a crescendo, as the soloists entered, followed by the conductor. He was a tall, fresh-faced man, with a balding head. The coughs died away into silence. The first chords sounded.

Polly hissed, 'Stop fidgeting!' and nudged Ran hard in the ribs.

'He's utterly gorgeous,' Justine said. 'No wonder you lost your marbles and left poor old Berry at the altar. Is the sex divine?'

Polly laughed. 'Utterly. I never imagined it could be this good.'

'Well, you always were a lucky cow.'

Justine would broadcast Ran's gorgeousness round every lunching place in London, and this was gratifying. On the whole, however, this evening was becoming increasingly vexing. It was the interval, and Ran had rushed outside to smoke, though he knew it was a habit Polly abhorred. Now the musicians were taking their places again, and only a few people remained at the back of the church, hurriedly draining their glasses. Hugo said, 'I suppose we ought to—er—'

'Yes, we won't wait for Ran.' Polly led the way back to their pew, pretending not to be furious that Ran had not rejoined them in time. She spent the second half of the *Requiem Mass* seething.

Afterwards, she found him among the knot of Hastys, holding his sleeping daughter in his arms. He did not seem to think he owed any kind of apology. 'Oh, hello,' he said listlessly.

She hissed, 'What happened to you? Where were you?'

'I needed a pee, and the queue was so long I nipped to the pub.'

'For God's sake! You might have told me.'

'Hmm. Sorry.' Ran's heavenly eyes were fixed on the people round Rose. Lydia, flushed and smiling, was introducing the conductor.

'Phil's been so kind,' she was saying. 'He refused to let me wriggle out of it, though I was petrified I'd squawk a duff note in the Sanctus.'

'She wanted to sell programmes, but I told her we're not so rich in good sopranos that we can afford to let her off,' Phil said, and they shared a laugh, weighted with their private history.

It was obvious to Polly that the man was smitten—and what a wonderful solution he might be, to the problem of the ex-wife and the child.

Ran had noticed, too. His angel's face was chillingly outraged.

Chapter Three

LINNET CHARGED INTO THE Melismate kitchen, clutching a battered piece of sugar paper. 'H'lo, Granny.'

Rose bent down, trapping the little girl long enough to plant a kiss on her head. 'One of your paintings? How lovely. This kitchen needs some good paintings.'

'It's some apples and a banana. It's called a Still Life, because there aren't any things that move in it. Can I watch *The Worst Witch*?' Not waiting for a reply, Linnet shrugged off her Pikachu rucksack and her pink cardigan and dashed out of the room.

Rose picked up the rucksack and cardigan, glancing round warily as Rufa came in. When Rufa lived at Melismate, she had worked hard to establish a proper routine for Linnet, religiously observing bedtimes, mealtimes, basic good manners and healthful food. But Rufa had not been here for weeks, and Rose was the first to admit things had got rather lax.

Rufa, however, did not appear to have noticed the video, nor the rudely dumped belongings. She hovered near the door, smiling—but miles away, Rose decided. Bathed in the light of some other planet.

Rose put the kettle on. 'Thanks so much for fetching her. It really got us out of a hole, what with the car languishing at the garage, and Ran off at the races. Polly wanted him to meet some friends of hers.'

Rufa smiled. 'She's not the sort of woman you disagree with. Where's Lydia, anyway? Isn't she here?'

'No, she's rehearsing with Phil Harding, and I wouldn't make her miss it for the world. Phil's choir has brought her back to life. She hasn't been this unzombified since she left Ran. Do sit down, darling.'

'Oh, I'm not staying, thanks.'

Rose turned to face her squarely. 'Rubbish. We haven't seen you in ages. I absolutely forbid you to leave without having a cup of tea.'

Rufa laughed. 'All right. A quick one.' She moved away from the door and sat down at the table, still clutching her keys.

Like a visitor, Rose thought. As if this house, and the people in it, no longer concerned her—and this was the girl who had offered herself as a sacrifice, to preserve them all.

'Tell me how you are.' Rose joined her at the table. 'I've missed you.'

'I've been busy,' Rufa said. 'There's such a lot to do.'

'Such as what?'

'At the moment, I'm making tomato chutney.' She laughed suddenly—a lightning flash of animation. 'We have a ridiculous glut of tomatoes, and Tristan picks the things faster than I can bottle them.'

'Oh, good. Roger adores your chutney. May we have a couple of jars?'

Rufa laughed. 'You can have a caseful. I thought I might sell a few dozen to that shop in Bourton.'

Rose sighed. 'Listen to us. A year ago, your cooking activities made a real difference. But, darling, you don't have to slave over a hot stove any more, so why on earth do you do it? Edward will have a fit.'

'No, he won't.' The light dulled. Rufa's face became tense and still. 'He likes me to be enterprising.'

Rose thought how transparent she was—you could always tell exactly what she was feeling, because it was written in those great, serious, radiant eyes. She wished to God that Edward would come home. He seemed to understand her better than anyone. Watching Rufa narrowly, she asked, 'How is Edward, by the way? Any nearer to getting home?'

'There's a good chance he'll be called next week. Once he's actually in the witness box, it shouldn't take long. He's not the only witness.'

'Why the delay?'

'Oh, apparently the dreadful man on trial keeps claiming to have terrible illnesses.'

'I never thought I'd hear myself saying it, but I miss Edward,' Rose declared. 'Apart from anything else, we had to call a plumber about the downstairs lav. Edward would have fixed it in a second.'

Rose waited for her daughter to protest that Edward was not the family's unpaid handyman. But Rufa had crossed back into the blessed safety of her secret realm, and only smiled.

The front door banged.

'Anyway, here's Roger,' Rose said. 'Which must mean the car has lived to fight another day.'

It was not Roger. The kitchen door opened. Selena, thin as a wishbone in jeans and a cropped T-shirt, dragged in a bursting rucksack.

'Hi, Mum. Hi, Ru.' She grinned at them shyly. 'Can you give me a hand with my bags?'

Selena had two large leather suitcases, both crammed with books. They were incredibly heavy. It took the combined muscle of Rose, Rufa, Selena and the taxi driver to heft them into the house. Rufa, jolted back into her usual energy, put the kettle on the range.

Linnet scampered into the room, shrieking with joy, and she and Selena wrestled on the floor like puppies. Once she had got her breath, Selena dug in her rucksack to produce a battered plastic bag. It contained a pink velvet handbag, ornamented with a red sequinned heart.

'Oh, *thanks*, it's lovely, lovely—' Linnet examined it reverently. She hugged Selena's legs. 'Are you back for ever and ever?'

'Not for ever,' Selena said. She glanced at Rose. 'For the moment.'

'Good. Do you want to watch *The Worst Witch*?'

'No, thanks. I'd like to talk to Granny.'

'All right.' Linnet ran off again, clutching the handbag to her bosom.

'She'd like to talk to me!' Rose murmured. 'Did you hear that, Rufa?'

'Do shut up, Mum,' Rufa said. 'Selena, have a cup of tea, and tell us what on earth is going on.'

Selena smiled lopsidedly at Rufa. 'Well, I've decided to try for Cambridge. I've decided that modelling is a crap career.'

'Seriously? Oh God, that's fabulous!' The old Rufa was thoroughly back with them now. 'I knew you couldn't be that brainy for nothing!'

'I've obviously died,' Rose said. 'And this is heaven. My problem teenager is giving me something to boast about, at long last.'

'Roshan's been nagging me for ages,' Selena said. 'But it was Max, in the end. I was complaining about the people I have to work with—the photographers who think they're God, the creepy women who talk about you as if you're not there. And Max said I should just admit I didn't belong. He said he didn't know what point I was trying to make, but he doubted it was worth wasting my whole life for.'

Rose asked, 'What point?'

'I don't know.' Selena was uncomfortable. 'Maybe I had to prove I wasn't the plain one.'

Rufa laughed softly. 'You've certainly done that—we've all been dining out on your *Vogue* cover.'

'Go on,' Rose urged. 'Did you decide there and then to jack it all in?'

'Nope,' Selena said. 'That was last night. I had my blinding flash this morning. I was wearing a mauve ballgown with a tulip skirt, and standing up to my knees in the Serpentine.'

'Good God—why?'

'For a shoot, obviously,' Rufa said, laughing. 'Why else?'

'It was for *Harpers & Queen*,' Selena said. 'The agency's going to be furious with me—I haven't told them yet. But I suddenly wondered what the hell I was doing there. I couldn't see a single person I respected, or even liked. Everyone treated me as if I was made of plastic anyway. And I knew the next job wouldn't be any better. So I thought, fuck it. I got out of the water, stripped off the dress, got back into my jeans and went back to Wendy's.'

'You couldn't have done it at a better time,' Rufa said. 'When did term start at St Hildy's? Mum, you'd better ring Mrs Cutting today.'

'I've done it,' Selena said. 'She was the first person I called after I cleaned the pond-muck off. She said she'd be delighted to have me back.'

'The woman's a masochist,' Rose said. 'You were an absolute torment to her before. Such a pity Tristan's at the other place,' she added, seemingly offhand. 'He's just the right age for Selena.'

'Who's Tristan?' Selena asked.

'I forgot you haven't met him. He's Alice's nephew. He's staying at the farm.'

Rufa looked angrily at Rose. She saw right through her mother's attempts at offhandedness. 'He's quite a bit older, actually. Nearly twenty-one.'

'Oh, there's not such a yawning gulf between twenty and seventeen.' Rose left the rest of the sentence—concerning the larger gulf between just twenty and nearly twenty-eight—to reverberate silently.

'He's very old for his age,' Rufa said coldly, knowing he was the exact opposite. 'I sometimes think he's more mature than I am.' She stood up. 'I must go now.'

'Wait—' Something made Rose leap up and hug her daughter fiercely. 'Come back soon, won't you, darling? Please don't leave it so long next time.' She could not shake off a sense of having lost her.

Rufa bent to kiss her without a word, and almost ran to her car.

'So the board voted to extend the scholarship,' Mrs Cutting said. 'The *Vogue* cover probably helped. I certainly didn't need to beg.'

'Thank you,' Rose said fervently. 'Thank you so much.'

The headmistress of St Hildegard's had called at Melismate directly after the governors' meeting, to bring Rose the news that despite Selena's behaviour over the past year, her scholarship was safe. Rose was weak with relief—she had dreaded having to beg Edward for the fees.

She had been very surprised, and rather alarmed, to find Mrs Cutting on her doorstep. Selena's headmistress was a handsome woman in her fifties, with a tidy cap of straight brown hair. She wore a soft blue shirt under a Fair Isle waistcoat, smart skirt, and black shoes with high heels. Rose, in her usual baggy sweater and balding corduroys, thought Mrs Cutting looked far more at home in the newly restored drawing room, with its thick Indian silk curtains and enormous Knole sofa, than she did.

'You've been wonderfully kind and miraculously patient,' she said. 'I really don't think she'll blow it this time.'

'I wanted to keep faith with her,' Mrs Cutting said seriously. 'It was perfectly obvious why she was so difficult last year. It was her response to the loss of her father.'

Rose sighed, suddenly acutely lonely for the Man—so not here, so left out of all their plans. 'I did my best, but it was impossible to reach her.'

'Mrs Hasty, I'm not saying any of it was your fault. I know you've all had a hellish time. Selena seems very focused and motivated now, and I'll be astonished if I can't get her into Cambridge. She's one of the ablest girls I've ever taught.'

The door opened. Selena herself came in, carrying a tray of tea. She set it down on the antique chest on the hearth-rug, and Rose tried to look as if this sort of thing happened all the time. Selena had made real tea, in a teapot, and unwrapped the new cups and saucers Rufa had bought at Heal's. Gravely, Selena poured the tea. Rose watched her, with the eyes of a stranger—this poised, graceful and entirely presentable teenager. It astonished her to see her daughters remaking themselves. The Man would not have recognised the green shoots that were springing from the ruins of his family.

'I'll go now, if you don't mind,' Selena said to Mrs Cutting. 'I promised I'd read to Linnet.'

'Of course I don't mind. See you in school on Monday.'

When the unrecognisable paragon had left the room, Mrs Cutting turned back to Rose. 'Do you know, she reminds me so much of Rufa, now those frightful studs have gone.'

'Yes, I suppose there is a resemblance,' Rose said thoughtfully. Until now, she had thought of Selena as an elongated version of herself and Lydia. But there was a definite echo of Rufa in the set of her head, and the coltishness of her long limbs.

'How is Rufa?' Mrs Cutting asked pleasantly.

'Fine!' Rose declared, with a shade too much enthusiasm. She could hardly tell her daughter's old headmistress that she strongly suspected Rufa of having a rip-roaring affair with her husband's nephew by marriage.

Mrs Cutting said, 'Rufa was the one I worried about most when your husband died. They were extraordinarily close, weren't they? I was afraid she wouldn't be able to cope with the shock.'

You were right there, Rose thought; you know her better than I do; she had me fooled for months.

'But she seems to have pulled herself through it really well,' Mrs Cutting went on. 'I've never seen such a stunning bride.'

Outside the window, beyond the silk curtains, they heard the sound of wheels crunching the gravel. Rose peered out into the deepening dusk. 'Rufa's car,' she said happily. 'Now you can ask her yourself.'

It was not Rufa. If Mrs Cutting had not been there, Rose would have shrieked aloud. *Edward.* What was Edward doing here? There was not enough light to see the expression on his face, but Rose read tension and anger into every line of him.

She heard him thumping on the heavy door. She heard Lydia, in the kitchen, calling, 'I'll get it.'

And, far too soon, Edward was in the room with them. He was sharp and clean and rigid, in his dark suit and regimental tie.

Mainly for the benefit of Mrs Cutting, Rose kissed his cheek. 'Edward, how terrific to see you. You know Theresa Cutting, I'm sure.'

Edward's dark grey eyes had a dangerous glitter. He did not acknowledge Mrs Cutting: a very bad sign in such a punctilious man.

'I think you know why I'm here,' he said. 'I want to speak to Rufa.'

'To Rufa?' Mindful of Mrs Cutting, Rose struggled to sound breezy. 'She's not here, I'm afraid. Wasn't she in, when you got home?'

Edward said, 'I arrived back at the farm about half an hour ago. There was a note on the kitchen table. Rufa's left me.'

'*What?*' This time, Rose did shriek aloud. 'Oh God, that idiotic girl!'

Mrs Cutting, her face a mask of discretion, quickly stood up. 'I must be off. So nice to see you.' She hurried out, without looking back.

'I saw it coming,' Rose groaned. 'Why didn't I say something to her? Darling, I'm desperately sorry. All I can say in her defence is that she's probably lost her mind.'

'Where is she, Rose? I think I'm at least entitled to an explanation.'

Rose scrabbled in the pocket of her trousers for cigarettes and matches. She lit one and threw the spent match angrily into the fire. 'For the last time, Rufa is not here. But I assume she's wherever Tristan is.' She glanced up at him, and realised she had shocked him profoundly.

'Tristan?' His voice was quiet, simmering with fury. 'But he's a boy!'

'He didn't look like a boy to me.' Rose's tone sharpened. 'What did you expect anyway? You bugger off abroad, leaving her alone in the house with a gorgeous young man—what did you bloody well expect?'

'I trusted her. The rest of you have the morals of alley cats, but I thought she was different. She's the Man all over again!'

'Oh, dear God—' She pressed both palms into her cheeks, forcing herself to be calm. 'Sorry, Edward. It's my fault. I let her marry you, when I knew she was clinging on by her fingernails. Oh God, what a mess.'

His anger had retreated. The whole room tasted of his anguish. 'I knew it too,' he said. 'She rang me two days ago, crying and begging me to come home. I pulled every string to get away—and I was too late.'

'The thing is, she does love you.' Rose took a step towards him, awkwardly touching his arm. 'Come into the kitchen and have a drink.'

'Is there any whisky?'

'Yes. I'll pour you a huge one.'

The situation seemed just as ghastly in the kitchen, but easier to digest. Fortunately, the kitchen was empty. Lydia, lately developing a most un-Hastyish tact, had withdrawn upstairs to keep Selena and Linnet out of the way. Rose poured Edward an enormous whisky.

'Medicine,' he said.

'It helps.' Rose poured herself a gin and sat down at the table. Edward dropped into a chair opposite, dazed with shock. There was a silence that seemed to stretch for ages.

Rose sighed heavily. 'Edward, I'm sorry—but did you really not suspect something was going on with Tristan?'

'No.' He frowned. 'That makes me a fool, I suppose. But I can't get my head round it. Any other woman—but not Rufa. Never Rufa.'

His pain wrung the blood from Rose's heart. She searched for words to cushion the truth. 'She's only a woman, not an angel. Sleeping with a gorgeous young man who's in your house is a very ordinary sort of crime. When I saw them together, she was acting as if she'd just discovered sex—perhaps,' she hastened to add, 'because she missed you.'

'Crap,' Edward said. 'We've done it once, as I dare say she told you.'

'She didn't, but I had wondered,' Rose admitted. 'What was the problem? I know it's a rude question, but she can't have turned you down—Ru's the soul of duty.'

'That's just it,' Edward said. 'I couldn't do anything when I even suspected she was acting out of duty.'

She nodded sympathetically. 'Rather a turnoff. It doesn't seem fair that you should be rendered impotent by your in-built sense of decency.'

'I am not impotent—bloody hell.' He was not annoyed now. He was even slightly amused by her tactlessness. He drained his glass. 'I don't know why on earth I want to tell you this, but I had been having a sort of relationship with Prudence. Nothing particularly serious. We saw each other when she was between marriages.'

'Did you tell Rufa?'

'I told her we'd had an affair after Alice died.' He was defensive.

'That was years ago,' Rose said. 'What about the sequel?'

'Look, it really wasn't serious—certainly not on my side.'

Rose was white with anger. 'No wonder the old bitch wouldn't come to the wedding. I suppose you went to Paris to break the news?'

'Yes.' Edward let out a heavy sigh. 'I honestly thought it had been over for months, but she acted as if I'd broken some kind of understanding.'

'Oh, come on, look at it from her point of view. Dear old Edward, always good for dinner and a screw, turns out to be just like all the others—he buggers off with someone twenty years younger.'

There was a silence.

Edward said, 'You think I'm an idiot.'

'No, I just think you're a typical man. Or you would have told poor Ru the whole story.'

'I didn't think there was anything to tell.'

Rose exhaled gustily. 'So you invited the bloody woman to her house.'

'Pru invited herself. I assumed, because I was finally married—'

'Well, I bet Rufa found out,' Rose said. 'She might be barmy, but she's not stupid. Think how it must have looked to her. She fails to have sex on her honeymoon, then her husband invites his old squeeze to stay.'

Edward winced. 'But it wasn't like that! Pru made it quite clear that she only wanted a shoulder to cry on—I'm sure she'd never have told Rufa.'

'I'm not,' Rose said, with a surge of bitterness. 'I remember what she was like when she dropped you for the Man—she couldn't stop rubbing my nose in it. It was the only time the Man and I ever rowed over one of his lovers.' She regretted saying all this when she saw the agony rake across his face. She lit another cigarette, tears trembling in her eyes. 'I don't understand you, Edward. This family has completely screwed you—I don't know why you don't get a sledgehammer and smash this whole house down. You'd be completely within your rights.'

He understood that she was serious, and answered her seriously. 'I think it must be because I love you all so much.'

'Because you love Rufa.' Rose sniffed, digging in her sleeve for a tissue.

'All of you. You've been a family to me—everyone needs some very annoying relations. Let's say I liked being annoyed. It stopped me dying of loneliness.' He had never made such an admission to Rose. Suddenly made awkward by the intimacy, he stood up. 'May I have some more?'

'Help yourself,' Rose said.

Edward returned to the table with a fresh glass of whisky, and passed the green bottle of gin to Rose. 'I'm going to get very drunk,' he announced gravely. 'Then I'm going to sleep here, on the strangely hideous new sofa Rufa chose for your drawing room.'

Rose giggled, wiping her nose. 'You're very welcome.'

He took a dose of whisky. 'Tomorrow I'll go to Oxford to fetch Rufa,' he said. 'I should never have let Prudence make me feel guilty. I'm going to apologise, and offer to start all over again.'

Rose, without knowing precisely why, did not like the sound of this. 'You're saying you've decided to forgive Rufa?'

'Of course.'

'Please, Edward, don't . . .' She paused. 'Don't forgive her too hard.'

Tristan's father had bought him a small terraced house in the part of Oxford known as Jericho. Dusty evergreens drooped in the window boxes. There was a cheerful, tattered air of well-heeled studentry.

Edward stood on the other side of the street, staring at the house. He could not connect it with Rufa. Suddenly, he was sick with longing for her. He cursed himself for never daring to tell her how passionately he had loved her.

In his rational mind, he did not hate Tristan—the baby Alice had adored, the callow oaf who had heedlessly blasted his marriage apart. He had already decided, while driving to Oxford, that there was no point in being heavy with Tristan.

He crossed the road and pressed the tarnished brass bell. He had crouched in shell holes under fire, and not felt as nervous as this.

There was movement inside the house and the door opened. He was gazing into Tristan's blue eyes. He looked ghastly. His face was pasty and swollen, his hair lank and unwashed. He was the incarnation of misery.

'Come in,' Tristan said. There was a hint of sullenness buried in the depths of his misery. 'Make your scene. I know what you're going to say.' He led Edward into the sitting room, and sat down at a littered desk.

Edward suppressed an urge to smack Tristan's head. 'Where's Rufa?'

'Gone,' Tristan said. 'It's over. She's left me.'

Edward struggled to process this. He had expected to find a lovers' bower, yet here was Tristan, as deserted and sorrowful as he was.

'It wasn't my idea,' Tristan blurted out desperately. His reddened eyes filled. 'I didn't make her run away. Yes, I fell in love with her. Yes, I had an affair with her. But as far as I knew, I was leaving her at the farm. I hated it, I begged her to arrange our next meeting—and she wouldn't. She acted as if she never wanted to see me again.' He looked away, withering under Edward's glare. 'She turned up here, out of the blue, the day before yesterday.' His lower lip buckled pathetically. 'Everything was different, because she—she'd found out she was pregnant.'

Edward gritted his teeth to stop himself roaring aloud. This was as cruel as death. He had lost a chance to have a child, as well as losing his wife. 'And what did you have to say to that?'

His tone made Tristan wince. 'I freaked out.'

There was a charged silence. Tristan waited for Edward to sketch out the rest. Edward said, 'You told her to get rid of it.'

'No, I wouldn't do that.' He sounded doubtful. 'Honestly. I just assumed, you know—I mean, does she honestly think I want to miss my finals, because I'm sitting in a maternity ward?'

The longing to deal him a mighty sock on the jaw, like Gary Cooper in a film, was so intense that it was almost erotic.

'She seemed to think I'd want to get married, or something.' Tristan rubbed his eyes wearily. 'Then she went cold on me. She said I didn't love her enough. I started swearing I loved her, but it was too late. She said I was making her choose between me and the baby.'

'And of course she chose the baby,' Edward said. 'You don't know her at all, do you? And she realised she didn't know you.'

Tristan nodded. He began to cry. 'She said she was an idiot to fall in love with me, because the man she loved had never really existed—she saw me properly now. And that was it. She went.' Another sob shook him. He buried his head in his arms.

Edward's mind was in a state of chaos. Rufa was somewhere in the world, pregnant and alone. She had run away from her husband, she felt rejected by the father of her child. The fearful surrounding darkness had come to claim her at last. He had to find her.

In the meantime, here was Tristan, weeping in the burnt-out ruins of his great passion. Edward found his anger had evaporated. He touched Tristan's shoulder awkwardly. 'Come on, think. Think of everything she ever said to you. Where would she go? Was she afraid I'd be angry?'

Tristan raised his head. 'She was angry with you. You hurt her.'

'Me? What the hell had I done?'

'You told Prudence about your sex life. Or rather, the lack of it.' Tristan was rallying, now that he had something to fling back at him.

Edward exhaled heavily. 'And Prudence told you.'

'Of course. What did you expect?'

Well, of course, Edward thought. He should never have let her coax him into confiding in her. Rufa would be thinking that he had betrayed her, and she would be right.

Tristan sat up. 'Edward . . .'

'MM?'

'I'm sorry.'

'You're apologising to the wrong person. But I forgive you, anyway.'

God, he looked so young, Edward thought. 'Don't let all this mess up your work, Triss,' he said, on an impulse. 'One day you'll look back on it, and realise what a complete little shit you were.' He rubbed Tristan's hair, affectionately and slightly contemptuously. 'So put it all down to experience, is my advice.' He left the room.

In Rufa's dream, the Man called to her. She saw herself, sitting beside the window of her bedroom at Melismate. At the same time she could see the Man downstairs in the sitting room, holding his head. Rufa could not make the self in her dream get up to go to him, though she knew he needed her. She sat and sat; the Man called and called.

She was suddenly awake, her face awash with tears. The woman on the other side of the little table eyed her sympathetically. Rufa turned towards the window. Outside, the undulating grey fields—the standard view from any train window in England—were darkening in the dusk.

'I'm just popping to the buffet,' the woman said. 'Can I get you a cup of tea? You don't look well.'

Rufa dredged up a laugh, grimly thinking this must be the understatement of the year. 'Oh, I'm fine—it's just—' The woman looked motherly and kind. On impulse, she said, 'I'm pregnant.'

Here was a perfectly satisfying explanation—one that even covered sobbing on a train. The woman smiled, relieved. 'Morning sickness? Oh dear. Isn't it hell? A good cup of tea is just what you need, then.' She stood up. 'It always worked for me.'

'I'd love one,' Rufa said, gratefully. 'You're very kind.'

'I remember how it feels.'

Left alone, Rufa took off the smile, which was painful. She would bet this woman did not know how it felt to run away from a husband and a

145

lover, carrying the lover's child. She thought how odd it was that she had cried for the Man, when she had not yet shed a single tear over the wreckage of her hopes.

Calm enough, at last, to look over the smoking ruins, Rufa thought back to the beginning of her descent into nightmare-land.

The summer heatwave had ended overnight. The lovers had woken one morning to a solid downpour. Rufa had built a crackling log fire in the drawing room. And, incredibly, Tristan had not wanted to make love to her in front of it. Still more incredibly, he had announced that he was feeling 'claustrophobic', and suggested they drive over to Melismate. He had refused to understand why this was out of the question. There had been a quarrel, a scratchy, bickering, irritable quarrel. Alarmed at how quickly he had been able to reduce her to tears, Tristan had repented and consoled. Now, she wished she had paid attention to his inability to face the future and admitted that it lay between them.

The nightmares had begun again that night. She had dreamt that she knelt on the floor of the small sitting room at Melismate, sweeping the fragments of something precious into a dustpan. The voice of the unseen Man had been around her, assuring her that she could fix it. Rufa, in her dream, had known this was something she could never fix. She had woken in tears, and, at the moment of awakening, had felt a pang of disappointment that Tristan was not Edward.

Tristan had been sweet, but his comforting was not up to the standard of Edward's. Throughout the following (also rainy) day, she had made great efforts to keep the atmosphere as light as gossamer. She had coaxed and flirted, until Tristan had been unable to help falling back into enchantment. The magic bubble had been sealed again.

On her last full day with Tristan, before he had to return to Oxford, the sun had returned for a final bow. They had taken last walks in their lovers' haunts, and he had begged Rufa to come with him, stay with him, live and die with him. At the time, she had thought it important to take formal leave of Edward, as if on her deathbed, but now she wondered if Tristan would have been less horrified by her pregnancy if she had gone with him and they had discovered it together.

Useless to speculate, of course. But once the incredible, unreal suspicion that she was pregnant had been confirmed with a pregnancy test, there had been only one course of action open to her. She had decided that regrets for Edward were irrelevant, because they had come far too late. For better or worse, she belonged now to Tristan—and that was all that had stopped her going out of her mind. She had felt such warmth, such love and joy about Tristan, and the beautiful child who would enter the world in the little house in Jericho. Perhaps it would be a boy, to fill the vortex in her heart left by the death of the Man.

The kind woman was swaying back up the aisle between the seats, carrying a small paper bag. 'I got you a couple of ginger biscuits, too. The minute you get one down you, you'll feel heaps better.'

Rufa smiled and politely took a sip of railway tea, and a bite of railway biscuit. To her surprise, they made her feel better. The giddy, weak feeling passed, and she felt ready to start thinking properly.

'Told you,' said the woman. Smiling, she picked up her magazine.

The windows were black mirrors, reflecting a cosy image of the lighted carriage. Rufa felt she now had nerve enough to start tackling the enormous mess she had made of her life since her marriage—since the death of the Man. All roads wound back to that. She wondered where she had been; what had driven her to forget herself so drastically.

For Tristan to overlook the unromantic question of contraception was understandable, if not forgivable. He was young, and had assumed that she would take care of it. But, until now, Rufa had taken a serious pride in her perfectly ordered life, and been scornful of weakness in others. What a starchy little cow I've been, she thought. Now she felt ashamed.

When she ran away from Tristan's house, she had managed to get herself and her suitcase to Oxford Station and onto a London train. She had intended to take refuge at Wendy's, but in the taxi on the way there she suddenly realised she could not face Nancy, Wendy or Roshan. Instead, she had told the driver to take her to King's Cross; the only mainline station she could think of through the internal tempest.

This train, to Edinburgh, had been on the point of leaving. Rufa thought Edinburgh had a sonorous, historical ring to it, which she liked. She remembered a dinner-party customer of hers, who had a house there. This amiable and well-connected lady might be a useful contact—she would need to work again. She would atone for her stupidity by building a life for her baby. It was oddly comfortable to be worrying about work and money again. But how frighteningly easy it was, she thought, to disappear.

Waverley Station was a maelstrom of lights and people. Rufa, a lonely speck in the crowd, considered what to do next. It was late and she had an urgent longing to lie down—the baby was giving the orders now. She accosted one of the guards and asked for the nearest hotel.

The man looked her up and down, taking in her Mulberry suitcase, her Prada handbag, the jewel on her wedding finger, and directed her to the Balmoral. She hefted her case out into Princes Street. The hotel was impossible to miss. Fortunately, she was too exhausted to worry that its solid opulence was unsuitable for a Fallen Woman.

At the gleaming desk, she showed her gold credit card. She had no idea how to avoid giving them her real name, and signed in as Mrs Reculver—it would surely be ages before anyone thought of checking hotels in Edinburgh.

The room was wondrously comfortable. The moment she had tipped the porter a pound and shut him out, Rufa shrugged off her coat and collapsed on the firm, fatly quilted double bed. Tomorrow she would think about finding herself a flat, and phone Diana Carstairs-McSomething, informing her that she was available for dinner parties.

Her hand strayed to her stomach. She closed her eyes. For the very first time she visualised a real baby, and was ambushed by a fierce, pagan joy that refused to take into account the Man's death, Tristan's hideous inadequacy or Edward's anger. The baby overrode them all. It would make her strong enough to laugh at her misery, and the misery she had caused to all the others. She began to sing to it, with the Man's voice in her mind, singing her to sleep in some lost, primeval era.

Rufa had always heard Edinburgh described as a beautiful city. The view from her window the next morning was bleak and forbidding. Roofs and spires were clustered round the hem of the Castle Rock, with the grey castle carved into its summit. Autumn had arrived here ages ago, unpacked its bags and settled in permanently.

The people in the street below wore thick coats and bent their heads against the wind. Rufa put on her cream cashmere sweater, soft and warm as an embrace, and went down to breakfast. She was still tired, but the sickness had receded. She ate porridge, bacon, eggs, a sausage and two racks of toast. The hunger attacks had started before she knew she was pregnant. You just had to hurl food at them, by the bucketload.

Once her stomach was full, she could think more rationally. She realised that Edward would know exactly where she was as soon as he saw her credit-card statement. If she were serious about hiding, she would have to take out a big wedge of cash, and live anonymously on that until she found work. The priority was a flat. Timidly, she asked the young woman at Reception.

She could see that the girl was puzzled by her urgency—why would this cashmere-clad Englishwoman want a cheap flat in a hurry? The girl gave her a local newspaper, in which there was a page of advertisements for letting agencies. Rufa chose the agency with the largest advertisement, and ordered a taxi.

Outside the hotel, the wind pounced on her like a tiger, stinging her eyes. The taxi carried her through streets of unrelenting grey stone and small windows staring in high, blank walls. There were no trees, no parks, no window boxes. The sterile chill of the city made her ache for the fat fields at home.

The letting agency was an office, in a depressing row of shops. Anxious-looking people waited on orange plastic chairs. Phones shrilled continually. Rufa found that nobody was interested in hearing what kind of flat she wanted. Once she had mentioned her price limit, she was handed a sheaf of typed papers.

She sank into a chair to study them. Her spirits plummeted when she read the descriptions of flats available. They seemed fantastically expensive, and though she did not know Edinburgh, were obviously ghastly.

She took the papers back to the counter. 'I'm awfully sorry, but these all seem to be shared. I was looking for something self-contained, with my own kitchen and bathroom.'

The woman at the counter looked (or Rufa imagined she looked) scornful. 'You'll need to pay more, I'm afraid.'

'Could you show me some details, please?'

This time, the woman looked at her more closely. If Rufa was prepared to take a short-term let of three months only, she said, she had something that might be more her style. The rent was enormous, but Rufa no longer cared. If the place was halfway decent, she would be buying herself three whole months of not having to face them all at home.

The flat was in a 400-year-old court off the Royal Mile, fifty yards below the castle. She liked being near the castle. Its stony solidity made her feel safe. The sentries said 'Good night' when she wandered past them. Sometimes she walked past on purpose, just to hear a friendly voice. She was desperately unhappy. I might have known, she thought, that Edward only meant to give me the money—not himself.

He belonged, in that sense, to Prudence. She now knew why their single night of sex had felt vaguely illicit—Edward had felt he was committing adultery. She hated herself for throwing such a tantrum about Melismate that Edward had felt compelled to rescue her.

She stayed in the flat until she could not bear the cold and the silence, then went for long walks through the steep streets of the blackened, beautiful, monumental Old Town. Little by little, she began to drag herself out of the slough. Diana Carstairs-McInglis, the kind hostess for whom she had cooked in London, would not be visiting her Edinburgh house until next spring, but she had promised to recommend Rufa to her friends. One of these telephoned soon afterwards, to engage Rufa for a large dinner party. She lived about an hour's drive from the city, but offered to provide transport.

Work proved to be the best medicine. Rufa spent a frantic day in the antiquated kitchen, but her cooking was a success, and she rediscovered her delight in producing perfect food. The game, and most of the vegetables, had come from her employer's estate. Rufa threw up twice while plucking the birds, but the result was a miracle of tenderness and flavour. She could still cook and she could still earn money.

There would be more dinner parties in the weeks before Christmas. Rufa could not think about Christmas. The longing for Melismate bit deeper every day, but she did not see how she could return as the old Rufa. They were all better off without her—Edward certainly was, though she was half ashamed of how cruelly she missed him. The baby, growing steadily inside her, gave her courage. She began to promise herself that she would go home when the baby was born. It would be a kind of passport back into their good graces, she thought.

One of her walks took her down some steps to a narrow street full of arty junk shops and boutiques. There was a café beside the Grassmarket where she sometimes had a cup of tea: a noisy, youthful place, where the students from the university sat for hours. Had Tristan really been this young when she fell in love with him? I was pretending to be as young as he was, she thought; maybe I was trying to have the youth I missed.

The café put a notice in its steamy window for a cook and Rufa applied for the job. After an exhausting night's trial she was hired, to make mountains of stovies (a delicious mess of mince, onion and potato) for the students. The work was hard and hot and swelled her feet, but it gave meaning and shape to the days, and she needed the money. She became friendly with Amy, the energetic middle-aged woman who owned the café. There were people around her. She began to hate herself a little less.

Knives tore at her innards. Rufa was aware of the pain before she was aware of being awake. Stupid with sleep, she told herself this was the worst period pain she had ever known.

Except that it couldn't be.

She fumbled for the light. Blood was pooling on the sheet underneath her. She stared at it for ages, refusing to accept what she saw. The knives twisted, intensifying the pain. Rufa broke out in howls of despair.

She had not been good enough. She was still being punished. She was suspended on the very edge of the world, with no more reason to exist.

Chapter Four

'I THOUGHT OF TAKING OUT the wall between the kitchen and the scullery,' Polly said. 'To make one big, warm room—rather like the kitchen at Melismate, though tidier, obviously.'

She came to Ran's side of the table bearing her white everyday Wedgwood coffeepot, and poured fragrant dark coffee into his deep cup of steaming milk. He grunted absently, turning a page of the *Guardian* with tremendous flapping that knocked a piece of toast onto the floor. He did not notice. Ran was incapable of doing more than one thing at a time, and reading the *Guardian* took all his concentration.

Polly stooped to pick up the toast. Rome—as she had to keep reminding herself—was not built in a day. The progress of her great renovation was painfully slow, but changes had been made. His squalid kitchen was, at least, clean. Polly had wrestled the ancient Aga into submission, and there were new chairs, china and pans.

She went on, in the sunny, positive tone she adopted when Ran needed chivvying, 'And while we're about it, we really should get rid of the wall between the sitting room and what you sweetly call the parlour.'

Ran, intent on his newspaper, blindly gulped coffee.

She sighed. 'I do wish I had a magic wand, and I could make it ready for tonight. I've done my best, but this is still a hostess's nightmare. The state of the downstairs cloakroom cries out to heaven. That's another thing I'm going to fix before winter sets in.'

The fog of incomprehension was clearing from Ran's dark eyes. 'Hang on, Poll—this is all going to cost a bloody fortune.'

She smiled, pouring coffee, enjoying the picture of serenity she made. 'I know it's a huge project, but I don't want to do it in stages. I might ask the Bickerstaffs to take it on. They're expensive, but worth it—that's what poor Rufa told me, only a matter of days before she vamoosed.'

Ran was not ready to move on to the topic of Rufa. 'It's going to cost a fortune,' he repeated. There was that stubborn glint in his lustrous eyes.

Polly made her voice caressing. 'Oh, darling, you don't have to worry about that. I can afford to make a few more improvements here—I think of it as an investment in the future.'

151

'But I can't let you spend your money on my house.' His perfect brows drew together ominously. 'If you want the truth, I don't fancy any more changes. I like it as it is.'

'Now you're being silly.' This was seriously vexing. Keeping her voice light and reasonable was an effort. 'You can't possibly like all this chaos.'

'Why do you want to knock all my walls down?' Ran was plaintive. 'This is my home!'

Polly's wedding dress was still hanging, in its protective blue body bag, on the back of the door. She did not think she needed to point out that it was her home, too. She smiled into his heavenly eyes. 'Sweetheart, I'm not trying to destroy your home, honestly. I was only getting flurried about tonight.'

'Tonight?' Ran echoed innocently.

She let out a peal of indulgent laughter. 'You've forgotten, haven't you? It's my dinner party for Hugo and Justine, and Hugo's parents.'

'Oh. Right.' Ran folded his newspaper. With the expression of a man facing a firing squad, he said, 'I'm really sorry—but I won't be here.'

The blood slowly drained from Polly's lips, leaving them white and compressed with unbelieving fury. This dinner party was meant to be her introduction to the local gentry. Hugo's parents were prominent among the squirearchy on this side of Gloucestershire.

'Of course you'll be here,' she said. 'Where else would you be?'

He looked unhappy. 'The thing is, it's November the 5th and Nancy's invited a few people over for a firework party.'

Bloody Nancy, Polly thought wrathfully; why can't she just go back to London? 'Well, she'll understand if you say you can't come.'

'I have to be there,' Ran said. 'Nancy arranged the party specially, to cheer Linnet up. She misses Rufa.'

'For God's sake,' Polly snapped. 'You're always rushing over to Melismate. I wish you'd just accept that you don't belong to the Hastys any more. Hanging around them just makes you look stupid.'

'I'd rather hang around the Hastys than that berk Hugo,' he said hotly.

'Oh, I know what this is really about—it's your obsession with Lydia,' she said. 'Just because she's joined a choir and got herself a life—'

'This is not about Liddy, all right?'

'I suppose I'll have to settle for a compromise,' Polly said icily. 'You can show your face for the first bit of the party—presumably it'll be early, because of Linnet. But you'll have to be back by seven.'

'I'm not coming back,' Ran said, with an unfamiliar steeliness. 'I'm staying for the whole party. I've bought sparklers.'

'You're coming back at seven!' Polly was fierce. 'I've invited the

D'Alamberts to meet us as a couple. I've told them unofficially about the wedding. If you're not here, it will look ghastly.'

'What fucking wedding?' Ran shouted. 'I wish you'd told me about it, while you were spreading the news far and wide! When did I agree?'

She stood up, holding herself rigidly to control the shivers of rage. 'Every time I do something you don't like, you try to ruin it by pretending we're not getting married. It's pathetically childish. I'm expecting you here at seven. If you're one minute late, you can sleep on the sofa.'

'I'll come back when I feel like it! This evening belongs to Linnet—you're always trying to come between us!'

He stormed from the room, slamming the door so hard that Polly's wedding dress leapt in its blue plastic shroud.

Nancy carried the plate of sausage rolls out to the old stableyard, where Roger had built the bonfire. The fire was now a ten-foot wall of orange flame, cracking out sparks like snipers' bullets. Drinks and snacks were circulating. Everything seemed to be going well, though Nancy still had her doubts. Quite apart from the awkwardness of everyone knowing about Rufa, she had never taken sole responsibility for a party before.

She halted for a moment, missing Rufa so intensely that tears rushed to her eyes. Since Edward had brought back the news from Oxford, Nancy had shed rivers of tears. Where on earth had the silly mare hidden herself? Rose had protested that she was bound to turn up in a few days, but Nancy knew her sister better. Rufa could be horribly stubborn. She felt shame far more acutely than anyone else in her family—she would never face them until she could face herself.

Nancy had fled back to Melismate, and insisted upon calling the police. Rufa was an adult, however, and there was nothing much the police could do. Their only hope was Edward. When he had opened Rufa's credit-card statement, and discovered she was in Edinburgh he had gone searching for her. He would let them know the second he saw her. Nancy did not see how she could have endured the anxiety, if Edward had not been on the case.

This party was an attempt to cast out fear. They were all frightened by the chasm in the family. The Man had always responded to adversity by throwing a party, and it was his spirit they were trying to invoke. Rose was wandering round the groups of guests, refilling wineglasses. Lydia and Selena had risen to the occasion magnificently. Selena had amazed Nancy by meeting her at the station in a neat white Golf. Since her return to Melismate she had passed her driving test, and now drove herself and Linnet to school. She was young enough to wipe out the nightmare year, and revert to being an ornament to St Hildy's, almost as if the Man had not died.

Lydia had been another revelation. She was as soft and as gentle as ever, but no longer so soft that she was running off the plate. Her excellent cooking had made the supper possible—she had produced gingerbread men, salads, baked potatoes and vegetarian hot dogs.

'Stop thanking me,' she had said earlier. 'This is your reward for cheering up Linnet. She hasn't let you speak in your own voice for days.'

'Listen, I'd happily speak like Egbert Ressany for the rest of my life if I thought it would cheer Linnet up.' It had cut Nancy to the heart to find Linnet sobbing every night for Rufa, and asking why she did not phone. She had dredged up all her storytelling powers to invent mad adventures for the Ressany Brothers, and fantastic narratives about Rufa's life in Scotland, full of ingenious reasons why she had not been in touch.

Watching Linnet now, Nancy decided the party had been a brilliant distraction. She had asked Terry and Sandra Poulter, who worked for Edward and had a child in Linnet's class at the village school. Another child, from the same class, had been brought by two of Lydia's friends from the choir. Nancy smiled at the three small girls, silhouetted against the flames, quivering with glee like hummingbirds.

How long is it, she wondered, since nice, normal people like this came to Melismate parties?

Lydia had made mulled wine, to the Man's old recipe. She looked charming, in new jeans and an oversized scarlet sweater. She had invited a dozen people from the Cotswold Chorus, and was listening to the conductor, Phil Harding, with a rapt and radiant face.

'Look at him,' Ran's voice said bitterly, next to Nancy's ear. 'Smarming all over her.'

'Have a sausage roll,' Nancy said, thrusting the plate at him.

'Are they organic?'

'Of course not.' She pulled the plate back. 'Do stop glowering, Ran.'

'He fancies her—it's disgustingly obvious.'

'And I can't help thinking she rather fancies him. Now go and light some fireworks,' Nancy said. 'Isn't that why you came?'

'I'm not letting that mimsy singing bastard out of my sight!'

Nancy left him scowling, and took her sausage rolls to the lively group round Lydia. It had to be admitted, the Man would have laughed at some of these choir people—so clean, so polite, so crashingly harmless with their spotless gossip and lame musical jokes. Well, why not? Nancy was ashamed of her sneering reflex. Left to herself, Lydia evidently preferred unoriginal niceness to the Man's alarming bohemianism. It was strange,

Nancy thought, how they were all beginning to seek out their real selves, outside the shadow he had cast.

Lydia broke away from her group to pour out a mug of mulled wine for Nancy. 'Go on—you haven't had a single drink yet.'

'Thanks, darling. Is it going well, do you think?'

'Wonderfully.' Lydia poured another mug of wine. 'Would you mind taking some over to Ran? He'll only get upset if I do it.'

'OK. Let's avoid a scene, at all costs.'

They both looked at Ran, standing with his arms folded, glaring at Phil Harding. 'He hates seeing me with my own friends,' Lydia murmured. 'He finds the friends I make for myself too threatening.' Her face was full of tender affection for her ex-husband.

'Liddy,' Nancy said, 'tell me you're not making him jealous on purpose!'

Lydia smiled. 'Course I am.'

'Why bother? Why pay any attention to him at all?' Even as she asked, Nancy knew these were pointless questions. Her foolish sister, besotted with Ran since the year dot, had aimed her transformation entirely at him. Did she imagine he would change?

Nancy took the mulled wine to Ran. 'This should lighten you up.'

'I'm not sulking. How typical of you not to acknowledge real pain.'

'Bollocks,' Nancy said, thinking this was the only reply he deserved. What was it with the Hasty girls and men? Rufa had practically arranged her own marriage of convenience, only to break her heart over Tristan. Lydia had stubbornly attached herself to the village idiot. Nancy herself had fallen in love with the one decent man to come their way—and Berry was in Frankfurt. Selena was their only hope. She took the empty plate back to the kitchen.

The telephone rang. She reached for the receiver. 'Hello?'

'Is that Nancy?' It was the voice of Polly, clipped and wrathful. 'I'd like to speak to Ran, please. Is he still there?'

'Hi, Polly—yes, he's still here. But he's outside, and it's a bit of a trek. Can I ask him to call you back?'

'Actually, I have to speak to him now. Urgently. We're giving a dinner party. He seems to have forgotten the time.'

'Silly old him.' Nancy tried not to laugh. 'I'll get him.'

Nancy sauntered over to Ran. 'Ran, Polly's on the phone. Apparently you're expected at a dinner party.'

'I hate her dinner parties,' Ran said. 'Tell her I'm not coming.'

'Tell her yourself. I'm far too busy to get involved in your sordid domestic wrangles.'

He suddenly clutched at her hand, his black eyes pleading. 'Don't you understand? Look at her!—rubbing herself against him!'

Nancy gently disengaged her hand. 'That's rich, considering you've rubbed yourself against half the female population of Gloucestershire.'

'Please, Nance—just tell Polly I'll be along later.'

She laughed. 'All right, but I somehow doubt she'll keep anything warm for you.'

Nancy returned to the kitchen to pass on the bad news. She found that she felt mildly sorry for the redoubtable bossy-boots. Polly had given up Berry, burned all her boats, only to discover that Ran was not nearly as malleable as he seemed. There was some comfort in the knowledge that even people who considered themselves experts at the Marrying Game could fall on their fannies at the last hurdle.

'Liddy—' Ran plucked urgently at her sleeve. 'I have to talk to you!'

'In a minute,' Lydia said. 'Have you had some stew? It's delicious.'

'How long are you going to keep this up? Oh, please!'

The kitchen was packed. Lydia, Selena and Nancy had just finished a production line of plates. There was a solid roar of conversation.

'I can't just walk away,' Lydia said reasonably. 'I ought to keep an eye on the girls, and make sure they eat something besides chocolate fudge.' Her sweet, delicate face lit up as she looked over at Linnet and her two friends, sitting round Linnet's miniature table on tiny chairs. The girls were giggling wildly and shrieking witticisms that contained the word 'bum'.

'They're fine,' Ran said. 'Please, Liddy—I really need to talk to you.'

The moment had arrived. Lydia felt surprisingly comfortable and calm. 'Can't we talk in here?' she asked.

'No!'

'Well, OK.' There were people in the kitchen, the drawing room and the Great Hall. 'We'd better go upstairs. Make it quick, though.' She led him up the uneven wooden staircase and into her bedroom. Flicking on the lamps, she said, 'So talk.'

Ran had not seen inside Lydia's bedroom since long before the renovation of Melismate, and was unprepared for this charming, chintzy, lamplit boudoir. 'I don't know you any more,' he said plaintively, bewildered. 'What's happened to you?'

'Nothing. I was always like this, if you'd ever bothered to find out. I like beautiful music and nice things. I like getting up in the mornings at a reasonable time, and sending Linnet to school in decent clothes.'

Ran paced distractedly across the polished boards and flowered rugs. 'You never liked all that stuff when you lived with me.'

'I loved you enough to put up with not having it.'

'This isn't you!' There were lines appearing on his beautiful face, and threads of grey at his temples. Like the Man, he could not fight time. Every year, he became slightly less flawless.

Lydia had put herself through a painful course of thinking and made some important decisions. One of them was not to let him turn into the Man. She sat down on the bed. 'I'm sorry you don't like all the changes. But you don't have any right to object to them.'

'I do when they affect my daughter,' Ran said.

Lydia had been expecting this line of reasoning, and was prepared. 'Linnet's never been better,' she said calmly. 'She's settled and secure. And now she's making proper friends at school. Nobody asked her home to play. Partly because her mother was a ragged depressive who lived in a dump. And partly because her father was a sex maniac—who also lived in a dump. Her only real friends were the Ressany Brothers.'

'Sex maniac?' In his trance of astonishment, Ran could only echo the key words.

She sighed. 'You were the one who wanted to talk, and I'm doing all the talking. Sorry.'

'You should have told me about Linnet,' he said softly.

'What would you have done?'

'I don't know.' He dropped to his knees on the rug. 'Tried to make things better. It kills me when she's unhappy. I hate myself for letting Polly come between us. Why am I such a stupid shit?'

She smiled. 'You grab things you fancy, without thinking of the dangers. Like Linnet chasing swans.'

He was neither tearful, petulant, nor self-justifying. 'I wish I could turn the clock back,' he said quietly. 'I've made some incredible mistakes.'

'Is Polly a mistake?'

'Poor thing, it's not her fault.'

Lydia repeated, 'Is Polly a mistake?'

'Yes,' Ran said humbly. 'Oh God, it's awful. You should see what she's done to the house. She thinks she's bought me. I can't make her understand that I don't want to marry her.'

'So are you going to tell her?'

Ran reached to take her hand. 'Yes. Even though she'll probably kill me, and squat in my house till I can pay her back all the dosh she's spent on it. I don't care. It's still better than hurting my baby.' Ran groaned gently, and laid Lydia's hand against his cheek. 'I've got myself into a huge mess this time, eh? And I look at you, and see what a bloody great fool I am for ever letting you go. I'm sorry I got angry tonight, but if you will go round looking so incredibly beautiful—and bombarding me with psychic messages that I can't ignore—'

'If you want me now, you have to want me for ever,' Lydia said. 'And if you want me for ever, the rules have to be different. You know what I mean.' She was breathless, forcing herself to make the speech she had rehearsed in her head so many times. 'You made me desperately unhappy when we were married. The first time you cheated on me, I thought I'd die. You told me I'd get used to it—'

'Oh God!' Ran winced. 'I didn't, did I?'

'But I never got used to it. Each time was another death. I never stopped hoping you'd want me again.' Tears brimmed in her eyes.

The years melted from him. For the first time that evening, he smiled fully. 'Do you still love me?'

'I don't know how you can ask me—I've never stopped loving you for a second—' Lydia's voice was fractured with sobs.

Ran sprang up, to gather her into his arms. 'Liddy, please forgive me and start again. I'm a stupid shit, but at least I've learned that I can't be happy without you. Or Linnet. I want my family back.'

Rufa waited at the crossing outside the Caledonian Hotel, bracing herself against the wind. Hard flecks of snow stung her face. Her hands ached inside her gloves.

Then, on the point of weeping, the strange feeling of dislocation stole over her again. The thundering traffic, the harassed crowds, the lighted Christmas windows—everything was unreal and two-dimensional, like a picture. She should have stayed at the flat, but she had to find a present for Linnet. This was a large project. The tea set she had bought for Linnet's birthday had involved hours of glassy-eyed wanderings round toy departments. She then had to find wrapping paper, a card and a Jiffy bag. Once, she could have accomplished all this in an hour. These days, everything seemed to take amazing amounts of energy. She had fainted in the queue at the post office.

The faint had been very embarrassing. The place had been thronged with nosy old ladies collecting their pensions, and it had been a struggle to get away. They had wanted to call an ambulance, but were distracted when Rufa lied that she was pregnant. Being pregnant seemed to explain away all kinds of medical horrors.

She had probably fainted because she was not eating. It was not that she disliked food—simply that the huge effort of pushing things into her face made her exhausted. This morning it had taken her a good hour of the *Today* programme to eat a single slice of toast.

She was fine, however, if she did not think too much about the wrong things. Such as the painful Christmas decorations, which pulled her heart towards home. The home she longed for no longer existed. She wanted the old Melismate, all grimy and chaotic and crumbling, where she could find the Man in the kitchen with Linnet on his knee—Rose in her drinking chair—the girls up in the old nursery. She had wanted to save the Man's home, and she had raped it.

Very distantly, Rufa saw that the green man had appeared on the crossing. The people round her surged across the road. The red man appeared before Rufa remembered that she had intended to cross too. Why was everything happening so fast?

There was a hand on her upper arm. 'Rufa? I thought it was you.'

She turned her head, and saw—of all people—Adrian Mecklenberg.

Adrian reacted with the impeccable consideration one would expect from a man dedicated to the pursuit of perfection. It was as if he was following instructions in some arcane book of etiquette—How to Behave When a Lady Known to you Faints in Princes Street.

He took Rufa into the Caledonian Hotel, installed her in a room and arranged for a private doctor to be sent. Then he departed for his meeting in George Street. The rational part of Rufa was mortified. To Adrian, a faint would be nearly as offensive as a loud fart—the unwanted attention, the fuss, the sheer lack of control.

The doctor was a young woman, no older than Rufa herself. Rufa answered her questions truthfully.

'You're anaemic,' the young doctor announced in conclusion. 'I'm prescribing you some iron. And it looks as if you have an infection, so I'm giving you a short course of antibiotics—but for God's sake, get yourself looked at properly. You should always get help for something like that. You might need a D and C, and I can't tell without a full examination.' She tore the prescription out of her book.

Rufa smiled, glad that the session appeared to be over. She held out her hand for the prescription.

The doctor said, 'Actually, I have to give this in at the desk. Mr Mecklenberg's arranged to have it collected and paid for. I believe he is waiting for you downstairs. Now, take it easy for a day or two and try to eat a good lunch.'

Rufa went down to the dining room, wishing she had dressed with more elegance. Adrian was particular, and he would not care to be seen lunching at the Caledonian Hotel with a woman in jeans.

Adrian stood up at the corner table where he had been reading the

Financial Times. Rufa dropped a chaste peck on his clean, smooth cheek. 'You've been so kind. I'm terribly sorry about all this.'

He tucked her chair underneath her, and sat down. 'Please don't apologise. Are you all right now?'

'Absolutely fine. I can't think what came over me.' Rufa found, to her surprise, that she was rather glad to see Adrian. He was less stressful to talk to when you were not trying to marry him, and she was famished for conversation. She had not had a proper conversation for weeks.

'You've been so nice to me, Adrian. Far nicer than I deserve.'

He was, distantly, amused. 'We won't go into that. I've ordered you the tournedos, because you look as if you need something substantial. Now, have a glass of wine and tell me what you're doing in Edinburgh.'

'Working, mainly,' Rufa said carefully.

'Where?'

'I'm still doing my dinner parties. And I've got a job at a café just beside the Grassmarket—Nessie's. You wouldn't know it.'

One of Adrian's eyebrows moved slightly upwards, indicating surprise. 'A café? What does your husband think of that?'

Rufa decided he had a right not be lied to. Briefly, sipping rich red wine, she sketched in the details of her catastrophic foolishness. She tried to keep her voice light and casual, remembering how Adrian liked his stories—neat, and to the point. She only faltered once, hurrying over her miscarriage. He listened impassively.

Their first courses arrived—a delicate terrine of smoked duck. Rufa admired hers, and made a determined effort to eat it. Chew, chew, chew, swallow. How did normal, fat people manage to do this all day?

Before she had finished, a man in a suit came to the table, with a white paper bag, which he handed to Adrian. 'Your tablets, sir.'

'Thank you.' He passed it across the table to Rufa. 'You ought to begin now, I suppose.' He looked away as she swallowed one of each type.

When she'd finished he said, 'I still don't quite understand why you're here. What on earth is stopping you from simply going home to your family?'

'I can't face them,' Rufa said. She knew this sounded feeble, and struggled to explain. 'The house—everything in it was paid for by Edward, you see. I made him do it, in exchange for marrying me. And now I've broken the agreement. I've dishonoured him.'

'I seem to have missed a segment of the plot,' Adrian said. 'I gathered that you wanted to marry me for my money. But I also gathered it wasn't as important as I had been led to believe. It seemed embarrassingly obvious that you were in love with Mr Reculver.'

'Did it?'

'I confess I was slightly annoyed to find that I had been used as a device to bring true lovers together.'

Rufa felt her face flaming. He made her sound cheap and silly, and he was right. 'I know you don't like apologies, but I am sorry for the way I behaved. I look back now, and I can hardly believe it.'

'So you turned out not to love Mr Reculver after all?'

'It's not as simple as that.' Rufa pushed a shred of duck round her plate. 'I love him and miss him more than anyone, but look how I treated him. He's really far better off without me.'

'Does he think that?'

'I expect so.' She risked a glance across at Adrian, and saw the same expression of tolerant amusement. 'Please . . . if you see anyone from home, don't say you've seen me.'

'I shouldn't dream of interfering.' He raised an eyebrow at a waiter. 'If you're not intending to eat that, I suggest you move on to not eating the entrée. I'm leaving for the airport at three.'

'Ah, Berry.' Adrian, still in his overcoat, stepped into Berry's office.

Berry jumped guiltily, conscious that he had been caught with a vacant expression on his face. 'Adrian. How did the meeting—?'

'This isn't to do with business.' Adrian shifted his briefcase to the other hand. 'Or pleasure, now that I think of it. Do you still see that barmaid sister of Rufa Hasty's?'

Berry felt his face turning a royal purple. 'Yes. She . . . she works at Forbes and Gunning. I do go in there sometimes.'

'Did you know Rufa had bolted?'

'Yes, actually.' A week ago, when he had rushed into the wine bar hours after his return from Frankfurt, the other barmaid—seeing how crestfallen he was that Nancy was not there—had told him the whole story of Rufa's disappearance. His darling Nancy had, apparently, spent a whole night crying her lovely eyes out when she heard.

'Well, tell her I've seen Rufa. I met her up in Edinburgh today, and had lunch with her. She's working at a café called Nessie's, in a street off the Grassmarket. I don't know which, but there can't be many.'

Berry tried not to gape. 'Does she have a phone number?'

'She didn't give it to me,' Adrian said. 'She made me promise not to tell anyone I'd seen her.'

'What made her change her mind?'

Adrian sighed. 'She didn't. I was lying to her. She looked so dreadful, I knew I would be forced to send someone to fetch her.'

'Is she ill?' This was alarming. Berry knew Adrian would never interfere unless he felt he really had no choice.

'Yes,' Adrian said crisply. 'When she saw me, she fainted. She has, apparently, had a miscarriage.' His eyelids wrinkled with distaste. 'The doctor thought she was anaemic, and tried to tell me about infections and depressions. The entire experience was deeply annoying.'

'Still,' Berry said boldly, 'it was awfully kind of you to take care of her.'

Unexpectedly, Adrian's expression thawed into a wintry half-smile. 'Don't you dare accuse me of kindness. I've been hijacked into it, against all my better instincts. May I now consider my hands washed?'

'Yes, of course,' Berry said quickly. 'I'll go round to tell Nancy at once.' He grabbed his jacket. 'And I'm sure she'll want me to say thanks.'

'Tell her to send that silly girl back to her husband,' Adrian said. He left the office without another word.

The bar of Forbes & Gunning was decked with silvered vine leaves and packed with festive drinkers. Berry saw Nancy's red head flashing between the rows of square charcoal shoulders. She was working like a Fury, cramming bottles and glasses onto trays, throwing notes into the till. Berry lowered his head and battered his way through the scrum.

Nancy beamed at him. 'Hello. What can I get you?'

'Nothing . . . hello . . . I need to talk to you—'

'What?'

With one more determined push through the shoulders, he leaned right across the bar towards her. 'It's about Rufa. Adrian met her up in Edinburgh today.' As concisely as he could, through the roar of male conversation, Berry gave her the news headlines. Nancy listened in perfect stillness. When he got to the part about the miscarriage and the fainting and the illness, her blue eyes flooded with tears. She said, 'I must phone Edward,' and hurried off.

Berry gamely held his position, battered by elbows and squeezed against the mahogany. Nancy needed him. He refused to leave her now—he was all the more determined when he saw her hurrying back, wiping her eyes. He asked, 'Did you get him?'

'Yes.' She smiled through the tears. 'I'm glad you're still here.'

Out of the corner of his eye Berry saw Simon, working in an apron alongside his troops, edging his way towards them. 'Get a move on, Nancy. No time for you to hold court today.'

'Sorry.' Two more tears dripped from Nancy's lashes.

Berry felt a soaring, exultant surge of power. He could have slaughtered a lion. 'Excuse me.' He tapped masterfully at Simon's arm with his credit card. 'Nancy's had some bad news. I think I'd better take her out of all this for a minute. Is there somewhere we can go?'

Simon shot a searching glance at Nancy. 'Oh, right. Sorry. I can let you have half an hour. You can go in the office, I suppose.'

'Thanks,' Berry said.

Simon opened a wooden flap to admit Berry behind the bar. Berry swept a protective arm round Nancy's shoulders. The softness of her flesh, warm underneath her thin black cardigan, sent his heartbeat into overdrive. Wiping her eyes, she led him to a tiny, windowless office.

Berry shut the door behind him. He folded Nancy in his arms, drawing her face down into his shoulder. 'Darling,' he murmured into her hair. 'My darling. It'll be all right.'

Her voice was muffled in his suit. 'I just can't bear to think of Ru having a miscarriage, and keeling over in front of Adrian. God, it's such a relief to know she's not dead!'

She drew away from him, sniffing and rummaging in her pockets.

Berry whisked out his handkerchief. He put it into Nancy's hand. 'But she'll be fine now. You've found her, and you can stop worrying.'

Nancy blew her nose. 'I can't get over Adrian playing the Good Samaritan.'

Berry laughed. 'The rather reluctant Samaritan.'

Nancy mopped at her face. 'Edward said he'll drive up to Edinburgh again tonight. I don't know if I should have told him first, but he's the one who deserves to claim her after all those times he's been up there searching for her. Oh, Berry, she'll be home in time for Christmas!'

She smiled properly for the first time: a radiant, brilliant smile that burned away the tears. She flung her arms round Berry's neck and hugged him fiercely. It was incredibly easy—and felt beautifully natural—for Berry to kiss her warm neck, her soft cheek, her ripe mouth.

He pulled his mouth away, keeping one hand on her breast. 'Look, I have to tell you,' he whispered, 'because I can't hide it any more—you're a goddess, you're an angel, and I've been completely crazy about you since the moment we met, when you made me look at your nipples.'

'Oh, darling.' Nancy's eyes were streaming, but her smile was beatific. 'I've been crazy about you since the moment you told me you didn't have enough money for that stupid Marrying Game.'

They fell ravenously upon each other's open mouths. Berry groaned softly, and whispered, 'You're still very upset. I'll tell your boss you can't possibly do any more work, and then I'll take you home, and then I'll make love to you in every imaginable position. It might take days.'

'Weeks.' Her wanton hand caressed his flies.

'Months. Actually, I'm afraid I may have to keep you for ever.'

Chapter Five

THERE WAS NO MISTAKING NESSIE'S. A jaunty purple Loch Ness monster cavorted cheerfully above its window. Edward halted as soon as he saw it, almost gagging with anxiety.

He had driven to Edinburgh straight after Nancy's breathless phone call, arriving at his hotel in Charlotte Square in the small hours.

The three previous trips to Edinburgh had only hardened his determination. He had interrogated the embarrassed but helpful staff of the hotel at which Rufa had used her credit card. One girl had remembered that she had been looking for a flat. Edward had doggedly begun to work his way through every letting agency listed in the phone book. He must have passed within a few yards of this café a hundred times.

Bracing himself for yet another disappointment, he crossed the narrow street and went to the window of the café.

His heart almost stopped. He saw her.

Rufa, wrapped in a striped butcher's apron, was stirring a vast saucepan in a kind of open kitchen. He was startled by the change in her. She was far too thin. There were poignant hollows in her cheeks and dark smudges under her eyes. She was unbearably beautiful. Tears of relief spilled down his face, instantly turning cold in the sawing wind.

She turned her head, and saw him. She froze, her eyes wide with shock. Edward blindly pushed his way into the café, strode right up to Rufa and threw his arms round her. He could not hold her close enough. Her bones felt sharp and fragile under several layers of clothes. Then he gently pushed her away, so that he could look into her face. 'My darling,' he murmured, ignoring the stares of the people round them. 'Say you won't run off again. Say you're glad to be found.'

Rufa said, 'I lost my baby.' A silent sob shook her. She flung her arms round his neck, and wept into his shoulder.

She did not cry for long. She pulled away from him, scooping the tears with the backs of her hands, scattering apologies. She insisted upon finishing her shift. Edward refused to leave her. He established himself at a corner table, pinning his eyes to her as if afraid she would fly away, seething with impatience. Finally, Rufa took off her apron, the café's owner brought out her coat, said something to her, and kissed her.

Rufa's flat was nearby. Once inside, she stopped pretending to be fine, and collapsed on the sofa with a gasp of relief. 'Stairs,' she said, trying to smile. 'Everything in this town is vertical.'

Since when had Rufa not been able to manage stairs? And how long did they have to pretend she was not ill? Edward bit back an impulse to lecture her about taking care of herself. 'I'll make some tea,' he said.

'That would be lovely.' She did not even try to protest about being waited on: a very bad sign.

He went into a kitchen the size of a coffin. He was dismayed to see that, apart from a few rich tea biscuits, there was no food.

When he carried the tea into the sitting room, Rufa—still in coat and gloves—was fast asleep. He spoke her name softly. She did not stir. Very gently, Edward raised her legs, found a duvet in the bedroom and draped it over her. Then he sat down to wait until she woke up.

The short afternoon darkened as he watched her. When he could no longer make out her face in the shadows, Edward switched on a lamp and moved silently to draw the curtains against the winter night.

He brooded over her face as she slept. Perhaps it was the softening effect of the lamplight, but it seemed as if some colour had crept back into her lips. Edward thought, as he often did, of the one night he had lost control in Italy. He blamed the brandy. He had been sloshed, and Rufa had been as drunk as a skunk, without an inhibition left in the world. He had felt ashamed of himself while he was doing it, but never in his life had passion made him so savage.

The memory mortified him. Since the death of the Man, Edward had been profoundly disturbed by Rufa's aching vulnerability. He would never have taken advantage of her by marrying her, if the poor creature had not been so determined to marry someone else. Thank God she had not—he felt he had grabbed her from the precipice.

Rufa sighed, and stirred. She blinked at the ceiling, and turned her head towards Edward. He was encouraged to see that the hunted expression in her eyes faded as soon as she saw him. 'What time is it?'

Edward came over to her, perching on the sofa beside her feet. 'Nearly seven.'

'What? Oh God—'

He put his hand on her shoulder. 'Relax. I'll make that cup of tea.'

'I'm glad you're still here. Otherwise I might have thought I'd dreamt you. I have dreams about you all the time.'

'Of course I'm still here. I'm not going anywhere.'

'Adrian gave me away, didn't he?'

'Yes, thank God,' Edward said.

'He was incredibly kind to me. Even though he thinks being ill is very bad manners.'

Edward made them fresh cups of tea with the last two tea bags. Rufa was sitting up when he brought in the cups. 'Thanks so much. How is everyone? Is Linnet all right? I hated missing her birthday.'

'Everyone's fine,' Edward said, sitting down. 'They'll be even more so when you tell them you're coming home.'

She bowed her head. 'I can't go home. Not after what I did.'

'My darling, that's all forgotten.'

'Not by me,' Rufa said, tears dropping from her eyes.

'Rufa, I haven't spent all this time searching for you because I wanted you to apologise. I should be saying sorry to you. I wasn't honest with you about Prudence. I assumed it didn't matter that I didn't tell you the whole story because it was all in the past. I'd forgotten what a stirrer she can be.'

'You told her about us,' Rufa said, her voice pinched with the hurt.

'I didn't have anyone else to talk to, so I talked to her,' Edward said. He sighed. 'I knew it was wrong at the time. I'm sorry.'

She looked up at him. 'Do you swear it's really over?'

'God, yes. It was over after we split up that first time.'

'After Alice died.'

'Yes. When we . . . well, afterwards, it was never the same. I won't say it meant nothing, but it was basically a friendly arrangement.'

'Prudence seemed to think it was a lot more than that,' Rufa said. 'Did you sleep with her when you went to Paris?'

'Yes. Even though I'd just got engaged to you.' He willed himself not to hide behind excuses. There were none. 'I won't say I couldn't help it. That would be ridiculous. But she offered, and I didn't turn her down.'

'We should have talked more,' Rufa said. 'But we never talked about sex. If I tried to drop a hint, you went outside and mended the tractor.'

This was so true that Edward laughed, though he despaired over the gulf there had been between them. 'If only you knew how much I wanted you. But I was terrified of forcing you into anything.'

'I thought you'd roll straight back into bed with Prudence, because she was good at sex and I wasn't.'

'Oh God.' He reached out to stroke Rufa's cheek with the tip of his finger. 'I wouldn't do that. I'm so madly in love with you that I'll do anything to keep you. When Nancy rang me yesterday evening to tell me you were alone and ill, and patently nutty as a fruit-cake, I had to come and bring you home. But you're not to worry that I'm going to expect you to do anything, just because you foolishly agreed to marry me.' He smiled, longing to comfort her. 'Those are your orders.'

Rufa's tired eyes brimmed with tears. 'It wasn't foolish. It was the most sensible thing I ever did. I don't know how to begin to say sorry.'

He sat down on the sofa beside her, gathering her into his arms. She clung to him, in a tempest of sobbing. He stroked the back of her head. 'Stop it, Ru. I refuse to drive all the way to Melismate with you beating yourself up. I can see you're sorry. You nearly died of being sorry.'

'I'm not ill—it's only since I lost the baby—' Rufa raised her head. 'Did you tell Tristan? He ought to know.'

'No.' Edward could not help bringing this out curtly.

Hesitantly, Rufa asked, 'Do you know how he is?'

'The last I heard, he was absolutely fine.'

'I'm glad.'

They were silent. Edward asked, 'Is that all you're going to say?'

'I couldn't bear it if I'd made him miserable,' Rufa said. 'I wish I knew what got into me. I thought it would kill me to be apart from him. He wanted me such a lot.'

Edward winced over 'he wanted me', with its implication that her husband had not. He spoke as neutrally as he could. 'I went to Oxford a few days after you did. I spoke to Tristan.'

'How was he?'

'Rather a mess.'

'Oh.'

'Do you want to go back to him?'

'No.' Rufa's body tensed in his arms. 'I can't go back to the way I felt about him. It was all based on—I don't know—fantasies. It all fell apart when I turned up on his doorstep, anyway.'

'I heard,' Edward said. 'He told you to have an abortion. That and the disgusting state of his kitchen tore the scales from your eyes.'

Rufa gave a brief laugh that was half a sob. 'Am I that predictable?'

'I know you rather well.' He gave Rufa a friendly kiss on the forehead and released her. 'I know you need to be at home. So, please, let's forget about the past. I'll forgive you, if you forgive me.'

'There's nothing to—'

'Good. Pack up your things. I'll let Rose know you're on your way.'

Edward made Rufa stay in the flat while he went out in the wind and the snow to fetch his car. By the time he had driven from New Town, the car was blissfully warm. Rufa lay back in the passenger seat with a sigh of pleasure that made them both laugh.

'I haven't been this warm for weeks,' she said.

As he steered into a long line of cars heading towards the motorway, he switched on the radio to catch the weather. Heavy snow was predicted on the eastern side of Scotland. There had been a pile-up on the motorway, which was causing long delays.

'We could always go back and leave it till tomorrow,' she suggested.

'I am not going back to that flat,' Edward snapped. 'I'd rather spend the whole night in a traffic jam.' She looked anxious. He smiled at her reassuringly. 'But it won't come to that. I'm sure I can find a short cut.'

She trusted him. It felt delicious to lie back in the warmth, and let him do the worrying about the dreadful driving conditions.

Before long, he left the crawling motorway and nosed along dark, narrow lanes and skirted isolated small towns. Rufa watched him, thinking how lucky it was that she had run into Adrian. Thanks to him (or rather, the doctor he had summoned) she now felt better than she had for weeks, even though the antibiotics made her a little woozy.

The car slowed, and halted. Edward put on the handbrake, and switched off the engine. They were surrounded by blackness, studded with a few distant specks of light.

Rufa, who had been dozing, murmured, 'Where are we?'

'God knows. I'm lost,' Edward said. 'I can't find Berwick-upon-Tweed. Give me another look at that map.' He unclipped his seat belt and leaned across her, to study the map on her knees.

His face was close to hers. She stroked his forehead. 'I do love you.'

For a moment, he was wary. He tried to laugh it off. 'Despite my hopeless orienteering?'

'I love you so much I don't mind being lost in a snowstorm in the middle of nowhere. It's still better than being alone, without you.'

'Without anyone.'

'You in particular. Why don't you believe me when I say I love you?'

This startled him. 'Of course I believe you.'

'No, you don't. I tried and tried. You just think I'm grateful, or something.' Rufa's heart thudded uncomfortably, but she was suddenly desperate to speak the unspoken. 'You've never let me show you. It's as if you didn't want me to love you—in that way, I mean. I wish you'd tell me what I did wrong.'

He let out a brief, angry laugh. 'Every time I went near you, you looked as if you were at the dentist's.'

'I did not!'

'That's how it felt to me. I can't make love under those circumstances.'

'You have too much pride.'

'You seem to expect some sort of apology from me, because I was too decent to rape you—'

'I do not!'

He gave a sigh. 'This is stupid. This time yesterday, sitting here with you would have been my idea of perfect happiness—and now we're arguing. Rather ironically, just like a married couple.'

'All I'm trying to say is that I love you,' Rufa said. 'And I loved it when you fucked me.'

'You were drunk.'

'I should have got my hands on more of that brandy, so you'd fuck me again.' She smiled, a little sourly. 'You don't like it when I say fuck, do you?'

'Not madly. It doesn't seem necessary, and it's not like you.'

'You seem to have this fantasy picture of what I'm like, and it's a real pain to live up to. You wouldn't fuck me, and I thought you didn't want me.'

'Well, you were wrong.' Edward grabbed her hand, and pressed it against his erection. 'That's how much I want you.'

Rufa's head swam. Her flesh suddenly ached to be touched by him.

He moved towards her, unfastening her seat belt. He kissed her hard on the mouth. Their hands tore at each other's layers of clothes. When Edward pulled away from her, they were both breathless.

'I might have completely the wrong idea about you,' he said, 'but I really don't think you'd appreciate being fucked in a car.'

'Braemar' was a detached mock Tudor house in a street on the edge of Berwick. It was profoundly dark, except for one ghostly light above the porch. A sign in the front window said 'Vacancies'.

'Only the best,' Edward said. 'Come on, let's wake someone up.'

He jumped out of the car, bracing himself against the wind, and opened Rufa's door. With one arm round her, he rang the bell vigorously. It shrilled somewhere in the depths of the house, and echoed away into silence. He rang again. 'Don't get cold,' he said. He wrapped Rufa in his arms. They were kissing again. She was almost ashamed of the strength of her desire for him. There was a confidence and firmness in his touch that reawakened all the hunger she had once felt for Tristan, and something else that reached right down to the innermost chamber of her heart.

A light snapped on in the porch, revealing a bulky pink figure behind the frosted glass. A woman with grey hair took a long time drawing bolts and turning keys, before she opened the door an inch. 'Yes?'

'We hate to bother you,' Rufa said, 'but . . .' She smiled up at Edward. 'But we're on our honeymoon.'

Edward experienced a rush of pure happiness. He put an arm round

Rufa's waist. 'Yes. We've only been married a few hours.'

Sympathy softened the woman's face. 'Oh, you poor things. And you've had this dreadful weather. Well, I can hardly turn you away at this time of year, can I? I'll let you have one of my en suites.'

The room was large, and loudly decorated. There was a framed print of Landseer's *The Monarch of the Glen* above the fat, quilted headboard of the double bed. It was very warm, and blazing with light. Once the woman had wished them good night, Edward switched off the monstrous chandelier. He asked, 'Is this place really all right?'

Rufa whispered, 'It's perfect.'

'And you? How are you feeling?'

'Wonderful,' Rufa said. 'Do stop asking me. I'm not going to pass out this time. I'm sober and in my right mind.'

'Well, I'm not. This is the most romantic thing I've ever done in my life.' He took her into his arms and began to peel away her clothes. He was inside her before he had reached the last layer. They sprawled half-clad on the nylon quilt, gasping at each of his hard thrusts. He whispered in her ear, 'Ru, my darling, I love you so much—you're so beautiful.'

They came together, rocking the mattress beneath them, both weeping with the relief of it. Afterwards, Rufa lay in a trance of happiness, holding his head between her breasts.

'I love you more than the world,' she said. 'And you fuck divinely.'

He laughed softly. 'It sounds lovely when you say it. I might even get used to it.'

'You'd better,' Rufa said, 'because I'm never leaving you again, not for a single day. You'll never get rid of me now.'

Chapter Six

'"AND IT WAS ALWAYS SAID OF HIM, that he knew how to keep Christmas well, if any man alive possessed the knowledge."' Rose sat in her drinking chair beside the range. Linnet was on her knee. Roger, Lydia, Selena and Ran were round the kitchen table, drinking cups of tea. She glanced up tearfully at her family. '"May that be truly said of us, and all of us! And so, as Tiny Tim observed . . ."' She lowered the book.

170

Everyone chorused, '"God bless Us, Every One!"'

The reading ended, as it had done so many times in the past, with nose-blowing and self-conscious laughter.

Linnet, supple as a ferret, slid off Rose's knee. 'When's Rufa coming?'

'Do stop asking, darling. The answer will be just the same.'

'Well, I don't care how late it is,' Linnet declared. 'I'm staying till she comes. Why is she taking so long?'

'Edward said they had some shopping to do,' Rose said. 'Go and watch your video of *Muriel The Little Mermaid*.'

'*Ariel*,' Linnet corrected her, with withering scorn.

'Go and watch whatever load of pants you're obsessed with at the moment—and you can have a chocolate from the tree.'

'Yesss!' The little girl danced happily out of the room, twirling the Ressany Brothers round her glossy black head.

The moment she heard the drawing-room door close, Rose said, 'What the hell are they playing at? I thought Edward was bringing me a distraught Niobe at death's door, and now they're going shopping. And God knows where Nancy's got to. She swore she'd be here by six.'

'Listen to Mrs Cratchit,' Selena said.

Rose was finding it difficult to sniff away her tears, but only because her heart—like Scrooge's—was laughing. Tomorrow morning, when she went to church to watch Linnet in the nativity play, everyone she loved on earth would be in the pew beside her.

Roger understood. He gently squeezed her shoulder, murmuring, 'Wouldn't he have loved all this?'

Rose could only nod. It was no longer painful to remember the Man. The memories that came into her mind still made her cry, but they were joyful and benign, as if scattered by the Man himself. He was present, in a way he had not been present since his death. Last Christmas they had been too raw with shock, too blind with grief, to notice him.

She could not stop marvelling over the changes. This time last year, Selena had been sullen and belligerent. Lydia had been passive and despairing. Now Selena had blossomed into a confident bluestocking who cooked and organised. And Lydia—whether one entirely approved or not—was alight with the happiness of reclaiming Ran. He had stayed at Melismate for a week after Bonfire Night, until Polly had dropped his house keys through the letterbox. Then he had carried his wife and child back to Semple Farm.

Polly, in her avenging fury, had removed everything removable that she had paid for. There were three chairs and one bed in the entire house, and no crockery. Fortunately, Ran had stuffed the attic with items

Polly had thrown away. They had returned to the early, blissful days of their youthful marriage—the dinner of herbs where love was, and bugger-all else, as the Man had once described it. Lydia was radiant. Ran was as transparently happy as Lydia, and although Rose doubted they had heard the last of his amorous adventures, at least he now had sense enough to keep his family together.

Selena said to Lydia, 'I hope you're staying for supper. I've made industrial quantities of toad-in-the-hole.'

'We'd love to,' Lydia said. 'Linnet's determined to see Ru, and she might as well get as tired as possible now—I don't much fancy being woken at five in the morning.'

Ran leaned over to kiss her, folding his hands protectively over her belly (pregnant! thought Rose). 'Don't tire yourself out as well.'

'I won't. Selena and I wrapped all the presents yesterday.'

A shriek rang out in the drawing room. The door burst open. Linnet dashed blindly through the kitchen, screaming, 'Rufa! She's come! Rufa!'

The windows of Melismate glowed with golden light. The snow had an eerie glimmer in the darkness. The headlights of the car caught *Evite La Pesne* on the gates as Edward turned into the drive.

He stopped the car in front of the drawing-room window, which was filled with the coloured lights of the Christmas tree. They heard a child's squeal of joy from inside the house, and the door-slamming tumult of her approach, and both laughed.

The great wooden door creaked slowly open, pushed by the small and impatient figure of Linnet. Rufa wrenched open her door, dropped to her knees on the snowy gravel, and clutched Linnet in her arms. Then the little girl was prised away, and Rose's arms were round her. The older woman rocked her daughter like a baby, crooning and soothing. 'My darling, my petal, my silk princess, it's all right now.'

'Mummy, I'm so sorry,' Rufa mumbled in Rose's shapeless woollen bosom. 'I'm so, so sorry.'

'Darling one, there's nothing to be sorry for.'

'That's what I keep telling her,' Edward said. 'She's been wearing sackcloth and ashes all day.'

'Well, take them off. We're having quite a party inside, and sackcloth is against our dress code.' She released Rufa with a resounding kiss, to be vigorously hugged by her sisters.

Rufa asked, 'Is Nancy here?' She was aching to see Nancy. They had volumes of talking to get through.

'On her way,' Rose assured her. 'Do you need help with your bags?'

'No, thanks,' Edward said crisply. 'Ru's not staying here.'

'Oh?' Rose's antennae were twitching.

'I'm going back with Edward,' Rufa said, ridiculously shy. 'We're—well, we've decided to give it another try.'

'Darling!' Rose almost drove the breath out of her with another hard hug. 'That's wonderful! And does that mean—?'

'Yes, Rose,' Edward said, laughing and putting an arm round his bride. 'Before you go into tactless overdrive, we've done it. All right?'

'How wonderfully typical of Ru,' said her mother. 'To have a steamy affair with her own husband.'

Everyone began to laugh and talk at once. They went inside and Rufa found herself in her mother's drinking chair beside the range, light-headed with warmth, dazed by so much happiness. When she glanced over at Edward, she saw her happiness reflected.

Linnet twined her arms round Rufa's neck. 'I live at Daddy's now,' she said comfortably.

'I heard.'

'Smelly's gone. She found Daddy in Mummy's bed.'

Rufa was too tired to make her usual attempt at a straight face, and could not help laughing. 'Oh dear.'

'Oh goody,' Linnet corrected her. 'I was pleased. They're doing their marrying all over again, and I can wear my bridesmaid's dress.'

'Really? You've set a date?' Rufa asked Lydia.

Lydia nodded. 'April the 1st. Don't you dare say that's appropriate.'

'Congratulations. I'll make you another wedding cake.'

'We'll save the top layer for the christening,' Ran said.

'Don't, Ran. It's not the right time to tell her.' Lydia turned radiant eyes to Rufa. 'Sorry. It's far too early to know properly, anyway.'

Rufa smiled, to show she could bear the news. 'Liddy, that's brilliant.'

'We'll have to see who gets there first,' Edward said.

Ran gave him a friendly slap on the shoulder. 'Welcome back to the family, Ed. You can't get away from these Hasty women—so you might as well make babies with them.'

Selena presented Rufa with her plate of gingerbread stars. 'I hope you and Edward are coming for Christmas lunch tomorrow. It's my debut, and I want lavish praise from someone discerning.'

Rufa was impressed. 'You're not doing it all by yourself?'

The elegant young lady suddenly grinned, turning back into a child. 'I could use some help with the turkey.'

Colour flooded into Rufa's face. She revived like a Japanese paper flower dropped in water. 'Have you got chestnuts for the stuffing?'

'Yes. Two tins.'

'I picked up a bag of fresh chestnuts at the grocer's,' Rufa said. 'I knew they'd come in handy. I'll bring them to church with me. Edward, what is it? Why are you laughing?'

'You're going to make me get up at dawn again, aren't you?'

'Yes. You can sleep in on Boxing Day.'

'He can't,' Roger said. 'What about the meet? We can't let old Bute think he's beaten us, just because we've lost the Man.'

Ran said, 'Count me in. I loathe hunting.'

Edward was thoughtful. 'There's a box of his old leaflets somewhere.'

Rose had another moment of intensely sensing the Man. She listened to the three men talking about the Boxing Day meet, as if he had blown the idea into their minds. It was good to hear deep voices in the house again. She watched her girls, talking and laughing round the range. Lydia and Selena were laying the table for supper, vying to tell Rufa about the defeat of Smelly. Rufa cradled Linnet in her arms, listening contentedly. Rose saw how often she glanced over at Edward, and how tenderly he glanced back at her. It was an amazing outcome, and Rose had a strong sense of things being in their right places, at last.

She had learned a lot about Edward over the past year. She had discovered that you could peel away layer after layer of his character, and find only goodness, right to the core. Rose shuddered to think where they would all be now, without his endless love for Rufa. He had ended up marrying the entire family, resigning himself to the fact that they would all be in his hair for ever and ever. Once Rose had wondered what was in it for Edward. Seeing him with Rufa made it obvious. He was a man reborn.

'The toad's ready,' Selena called. 'Sit down.'

The door into the Great Hall creaked open. Nancy burst in, loaded with paper bags, and with milky mistletoe berries pinned in her blazing hair. 'Merry Christmas—where's Ru?'

'Hark, the herald angels sing, pom-pom, pom-pom, newborn king!' sang Berry. Nancy lay lushly asleep in the passenger seat, filling the car with her perfume. Berry ordered himself not to get an erection while driving. Back in the plump, cushioned life with Polly, he had sometimes fantasised about having a single night with Nancy. He now knew there was no such thing as enough, where Nancy was concerned. They had been making love every four hours for the past two days, in every conceivable position. Berry had never been so ridiculously, beamingly happy in his entire life. When he made love to Nancy, he became a

174

sexual swordsman, a Casanova, a king. She loved him, and life looked piercingly beautiful from the inside of her warm heart.

He smiled to himself, remembering how they had shamelessly snogged in the taxi on the way to Wendy's, that first night—he had given the driver an enormous tip. Then he had been inside her, with his lips and tongue round one pale pink nipple, coming and coming, pouring himself into her. He had proposed to her immediately afterwards. He had declared that he would buy her a diamond as big as the Ritz, and tell the whole world, before she could change her mind.

Nancy had said, 'As if I'd change my mind, when at last I've found the world's most perfect man—a model of chivalry who can also make me come like the *Flying Scotsman*.' They had ended up making love again after that.

The following day, oblivious to the jostling Christmas crowds, Berry had taken Nancy to Boodle and Dunthorne in Sloane Street, and chosen her a beautiful, vastly expensive diamond ring.

She had worn the ring that evening, when he had taken her round to his sister's flat in Clapham. His parents had been staying there, and he was impatient to introduce them to the future mother of his children (Berry had already decided four would be nice). Nancy had looked gloriously beautiful in the taupe jacket from the campaigning wardrobe. Annabel had muttered, 'God almighty, she's sensational— what on earth does she see in you?' And his father had drawled, 'I *say*,' in his Terry Thomas voice. They had loved her.

Berry turned his BMW down the lane that led to the gate of Melismate. 'We're here.'

Nancy stretched luxuriously. 'Mmmm. I was having such a rude dream about you.'

'What was I doing?'

'I'll show you later. Wait and see.'

He stopped the car and kissed her. 'Are you as happy as I am?'

'Absolutely delirious. I can't wait to tell Rufa.' She opened her door. 'Isn't it ironic? We were both ready to renounce everything for love, and we couldn't have married better if you'd paid us.'

The future Lady Bridgmore had a diamond ring. Better than that, Rose thought, she was very obviously madly in love. She was electric with it; more herself than she had been since the Man's death. Berry, who had spent the previous Christmas Eve with his eyes pinned hopelessly to her curves, now had difficulty keeping his hands off them.

Ah, that blissful first stage, Rose thought nostalgically; the grappling and sobbing, the moonstruck passion. She had not left the house for nearly three weeks when the Man first brought her home to Melismate. Love like that never died—it only went underground, to be endlessly re-created in the faces of the next generation.

All talking, laughing and shouting at once, they ate toad-in-the-hole and drank red wine. Selena showed off to Rufa, producing a queen of puddings, scientifically browned and perfect in every detail.

'I've been reading Sir Kenelm Digby,' she said coolly. 'He made me want to experiment with traditional English cooking.'

'She thinks her sisters are total fools,' Nancy said. 'Well, she's right. What a good thing we've all bagged husbands.'

Rose said, 'That cranking sound is Mrs Pankhurst turning in her grave. Did feminism pass you by completely?'

'It didn't pass Liddy by,' Ran said, his great eyes mournful. 'Independence. Singing in that bloody choir. Going to bloody church. Since she came back, she treats me like an inferior being.'

'I like church,' Linnet said. 'Nancy, guess what, I'm the innkeeper's wife in the nativity play. I have to say: "Husband, what about the stable?" Mummy sewed me a costume made of tea towels.'

'Hmm,' Nancy said, lazily feeling Berry's leg under the table. 'I bet you're tremendous.' In a deep, Ressany voice, she added, 'Yes, she is, but she doesn't do a dance or show her bum.'

Linnet, whose eyelids had begun to droop, giggled and snapped back into wakefulness. A Stilton was produced, smelling out the room like the essence of a thousand old socks. Roger made ten large mugs of strong tea, and a cup of juice for Linnet.

'Look,' Edward said, nodding towards the clock above the range. 'It's been Christmas Day for twenty minutes. Merry Christmas, everyone.'

There was more kissing, more filling of glasses.

'I'm so happy I need to dance,' Nancy declared. 'I wish we had the Man's party tape. He made a tape of all our favourite songs,' she explained to Berry. 'He used to bring it out at the drop of a hat. He'd certainly have played it now, wouldn't he, Mum?'

'God, yes,' Rose sighed. 'All this fabulous news would have merited "Cum on Feel the Noyz" at the very least.'

'Or even the Funky Chicken,' Rufa said.

Selena stood up. 'I might know where it is. All the stuff from his desk went into a box under the stairs, and I'm sure I saw it when I got out the Christmas lights.'

Lydia, tipsy and giggling, went with her to search for it in the dusty glory hole under the main staircase.

'Anything we can dance to,' Rose called after them. She got stiffly out of her chair. '*The Best of Abba* will do.'

Roger bowed and kissed Rose's hand. 'May I have the pleasure?'

'Darling, of course.'

'Got it.' Selena and Lydia entered in triumph. Selena was rubbing a cobwebby cassette against her jersey. 'The famous party tape.' She slotted it into the ghetto blaster on the counter, turning up the sound. As the Man had done, she announced, 'Ladies and gentlemen, please take your places for "Hi-ho Silver Lining".' She pressed the Play button.

There was a hissing sound, then a loud chord—then the music suddenly stopped.

The voice of the Man filled the room. 'Hello, girls. I hope you're playing this because you're having fun.'

Selena snapped it off, as if stung. They stood in awed silence, staring at each other's white faces.

Rose whispered, 'Of course, of course. I should have guessed. I knew there had to be a message.'

Gently pushing Selena aside, she reached out a shaking hand, and wound the tape back to the beginning. Edward put his arm round Rufa's waist. Lydia sat down, scooping a large-eyed Linnet onto her lap. Deep silence settled around them all, as they prepared themselves to hear the voice from another world.

'Hello, girls. I hope you're playing this because you're having fun. I hope it means you're not too sad. I'm sorry about all this, and I won't give you the reasons why I have to leave you. I just wanted to tell you how much I love you all. And I'm recording over my tape because this is exactly how I want you to remember me. Only the fun bits, all right?'

There was a pause, during which they could hear him humming to himself, as he did when thinking deeply. 'This feels rather like the Oscars,' the voice went on, eerily close and familiar. 'Rose, Rufa, Nancy, Liddy, Selena, Linnet—goodbye, my darlings—my silk princesses.' His voice faltered. He cleared his throat. 'And I ought to mention Rodge and Edward, because I'm expecting them to take care of you. I think that's all, and I'd better get going—oh, while I think of it, please don't play "Seasons in the Sun" at my funeral.'

Another pause. They waited breathlessly, feeling him among them.

'Forgive me, and be as happy as possible. Sorry to record over "Silver Lining".' His voice suddenly became brisk and humorous. 'And sorry to put a crimp in whatever party you're having—I hope it's a corker. Ladies and gentlemen, please take your places for "Wig Wam Bam".'

The song began. The Man had made his bow.

177

Rose switched off the tape. They were all mute, and all in tears. After a long silence, Rose said, 'Yes, it's a corker all right.'

These tears did not hurt. There was a great calm in the room.

Nancy lifted her wet face off Berry's shoulder. 'Didn't you hear him? He wanted us to dance—switch it on!'

Suddenly, they were all smiling round at each other, their eyes unfocused, as if they had shared a miraculous vision and it had blessed them like the Spirit of Christmas. Selena switched on the music and grabbed Linnet's hands. Ran swept Lydia into the middle of the kitchen floor. Berry convulsed Nancy with his uncoordinated attempts at grooving. Rose danced extravagantly, clearing a large space round her. Edward leaned against the table, clasping Rufa protectively in his arms.

'After he did it, I thought I'd never be happy again,' Rufa said. 'But this is the happiest night of my life. I feel as if I've come to the end of a long, long journey—only to find myself back on my own doorstep.'

He kissed the nape of her neck. 'Welcome home.'

KATE SAUNDERS

'Writing *The Marrying Game* was such enormous fun,' Kate Saunders told me, 'because I love to write the sort of yummy novel I want to read.'

Having left school at sixteen, Kate was an actress for ten years. 'My most famous role was appearing in one episode of *Only Fools and Horses*,' she says, with a self-deprecating smile. 'I still get recognised by very nerdy, obsessive cult followers of the series.' She also appeared at the National Theatre for two years, 'until I got into the world of print and discovered that it was better paid. I was very lucky,' she admits. 'I was just in the right place at the right time—in the eighties newspapers were falling over themselves to find writers to fill their pages. "Can you hold a pen?" "Yes I can." "Can you write a feature?" "Yes I can."'

One of Kate's many assignments as a journalist was working for the *Sunday Times* Style section, an experience she enjoyed weaving into *The Marrying Game*. 'In the novel, I very much wanted to contrast the truly snobbish event, where they don't let anybody in, with the tarty party, where they just want to make money and don't care who comes. Awfully vulgar but great fun, especially if you are from the press because everyone wants to talk to you and you can be as nosey as you want!'

Like the Hasty girls, Kate was brought up in a large house, one of six children, without a lot of money. 'It was a very different life to that at Melismate, but very much in my subconscious when I was writing. And I

knew people who were like the Hastys, especially the father, "The Man". I just couldn't have invented him.'

For Kate, writing is a wonderful retreat into another world; one that she is always sad to leave when the novel ends. 'The fun part about being a writer comes when you put together a good story: sniffing to yourself when you write something sad or sentimental, smiling to yourself when you pen something funny. That's the lovely, gorgeous bit. Then you write THE END, and you think that's that. But then comes the frustrating part, going back and editing where it sags, or rewriting a character that doesn't work. It's like a jigsaw puzzle, making everything fit.'

When I asked Kate if she thought women still married for money, she replied without hesitation. 'Of course they do. People marry for money in every society and it's a well-known fact that love can be helped along by a healthy bank balance. They may end up rich, but are they happy?'

Kate and her son live in London and when I met her they had just returned from a short break to the Isle of Wight. 'It's a wonderful place,' she enthused, 'but you can't get a decent cup of coffee for love nor money! And I need my coffee fix. My two staple necessities in life are good coffee and John Lewis. I'm never out of the place. You can always find me either in the basement, kitchenware, or on the fourth floor for school uniform.'

Jane Eastgate

Long Division
Sarah Harvey

It has taken Fliss Blakeney exactly one year, eight months and six days to work out that if she marries Richard Trevelyan she will be making the biggest mistake of her life. But with the wedding just three months away, the church and reception booked, her meringue dress hanging on her bedroom door, and the flowers and cake ordered, just how in hell is she going to tell her wedding-groupie mother that it is all off? That's going to be far worse than telling the groom.

CHAPTER ONE

LIFE IS A PEPPERED STEAK, I muse, toying with the charred remains of cow on my plate. You think you want all the crap on top, all the garnish, but does it actually make the thing taste any better?

I look up, up and across at my fiancé Richard sitting opposite me.

He is talking down to the waiter.

Richard talks down to everybody, an excellent trick for someone who is such a small person. Small in stature, small-minded, and, dare I say it, small . . . Well, let's just say small in other *rather* important departments.

Richard is my pepper sauce, my garnish, my piece of curling lollo rosso lounging on the side of the plate. Looks appetisingly good to the eyes, but tastes remarkably bitter. As a small person Richard likes to surround himself with large things. Large apartment (penthouse, of course), large car, large wallet, and large matching ego.

He is a prat, but my mother loves him. It has taken me exactly one year, eight months, six days to realise that I do not. I look at my watch. Make that one year, eight months, six days, three hours and thirteen minutes. I won't go into seconds, I've wasted enough time already. I stand up and reach for my handbag.

Richard looks away from the waiter and smiles briefly, anticipating another trip to the Ladies in order to titivate for his pleasure. He is what I would describe as an ego-hedonist, interested only in his own pleasure. He has dedicated a lifetime to pleasing himself, and expects those around him to follow his example and please him.

Titivate: the word pleases him, arouses him. This whole scenario, the candlelit restaurant, the expensive wine, is the charade he believes is his key to the important part of the evening, his reward for enduring the tedious niceties of courtship. That is, the sex part of the evening, where I usually have to attempt to coax Richard's small prick into being Richard's slightly bigger prick while he lies back with the same smug look on his face, as though he is bestowing a great favour by allowing me to do this.

My resolve deepens. I open my handbag. I take a deep breath, feel in my bag for the keys to Richard's place, the keys to Richard's life.

'Richard,' I rehearse in my head, 'I don't love you, and I'm leaving.'

I open my mouth. 'Richard . . . I don't . . . er . . . I don't.'

'You don't what?' he snaps at me, annoyed by my dithering.

I open my mouth but this time no words come out at all.

'Well?' he presses irritably.

'I don't want any dessert, and I'm going to the Ladies.'

The words come out in a breathless rush as I push back my chair and stride across the restaurant, my cheeks burning.

Inside the Ladies, I press my hot forehead against the mirror and watch my breath form warm pools on its smooth, immaculately clean surface. Through the vaporous reflection I can see my face, familiar yet totally alien. I stare at the strange dark eyes, which stare rather hazily back at me. Is that really my face? The only thing I recognise is my own fear. A fear of being single.

As part of a couple one is regarded as a normal human being. What would life be like without Richard? Like life after death, this is an unknown phenomenon. There may well be life after Richard, but if I attempt to explore this unknown terrain, then my mother will kill me.

I think I have the standard disease of the decade. I know I want something, but I don't really know exactly what that something is. Something better? Something different?

I ponder for a moment. Somebody better, something different . . . definitely something bigger! I snigger aloud at this thought.

The Ladies' attendant, having replenished the loo roll in number two cubicle, is now sitting in her dainty paisley-upholstered Queen Anne replica chair, engrossed in her favourite Barbara Taylor Bradford novel. She glances up upon hearing my snort of laughter, and glares at the dark-haired girl loitering in her scrubbed and lemon-scented domain.

I rummage in my voluminous handbag for a lipstick as a ruse to appear unaware of the attendant's disapproving gaze. Life is so restrictive, I muse as I run Beautiful around my mouth. You can't even laugh out loud nowadays without someone looking at you like you're mad.

Perhaps you are mad, my reflection mocks me, mad to want to give up a comfortable secure future for the unknown, in the hope of finding something better. But then again, any future is unknown, even the anticipated one. I ostentatiously place a £5 note in the attendant's small white saucer. For some reason, this makes us both feel better.

I return to the table. My pepper sauce has cooled and congealed, just like my love life really. It's now or never. I take another swig of Burgundy, steel myself, and open my mouth.

'Richard . . .' I begin again.

'Richard? Richard Trevelyan!'

A sleek brunette dressed head to toe in Versace, in the process of being shown to her table by a waiter, stops mid-sashay and peers across the dimly lit room towards our table.

'Why, it is, isn't it?' With a toss of her raven head, she pushes past the waiter towards us, dragging a rather good-looking, obviously embarrassed man in her wake. 'I thought it must be you,' she gushes. 'Well, long time no see . . .'

She swoops down upon Richard and kisses him firmly just to the left of his mouth, leaving a big red lip imprint. She'd have caught him full on the lips except for the fact that he moved his head slightly. I know he only did this because he's been eating garlic. It's OK to blow it all over me, but never another member of the female sex.

'How *are* you, darling? Still a dangerous shark in the sea of corporate law?'

She laughs, one of those cultivated laughs that's supposed to sound all light and melodious, but is as false as the nails on her slender elegant hands. Richard laughs too. He also has a false laugh, a sort of boom, one of those deep, hearty, I'm-a-jolly-good-chap-really laughs, the kind that resonates around a room like a rubber ball.

'Well, I never, Katherine the Great—what a wonderful surprise. You look bloody marvellous, but then again you always did.' Richard makes a show of getting to his feet and kissing her hand. (The garlic again, he's not at all chivalrous usually.)

'And, Alex. How are you, old man?' Richard turns to her companion, taking his outstretched hand and pumping it vigorously. 'So good to see you both. It's been far too long.'

The man called Alex is smiling at me, waiting to be introduced, but Richard isn't that polite.

Curiosity is obviously too much for Alex's wife, however.

'Who's your little friend then, Ricky?'

Ricky! Despite the fact I've just been interrupted at a pretty important moment in my life, I only narrowly suppress an outburst of laughter.

'This is Felicity,' he says.

The woman's elegant hand is extended graciously. I notice she has rings on all of her fingers. There are so many diamonds she must be wearing a whole field full of carats. It gives the effect of an outrageously extravagant knuckle-duster.

'My fiancée,' Richard continues.

The hand immediately shoots back and, flustered, toys with her dark brown hair which is so glossy she could be on the vitamin pills my father feeds his labrador. I can see genuine shock on the girl's far-too-perfect features, but it doesn't take her long to regain her composure.

'Why, you sly old dog,' the affected lightness has returned, but the voice is noticeably strained, 'and you always said matrimony wasn't for you.' She tries the laugh again, though it's even more false than the first time. 'But I knew you'd get caught sooner or later.'

Richard is smirking. I don't know why but I get the feeling there's an exchange going on here that isn't purely verbal.

'Every dog has his wedding day,' he says brightly, trying to be witty. 'You know, it really is great to see you, Kat. Tell you what, why don't you join us?'

I groan inwardly. I can hardly announce I have no intention of marrying Richard before an audience.

To my horror, Katherine beams. 'Oh, what a lovely idea . . .'

This time her companion steps in. He must be more intuitive than her; either that or he spotted the look of dismay on my face. 'Thanks, Richard. It's really very kind of you but perhaps on another occasion,' he says. He has a nice voice, warm but not too hearty, educated but not clipped or false.

'That would be nice,' I say, smiling gratefully at him.

'Yes, we really ought to get together some time.' Kat addresses Richard. I get the feeling the invitation doesn't include me. 'It's been *far* too long.'

'That would be *nice*.' Richard echoes my words, but the tone of his voice is very different. 'In fact,' he looks over at me, his smirk so wide that by rights his oh-so-chiselled jaw should begin to crack, 'I've just had the most marvellous idea. Why don't you come to the wedding?'

'Wedding?' The laser beam smile flashes on and off again.

'Well, that's what usually follows an engagement.' Richard laughs.

If only you knew, I think to myself.

'August the 25th—only seven weeks to go, eh, Fliss darling?' He smiles at me affectionately. Now I know there is something very odd going on here. 'You must come, I insist upon it. If you give Fliss your address she'll send an invite through, won't you, darling?'

Two darlings in the space of twenty seconds. This isn't the Richard I know and loathe.

'Alexander and Katherine Christian, 16 Belvoir . . . very nice address.' I read the card a very disgruntled Katherine Christian presented to Richard with a whispered 'Call me' that could be heard by her husband, half the restaurant and myself.

'Nice girl, don't you think?' says Richard, as soon as they are out of earshot.

I don't think, but I'm not going to give him the opportunity to misinterpret my instant dislike of Katherine Christian as jealousy by saying so.

'Who is she, Richard?'

'An ex.' He attacks his *haricots verts* with surgical precision.

Well, that much was pretty obvious.

'How ex?' I'm not bothered, just curious.

'Oh, a few years ago now. She wanted more than I was prepared to give at the time.' He looks up at me with clear brown eyes, his mouth full of beans and sole. 'She was devastated when I finished the relationship,' he adds.

He's waiting for a reaction. I refuse to give him one and stay silent.

He tries again. 'She used to worship me, you know.'

If you're that wonderful then why did she marry someone else? I think furiously.

'Of course she married on the rebound,' he states smugly, unconsciously answering my unspoken question.

I look over towards their table; Alex Christian catches my gaze and smiles. He has a very nice smile. He also has a very nice face, fit body—lean and muscled—and is wearing an impeccably cut dark grey Armani suit extremely well.

'He looks very nice,' I challenge, sneaking another look and deciding that I wouldn't mind rebounding from Richard on to someone like Alex Christian. How on earth did Katherine manage it? Yes, she's beautiful, but from what I can make of her in the short space of time I've known her, that beauty is about as deep as the lightest of paper cuts. I suppose it's not really fair to make snap judgments about people you barely know, but my first impressions of people are usually pretty spot-on. Although I have been known to be wrong. A major example of this is currently sitting opposite me.

'Oh, he is,' concedes Richard. 'Decent chap really, quite successful, runs a small but rather good publishing company.'

'Why on earth did you invite them to the wedding?'

'Why not? Don't you want one of my exes at our wedding? You're not jealous, are you?'

Oh, he'd like that, I can tell you. A little jealousy always bolsters his self-esteem which is already unwarrantably high.

'She's a stunning girl, isn't she?' He's really stirring now. 'Quite a beauty.'

'If you like that sort of thing,' I murmur nonchalantly. 'I actually thought she seemed a little bit plastic. A bit false. You know: false nails, false eyelashes, false laugh, false smile.'

'Ooh, we are jealous, aren't we!' he crows happily, then adds rather patronisingly, 'Never mind, darling, you've just got to remember that it's you I'm marrying.'

'That's what you think,' I long to shout back at him, but my already wavering courage has gone as cold as my rejected peppered steak and the moment for revelations has therefore passed. I steadily drink my way through another bottle of wine as I wait for Richard to finish the rest of his meal. He always chews his food a hundred times before swallowing. He reminds me of a square-jawed bovine monotonously chewing cud.

Finally, after pudding, which I didn't have, and coffee, which I should have had considering the amount of wine I managed to consume, Richard signals for the bill. He hands the waiter his platinum card with a flourish, and then states that he's just going to say goodbye to Katherine and Alex.

I can see him smoothing his very clean brown hair in the large gilt mirror on the far wall as he makes his way through the tables towards them. Richard has a major league love affair with mirrors, and spends more time in the bathroom getting ready to go out than I ever do.

I can't deny that he's a very attractive man—as he walks across the room several female heads turn to look. The problem is I find him about as attractive as week-old cottage cheese. What are you doing with the man? I hear you say.

Well, apart from pointing out that we all make mistakes and what girl hasn't got a few embarrassing exes in her closet, all I can say is it hasn't always been this way.

When I first met Richard he really kind of swept me off my feet.

Richard is a barrister. I'm a teacher. I'm also a terrible driver. He represented me when a minor car accident turned into a major lawsuit. By the final court hearing, he'd somehow managed not only to convince the judge that I was the innocent and injured party, but also to convince me that I should promptly fall into bed with him as a jolly good way of expressing my gratitude.

I have to admit he's very impressive in court. Shame he wasn't so impressive in bed, but at the time I was so swept up by the whole knight-in-shining-armour thing, I was even prepared to overlook the fact that the first time we hit the mattress together he kept on not only his socks but his stupid curly white wig as well. Despite this, and the fact that his come-to-bed line was a pretty crass 'the courts may have found you innocent, but I find you guilty of stealing my heart', which at the time I thought was dreadfully romantic but now makes me cringe, I am ashamed to admit that I was a pretty easy lay.

The ease with which Richard lured me into bed might also have had something to do with the fact that I was always the girl at school who never got the boys.

Going to an all girls' school didn't help, but considering I left when I was eighteen, and at twenty-six Richard was really the first man ever to show more of a permanent interest in me than, say, the odd drink and a quick grope to follow on a second date if I got lucky, then maybe I couldn't be blamed for thinking that there was something wrong with me (an opinion regularly voiced by my wedding groupie mother). No wonder I jumped at the chance of a relationship with someone who on the outside at least seems to have everything a girl wants.

For the first time in my life I was able to bask in the warm glow of maternal approval, an emotion never really radiated by my mother before. Not in my direction anyway. Her overweight, underachieving daughter had finally got herself a man. And not just any man, but one who could actually be boasted about to friends and family.

Unfortunately, although Richard seems to have everything a girl wants—looks, charm, wit, success—none of it has ever really been aimed in my direction. He's the kind of guy who will lead you onto the dance floor and pull you into his arms to smooch to a slow romantic record, then spend the entire song gazing over your shoulder at some-one else.

I don't suppose I can put all the blame on him. After all, as they say, it takes two to tango. Maybe I haven't made him as happy as I could have done. Maybe I didn't turn out to be quite the person he thought I was either.

Maybe it's him, maybe it's me. But there are no maybes any more when it comes to whether we should be together. That, my friends, is a definite no.

He takes half an hour to say his goodbyes. I'm getting crosser by the minute. You can hear the false tinkling laugh and the false hearty boom simultaneously at regular intervals. Alex Christian is noticeably quiet. Finally Richard returns to our table, smiling like a Cheshire Cat.

'Nice couple, shame we lost touch. Must have them round for dinner some time.' He picks up their address card, which is sitting by my empty glass, and puts it in his pocket.

I'd love to have Katherine and Alex Christian round for dinner. I could pot-roast her, and eat him.

I lie back and think of Richard Gere in a white uniform. He is carrying me into the bedroom, all ten stone of me, without a murmur. He lays me back upon the king-size bed and admires my magnificent body (cellulite does not exist in celluloid). He bends to kiss me.

My eyes blink open, the real Richard trembles for a moment above me like a persistent Jack Russell mounting a red setter. He tenses, sighs, and then falls away. He is asleep within seconds, leaving me gasping in frustration. It may be madness to give up something good, but it is utter stupidity to hold on to something bad.

I reach for the glass of wine beside my bed. I don't smoke so I allow myself the vice of drinking too much on occasion. Tonight is one such occasion. Two shared bottles of excellent Burgundy over dinner, and now halfway down a bottle of Sancerre, I am beginning to feel marvellously brave, ready to throw off the shackles of boredom and compliance to convention, and head for freedom.

I reach for my ever-present tardis of a handbag, which is at the side of the bed. I don't have a pen or paper, but I manage with a credit-card bill envelope and a dark pink lip-liner.

I'm not sure what to write. After rehearsing the words in my head for weeks my mind has now gone rather blank. I'd made up this speech about different values and a better future for both of us if we went our separate ways, but that all sounds terribly trite. And far too kind.

Like a typical woman I usually take the blame for everything that has gone wrong and apologise profusely when I'm sober. But at the moment I'm far from sober and ready to blame the whole banality of our relationship on him, fair or not.

Richard, you are the weakest link. Goodbye.

The final message is short but satisfyingly sweet. I snigger to myself.

Getting quietly from the bed, I pad across the shagpile carpet. Richard's bedroom is opulent yet impersonal, dominated by the king-size oval bed which sits in the centre of the room on the sort of dais you expect to see a pair of thrones mounted upon. A door pretending to be a cupboard door actually leads to a white bathroom with gold fittings. It's very sparse. Safari for Men, in various guises, sits upon the glass shelf below the large bathroom mirror: aftershave, deodorant, body lotion, shower gel. These bottles and several thick white towels are the only proof of human existence within the room. There are no hairs blocking the plughole in the basin, no abandoned underwear bundled in a corner.

I splash cold water on my face and rub a finger laced with toothpaste across my front teeth, then purely for the hell of it wipe my still plum-coloured lips—Richard rarely kisses—across the snow white of a virgin towel.

I go back into the bedroom and pull on my clothes. As I sit down on the bed to put on my shoes, Richard rolls over, pulling all of the duvet onto his side of the bed, and farts noisily.

It's gone three in the morning. The streets of Oxford are practically deserted. The Indian taxi driver plays Bhangra music all the way back to my place. My head throbs in time with the frenetic bass beat. I live just on the outskirts of Oxford in what used to be a village but has now been swallowed up by urban sprawl—a small fish living in the belly of a whale. My flat, my home, is the total antithesis of Richard's apartment; it is small yet very personal. The place is a mess. I don't really like it that way, but after twenty-eight years of an oppressive mother-dominated life, untidiness is an easy way to assert one's own independence.

Feeling guilty but liberated, I collapse onto my bed fully clothed, eating a cold Mars bar straight from the fridge. For some reason I'm always ravenous when I'm pissed. I ignore my usual ritual of showering and religiously removing make-up. For once I don't care. Sod the regime of trying to retain my looks for the sake of my love life and future happiness—what I have of looks anyway.

Some kind soul once said to my mother, 'Fliss could never be called pretty, but there are moments when she looks beautiful.'

Isn't it funny how some comments, no matter how carelessly voiced in the first instance, can stick with you for a lifetime?

I've tried to re-create these rare moments when I could be described as beautiful at will, but it never works. You'd think I'd have had more luck recently what with all the pampering I've been subjecting myself to in preparation for the 'Big Event'. Manicures, cathiodermie, anti-cellulite massages, increasingly more intimate waxing, seaweed wraps, the agony that is tweezing . . . hell, my mother even tried to persuade me to go for a course of Botox injections a couple of weeks ago.

She has been attempting to train me for my wedding day since birth. It was her idea to call me Felicity, a girlie name if ever I heard one. It doesn't really suit me, I'm not a girlie girl.

I think this is probably one of the main reasons why we've never really got along. She wanted a little doll she could dress in pink, with curls and an angelic smile. Someone she could be dreadfully proud of, and take to ballet lessons.

Instead she got an ungainly tomboy who lived in jeans, and who rebelled at just the thought of pink, organza or gingham, singing lessons, piano lessons, deportment, and practically everything else that Mother thought the right ingredients for a proper girlie childhood.

My mother was brought up in an era when women were expected to finish school then marry. That was it, no career, no choice, and no particular say in the future of the one life you had been given. Women were good for only one thing. Marriage.

Well, most women anyway. I'm a different story. My mother has always despaired of ever getting rid of me.

Unlike my younger sister, Sally-Anne, who is pretty, delicate and feminine in every way, and has had a string of male admirers since first learning to flutter her long black eyelashes at the tender age of three, I am slightly too tall to be fashionable, totally addicted to chocolate, which I store in my fridge and on my hips, totally devoid of feminine guile and, according to my mother, a hopeless case.

That's why she loves Richard so much. It's like entering your daughter in a beauty contest expecting her to come in a dismal last, and then finding out she's actually won first prize. My mother couldn't believe her luck. Richard has everything she thinks a man should have. She loves him, Sally loves him, my wonderfully sensible father thinks he's an arsehole, but since when has Dad's opinion ever been taken into account? I think my mother would marry Richard herself if she could.

What was I doing agreeing to marry the man, I hear you ask, if just the thought of him breathing makes me want to punch his lights out? I think part of it is my lack of self-esteem. I'd actually begun to believe that nobody would ever want me, my mother had drummed it into me for so long. So when Richard proposed, I grabbed the opportunity with both hands, and when you want so very much to be in love, it's so very easy to convince yourself that you are.

And why the change of heart now? Self-preservation has a lot to do with it. I'm like my little village being swallowed up by the whale of the town, losing its own individuality. Only somebody threw me a life belt and hauled me to shore.

That somebody is Caro.

I've been a teacher at the local girls' high school for about four years now, tutoring a reluctant upper-fifth through their English GCSEs. Caro is the new drama teacher. She is also a very old friend, last seen before our recent reunion as a skinny, horse-mad eleven-year-old. I lost touch with her when her father took a posting to Hong Kong. She is four years older than me, and used to boss me around dreadfully, but I adored her with a reverent passion. Things haven't changed very much since our childhood, only now she is not so much bossy as emboldening.

Since her return into my life Caro has given me a new outlook on things. She is now very happily married herself to a wonderful man called David who farms on the border of the Chilterns. He is fifteen years older than Caroline. Together they have two teenagers from his previous marriage, one dog, and the most idyllic partnership you could ever imagine.

They are the best of friends. They tease, they talk, they complement each other—Caro is outgoing, vivacious, artistic; David, solid and reliable yet sensitive and imaginative. They go together like pepper and salt. Just seeing them together made me realise I want more.

The last time I stayed with Caro and David it was a hot, balmy summer's night, the sort where you throw off your duvet at midnight and lie with the window wide open, listening to the gentle sounds of the night. Well, that night the gentle sounds were interrupted by the sound of Sarah Vaughan playing on an old gramophone. When, enticed by the music, I leaned out of the window, there they were, in each other's arms, dancing in the orchard, illuminated by the light through the open French doors like a spotlight on the star couple in *Come Dancing*.

David was stroking Caro's golden hair, singing 'Misty' to her, along with the record. The orchard was raining blossom on their heads like confetti at a wedding.

Corny? Maybe. Appealing? Definitely.

It was at that moment I made my decision. I want someone who'll dance with me at midnight to old songs, who'll sing sweet words to me, who'll treat me like a friend and a lover, the most precious object in their world. I know now that Richard and I don't have that, and that I'm worth more. More, anyway, than a no-hope relationship with someone whose idea of a balanced relationship is ninety-nine per cent to one.

Now I've made my decision, it's as though a whole hundredweight has been lifted from my shoulders. My mother always nags me not to stoop, but I'm sure it was the weight of all my worries that made my shoulders bow. Do I stand taller now? I get up rather unsteadily from the bed and, stripping, stand naked in front of my full-length mirror.

I throw back my shoulders and my head. My long brown hair falls against my shoulder blades. My skin looks darker in the lamplight. Brown hair, brown eyes, brown skin . . . like a Gypsy. Slightly overweight but not unattractive: full boobs, plump arse, long legs. Not bad at all, I decide, pissed and in a low light.

I draw myself up, inducing the mirror to reflect my new resolve. Yes, I'm sure I'm a full inch taller now. Tomorrow I shall look Mother straight in her ice-blue eyes and tell her that the wedding is off. She will see a new Fliss, a strong Fliss, a Fliss who doesn't give a damn whether her mother approves of what she does . . . a Fliss who is at this very moment contemplating a quick hike back to Richard's place to retrieve the hastily scribbled missive that will rocket her life onto a very different course.

The wonderful drunken abandon is beginning to wear off, and a horrible feeling of panic starts to set in. I'm torn between hiding away in sleep or opening another bottle of wine. Oh, sod it, I won't be able to sleep now anyway. I head for the kitchen, and open a bottle of rather nice Australian Shiraz.

The cat, who is already disgusted that I got in late and could only offer a week-old tin of pilchards in tomato sauce for dinner, looks at me out of the corner of one sleepy green eye.

If she had eyebrows she'd raise them to heaven. If she had a voice, she'd chide 'drunk again'. Instead, she stalks off and takes revenge by throwing up said pilchards in my slippers, and then wiping her face on my bed linen.

CHAPTER TWO

I'M WOKEN AT SEVEN THIRTY by the sound of the telephone. There is only one person who would call me this early on a Saturday morning. One person who has found an empty bed.

'Fliss, is that you?'

I have a throbbing head, cat sick in my hair, and a very vague recollection that I've done something outrageous.

'No, it's the Chinese laundry.'

I cringe as I pull the offending section of my hair well away from my face and, clutching the hands-free, stagger into the bathroom.

'Don't be flip.' He sounds annoyed. 'What the hell's going on? Why aren't you here, and what on earth is the meaning of this note?'

Note? *Oh, yes.* My memory wakes up. I left a note, didn't I? But I can't for the life of me remember what exactly I wrote.

Sticking the left side of my head under the shower nozzle, I begin to babble.

'Well, I think it's pretty self-explanatory, don't you?' I offer lamely.

'Felicity!' His voice rises an octave in indignation. 'I demand to know what is the meaning of this note?'

I think hard. Oh, yes, it's coming back to me now. My hangover-befuddled mind suddenly flashes last night's missive across my mind in big red neon letters.

Did I really write that? I'm rather surprised to find that instead of being horrified, I'm more than a little pleased with myself.

'Felicity!' He's roaring down the line now. I'm sure if it were possible he would put his hands down the receiver and throttle me.

'Well, Richard,' I begin. I waver for a moment, but the moment's very brief. It's now or never, the point of no return. I take a deep breath. 'It means that we're through, Richard, kaput, finito, end of story, finished. I don't want to marry you.'

I'm getting to the point now, thank goodness, it's taken me long enough.

'What?'

'The wedding's off. I'm not going to marry you—'

'This is utter madness. You're ill, aren't you?' he cuts in. 'That must be it. I'm coming round.'

'No! I don't think that's such a good idea . . .' I begin to protest, knowing a face-to-face onslaught to be beyond my capabilities at the moment. But it's too late, I'm talking to the buzz of a hung-up receiver.

Help!

I run round the flat in a panic, like a wasp trapped inside a lemonade bottle. I can't face Richard. If I could have faced dumping Richard, I wouldn't have left a bloody note.

I grab the phone and dial Caro's number. She will tell me that I've done the right thing, and then hopefully tell me what to do now. And then I remember that she has made the most of the end of drama lessons due to end-of-term exams, and sodded off to the South of France.

Perhaps that's what I should do. Perhaps I should just go away for a while, until everything cools down. Outer Mongolia is supposed to be nice at this time of year. How long will it take me to pack?

After twenty minutes I have packed and unpacked a suitcase twice. Decided to make a run for it twice, and to stay and fight it out twice. I'm currently on the stay-and-fight-it-out phase, but my courage falters alarmingly when I see Richard pull up outside.

To my utter horror I see that his large iron-grey BMW is full to capacity. He has summoned the troops.

My mother glowers in the front seat, like a small malevolent bird, her feathers well and truly ruffled. My sister sits behind Richard, her cheeks flushed in concerned agitation. Even poor Dad has been dragged away from the breakfast table. He's still wearing his tartan slippers.

I can't believe Richard brought them all with him. I'm very tempted not to let them in. Alternatively I could just pretend to be out.

I decide that this is by far the best option and scurry to the rear of the flat to hide out in my bedroom.

After leaning on the main-building door buzzer for five minutes, Richard remembers he's got a key and lets himself in. I hear them ascending the wooden staircase towards the first floor, like an advancing militia.

I tug desperately at the painted lock of the bedroom window, a stubborn obstacle between me and the fire escape and freedom.

They've reached the front door now. In full flight, the ominous descent of the circling vulture, Mother marches into the flat calling my name in a harsh contralto voice that holds more than a hint of Margaret Thatcher. At last the window sash releases.

As Richard and company troop into the bedroom, I greet them with a weak smile, precariously balanced astride the window ledge. I'm still wearing my dressing gown, which is gaping most revealingly, and I'm not wearing any knickers. Mother's acid glare says more than a thousand abusive words ever could.

It's a long session.

Richard is patronising and totally disbelieving.

Sally is tearful, tender-hearted and totally disbelieving, torn between a desire to comfort me and what appears to be a slightly stronger desire to comfort Richard, who is acting every bit the severely injured party.

Mother is initially gobsmacked and speechless, which is a definite first, and Dad's surreptitiously watching the Wimbledon highlights on the portable in the kitchen while making us an umpteenth cup of tea.

I'm trying very hard to convince them all that I really don't want to marry Richard, but at least two members of my family, and of course

Richard himself, are finding this very difficult to come to terms with. I should have known that Mother and Sally would take his side in this. Richard has insinuated himself into their affections with the ease of a tapeworm into an intestine.

Mother, who unfortunately regained her power of speech, is banging on about calling a doctor because I'm obviously suffering from a bout of temporary insanity, so I turn to Sally-Anne who will hopefully be slightly more receptive.

'Honestly, Sal, you've got to believe me, I really don't want to get married.' I plead with her to grasp what appears to be an ungraspable concept.

'But why ever not?' Her fine eyebrows are arched like question marks on her smooth pale forehead.

'Well, to be perfectly blunt, I don't love Richard.'

'But why ever not?'

'Well . . .' I try to be polite here. 'I just don't think we're compatible.'

'But why ever not?'

She's starting to annoy me now. 'Do you want a list?' I snap.

Sally beats a hasty retreat. 'Er, I think I'll give Dad a hand with the tea.' She escapes to the kitchen.

This leaves me, Mother and Richard.

'Well, I think this is absolutely insane!' they blurt out at the same time.

How clever: synchronised barracking. They even have the same mixed expression of mingled disbelief and annoyance on their faces. Now I know why I can't marry Richard: he reminds me of my mother. That's probably why she likes him so much, he's a mini Miriam Blakeney. Where she left off dominating my life, and making it a general misery, he will take over.

My resolve deepens. As Dad and Sally come back into the room bearing tea and biscuits, I take a deep breath and make my stand.

'Look, I really am sorry. I know I'm causing a lot of upset and inconvenience, but I really do think it would be a big mistake for both of us to go ahead with the wedding.'

Dad puts the tray down and lays a reassuring hand on my shoulder. 'It's all right, darling, we understand.'

'No, we do not!' storms Mother. 'The wedding is in seven weeks' time, you can't call it all off now. I really can't believe you're even contemplating such stupidity!'

'Surely the stupidity would be to go through with it, when I really don't want to get married?'

'But why ever not?' says Sally again.

Honestly, as much as I love my sweet-natured little sister, I'll swing for her if she doesn't change the record.

'Because, I'm sorry, but I'm not in love with the man I'm supposed to be marrying.'

'Don't be preposterous,' says Richard, as though not to be in love with him is an inconceivable idea.

I try to explain. 'There's no passion, no poetry, no romance.'

'There's more to marriage than *romance*,' Mother says contemptuously.

'I know that, I'm not totally stupid. Look, I'm sorry, Richard. If it was just a case of missing romance, perhaps I could have carried on, but there are so many other things missing as well.'

'Such as?' he asks indignantly, completely unaware of any personal shortcomings.

'Well . . .' I look down at his crotch, home to exhibit 'A', and then look at my mother. This is ridiculous. 'Look, do we have to do this in front of an audience?'

'Quite right, quite right,' says Dad in relief. 'I think we should go and leave them to it, don't you?'

As he heads for the door, I decide the last thing I want is to be alone with Richard, and wish I'd kept my mouth shut. But there's no need to worry, Mother has absolutely no intention of leaving.

'Sit down, Drew, Richard wanted us to be here.'

Dad sits down.

'Look, I really am sorry,' I say for the hundredth time, 'honestly I am, but isn't it better for me to realise now rather than six months into married life? I know it seems appalling of me but it's the right thing to do, really it is.'

Richard has tried indignation and anger already. He adopts a different tactic.

'Well, really, Felicity, I just don't understand,' he purrs, using the little-boy-lost look he adopts to charm indecisive juries. The look he used to first charm me into bed, gazing up at me with big brown eyes from under thick black lashes. It used to make my knees melt. Now it just annoys the hell out of me.

'I don't respect you, Richard. How can I marry someone I don't respect?'

'But he's a barrister,' says Mother as if this fact alone commands that missing factor instantly. 'My goodness, girl, what's wrong with you?' She's beginning to sound hysterical. 'Richard is a brilliant, wonderful, talented man. He's also a perfect gentleman. You obviously don't know how lucky you are to have found him.'

Sally nods in agreement. I've had enough.

'And he's a perfect wimp! The perfect gentleman is able to fight his own battles, not come in hiding behind the skirts of his future mother-in-law. Sorry, former future mother-in-law.'

'How dare you speak to me like that?' she storms. I flinch away from the murderous impulse in her eyes.

Rescue comes from a very unexpected quarter.

'It's all right, Miriam.' Richard gets to his feet. 'Thank you for defending me, but I think Felicity has made her feelings perfectly obvious. The futility of continuing this conversation is blatantly clear.'

I gape at him in surprise. That must be the fastest U-turn in history!

He is oddly dignified, and holds out a hand.

'I can respect Felicity's decision even if I cannot for one moment understand it. Goodbye, Felicity.'

I take it meekly. His grip is firm, his hand is warm, his gaze is steady. For a second I wonder if I'm doing the right thing, but then he reverts to true Richard form.

'Just don't expect to come crawling back when you realise what a horrendous mistake you've made.'

He strides towards the door. I'm finally seeing the back of him in every sense of the word. With a look of pure disgust, my mother, closely followed by Sally, rushes after him.

'Well . . .' I look sideways, at Dad, seeking approval I suppose from the one person whose opinion really matters, because he is the one person whose opinion will be based on concern for my welfare.

I am relieved to see a wide smile spread across my father's face.

'As long as you're happy, eh? Never did like the man much anyway.' He envelops me in a long-armed hug, drops an affectionate kiss on the top of my head, and then follows after my mother.

God bless my father.

Richard departs rapidly, loudly squealing his tyres all the way up the avenue. Although he brought my family here, he obviously has no intention of taking them away again.

Dad comes back in to call a taxi. Mother refuses to let me drive them home, and won't come back up to the flat. I can see her glaring angrily up at my window. As she waits for the taxi to arrive it begins to rain. No doubt I shall take the blame for that as well.

The flat seems strangely quiet after they've gone. Sort of like the moment after a party when the last guest has just left and you don't know whether to start clearing up the mess or go to bed. I certainly don't feel like clearing up the mess I've just apparently made of my life (according to Mother) so I concentrate on the tangible mess in the mirror, and run a bath.

I feel sort of drained, empty. I try to concentrate on my exciting new future, and then realise I spent so long planning the end of the old life, I haven't even contemplated the new.

The phone is ringing. I haul myself out of my bath, foam bubbles sliding soapily down my wet body, and slip out to the hall.

I stand and look at the telephone for a moment. It could be Richard or worse still my mother—then the doorbell begins to ring. I take the lesser of two evils and pick up the phone. To my surprise it's Sally.

'Hi, Fliss. Look, I just wanted to say I think you've done the right thing. You and Richard were never suited. Don't worry about Mum, she'll get over it. What's happened is definitely for the best.'

'Oh, Sal, I'm so glad you said that,' I sigh in relief. 'You wouldn't believe how much better it makes me feel, Sal. I thought I'd lost one of my biggest allies . . .'

'Don't be silly, I'll always be there for you, Fliss.'

I'm so relieved that I open the door without thinking, and give the milkman a big surprise. He takes in my wet, naked soapy form, and a huge grin spreads from ear to ear over his weathered old face.

'That'll be four pounds twenty, please, darlin',' he cackles. 'Cash'll do, I'm getting a bit too old for payment in kind.'

Come Monday I'm back at school for the last week of the summer term. It drags by. My news quickly spreads around the staff room, but fortunately not around the girls themselves. Reaction differs. Some think I'm totally mad, others very sane, but all, whatever their opinion, remain commendably discreet.

My two closest friends are also united in their opinion. Caroline never rated Richard at all and never made any particular effort to hide this fact. Sensible Sasha leaves me a message on my answering machine.

'Fliss, it's Sash. I've heard a funny rumour that you've finally seen sense and ditched the vile Trevelyan. Give me a call and let me know if it's true. If it is true then well done. And call me, you old tart, before you get the chance to change your mind.'

I always believed Sasha liked Richard. If I'd known he wasn't as high as I'd thought in her ratings, I might just have been bold enough to make my escape a little sooner. It's great to know there's one person less who'll hate me for what I've done. Isn't it sad how many restrictions you put on yourself when you fear the wrath of others?

In fact, thinking about it, there are only two people at the moment who are still very anti-me: Richard, of course, who has quite typically announced to the world that he dumped me rather than the other way round, and my mother.

While I've tried very hard to push Richard to the back of my mind, telling myself that my life is now a Richard-free zone, it's harder to ignore the fact that my own mother is still refusing to speak to me.

I've tried being conciliatory on several occasions, but it's hard when the person you want to be conciliatory to refuses to acknowledge your existence. As Henry VIII would have been the first to point out, excommunication does have its advantages, like total autonomy in his case, and in my case the freedom to do whatever I want without fear of in-your-face disapproval. I, however, am fairly realistic in recognising that it's not an ideal state of affairs. Still, the fact that no one can say I haven't tried does a lot to ease my conscience on this score.

On the very last day of term, I prepare to make a swift and silent exit. Unfortunately, as I am attempting to sidle out of my classroom and head for the car park with a box of papers, I am accosted by a deputation of smiling fifteen- and sixteen-year-olds. My girls, Upper Five B, have bought me a wedding present, carefully wrapped in ribbons and presented with a well-rehearsed speech.

I could die.

They are insistent that I open their gift straight away, they want to see my face and share my pleasure. I open my mouth to explain but Mrs Monkton, the headmistress, who is witness to the occasion, shakes her head so I just mumble a tearful 'thank you'.

They observe my choked expression, and thankfully decide it's because I'm touched and overwhelmed by their kindness. Full of the joy of giving, and of finally reaching the summer holidays, they depart with much banter and backward calls of good luck, voices heavy with insinuation, shouting laughing comments about honeymoons.

Mrs Monkton and I are left alone in the classroom. She is a little queen bee of a woman, with steely grey hair, matching eyes and personality. But she is kind and wise. She puts a small, wizened hand on my arm, a conspicuous display of affection on her part.

'Now is not the time for explanations, Felicity,' she says quietly. 'Relax and enjoy the break, see if you can get away for a while. Come autumn everything will seem so much better. The start of a new term—out with the old, in with the new.' She smiles encouragingly at me.

Out in the car park I load the box full of papers and books I'll need over the summer holidays into the boot of my car. As I climb in and grip the steering wheel to stop my hands from shaking the sun catches the stones embedded in the platinum band on my wedding finger and I realise I'm still wearing my engagement ring.

The Beeches, Clayton Avenue, is an old and sturdy house built in the reign of the old and similarly sturdy Queen Victoria. I was born here, twenty-eight years ago—a painful birth that lasted a phenomenal three days according to my mother. She has since made me pay for that pain threefold. We've never got on, and after I so thoughtlessly and callously rejected Richard, her far-from-quiet dissatisfaction with the way I have led my life so far, rebelling against everything she values, has turned to vengeful hatred. It has taken me all weekend to pluck up the courage to come round. I'm supposed to have left for Caroline's an hour ago, but I know if I don't do this now, I'll lose my nerve and never will.

I knock timidly on the front door. Fortunately, as I'd hoped, Sally-Anne has got the day off to Mother-sit. She looks out of the front window, then hurries to let me in.

'Is she in?' I whisper quite unnecessarily.

My mother is always in at this time of day. She has never worked, although she is the most efficient secretary the local branch of the Oxfordshire Women's Institute has ever seen. My father took early retirement from a civil engineering job two years ago. They don't have much of a social life. Dad is rarely in the house. He still has his gardening and his fishing, and Roger, Dad's fat but eager black labrador, seems to get taken on an awful lot of exceptionally long hikes in the country.

Sally puts a finger to her lips, and points upstairs. Since the previous Saturday afternoon Mother has been threatening us with a nervous breakdown, and has taken to her bed like Jane Austen's Mrs Bennet, refusing to come downstairs, taking all her meals on a tray, and generally berating life and decrying me.

Sally squeezes my hand. 'Come into the sitting room,' she says in hushed tones. 'It's best if we don't disturb her, she's still in the most awful mood.'

We go through to the sitting room. I sit down on the 1950s chintz sofa, which is the most modern item in the room. Sally, who has been making afternoon tea, pours some into bone china cups.

'I've just called round to let you know I'm going away for a while,' I tell her, accepting a steaming cup gratefully. 'Caro's back, she called me earlier and asked me to go and stay so I'm going down to Angels Court for a few weeks. Give everything and everybody a chance to settle down, get back to normal.'

'What's your definition of normal?' Sally laughs wryly.

'Mother being just plain horrible to me, rather than completely and utterly obnoxious,' I say sarcastically.

Sally looks fearfully above her head as though Mother could be listening in at this very moment.

Putting my teacup down on the coffee table, I delve into my handbag and locate a small black leather box. I hold it out towards Sally-Anne.

'I need a favour, Sal. Would you give this back to Richard for me . . . please?' I falter. 'I can't face him at the moment—not that I think he'd want to see me anyway. He was absolutely furious, wasn't he?'

'He wasn't too happy, no, but he seems all right now,' Sally murmurs, taking the box. Opening it she removes the ring and holds it in her hand.

'You've seen him?' I ask in surprise.

'Mmm,' she nods, casually sliding the ring onto her finger, watching the diamonds catch the light. 'He came round last night.'

'He came round?'

'I think he wanted someone to talk to.'

Sally smiles in a slightly embarrassed fashion, and puts the ring back in the little leather box which snaps shut with a sharp crack.

'About what?'

'Well, about what happened, of course,' Sally replies, raising her eyebrows at me, 'among other things . . .'

She is obviously surprised by the fact that *I'm* surprised Richard felt the need for a heart-to-heart. He never really gave me any cause to believe he would be overly upset not to have me around. I'd always secretly thought that his proposal was the result of his getting carried away in the heat of the moment. As far as I was concerned, Richard and I weren't getting on too well at the time. He'd been coming up with some pretty dodgy excuses for breaking dates and I hadn't really seen that much of him.

For the first time in ages we'd had a good evening together. I think this might have had something to do with the fact that we'd both had quite a bit to drink before meeting up, so we'd had a laugh. But to be honest, when he moved in close and said he'd got something to say to me, I was expecting a push-off rather than a proposal. It was also unfortunate we were with my family at the time. That before you could say 'Forget it, I was pissed', my mother had announced it to the world in the local papers, and organised a family party complete with engagement presents, and we were steamrollered into formalising a relationship I thought had already hit the rocks. I really hadn't thought that once the break was made Richard would be that reluctant to move on with his life.

'What did he say?' I ask uneasily.

'He seemed really sad, Fliss.' Sally smiles sympathetically.

'Of course,' I reply bitterly, 'I can just imagine it now, the wounded-dog act, guaranteed sympathy puller. Make me look even more horrible than everybody already thinks I am.'

'No, it wasn't like that, Fliss, honestly. Far from it really. He seemed to be blaming himself more than you. Wanted some assurance it wasn't all his fault.'

'Oh, yes, and I suppose Mother laid the blame entirely at my feet?'

Sally shrugs embarrassed. 'Well, you know what she's like.'

'All too well.' I sigh. 'Is that all he said?'

Sally shrugs, embarrassed. 'Well, he did say that just because he wasn't with you any more, didn't mean we should lose touch.'

'He said that?'

'Yes, he said that!' snaps a familiar voice.

I look up with a start. Mother is standing in the doorway.

'I don't know why you find it so surprising.'

I really wish I could conquer the sick feeling of panic and apprehension she always induces in me. I am, after all, an adult, so why does she have this infallible ability to make me feel like I'm ten years old and due for a severe telling off?

She looks pale, and is resting the back of her hand against her forehead, drama-queen style. She is still in her dressing gown. Funereal black. Very appropriate.

She stalks across the room, an ominous crow come to pick the bones of a dead subject.

'He cares about us, Felicity. He'd come to look upon us as his family, and then you took it all away from him,' she croaks hoarsely. Ignoring the tea on the table, she pours herself a large brandy. 'I'm surprised you dare to show your face around here.'

'You're *my* family,' I breathe indignantly, 'I can't believe you'd side against me. I need your support at the moment. This has been traumatic for me too, you know.'

'Don't expect any sympathy from me.' She takes a sip from her drink and pulls a face. She's never been a drinker. I imagine I'm supposed to have driven her to it.

'You've made your bed . . .'

'And now you're going to suffocate me with one of the pillows!' I get up. 'I can see it was a mistake coming here.'

'You've made rather a lot of mistakes recently, haven't you, Felicity?' she says nastily. 'But then, what more should I expect from you? I suppose it was only a matter of time before you and Richard split up. You were never good enough for him. In fact, I'm surprised your relationship lasted so long, especially after what he said to Sally-Anne last night!' She glares at me challengingly.

'What are you talking about? What did Richard say?' I turn to Sally.

'Nothing,' she whispers, shaking her head. 'She's upset, that's all.' She takes my arm and starts to usher me out of the room. 'Just ignore her, Fliss, you know what she's like, she's upset, it's best to leave it for now.'

'Yes, leave it for now, Fliss,' Mother calls after me mockingly. 'Run away from this like you do from everything else.'

I pull away from Sally and face Mother. 'I am not running away! I'm trying to do the right thing for me, can't you understand that?' I plead, searching her face for one iota of compassion, of understanding. It is as cold, hard and closed as the lid on a chest freezer. 'Don't you want me to be happy?' I persist, but I already know the answer to that one. Duty, social standing, financial security; all are far more necessary for a good life than happiness. 'Would you rather I made the biggest mistake of my life, married Richard, no doubt divorced Richard, and end up a lonely, embittered old bitch like you?'

She walks up to me, eyes blazing angrily. She hurls the brandy at me. I feel the sting as it hits my eyes and runs down my face to mingle with the steady stream of salt water already flowing.

CHAPTER THREE

EVENING IS FALLING as I finally reach Angels Court. The crumbling old stone farmhouse looks familiar and reassuring. A huge yellow sun is gradually disappearing below the line of ridge tiles at the summit of the roof, casting pointed fingers of light against my windscreen.

I'm on the proverbial emotional roller coaster. On the drive down, I have been alternately singing and sighing, ecstatic and sobbing. The recent confrontation has thrown me. My life is on a totally different course. This is what I wanted, so why do I suddenly feel so empty inside?

Caroline is waiting at the drawing-room window, looking out for me, no doubt worried. The drive, which should only have taken an hour, has taken me two. I kept missing turnings due to lack of concentration.

'Fliss, where the hell have you been?' Caro hurries out of the front door towards me, first scolding and then hugging me, enveloping me in affection and the warm waft of Chanel and clean blonde hair.

'My goodness, you're a wreck! Look at the state of you.'

She pulls away, holding me at arm's length for inspection.

'You're all sticky! You smell like a brewery. You haven't been drinking, have you? Oh, Fliss, you know never to drink and drive.'

I shake my head. 'Of course not. I'm not that stupid. I made the mistake of going round to see Mother before I came down here. She'd been hitting the medicinal brandy, and threw a full glass of Rémy Martin in my face.'

'Why, the old cow!' Caro's eyes are wide with outrage. She takes my arm. 'Well, you're among friends now. The only alcohol we'll be throwing is down your neck. You come along inside, we'll send David out to fetch your cases.'

'Oh, yes, cases,' I muse. 'I knew I meant to pick something up before I left.'

Caro leads me into the house and takes me upstairs to one of the guest rooms. The room is comforting and welcoming with antique pine furniture and its warm terracotta walls turned honey-gold by the last rays of the sun streaming in.

As it is summer, the open fireplace is filled with a heavy copper pot brimming over with sweet peas, their delicious scent hanging lightly on the warm air. White gauze curtains flutter at the open windows in the slightest of breezes. I can hear birds' evensong from the orchard just beyond the garden. Angels Court is so beautiful, so peaceful, a little corner of Eden in which to rest and recuperate.

I collapse heavily onto the wrought-iron bed, and Caro disappears into the bathroom. I can hear the thunder of water filling the old cast-iron bath, and the smell of lavender as she shakes salts into the foaming water. I curl into a ball, knees to my chest, like a baby in the womb. For the first time since my confrontation with my mother I feel my hands cease to tremble.

I emerge from my bath feeling decidedly more human. Caro has left me one of her sweaters and some clean jeans on the bed. The jeans are a touch too tight, she has always been enviably slim. The sweater's dark blue angora. Despite the mildness of the evening, I'm glad of its warmth, and its length covering my midriff which protrudes a little too much over the tight waistband of the jeans. I sigh. Perhaps my new life could incorporate a new figure. Then again I'm still on official comfort eating time.

Downstairs, I find Caroline and David in the kitchen, sharing a bottle of wine. Caro is hovering over pans on the Aga, listening to Radio Four. David is seated at the kitchen table, shelling peas, dark head bent, half-moon glasses perched on the end of his long nose, reading yesterday's *Sunday Times*. He looks up as I enter and smiles warmly.

I slip into one of the seats at the long scrubbed kitchen table. Darius, David's labrador, rises from his basket and, plumy tail wagging so hard it shakes his whole backside, pads across the red flagstone floor to me and thrusts a wet nose under my hand, urging me to stroke him.

I stroke his silken head. 'At least someone loves me,' I whisper.

I can feel my bottom lip begin to tremble again.

David the diplomat, no doubt primed by Caroline, makes his excuses and heads towards the study. Caroline turns to me with a wide smile.

'Feeling more human?' She hands me a glass of wine.

I nod slowly.

She raises her own full glass to me. 'Well, congratulations, you did it, you did it. You're finally free.'

I obviously don't look too ecstatic.

She peers more closely at me. 'Fliss . . . earth calling Fliss, are you all right? You're not regretting it, are you? Thinking about the wedding?'

I leap out of my wineglass like a salmon jumping upstream. 'Oh, my goodness, the wedding!'

Somehow in the whole drama of everything I'd forgotten it. I hadn't forgotten the marriage—I mean, that's what the whole damn argument was about—but the actual mechanics of getting married, the church, the flowers, the reception for 200 people. The empty paranoid lethargic feeling turns to blind panic.

'I must start cancelling things or people will turn up expecting to see a marriage!'

'Calm down, Fliss.' Caro sloshes another litre of red into my bulbous gallon-sized glass. 'It's not for another six weeks. Besides, I'm sure Miriam will be taking care of all that. Why don't you give her a call just to put your mind at rest?'

I lay my poor aching head down on the kitchen table. The old wood is smooth and warm. Comforting.

'She's not talking to me,' I groan. 'You know how much she idolised Richard. She's in mourning as we speak. I can just see her retiring to a darkened room, complaining bitterly about her errant and ungrateful elder daughter, and being waited upon hand and foot by poor old Sally-Anne.'

'More likely making wax effigies, calling them Fliss, and doing unspeakable things to them with pins,' says Caro. 'Oh, and you forgot stupid.'

'What?' I lift my head from the table and look at her in confusion.

'Her errant, ungrateful, and unspeakably *stupid* daughter.'

'You don't think I'm stupid, do you, Caroline?' I wail. 'Please tell me you don't think I've made a huge mistake?'

'Certainly not!' she replies adamantly. 'That's not what you think, is it, Fliss?'

'I don't know,' I wail, 'I'm soooo confuuuused.'

The tears that have been switching on and off all evening like the stop and go sign on a pedestrian crossing begin to slide down my face again. It must be all the alcohol I've drunk over the past few days; I need to lose some liquid from somewhere. Caro comes to put a comforting arm round my shoulders.

'There, there . . .' She has her teacher's voice on. 'Let it all out.'

'I'm not crying for him,' I sniff. 'I'm crying for me. I'm nearly thirty, and look what I've gone and done . . . I've just turned my whole life upside-down. I'm too old to change everything, I shall become an ancient lonely spinster . . .'

'That's the Châteauneuf-du-Pape talking, not you, and you're twenty-eight—I'd hardly call that ancient now, would you?' Caro sits down in the chair next to me, and takes my hand. 'Now, Fliss, do you love Richard?'

I stop crying, and look up at her. 'No. No, I don't.'

'There now, you didn't even hesitate. And if I were going to marry somebody I didn't love, and I had these massive doubts and came to you for advice, what would you say to me?'

'I'd tell you not to go through with it,' I answer slowly, registering my own words. How come Caroline can always put everything back into perspective so easily?

'So, tell me, do you really think you've made a mistake by calling the whole thing off, or do you want to spend the rest of your life being married to some pompous twit who only wants a woman to stroke his ego?'

'Well, his ego is the largest thing he's got. I'd rather stroke that than certain other parts of him.' I begin to giggle.

Caro smiles brightly at me. 'See? At least you've got your sense of humour back now.'

David sticks his head round the door. 'Is it safe to come in?'

'I think the patient is well on the road to recovery.' Caro indicates me, still slumped, but giggling. 'She seems cheerful enough now.'

'Well, I'm glad you're feeling better, Felicity dear. You *are* feeling better, aren't you?' He peers at my reddened eyes.

I nod.

'Good, 'cause your mother's on the phone for you.'

I'm shaking as I pick up the receiver. The last thing I need right now is another torrent of abuse.

'Hello?' My voice is a whisper.

'Fliss, is that you?'

My heart does a yo-yo action, dips to my boots and then boings back up again as I realise it's not Mother, it's Sally.

'Oh, Sally,' I sigh in relief. 'Thank goodness it's only you. David just said you were Mother. How is she?'

'She's gone to bed . . . she didn't mean to be so awful, Fliss, not really, she was just very upset.'

'I'd never have guessed,' I say sarcastically.

Sally pauses for a moment.

'About the wedding . . .' she offers tentatively.

'The wedding that was but isn't any more? I was just saying to Caro that I ran off without even thinking about the wedding. I'll have to contact all the guests, return the presents, cancel the caterers . . .' My voice begins to rise in panic at the enormity of the task in hand.

'Look, Fliss, that's one of the reasons I'm calling. I know how upset you are at the moment—the last thing you need is to have to run around like an idiot cancelling a wedding. I don't want you to worry about a thing. I want you to leave it all to me. I'll do whatever has to be done, OK?'

Such a tempting offer, to be able just to forget the whole fiasco. Unfortunately, I'd feel far too guilty to offload the burden onto Sal, especially when she has everything else to cope with as well. I ran away from the flak, she's still slap-bang in the middle of it.

'Are you absolutely sure?' I ask her. 'It's such a burden to put on you, and there's so much to cancel . . .'

'Positive. I want you just to relax and forget about everything, do you hear me?'

I'm suddenly desperately grateful to my little sister. 'Well, if you're sure . . .'

I return to the kitchen in better mood. Sally-Anne has lifted a big weight from my shoulders. I'm surprised at her really. We've always got on well but we've never been what you would call close.

I was seven when Sally was born. I was perhaps a little jealous to start off with, but I soon came to realise that instead of a rival I had an ally. Sally's always been able to handle Mother's moods far better than I. Probably because I always seem to be the one to cause them, whereas Sally has fitted happily into my mother's image of the perfect child right from pink dresses through to becoming an assistant bank manager. Mother's idea of a perfect career.

Sally also models part-time. She's one of those wholesome, healthy, pretty girls with perfect teeth who you see smiling happily out at you from the front cover of *Woman's Weekly*. She's the human equivalent of a kitten on a chocolate box. Totally adorable.

Come to think of it, I always thought if Richard had met her first he wouldn't have given me a second glance.

'Well?' Caro is curious. 'What did Mater say? You look surprisingly cheerful.'

'It wasn't Mother, it was Sally.'

'David!' Caro chastises her husband. 'That wasn't a nice thing to do. Honestly, darling, your sense of humour has no sense of timing!'

He holds up his hands and backs away. 'But it sounded like Miriam, honestly,' he defends himself, 'I wouldn't be so cruel . . .'

Caro returns to her stew, stirring it gently. She holds out the huge wooden spoon for David to taste some. 'More salt? What do you think?'

He shakes his head. 'Perfect as always, darling,' he replies, kissing her forehead. 'Just like you.'

Here most people would reach for the sick bag, but David's not being nauseating, he's just being nice. The sincerity saves the sentiment.

I say enviously, 'Tell me, what is the secret of such an idyllic marriage? I think I ought to watch and learn.'

'Idyllic!' Caro laughs, as does David. They share a look.

'Come on, I want to know. I wouldn't mind a shot at happy families myself some day. With the right man, of course,' I add hastily. 'Don't want to make another mistake like last time.'

'You want some lessons in family life?' Caro asks. 'Good, the kids are arriving at the end of next week, you can entertain them. Maura's going to some retreat in Scotland or something, so we've got them for six days.'

I walked right into that one.

Maura is David's ex-wife, an ageing hippy who believes in alternative medicine, alternative religion, and alternative ways of bringing up children. Hannah, just sixteen, and Charlie, nearly eighteen, are good kids but rather wild. Used to a total lack of discipline from their mother, they find even the relaxed regime of Angels Court restricting. David tries to overcompensate for Maura's lax attitude and tends to lay down the law with them, but just ends up wound-up.

'A retreat?' I laugh halfheartedly. 'Any spare places? I could do with retreating somewhere nice and peaceful myself.'

'I thought that's why you'd come to us?' says Caro indignantly. 'Don't worry, David has promised to be relaxed and to just let everything float over his head, haven't you, darling? Besides, you don't want peace and quiet, you want life and action. You need to see what you've been missing out on so you don't look back with regret. It's very easy to paint the past with a rosy glow, you know.'

'Nothing could make me recall Richard as a glowing memory. You know, that's a lovely thing to be able to call him.'

'What's that?'

I raise my glass. 'A memory.'

I spend the majority of the next week sleeping.

I wake only to eat and play the odd game of chess with David. I soak indulgently for hours in lavender-scented baths, and wander gently through the beautiful countryside with Darius. Caro is waiting on me hand and foot, and I am unashamedly and unadulteratedly making the most of it all.

I know I've got to think about my future, but the forward-planning, practical-thinking part of my brain has gone on a long holiday.

I decide to go with the flow. Whatever life throws at me, I shall conquer. A very easy philosophy to adopt at Angels Court, where the only decision to make is red, white or both at dinner.

It's wonderful to be with people who totally laud my decision to leave Richard. Even when you're sure that you've done the right thing, there are always the 'what ifs' to contend with. Caro washes these away with bitchy, wonderfully witty comments about him. If I start to view the past with rose-tinted glasses she quickly swaps them for a microscope under which Richard the Toad can be easily dissected and seen for what he really is.

Oh, the danger of beginning to enjoy oneself too much.

Just over a week into my stay, and Caro and I are enjoying another idyllic summer's day stretched out on rickety old wooden sun loungers in the garden. Darius is chasing the small rosy apples which fall from the trees, the ring doves that congregate on the roof of the house are cooing softly to each other, the air is tinged with the smell of warm grass, lavender and old roses—and typically, where most normal people would surrender their minds to the near nirvana surrounding us, my overdeveloped sense of guilt kicks in to ruin everything.

I begin to think of the chaos and confusion that Sally-Anne has been left to clear up. I breathe in the fresh, sweet, flower-filled air and sigh heavily as guilt wins over self-indulgence.

'It's no good. No matter how much I don't want to, I really must go home,' I announce to Caro, who is sun-worshipping beside me. 'I know

Sally said to leave everything to her, but it just isn't fair. It's my mess, I ought to be there to clean it up.'

'I wouldn't worry.' Caro stretches and turns over to get the sun on her back. 'I'm sure Miriam's doing a wonderful job of sweeping the whole thing under the carpet. Besides, you can't go yet, you promised to help me with the kids.'

'I know, but I'm running away from my responsibilities, Caro. I can't leave it all to poor old Sal.'

'Sally-Anne wouldn't have offered if she didn't feel she could cope,' Caro replies matter-of-factly.

'I suppose so, but I still feel like I should—'

'Fliss!' She holds up one elegant hand, like a traffic policeman stopping cars. 'Stop right there! I'm not going to let you ruin such a beautiful day by going on a guilt trip.'

'Sorry, but I can't help it. Every time I close my eyes I get visions of wedding cakes and flower arrangements arriving at The Beeches. Something like that would give Mother a heart attack.'

'Every cloud has a silver lining!' Caro laughs. 'No, seriously, forget about your mother and the wedding and Richard and Sal. Try and think about something else.'

'Such as?'

'Well, I certainly have different fantasies when I close *my* eyes.' Caro smirks. 'I don't know, think about what we can do with the kids for six days. You know how bored they get down here. It's far too rural for them after the bright lights and excitement of London.'

'I thought all kids loved the countryside, especially farms?'

'Well, they used to love it, but I suppose they're not really kids any more, Charlie especially.'

'We could organise something—a trip down to the sea perhaps?'

'Would they appreciate organised events? You know what they're like if they think they've got to do something someone else wants them to, rather than something they chose themselves. And you know what Hannah's like at the moment. Everything you suggest is "so juvenile".' She lapses into a fair impression of Hannah's bored drawl. 'The only thing she likes down here are all of the horses and some of the farm hands . . . oil my back for me, darling.' Too lazy to move, she points to the suntan oil with her foot. 'At least we won't have them stuck indoors all the time. You know, it's so hot, it's almost like being in the Med.'

'Apart from no beach, no cheese and wine, and no tasty bronzed Frenchmen?'

'Well, we can supply the cheese and wine, no problem. We might even run to some men, if you like. In fact, I think that's probably what you need to keep you amused. We could keep you and Hannah happy at the same time.'

'Eighteen-year-old farm hands are hardly my scene.'

'Have you actually seen the eighteen-year-old farm hands that run around this place?' Caro looks mischievously at me. 'Young, tanned and bulging with bronzed muscles.'

I try to get excited about young, tanned, bronzed and muscled, but find that I can't.

'I think I'll give Hannah first choice,' I say drily.

'Well, we could always find you something older and more sophisticated, if that's what you want?'

'Caro, at the moment I don't want anything. I've had my fill of men.'

'Are you sure?' she asks wistfully. 'I love playing Cupid.'

Stupid Cupid, who needs him? I'm too tired for men at the moment. No, rephrase that. I'm too tired *of* men at the moment.

'No, Caro,' I plead, knowing full well how much she would enjoy fixing me up. 'Promise me, no playing Cupid? Please.'

'Not just a teensy bit?'

'Not at all, promise me? No men, OK?'

She rolls her eyes to heaven. 'OK. No men.'

The next Sunday I return from one of my self-indulgent solitary walks, to find that Hannah and Charlie have arrived.

David, who had to go to town to pick them up from the station, has also thoughtfully retrieved my suitcase from the hallway of my flat so—bliss—I now have some clothes of my own to wear.

I haven't seen Hannah and Charlie for over six months, since Christmas actually. Charlie has grown about a foot since I last saw him. He is the image of his father, tall and dark with hooded sleepy eyes that never betray too much emotion. Hannah is the complete opposite of Charlie, small and lithe, with amazing hair the colour of the sun setting over a field of ripe corn, strange but very beautiful.

David has obviously filled the kids in about Fliss and her recent cock-up, as they are initially far too polite to me, making me endless cups of coffee and offering me first choice of which radio station we tune in to while making Sunday lunch.

This solicitude doesn't last very long, however.

'What you need is another man,' announces Hannah out of the blue when we finally sit down to dinner.

'That's the last thing I need!' I choke over my iced water.

'Take it from me, Fliss, the best way to get over one man is to find yourself another.'

'Such words of wisdom from one so young,' mocks David.

'Oh, shut up, Daddy. Just because you're far too old to know about these sort of things.' Hannah yawns purposely to annoy her father.

'I was over Richard a long time ago,' I state adamantly.

'Then why are you hiding out here?' she challenges.

'I need to get over the consequences of getting over Richard.'

'She's avoiding her mother,' adds Caroline.

'Honestly, Fliss, it's so pathetic to be frightened of one's mother!'

'Hannah, don't be rude!' snaps David.

'Mum believes in freedom of expression.' Charlie grins.

'Is that what you call it?' The sarcasm in David's voice is heavy.

'She doesn't want us to stifle our true selves, believes our personalities should be free to grow and develop without harmful parental interference,' Hannah explains.

David shudders.

'Don't deliberately provoke your father,' Caro chastises gently. 'Think of his blood pressure. These old wrinklies have to be kept stress-free.'

Hannah laughs. 'Yes, I keep forgetting that Dad's past it,' she says. 'When are you going to have children, Caro? You'd better hurry up or Dad won't be able to manage it any more . . .'

David opens his mouth to argue, looks at Caroline, shakes his head and then closes his mouth again.

'I'm not having any children,' states Caro firmly, stacking pots in the large white enamel butler's sink.

'Why ever not? I want at least six.'

'Six!' splutters Charlie. 'I don't think so. You can't look after yourself, let alone six kids.'

David gives them both a warning look. 'Just drop it, OK?'

Caro suddenly looks pale and tired.

David looks pointedly at his children again and they lapse into silence. Caro finishes clearing the table.

'Sit down, Caro. Hannah and Charlie can do the dishes,' David tells her.

'But we're taking Fliss out for a walk.' Hannah protests. 'You said we'd got to look after Fliss.'

'Dishes first,' says David emphatically.

Charlie the peacemaker steps in. 'I'll do the dishes. It doesn't take two of us to stack the machine.'

Hannah takes my arm as we step out into the warmth of the evening.

The sun is sinking slowly over the edge of the dark green woods that lie beyond the fields surrounding the house. We follow the sun and walk towards them.

As we reach the edge of the field beyond the orchard, where the beech trees begin to grow in a tangled mass of thick brown and mossy green roots, Hannah dives ecstatically into the smoke-scented gloom of the wood, drawn by the deep pink sea of densely growing wild rhododendron. She runs through the trees, gathering flowers, like a maenad, her web of golden hair fluffed about her face like a halo.

She makes me feel so old, yet it feels like only yesterday I was a teenager. Was I that self-confident at her age? I don't think so.

Hannah dances back to me, her arms full of already wilting petals, which she proceeds to scatter like confetti along the path before our feet.

'Did you know Caroline's arranging a party on your behalf?' she laughs, skipping backwards so that she can see my face as she talks. 'Daddy let it slip on the way back from the station. I think they've got some man lined up as a prospective boyfriend. I'd be careful if I were you, Caro has suspect taste. After all, she married *him*, didn't she? Do you know, he's nearly sixteen years older than her? Your bloke's probably sixty, with a receding hairline and a fat belly. Then again he might have a fat bank balance as well. I want a rich man, someone who can keep me in the lifestyle to which my parents are determined I won't become accustomed. If I get a rich and old man then I can kill him off with lots of sex and be a very merry widow.'

'Hannah!' I shriek, amused but slightly shocked. 'There's more to life and love than a full wallet.'

'I know that,' she says wearily. 'I'm not stupid. An older man has a lot of other things going for him as well. He would be more experienced sexually for one thing. I want to be initiated by someone who knows what they're doing. Was Richard good in bed?'

'Hannah!'

'Well, if I don't ask I won't learn, and the best way to learn is from other people's mistakes.'

'Well, Richard was certainly one of those. As far as I was concerned anyway.'

'Mmm,' agrees Hannah. 'You haven't answered my question.' She looks at me slyly. 'Was he good in bed?'

She's not going to give in, so I decide on honesty being the best policy.

'Frankly? He was bloody useless. One word of advice, Hannah. Whatever you do, avoid selfish men.'

'Well, that goes without saying,' she replies, snapping a branch from our path. 'I want a man who puts me before anything else. Was that why you got shot of him then, 'cause he was a failure in the sex department?'

'That was one reason, not the most important,' I answer truthfully. 'I just decided it wouldn't be a good idea to spend the rest of my life with someone I didn't particularly like. And I realised that I didn't have to settle for second best. Actually, no, Richard wasn't even second best, he was lousy last.'

'Was he really that awful? You must have liked him at some point. I mean to . . . you know . . .' She giggles. 'To go to bed with him.'

'You don't have to like someone to love them,' I answer carefully.

She digests this for a moment, and then nods her head slowly. 'I suppose so. I mean, I absolutely detest Charlie at the moment, but I suppose I do love him really.'

We walk in silence for a while as the path dips down a bank. At the bottom lies a stream, clogged thickly with bulrushes.

'I wonder what your next lover will be like?' Hannah muses. 'That's if you can bag yourself another one,' she teases. 'I mean, you're getting on a bit now, aren't you?' She takes the rest of the bank at a run as I throw a handful of leaves at her, and collapses in a fit of giggles, flopping down on the long grass at the edge of the stream.

'Perhaps Caro's man will be your dream man,' she murmurs, eyes shining excitedly. 'Wouldn't that be romantic? Your eyes meet across a crowded room, he's drawn to your side . . .'

'Please!' I hold up my hands, pleading for her to stop. 'I made Caro promise me that there would be no matchmaking.' I sit down next to Hannah, who is stripping a reed.

'She was probably crossing her fingers,' she replies.

'Lying, you mean?'

'Not at all. It's perfectly legitimate to cross your fingers when making a promise under duress, it just means you don't have to carry it through.'

'Well, she'd better not have been,' I state crossly. 'I meant it when I said no men. They're a complication I can't cope with at the moment.'

'I've never heard them called that before.' Hannah laughs.

'Give it another few years and you'll understand what I mean,' I promise her.

We make our way back to the house via the stable yard. The sun has fallen beyond the horizon yet still spreads a warm glow up through the sky, blazing orange, pink and red like a raging field fire.

Jake, the son of Angus Macready the farm manager, is wielding a pitchfork in the end stable. He is stripped to the waist, his muscular torso brown from the sun and gleaming with fresh sweat. As we clatter noisily across the cobbled yard, he pauses and looks up. His eyes flick over me, he smiles in greeting, and then he looks over at Hannah.

They haven't met before. Jake has recently come down from a three-year degree course at Oxford.

His large dark eyes register extreme interest now. She smiles coquettishly, looking at him with her strange grey eyes, as he incredulously takes in her willowy body, pretty face and amazing silken cornfield hair. When she is sure she has his full interest, she turns away and, completely ignoring him, walks over to one of the boxes, swinging her hips seductively.

Mac, David's handsome chestnut hunter, sticks his thoroughbred head out of his loose box and, recognising a friend, blows affectionately in Hannah's hair. She reaches in the pocket of her bleached denim cut-offs and pulls out a half-eaten packet of Polos. His thick whiskered lips mumble against the palm of her hand as he delicately consumes the half-dozen she proffers.

The other horses watch her impatiently, hungrily, as does Jake. I have a feeling she could have him eating out of her hand just as easily as Mac.

Two evenings later, Caro and David have gone to a dinner party that was arranged months ago. I'm kid-sitting.

It's one of those slow, quiet nights, where boredom prowls around the perimeter of the room like a fox around a chicken coop. Charlie is bringing new meaning to the word apathy. The video I got from the local shop is rejected as rubbish. There's nothing interesting on television, and a game of cards soon broke down into a screaming match between siblings.

I've given up being entertainment manager and referee rolled into one, and retired behind the latest issue of *Cosmo*. Charlie is trying to shunt a cigarette straight from the packet into his mouth, but keeps missing. Hannah is pacing restlessly about the room.

'It's really not fair to go out and leave us,' she complains about her parents. 'We're only here once in a blue moon. You'd think they'd want to spend the time we're here actually with us, wouldn't you?'

'They can't spend every waking moment pandering to you,' mumbles Charlie, as he finally manages to chuck a B & H into his mouth.

Hannah looks at him in disgust. 'There's nothing very clever about smoking,' she sneers at him.

Charlie makes a discreet but very obvious V sign at her.

'What are you reading?' she asks, staring at the feature headlines on the front cover of my magazine. '"Sex Fabulous Sex"? "The Perfect Summer Diet"? Have they got an article on combatting extreme boredom?'

'I'm reading an article on how to find the perfect man,' I answer her without thinking.

'I thought you didn't want one of those at the moment?'

'Not especially,' I put down the magazine, 'but I thought I might pick up a few tips for when I'm ready to go back into circulation.'

'What sort of qualities would you want in a man for him to be perfect for you?' Hannah urges.

'Well . . .' I muse. 'I want someone with a sense of humour.'

'Oh, so do I,' agrees Hannah. 'A sense of humour is very important. Go on.'

'I suppose it would be nice to have someone who's interested in what I do. Richard only ever thought about himself. If something didn't affect him, it didn't interest him. I'd like someone I can talk to. You know, not just trivialities like what do you want for dinner, but a proper, interesting conversation.'

'Mac has all the qualities I'd want in a man.' Hannah smiles thoughtfully. 'He's well bred, good-looking, a real gentleman, and terribly clever and funny. You talk to him and you can tell he's really listening to you, but best of all he never answers back.' She laughs.

'He's a horse,' shrieks Charlie derisively. 'I always thought you were weird, and boy was I right!' he taunts.

'You know that's not what I meant!' Hannah screams back at him.

'Wouldn't you prefer Mac's groom?' I tease her, trying to defuse yet another row.

Hannah looks coy. 'Perhaps . . . perhaps not.'

'Women!' snaps Charlie more derisively this time. 'The things you talk about! I'm bored out of my *skull*, I'm going down the pub.' He shrugs on his leather James Dean-style jacket. 'Lend us a tenner, Fliss?'

'You're not old enough to go to the pub, Charlie.'

'Oh, come on, my birthday's in three weeks. What's the difference? Mum lets me drink anyway.'

I turn to Hannah. 'Is that true?'

She nods reluctantly.

'Oh, go on then, but I don't know you're there if your father asks, OK?'

'You're a doll, Fliss,' he replies, grinning. He pockets my proffered ten-pound note. 'See ya later!'

Hannah watches him go and then turns petulantly to me.

'Well, if he gets to go to the pub, I'm going to have a drink too,' she announces, making her way to the rosewood cabinet that houses David's collection of malt whiskies.

'Hannah, you're *definitely* not old enough!'

'But you let Charlie go to the pub!' she cries in outrage.

'He's nearly eighteen,' I protest weakly. 'It's very different from being only just sixteen.'

'Why does everybody treat me like a child?' she wails.

'But, Hannah . . .'

'I also detest hypocrites,' she accuses me with a glare, and stamps noisily out of the room.

I hear the back door slam. Darius, who has been slumped on his own personal clapped-out chintz-covered chair for the entire evening, opens one eye and looks at me accusingly.

'Don't you start,' I snap unjustly at him. 'I wasn't being unfair, was I?'

Double standards, he answers with his eyes, or are they simply reflecting my own thoughts.

I go outside in search of Hannah, taking a bottle of low-alcohol wine, two glasses, and an apology. She's not in the garden, but I have a good idea where she'll be. I walk round the side of the house, through the small kitchen garden and under the stone archway into the stable block.

In the dim light I can see Hannah leaning over the edge of the half-open door into Mac's loose box. I can hear the low sound of her voice as she whispers to him.

I'm just about to call after her when a figure slips out of the shadows opposite me. It's Jake.

Hannah turns quickly, alarmed at his footsteps, then, recognising him, smiles softly. I'm torn between friendly discretion and surrogate parental concern. Discretion wins, as I'm still in the mood to make amends, so I slip back through the archway and return to the house.

Big Ben is just striking for *News at Ten* when I hear the back door again. Hannah sticks her head round the drawing-room door, and grins sheepishly at me.

'Hi, Fliss, sorry I was such a brat earlier. It's no excuse, I know, but I'm really tired and that always makes me ratty, so I think I'll just go to bed, OK?'

Charlie arrives home just over an hour later, also in a better mood. We take a cross-legged Darius for a quick walk in the moonlight and then he helps me to lock up.

I hear Caro and David return. It's about two o'clock in the morning. They are obviously very drunk. Caro is singing softly, David is shushing her loudly. I'm just drifting back to sleep when I hear the faint click of the back door being opened and shut very quietly. Immediately I'm as alert as a hound on the scent of a fox.

I sit upright, listening, as footsteps softly ascend the bare wooden staircase. Sliding out of bed, I grab a poker from the fireplace and edge towards the door. Slowly, quietly, I pull the door open towards me, raising the poker above my head so that I can easily bash any burglar before he can bash me. There is a figure at the head of the stairs, paused in mid-step, like a trembling whippet listening for its master's whistle.

I'm trembling slightly too. Angels Court is reputed to be haunted, and although I refute this as ridiculous, it always seems more plausible after midnight. Ghosts, however, don't creep around the house carrying a pair of worn red Kickers in their right hand.

'Hannah!' I hiss, relief turning to outrage. 'I thought you'd gone to bed hours ago.'

She looks at me, and then at the closed door of Caro and David's bedroom, which is next door to mine. Bed springs creak as someone stirs inside. We both shoot like conspirators into my room.

'Where have you been?' I whisper crossly, closing the door softly behind me.

She sits on the end of my bed. 'What would you say if I told you I was in love?'

'I'd say you still hadn't answered my question.'

'I've been up at Woodsman's Cottage.' Her eyes are bright, pupils dilated, she looks like she's been drinking.

'With Jake?'

'With Jake,' she confirms, trying to look sheepish but failing dismally, a broad grin on her pretty face.

'And I suppose that's who you think you're in love with?'

'I don't *think* I'm in love with him. I *am* in love with him.'

Oh, the certainty of youth. 'You've only known him five minutes!'

'Nearly three days actually.'

'Oh, and that's a really long time, isn't it?'

'I didn't realise time was a prerequisite for falling in love with someone,' she answers indignantly. 'Honestly, Fliss, I thought you of all people would understand. You usually treat me like an adult. I thought you'd be able to give me some advice about . . . well, sex and stuff.'

I swallow hard. The only advice I could happily give Hannah at the moment is *don't*.

'I'm probably not the best person to ask about this sort of thing,' I mutter, 'you know me, an embittered old cynic. Shouldn't you really be talking to Caroline about this?'

'Why? She's not my mother.'

'Well, what about your father then?'

'Oh, I know what he'll say. That I'm far too young to form any sort of relationship, and that Jake is too old for me.'

'Don't you think that might be right?'

'I believe age is irrelevant when it comes to love,' she sighs.

'How old is he, Hannah?'

'Oh, he's getting on,' she replies. 'He'll be twenty-three at Christmas. But I think I prefer older men.'

'Well, David can hardly say anything when he's sixteen years older than Caroline, now can he?' I say without thinking.

A smile slowly spreads across her face. 'No, of course, I hadn't thought of it like that. Thanks, Fliss, you've been a big help.'

She slides off my bed and slips silently out of the room before I can say anything to redeem the last statement.

Oh dear. She may think I've been a big help, but I don't think Caro and David would look at it that way. She's taken the gun, and I've just handed her the ammunition.

Breakfast next morning is a sombre affair. Hannah is quiet, pleading with me using her black-shadowed eyes not to mention last night's escapade.

Fortunately Caro and David are far too hung over themselves to notice Hannah's state. Caro is slumped at the kitchen table nursing a mug of black coffee; David is struggling to pull on and strap up his boots, and complaining that he's desperately late to meet Angus Macready down in Far Meadow.

Charlie, still in excellent spirits from his trip to the local, whistles while he fries spitting bacon and runny golden-yellow eggs in a huge black pan.

I'm fighting yet another battle of conscience, I'm worried about Hannah. Worried she might do something silly—sixteen is a good age for that. I remember when I was sixteen, I was old enough to get into mischief and too young to worry about the consequences. A dangerous age.

Charlie slides the greasy mess from the pan to his plate, and slaps the whole lot down on the table.

David visibly gags and shoots out of the kitchen door. Caro takes one look and sprints off to the downstairs loo. She comes back five minutes later looking decidedly ill. Her skin has the pallor of a corpse and her hands are visibly trembling.

'I'm going to go back to bed,' she just about manages to utter, 'I think I've got a touch of food poisoning . . .'

'Don't you mean alcohol poisoning?' says Charlie politely.

'I don't know what you mean,' she replies indignantly, but flatly refuses to meet his mocking eyes as she beats a hasty retreat.

Laughing, Hannah puts down the piece of toast she's been staring at but not actually attempting to eat for the last ten minutes. 'Well, I'm off out, see you later.'

And with that she's gone. I don't have to ask where.

'Are you OK, Fliss? You look a bit down.' Charlie moves to the seat next to mine. 'You're not still brooding about Richard the Turd, are you?'

Just taking a sip from a cup of coffee, I choke over the new nickname, trying very hard to look disapproving and suppress the smile that's blossoming instead.

'Actually I'm a bit worried about your sister,' I confess to him.

'Aren't we all?' he sighs. 'Still, the doctors said she'd never be normal.'

'No, seriously, Charlie. I really am worried.'

'About her and Jake?'

'You know?'

'Of course. I may look innocuous, but I see all and hear all,' he jokes. 'Don't worry, it's only a stupid crush, she's had tons of those before and lived to tell the tale.'

'Maybe. But this one worries me. She's so serious about the whole thing. I think I should tell your father and Caroline what's going on.'

'And have her fall out with you big time? What's the problem? Why not just let her get on with it if she's keen on him?'

'But she's *too* keen on him, Charlie, I'm frightened she'll do something stupid.'

He pushes his floppy black fringe out of his eyes and grins easily at me. 'You worry too much. She'll be all right, let her work it out for herself. Hannah won't thank you for interfering, and Dad's got eyes in the back of his head, I bet he knows already. Anyway, we're only here for another three days. We'll go back to London and she'll forget all about him. Besides that, she's far too young for him. If Jake's got any scruples, he won't take advantage of the fact she's totally dotty about him.'

'Twenty-three-year-old men don't have any scruples when it comes to sex.'

'Don't they?' says Charlie, his eyes brightening perceptibly. 'In that case, roll on twenty-three!'

Over the next few days Hannah is quiet and miserable, and finally admits to me that Jake seems to be avoiding her. I hate to see her unhappy, but I guiltily heave a sigh of relief.

When Sally-Anne phones again it almost feels like an intrusion. I've managed to push all thoughts of Richard and Mother and the cancelled wedding quite out of my mind, and I like it that way. Speaking with my sister only brings it all back into too-sharp focus.

She sounds rather odd, but when questioned puts it down to stress. My guilt increases tenfold as I'm pretty certain any stress Sally is under has one direct cause—me.

When pushed she tells me that my name is still pretty much taboo in the Blakeney household, but that Mother seems to be surfacing from her me-induced misery incredibly well. What precisely has caused this miraculous recovery escapes me, and Sally seems almost reluctant to offer an explanation, simply pointing out that I should be grateful. At this rate I'll be allowed back into my mother's life in say . . . five years' time. Sal then informs me that my poor put-upon father has moved into the potting shed on a pretty much permanent basis, when he's not off night fishing with Roger.

Although Sally is adamant that she's coping pretty well, I decide for her sake and my father's that I really must go home. When I announce this intention to Caro, however, she goes to great lengths to persuade me to stay till the end of the week. She apparently has a surprise for me.

I remember Hannah's warnings about men and parties and this only deepens my resolve to go. I'm feeling 100 per cent better but I don't think I'm up to surprises just yet. However, after much good-natured grovelling on her part, I agree to stay.

The night before Hannah and Charlie are due to return to London, Caro has arranged a trip to the local theatre.

Charlie, who has been forced out of his usual uniform of jeans, white T-shirt and leather jacket, and into a suit, is making rude comments about local culture or rather lack of it and pulling agitatedly at his tie and collar as though they are actively trying to asphyxiate him.

'I don't know why you made me get all topped and tailed,' he complains. 'Market Atherton is hardly West End.'

'Stop moaning, you heathen,' David replies, grinning broadly. 'A bit of culture will do you good.'

'Flisssss,' hisses a voice. I turn. Hannah is standing in the shadows by the doorway, beckoning to me in a conspiratorial fashion. I sidle over.

'Guess what!' she whispers, excitedly. 'Jake wants me to meet him.'

She's beaming broadly, her eyes shining. 'Will you cover for me, Fliss?'

'But we're all supposed to be going out. I really don't know that I should . . .'

'Please,' she begs, anguished. 'Would you stand in the way of true love? I may never see him again, Fliss, this could be our last evening together. Pleeease.'

'Oh, OK,' I sigh. 'What do you want me to do?'

'Fliss, you're an absolute angel!' She kisses me warmly on the cheek.

'I'm not, I'm a fool.' I shake my head. 'I can't believe I'm doing this.'

'Just tell them I feel ill and I've gone to bed. I'll be back before you get home, I promise.'

I crumble. 'OK, but Hannah . . .'

'I know, I know, don't do anything you wouldn't do!' She winks lasciviously, blows me a kiss and is gone.

Caro, David and Charlie have made their way out to David's Range Rover.

'Now all we need is Hannah,' says Caro as I walk out of the front door. 'Where is she? Don't tell me she's still in the bathroom?'

'Er . . . she's not coming.' I can feel my face going red. I hate lying, especially to Caro. 'She said she doesn't feel too good.'

'Oh dear! Really! I'd better go and make sure she's all right,' says Caro in concern, turning back towards the house.

'Oh, she's fine,' I blurt out quickly, practically rugby tackling her away from the door. 'Just a bad headache, thought sitting in a stuffy theatre all night might make it worse. She said she wanted to be left on her own . . . You know, a couple of hours in a dark room.'

Caro stops. 'Typical Hannah. She's probably in a bad mood because she's got to go home tomorrow. Never mind, if she wants to miss out on tonight as well, then so be it.'

'That was total crap,' moans Charlie as we pull back into the drive, nearly three hours later. 'If it had gone on for even one more millisecond, I'd have died of complete and utter boredom.'

'Heathen,' mutters David, but he's smiling.

'Actually it finished a lot earlier than I thought it would.' Caro looks at her Cartier watch, an anniversary gift from David.

'Hannah knew what she was doing welshing out.' Charlie is still moaning as we enter the house, which is in darkness.

'Actually, I'd just better go and make sure she's OK,' says Caro. 'David, be an angel and get me a large G & T while I check on your drama queen of a daughter.'

I follow her upstairs, praying that Hannah has got home before us.

Sure enough, she's in bed, duvet pulled up to her neck. I send up a silent prayer of thanks.

'Feeling better?' Caro glides across the room, and flicks on the bedside lamp. 'Actually you do look flushed. Are you running a temperature?' She puts a cool hand on Hannah's forehead. 'Would you like anything? Some aspirin, or a hot drink perhaps?'

Hannah shakes her head. She's trembling, she actually does look ill, but I know she's not.

It's then that I notice the reason. A pair of boxer shorts lies on the floor just behind Caroline, who is sitting on the edge of Hannah's bed.

Hannah's eyes keep darting from them, to Caroline, to me. Rescue me! they plead.

I surreptitiously slide down the wall and, picking up the offending article, hold it behind my back.

'Well, if you're sure you're OK?' Caro stands up.

Hannah nods again, not trusting herself to speak. I can see relief flood her elfin face as Caro leaves the room, closing the door behind her.

'Well?' I demand, waving the boxer shorts at Hannah.

In response her cupboard door creaks open three inches, a hand slides out of the gap, takes the shorts and slides back in again. Hannah can contain herself no longer. Suppressed laughter explodes from her mouth like Coca-Cola fizzing from a shaken bottle.

Hannah and Charlie's last day. I decide I'm not even going to mention last night to Hannah, who grins all through breakfast. Lectures are futile. The horse has already bolted.

It turns out Hannah and Charlie's last day is also the day of the previously threatened party, which is Caro's not very surprising surprise. She expects me to be pleased about it, so I do try to be, but I'm not. I've never been party hearty, all that small talk and polite conversation, I'm not really very good at it.

One and all are gathered in the kitchen. David is doing amazing things with a blender while Caro is polishing wineglasses. I have embarked on the ambitious construction of a rich chocolate torte for this evening's soiree.

'We're only having a light meal,' David protested, when I announced my intentions. 'Soufflé, seafood, that sort of thing.'

'Are you saying my torte will turn out like a brick?' I ask indignantly.

Hannah, shelling peas, seems much happier, much brighter. I notice she's wearing Jake's signet ring on a chain about her neck. Her only gripe at the moment is that she will miss the party.

'I really don't think it's fair,' she complains. 'Get us to do all the hard work, clean the house, peel the veggies, and then ship us back to Mother's.'

'It's an adults only dinner party,' states Caroline firmly. 'Strictly no kids allowed.'

'I'm not a kid!' Hannah gives her usual disclaimer, but this time she is serenely smug.

'I'm sorry, Hannah, but your mother's coming to collect you,' says Caro.

'You could phone and put her off.'

'She'll already have left, it's a long drive from Scotland.'

Hannah's face falls in disappointment, but I know it's not really the party she wants to stay for. I sigh heavily. I really hope they were careful.

'That woman drives me round the bend!' Caro clenches her fists in exasperation. 'I thought she'd never leave! It's all your fault, Fliss, you and your bloody cracked aura, she was banging on about it for over half an hour.'

Maura has finally carried Charlie and Hannah back to the civilised capital in her Mercedes convertible. Very bourgeois for a self-proclaimed communist. I thought hippies drove VW campers.

'Starting her own healing workshop!' David collapses into a chair and shakes his head in amusement. 'Whatever next?'

'She could call it Maura's Auras,' I suggest, laughing. 'Cracked auras and crackpots a speciality.'

'Well, I don't think it's very funny,' Caro snaps, beginning to panic. 'We've got a dinner party to organise, and the guests will start arriving in an hour.'

'Don't worry, darling, everything's just about ready anyway,' David says soothingly. 'The food's prepared, I've chosen the wine. All you have left to do is make the table look beautiful and work the same magic on yourself.'

'You haven't forgotten we're eating earlier than usual tonight, David?'

They exchange a look. Caro's passing eyeball messages, like Morse code with her eyebrows. David deciphers.

'Oh, yes, of course. Don't worry, it's all in hand.'

I wish I could decipher that little exchange. Perhaps Hannah's right, perhaps tonight is a set-up and I shall find myself besieged by some pot-bellied businessman or pink-faced farmer. I feel the first stirring of nerves, butterflies drifting to and fro in my stomach.

By seven, I'm dressed, coiffured, and seated at the dressing table, painting my face. Such is the freedom here at Angels Court, the blissful isolation, I haven't worn make-up for three weeks. There's been no need. Caro, David and Darius don't care if my eyes look like two shrunken raisins in the head of a gingerbread man, and my lips are paler than a ghost's. I've almost forgotten how to apply it. It takes three attempts to get my lip-liner straight, not just through lack of recent practice but from my nervously trembling hand.

I can hear people arriving. Cars pulling slowly down the long gravel drive, doors slamming, David playing genial host-cum-butler in the hallway, Puccini drifting up the stairs.

There seem to be an awful lot of people arriving. The long table in the dining room seats at least twenty, but surely they haven't invited that many? As a newly single person I would prefer to be eased back into society gently rather than thrown in at the deep end with a full-scale party. Can I remember how to socialise? Do I *want* to remember? I think what I really want to do is curl up in bed with a bottle of wine and watch *Blind Date*.

I force myself to make my way downstairs. I look through the double doors that open into the lemon-coloured drawing room. Glamorous people are standing in groups, talking. The combined noise sounds like the babble of geese in a field.

I baulk at the numbers. There *are* over twenty people in the room. Perhaps I should feign a headache and return to the safe haven that is my bedroom.

I'm just backing out of the doorway when David appears at my side, whispers encouragingly that I look 'Bloody marvellous' and guides me across the room.

I recognise some of the group he's introducing me to from previous forays to Angels Court. Caro and David are sociable people, always throwing dinner parties.

I have already met the oh-so-glam blonde bombshell Eloise Gray who is talking to Caroline. We've never really hit it off. She's a bit of an ice queen, and also weirdly possessive of Caroline. Like she's not allowed to have any other friends. I therefore am not Eloise's favourite person. She raises eyebrows plucked to the point of extinction in greeting, but continues with her conversation in a manner that pointedly excludes me.

David introduces me next to an incredibly pretty and petite woman. She's like a little doll with enchanting eyes, wide and fawn-like and thickly fringed with long black lashes, a little rosebud mouth, which is painted a glossy cherry red, and a tiny tip-tilted nose. As far as her figure is concerned, God may have stinted in the height department, but she has the largest chest I have ever seen outside of *Treasure Island*. How can such a small person carry such a large front without overbalancing? Then again they appear to defy gravity. Perhaps they're weightless, like balloons filled with helium, and it's only the material of her low-cut bodice that is actually stopping them from floating right up to the ceiling.

She catches me staring. I blush as crimson as her mouth, but she simply smiles. I suppose she's used to a lot of attention.

'This is Sukey.' David smirks at my fascinated expression. 'She breeds horses.'

'No?' I can't imagine her doing anything more manual than filing her fingernails, let alone getting down and dirty in a loose box.

Sukey laughs lightly. 'This is my husband Bob,' she says, putting a hand on the arm of the man standing next to her. Husband Bob is thin, plain, straight-faced and unprepossessing. The boring but necessary bamboo cane supporting the wonderfully exotic bloom, I suppose.

'Bob's a chef,' says David, 'so my soufflés will have to rise to the occasion tonight.'

'Among other things!' Sukey giggles.

They all laugh as though this is some kind of 'in' joke.

Bob doesn't look creative enough to be a chef, although his face does have the quality of an unrisen loaf.

A tall, rangy, blond man who has been standing quietly at the edge of the group, elbow resting casually on the mantelpiece, steps forward and raises his eyebrows at David.

'Aren't you going to introduce me then?'

'Fliss, darling, I'd like you to meet Gwillem Davies.'

Gwillem takes the hand I offer him but doesn't shake it, preferring instead simply to squeeze it gently while holding it for a fraction of a second too long.

'Gwillem's a very old friend of ours from London,' David continues. 'He's an artist, you know. He painted the portrait of Caroline that hangs over the fireplace in the sitting room.'

'Oh, but that's wonderful.' I'm genuinely impressed. 'It's such a good likeness.'

'Unfortunately he is now far too popular and well known ever to paint for us again. We could never afford him!' Caro, angelically beautiful in cream silk, has left Eloise to join in our conversation. She squeezes Gwillem's arm affectionately.

'Caro is an unadulterated flatterer!' he laughs. His voice is low, with just the softest trace of a Welsh accent.

Reaching out, he takes my hand again. I notice that his fingers are very long and his nails perfectly manicured.

'So pleased to meet you. I keep telling Caro that we could do with some new blood in the group.'

He holds my hand and my gaze for longer this time. I don't know whether to feel flattered or uncomfortable.

I find myself seated next to Gwillem at dinner. I wonder if this is the potential date that Hannah warned me about. I don't normally go for blond men, but I have to admit that Gwillem is very good-looking.

I estimate that he's either in his late thirties or early forties. Tall and golden, he's like a rangy lion, far removed from Hannah's balding, fat fifty-year-old. He can also hold an intelligent conversation, a rare trait, much appreciated after the barren wasteland of unused intellect I previously shared with Richard the Turd. He also seems flatteringly interested in me. There is a stunning redhead to his other side, but apart from a polite hello when we first sat down to eat, he has almost completely ignored her in favour of me.

The food as usual is superb, a combined effort between the gourmet David and the artist Caroline. Caro's artistic skills have come into play with the table. The lobster bisque is served against a backdrop of white and palest pink roses on white linen. Candles flicker in silver Art Deco candlesticks that twist and turn like entwined lovers, casting golden flickers of light across the room. The room is all flesh pink and white like a luscious Rubens lady, sensuous, flirtatious.

'How long have you known Caroline?' asks Gwillem, passing me a bread roll.

'Since I was a child, but we lost touch,' I reply. 'Only found each other again last year when Caro started to work at the same school.'

'A happy coincidence . . . so you're a teacher?'

I nod unenthusiastically. Teacher sounds so boring, so worthy. I want to be exciting and unconventional like the rest of them. Gwillem, as you know, is a painter. Eloise is an actress. The man beyond her, Blakesley Hardington, apparently a rather well-known poet, is being flirted with by an opera singer.

'You don't look like a teacher,' muses Gwillem, assessing me.

'Oh, yes, and what are teachers supposed to look like?'

He laughs quietly. 'I don't know. I suppose I always have this rather clichéd picture of Maggie Smith as Miss Jean Brodie, but you're nothing like that at all.'

I begin to feel awkward again under such close scrutiny and look around the table for rescue. Angus Macready is sitting opposite me. He is a handsome man, with dark hair greying elegantly at the temples, his face and hands tanned from the outdoor life. This is the first time I've seen him without a tweed jacket and a flat cap. He always wears a tie, although tonight the usual brown knit has been replaced by a far more flamboyant multicoloured silk.

'Is Jake as devastated as Hannah at their enforced separation?' I ask him.

Angus smiles but shakes his head. 'He liked her well enough, but he's a young lad. I'm afraid they don't take things so much to heart as girls, do they? He'll be moving on soon.'

Moving on? Physically or emotionally? Another day, another woman. Bastard.

'I see,' I answer, smiling through clenched teeth. Poor Hannah.

'We're not all as fickle.'

'I'm sorry?' I turn back to Gwillem who, leaning towards me, his chin resting in his hand, is gazing at me rather unnervingly.

'Men. We're not all as fickle in our affections.'

I smile nervously, unsure of what to say. He's like headlights on full beam, approaching well over the usual speed limit.

'Try this, it's wonderful.' He holds out his fork to me.

I decide that I haven't known him long enough to share his cutlery. I lie to him that I'm so full I couldn't swallow another morsel, which is unfortunate as, in order to keep up the pretence, I have to refuse dessert. I hate to refuse dessert, especially as no one else seems remotely interested in the chocolate torte I made and I'd be more than happy to lay into a massive piece.

To my surprise, there is no lingering over coffee at the end of the meal. Everyone is getting up and adjourning to the sitting room. There's a hurried scraping of chairs, an air of excited anticipation.

'What's going on?' I ask Caro.

'Party games,' she replies.

I look confused.

'It's a tradition at Angels Court,' says Gwillem, smiling at me.

'Is it?' I've never been party to it before when I've visited.

'When *we* all get together, yes,' he replies.

'Why don't you take Fliss for a stroll round the garden while we set up in here?' says Caro, a mischievous gleam in her blue eyes.

Hannah was right, I do believe Caro is matchmaking.

'I've seen the garden before!' I protest. Gwillem seems very nice, but intense and unnerving. I'm not at all sure I want to be set up.

She raises her eyebrows at me, warning me not to be obstructive.

I follow Gwillem out into the garden. The air is still warm, and scented with night stock and old roses. Billie Holiday starts to sing on the old gramophone.

'Would you like to dance?' Gwillem holds out a perfectly manicured hand.

I think he's been primed in the right seduction techniques by Caro. Without waiting for an answer, he takes my hand, pulls me onto the lawn and begins to waltz across the dew-strewn grass.

I finally get to dance in the moonlight.

It's nice but I'm stiff as a board from sheer nerves. I try to follow his feet without actually treading on them, which is rather difficult. I finally get the rhythm and look up. He is gazing down at me. His eyes are the colour of amber, bright shining stones amidst that mane of golden hair. He's so dangerously like an animal, I almost expect to hear him begin to roar at the moon above us. He's attractive, but unattractive. Appealing, and yet invidious. Like the lion, whose beauty captivates and whose savagery repels.

'What are you thinking?'

I realise with embarrassment that I have been staring at him and quickly look back down at the short damp grass we are slowly trampling underfoot.

'You look so deep in thought,' he continues. 'I know you must be thinking something interesting. I'd love to be able to paint people's thoughts. Now that would be fascinating. What would yours be, I wonder? Do you have a twisted mind? Would you be a Chagal? A Breughel? Or perhaps something a little more erotic?'

'More like a Rubens with their plump thighs and dimpled bottoms,' I say without thinking.

He smiles lasciviously at me. I flush pink.

'You have a lovely skin tone,' he whispers into my hair. 'Perhaps one day you would let me paint you.'

My heart skips a beat. I'd forgotten how enjoyable it is to be chatted up. I relax a little. Gwillem notes that I am no longer stiff and pokerlike, and takes his chance to pull me a little closer. His arms around me are warm and strong. He smells nice, of some clear as crystal and obviously very expensive aftershave. He whispers very flattering things in my ear.

I think I'm beginning to warm to him a little. Maybe even enjoy myself.

'I can feel your heart beating,' he murmurs. 'Boom, beboom, beboom.'

I try hard to suppress a laugh and fail dismally. I'm instantly reminded of that cartoon where the skunk falls in love with the black cat whose tail is somehow painted with a white stripe.

Gwillem's murmurings cease to be romantic. The whole thing—the moonlight, the music, the dancing—simply reminds me of some bad film *d'amour*.

The music slowly winds to a halt. We can hear shrieking and laughter coming from the house.

'The games have commenced,' says Gwillem, smiling, obviously completely unaware that his rating, which was rising, has just sunk to an all-time low. 'Shall we go back in and join in the fun?'

I agree enthusiastically, trying to hide my relief that I have a chance to escape being alone with him. I've been twitchy all evening, struggling to overcome the faint feelings of dislike, distaste even, that he arouses in me. I'm faintly embarrassed that I dropped my guard even to let him in a few millimetres.

I've learned one thing on my search for happiness, though. The romance in a relationship just doesn't work properly if you're with the wrong person.

Gwillem's all wrong.

Back in the sitting room the lights have been dimmed. When my eyes adjust to the low light, I blink as though I'm trying to focus properly. I close my eyes and then open them again, wide, very wide, until they almost pop out onto the carpet.

Am I imagining things or are there naked people on the floor?

It takes a few moments for my shell-shocked mind to acknowledge that we have walked into a full-scale orgy.

Blakesley Hardington's little white bottom rises like the full moon from a pile of maroon cushions in the corner, and then sinks as he buries his face between the plump pink cushions of Sukey's plentiful bosom.

Her husband Bob, no longer sporting a face the consistency of dough, and certain parts of his anatomy fully risen like a yeast-fed loaf, frolics happily with two half-naked girls upon the chaise longue where in recent weeks I have happily reclined with a good book.

Angus Macready, his weathered face and brown arms a strange contrast to the lily-white hue of the rest of his body, is running a weathered hand along the creamy white flank of the local Master of Foxhounds's wife, as he does with horses to test that they're sound enough to ride.

Open-mouthed, I look round for Caro and wish I hadn't.

She is kissing Eloise. Slow, tongue-entwined kissing. Her left hand is clasped firmly around the flesh of Eloise's right breast; Eloise, who is naked, is struggling with the buttons of Caroline's blouse.

David is seated in an armchair, like a king indulgently surveying his subjects. He is watching them in fascination, smiling. All around, people are abandoning clothes and inhibitions.

I look incredulously at Gwillem, but he doesn't seem at all fazed. He smiles at me, eyes bright from drink and arousal, and begins to unbutton his shirt.

Party games! I was expecting charades.

I start to giggle hysterically until Gwillem, divested of his clothes, begins to try to divest me of mine, and then the hysterical giggle turns into a loud scream.

Pulling away, I stampede across the room, trampling bodies as I go. The opera singer hits the highest note of her career as my high heel engages with the flabby cushion of her backside.

My handbag and car keys are on the dresser in the hall. I grab them and head for the door.

As I leap in my car, fire up the ignition and speed up the drive, I see Caro in my rearview mirror, chasing after me out of the house, her boobs, which Eloise obviously succeeded in freeing from her blouse, bouncing elegantly in the moonlight.

CHAPTER FOUR

AFTER NEARLY THREE WEEKS, I drive home from Angels Court in pretty much the same state as I drove down to it. Looking back I'm not quite sure how I managed to get home, because I certainly wasn't taking much notice of where I was going. I somehow managed to make it back to the flat without ending up in a ditch.

The phone's ringing as I insert my key in the lock of my own front door. I take the emotional coward's way out and unplug both my handsets.

Home doesn't really seem very homely. It smells cold, damp and empty. I turn up the central heating and run round the flat switching on lights and lamps until the place has a rosier glow. Then, raiding the fridge for my supply of comfort Mars bars, I retire to my duvet.

I stuff a Mars bar in my mouth, and try to find something trashy on the TV to take my mind away from the pretty pornographic scenes that are filling it at the moment.

It doesn't work. I may as well tune into the Fantasy channel, all I can see are pictures of Caroline and Eloise.

Who'd have thought it? Certainly not me!

I mean, I know Caroline and David have a pretty healthy sex life. Girls chat, don't they, and Caro and I are no exception. But she's somehow managed to forget to mention the fact that their pretty healthy sex life is so sociable it includes half of the local neighbourhood as well.

A brand new meaning to the Chiltern five hundred.

Totally knackered, I try to sleep, but my mind's too full for rest. I feel very alone. I really need to talk to someone. Of course I have other friends, I'm not a total Billy No Mates, thank heavens, but Caro's the one I'd usually call at three in the morning when I'm feeling like hell. The one person I really want to talk to is the one person I really want to talk about, so I'm at a bit of a stalemate, aren't I?

I finally emerge from my bedroom after dark the following evening. I feel like a vampire venturing out of the crypt. It's only my stomach that's managed to force me from my self-inflicted purdah, insisting that if I force-feed it another Mars bar it will explode. As my fridge is pitifully empty, at this time of the evening I have a choice of heading for yet more junk food, that, while still calorie–laden, at least isn't sweet and covered in chocolate.

However, halfway towards McDonald's, I suddenly find myself heading for Clayton Avenue, The Beeches, and my father. A sort of homing instinct that tells me I need a kind of sustenance other than food. I look at the car clock. It's nearly ten o'clock. Dad will be in the potting shed at the bottom of the garden, avoiding Mother.

I'm in desperate need of his calming influence and reassuring normality, but I'm not keen to face her. Still, I can't avoid her for ever. It's been over three weeks, she may have calmed down a bit by now. Nevertheless, I give in to my cowardice and take the bumpy track that runs along the back of the avenue, entering the long rear garden through the back gate. Roger appears out of a clump of heavily overgrown delphiniums, his stumpy tail wagging enthusiastically.

If Roger is wandering loose in the garden, then where's Dad? They're normally tucked up in the shed together, Roger KO'd on a smelly old horse blanket and Dad sucking his pipe on some ratty old deck chair, Radio Two crackling out of the old prewar wireless.

There's no telltale glow of a gas lamp from the shed so I head up the garden path towards the house. It's a beautiful evening, but I'm still shaking like a leaf.

The heavy blue velvet drapes that usually cover the French doors into the dining room are still tied back. I can see the incandescent flickering of candlelight, and my father sitting at the head of the table. My mother is seated to his left, and to his right is Sally-Anne. At the end of the table, with his back towards me, sits a man.

His outline looks vaguely familiar.

I stumble up the three steps that lead onto the patio, and press my nose up against the window to get a better view.

Bloody hell! I don't believe it!

It's Richard!

I'm about to beat a hasty retreat when suddenly someone screams.

'There's someone in the garden! I can see them staring in at us!' It's Sally, shrieking at the top of her voice.

Dad drops his dessert spoon, which was halfway to his mouth bearing sherry trifle, and rushes to the doors brandishing the carving knife. His face is so red he looks like a Native American on the warpath. He cautiously pushes open the door and steps out into the night.

'We know you're out there!' he bellows gruffly, the blade flashing ominously in the moonlight, 'Come out, you swine . . . show yourself!'

Roger joins in the foray by beginning to bark.

At Sally's scream I had instinctively stepped back into the shadows. Now Dad peers through the darkness and catches sight of me. 'Felicity?'

I smile sheepishly.

'Fliss!' He stops brandishing the knife and puts a hand on his chest. 'Oh, my goodness, you nearly gave me a heart attack!'

'Drew! Drew!' my mother calls out to him. 'What's going on?'

'It's OK, everybody,' he calls back. 'It's only Fliss! Goodness, girl, what are you doing lurking out here?'

'Dad, what's going on?' I echo my mother, indicating Richard who is still seated at the table; trust him to let my father face intruders alone. Dad follows my gaze as I take in the best china, the silver cutlery, the candles.

'Look, Fliss, I think we'd better have a private chat,' he says, biting his bottom lip. He takes my arm and starts to lead me away from the house, but is pre-empted by Mother who, composure fully regained, sails out of the dining room and grabs my other arm.

'Felicity, how nice to see you.' She smiles at me. 'I was just saying that all we needed to complete the evening was Felicity, wasn't I, Sally?'

I've got Dad pulling me in one direction, Mother pulling me in the other. Plus I'm still in shock from earlier events and it takes a while for this unexpected pleasantness to register.

I look back at Dad, who looks at the floor and then at Sally-Anne, who also looks away as Mother leads me into the candlelit room. Richard is leaning back in his chair, looking far too relaxed and happy for my liking.

'Hello, Felicity.' He smiles at me, sweetness and light, a world away from the glowering, angry man I last saw almost a month ago.

'What's going on?' I ask cautiously, not at all sure that I want to hear the answer.

Mother and Sally return to their seats. Dad draws up another chair and gestures for me to sit down.

'We're having a little celebration.' Mother is also smiling far too much for my liking. 'In fact, we were just about to propose a toast. Drew, give Felicity a glass of champagne.'

'Miriam, this really isn't . . .' Dad begins to object, looking thoroughly uncomfortable.

'Champagne, Drew!'

She waits while Dad pours me a drink. I realise he's actually handed me a glass of brandy. I've got a horrible feeling I'm going to need it.

Mother gets to her feet. 'To Richard and Sally-Anne . . .' The pause is long, drawn out, yet I recognise, for my mother, triumphant. 'On the *wonderful* occasion of their engagement. Congratulations!'

Sally and Richard? It can't be true. 'This is a joke, right? You're winding me up.'

I just about resist the urge to pinch myself to test if I'm asleep and having a nightmare. That's what it is, you know. This is all some terrible Freudian dream. It was the Mars bars. Nobody can consume that amount of serious glucose and get away with it. I'm going to wake up any minute now and laugh about the whole thing.

Roger, sensing my unease, thrusts a warm wet reassuring nose into the palm of my hand and licks, in a doggy attempt to comfort. The touch is very soggy, and very, *very* real.

I look at the faces surrounding me. Mother, smiling orgasmically. Richard, smiling smugly as usual. Sally looking pained and not quite meeting my eye. Dad silently oozing sympathy and helplessness from every pore.

I look over to Richard and Sally-Anne again and notice that they are holding hands.

'Oh my God, you're totally serious, aren't you? Sally, how could you!' I stare incredulously at my sister.

To her credit she looks highly embarrassed. 'I'm s-sorry, Fliss . . .' she begins stuttering wildly.

'Don't be ridiculous! You've got absolutely nothing to be sorry for. Felicity has made her bed and she must lie in it.' Mother is crowing like a cockerel. 'You shouldn't let petty jealousy spoil your sister's good news, Felicity. You had your chance, now it's Sally's turn.'

She makes Richard sound like a fairground ride. I've just got off, now it's Sally's turn to take a spin.

'I'm not jealous,' I snap. 'Just completely and utterly . . ..' I struggle for a word that will describe how I'm feeling. I'm still struggling with major disbelief. This wasn't exactly what I thought Sally-Anne meant when she said she'd take care of everything.

I look from face to face. We are all silent.

Finally I look quizzically at my sister. 'Sally, are you sure this is what you want? Richard isn't exactly a hand-me-down pullover that you're obliged to wear because I've grown out of it.'

'It's what I want, Fliss.' Sally still won't quite meet my eye.

'Honestly? This is really what you want?'

'I don't know why you find this so hard to believe,' Richard says indignantly. 'In fact, my marrying Sally-Anne is a far more plausible prospect than my marrying you ever was. We're much more compatible, aren't we, darling?' He squeezes my sister's hand, and smiles warmly at her.

Darling? I think I'm going to throw up.

Sally returns his smile with equal warmth.

'In fact I should be thanking you, Fliss. It was you walking out that threw Sally and me together, gave us a chance to realise our true feelings for each other.'

'This is madness. How can you decide you want to spend the rest of your life with someone after only three weeks?'

'We've known each other for as long as you and Richard have been together. Besides, I've always carried a torch for him. Of course, I would never have acted on my feelings if you'd gone ahead with the wedding, Fliss, but when you ran out . . . well, Richard needed someone to talk to. It's just grown from there really . . . You'd made it pretty clear you didn't want to marry him.'

Yes, I can't deny that. My brain, which has been struggling to fit the concept of my sister marrying him into the compartment called 'reality', gives up the fight and surrenders unreservedly. It's really had far too much to cope with in the past few weeks. A fight is definitely beyond its current capabilities. I wave a verbal white flag.

'Well, if this is really what you want . . .'

'Oh, it is!' chorus Sally-Anne and Mother in unison.

'So when are you actually going to get married then?' I sink back into my seat, completely exhausted mentally.

This time Sally definitely can't look at me. It's left to Richard to answer, and he does so with a noticeable amount of pleasure.

'At the end of the month, the 25th.'

'But that was when we were . . . the date that . . .'

Dad hands me another brandy.

'Well, everything was already booked, it seemed such a shame to have to cancel it all and then rearrange everything,' Mother says cheerfully. 'All we've had to do is notify the Reverend Parsifal, reissue the invites, and get the dress altered. Sally is a tad more slender than you are, Felicity dear.'

I decide I *am* asleep and having a nightmare after all. 'She's wearing my dress!'

'Well, she did help you choose it, didn't she? And she looks so lovely in it. I always thought it was a touch too fussy for someone of your stature.'

I'm completely outraged. I hated that meringue concoction, but it was still *my* dress, for *my* wedding. I feel like the female lead in a play. I bow out and the understudy steps straight into my shoes to rounds of rapturous applause.

'You don't look too happy, Felicity. Surely you don't begrudge your own sister . . .'

Mother's fishing. There's nothing that would make her happier at this moment than for me to express regret, jealousy, then she could do the I-told-you-so routine and really rub my face in it. Richard would like that too. He's playing from a superior position now, and he knows it. I hope to God he's not doing this just to get back at me.

I force the widest smile I think I can get away with, and raise my glass. 'If Sally is happy, then of course I'm happy too. Congratulations to you both.'

If I'm being honest, I certainly don't mean that, but a toast is a good excuse to knock back my brandy.

Dad gives me an approving look.

'That's the spirit!' he whispers so that only I can hear. 'Don't let her think that you're upset.'

Richard looks disappointed.

I'm forced to endure another hour of lingering over coffee and brandy. My timing is so lousy. Why couldn't I have turned up after dinner instead of during? Or not turned up at all. I could just have stayed under my duvet for the rest of the summer holiday. Hell, the rest of my life maybe. As it is I can't just leave, that would look too much like sour grapes, and if there's one thing I'm determined to do, it's to show Richard I don't give a fig that he's not marrying me.

I don't, you know. I feel absolutely no pangs of regret that he suddenly belongs to someone else. The only regret I do have is that it's my sister.

The only consolation I have is that this new shock has taken my mind off the earlier one.

I eventually manage to escape to the kitchen by offering to wash up. Mother's gone the whole hog with this meal. Dirty pots and pans litter the side; a roasting dish swimming with grease is floating in the sink. This must be the only occasion in my life I've been pleased to see so much washing-up. I wash everything, slowly, meticulously, scrubbing, scrubbing and scrubbing. I pretend one particularly obstinate food stain is Richard, and take great satisfaction in obliterating it with Vim and a scourer. I just wish I could wash all my current problems down the plughole, along with the dirty water.

The others have gone out onto the patio with more brandy. I can hear Richard talking. Dad and Roger join me in the kitchen. Dad silently takes a tea towel and begins to dry the dishes.

'I'm sorry, Fliss,' he finally says, 'I only found out myself tonight. I knew something was going on, but I had no idea that this was what they were planning. I tried to phone you earlier as soon as they told me, but Caroline said you'd left yesterday.'

'You spoke to her? What did she say?'

Dad looks at me sideways. 'She asked me to get you to call her, sounded quite insistent about it. Is everything OK, Fliss?'

I am assailed by a vision of Blakesley Hardington's little white bottom. Ugh!

'Not really,' I answer carefully, 'but never mind that now . . . what on earth are we going to do about Sally-Anne?'

'What can we do?' Dad shrugs. 'She seems determined to marry the chap.'

'It just seems so surreal, I keep expecting to wake up and find out the whole thing's some strange dream.'

'I hate to say this, but when they told me I wasn't completely surprised. Sally's always had a pretty obvious soft spot for Richard—I would have thought you'd have noticed before.'

I shake my head. 'Too wrapped up in my own feelings, I suppose. As usual.' I can feel the tears welling up. I tell myself it's the stress. I hate weepy women.

Dad's the picture of concern. 'You don't still love Richard, do you?'

239

'No.' I wipe my eyes on the tea towel. 'But I do love Sally. I want her to be happy.'

'Sally loves Richard, she is happy.'

'Do you really believe that?'

'I've got to believe it.' He shrugs, hanging up the tea towel and looking out onto the patio at Richard. 'It's the only thing that stopped me from carving him up instead of the roast.'

I finally arrive back home at midnight, remembering at last to collect my struggling angry cat who really does not want to come back home, thank you very much, from the girl in the upstairs flat who never seems to go to bed, and fall back into my own in a daze.

Life is so confusing. I think I've finally got Richard out of my hair once and for all, and now the bastard has made sure he's there to stay. I suppose brother-in-law is better than husband, but I'd still rather there was no connection whatsoever.

I'm really very concerned about Sal. What's got into her? I know there is such a thing as a whirlwind romance, but this is ridiculous! I'm just so worried for her. I can't believe Richard's motives for this are purely romantic.

If you think about it, this is the ultimate revenge. If he'd spent the rest of his life trying to think of something that would really piss me off, he couldn't have come up with anything better than this.

I feel so guilty. Sally is about to throw herself away on the egotistical, self-centred scumbag and it's probably all my fault.

Good old guilt has now become a permanent fixture in my life. If only I'd done everything differently. For example, instead of leaving Richard in bed when I walked out on him, I should just have smothered him with one of his pillows. Problem solved. A long stay in Holloway would have been a small price to pay, wouldn't it?

I feel like I'm in prison at the moment anyway. Maybe without the dodgy food, drug abuse, lesbianism and lock-up time, but I'm definitely becoming a recluse. My own form of solitary confinement. I leave the flat once in the next few days to buy cat food. I spend the rest of the time holed up in the sitting room with the phone off the hook, watching mindless television and eating junk food, and struggling not to think too much.

If I think, I get depressed. Mainly because I know I'm being a totally sad git who should really pull herself together and get on with what she had promised herself would be a wonderful new life if only she could get up the guts to make a break for it. I knew I'd have to suffer whatever consequences arose from that break. Unfortunately, in all of the imagined post-Richard scenarios, the one about him marrying Sally-Anne never actually came up!

On the Thursday morning Richard and Judy do a slot about people who spend their lives holed up on their own watching television and eating junk food, and I decide that enough is enough. Life is a bitch, but I'm not going to let it get the better of me.

I go shopping.

I return home three hours later feeling decidedly better. Why is splurging on one's credit card so incredibly therapeutic—at least until the bill comes in?

As I push the key into the lock I can hear the phone making up for its enforced silence by ringing itself off the hook. I dump my six million carrier bags on the hall floor and force myself to answer it.

'Hello?'

'Fliss, it's me, I've been trying to get you for days. Look, will you meet me? I think we need to talk.'

'Really there's no need, Sally.' I'm still on a shopping high. 'Just as long as you're happy that you're doing the right thing, then everything's fine by me.'

This is what I managed to convince myself halfway round John Lewis anyway. My new mantra, quoted twenty times in each department, so that I looked like a madwoman muttering to myself constantly.

Although I've managed to convince myself that I mean it, I don't think Sally-Anne's very impressed by my sincerity.

'I wish I knew that you really meant that, Fliss . . . I really do think we should meet up. Please, I'd like a chance to explain what's happened. I think it would help put your mind at rest.'

'OK,' I sigh, 'when?'

'How about tonight? We could go for something to eat.'

'Where?'

'Eduardo's is supposed to be nice.'

Eduardo's? Oh dear, Richard's favourite haunt. Do I really want to spend any evening there? Still, it's a good restaurant.

'OK, what time?'

'About eight thirty.'

I arrive at the restaurant early. It's Sod's Law that when you allow yourself plenty of time to park in what is usually a car-parking battleground, you find a space straight away. As usual the restaurant's incredibly busy.

I manage to find a dark corner at the end of the bar, and I settle down on a stool with a gin and tonic.

I can hear lots of hearty 'Richard' laughing coming from the group of dark-suited businessmen at the other end of the bar. Why is a bar man's natural domain? I've always envied men their ability to be completely at ease when on their own in a bar or pub. It's so hard to escape the myth that a woman on her own is just waiting to be picked up.

I'm obviously giving that impression right now. One of the not-quite-so-raucous suits keeps looking over at me. I gaze at my reflection in the mirror behind the rows of bottles, determined not to look back, but the next minute he's heading in my direction.

'Excuse me, but I know you, don't I?'

Oh dear, corny chat-up line number one.

I turn to face him, semi-polite rebuff at the ready, but the face is actually quite familiar. The man's eyes widen in friendly recognition.

'It's Fliss, isn't it? Richard's fia—I mean, we met here, when you were with Richard Trevelyan. Alex . . . Alex Christian.'

Ah, the nice husband of the horrible ex-girlfriend.

'Of course. How nice to see you again.'

He runs a hand through his short brown hair and smiles. I remember that smile, warm and open. He holds out his hand. That's warm too. We shake rather self-consciously.

'I take it you're waiting for someone?'

'My sister actually.'

'Ah, yes, Sally-Anne. We met last week.'

'You did?'

He looks slightly uncomfortable. 'An evening Kat, my wife, arranged. Look, can I buy you a drink while you're waiting?'

I'm just wondering whether to accept when I hear my name being called. It's Sally-Anne.

I turn to Alex. 'Thanks. That would have been nice.'

'Perhaps some other time then?'

He returns to his party, stopping briefly to say hello to Sally on the way.

'Fliss!' Sally pushes her way over to me, hugs me, kisses me gently on one cheek and then steps back a little awkwardly.

'I didn't know you knew Alex?'

'I've only met him once before.'

'He's really nice, isn't he?' she says enthusiastically.

'Yeah, he seems to be.' I glance over at him. He catches my gaze, and his smile broadens.

'Have you met his wife? Katherine . . . Kat.'

'Unfortunately, yes.'

'Unfortunately? You didn't take to her then?'

'Not really, no. She seemed a bit false if I'm being honest.'

'And I thought it was just me,' muses Sally. 'I thought I was being a bit bitchy because she's an ex of Richard's.'

Oh, so either he or Kat's got that piece of information into play already.

'She's very . . . um . . .'

'In your face?' I offer. 'Or perhaps I should say in Richard's face?'

'You noticed that too?' She catches the barman's eye and orders a white wine. 'She's a bit over the top, isn't she? She spent the whole of the evening fluttering her eyelashes at Richard. They were batting so hard she could have turned out for the England cricket team.'

'Oh, yes? And was he encouraging this sickening display of affection?'

'Of course he wasn't,' says Sally indignantly. 'He only had eyes for me. Come on, our table's ready.'

She slips into the seat opposite me, and smiles nervously.

'You know, I'm really glad you agreed to come tonight. I wasn't sure if you'd still be speaking to me.'

'Yes, well, it was rather a shock to arrive home in the middle of your engagement party, especially when your fiancé turns out to be Richard,' I reply, unable to keep the sarcastic note out of my voice.

'I'm sorry. It was rather bad timing, I know, but Mother insisted on a family celebration. She was so ecstatic.'

'I bet she was. Look, I'm sorry, but I've got to ask this—you do love him, don't you?'

'I think so.'

'Only think? That doesn't sound too promising.'

'I only said "think" because I've never been in love before. I'm not quite sure how it should feel.' She looses her linen napkin from its ring and begins to twist it, looking at this rather than me as she speaks. 'Do you believe in love at first sight, Fliss?'

'Well . . .' I muse, 'that's a tricky one. I suppose it is possible, yes, but I think it takes a bit longer than thirty seconds to really, *truly* fall in love with someone. I mean, how can you profess to love someone when you couldn't possibly know anything about them?'

'Well, I think I fell in love with Richard the first time I saw him.'

'Really?' I ask in astonishment.

'Really.' Sally smiles nervously. 'I used to be so jealous of you, Fliss. You know, I couldn't believe it when you said you didn't want to marry him.'

'So I noticed,' I say, recalling Sally's disbelief at that time.

She laughs. 'And then when he started showing an interest in me . . . Don't get me wrong. It may look a bit suspicious, everything happening so quickly, but honestly, nothing happened until after you two split up. I thought it was important I should make that clear.' She takes a big gulp of her wine, and then looks at me coyly from under her long lashes. 'I remember the first time he kissed me,' she muses happily.

'You threw up?' I smile evilly.

'Fliss!'

'Sorry. Do go on.'

'It made my tummy go all funny . . . You know, butterflies in the stomach, going weak at the knees.'

'That doesn't mean you're in love. You could just have been going down with a bout of 'flu or something.'

'Oh, Fliss, do stop being flip, please.'

'I'm sorry.' I smile weakly. 'I've had a rather stressful few weeks, that's all.' I pause and look at my sister. She's so young. She's only twenty-one, she doesn't need to get married yet. 'Please, Sal, just tell me you're doing the right thing.'

'I'm doing the right thing,' she answers easily.

'And that Richard loves you?'

'Of course he does. Do you think he'd be marrying me otherwise?'

'Ah, that is the question.' I shake my head slowly. 'Sally-Anne, I'm sorry, but I can't help thinking he's only doing this to get back at me.'

'Well, thank you very much!' she spits. For the first time this evening her pretty face is actually clouded with anger. 'It's not possible he could love me, is it? Life doesn't revolve around you, Fliss. Can't you just accept that Richard and I are in love?' She takes a deep breath. 'Look, I'm sorry, I shouldn't get angry with you. I really don't want Richard to come between us, Fliss.'

'Well, don't marry him then!'

'Yes, but I am marrying him, aren't I?' She looks beseechingly at me. 'I'm not asking for your blessing . . . well, I suppose I am really.'

'I don't know if I can give it,' I state miserably, snapping open my menu, ostensibly to choose my meal but in reality so that I can hide behind it.

'Fliss, please . . .' Sally begins, but is pre-empted by the arrival of the waiter to take our order. I look at the menu. One thing is for sure, I definitely won't be having a peppered steak. Sally orders tomato salad followed by salmon. I take the easy option and ask for the same. She also orders a bottle of Chablis. I'm tempted to ask for one of those too.

The waiter leaves. Sally looks at me with puppy-dog eyes.

'Please don't be horrible, Fliss.'

'Horrible?' I mutter. 'I'm not being horrible. If I really wanted to be "horrible" I could say that you said to leave all the wedding cancellations to you because you had absolutely no intention of cancelling anything. Richard just needed to find a replacement bride and you conveniently offered to fill the vacant position!'

'It wasn't like that, Fliss. Honestly, I really wanted to help—I could see how upset Mother made you, that's why I offered to cancel everything for you. I didn't know what was going to happen, believe me. I mean, nobody could anticipate that we would decide to get married so quickly.'

'You said it.'

There's a long silence. She's tapping her long fingernails agitatedly against her now empty wineglass. The waiter returns with our starters.

Sally leans back in her chair and looks at me through narrowed eyes. 'I know you don't approve, but do you really mind me marrying Richard, Fliss? I want the truth now.'

I know what she's implying, the same thing that's on everyone else's lips and minds: do I still want him for myself? Is that where my objections to this farce stem from? I choose my words carefully.

'I don't regret for one minute that I'm not marrying Richard. But seeing you together as a couple will take some getting used to. And it just all seems so rushed. Do you have to get married? Why don't you just try being together for a while, see how things work out? Believe me, it's never too late to back out! As you know, I'm speaking from experience.'

'Honestly, I'm happy with the way things are, I want to get married.'

'Are you sure?'

Silence.

'Look, I'm not saying don't be with him. If that's what you want then I certainly won't stand in your way. What I'm saying is that it took me nearly two years to decide that Richard and I weren't right for each other. Why don't you give yourself a bit more time to get to know each other first before you actually get married?'

'I've known Richard for almost as long as you have.'

'Yes, but not in the same way. He's a completely different person as a lover. He's very selfish, Sally. He made me so miserable sometimes. Believe it or not, I do want you to be happy.'

'Please don't use your relationship with Richard as a measure for my relationship with him.' She pushes her untouched plate to one side. 'Are you saying that he can never make another woman happy because he couldn't make you happy? How would you feel if he said that about you?'

I digest the logic in this.

'I suppose you're right,' I say slowly. I can see that she is determined to marry him, and I'm only going to make things much worse by taking a stand against that decision. Besides, like Sally said, I wouldn't want people to write me off because of one failed relationship, so it's hardly fair to do the same to Richard. Maybe he can make her happy. I know it's hard for me to contemplate, but it is possible.

I admit defeat. I don't have a white flag so I wave my napkin instead. 'Peace?' I offer sheepishly.

Sally laughs in delight. One of her many good qualities is that she can never stay cross for long. Really my sister is a beautiful person, not just externally but inwardly too. Why would I find it hard to believe that Richard would want to marry her simply because she is so lovely? Perhaps I don't want her to succeed where I have indeed failed quite dismally. Perhaps I am jealous of her easy ability to find good and love in those around her.

I must be more magnanimous, less egocentric.

'If it's what you really want, then I wish you nothing but the best.'

'Oh, Fliss, that's so wonderful! This is definitely a cause for celebration. We need champagne!'

She calls to a nearby waiter, who hurries away and returns with a dusty bottle. Picking up on Sally's excitement, he opens it with all the dash of a Grand Prix driver celebrating a victory. The cork shoots towards the ceiling. Fortunately he doesn't spray us Damon Hill-style, but manages to find our glasses before losing any of the precious liquid.

'Cheers!' Sally raises her glass.

'To a happy future,' I offer, and drain mine in one go. I put my hand over it as the waiter hovers nearby with the bottle, waiting to refill. 'No more for me, thank you. I'm driving.'

'Oh, come on, you can pick your car up in the morning, we'll give you a lift home.'

'We?'

'Richard's picking me up.' She smiles happily.

I take my hand away from the glass. 'On second thoughts, I think I will have another drink. But I'll get a cab.'

'Don't be like that, Fliss, we've all got to learn to get on.'

'I know,' I sigh, 'but I don't have to start learning tonight, do I?'

We slowly work our way through the rest of the bottle, and the rest of our food. Sally is happily talking wedding plans. I pretend to listen, nodding and smiling at what I hope are appropriate moments. She is so carried away with excitement she doesn't notice that I may be with her in body but not in spirit.

After Sally has eaten all of her main course and most of mine, consumed a pudding that is far too large and fattening for someone so slim and svelte, she finally looks at her watch.

'Oh, my goodness!' she trills. 'It's gone eleven, Richard will be waiting for me. I'd better get the bill. No,' she waves away my money, 'I told you, this is on me. Well, on Richard really.'

I look on incredulously as she pulls out a credit card.

'He gave you a platinum card?' I breathe in surprise. 'Maybe things *will* be different for you.'

Sally smiles at me. 'Trust me. I know how difficult this must be for you, Fliss, but I honestly think things will be different for Richard and me. Vastly different . . . *amazingly* different!' The smile broadens and her eyes begin to glow with happiness.

Sally calls over our waiter and hands him the card. The waiter waves his arms in the air, and hands the card back to her.

'No, no, Mademoiselle, ees not necessary.'

'Sorry?'

'The bill ees already paid, Mademoiselle. Mr Alex Christian, ee take care of eet. Ee ees very insistent.'

Sally goes pink with pleasure. 'How terribly kind. Where is he? I must thank him.'

'Ee just leave, Mademoiselle. You miss him only by five minutes.'

Richard is waiting outside when we leave. I'm surprised he's not revving the engine of his car, he used to do that purposefully to infuriate me if I ever dared to keep him waiting.

'Hello, darling, did you have a good evening?'

He gets out of the car and presses his lips to Sally's cheek, looking smugly in my direction as though he's thumbing his nose at me.

'Fliss, are you well?' He turns to me. 'You're looking rather run down. Don't you think so, darling?'

'Do you think so?' Sally turns to me in concern. 'You do look tired actually, Fliss. Are you sure we can't take you home?'

'I'll make my own way, honestly, I'll be fine,' I state firmly.

'Thank you for coming.' Sally touches my arm. 'I'm so glad we've had a chance to talk and sort things out.'

I watch them drive away together. We haven't really sorted anything out. I still loathe Richard with a passion. Loathe the idea of Sally marrying him with a passion. I suppose I have just come to accept the inevitable, like a prisoner on death row without appeal.

I'm just about to go back into the restaurant to phone for a taxi when a long, dark blue Aston Martin pulls up next to me. The driver's window winds down. A tousled brown head appears. Through the gloom I recognise Alex Christian.

He smiles. 'Are you OK? Can I give you a lift somewhere?'

'No, thank you, I'm fine. I'm just going back in to call a cab.'

'You don't need to do that, let me take you home.'

'Thank you, but I'm OK, honestly.'

'I can't leave you here alone in a darkened street.' He grins. 'Anything could happen to you.'

'And I can't accept lifts from strange men.' I smile back at him. 'Anything could happen to me.'

'I'm not strange,' he laughs, 'just mildly psychotic. Why don't you hop in? I promise not to butcher you horribly down some darkened alley.'

He's more likely to get butchered that I am. I'm in rather a murderous mood.

'I'm probably completely out of your way,' I mutter ungraciously.

'I really don't mind.' He gets out of the car, and walking round towards me, opens the passenger door.

'OK, thank you.' I give in and clamber rather ungracefully into the low-slung car, settling back against the cream leather as he shuts my door gently then climbs back into the driver's seat.

'Where to?'

'Laurel Road,' I say.

As he pulls away, Mahler begins to play softly on the CD player. His car's so quiet you can't even hear the engine running. It makes the silence between us seem even more noticeable.

Finally I think of something sensible to say to him.

'It was really very kind of you to pay our bill.'

'Think nothing of it.'

'Sally wanted to say thank you as well, but we just missed you. It was very kind . . .' I repeat a touch nervously, the situation, being in a car with someone I don't really know, making me feel a little awkward.

'Well, it was a celebration, wasn't it? Of Sally and Richard's wedding? I just wanted to congratulate her.'

It's more usual to send a card than pick up a tab for a £200 meal. What sort of man is Alex Christian? A wealthy one very obviously. I'm too cynical to accept that such a generous gesture could be born of kindness rather than self-interest. I remind myself that I mustn't go through life holding Richard as my standard for the male sex.

'We've received an invitation to the wedding,' he says conversationally. 'Are you going?'

'Wouldn't miss it for the world,' I say drily.

We travel in a more companionable silence for a while.

In the intermittent beam of the street lamps I study him curiously. He has slanting eyes, exotically opalescent blue-green, with thick dark lashes that most girls would commit murder to possess. He also has a beautifully shaped mouth. To my infinite surprise I find myself wondering fleetingly what it would be like to kiss.

Unfortunately, he chooses this moment to look across at me, and catches me staring. I look away in embarrassment.

'You hear of people changing the venue or the dress at the last minute, but never the bride,' he says quietly after another moment's silence.

'Oh, the dress and the venue are the same all right,' I mutter.

He looks sideways at me. 'I'd be lying if I told you I wasn't curious.'

I look across at him again. He's smiling.

'Didn't Richard give you the details? He's not usually backwards in coming forwards, especially when it comes to safeguarding his own reputation.'

'Oh, yes, I heard *Richard's* version of events,' he says. 'I don't know Richard that well but somehow I got the feeling it wouldn't be exactly the same as yours?'

'How perceptive of you. How long have you known him?'

'About three years. For as long as I've known my wife really.'

'I'm surprised we never met before.'

'Well, Kat and Richard had been . . . er . . . friends for some time, but I think they kind of fell out when she met me.'

'Friends?' I raise my eyebrows at him.

'Very good ones. Yeah,' he admits. 'On and off. They were on a big off when I met her. I think I made it a more permanent off than Richard actually wanted it to be.'

We pull up outside my building. He gets out to open the door for me, offering me his hand as I step from the low seat. Briefly his thumb brushes softly over the back of my hand, as he helps me to stand. We're face to face.

He looks at me; I look back at him, suddenly feeling kind of awkward again.

'Thank you for the lift.' I break the silence.

'Any time.'

'Well, I'll see you at the wedding then.'

'I hope so.'

I've bought myself one of those phones that displays the number of whoever is calling you. It's The Beeches. My mother hardly ever calls me, so it's a pretty even bet that it's either Dad or Sal. I feel safe enough answering.

It's Sal. She sounds excited.

'Fliss, are you free on Saturday night?' she bursts straight in without even a hello.

'I think so,' I reply cautiously, 'why?'

'Because we're going out. It's my hen night!' she cries enthusiastically.

'Oh, right.'

'You're going to come, aren't you? Don't tell me you'll turn down a night of drunken debauchery and general bad behaviour?'

I only hesitate for a moment.

'Of course I'll come,' I tell her determinedly.

'You will?' She sounds kind of surprised.

'Yeah, if you're sure that you want me to? You sound like you were expecting me to say no.'

'Well, I was, sort of,' she replies honestly, 'but of *course* I want you to come, it wouldn't be the same without you.'

Things don't seem as bad as they did. The times that I have seen Richard and Sally-Anne together, I've actually been impressed by the way they seem to be so comfortable and happy with each other. Even Dad says that Richard's far easier to get on with than he ever was when we were together. Maybe it was just me, maybe I brought out the worst in him. Perhaps with Sally he's a better person.

They seem to be far better for each other than Richard and I ever could have been. Perhaps my reasons for opposing this marriage are more selfish than I'd admit to. I did want Richard out of my life for good, I felt that this was the only way I could move forward properly, and I've been allowing the fact that he's now in it permanently to over-shadow all my plans for the future. Knowing there is after all a strong possibility that Richard and Sally will be happy together makes me feel that perhaps, once the wedding itself is out of the way, things could start to move on in my own life.

I'd be lying if I said that I was looking forward to the actual day. I wish I was. I mean, it's my little sister's wedding day, and it should be a major celebration, a happy day, but unfortunately I just know it's going to be overshadowed by the fact that, as the song goes, 'It Should Have Been Me'.

Not that I want it to be me, but you know what people are like. It's going to be the main topic of the day, isn't it, and by rights it should be

Sally's day. A little part of me thinks that maybe it would be better if I didn't go, but I'm not sure which would make it worse for her—my being there or not being there.

There's no way I'm going to miss the hen night, though, although I think some back-up would be a good idea.

I pick up the phone and dial.

''Lo.' It's Jack, Sasha's toddler, who is slap-bang in the middle of the terrible twos.

'Hello, Jack, is Mummy there?'

There's a long pause while I can hear him ignoring the telephone and giggling at something on television.

'Jack . . . Jack, is Mummy there?'

'Mummy's head down toilet . . .'

'Oh dear, is Mummy sick, Jack?'

Fortunately I can hear Sasha's voice in the background.

'Give Mummy the phone, Jack . . . hello?'

'Sash? Are you OK?'

'Fliss! Mummy was just cleaning the bathroom actually. Kids, honestly! Do you know, he told my boss that Daddy and Mummy were playing Doctors and Nurses in the bedroom the other day!'

'And were you?'

'Chance'd be a fine thing! Niall was in bed with flu, the childminder was off sick, and I had to take the day off to play nursemaid to the kids and my husband. Anyway, enough of my troubles. Where the hell have you been, you old trout? I've been ringing and ringing and you never answer the bloody phone. Your mobile's always switched off. You never respond to my messages. I'd nearly given you up as a waste of energy and struck you off my Christmas list.'

'You'd never do that,' I interrupt the flow of recriminations.

'Yeah, and don't you know it? That's why you take advantage of my good nature and keep me waiting for a month before you contact me.'

'I know, Sash, I'm really sorry, honestly I am.'

Sash sniffs, but any pretence at being cross with me never really lasts for very long.

'Well, I suppose you have had a lot on your plate recently, haven't you, what with cancelling the wedding and everything? I just wish you'd phoned me. I could have helped, you know, that's what friends are for.'

'I know,' I repeat. 'But everything's been a bit strange recently . . .'

'I can imagine,' Sash says drily.

She pauses for a moment. I can almost hear the radar working overtime down the telephone line. 'Something else has happened, hasn't it, Fliss? Come on, I recognise your tone of voice.'

'Well, yeah, there is something I need to tell you. But first, I don't suppose you fancy a night out?'

'A night out! Do I fancy a night out? What's one of those then? Oh, yes, I remember, it's what people do when they don't have children, isn't it?'

'Does that mean you'll come?'

'With bells on. When? Where?'

'Next Saturday. Sally's hen night,' I reply slowly.

'Sally? Your sister's getting married? Since when? I didn't even know she was dating. Well, who's the lucky man then?'

'Er . . .' I pause. 'Well, you know I said that there was something else I needed to tell you . . .'

As part of the activity tradeoff we need to do to get Sash out for the evening, I end up taking Niall's place on a shoe-shopping trip with the kids. I also feel a touch guilty, as Sash is right and I really don't see enough of her. She may joke with me but it's true that I'm pretty confident of the fact that when I do see her, there won't be any real recriminations about my neglect of our friendship. This doesn't make it right for me to take it for granted, though.

When I split up with Richard I promised myself I'd see more of my mates. So far I've done nothing, wasting most of the summer holiday slouching round my flat instead.

We not only manage to find two pairs of shoes for Jack without any major tears or tantrums, but we also manage to squeeze in a few clothes shops on our rounds.

We do a running handover of the kids to Niall, like a tag team in the Olympics passing the baton, and then head back to my house to get primped, preened and pampered for our big night out.

An ecstatic Sash spends more than half an hour in the bath.

'This is absolute bliss!' she sighs, wiggling her toes happily in the bubbles. 'I don't think I've had a bath on my own for the past two years.'

Taking pity on her, I complete the idyll by taking her a glass of wine and offering to scrub her back for her.

Sash is almost purring as I attack her shoulders with my loofah. 'Careful,' she laughs, 'you're the first person over eighteen to touch me for at least a month. If you turn me on I might have to jump you.'

'Are things really that bad?'

'Worse. What about you? Have you had any offers?'

'Well, only if you count Caro's party,' I reply without really thinking.

'Oh, yes? What party was this then? Tell all.'

'Nothing much to tell really,' I bluster, wishing I'd kept my mouth shut.

'Come on, Felicity, spill the beans.'

Under Sash's gentle yet enquiring gaze, I suddenly find myself confessing all about that night at Caro's.

To my surprise Sash bursts into peals of laughter. 'Oh, my goodness, how wonderful! And you just walked out? I wish I'd been there.' She stops as she realises that I'm staring at her open-mouthed. 'You've got to see the funny side, Fliss.'

'I have?'

'Yeah, and think how fortunate you were to be there in the first place. Do you think you could get me an invite to the next one?'

'Honestly, Sash! Well, I suppose looking back it's kind of funny, but the hard part is how am I ever going to face Caroline again? I'm too embarrassed. I feel really bad, she keeps calling and leaving messages, but I haven't got back to her.'

'I know the feeling.' Sash smiles wryly.

'I know, I know, I'm sorry . . .'

'Stop apologising and pass me a towel. I suppose I should get out, I'm not going to pull if I go out looking like a sun-dried raisin, am I?'

'Oh, so you're out on the pull tonight then?' I tease her. 'Does Niall know this?'

'I don't think Niall would notice if I took Robbie Williams home and shagged him on the living-room carpet right in front of Niall's face. As long as I wasn't blocking his view of the football on TV, that is.'

'Are things really that bad at the moment, Sash?' I ask her for the second time.

She looks up at me from under long dark eyelashes, her equally dark brown eyes narrowed.

'I've been pregnant for two years out of the past three. Now I'm either working, potty training, or watching *Postman Pat*. I mean, what sort of life is that?'

I shake my head in sympathy.

'All Niall and I talk about is the kids. We're too tired for sex. Either that or we've just got to the point where we can't be bothered. It shouldn't be like this, I'm not even thirty yet. I should be standing in the middle of the bedroom in my thigh-length boots with a whip in one hand and a King Dong vibro in the other, with Niall tied to the bed head, spread-eagled and helpless . . . not curled up under my duvet by nine thirty with a cup of hot chocolate and a trashy novel.'

'Do you still fancy him?'

'I don't know. It's so hard to see him as a love object when he's fast asleep on the sofa, dressed in an old sweatshirt with baby sick on one shoulder and three days' growth on his chin. I can't remember the last time I saw him looking anything other than knackered.'

'So now you're tempted to go out and find someone else?'

'Is it better to do something that you regret, or to regret something that you haven't done? I really don't know, Fliss. I suppose it would be nice to see if I can still pull.'

Half an hour later, I'm squeezed into the new outrageously sexy dress that Sash persuaded me to buy in town. It's a cobalt-blue sequinned tube that holds me in and pushes me out in all the right places. I wouldn't even have picked it up if I'd been on my own.

'Wow!' Sash says as I head back into the bedroom.

'Is that a good wow or a bad wow?' I ask, nervously tugging at the hem which seems to be at least three inches shorter than I remember it being in the shop.

'Oh, a good wow.' Sash nods. 'Definitely a good wow.'

'You haven't scrubbed up too badly yourself. You look a total babe,' I tell her. 'Really hot.'

Sash pushes at her gorgeously glossy short-cropped curls before applying another liberal dose of hair-shine spray.

'Really? Thanks, Fliss. At home I'm always a mummy, never anything else.' I detect a wistful note in her voice. 'Tell you what, let's just relax, forget about our woes and have a really good night, yeah?'

The plan is that we're to meet Sally and the others in Dune, one of Oxford's newest nightclubs.

Nine o'clock may seem ridiculously early to head into a nightclub, but it's one of those places where they have a fairly decent restaurant, and Sally has arranged a table for twenty.

Sash and I hit the bar first and knock back a couple of quick doubles before heading into the restaurant. I'm glad I did when I see who's seated to Sally's left.

Mother.

I've never, ever been in a nightclub with my mother before.

I don't know which surprises me more, the fact that she's actually there, or the fact that when I walk in she gestures for me to go and sit next to her, and then stands up to greet me, pressing her lips against my cheek, before I collapse into my chair in shock.

Even Sash looks wide-eyed and surprised at this unexpected show of affection and has to grab a glass of wine quickly.

'I've bought Sally a little pressie,' she tells me, eyeing my mother nervously. 'The only problem is I'm not sure that I can give it to her in front of your mother.'

'Me neither.'

Mother starts the gift giving with an exquisitely beautiful gold locket, then looks expectantly at me.

'Er, just got to get mine out of the bag . . .' I prevaricate. 'Why don't you move on to Sash first?'

Mouthing 'Rat' at me, Sash places a long thin parcel in front of Sal.

'You might want to wait until you get home before you open this one.' She smiles.

'No way!' roar Sally's mates.

Laughing nervously, Sal tears the bright pink paper from the box. Opening it gingerly, she gives a shriek of laughter and pulls out an eight-inch, flesh coloured, throbbingly veined dildo.

'Don't assume that just because you're getting married, you'll get a constant supply of the real thing,' Sash tells her.

Sally blushes such a bright shade of pink you can see her glowing, even in the gloom of our corner table.

Feeling slightly more emboldened now that Sash's present has been greeted by my mother with laughter, I hand Sal my gift.

Everyone watches as Sally unties my parcel, before pulling out a pair of black velvet-covered handcuffs, a bullwhip and a blindfold.

Eyes and cheeks still glowing, she reads out my card. '"Just so you can let him know who's the boss!"' she giggles. 'Thanks, Fliss.'

'Well, it's always best to start out as you mean to go on,' I reply.

It seems that nearly everyone's bought her sex-related gifts, apart from Mother, of course, and Sally's best friend, the ever-practical Erica, who's bought her the latest Jamie Oliver and a pair of oven gloves. As well as my and Sash's little offerings, Sal ends up with edible panties and lickable body lotion, a full-colour photographic *Kama Sutra*, several sets of rather racy undies and a large chocolate willy.

The *Kama Sutra* is currently doing the rounds to many gasps of amazement and amusement. Even my mother's laughing and exclaiming. She's been an entirely different person tonight, happy and chatty all the way through dinner, and then straight out on the dance floor when we head into the club afterwards.

She's giddy. Like a little girl on her first outing to the fairground. Her eyes are bright, her face is shining, she's dancing, and drinking, and laughing. If I didn't know her better I'd say she's popped something illegal. She's definitely drunk. I don't quite know how to handle this.

Not that I'm having too bad a time myself this evening. Sally's friends are a really great bunch, like Sal really, easy to get on with, all out for a good time, especially the ones from the bank. Boy, do they know how to party. I suppose it comes with having to be strait-laced and disciplined during the day, they let their hair down with a vengeance at night.

The club is pretty packed as well, and I've even had a few eye meets with some pretty tasty men. I'd also forgotten how much I enjoy dancing. I used to embarrass Richard with my enthusiasm for a good boogie. It's lovely to be able to strut my funky stuff without someone looking on in disapproval.

Unfortunately, my enthusiasm dies a death at about eleven thirty when I realise that there was one aspect of this evening's festivities that Sally neglected to mention to me.

The stag party.

Having spent the past three hours on an extended pub crawl, it has now just staggered en masse into our nightclub.

Why didn't Sal tell me they'd arranged to meet up later on? Well, I know why Sal didn't tell me.

As Richard and his cronies walk in one door, I just about manage to restrain myself from walking out of another.

I look around for back-up, but Sash has disappeared, and as a temporary escape measure I head for the loos instead.

I find her inside, trying to hold a mobile phone conversation with her husband over the muted noise of the club music.

She catches sight of me and rolls her eyes.

'Honestly, Niall, can't you cope with them for one evening on your own? . . . Well, he's a baby, that's what babies do . . . What was that, darling? Shhhhhhhhk . . . I can't hear you . . . Sorry, I think my signal's going to f—'

She presses the end button on the phone and sighs heavily. 'Honestly, you leave them alone for one evening!'

'Guess who's here?' I cut in agitatedly.

'Er . . . don't tell me, Tom Cruise, and he wants us to go back to his bachelor pad for a threesome?'

'I wish. Think of something less appealing.'

'Richard.'

'Bang on.'

'You're joking, aren't you? What's he doing here?'

'I think it was all prearranged. You know, go out separately and then meet up later. Only for some reason Sal forgot to mention that part to me.'

'What do you want to do, go home?'

'That'd look a bit off, wouldn't it? Besides I don't want to go, we were having a good time.'

'We still can.' Sash links her arm through mine. 'This is a big place, we can avoid him if we want to.'

When we go back out my mother is dancing with Richard.

The two groups have intermingled. Some of Sally's friends' other halves are out on Richard's stag do, and vice versa. They've all taken over a group of chairs and sofas on the edge of the dance floor.

Sally spots Sash and me emerging from the loos and waves for us to go over, probably thinking that if she doesn't collar me straight away I'll be heading for my coat and home.

Sal smiles sheepishly at me. 'Surprise!' she mumbles weakly.

Determined to be magnanimous—it is Sally's night after all—I return her sheepish smile with a halfhearted 'Don't worry about it' one of my own.

Someone has ordered a dozen or so bottles of champagne, which is now flowing freely. Sally hands us a glass.

'Sorry, Sis, but I thought you wouldn't come if I mentioned that we were meeting up, and I really wanted everyone here.'

'It's not a problem, Sal.' I shrug. 'Honestly.'

Amid the large group of men is a woman, smiling happily like a lone cow that's just stumbled away from the herd and into the bull's enclosure. I recognise the immaculate make-up, glossy hair and expensive clothes instantly.

Katherine Christian.

She wasn't with us, so she must have come in with Richard's party. What on earth is she up to? I notice that Sally is watching her as well.

'I thought stag nights were men only?' I murmur.

Sally sighs heavily. 'So did I. Richard suggested I should invite her to the hen night, but I couldn't bring myself to. Awful, aren't I? But I got my just deserts because she just tagged along with Alex and went to the stag party instead,' Sal says a touch sourly.

'Who's that then?' Sash asks, as she looks over to where Kat is holding court among a group of semi-pissed men, mesmerised by the way she keeps crossing and uncrossing her long legs.

'An ex of Richard's.'

'Really?' Sash looks from me to Sal and then back again, taking in the way we're both gazing sourly at Kat Christian. 'What's she done to upset you then?'

'It's not what she's done . . .' Sally murmurs.

'It's what she might do,' I finish for her.

'You get that impression too?' Sal turns to me.

'It's hard not to. Maybe that's just the way she is though,' I try to reassure my sister. 'Anyone can see she's a big fat flirt, and not just with Richard. Besides, this time next week you'll be dancing at your wedding reception . . .'

'You're right.' Sally relaxes, the frown replaced by a smile. 'I'm being ridiculous, aren't I? The jealous little wife.' She giggles with pleasure as she awards this title to herself. 'Oh, my goodness, I'm getting married next week!' The giggle broadens into a wide happy grin.

'Yeah, well, I suggest you go and rescue your husband-to-be from the clutches of his future mother-in-law, before he changes his mind about marrying into a family where madness is so obviously in the genes,' I warn her, watching as Mother attempts an enthusiastic, if somewhat ungainly, reggae grind against a worried-looking Richard.

'You don't think Kat's after him, do you?' Sash asks me as Sally rescues a relieved Richard from my mother.

'I don't know. But I was with Richard for nearly two years and the woman never figured in our lives. Now that she's returned, she seems to have returned with a vengeance.'

After the odd scene of my mother dancing to trance, garage and jungle, you'd think it would be easier watching Richard smooching with my sister. Well, it is easier on the eye, but it's also really strange.

'This is so weird, seeing Sal with Richard instead of you,' Sash muses, echoing my thoughts, as Richard wraps his arms round Sally-Anne's waist and pulls her to him.

'You're telling me. Do you think they look happy?'

'Well, I suppose so.' Sash shrugs.

'Good.'

We're silent for a moment as we watch Richard lean down and whisper something in Sally's ear.

'Tell you what, why don't we hit the bar? This champers is nice, but it's not really hitting the spot,' Sash says.

We skirt round the dance floor and manage to find ourselves a couple of vacant stools right at the far end of the long stretch of oak. Sash manages to attract the attention of the barman.

'Another vod? Double?'

'Is there any other way to drink it at the moment?'

'Yeah,' Sash grins, 'straight from the bottle.'

'I don't think I'm feeling that desperate.'

'Glad to hear it. But you are pissed off, aren't you?'

'Well, yes, I am a bit fed up. I dumped Richard because I wanted him out of my life. But he's still going to be in it. Permanently. I'm really worried Sally's not doing the right thing.'

'Maybe, but you have to let her make her own decisions, don't you?'

'I suppose you're right.'

'I'm always right,' Sash jokes. 'Anyway, enough of this. What do you want first? Booze, boogie, or how about a good old flirt with a bonkable bloke?'

'And where are we going to find one of those then?'

'Heavens, Fliss, we're in a nightclub. That's like asking "Haven't you got any chocolate?" in a sweetshop. We're surrounded by men.' She waves an arm around expansively. 'In fact,' the arm stops mid-wave and she peers over my shoulder, her eyes lighting up, 'there's a pretty tasty one heading right for you at this very moment!'

I follow the inclination of Sash's head to see a good-looking man with short brown hair and smiling blue-green eyes approaching me.

It's Alex Christian.

'Hi, Fliss. How are you doing?'

Suddenly I feel a little nervous and only manage a very high-pitched squeaky hello.

'I was going to say that I'm surprised to see you here, but actually I'm not.'

'I know,' I trill. 'Wherever there's a bar . . .'

'That's not what I meant.' He smiles good-naturedly. He's standing between Sasha and me, turned towards me.

She purses her lips together in a kissy movement and mouthing 'Phwoar!' at me, while making squidgy movements with her hands in the vicinity of his very tasty backside, as though she's going to reach in and squeeze it.

Throwing her a 'Will you behave?' look, I introduce him.

'Alex, this is my friend Sasha. Sash, this is Alex.'

As he turns to say hello, Sash hastily rearranges her features into something that doesn't resemble a leer. She takes his hand and smiles seductively.

'Alex Christian, Katherine Christian's husband,' I add.

Sasha's eyebrows shoot straight up her forehead. 'Really?' she breathes, glancing significantly at me. 'How *nice* to meet you.'

Sash and I have been watching Kat Christian with a mixture of amusement and consternation. She appears to be following Richard everywhere he goes, like a little tugboat bobbing after a docking cruise liner, anxious to shepherd it in precisely the direction she wants it to go.

And I thought my mother was bad.

When I look back over at Sash, expecting her still to be drooling over Alex, I find that she's looking at Richard. He's still on the dance floor, smooching away to a slow romantic ballad, but the woman he's got his short arms wrapped round is most definitely not my sister.

It's Kat Christian.

So he's dancing with an old friend? Big deal. At least it would be nothing if she didn't have her head resting tenderly on his shoulder, and her hands resting under his shirt and inside the waistband of his trousers, fingers down out of view but easily far enough to be touching a great deal of his arse.

To Richard's credit he does look a little uncomfortable. He's certainly not hanging on to Kat with the same intensity or intimacy.

I peer across the room looking for Sally. She's spotted them, and is watching with a strange expression.

Alex is watching them too, the usual ready smile replaced by a heavy frown, but he doesn't make a move until he too spots Sally-Anne's concerned expression.

'Would you excuse me a moment?'

''Ere we go,' Sash nudges me, as Alex heads towards the dance floor.

I watch Alex make his way to Sal. After a moment's conversation he pulls her out onto the dance floor. I can see him now, whispering in her ear and making her laugh. He dances with her for one record.

Then, when the next record starts, he moves so that they are closer to Kat and Richard and engineers a swift excuse-me so that the right partners are back together again.

Very smoothly done.

I find myself wondering if Alex did it for himself or for Sal. Both probably. Richard wasn't really doing anything to merit an outburst of jealousy, and Alex didn't make a move until he spotted Sally's miserable face, but it can't be that much fun watching your wife run around after another man.

To my surprise, however, instead of staying on the dance floor with Kat, he immediately leads her back to the group lounging and drinking in a corner, deposits her in an empty chair, and heads back to where Sash and I are standing at the bar.

'Mind if I join you?' he says with a lopsided smile.

'Not at all,' Sash smiles, winking surreptitiously at me.

'Large brandy, please.' He waves a twenty at the barman. 'Are you ready for another one?'

'Thanks, but we'll get that.' I grin at the barman. 'Add two large vodkas onto that as well, please, will you?' I turn back to Alex. 'I think I owe you a large drink for what you just did.'

'I think I need a large drink for the fact that I had to do what I just did.'

'The Kat's in the doghouse then, is she?' Sash grins at him. She is too pissed to be subtle. I elbow her swiftly in the ribs.

'Ouch, Fliss, you big meany—what did you do that for?'

'Because sensible Sash is now sozzled-can't-keep-my-mouth-shut Sash, that's why!' I hiss at her.

Alex laughs. 'It's OK, I hardly think subtlety is the key word for anybody this evening, do you?'

'Well then, if we don't have to be subtle can I ask you something?'

'Sure,' he replies, looking at me cautiously.

'What the hell is your wife up to, running around after Richard like that, in front of everybody?'

He hesitates for a while, and I start to regret the question.

'Sorry, I shouldn't have said that.'

'No, it's OK.' Alex's mouth twists into a wry smile. 'I think she always wants something that much more when she thinks she can't have it.'

'I'm like that with chocolate,' I sigh.

Sash reflects for a moment. 'I'd be more than happy to turn the tables for you and help make your wife jealous?'

She winks heavily at Alex, who I can see is unsure whether to laugh or run away very quickly.

'It's all right,' I tell him reassuringly. 'She's only joking.'

'No, I'm not!' Sash cuts in indignantly.

'She's just had a bit too much to drink, I think,' Alex replies.

'Well, I might have had a few . . .'

'I meant my wife, not you.'

He leans in and kisses Sash gently on the cheek. 'Thanks for the offer, it's the nicest one I've had all night, but I think I should probably take Kat home.' He drains his glass and smiles a little grimly at us. 'Well, it was lovely to see you again, Fliss, and very nice to meet you too,' he adds, as Sash leans in and drunkenly lands a wet kiss on his cheek.

'Why can't he take me home instead?' she asks wistfully as she hungrily watches Alex's retreating backside. 'What a lovely bloke. How on earth did that woman get her claws into someone like him?'

'Well, I'd say Kat Christian was restrained compared with you just then,' I say drily.

'Oh, come on, darling, you've got to agree that Alex Christian is a bit of all right?'

'I hadn't really thought about it,' I lie.

'Yeah, and I'm a virgin.' She raises her eyebrows in disbelief.

'OK,' I admit, 'yes, he's lovely, but he's married, isn't he?'

'Trust me, babe, that means bugger all to some men.'

'Yeah, but if that's what Alex is like, I wouldn't be interested anyway.'

'Not into the thought of some extramarital sex then? You know, a nice bit of no-strings nookie?'

'Not really.'

'Does that mean I can have him?'

'No, you can't!' I howl.

'Ah, so you *do* want him for yourself,' she teases me.

'It's not that and you know it. It's just that I really want to believe in the sanctity of marriage at the moment and nobody's helping me do that really, are they? Especially not you, you old tart,' I tell her affectionately. 'Banging on about banging someone else.'

'I didn't know that sanctity meant total chastity.' Sash's big eyes make her resemble a puppy by a door, desperate to be let into the garden.

She follows my gaze to where Alex has collected Kat and, with a firm grip on her arm, is saying good night to everyone.

'Don't worry about your sister, they stand as good a chance as any of us at getting it right.'

'With a few other detrimental factors thrown into the equation,' I sigh, watching as Kat makes a point of saying a prolonged good night to Richard before they leave.

'Well, he'll be a married man this time next week.' Sash smiles encouragingly at me. 'Hopefully that'll be the end of it.'

'Yeah,' I sigh uncertainly. 'Either that or the start of something worse.'

CHAPTER FIVE

THE DAY OF THE WEDDING dawns bright and clear. Rain would have suited my mood better. I lie in bed for far too long, hoping that some miracle will occur that excuses me from going, or better still results in the permanent cancellation of the whole thing. Earthquake, flood, hurricane . . . I don't mind which.

The last three weeks have been a nightmare. I thought it would be nice to see Mother happy for a change. What I didn't realise was that a happy Miriam Blakeney is even more intolerable than a miserable and martyred Miriam Blakeney. She has gone into wedding overdrive.

I had hoped that, owing to the rather unusual circumstances, I might be spared the usual rigours of the pre-wedding party, but Mother is determined I'm not going to miss a thing. I have my orders to be at The Beeches for 10.00am sharp to supervise the arrival of the bridesmaids, the flowers and enough booze to sink the *Titanic*. I suppose things could be worse: Sally-Anne had tentatively suggested that I might like to *be* a bridesmaid. Fortunately she didn't push the point.

I finally drag myself out of bed and end up arriving at The Beeches an hour late, but fortunately Mother is on too much of a wedding high to notice. Sally-Anne has six bridesmaids. Two friends, two cousins and two of Richard's nieces. They range from age six to twenty-six. The six-year-old is the only one who is treating me normally. Nobody else knows what to say.

Of course rumours have been rife, ranging from the sublime to the ridiculous. I can just about cope with people thinking that Richard left me for Sally-Anne. What I can't handle is the quiet sympathy, the looks, the whispers when they think I'm not listening.

Up in Sally's large bedroom all is mad activity. The hairdresser is valiantly attempting to pin, curl and coiffure eight people within two hours. Mother's swooping around the room interfering with everything, like an excited budgie let out of its cage. Seated at her dressing table, long brown hair in papers, Sally-Anne smiles happily, serene amid the chaos.

I escape to the kitchen where I valiantly make enough sandwiches for fifty people in half an hour. Somehow I feel more comfortable brandishing a huge carving knife. It's a brilliant way of relieving tension.

There is one particularly awkward moment when Dad's dotty sister, Aunt Vera, arrives. She obviously hadn't received an amended invite, and proceeds to make a great show of congratulating me and giving me her wedding gift.

Dad, God bless him, manages to steer her quietly away and explain the new turn of events. She strides back to me and says in her booming voice, 'Drew says you're not marrying the man. Glad to hear it, never liked him. Don't know why Sally-Anne has to step in, though, but then again you've always had more sense than her.'

She thrusts the present at me again. 'Bought this specifically for you so you may as well have it. Sally-Anne'll be getting plenty. Besides, now you're young, free and single again, you need it more than her.'

Blushing crimson, I open the beautifully gift-wrapped box. It contains the most wonderfully luxurious, racy-lacy set of Janet Reger.

'Find yourself a man who'll appreciate it.' She winks one heavily blue-shadowed eyelid.

'I'd rather find a man who appreciated me,' I say wistfully.

'Impossible. All men are pigs,' she snorts, and strides off into the garden dragging my father with her.

The little bridesmaids, bored with waiting around in their underwear for the appropriate moment to be dressed in their frilly pink outfits, descend on the kitchen like a flock of hungry young vultures and start to make mincemeat of my platefuls of sandwiches.

They look at me in my blue-striped apron worn to cover my Ungaro suit—an extravagance that ironically should have been my going-away outfit—a whispering little clique.

Eleven-year-old Lucy, my cousin's eldest daughter, is elected spokesperson.

'Auntie Fliss? Is it true that you were supposed to marry Uncle Richard?'

'Well . . . yes, that was what was going to happen.'

'So why is Auntie Sally marrying him instead?'

That's a good question, but what would be a good answer to give an eleven-year-old?

'Um, because I don't want to,' I offer.

'My mummy always makes me do things I don't want to,' she replies. 'Like have a bath when Disney's on, or eat liver. I hate liver but I can't give it to Emma,' she gestures towards her younger sister, 'because she doesn't like liver either.'

'Well, I didn't exactly give Sally-Anne Richard because I don't like him . . .' I start to say, but am saved by the appearance of mother's best friend, who bears them away for final preparation.

More close friends arrive. I busy myself handing round drinks and canapés, and trying to look pleased to see everyone. My sandwiches are beginning to curl at the edges in the dry heat of the day. I feel like I'm beginning to curl at the edges too. The false bright smile I've been wearing all morning is beginning to slip, and if one more person touches my arm and smiles sympathetically I'm sure I shall crack and hit them.

Dad, looking handsome yet somewhat funereal in a grey morning suit, with a grey mourning face, appears at my side.

He hugs me. 'You're a real trouper, Fliss, the way you've handled this. I'm really proud of you.'

'The worst is yet to come,' I mutter gloomily.

I've elected to drive myself to the church, that way I can arrive unannounced and slip away if desperate. I slide in as inconspicuously as possible, and ignoring a frantically signalling usher, slip into one of the rear pews, just behind a well-placed pillar. I chose my lampshade-style hat specifically to hide my face. If I could have got away with it I would have worn a veil as well, not through some misplaced desire actually to be the bride but so that I could remain anonymous throughout.

Huge arrangements of pink and white carnations, white roses, pink roses and cloudy gypsophila flank the altar. Smaller posies are throwing sweet scents from the end of each pew. Garlands of dark ivy are wound round each pillar like serpents climbing to the vaulted roof.

Richard emerges from the vestry with his best man, James, who's actually a really decent guy, and the Reverend Parsifal. I suppose right up to this moment I still thought that the whole thing was just a ruse to piss me off, but there is Richard in his grey morning suit actually looking like the nervous husband-to-be. He keeps looking around, seems agitated. Perhaps he's worried that Sally-Anne might actually come to her senses and stand him up.

Mother sails in with Aunt Vera. She's wearing a hideous pink creation with a wide-brimmed hat trimmed with flowers to match the ones in the church. Fortunately, she doesn't notice me. She's too busy nodding regally to friends and relatives as she makes her way up the aisle and into the front pew, waving graciously like the Queen. The few people who notice me don't know what to do. A few smile nervously or sympathetically; some look away quickly, pretend they haven't seen me. None of them dares to sit in the same pew as me. Is this an indication of what the rest of the day will be like, being treated as though I have some frighteningly contagious disease?

Ollie Barton-Davis, Richard's hideously oily head of chambers, comes in.

I call him Ollie the Octopus. He's short, fat and stumpy but you'd think his arms were eight feet long, the places his hands always manage to end up. He has been harassing me since the first day we met; inane comments, sexual innuendo that's always accompanied by the laughter and 'it's only a joke, darling' exterior that protects him against rejection or particularly nasty harassment cases.

For one horrible moment I think he's going to come and sit next to me, until he's accosted by an usher and made to sit on Richard's side of the church.

The click of high Russell & Bromley heels on the stone floor heralds the arrival of Kat the predator, ex-fiancée, the clothes horse in the closet.

She is looking decidedly chic in a very expensive Chanel suit. She and Alex edge into the pew opposite me on Richard's side of the church. Alex looks over, tilts his head sideways as though he has to look under my hat to recognise me, and mouths 'Hello'.

The choir slow-step down the aisle to the sweet strains of 'Jesu, Joy of Man's Desiring'. They file into their designated pews and sit down.

Two minutes later the organ begins to play the 'Wedding March'.

There are gasps as Sally enters the church and floats up the aisle on Dad's arm. She really does look beautiful, ethereal even. Where I looked like a dessert in that dress, she looks like a fairy princess.

Richard turns to greet her. I strain to see his face. Does he look proud? He should. I send a fervent prayer to God that he really, truly loves her.

Dad hands his younger daughter to her future husband.

'Dearly beloved . . .' the Reverend Parsifal intones, his voice reverberating round the building.

Richard is hidden from my view partly by the pillar, and partly by a huge arrangement of flowers which is almost indistinguishable from Mother's hat. I'm not complaining.

'Let him now speak, or else hereafter for ever hold his peace.'

Am I imagining it or do all eyes turn to me at this point? I tell myself I'm imagining it. The moment passes.

James the clown pretends to have lost the rings. Oh, that he had for real. Like a magician, he produces them with a flourish from his silk handkerchief. A bubble of laughter rises around the church. The rings are exchanged.

The vows are complete.

Richard and Sally-Anne are married.

How do I feel about this? I ask myself. Bloody awful comes the answer.

Mother is dabbing her eyes with a small lace handkerchief. Kat is biting her bottom lip so hard, it's white. Dad blows his nose noisily on a man-size tissue. I think it's time to go.

I chose Adesley Hall for the reception because it is so romantic. A long honey-coloured stone building that basks at the bottom of the Whystone Valley, it automatically assails one with visions of heroes climbing the rambling vines that clutch its crumbling walls, to rescue some fair maiden stuck in one of the two towers which flank the porticoed main entrance. That romantic beauty now mocks me silently.

I've driven like the devil to get here before everyone else so that I don't have to walk in through a sea of wedding guests.

The great oak-panelled reception room is empty of people as yet. 'Richard and Sally welcome you' announces the board that displays the seating plan, more argued about, thought out and prevaricated over than the Magna Carta. The tables are set with pink and white flowers, and pink and white linen, and pink and white place cards with gold writing, and a little gold cherub is drawn in the top right-hand corner of each menu (not my touch, I can assure you).

The room is all pink, fluffy and cosily romantic, my original ideas transformed by Sally's very feminine touch. I'm a romantic too, definitely, but more of a Heathcliff and Cathy-type romance, wild and breathtaking, not the chocolate box, Valentine card kitsch this room now resembles.

I manage to get out of the official greetings line-up by hiding in the loo. I hole up for long enough to sneak to the end of the line just as the last few people are coming through the foyer, and therefore only end up having to kiss some dotty old Great-great-aunt thingummybody, who always used to get Sally and me confused anyway, and, just my luck, queen of the late entrances, Kat Christian.

Kat seems to have perfected the lips hitting the air to either side of your face style of greeting. I can see her waving her crimson-painted mouth in the vague direction of Sally's cheeks. She lingers over Richard. Her lips somehow manage to hit flesh this time. Her lipstick's so thick and glossy it will probably take him half an hour and a tin of Vim to scrape off the crimson marks she's left behind.

Alex, who seems embarrassed by their tardiness, continues ahead of her down the line, charming my decrepit relatives with his easy manner. He reaches me and stops.

'Hello again.' He gently takes my automatically outstretched hand. 'I won't shake, I should imagine your arm will drop off if one more person tries that manoeuvre.'

'Actually,' I confess, suppressing a small smile, 'I cheated.'

I tell him about hiding in the loo, and he bursts out laughing, earning me a reproving glare from Mother for daring to hold up the line, despite the fact that Kat is still hovering by Richard.

Casting a hard-to-read backward glance at his wife, Alex squeezes my hand gently and walks on.

Richard's speech is smug and self-congratulatory. Dad's is very brief. Sally, I'm happy to report, is smiling and radiant.

Mother is also grinning like a gargoyle, her smile so wide she could swallow the whole of the garlanded top table and its occupants.

Richard, despite the fact that he is the world's most natural bastard, actually has two parents. They are divorced. They haven't spoken for eight years. They clearly want to kill each other. They are currently attempting this with looks. Apparently they fell out over who should keep the family silver. I think the truth of the matter is each blames the other for producing a child like Richard.

I'm seated at a table reserved for antique and distant relatives. I'm relieved that I'm here, though, tucked out of the way with a bunch of people who aren't really sure who I am.

After the speeches the huge four-tiered cake is wheeled in to gasps of astonishment. The cake is indeed a marvel of modern cake engineering and it has more flowers than the church.

Richard stands up and takes Sally's hand. They walk regally round to the front of the table, smiling, happy. They take the long silver knife, Richard's hand protectively over Sally-Anne's.

Cameras begin to flash as the blade slices cleanly through the white icing. Sally-Anne gazes up at Richard in adoration. He looks over to where Kat Christian is sitting and raises his eyebrows. This one's for you, he seems to mock her silently.

As the tables are wheeled away and the disco is wheeled in, and people begin to circulate, I adjourn to a chair in a dimly lit corner. I feel like a charity collector waving her tin. People are taking obvious alternative routes to avoid me. You certainly find out who your friends are at a time like this. Most of mine were struck off the amended guest list. They could at least have left me one crony for moral support. I think of Caroline. She was going to be my matron of honour. Or matron of dishonour maybe.

Perhaps another drink would be a good idea.

'It must be so weird being a guest at your own wedding.'

I look up in surprise as a waft of Poison assails my nostrils and find that Katherine Christian is standing next to me.

'I'm sorry?'

'Are you?' she replies quizzically.

She is trembling, like the taut string of a bow preparing to launch an arrow. Why do I get the feeling I'm her target? She grabs a glass of champagne from a passing waiter and, totally uninvited, sits down next to me.

'I must say, it's very brave of you to be here. It must have been so difficult for you, being dumped by Richard. Of course, don't take this the wrong way, darling, I wasn't surprised when I heard he'd called the whole thing off. I knew you couldn't hold on to him the moment I saw you. I think I know Ricky better than any woman and I could see straight away you weren't the one. "Now that couple," I said to Alex, "are not happy together."'

The front of the woman! I'm torn between being rude back or reluctantly tolerant. I decide that I'm still coping just about well enough to be tolerant.

'Well, you're right about one thing, we weren't happy together. But Richard did not dump me for Sally-Anne, I simply decided that I couldn't marry him. His relationship with Sally developed after we split up.'

Kat looks at me incredulously. She obviously finds it hard to believe that lowly old me could ever decide I didn't want glamorous, wonderful Richard.

'You know he wanted to marry me? Was desperate to, actually, but I turned him down. I felt I was too young to settle down then. He was devastated when I left him.'

A similar but noticeably different version of the story I had heard from him. Somebody's telling fibs. I wonder who?

'Oh, yes? That's funny, in all the time we were together, he never mentioned you,' I tell her, looking sideways to gauge her reaction.

I get a lot more than I bargained for.

'I know that Richard didn't dump you for Sally-Anne,' she says slowly, still not looking at me, 'because he left you for me.'

She turns to look at me, obviously expecting some dramatic reaction. My mind shrieks in outrage, but I manage to control the rest of me.

'I'm sorry, Felicity. I wasn't going to say anything, but I think you deserve to know the truth. It was that chance meeting in the restaurant, you see. It just awoke all the old feelings he had for me.'

Well, this is a turnup for the books. The woman's obviously completely mad, or totally deluded.

'Richard did not dump me for anybody,' I repeat slowly, hoping that this time it will register. '*I* called off the wedding.'

She looks at me calmly without blinking. 'He wrote to me last year when he heard that I was getting married, begged me not to go through with it, and to come back to him,' she says. She waits for my reaction again, but I'm not going to give her the satisfaction of betraying my surprise by even a flicker of my eyelids, so she continues. 'Last June to be precise. I still have the letter. It's quite touching really, he offered to give up everything to be with me . . .' She looks sideways at me, a flash of triumph in her pale blue eyes.

Last June? Richard asked me to marry him last June.

Kat can see she has struck home, and smirks happily.

'I very nearly gave in to him, he was so insistent and the flame between us, of course, can never be extinguished. You know, that special kind of love that's bigger than both of you . . .' She glances at me again from under her curling black eyelashes—I'm sure they're false—looks me up and down appraisingly. 'But I was due to marry Alex in only two weeks, and I'm not the sort of person to run away from my responsibilities.'

'Or a very large bank account,' I snap.

She doesn't rise to this. 'Certainly Alex is a very wealthy man, but I didn't marry him purely for his money. He has other attributes.'

He certainly has. If I'm totally honest with myself, Alex Christian's face has returned to haunt a few of my dreams.

'Of course, you had a lucky escape really. It's Sally-Anne who I feel sorry for.'

I snap out of fantasy mode. 'Richard has married Sally because he loves her.' Who am I trying to convince, her or me?

'He's only done it to get back at me.'

'That's funny,' I say quietly, 'for a while I thought he was doing it to get back at *me*. I would have been worried apart from the fact it's so screamingly obvious he's crazy about my sister.'

'He called me the day after we met in the restaurant . . . said that he'd call it all off with you if I went back to him.'

Why, the sneaky rotten . . . No wonder he was so quick to concede defeat that day I told him it was all over. He thought he could walk straight into the arms of Katherine the not so Great!

'We had a huge row,' she continues, pouting. 'He was trying to pressurise me into leaving Alex. He was using his marriage to you as a threat. Of course, I knew he wouldn't go through with the wedding. You can hardly demand a ransom from someone when you have no intention of taking a hostage.'

Or when the hostage has escaped in the nick of time, I think crossly. 'You're right.' I smile at her, but my smile is about as sweet as a lemon. 'When he phoned you, Richard knew he wouldn't marry me, because I'd told him so that very morning.'

She starts to protest.

'I have witnesses,' I add quickly.

Her glossed mouth opens slightly. Is this a sign that her brain's working? I think what I've been saying is finally sinking in. I hope so, it's taken long enough to get the message home.

'You mean, you really did finish with him?' she asks weakly.

I nod. 'It must have been quite convenient for him, bumping into you the night before, softened the blow really. He thought he had someone to fall back on.'

'Fall back on! He doesn't want to fall back on me. It's me Ricky loves . . . do you hear me? ME!'

'Oh, yes, that's obviously why he's just married someone else!'

'He threatened he'd do something drastic if I didn't take him back. He left you for me, and when I turned him down your sister was just waiting to snap him up. He loves *me*, not your sister.' Her eyes are ablaze as she gets up, repeating insistently, 'You'll see, he only married her to get back at me . . .'

'Oh, yes? I thought you married someone because you loved them!' I shout after her. 'But I was obviously totally wrong.'

Everybody turns to look, and then realising it's me yelling they quickly turn away. Of course it's just the jilted fiancée having a tantrum, they all knew her calm and placid acceptance wouldn't last for ever.

I rest my head in my hands.

Kat has finally drained the last of my strength, renewed my myriad doubts over Richard's intentions towards Sal. I reach for my glass but it's empty. Typical!

'I do hope my wife wasn't being too obnoxious?' says a low calm voice amid the babble.

I look up to see Alex Christian smiling down at me. He hands me a glass of champagne. 'Do you mind if I join you?'

'Are you sure you want to? Everybody's avoiding me today. They are too embarrassed to speak to me. Everyone except your wife, who, by the way, *was* completely obnoxious.'

'I'm sorry,' he replies uncomfortably.

'No.' I shake my head. 'It's I who should be apologising, I didn't mean to take it out on you, it's just been a very stressful day.'

'I can imagine. I should think you're having a pretty lousy time, aren't you?'

I look at him. He's got such a kind face, you can tell he'd be a good listener. I've got this incredible urge to tell him everything. The only problem is he's married to Kat, so how can I?

'I do know about Richard and my wife,' he says as though he can read my mind. 'Kat likes to tell me all about it.'

'Well, she's just told me all about it too. Not very discreet, is she?' I complain, and proceed to be completely indiscreet myself.

The whole story comes pouring out. Words flow well on champagne. He sits, gaze steady, listening quietly. He doesn't interrupt and his eyes don't glaze over. When I finally stumble to a halt, he reaches over and squeezes my hand.

'You poor old thing.' He's laughing at my tragicomedy, but he's not taking the piss. 'I'm sorry she had a go. I'm not making excuses for her, but she's finding this very hard.'

How can he be so understanding about this?

'I think she thought she'd have Richard twined round her little finger for ever,' he continues.

'I'm really surprised you're so calm about all of this. If I were in your situation I'd be fuming.'

He shrugs. 'Kat is the queen of melodrama, her whole life's one long play with her centre-stage. It's all an act, her and Richard. It's pure *Romeo and Juliet* syndrome. Do you think their romance would be quite so intense if they were allowed free access to each other?'

'If they were so *madly* in love,' I say sarcastically, 'then why did they split up in the first place?'

He shrugs. 'I don't really know, I think it's the sort of relationship where they can't live with each other and can't live without each other.'

'So they have to go off and make other people miserable instead?' I mutter angrily, glaring over at Richard who is holding court at the bar. Alex misinterprets my unhappiness.

'Fliss, you never did tell me your side of things. Did you love him?'

Oh dear, the note of sympathy again.

'You know, I feel like wrestling the microphone off the DJ and announcing I wasn't dumped by Richard, that in fact I'm absolutely ecstatic we're no longer together. The only reason I'm miserable today is that I'm worried he doesn't really love my sister.'

He smiles. 'Sorry. Point taken. But what makes you so sure he doesn't love Sally-Anne?'

'Well, it was a bit of a whirlwind courtship, wasn't it? And what with Kat's claims about their relationship . . . oh, the whole thing's such a mess, and I feel like it's all my fault!'

Alex reaches across and to my surprise takes my hand, squeezing it reassuringly. 'Sally's a lovely girl, any sane man would be over the moon to find someone as patient and understanding and beautiful as her.'

'That's true,' I agree, gazing affectionately at my sister who with typical unselfishness is dancing with a rather old and smelly relative who everyone else has been avoiding.

'Can you honestly see Richard marrying Sally if he doesn't have any feelings for her?'

'If it benefits him, then yes I can. I mean, what a spectacular way to try to get Katherine back. If the only thing that turns her on is his unavailability, then getting married was one clever move.'

'But who's to say your sister will be hurt? It's all a game. Richard's devotion makes Kat feel good, and she likes to think she makes me jealous, which makes her feel good too.'

'Does she make you jealous?'

He bites his bottom lip and exhales. 'Not really. Kat's an egotist. She loves herself, and wants to feel infinitely desirable to all men. She wants me and Richard to feel insecure. She feels her indifference is the only thing that keeps us hanging on. The irony of it all is that she's fuelled by her *own* insecurity. Now Richard has married your sister, she wants him. It's Richard's indifference that spurs her into winning him back.'

'She's a bitch then,' I say without thinking. 'Whoops, sorry.'

'That's OK,' he replies, mouth curling into an almost imperceptible smile. 'She *is* a bitch.'

We smile slowly at each other.

'Why did you marry her?' Suddenly I'm very curious. The more time I spend with Alex, the more I like him. 'How did someone as nice as you marry someone as horrible as her?'

He goes quiet.

'Oh dear, I'm really sorry, that was such an impertinent question . . .'

I blush, then realise that he's looking at me with an amused expression on his face, indulgent almost.

'You know, that's a question I frequently ask myself.' He smiles wryly. 'I think it was one of the few things in life I've ever rushed into. When you first meet somebody it's really hard to tell whether what you're seeing is the true person. Everybody puts on an act, don't they? I just didn't realise how different . . .' He stops talking, looking at the floor instead. It's my turn to squeeze his hand, which is for some reason still holding mine, feeling so comfortable I'd almost forgotten it was there.

'Why do you put up with her?'

He shrugs. 'Marriage is a big commitment, and I feel I should work at it. Why did you put up with Richard for so long?'

'Oh, I can answer that one quite easily—cowardice. Too scared to make the change. Almost convinced I didn't deserve any better.'

'Well, I can tell you, you definitely deserve better than Richard,' he states. 'A lot of men would give their right arm for a girl like you.'

I look at him in surprise. No, he's not taking the piss. I think he's just a genuinely nice guy. I tell him so.

'I know,' he replies. 'And nice guys always finish last, don't they?' He turns and looks at me. The laughter lines around those amazing aquamarine eyes deepen as he smiles. It suddenly hits me like a fist in my face. This man is gorgeous! I get this almost irresistible urge to run my fingers through his short dark hair. I must be blushing because he asks me if I'm hot and heads across to the bar to find us another bottle of champagne.

On the darkened dance floor, Richard is dancing with Mother, while Sally-Anne is dancing with Dad. As the music changes to a slower number I watch Kat march across and tap Mother on the shoulder. For a moment I think they're going to fight for him, and then Mother concedes and stalks indignantly back to her seat.

Alex returns with a full bottle. We watch as they float round the dance floor. Their feet are in perfect sync but you can see them talking heatedly through pursed lips. It's obvious they are arguing. Fortunately Sally-Anne is too preoccupied to notice.

'Just look at them,' I murmur bitterly. 'Poor Sally-Anne. I thought I'd managed to overcome my doubts.'

'Kat doesn't look very happy, he's probably fending her off.'

'Yeah, sure,' I say belligerently, totally unconvinced.

'No, seriously, the guy's just got married, Fliss, to a fantastic girl. Your sister's seriously beautiful and seems like a really great person too . . . Don't write them off before they've even got started. You have to give them a chance.'

'Oh, I'll give them a chance, no problem, but do you think your wife will? Look at her!' I round on him angrily. 'You know, perhaps if you were dancing with your wife, Richard might be dancing with his.'

He stares at me. I'm surprised to see a small smile play across his lips. 'I'm afraid it doesn't work like that. The more interest I take in her little games, the worse she gets. She'd love it if I stormed over there and dragged her away. She feeds off the attention. Therefore I shall remain perfectly calm and controlled . . .' the smile flickers back again '. . . because I know it irritates the hell out of her.'

He leans forward and slowly wipes a smudge of mascara away from my cheek with his thumb.

'Would you like to dance?' He gestures to the dance floor.

It's only when I stand up that I realise how much I've had to drink. 'I'm not sure that I can,' I reply, surprised at how legless I feel. 'My legs seem to have divorced themselves from the rest of my nervous system.'

'Well, you can just lean on me then.' He smiles that lovely slow lazy smile, and my legs go even weaker.

He leads me onto the dance floor. We're being watched from all sides. Everybody's been waiting for me to crack.

'You're very brave dancing with me. Everybody's watching us,' I murmur, resting my head against his collarbone.

'Let them,' he says.

'I can just hear the gossip now,' I whisper into his ear. 'Awful old Fliss, jilted by what should have been *her* husband so now she's out to nab somebody else's,' I giggle.

'Shall we give them something to really gossip about?' Alex laughs and pulls me closer.

Kat catches sight of us over Richard's shoulder, and her eyes narrow.

'Your wife is glaring at me,' I murmur in his ear.

'She's probably jealous.'

Psychology never was my best subject. I struggle to find the logic of this one. 'So, let me see if I've got this right. Basically she wants Richard, but only if she thinks she can't have him. But she also gets jealous of you?'

'Correct, but only when she thinks I'm losing interest.'

'So if you and Richard were both totally devoted one hundred per cent of the time, she wouldn't want either of you?'

He laughs. 'I suppose it might work like that, yes, I hadn't really thought of it before.'

'So if you were both being indifferent she'd probably want you both at the same time. Therefore, because Richard has just got married and you have spent the past half an hour giving your undivided attention to lucky old me, we have one unhappy shitty Kitty, sharpening her claws as we speak, who doesn't know quite whose flesh to stick them into first. This could get complicated.'

'I think it already is complicated,' says Alex. 'She wants to have her cake and eat it too.'

'No, no, no,' I slur. 'She wants to have her cake, eat her cake, and then have somebody else's cake and eat *that* too. You know, she must have a screw loose or something, even to *think* about old Dickhead over there when she's got you.'

I flush as I suddenly realise what I've just said, but, when I dare to look up into his face again, he's laughing softly.

When I start to laugh too, I realise that I'm very drunk. I'm actually at that awful point of drunkenness where you're still lucid enough to know you'll end up doing something stupid if you carry on drinking, but where you're also drunk enough not to give a damn.

Dangerous.

Especially as I'm finding Alex more attractive by the moment. Holding him close, feeling his flesh under his clothes, under my touch, being able to bury my head in his chest and breathe in the scent of him.

I try to drag myself back to reality.

Kat is still dancing with Richard so I look around for my sister. She's sitting at the side of the floor with my father, both of them watching Richard and Katherine dancing together, Sally looking unhappy, Dad fingering his unused butter knife.

Sally shouldn't look unhappy on her wedding day.

Alex sees me frowning, and turns to look at Sally-Anne as well.

'I'm going to ask you to do something that might be a bit difficult for you,' he murmurs in my ear. 'Feel free to say no if you want to.'

'It's OK,' I tell him, 'I'd already had the same idea. Go for it.'

Overcome by a feeling of total revulsion at what lies ahead, I think of Sally-Anne as we manoeuvre our way across the dance floor towards Richard and Kat. A swift excuse me, and suddenly she is safely back with her husband, and *I* am dancing with Richard.

I think Richard is as stunned as I am.

He opens his mouth to say something, then for once just shuts it again without speaking. The fact that I'm having to dance with him for Sal's sake is suddenly made worthwhile for me too, just to see him speechless for once.

Everybody's staring, so I force a smile onto my face.

'Congratulations,' I tell him.

Richard's eyes open even wider in surprise.

'I hope you'll both be very happy together. You're a lucky man, Richard Trevelyan. Sally-Anne is one of the best people I know, and I really do hope you have a good life together.'

'Well, thank you.' Richard is obviously taken aback. 'It's nice to know that you can be so . . . er . . . magnanimous.'

Taking the lead, I rather inelegantly dance him back over towards my sister.

'Oh, and just one more thing . . .' I whisper as I hand him over to Sally-Anne. 'If you *ever*, I repeat *ever*, hurt her, I will personally make certain that you have to keep *little* Richard,' I waggle a finger in the direction of his crotch, 'in your inside jacket pocket instead of in your Y-fronts.'

Pausing long enough to see Sal and Richard safely out onto the floor together, I head back to my darkened corner, rescue the remainder of the champagne and head towards the French doors which lead onto the long stone terrace. I'm suddenly in desperate need of some fresh air.

I slip across the spotlit terrace, which is dotted with couples enjoying the gorgeous velvet warmth of the evening, and flit across the lawn to the lake at the end of the bottom lawn.

I plonk myself down at the water's edge and kick off my shoes, dangling my feet in the dark inky water.

So that's it. Sally-Anne has married Richard.

I meant what I said to him. I do wish them well. In fact, I will probably do an awful lot of praying that things will work out for them. I may not love Richard, but I do love Sal.

I look up at the clear dark sky and try to find the biggest star I can wish on. My head spins as I throw it back and gaze into the heavens, so much so that I find I simply have to lie down, feet and ankles still dangling in the water, head resting on the grass, which while slightly damp is also still warm from the very last rays of the sun.

Suddenly I feel a shadow fall across my face, and then a dark figure blocks my view of the Plough and Orion's Belt.

'What on earth are you doing?' a familiar voice asks.

'I'm wishing on a star,' I murmur.

'And what are you wishing for?'

'True love and happiness,' I reply, thinking of Sally-Anne.

'Is that what you want?'

'Don't we all?' I murmur. 'But no, for once I wasn't wishing for myself.'

I look up at Alex who is gazing across the water like a beautifully carved figurehead on the prow of a ship.

'Think I see a frown,' I murmur, lazy with alcohol. 'Is getting married always a mistake?'

'It is when you marry someone you don't love.'

'True.' I nod.

'Or someone who doesn't love you,' he adds quietly.

'If Kat didn't love you, then why would she marry you?'

'Perhaps she was on the rebound from Richard.' He is not being self-pitying, he is merely stating what he believes.

'She's an idiot then,' I exclaim. 'You don't rebound onto someone like you from a prat like Richard. You rebound onto someone like Richard when someone like you dumps you!'

How much have I had to drink?

'I think there was a compliment in there somewhere,' he says drily. 'I'd need an interpreter to verify it, but thanks . . . I think.'

'Do you love her?'

'That's an impertinent question.'

'I know, but I'm in an impertinent mood. Well, do you?'

He shoves his hands deeper into his trouser pockets and looks up at the still starlit sky. 'Oh, look, I can see the Great Bear.'

'Do you?' I insist. I'm not going to let him change the subject.

He thinks for a moment. 'I suppose so.'

Oh boy, I didn't want him to say that. Did I really expect him to say 'No, I don't love her'? I suppose I did, he seems so indifferent to Kat's flirtation with Richard. If I loved someone, and they behaved the way she did, I'd be spitting nails.

Isn't it funny how emotions can creep up on you? Why did it hurt so much to hear Alex say he loved his wife?

'She's been acting like a complete bitch, though,' he adds, which makes me feel a bit better. 'I don't know what I see in her.'

'She's very beautiful,' I say wistfully.

'You know, you're very beautiful too.'

I look at him through narrowed eyes. 'I may be drunk,' I slur, 'but I am *not* stupid.'

'No, I mean it,' he insists, slumping down on the grass next to me.

'In that case, *you* must be drunk.' I offer him the champagne bottle.

'Perhaps I am,' he agrees, taking the proffered Krug and raising it to his lips with the careful precision of someone who *has* had a good few too many. 'But you're still beautiful. Inside and out, and that's a rare quality.'

He smiles at me with his wonderful mouth, and with his glittering blue-green eyes. They're as liquid as an aquamarine swimming pool, inviting me to strip off and dive in.

The desire I've gradually recognised I feel for this man suddenly hits me full strength. He's so close I can feel him breathing. I reach forward with one hand and, taking hold of his shirt, pull him towards me.

Our lips meet.

I think I'm going to pass out. Is it through passion or alcohol? I'm not quite sure, I just wish I was sober enough to enjoy the moment properly and to be able to remember it clearly afterwards, but I'm concentrating too hard on remaining conscious throughout the length of the kiss actually to register the kiss itself.

Then I have the most sobering thought possible.

He's married. Somewhere inside that beautiful house behind us is a beautiful wife. She's a mega-bitch of the first degree, but she's still his wife.

A burst of sound as the doors onto the terrace are opened. Voices, laughter, people coming out of the heat of the disco into the gentle, beautiful warmth of the night. The moment fades, reality reasserts itself.

We break apart. He looks away guiltily and gets hastily to his feet to head for the house.

He looks back once, I think, but I'm blinded by the hot wet tears that are brimming in my eyes. Tears of frustration, anger, helplessness. Why did I do that? I'm such a bloody fool. The whole damn day has suddenly jumped upon my back like a demon, its hands slowly closing around my throat and squeezing the life out of me until I can't breathe.

I have to get out of here. Lurching unsteadily across the lawn, I make my way to the front of the hotel and fall into a taxi that was waiting for someone else, swearing blind that, yes, I am definitely the Mrs Hayes who ordered the cab.

We finally arrive home. I hand the taxi driver a twenty-pound note for an eight-pound fare, and stagger blindly up the stairs to my flat.

Once the front door is locked and bolted behind me, there is only one thing left for me to do, and if I do say so myself I think I do it with great aplomb—I pass out.

CHAPTER SIX

I WAKE UP WITH A START. I'm on the floor in the kitchen, still fully dressed apart from the fact that I've lost my shoes, and hugging the empty Krug bottle to me like a comforter. The cat is licking my toes. The kitchen clock tells me that it's 11.30am. The thought, Alex, slides briefly through my mind.

It hurts more than my hangover. There's a blinding ache behind my eyes, and this awful ringing in my ears which I eventually realise is the telephone.

Clutching the kitchen table for support, I clamber up, stiff and cold from the floor, and stagger out into the hall. I put the receiver to my ear with trembling hand.

'Fliss, it's Dad. Are you all right? You left so suddenly last night, I was worried.'

I think hard, and decide that, no, I'm not really OK. 'I was tired . . .' I say, not altogether untruthfully.

'You missed Sally's departure. She and Richard left half an hour ago. Your mother went with them to the airport.'

'She'd be going on the actual honeymoon if they'd let her,' I snap.

'You're not all right, are you?' says Dad. 'You don't regret it, do you, Fliss? Not marrying him?'

'Heavens, no. Honestly, Dad. My only regret is that my poor little sister ended up lumbered with him. No, I've got other problems, I'm afraid.'

I think back to last night, and physically feel this little pain, deep in my stomach. What is it? Longing? Guilt? I'm not sure, but it hurts.

'Anything I can help with?'

'Thanks, but I think I've got to work this one out for myself,' I murmur.

'Look, darling,' Dad's voice is hesitant, 'I know this is probably lousy timing but I really need to talk to you.'

He sounds strange. I've been so wrapped up in my own warped thoughts that I didn't notice at first. Guilt and concern flood through me. 'Dad, what's wrong?'

'Well, I'd rather not talk about it over the phone. Can I come round and see you? Is that all right?'

Now I'm worried. I pace the floor until he finally arrives. It's a fifteen-minute drive at Dad's usual pace, but it takes him over half an hour today by the end of which I have no nails left.

I go to open the door and Dad staggers up the stairs. He looks tired. He's always been tall and gangly, now he looks gaunt. I feel guilty for not noticing before. He carries an air of doom about him, as though he's about to tell me something really awful.

'Coffee?'

I sod the instant, and go for the strong stuff. Leaving the percolator bubbling and spitting like a little glass geyser, I edge back into the sitting room.

Dad's sprawled on the sofa. He's fidgeting like mad, and won't look me in the eye. Finally he stops pulling at his shirt collar and speaks.

'Fliss, I've got something to tell you.' He studies his feet, looking at his reflection in his highly polished black shoes.

'Don't tell me, you've finally snapped and murdered Mother?' I laugh halfheartedly.

He sort of smiles. His face is too unhappy for it to be a proper smile. 'If only it were that simple,' he says quietly.

He looks so sad, I sit down at his feet and rest my chin on his knees. 'Dad, you're scaring me, what's wrong?'

He doesn't answer.

'Come on,' I wheedle, 'it can't be that bad, surely?'

'Fliss, I'm in love with someone else.'

'What?'

'I'm in love with someone else . . . I've been seeing someone else.'

The words take a moment to sink in, and then they hit the part of my nervous system that controls my jawbone. It drops to the floor like a broken lift.

I thought I knew him like the back of my hand. Completely in shock, I manage to realign my mouth and move into speech mode.

'How long?'

'Seven years.' He looks at me, trying to gauge my reaction.

'Seven years?' I repeat incredulously.

'It started not long after you moved out. I'd never have got away with it if you'd still been there, Fliss, you'd have noticed.' Now the dam gates have opened the words are flooding out. 'I've wanted to tell you for so long. Your mother never loved me, Fliss, our marriage was a sham. I stayed for your sake and for Sally-Anne's. I can't do it any more. As soon as Sally walked out of that front door this morning, I just knew I couldn't spend the rest of my life alone with your mother. Florence is so sweet and kind and loving . . .'

'Florence?' I query.

'Sweet, sweet Florrie . . .' His face softens for a moment, the tension slips away fleetingly. 'She gives me everything your mother never could or would. You don't know how hard it is to continue in a relationship that's totally barren, devoid of any real affection.'

'Do you love her?'

He nods.

'Then I'd like her,' I decide. 'It's all right, Dad, I understand.'

'You do?' There's a spark of hope in his weary grey eyes.

'Of course I do. My only wonder is that you managed to stick it out for this long. Oh, Dad. I knew you were unhappy, but not to that extent. Why didn't you ever tell me?'

'I wanted to be the perfect father, God knows I owed you that much. I tried to make up for the way your mother treated you, Fliss. I should have stood up to her, stopped her bullying you and manipulating Sally-Anne, but I never did, did I . . .?' He trails off, voice too choked to speak. He rests his head in his hands and his shoulders begin to shake.

Gently I pull his hands away from his face. His eyes are glazed with unshed tears.

'You *are* the perfect father,' I say soothingly. 'To me you always will be.' I squeeze his hands and he hangs on tight.

'I thought you'd hate me.'

'Why should I hate you for trying to find some happiness?'

He smiles hesitantly. 'I think I've finally found happiness, Fliss. Do you think I'm selfish for not wanting to let it go?'

I shake my head. 'Not at all.'

'Do you think I'm doing the right thing?'

'What *are* you going to do, Dad?'

281

He takes a deep breath. 'I'm going to go and live with Florrie. I'm leaving your mother. I'll wait till Sally comes back from Mauritius and then I'm going. I really can't go on.'

I spend the next four days holed up in my flat, pretending to work on assignments for next term. My heart's not really into *A Winter's Tale*. I decide to go out for a walk. I really should get a dog, the amount of walking I've been doing in the past few days. Why is walking conducive to thinking? Is the pace of one's brain connected to the pace of one's feet? I don't think so. Outside, summer has taken a breather after a lengthy debate on whether it should make way for autumn. The weather has changed more quickly than someone in a communal changing room wearing their greyest undies. The intense heat has given way to long bouts of rain and grey cold skies.

This summer has certainly been memorable. I'm still reeling from Dad's revelation. I wasn't surprised but I was, if you know what I mean. I know how unhappy my father has been but even though I always expected Dad eventually to find someone else, it was still a shock when it actually happened.

Life is so confusing. I think of Alex all the time although I know I really shouldn't. When I think of what I did I could almost die of embarrassment, but underneath that emotion is something else. That first faint thrill of excitement, of knowing that you've found someone who really could make a difference to your life.

I try to tell myself very sternly that I'm not interested in him, but I don't believe me. I try to tell myself very sternly that he's probably not interested in me, and I unfortunately find that far more believable. What shared ground do we have? One evening of confessions, and one wonderful if rather drunken kiss. Hardly the basis for the all-consuming, undying love I'm ready to declare.

You see, that's the emotion that crept up and hit me in the face with all the subtlety of Barbara Cartland's wardrobe.

Love.

Why does Cupid always strike when he really shouldn't? I think I'm falling for Alex. Alex is married to Katherine. Katherine is in love with Richard. Richard is married to my sister. Why is life so complicated?

Back to school next week. Time to face another trauma: Caroline. When I get back home there's another message on my answering machine from her. She's been desperately trying to contact me since that night. I won't phone her back. I don't know what to say to her. I'm still in shock from the sight of her sprawled on the floor, her hands full of Eloise Gray.

So that was the secret to their happy marriage. Free love. And they used to take the piss out of Maura for being so seventies!

I'm beginning to wonder if the words 'happy' and 'marriage' are at all compatible, what with Caro and David, Mother and Dad, Sasha and Niall, Sally-Anne and Richard, Kat and Alex . . .

Every time I think of Alex I feel so sad. If this is love, who needs it?

Being a perverse sort of person, the apparent onset of autumn makes me feel like spring-cleaning. Tonight I am blitzing. Unable to control my life, I have decided that I will control my surroundings. I am determined that my untidy home will become my tidy home. Anything movable has been bin-bagged: clothes I was determined to slim into, magazines I was keeping to cut recipes out of and never have—all destined for black plastic bin bags. Having denuded and scrubbed my flat to within the last inch of its life, I start on the washing.

I have a running battle with my washing machine. If I'm desperate for it to work properly, it won't. I have to load it casually, appear nonchalant, make it think that I don't care if it won't work. If it so much as gets a hint of the fact that I need my best blouse for the next day, then it will seize up on me instantaneously.

It's just managed to turn my best white undies the dingiest blue-grey, when I hear the doorbell and stop in mid-swear word.

I'm not expecting anybody. It must be the milkman. At least this time he's caught me with my clothes on. I grab my purse and head for the door.

Standing on my doorstep is Alex Christian. He smiles at me. I just stand there, my bottom lip detached from the top by about half an inch. Does desire always immobilise one's brain?

'You don't do anything by halves, do you?' he finally ventures. He holds out a pair of shoes. 'Cinderella managed with one, you had to leave a pair.'

'My shoes,' I say stupidly.

'Well, I don't think they're mine.' He smiles gently. 'I rescued them from the hotel garden.'

'Thanks.'

That means he came back to look for me. I manage my first smile in a week.

'My pleasure.' He looks at my purse. 'You don't have to reward me, at least not with money anyway.' He laughs wryly.

I blush.

We're at that stage again, conversation running dry. We just stand there gazing at each other.

'Look, I'm really sorry about . . .' we both say at the same time.

We both start to laugh as well, and the ice is, well, not entirely broken but fractured. I stand back and pull the door wider.

'Do you want to come in?'

He follows me into the sitting room and looks about him. Thank goodness I've just had a major clearout. The flat actually looks really good. Minimalist chic.

He's wearing faded Levi's and a loose collarless white shirt. His hair is tousled and he has dark circles under his eyes, but he still looks amazing and disgustingly desirable.

I'm suddenly acutely conscious of my old ripped jeans and faded blue T-shirt, my clearing-out gear, and of my unmade-up face.

We stand facing each other for a moment, awkward, silent, then I remember my manners and ask him to sit down.

I can't look at him, keep darting surreptitious sideways glances at him, like looking at the last cream cake on the plate, pretending you don't want it really but fighting the saliva that's gathering in full flood on your tongue.

He starts talking about the wedding, but I'm concentrating too hard on fighting my own discomfiture really to listen. The atmosphere's so charged I can almost hear it buzzing.

'Coffee?' I suddenly blurt, my mind finally fixing on something normal.

I leave him sitting uncomfortably on the sofa in mid-meaningless sentence and escape to the kitchen. I attempt to refill the percolator, but my hands are shaking.

'Fliss?'

I jump at the sound of his voice.

'I'll be with you in a minute . . .'

'I don't want any coffee.'

I turn round. He's standing in the doorway.

'Look, it's no good, we've got to talk about what happened on Saturday night.'

'Don't worry about it.' I try to smile brightly at him. 'It was just a kiss.'

'That's the problem, it was more than just a kiss and we both know it.' He falters, looks away and then back at me again. 'This is going to sound completely insane. I mean, I hardly know you, but I've never felt this way about anybody before. There's just something . . .' He shrugs, at a loss for words. 'It's just there, a feeling, a very strong feeling that I've got to be with you. Don't you feel it too?'

I look at the floor. Talk about inner conflict!

Dear Auntie Ruth, I met the man I want to marry at what should have been my wedding, the problem is he's married. I've tried to forget him, but I can't get him out of my head. Every time I see him, I just want to rip off all of his clothes. What do I do?

I decide the best form of defence is attack. 'Why did you run away from me then?' I accuse him.

'Infidelity isn't exactly my forte.'

'No, you leave that to your wife,' I quip without thinking.

He's silent.

I kick myself mentally. Very hard.

'Besides, when I came back you'd done exactly the same thing.'

He walks over to me.

I back away. I can feel the table top jutting into the small of my back. I suddenly find the floor tiles very interesting.

'You normally run and hide from people you dislike.' I'm whispering, but he's close enough to hear me easily.

'Or people you like too much,' he answers softly.

His face is so close. My senses are so heightened, I can feel the warmth of his skin even though he's not quite touching me.

'Fliss?' His voice is quiet, uncertain, questioning.

He reaches out and pushes a stray tendril of hair away from my downturned face. As he touches me I realise that no matter how much I want to fight this I can't. Just the sensation of his fingertips against my face carries pure electricity.

I want him. Oh *boy*, do I want him.

He's married.

How can something so wrong feel so right?

His kiss is as soft as thistledown. This time I want to remember every single minute detail.

He follows the contour of my neck with his lips. The warmth of his breath against my skin makes me shiver. As he kisses me again, my stomach begins to churn like the washing machine which is now stuck on spin.

My hands slide under his shirt, feel the warmth of his skin, the smooth firm curve of his back. He pulls me closer, fingers tracing the length of my spine, tangling with my hair. I revel in the weight of his gloriously fit, lean body pressing against me. The kiss gets harder, less tentative, more passionate, and this little voice in my head begins to nag.

It's just no good, I can't do this. It's like indulging in too much of your favourite ice cream. No matter how good it tastes at the time, the guilt afterwards takes away the majority of the pleasure.

Reluctantly, very reluctantly, I pull away. 'This is wrong.'

'It doesn't feel wrong.'

'I know, but you're married. I don't want to break up a marriage.'

'Even if that marriage is turning out to be a total farce?'

'You said yourself, it's a commitment you have to work at.'

He backs away and leans against the kitchen table.

'If you don't feel the same then just say so, don't hide behind false guilt.'

Oh, that it were. Guilt is an emotion I can rely on to be with me all my life, never to leave my side. I should have been Catholic I'm so good at it.

He's upset. His face is drawn, and he won't look me in the eye. All I can think is how much I long to kiss that angry mouth again.

'I think I'd better go,' he mutters.

'It's for the best,' I force myself to say. How trite those words sound.

'I suppose so.'

As he leaves, he looks back. I have to look away and cram my fist into my mouth to stop myself calling after him.

Love is supposed to make you feel on top of the world. I feel like I'm at the bottom of a pit.

'He's married,' says my head rather bluntly.

My heart keeps telling me not to get hung up on technicalities. Kat is hardly keeping to her marriage vows, now is she?

'But,' says my head, 'that doesn't mean I should sink to her level. Somebody's got to have some standards around here.'

'Why, oh, why, does that somebody have to be me?' answers heart despondently.

'It's that guilt thing again,' sighs head sympathetically.

It's been three days now since I sent Alex away. Three whole days of thinking of nothing but him. And what could have happened if I'd let him stay.

I pick up the phone about ten times in one day and then put it back down again. I am desperate to talk to him. Even if I could pluck up the courage to call, what the hell would I say to him? Besides, we keep coming back to the inescapable, unshakable truth—he's married.

And look who he's married to as well. A whole bloody chain reaction could be set off if I give in to the feelings I have for this man.

No, I can't call him. I keep telling myself this as I sit by the phone hour after hour. Perhaps he'll call me.

As the days drag by with no contact, I get more and more depressed, mooning around, staring at the walls, climbing the walls, staring out of windows, contemplating throwing myself out of said windows. I can't work, I can't settle to anything. A momentary high every time the phone rings, then sadness when I answer and it's not him.

The sensible little voice that keeps nagging me just to forget about Alex and get back to reality, and therefore back to relative normality, is gradually getting more and more subdued. The longer I go without seeing him the worse it gets. One day very soon, reason may pack its bags and bugger off completely on an extended holiday, and then what do I do?

Sash doesn't help.

She calls round midweek for a coffee and to flick through the wedding photographs my mother insisted on dropping off as soon as she'd done showing them off to her cronies.

'You should just go for it, Fliss,' she urges, drooling over a photograph that, oh, cruel fate, actually has Alex in it. 'I know I would. A little of what you fancy and all that.'

'Things still bad at home then, I take it?'

'To be honest it's worse. Niall's cock's got a "No Access" sign on it at the moment. Do you know, I put my hand on it the other night in bed, just to say hello, see if it was still talking to me, and you've never seen anyone jump so high or so fast. It's the biggest display of energy I've seen from him in months. Maybe it's not sex he's gone off, maybe it's me.'

'Oh, come on, Sash, we all know how much Niall loves you.'

'Well, yes, I know he loves me, Fliss, but does he still fancy me? Some men are funny like that, you know. You have children and suddenly cease to be a sex object. It's so frustrating.'

'Don't talk to me about frustration!' I grin at her.

'I know. Actually . . .' Sash looks sideways at me under her eyelashes, a small smile playing about her red lips. 'I've got a confession too.'

'Oh, yes? Tell me all.'

'I've been asked out for a drink by this new guy at work . . .'

'You haven't?' I breathe, intrigued. 'You're not going to go, are you?'

'I don't know, I'm tempted. He's gorgeous, and he's only twenty-two.'

'Well, he's past his peak then. Don't they say a man's at his best at nineteen?'

'Oh, well, in that case I'll definitely stand him up.'

'Don't tell me you've already agreed to go out with him?'

Sash nods. She looks guilty but happy at the same time.

'When?'

'Well, that's the difficult one. Finding an excuse to get out.' She pauses. 'Fliiiisss . . .' she wheedles. 'Will you be my alibi?'

I hesitate. I really like Niall, but Sash is one of my best mates.

'Please? Can I tell Niall we're going out for a drink or something? I mean, I haven't actually decided whether or not to go ahead with it, but if I do, will you cover for me? You could look upon it as helping our relationship . . .'

'Oh yeah, and how do you work that one out?'

She grins. 'Well, if I don't get my leg over soon, I'll probably end up murdering him.'

A slight respite for my sanity is my return to school. Here *I* am in control, a rare feeling lately. I say slight respite, however, because now I have to face the music as far as my girls are concerned.

They say that curiosity killed the cat. Curiosity, however, does not kill fifth-formers. It fuels their overeager minds like dry moss on a campfire. It's not long before news of my spectacular lack of a wedding ring filters down from the upper echelons of the school hierarchy.

Rumours abound, my personal favourite being that I discovered Richard in an après-stag-night clinch with the male stripper from *my* hen night. Where this particular little beauty came from I don't know, but as a counter to the other rumours flying around like Chinese Whispers at a sore throat convention, it was a moment of exquisite light relief from the heavy burden of being the most talked about person in the whole school community.

I try to keep my mind looking forward to the inevitable day when I'll be yesterday's news. The imminent arrival of a new, young, attractive, *male* sports coach gives me hope that this will be sooner rather than later as the girls' attentions are transferred. Unfortunately, another confrontation awaits me, another problem on my long list.

Caroline.

I can't deny it, I've really missed her wicked sense of humour and unswerving loyalty. I feel a git to have avoided her over the last four weeks. I just wish they hadn't tried to involve me in their sex life.

I don't think I'm a prude, not really, but orgies I cannot handle. I mean, it's all very well displaying your flabby bits on a one-to-one basis, but not in front of your friends. No, orgies are definitely not my scene, and not just because I'm slightly shy. I've always been a very giving person, but there are limits to what I'm prepared to share.

I'm not condemning Caro and David, not really, let he who is without sin and all that, but really what do I say to them? I can't pretend the whole thing never happened, so how do we get back to the lovely easy friendship we shared before?

I manage to avoid Caroline at first, timing my visits to the staff room so that I don't bump into her.

Once I even duck into the gents' loos to avoid her. You'd think with the shortage of men there naturally is at an all girls' school, I'd be fortunate enough to find it empty. Not so. Mr Carver, the wrinkled old Latin teacher, is leaning against a stall, pointing an equally wrinkled old John Thomas towards the urinal. He looks over at me and sighs.

'*Nil bastardo carborandum,*' he murmurs.

I don't know whether he's talking to me or to himself.

My avoidance tactics can't last for ever, though.

Caro eventually corners me in the empty staff room.

'Fliss, we have to talk.' She smiles uncertainly at me.

'Can't stop, double English, Upper 5B. Must rush,' I garble with false brightness. I know, I'm a big fat coward.

'Fliss, pleeease. We have to sort this out.'

'Nothing to sort out really.' I smile inanely at her.

I feel I should be sophisticated enough to cope with one little orgy but I'm not. I was, well, quite frankly shocked. And the feeling that followed was acute embarrassment. I don't know how to handle the situation.

'Er, did you have a nice break?' I suppose that's a start.

'So you're just going to pretend that nothing happened?' she asks bluntly.

That sounds like a very good option to me. I deliberately drop my file, so that I don't have to look her in the face, and flounder round on the floor after my papers.

'Fliss!' she says exasperatedly. 'I need your friendship, Fliss, please don't shut me out.'

I always thought it was I who needed her. Caro, my friend, my rock, my other sister. I always knew she liked me, loved me even, but needed me? That's a new one.

'Hannah's pregnant.'

That makes me listen. I stop grovelling on the floor and look up.

'You're kidding!'

'Afraid not, we've just found out.'

'Who?'

'Who do you think? Jake.'

'Jake?'

Oh dear. With a rush of guilt, my ever-present companion, I stumble to my feet, clutching my file to my chest.

'Oh, Caro,' I whisper, 'I'm so sorry. It's all my fault, I encouraged her to see him.'

She shakes her head. 'Hannah only does what Hannah wants to do . . .
It's not your fault.'

'How is she?'

'Remarkably all right actually, after the first round of hysterics. She
now seems amazingly calm about the whole thing.'

'I suppose Maura the free spirit is overjoyed?'

Caroline shakes her head. 'Actually she's furious. She threw Hannah
out.'

'You're joking?' I'm outraged. 'Of all the hypocritical . . .'

'Don't worry, we're looking after her now.'

'What will she do?'

'Well, she's adamant she doesn't want to get rid of it. She doesn't
believe in that. David and I . . . well, we've offered to look after the baby
for her. Hannah's really happy with the idea. She doesn't want to get rid
of it but she doesn't want the responsibility either . . . she wants to go to
university . . .'

I gaze incredulously at my friend. 'But you don't like children.'

'That's what I'd always tried to convince myself, Fliss, but only
because I knew I could never have any.'

'You never told me that . . .'

'I haven't known myself for very long, I don't suppose it had sunk in
enough to be able to talk about it.'

'So that's why David got so touchy when the kids were winding you
up about babies?'

She nods. 'Now a new child is joining the family . . . well, it's made
me realise how desperately I really wanted one. Not that I intend to take
him or her away from Hannah,' she adds hurriedly. 'It will always be her
son or daughter even though David and I will be bringing the child up.
And when I'm a surrogate mother that means I'll have to behave . . .' she
pauses and looks meaningfully at me '. . . more responsibly.'

I digest this last.

'And you, Fliss, how are you?' she asks quietly. 'I heard about Sally-
Anne and Richard. It was a shock for me, so goodness knows how it
made you feel. I did try to call . . .'

'I know,' I hang my head in shame. 'I'm sorry.'

'It's all right, I do understand. How do you feel?'

'Confused,' I answer. 'I just hope he makes her happy.'

The bell heralding the start of class begins to ring.

'You know, we all would love to see you. We miss you. I miss you.'

'I've missed you too, Caro,' I murmur.

'Then come and see us . . . please?'

Sally and Richard arrive back from honeymoon. They are brown, relaxed, and seem very happy. I am summonsed to a celebratory sherry and photos session at Mother's where Richard is attentive and loving towards Sal in a manner that even I cannot fault. To some extent my fears are allayed.

In fact, for the first time in ages I can react to Richard as if he's a normal human being. He spends the evening focusing more on Sally-Anne than anything else and being, for want of a better word, *polite* to me. I was expecting the usual arrogant, pugnacious attitude, but it's like he's a different person. Or perhaps I'm just seeing him in a different way now. That's probably what I need to do, give him the same opportunities I would if I were meeting him for the first time, not as my ex-fiancé but as Sally's husband.

Dad waits over a week after Sally has moved her final suitcase into Richard's apartment, then finally he tells Mother that he's leaving.

She seems strangely unaffected by his decision to go.

My mother is someone who always does the socially acceptable thing. I think she got married because that's what girls were supposed to do, but her life has been tainted by the inevitable disappointments that this entailed when it was never really what she wanted in the first place.

I don't think Sally-Anne's surprised at Dad's decision. Like me, she has grown up in a family where only an idiot would fail to notice that the parental unit is far from unified and less than happy. She can't help but be desperately upset, however. The beginning of her marriage has heralded the end of her parents'. She can't help but associate the two events and wonder if this is some sort of omen.

Sally and I help Dad to pack. It's amazing really how few of the things in this house belong to him. Just bits from the shed, one small suitcase, and Roger. After all these years you'd think they'd have some shared history, some treasured memories. That's the saddest part of all, that they've lived like this, in an emotional, loveless void for so long.

It's Monday evening and Mother is playing St Joan at the stake. She sits on the sofa, glowering like a malevolent old crow, watching with sharp eyes to make sure that Dad doesn't take anything she feels he shouldn't.

She enjoys playing the martyr, it's a role she has perfected over the years. As far as my mother is concerned Dad is an unnecessary part of her life. To her it's rather like having a wart removed. You may have got used to it being there, but you're certainly not going to profess you miss it after it's gone. The only time she shows any emotion is when Dad starts to wrap up a rather valuable painting given to them as a wedding present by his family.

'Put that back, Drew!' she shrieks. 'It was a present to us both. You must give me half the value if you want to take it.'

We wave goodbye as Dad and Roger drive down the road.

Sally is crying quietly.

'It's for the best,' I try to reassure her. 'They weren't happy together, Sal. At least now they've got a chance to find some joy.'

'I know, but things will never be the same for us again, Fliss.'

She takes my arm as we walk slowly back into the house.

'Well, thank goodness that's all over,' my mother says, as though referring to the end of a rather boring television programme.

'Today or your marriage?' I can't help snapping at her. 'How can you just let him leave like that?'

I know it seems an odd question, me being an advocate of their separation, but I've never really understood why my mother has always been so careless of my father's feelings.

'I'm not going to beg him to stay,' she replies, staring icily at me.

'Because you're too proud, or because you simply don't care?'

She doesn't reply, merely continues to glare at me, her eyes as cold as her seemingly frozen heart.

'Did you ever love him?' I persist.

'I've told you a thousand times before, there's more to marriage than a foolish ideal of love and romance.'

'Yes, there's trust and respect, but you never had those either, did you?'

'You may think you know everything there is to know about life and love, Felicity,' she hisses, 'but you've got an awful lot to learn, I can tell you. I've tried to teach you, but you never listen to me. You just can't understand the true value of security and stability. Love is a fickle emotion with no substance. You can't build a good life based on love.'

'You call what you've had a good life? You want me to model myself and my future happiness on your example! Well, you've made me determined I shall never lead an existence as miserable as yours!'

I run out of the front door. I'm so angry I'm shaking. Sally follows me out, puts her arms round my waist.

'It's a difficult time for us all,' she murmurs. 'She's not like you, Fliss, she has a completely different set of values. Don't hate her for it.'

'Hate her?' I turn to Sally, my eyes damp with tears. 'I don't hate her. Do you know, I actually feel sorry for her.'

The one good thing to come of this whole mess, is the fact that Sally-Anne and I have become a lot closer. Although we'd always rubbed along well, with Dad gone we need and appreciate each other a little more.

Mother is driving Sally round the bend. Sally has moved in with Richard and it seems that Mother is determined to follow suit. She's practically decamped into their spare room. Every time she goes to stay, which has been about ninety per cent of the time since my father moved out, she moves something else over. It's a slow and devious process of infiltration.

Sally has started to retreat to my flat just to get away from her.

'I know Mother must be lonely on her own, but we've only been married five weeks,' she frequently sighs. 'I really don't think Richard relishes the idea of turning our guest suite into a granny flat just yet.'

I feel guilty for the fact that I don't get on well enough with Mother to take some of the burden off Sally. I would if I could, but even if I asked her over to stay with me, she'd probably just laugh in my face.

It's kind of sad really. Then again, I've always been so close to Dad, I've never really felt I was missing out that much.

He has been gone for three weeks now. It seems like for ever. We speak a lot on the phone, but it's not the same as having him fifteen minutes' drive away. The elusive Florrie lives in Kent, which explains the amount of time Dad spent there 'fishing' over the past years.

I haven't heard from Alex at all either. Not that I really expect to. I had my chance and I blew it. I know that's what I *should* have done, I just didn't realise how lousy it would make me feel. What was it Sash said? Is it better to do something you might regret than to regret something you haven't done? She and I are both still undecided on this front.

Apparently she's still being pursued by the gorgeous twenty-two-year-old. She hasn't succumbed yet, but it's doing her ego the power of good. Maybe I need to be unashamedly lusted after by a gorgeously fit, sexily single twenty-two-year-old. Unfortunately the only thing I want at the moment is to be pursued by a gorgeously fit, maddeningly married thirty-five-year-old.

Sally calls to invite me to dinner. I decline as graciously as possible. I do seem to be getting over my self-destruct mode. I don't spend my evenings watching crap on the box, and amazingly the fridge has been empty of Mars bars for two weeks. At the moment, however, I don't even want to go out to the supermarket, let alone to a dinner party which will no doubt be graced by the presence of my sister's horrible hubby and several of his equally awful friends. I feel about as sociable as a virgin at a vampire's birthday party.

Unfortunately Sally is not to be dissuaded, and since an oven chip would have far more force of mind than me at the moment, I soon find myself crumbling.

'Oh, Fliss, it's my first dinner party, I want you to be there.' Her voice holds just the right note of pleading.

'Honestly, Sal,' I groan. 'I'd rather not, I'll feel such a gooseberry.'

'Don't worry about that, we'll find you a nice man.'

'In that case I'm definitely not coming,' I reply belligerently.

'Pleeeease, Fliss!' Sally-Anne begs. 'I need you there, I really do.'

She sounds strange.

'Sally, is everything OK?'

She goes quiet for a moment.

'Yes, of course it is, I just want some moral support, that's all.'

'Moral support? For any particular reason?'

'No.' She's not quite convincing enough. 'Just first-night nerves, I suppose. Say you'll come, Fliss, please?'

I give in. 'OK, but promise me you won't try to fix me up?'

'You're the one who said you'd feel like a gooseberry on your own. Trust me, Fliss.'

Why is it that when people say 'trust me' your instinctive reaction is to do exactly the opposite?

'Fine, just not one of Richard's stupid friends, OK?'

'Richard's friends aren't all awful. You like James, don't you?'

'Everybody likes James. But that doesn't mean I want to be fixed up with him.'

'Don't worry,' Sally laughs. 'I've already got him earmarked for someone else.'

'He will be pleased,' I remark drily, thinking back to the wedding and Erica's dogged pursuit of him. 'Sal, promise me you won't try to fix me up? I don't mind sitting next to someone and making polite conversation, but no matchmaking, please.'

'Oh, OK,' she sighs.

'Can I bring anything?'

'Just yourself,' she says pointedly.

'Don't worry, I'll be there. What time do you want me?'

'Well, dinner's at eight thirty, but if you could come a bit earlier I'd be eternally grateful,' she wheedles. 'It would be nice to know you're there if the doorbell rings while I'm trying to flambé something.'

'To be on hand to call the fire brigade?'

'Something like that. I'll see you about seven thirty?'

Saturday night. I arrive at Richard's apartment—sorry, Sally and Richard's apartment—at seven thirty on the dot, resplendent in obligatory little black dress and fetching blue-and-white-striped butcher's apron. This is the first time I've been round since they got married.

When Sally answers the door, I get this urge to say, 'What are you doing here?' It seems so strange to see her in this setting.

Sally is similarly attired to me, only she's forgotten the dress. She is wearing pale pink silk undies beneath her pink floral apron, and nothing else. She is flushed, her long dark hair which is curled and pinned is starting to come loose, and she is waving a wooden spoon, burnt black, in her right hand as though she's going to hit me over the head with it.

'Oh, Fliss,' she burbles breathlessly, 'thank goodness you're here, everything's going wrong. It's all a complete disaster . . . I've spilt seafood sauce on my new dress and burnt the potatoes. And worst of all—oh, Fliss, it's horrible—the first course is still alive!'

'I beg your pardon?'

'The first course,' she wails, 'it's alive and walking round my kitchen! Fliss, you've got to do something!'

'Er, what exactly are we having to eat?'

'It was all Richard's idea,' she snivels. 'And of course he's been into work today and he's late home, and I'm left to massacre it. It's bloody huge, I've never seen one this big!'

Well, she's definitely not talking about what Richard keeps down his trousers.

'What is it, Sally?'

If she gets any more hysterical, I shall have to slap her.

Sally edges towards the kitchen, ushering me in front of her. Then she spots it, shrieks and jumps onto a chair.

'It's under there, Fliss, it's under there!'

I crouch down and stare under the kitchen table.

A pair of beady black eyes stares back at me out of a hard brown face. The largest lobster in the universe is squatting under Sally's kitchen table. It waves a threatening pincer at me.

'It's supposed to be the centrepiece, we're having seafood pancakes. But when I opened the box I got such a shock, I thought the thing would already be . . . well, you know . . . dead.'

'It looks a bit like Richard,' I comment, staring at its hard little brown face and mean little eyes. 'I shall enjoy boiling it alive!'

I'm joking, of course. Even I don't relish the thought of cooking something while it's still moving.

'I'm sorry, Sally.' I admit defeat as, having finally managed to recapture the blasted thing using a pair of salad tongs and a dustpan and brush, I chicken out of dunking it into the boiling cauldron on the stove. 'We're going to have to think of another way.' I dump the lobster back in its coffin of a wooden crate, and pour us both a very large G & T.

Three further very large G & Ts later we're a lot more relaxed, the lobster's been grandly christened Ethelred the Unready-cooked, and we're still no closer to a solution as to how to humanely kill the bloody thing.

'We could drown it in the bath?' Sally suggests tentatively.

'Drown it? Honestly, Sally, where do you think the thing has lived for the past goodness knows how many years?'

After another large gin, we hit on the bright idea of trying to suffocate it, but the sight of a lone Waitrose bag running around the kitchen floor is pretty disturbing after drinking so much. In the end we dunk it in a bucket of whisky and water, and stick it in the oven with the gas on, which amazingly seems to do the trick.

'At least it died happy,' says Sally, waving her glass in the air. '*Salute*, Entrée.'

'Cheers,' I agree, making a mental note to go vegetarian, if I can only beat the bacon sarnie cravings.

I send Sally-Anne off to the bedroom to find something else to wear, and manage to get the meal back on course. By ten to nine, I'm sobering up, there's still no sign of Richard the Turd, but everything is cooked and waiting. The lobster is resplendent on a silver salver, resting on a bed of lollo rosso.

The doorbell chimes.

'Fliss!' Sally-Anne calls plaintively from the bedroom.

'Don't worry, I'll get it.'

The first arrival is Sal's best friend, Erica, who I haven't seen since the wedding. She was chief bridesmaid. I think she secretly harboured the hope of continuing the tradition of best man and chief bridesmaid getting together, for she flashed her large coltish teeth at James at every possible opportunity. She has obviously made a big effort to look good. At the risk of sounding a total bitch, it's a real shame it didn't work. Her foundation is not so much pancake as Yorkshire pudding, and her blusher is a hard streak of red across her non-existent cheekbones. She's wearing a killer dress, a little red number that swoops down low like a bird of prey at the front and at the back as well, and her pillar-box lipstick matches her outfit exactly. She is grinning in excited anticipation.

Five minutes later the doorbell goes again, and James is standing there holding a single red rose.

'For Erica?' I ask him. 'How appropriate.'

'Er, no.' His face falls. 'For Sal, actually.' He whispers nervously, 'Erica's not here, is she?'

I nod.

Sally-Anne emerges from the bedroom.

'James, so glad you could make it!' She kisses his cheek and leads him into the sitting room like a lamb to the slaughter.

If poor old James has been lumbered with Erica against his will, then who am I going to get?

Sally has dumped James on one of the long black leather sofas, next to Erica. I can hear him squeaking his way up to the far end as he surreptitiously tries to manoeuvre as far away from her as possible.

I follow Sally over to the drinks cabinet.

'Er, Sally darling, you know you said you'd find me a nice man? You were only joking, weren't you?'

'Well, we had to get someone to make up the numbers, Fliss,' she murmurs noncommitally.

'And who exactly will be making up the numbers?' I ask.

The doorbell rings again.

'Saved by the bell,' mutters Sal. 'That'll probably be him now. Why don't you go and see for yourself?' She whisks away.

I make my way somewhat hesitantly to the door.

'Feliiiicity . . .' growls a deep voice, tongue running lasciviously over the consonants of my name like a child licking an ice cream.

I've died and gone to hell. This must be punishment for my part in the murder of an innocent lobster. There, lounging against the door frame, is Ollie Barton-Davis.

Ollie the Octopus. Fat, balding and fifty, he thinks he's God's gift to women. He is a lech of the highest order—the sort who as a child would lift your skirt and twang your knicker elastic to get his kicks. Come to think of it, he's the sort who as a man would lift your skirt and twang your knicker elastic to get his kicks.

I can't sit next to him all evening, it's not nice, and it's certainly not safe. Not unless I put a mousetrap in my knickers.

'You're looking par-tic-u-lar-ly lovely, my dear. When Richard said you were in need of a partner, I leapt on my charger and galloped on down. Haw-haw-haw! Actually I leapt in dear old Richard's BMW really, he's just parking. I was *panting* to see you . . . now that we're both young, free and single, eh?' He winks heavily.

Forget the lobster, it's me that's been served up on a platter. Trust Richard to toady to the boss by offering me as a company perk.

Ollie leans forward and takes my hand and kisses it. I suppress the urge to shudder, but only just. He has rubber lips. Not Mick Jagger-style rubber lips, more like Planet of the Apes-style rubber lips, all pale and limp and trembling. The feeling of them running slowly across my hand and up my arm is not dissimilar to that of a pair of slugs trailing slimily across your body.

Removing his lips from my shoulder, I reluctantly take him through to the sitting room.

Five minutes after Ollie's unwelcome entrance Richard arrives, smiling happily and rubbing his hands in eager anticipation of the evening to come. I doggedly follow him and corner him in the kitchen.

'You little toad!' I hiss venomously at him. 'How dare you set me up with that slime ball!'

Richard grins infuriatingly at me.

'My, my, the worm turns,' he mocks. 'You used to be such a compliant little thing, Felicity.'

He reaches into a cupboard and takes out a bottle of twelve-year-old malt. James got Bell's. He pours the golden liquid liberally into a cut-glass tumbler.

'Be a dear and take this to Ollie.'

The doorbell rings.

'Sorry,' I smile sweetly, 'I'm on door duty.'

I turn and march away. Whoever it is, I reassure myself with the fact that it can't be any worse than Ollie Barton-Davis. I paste a welcoming smile onto my face and reach for the door handle.

I open the door to find Katherine Christian waiting there, immaculate in a shocking-pink Escada suit. Just behind her, stands Alex.

The moment I've been alternately dreading and longing for. I knew we'd eventually meet again. Somehow our lives seem to be inextricably entwined. I'd played out the different scenarios in my head so many times. They usually involved me starting out resistant and good, but always seemed to end up with me naked and in bed. Kat never featured in any of them, though. But here she undeniably is, as egocentric and obnoxious as usual.

'The guest of honour has arrived,' she announces without quite enough light-heartedness to save the statement.

Richard has emerged from the kitchen and kisses her far too casually on both cheeks.

'Kat darling, so glad you could make it.'

Let the games commence.

Richard's apartment is still the same as it always was, Sally has yet to make her mark upon any room except the bathroom where her Dune now sits neatly next to Richard's Safari, and the kitchen, which Richard has always believed is a woman's domain. The other rooms are redolent of Richard's taste alone, although the connection between Richard and actual taste is a dubious one.

Apart from the two long black leather sofas that dominate the sitting room there is little other furniture. The room is sparse in its decoration: no pictures, no plants, not even a framed photograph of the happy couple on their wedding day. A long window dominates the far wall, looking out over Oxford's dreaming spires. In relief against this window is a black and chrome structure which houses Richard's collection of electronic gadgets, hi-fi, speakers, TV, a whole tower block of CDs.

Richard is leaning against the black marble fireplace, playing man of the house. He has an arm draped casually along Sally's shoulders, is rubbing the back of her neck with the ball of his thumb. I think he's doing it to wind Kat up.

If it's not working on Kat, it's working on me. This totally un-Richardlike behaviour is just confirmation that Sally is being used as a pawn in a game. To make matters worse, when she goes back out to the kitchen, Richard tries to introduce me to Alex. Erica and Ollie are talking on the sofa, so this is presumably so that Richard can chat to Kat undisturbed.

'This is my *sister-in-law*.' He laughs, enjoying my discomfort.

'We've met before,' I say quickly. As you bloody well know, I want to shout after him when he and Kat move away from us.

Alex and I have a very stilted conversation.

'It's good to see you again,' I say quietly.

This roughly translates as 'I've missed you like mad', but I'm sure it doesn't come across that way.

'How have you been?' he says, not quite meeting my eyes.

We shoot apart like two magnets with the same polarity.

James sidles back into the room and comes to stand next to me.

'You don't look very happy,' he says, observing my glum face.

'Well, this isn't exactly my idea of a fun evening.'

'Then why did you come?'

'I promised Sally.'

'Me too. She doesn't deserve such loyalty,' he says darkly, casting a fearful glance in Erica's direction.

'I agree.' I follow his gaze. 'But I think your date is a little more acceptable than mine.'

Erica rises from the sofa and attempts to sashay towards us in her unfamiliar high heels.

'Must go to the bathroom,' he mutters.

'Again?' I mock him. 'Feeling a little weak-bladdered, are we?'

Richard slides on a CD. He's a Phil Collins man.

'That's our tune,' sigh Sally and Kat in unison as 'A Groovy Kind of Love' begins to pulse out of the speakers. Fortunately, although I hear both, neither hears the other.

It's Richard's tune actually, I want to tell them.

The one who loved him least is the one who knows him best. He used to play it nonstop when I first met him. He just shares this particular record with whoever happens to be in his life at the time. Makes it easier on the few brain cells he possesses, I suppose.

Although James is still in hiding, Erica seems to have attracted some interest from another quarter. Ollie is smouldering at her.

'I think you have an admirer,' I tell her, indicating his pouting lips and come-hither eyes with an inclination of my head.

'Do I?' She seems surprised but pleased.

'Isn't it obvious? Just look at the way he's looking at you.'

Erica casts a shy glance in Ollie's direction, and is rewarded with what is for him a rather nice smile.

Erica turns pink. She's obviously pleased to be admired. 'Ollie is rather sweet, isn't he?' she murmurs, toying nervously with an earring.

Sweet is not a word I would normally use in association with Ollie Barton-Davis.

'It's just a pity he's not the right person,' she sighs.

'Oh, yes. James,' I say. 'Are you sure he's the right person for you?' I say tactfully.

'Oh, yes, *he* just doesn't know it yet. Still, the course of true love never did run smooth,' she adds philosophically.

'I've always found it such a waste of time and energy wanting someone who doesn't want you.' This is the most tactful way I can think of telling her that James is definitely not interested. 'True love stands a better chance when nurtured by both parties. Trust me, I speak from experience.'

Erica follows my gaze. Richard is showing Alex his hi-fi.

'Yes, um, I never did say . . . that is . . . I'm sorry about what happened between you and Richard. You must have been very upset,' she blusters, misunderstanding.

'I was,' I reply, but I'm not thinking about Richard.

I want desperately for Alex to acknowledge me, but he doesn't. It's so frustrating. We may not be able to have a relationship, but I can still offer him my friendship, can't I? I must convince myself that this is all I want to offer.

Sally sees me frowning and thinks I'm angry because of Ollie. She decides to placate me.

'Dinner's ready, everybody . . .' She touches my arm. 'You go and sit down. You've done enough to help already. I want you to relax and enjoy the rest of the evening.'

How the hell am I going to enjoy the rest of the evening sitting opposite Alex and the delightful Katherine?

Kat is, of course, seated at right angles to Richard.

I slide into my seat. James hurries in, hotly pursued by Erica.

'Do you mind if I sit next to you?' he hisses.

Poor old Erica. I don't know about the eternal triangle, this table is home to the eternal octagon, everybody wanting the wrong person.

I really should say no to James, for Erica's sake. I am ashamed to say that selfishness gets the better of me. I really cannot stand the idea of sitting next to Ollie all evening..

You never know, I tell myself, determined to assuage the guilt, Oliver and Erica might just hit it off. I can see him gazing in admiration at her ample cleavage, while she shoots daggers at me for monopolising James.

'James!' Sally hisses, nodding her head in the direction of the empty chair at the bottom of the table next to Erica.

'I want to sit next to the beautiful Fliss,' he announces, and firmly parks his chino-covered bottom in the seat next to mine.

Everyone glares at James, except for Ollie who is obviously highly delighted at this announcement, sliding into James's unoccupied seat next to Erica and beaming broadly.

Kat, who has already suffered the slug treatment from Ollie—'a very old friend, darling'—has been waiting for James to acknowledge her like the Queen on deb day. She finally realises she has to make the first move, and flicking her long, dark, far too glossy hair back over her shoulder, smiles seductively at James.

'James, darling, how are you?'

'Kat.' He nods curtly in her direction.

'You look surprised to see me here?'

'On the contrary, you always come back, Katherine. Like the proverbial bad penny.' He turns back to me, cutting dead any chance of further conversation.

'That was rather rude,' I whisper in admiration.

'I don't like her. She's a bad influence on Richard,' he snaps.

'I always thought you were the bad influence on Richard,' I tease him.

'I may encourage him to go out and enjoy himself but never to lie and be deceitful, especially not to Sal.'

Alarm bells start ringing again. 'Oh, yes. Do you know something I don't?'

He turns away. 'Forget it,' he mutters gloomily, 'I shouldn't have said anything.'

'Look, James, I know their history. If there's something going on I want to know. It's not fair on Sally-Anne.'

He looks at me. He decides to confide in me. 'I don't know if there is anything going on . . . yet. I'm just going on past form,' he whispers.

'Past form?'

'Well, they were always bouncing off each other like a pair of rubber balls. I'm just worried they're going to collide again.'

A thought which had never really occurred before suddenly hits me. 'He cheated on me with her, didn't he?'

James doesn't reply.

'Didn't he?' I demand in a harsh whisper.

He won't look at me. That's answer enough. How could I have been so blind? I feel a fool. Richard gets an extra point on my bastard rating.

'Look, there's nothing Richard can do to hurt me. It's Sally I'm worried about.'

'Don't worry, Fliss, I'll always look out for Sal,' he says tenderly, gazing over at her, his expression softening.

'This lobster has a very unusual flavour,' comments Ollie.

Sally chokes on her wine. We trade a glance. I can see her mouth curling up at the corners as she fights the urge to laugh.

'You'll have to give me the recipe. I hope it's not complicated, I'm an atrocious cook. What I really need is someone to take care of me.' He gazes meaningfully at Erica.

Am I imagining things or is she fluttering her eyelashes back at him?

'I think those two may have hit it off,' I whisper to James.

'Thank you, God,' he replies. 'If she gets it together with Ollie the Wally, she might just leave me alone You know, I always hoped Sally and I might . . . you know.' James gazes into the bottom of his glass and sighs, then looks back up at me and grins. 'But *que será será* and all that.'

'Sally? Really? I'm sorry, I never knew.'

'I kept my feelings well hidden.' He laughs wryly. 'Too well hidden. I had this little fantasy of making my move at the wedding, best man and chief bridesmaid and all that, but obviously that wasn't appropriate in the end, was it, what with the sudden change in roles.'

'Well, you'd certainly be better for her than he is!'

I think one of the reasons that I currently feel so bloody angry with Richard is that he nearly had me fooled. The way they've been together since the engagement party, I really thought he and Sal could be happy together.

This evening he is chatting up Kat, leaning towards her so that no one else can hear what they are saying. His right hand is under the table.

James follows my gaze.

'I wonder what his hand is doing? You know, he may be my best friend but he can be a right arse at times!' growls James, pouring more wine into his glass and then mine.

Lounging next to me at the end of the table, licking those fat escargot lips like a lascivious lizard, sits Ollie, Erica to his left.

'So tell me about yourself?' He smiles cheesily at her. 'What do you do all day, apart from look beautiful?'

'I'm a PA,' Erica giggles.

'I bet that stands for Perfectly Adorable?'

I cringe, but Erica is obviously unused to unadulterated, unappetising flattery. She goes pink, and attempts a coy smile.

'I need a new PA,' he continues, leaning in towards her. 'Perhaps you could come and work for me. You could sit on my lap and take down my particulars.'

He laughs. It sounds like a small donkey with a large pair of lungs. Hee-haw, hee-haw. He brings a new meaning to the word asinine.

Erica giggles. It's a good job she finds this funny, I'd have slapped the little toad in the face by now.

Richard laughs because Ollie is laughing. Alex and I look at each other. He shakes his head in semi-amused consternation, and I relax a little. At least we're not desperately avoiding each other's gaze any more like infatuated teenagers.

'So what's it like rejoining the world of work after your nice long summer hols then, Fliss?' Richard leans back in his chair at the head of the table and looks at me. 'I don't know why teachers are always complaining about pay when they only have to work for eight months of the year. And let me see now, I do believe it's half-term next week. You must be worn out after working such a long period of time in one go . . .'

I totally ignore him. I know it's rude, but I'm not going to give him the satisfaction of rising to his pathetic little jibes.

'I've always thought it must be so rewarding to pass on knowledge to eager young minds,' sighs Erica. 'What are you doing at the moment?'

'I'm helping ninety-eight puberty-stricken teenagers murder Shakespeare,' I reply far from enthusiastically.

'Oh, I love Shakespeare!' Erica claps her hands together like a child, a movement which makes her boobs judder like two basketballs hitting the hoop at the same time, and Ollie's eyes nearly pop out of his billiard-ball of a head. 'Which play are you doing?'

'*A Midsummer Night's Dream*, but it's more like a Midsummer Nightmare. Every time you say Bottom or Titania, they all collapse into fits of immature giggles.'

'I used to be a bit of a thespian myself,' announces Ollie.

'Until you had the sex change!' guffaws Richard. They laugh heartily. Honestly, they're worse than my upper-fifths! They've perfected this pathetic non-comic double act over the years.

'Methinks I was enamoured of an arsehole,' I murmur.

Alex doesn't look very happy. He's stuck between Kat who is monopolising or being monopolised by Richard, I'm not quite sure which way round yet, and Erica who is being unbelievably attentive to the awful Ollie.

I smile at him.

He raises his eyes to heaven, and smiles back.

The tension's finally broken, but now I can't tear my eyes away. Alex has what Sally and I used to call nuclear eyes. They cause an immediate reaction resulting in total meltdown of your entire body and any living brain cells.

'It's rude to stare,' says James loudly.

I blush and turn away. Alex takes a sudden interest in the tablecloth.

'How's everything in the world of publishing, Alexander?' Richard asks, dragging himself away from Kat. 'I personally think the standard of literature has deteriorated radically in the last decade . . .' Richard launches into this long diatribe about the merits of the latest books. Alex is politely trying to maintain interest.

James leans confidentially towards me. 'I saw you, Fliss Blakeney, making eyes at Mr Christian over there,' he teases me. 'I think I should warn Kathrin' Bligh to watch out, there's mutiny afoot.'

'Don't be so ridiculous!' I snap. 'You're imagining things.'

'"The lady doth protest too much, methinks,"' he quotes. 'Now which Shakespeare special was that from? *Romeo and Juliet* perhaps?'

'You know perfectly well it's from *Hamlet*.'

'I know.' He grins. 'But *Hamlet*'s not quite so apt, now is it? So what gives, Fliss?'

'Absolutely nothing "gives", as you so quaintly put it.' I force a smile, trying to sound as normal as possible. 'Honestly.'

Well, it's the truth, isn't it? Alex is married so nothing can happen, right?

'Good, that means I'm completely at liberty to chat you up.'

He proceeds to do this loudly and unashamedly throughout the main course. I think he must be fuelled by alcohol. James has always drunk like a fish.

James's hand slips beneath the table and along my thigh.

'Silk stockings,' he murmurs lecherously, 'my favourite. Owwww!'

The exclamation of delight turns to a scream of pain as I stick my fork in his hand.

'Er, right, has everybody finished?' Sally tries to re-establish some order by starting to remove empty plates from the table.

'What did you do that for?' James grumbles.

'Do you see "Public Access" printed across my forehead?' I stare haughtily at him.

Sally comes back in bearing dessert: passion fruit ice cream smothered in a wickedly delicious-looking raspberry and orange coulis.

'Everybody for pudding?'

Kat starts virtuously protesting. 'Oh, no. It looks wonderful but I shouldn't. I really ought to be thinking of my figure . . .'

'You've got nothing to worry about,' purrs Richard. 'You've always had a wonderful figure.'

She smirks happily. 'Then I might just succumb.'

'Suck what?' says James, deliberately mishearing, then roaring with laughter.

'Have another drink.' He sloshes more wine into my glass. 'Has anybody ever told you how attractive you are? How about you and me cutting out and going back to my place?'

I look across at Alex.

His face is as frozen as the homemade passion fruit ice cream.

'Oh, this looks wonderful, doesn't it?' I say brightly, accepting far too much ice cream.

'Stop changing the subject.' He looks sideways at me, and grins wickedly. 'Now that Sally is no longer available perhaps you'd care to console me on the loss of what could have been a beautiful relationship?'

James, despite being a terrible lech at the moment, is very attractive. He is also single, solvent, fun to be with. But even I, usually too deeply immersed in Fliss World to spot unhappiness in other people, can tell that he is getting drunk and making advances to me because he's miserable about Sally-Anne. I don't want to try to take my sister's place in his affections. I want to be somebody's first prize.

Unfortunately I know what I want. Alex. But Alex is a forbidden fruit, that ripe juicy delicious pear dangling just beyond your reach on a tree in someone else's garden. James is a good friend, but he's missing that

X-factor that turns a man from a friend into an object of desire. Alex has my desired X-factor in overly large quantities.

It's not fair.

It's only when I stand up to go to the loo that I realise exactly how much wine I've drunk in the past two hours. It's not my fault. Every time I've put my glass back down on the table, James has refilled it. I head fairly unsteadily for the bathroom. Kat is just coming out.

'Oh, it's you,' she says disappointedly upon bumping into me in the narrow dark corridor. She was definitely hoping I'd be Richard, hovering in the hope that he'd follow her out.

'Are you having a good evening?' I can't resist the opportunity to dig for dirt, and Kat's usually happy to dish it.

'Oh, it's lovely to see old friends again, isn't it?' She smiles but this too is false. 'And to see the old place. It hasn't changed very much since I was last here.'

Now that is definitely a barb. Richard moved in here two months after he and I first started seeing each other. Again, I tell myself, I shall rise above it.

'Although I don't know what's wrong with Alex,' she continues. 'He's in such a foul mood.' She smiles smugly. 'I suppose it was rather cruel of me to bring him here when he's aware of the history Richard and I share.'

'Alex is well up on history and *current* affairs,' I say idly, but she's off, back down the corridor.

I lurch into the bathroom and lock the door, peer at my face in the mirror and redo my lipstick. My eyes are bright and my cheeks are flushed. James may be a rebounder, but it's still very nice to be chatted up by him. A boost to the ego and libido.

The thing is, what am I going to do about Kat and Richard? I can't just sit back and let Sal take all the flak. I walk out of the loo and shriek as someone steps out in front of me in the darkened corridor. It's Alex.

'You scared me half to death . . .' I breathe.

He's leaning against the wall, hands in pockets, eyes glittering dangerously in the dim light.

'What the hell do you think you're playing at, Fliss?' he hisses.

'I beg your pardon?'

'With James—what are you playing at?'

'I'm trying to have a good time.'

'Oh, yes, and is your idea of a good time letting some drunk crawl all over you?' He rubs his forehead agitatedly. 'You're driving me crazy, Fliss. Do you think I want to watch you publicly get off with another man?'

'Look, James is just a friend, that's all. If you must know, he's got a thing for Sally-Anne, not me. And besides, who are you to lecture me? You're married, I'm not, I can do what I bloody well want to.'

'I know, I know.' His voice is strained, his eyes narrowed. 'I can't help it, Fliss . . . I can't stop thinking about you.'

Why did he have to say that? This is so difficult. I just about manage to resist hurling myself bodily into his arms.

'What do you want from me, Alex?' I ask, drawing back a little just in case my self-control snaps and I make a lunge for his underpants.

He appears to regain some of his composure. 'More than I should,' he replies. 'Look, I'm really sorry, I shouldn't have had a go at you. You're right, I've got no claim on you.'

'No, but you've got a hold on me, haven't you?'

'Have I, Fliss?'

'I don't have to spell it out, do I? Surely you know how I feel about you?' I mutter reluctantly.

'No, I don't know how you feel! That's the bloody problem. One minute you're all over me, the next you're pushing me away.'

'You really want to know how I feel? I think about you every day. You're always in my head . . . it's driving me crazy. There's hardly a moment goes by without me wondering where you are, what you're doing, whether you ever think of me. And all the time, I know that it's so unbelievably wrong for me to feel this way . . .' I can hear my voice beginning to rise hysterically. I stop, take a deep breath. 'Look, I'm sorry,' I mutter, shaking my head, hardly able to look at him.

Alex shakes his head too, but he's half smiling. 'How come whenever I see you, you're either drunk or apologising?'

'Or both,' I laugh shamefacedly. 'I'm sorry, I'd better stop drinking.'

'No, I'm the one who should say sorry.'

'For what?'

'For this . . .'

He puts two fingers under my chin, gently tilts my face upwards, and kisses me.

'You shouldn't have done that,' I murmur.

'I know, that's why I apologised.'

I reach out and run my fingertips gently down his cheek.

'I think you should apologise again.'

We slide conspicuously out of the corridor and bump straight into Sally-Anne. She looks at my flushed and guilty face, and then at Alex.

'Do you know, you're wearing more of Fliss's lipstick than she is,' she murmurs.

I grin sheepishly. Alex frantically wipes his mouth. We both look back at Sally. It's her move.

She winks at us and carries on into the kitchen.

Sally obviously knows something about Richard and Kat or she wouldn't have just let that go. I follow her into the kitchen.

'Sally?'

She is bending over the open dishwasher, stacking plates. She looks tired. 'Don't ask,' she sighs heavily.

'What do you know?'

'You'd have to be blind and stupid not to miss my husband and Kat falling all over each other all evening. They're playing games with each other at my expense, and I don't like it.' She slams the door shut on the dishwasher, and turns back to face me. 'You warned me, Fliss, but I wouldn't listen to you, would I?'

'Well, we don't know that there's anything going on between them, do we? They've always been flirty with each other. I suppose the fact they're doing it to your face . . .'

'Means they're not doing it behind my back?' She raises her eyebrows.

'This is probably just an ego boost. Richard has such an enormous ego it needs a lot of boosting, believe me,' I offer in an attempt to be light-hearted.

Sally laughs quietly, but she's still not entirely happy.

'And what about you, Fliss?' She puts a hand on my arm. 'What if you get hurt?'

'Me?'

'Don't come the innocent with me, I know what I just saw. What's happening?'

'I'm damned if I know.'

I help her carry the coffee through to the lounge where everyone has adjourned. Ollie is knee to knee with Erica on the sofa. Alex and Richard are talking. Kat is sulking because Richard isn't talking to her. James is pouring himself another whisky. His hands are far from steady.

'Fliss, my angel, where have you been?' He careers across the room towards me, swaying dangerously. 'Come, my darling, I'm taking you home for some coffee and liqueurs. Your car or mine?'

'Don't be so bloody stupid,' Alex glares at him. 'You're in no fit state to drive, and neither is Fliss.'

'Then even better we shall share the back seat of a taxi.' James leers at me and slips an arm round my waist..

'I'll take Fliss home,' Alex says firmly, taking hold of my arm. He stares coldly at James, who quickly releases me.

'Well, I'm not ready to go yet,' says Kat petulantly. 'I want to go through some old photographs with Richard.'

'Why don't you take Fliss and I'll run Kat home later?' Richard smiles at Kat, who stops looking put out and smoulders back at him.

I look at Sally who is pale and drawn. James is looking at her too. He turns to me, takes in Alex's hand on my arm, and winks slowly at us.

'Well, if that's the case, I shall stay and help Sal with the washing-up,' he announces. 'Come along, my darling.' He ushers her into the kitchen.

Richard ushers Kat towards his study, and Alex frog-marches me towards the front door. As we leave, we pass Erica and Ollie necking enthusiastically on the sofa. At last Cupid's arrows have hit the right targets. Both single, they are free to share an uncomplicated and wonderful love affair. I suppress the desire to applaud them.

Alex and I stand silently together, his hand still on my arm as though he's afraid I'm going to bolt, while the lift descends to the ground floor. I half expect a little red light to appear on the display panel, below B for Basement. A big H for Hell, 'cause I'm going straight there.

'I'm supposed to be morally supporting Sally,' I murmur as he shepherds me towards his car. 'How can I morally support someone when I've got no morals of my own?'

We drive back to my flat in silence.

Despite my protestations, I'm savouring every moment, just gazing at his profile as he easily manoeuvres the large car through the dark silent streets. The sheer scent of him is erotic. Isn't it funny how smell evokes more memories than any other sense? Not sight, not sound, but smell.

When we reach my place, he pulls to a halt and switches off the engine. He stares straight ahead. There is silence for what seems like an eternity, and then he begins to speak.

'Do you know how much self-control I've had to exert to stop myself from contacting you?' He turns and looks at me with those amazing eyes, liquid, intelligent, and burning with warmth. 'In fact, I've exercised so much self-control, I don't think I have any left.'

His tense expression softens to a smile as he pulls me towards him.

I suppose this was inevitable really.

The bedroom curtains are open. The room is illuminated by moonlight. He slowly pulls down the zip at the back of my dress, pushes the material away from my shoulders so that it slides easily from my body and falls in a crumpled heap on the floor.

Silently, slowly, I undo his shirt, button by button, until this too falls in a crumpled heap next to my discarded dress. He is obviously not a seasoned adulterer. Surely on the list of adultering do's and don'ts is the use of a coat hanger to ensure clothes remain crease- and evidence-free.

I'm surprised at how shy I suddenly become, but finally, with a little help from Alex, we fall naked together onto the bed. Laughing, caressing, kissing slowly.

He is lean, firm, brown, well built, well hung. His skin is beautifully smooth.

I've wanted him so much for so long.

His fingers slide over my breasts and down my belly, and I'm convulsed with a desire stronger than anything I've ever experienced before.

'I don't normally go to bed with someone on the first date,' I whisper as his tongue follows the route his fingers have just taken.

'We haven't even had the first date,' he murmurs.

'Oh. No, we haven't, have we? Although I suppose this is sensible. If the sex is totally useless we haven't wasted any time or effort going out with each other first.'

He pauses, draws level with me again and smiles, amused.

'Fliss.'

'What?'

'Shut up.'

He silences me with a kiss.

CHAPTER SEVEN

I WAKE ENVELOPED IN A golden haze of well-being. The pillow is still dented where his head lay. I can smell him on my sheets and on my body.

Gazing hazily at the clock on the bedside table, I'm surprised to see that it's gone ten. To think that only nine hours ago he was still lying beside me. I stretch luxuriously, indulgently, running my hands across my own flesh, reliving the feel of his touch. Lazy and hazy with pleasure I feel almost ethereal, like I'm dreaming while I'm still awake.

These pleasant thoughts are unpleasantly disturbed.

The doorbell is sounding frantically. Sighing, but still grinning like an idiot, I slide on my robe and pad barefoot across the room and out into the hall.

A small shaking figure is standing outside my front door, hair slicked back from the rain, face white, eyes puffy and swollen with tears.

'Oh, Fliss,' Sally sobs, falling through the doorway and burying her stricken face in my shoulder. 'He's going to leave me and I can't bear it.'

I park a shaking, sobbing Sally-Anne on the sofa, and wheel out the brandy.

'What happened?' I probe gently.

Sally takes a sip of her drink, pulls a face, blows her nose on one of my tissues, and stops sniffing for long enough to speak.

'Last night, after you went, it was awful, Fliss, really awful. Ollie and Erica shared a taxi home. Richard was nose to nose with *her* on the sofa. James left at two and they were still reminiscing, laughing and touching all the time. I felt like a gooseberry. *Me*, his wife!' She shakes her head in disbelief. 'She stayed for hours!'

'Hours?' I query, ashamed to feel a certain relief in the knowledge that Alex would have got home before Kat.

'Well, of course Richard had to take her home, didn't he?' Sally spits. 'He wouldn't hear of me calling a taxi. It was gone four when he finally came to bed. It doesn't take an hour to drive across town, now does it? And then this morning he made some lame excuse and went out. He said he had to go into work. He never works on a Sunday, Fliss, never, but when I challenged him, he got so angry. Said that he had an important case on and if I didn't believe him I should phone Ollie.'

'And did you phone Ollie?'

'What was the point? Ollie would back up whatever Richard says, and I'd just end up looking like the stupid jealous wife. But then again, I suppose that's what I am, isn't it? The stupid, stupid, jealous wife.' She rubs a hand over her eyes, screwing them up in anguish. 'I know he loves me, Fliss, we just need a chance. If everybody would just leave us alone!'

She knocks back her brandy, and putting the glass on the coffee table begins agitatedly twisting her wedding ring round and round her finger.

'Bloody, bloody Katherine Christian! I've never hated anyone in my life, Fliss, but I loathe that woman. We were fine until she stuck her oar in. Happy, really happy. But now, because of *her*, I'm just waiting for him to go. Any excuse and he'll run to her, Fliss, I know it. If she were free he'd go to her like that.' She clicks her fingers. 'If Alex were to find someone else . . .' She pauses and looks at me.

She doesn't need to go on. I understand what she's trying to say.

As Sally is leaving, the phone begins to ring. It's Alex.

'We need to talk, I'll pick you up in half an hour.'

Just the sound of his voice makes my stomach flutter with desire. I'm sharply aware of the contrast between my happiness and Sally's misery.

He arrives early while I'm still showering. He pulls me against him, kisses me slowly. His hands slide inside my bathrobe, pull me closer. I respond hungrily, but Alex pulls away.

'Get dressed,' he laughs, 'I'm taking you out for lunch.'

'I'd rather stay in,' I murmur in disappointment.

'What about that first date?' He smiles. 'I don't want you to feel like you're missing out.'

Despite a very strong desire to take him back to bed, I smile, touched by the sentiment.

'Where are we going? Somewhere dark, where no one will recognise us?' I joke, rummaging through my wardrobe. 'Where we can hide away in an alcove or duck out of the back door if someone we know comes in.'

We pull up outside an old hotel on the outskirts of the other side of town, The Three Swans. An old coaching inn, still with its high arch leading through to the stables that have now been converted into a very good and very private restaurant. The restaurant consists of a main central area, providing room for about twelve small round tables, and several more discreet booths round the walls, divided by the old wooden stalls topped with iron bars where the horses were housed.

We are led to one of these booths. The table has two cane chairs to one side and a wooden bench seat running along the back.

'This is very secluded for someone who didn't want to hide me away,' I tease Alex.

He smiles and rubs his thumb across the palm of my hand, which he had been holding quite openly. 'I want to be alone with you.'

I slide onto the bench at the back of the booth. Alex sits opposite me with his back to the room, shielded partly from view by the largest aspidistra ever to emerge from soil. The smiling waiter hands us menus. Alex asks for a bottle of Pouilly-Fuissé.

My eyes flick across to Alex, greedily devouring the sight. I long to reach out and touch him. He catches my gaze and holds it. Suddenly embarrassed I look away.

Our waiter is returning, carrying a silver ice bucket and two glasses. As he passes one of the other booths the occupant calls out to him. He pauses, and balancing the glasses on top of the ice in the bucket, pulls a tab of matches from his pocket. As the match flares, the girl takes the man's wrist to steady it as she lights her cigarette, and the orange glow illuminates her face.

'I don't believe it!' My mouth falls open. A feeling of panic begins to rise from my stomach.

'What's the matter?' Alex asks anxiously.

I can only respond by sliding further down in my seat, putting one hand up to cover my face and pointing with the other to a table in an alcove behind us.

Alex turns. It's dark in the restaurant, but the long shining tresses and slender back of Kat Christian are unmistakable. She is wearing a cherry-red jacket belted at the waist and a short skirt which stops halfway down her thighs to expose an expanse of long tanned leg, at the end of which is a Bally court shoe tapping irritably against the floor.

She is sitting with her back to us facing into the booth, but every time the door opens she turns. She is obviously waiting for someone.

'She must have come in just after us,' I hiss. 'What do we do?'

He slides across from his seat onto the bench next to me. 'Of all the bars in all the towns.' Alex smiles wryly at me.

But I'm not laughing, I'm staring at the door, just like Kat, at the person coming in. She stands up as he reaches her. He kisses her lightly on the cheek, then stops, looks deep into her eyes, and leans forward to kiss her on the lips. She responds by twining a hand round the back of his neck and pulling him closer. Self-consciously they break apart, and together Kat and Richard slide into the shadows at the back of their booth.

'What the hell is *he* doing here!' Alex growls, then shakes his head. 'I might have guessed.' The waiter, who has been opening our bottle of wine, pours a little into Alex's glass and waits for approval.

'It's fine, thank you,' Alex dismisses him, looking back over to where his wife and her lover are seated, entwined in the shadows. Richard and Kat are openly necking now. I watch in horrified fascination as he slides his hands under her blouse and begins to knead her full breasts like dough. I can't believe what I'm seeing. It may be dark and secluded, but it's still blatantly obvious what they're doing.

'Come on, we're leaving.' Alex stands up and throws a wad of notes down on the table without even counting them.

'We can't! What if they see us?' I panic.

'Do you think they'll notice anything but each other?' he growls.

He grabs my hand and pulls me after him, striding quickly across the crowded room to the fire exit which is closer than the main doors. The heavy door falls silently to behind us, and we find ourselves in an alleyway at the side of the restaurant.

It's raining heavily now. The gash of sky above us, an eight-foot gap between buildings, is smoke-grey and dirty.

Alex pulls me round to face him. It's hard to read the mixture of emotions registering in his eyes and across his face but suddenly I feel desperately unsure of everything. He puts out a hand and pushes my already soaked hair away from my face. I can see fine droplets of water clinging to his eyelashes.

Hesitantly I reach out to him, pull him close, press my lips against his. He returns the pressure, kissing me softly, slowly. All the time his eyes are looking into mine as if searching for something. Abruptly his kiss gets harder. He backs me up against the wall, hooks his thumbs under the hemline of my skirt and pushes it up over my hips. I can feel the hard pressure of his thigh insinuated between my legs.

The wall against my back is harshly abrasive through the thin material of my shirt. He's kissing me so hard I can't breathe, his fingers pressing into the bare soft flesh at the top of my thighs.

I can't help responding. My mouth falls open under his; my fingers caress the back of his neck. Just as suddenly his touch becomes more gentle, his kiss less urgent. I'm almost collapsing with desire, my legs are trembling . . . and then I think of Sally-Anne, silently begging me with her huge sad eyes. I think of Alex's face at the sight of Richard with Kat, ablaze with anger . . . or was it jealousy?

I pull away.

'Was that for me or for Kat?' I whisper.

'What?'

Suddenly desperately insecure, I have to ask. 'Do you want me, or do you just want to get back at your wife? I want you to be honest with me.'

He steps away and looks at me in disbelief. His eyes are hard with disappointment. 'Have you any reason to think I never have been?' he asks me.

'I want to know whether you really care about me or whether you're just playing games like Katherine? Am I a bit of tit for tat? I saw how angry you were in there.'

'You think I'm like Kat or Richard, that I'm only using you? Is that how you see us, Fliss, as a sordid little affair?'

'I don't know,' I wail plaintively.

'You're the one playing games with me, Fliss. You can't keep pulling me in and then shoving me away, you've got to make up your mind what you want.'

'I know what I want, but . . . but . . . I want to do the right thing.' It sounds so bloody trite.

'And what the hell is the right thing anyway?' he mutters angrily.

'I don't know. I just know you're married so this is wrong.'

'Married!' He almost spits the word. 'After what we just witnessed, you still think my marriage means anything? Come on, Fliss, if you don't want to see me, at least tell me why. Be honest with me, you owe me that much.'

'I am honest with you.'

'Honest with me? I'm not sure you can even be honest with yourself.'

He turns and begins to walk away. I stand rooted to the spot, in a tumult of emotion. He's right. How long has it taken me to admit how I feel about him? And now I'm letting him walk away again. I'm shaking from cold, frustration, helplessness, fear.

He's only gone a few paces when he turns back to me.

'Come on, I'll take you home.'

We drive to my flat in silence.

As he pulls in to the kerb, he grabs my hand.

'Fliss, I need to know how you feel about me. What you want from me. What you want *us* to be.'

I look at him sideways, and feel desperate with wanting him.

'All I know is I've never felt this way about anybody before, but everything's just so bloody complicated.' I can feel the tears flooding down my cheeks, and turn away in embarrassment.

'Please don't cry.' His voice is gentle and full of anguish. He pulls me close, stroking my hair, soothing me like a child.

'I thought, because you were so angry, that you were jealous of Kat and Richard,' I sob.

'No.' He shakes his head. 'I wasn't happy, but I wasn't jealous. It just brought it home to me, that's all. Fliss, I don't want clandestine meetings in secluded restaurants or soulless hotel rooms. What I feel for you isn't something wrong and dirty, to be hidden away like some dark and disgusting secret.' He looks at me warily under soft dark lashes, his eyes cloudy and uncertain. 'I know what I want. I'm going to leave Kat, Fliss.' He kisses me with infinite tenderness.

My stomach dissolves like Alka-seltzer in a glass of water. Bubbles of lust rise from my groin to my throat, and escape in an involuntary moan of pleasure.

'Do you know what you want, Fliss?'

I know what I want. I want this moment to be frozen so that I can stay here for ever, being held by him, so close. And then I think of Sally-Anne, silently begging me not to give Kat the push she needs to take Richard away for good.

I draw away from Alex. 'I want you to go home, Alex, go back to Katherine, make it work if you can.' The words almost choke me and the pain as I see the surprise and hurt in his eyes is almost unbearable.

'What? But I thought . . .'

I put two fingers to his lips to silence him.

'It will be better for everybody. I know Kat must love you, Alex.' I force a smile. 'How could she not?' I pause. 'And Sally-Anne loves Richard . . .'

He nods slowly, registering this last, and then exhales deeply, audibly, a long, sad sigh of resignation.

'I think I understand.'

'Do you, Alex? I really need to know that you do.'

'Sure.' He strokes my cheek. I can feel his hand trembling.

I wake the next day feeling empty and horrible. I'm all cried out, but my spirits are leaden. They lie like a dead weight in the pit of my stomach, physically hurting. Can you understand what it's like wanting someone so badly, needing someone so much that every second spent without them feels like a lifetime? The rain has stopped and a pale yellow sun is smiling weakly in a cerulean sky. I want the black clouds to come back, they suit my black mood.

When the phone rings I pounce upon it like a starving man on a crust of bread.

It's Dad.

He's happy, he's relaxed, he's enjoying life. He wants to share this with me, especially when he realises that I am currently wallowing in the exact opposite frame of mind.

'It's half-term this week, isn't it? Why don't you come and stay, Fliss? I miss you, and it will do you good to get away from everything for a few days. Besides, I want you to meet Florrie.'

Sure, but does Florrie want to meet me? I finally give in and agree to visit. As usual I'm running away. When the going gets tough, Fliss gets going. I head into town to buy a suitcase—my only decent one's still at Caroline's along with half of my clothes. I think she's holding it to ransom to make me visit.

When I return, halfway through packing the phone rings again. A surge of hope, but it's not Alex.

Why should I expect him to call when I was the one who sent him away? Reeling him in and then out like a yo-yo tied to my finger.

This time it's Sash.

'Hiya!' Her cheery voice rings painfully in my miserable ear. 'How are you doing, you old tart?'

Well, of course, it all comes flooding out, doesn't it? Running true to form as a bloody good friend, she listens until I'm totally whinged out, and then announces that she's coming round.

'But you're at work,' I sniff.

'Well, I've suddenly developed severe PMT. My boss is terrified of PMT, he'll send me home straight away.'

Sure enough, Sash is round in half an hour, bearing a bottle of brandy.

'I want all the gory details first,' she demands, making us both a coffee and tipping a liberal dose of Napoleon's finest into each mug, ignoring my protests that it's only three in the afternoon.

'You mean the sex, don't you?'

'Of course. Come on, Fliss, neither of us has actually had any for so long, talking about it is almost as good as the real thing.'

I can't help it, a slightly smug smile spreads slowly over my face. 'Well, let's just say up until Saturday night I might even have gone so far as to say talking about it is actually *better* than indulging . . .'

'But not any more?' she prompts me.

'Definitely not any more.'

'That good?'

'Oh yes. In a way it would have been better if it hadn't been so good, then it would have been easier to give it up. Oh, Sash, it's all such a mess.'

'Well, I hate to harp on about one thing, but at least now you know what it's like to have great sex.'

'True, but that definitely makes it worse. I may never have mind-blowing, all-consuming, let's do it straight away, great sex ever again.'

'Well, I can sympathise on that front.'

'Oh, Sash, I'm sorry. Here I am moaning away when you've got plenty of problems of your own, and I haven't even asked about them once.'

She shakes her head. 'Don't worry about it, babe. I should be thanking you, actually.'

'For what?'

'Well, one of the reasons I phoned today was to call you in on that favour I spoke to you about.'

I bite my bottom lip. 'Yeah, right, you wanted me to be your alibi, didn't you?'

'Well, I did, but actually I've changed my mind.'

'Why?'

'You've made me realise how lucky I am. Life has seemed so mundane recently. All kids, and work, and bills, and a husband that I love but know just a little bit too well at the moment. I've been craving excitement. And you've made me see that excitement can sometimes be overrated. I don't really want to lose what I've got. If I start playing around then there's a very strong chance I will, and just end up being miserable instead of frustrated, or both. No, I think if I just spice up my own life a little, I could be very happy. Sod the twenty-two-year-old, I think a trip to Ann Summers and a baby sitter will do nicely as a starter.'

'Instead of a raging affair with some young stud?'

'You've hit the nail on the head.'

'Glad I could help.'

'I should think it's nice to know that your own dreadful mistakes can have a good effect on somebody else.'

The following morning I set off for Kent, leaving an answering-machine message that will give my mobile number in case of emergency.

As I carry the cat up to the flat above, she begins to purr again for the first time in weeks.

'I think you'd better keep her, you obviously belong together,' I say ruefully to the girl upstairs.

They both look highly delighted.

'Never did like cats anyway,' I mutter as I descend the stairs two at a time in a fit of reckless pique. 'I think it's about time I got that dog.'

Half an hour later, still not quite believing that I'm actually doing it, carefully sidetracking all the practicalities of dog ownership like the fact that I live in a flat and work full-time, I'm walking along cell block H of the local dog rehoming centre. Row upon row of unwanted, unloved, sad, excited dogs.

'Can I have them all?' I ask the handler who's showing me round.

She smiles indulgently. She's obviously used to mad lonely women looking for a man substitute.

I walk up and down the corridor, like an expectant father awaiting the birth of a child, filled to the brim with indecision and compassion.

And then I see him.

He's brown, he's fat, he's completely unrecognisable as a breed. He's sitting right at the back of a large cage on his own, while the rest of the pack clamours at the wire for me to notice them, and he looks miserable.

I look at him. He looks at me.

'That's the one.' I don't point, it would be rude.

'Are you sure?' The assistant looks at me as though I'm stupid.

I nod enthusiastically. 'He's mine.'

'He's only a puppy, he'll grow bigger.'

'Bigger than that?' I say incredulously.

'I thought you wanted a small dog, madam, due to lack of space?'

'I'll move,' I say adamantly, and mean it.

I recognise something in those doleful, hopeful brown eyes. Myself.

I crouch down and wiggle my fingers through the wire mesh. He looks over at me, looks around as if to say, Surely she can't mean me, she must be wiggling at someone else, and then sort of shrugs and ambles over trying not to look too hopeful. He sniffs my fingers cautiously then looks up at me with the cutest brown eyes, and grins.

I fall in love instantaneously.

'Can I take him now?' I ask the assistant.

On my way out of town, with Eric the dog on a blanket on the back seat, I realise I have taken the route that leads past Alex's office. I can see his car in the car park. I wonder which of the many windows blinking hazily in the morning sun is his. I wonder what he's doing, what he's thinking. Does he think of me as often as I think of him? Does he feel the same dull pain, born from the futility of wanting someone you can't have?

I shiver, although it's far from cold, and angrily brush away a tear that's dared to slide from my right eye.

Eric, who is pretending to sleep, hears me sniff and opens one eye. He squeezes between the two front seats and clambers onto my lap, settling down with a deep contented sigh. He must weigh about three stone, and every time I change gear he almost slides down my leg and jams against the throttle, but he's warm, and solid, and comforting.

He must be uncomfortable with his head in the side pocket and his fat backside hanging over the handbrake, but he shows no inclination to move, and I have absolutely no inclination to make him. It's very nice to be unconditionally adored for a change.

CHAPTER EIGHT

THE ROUTE TO FLORENCE'S COTTAGE takes me through the Chilterns, practically straight past Angels Court. I drive one mile further on, before exhausting every argument against it and turning back. When I get to the gates that lead to the house, I hesitate.

It's nine thirty. David will have gone off at least four or five hours ago to toil away on his beloved farm, so at least I shan't have to face both him and Caro at the same time, which should make things a little easier.

I drive slowly down the gravel driveway and pull to a halt next to Caro's immaculately clean Golf GTi. I've always wondered how she can keep her car so clean living in the country, but then she's always been more lady of the manor than Farmer Giles's wife. Or should that be Lady Chatterley? Then again Lady Chatterley restricted her extramarital bonking to just the gamekeeper, didn't she?

Looking in the mirror, I'm surprised to catch myself smiling.

As I step from the car the sun beats down upon my bare head. A lone bee is skimming the great clumps of buddleia and roses massed round the front lawn, and a pair of bluetits dart across it. An Indian summer has crept up on us, drying the damp grass.

I hesitate before pushing the doorbell. Taking a strong mental grip, I manage to connect with my finger and press.

Caro swings open the door. She is wearing an old shirt of David's spattered with yellow paint, cut-off jeans and faded espadrilles. Her golden hair is loosely secured at the back of her neck, and her face is bare of make-up. She looks totally amazing as usual.

'Hi.' I smile tentatively.

The surprise on her face changes instantaneously to delight.

'Fliss! How lovely!' She reaches out to hug me, hesitates and takes my hand instead, drawing me inside.

'Hannah's out, she'll be so disappointed she missed you.'

'I can't stop long.' I point to where Eric is hanging out of the back window of my car. 'Can't leave him in there. I'm just on my way down to visit Dad.' Eric is already proving useful in the excuse department.

'You've got a dog? When did you get a dog?' Caroline exclaims.

'About an hour ago.'

'Why on earth have you got a dog? You don't even have a garden, Fliss.'

'I know. Don't worry, I'll figure out the practicalities as I go along. I think I'd like to move to somewhere bigger anyway, and Edwin the caretaker at school brings his dog into work every day, so perhaps I could too.'

'Sure, but that's a bit different. He spends a lot of time outside, you're stuck in a classroom.'

'Well, Eric's very good at looking attentive. I can sit him at the front of my class as a good example, and teach him Shakespeare. He'll probably grasp it better than most of my pupils.'

'What about the cat?'

'We decided an amicable separation would be best for both of us,' I reply.

Caro laughs. 'Fliss, you're mad. Absolutely barking!' she jokes.

I hang back, unsure what to do or say, but she has no such reticence. 'Come and see the baby's room, I'm dying to show it off to someone.' She takes me upstairs to the room beyond theirs.

'I know I'm ahead of myself, but I thought I may as well get started.'

'It looks like you've nearly finished.'

The spare bedroom has been transformed into a nursery with lemon walls, enough toys to start a creche, mobiles dancing lightly in the breeze that blows through the open window, and a lemon-washed wooden cot and matching wardrobe.

'Well, you know me, once I get an idea into my head . . . I know it's early days yet with Hannah, anything could happen really.' She superstitiously touches the wooden edge of the cradle. 'But David and I have made a decision that if this doesn't work out, we're going to try for a baby of our own.'

'But I thought . . .'

'IVF, adoption, whatever it takes. I never realised how much I wanted a child until now,' she says wistfully, then, forcing a smile onto her sad face, she surveys the room with pride. 'It's all my own work, you know. I think I have quite a flair for this sort of thing.'

'It's great,' I agree, 'very professional.'

'Could make a good sideline for when I'm not changing nappies, don't you think? Caroline Hunter Interiors has quite a ring to it.'

'What about school?'

'Well, actually, I wanted to talk to you about that. I think it's time I had a change,' Caro continues bluntly, 'so I've decided to leave.'

'I thought you might,' I reply. 'I shall miss you.'

'Will you?' She looks at me sideways.

'Of course I will.'

'Good,' says Caro. 'But of course you'll come to visit often, won't you?' She looks at me, eyes hopeful and questioning.

'Of course I will,' I agree, and she smiles in relief.

There's a moment's silence.

'You look great,' I venture. 'Hannah's pregnancy suits you.'

'I can't believe how excited I am about this.' She smiles and then looks anxiously at me, peering at the dark circles under my eyes, pursing her lips in concern. 'But how are you, Fliss? I must say, you look tired.'

There's a sign up at work. 'Do you feel most of the following?' it asks. I ticked them off one by one. Loss of energy? Yes. Tearfulness? Yes. Guilt? Yes. 'You could be depressed,' it announces happily at the end.

'Life is rather complicated at the moment,' I offer, but I'm not in the mood for a heart-to-heart, and Caro is far too intuitive to press for information at the wrong moment. Feeling comfortable enough to forget the excuse that I'm in a hurry, we take a jug of weak Pimm's out onto the lawn and sit on wrought-iron chairs under the apple trees, as we did earlier in the summer.

Eric, released and watered, wanders round the vast lawn incredulously sniffing as though never having seen such exciting things as trees and grass before, lifting his legs in a very wobbly amateur way against anything upright, peeing as though he'll never get another chance.

'He's just been sprung from canine jail,' I explain to Caroline, who smiles indulgently, though whether at me or at Eric I don't know.

'Who'd have thought we'd have weather like this at the end of October?' she breathes happily. She turns and puts a hand over mine, her blue eyes direct and warm with affection. 'I'm so glad you came, Fliss. Really I am.'

'So am I,' I agree, squeezing her hand. 'I think I've laid a few ghosts.'

'Well, I suppose that's better than laying the neighbours!' she laughs.

I finally head off just before midday, cruising fairly well down the M40, then crawling my way along the hideously busy M25, which is bumper to bumper with half-term holidaymakers, finally hitting the civilised beauty of Royal Tunbridge Wells just after three.

Ten miles on and things are getting pretty rural. The road I'm following is little more than a track; I have to stop every five minutes to open and close a gate. Eric thinks it's a great game to leap out of the car every time I do and let me chase him round the fields before we get back in again.

The dog obviously has a warped sense of humour.

I think I like it.

I reach my destination as the church clock strikes five. Bishops Cross is a tiny hamlet, hidden at the bottom of a valley, surrounded by a mantle of woodland. Apart from the church, which is situated in the grounds of Wakeley Hall, there are a few stone cottages dotted round a handkerchief-sized village green complete with pond and obligatory ducks. There is also a picture-postcard pub—Dad wouldn't live in a place that didn't have at least one of these—and a small post office, hung with riotously coloured hanging baskets.

It's so gorgeously quaint I almost expect to see Noddy and Big Ears tootling down the main street in their little red car. It's the sort of place that instantly makes you feel better about the world.

Florence's house is hidden away down some back lane that seems to wind on for ever under a canopy of dark golden beech trees. I finally pull up outside Bluebell Cottage.

I'm suddenly so nervous it's untrue. I'm overcome with shyness.

I manage to get out of the car only to sit on the bonnet for another ten minutes, trying to pluck up the courage to go and knock on the door.

What if I don't like the love of my father's life? Worse still, what if she doesn't like me?

Bluebell Cottage is long and low, and made of crumbling yellow stone. Ivy crawls up its walls. A lone swift is catching the flies that hang in a cloud above me. She swoops and snaps, flies away to disappear under the eaves, and moments later circles back, accompanied by another of her dark sleek ilk.

I look closer. There are several muddy brown upturned igloos nestled under the eaves.

'I see you're admiring my swifts? They've normally left me by now, but perhaps they knew this glorious weather was on the agenda.'

Florence walks towards me across the immaculate lawn.

It has to be Florence. Dad told me that she is beautiful, and it would appear that he wasn't exaggerating in the way that you do when you're in love with someone and everything about them seems attractive. The sun seems to follow Florrie across the garden, lighting on her white-blonde hair like a halo. She moves a little stiffly, yet gracefully. As she comes closer, I can see that her face is lined, her smile easy, and her bright eyes the colour of a bluebell.

'You must be Fliss. Do you mind if I call you that? Your father talks of you so often, I feel as though I already know you.' She extends a slim hand. 'You must call me Florrie. We're in the back garden, your father and I, making the most of this miraculous weather.'

She leads me round the side of the cottage. The rear garden is a riot of autumn flowers, sadly battered by the recent storms but now recovering in the gentle Indian summer sunshine. Dad is seated at a white wrought-iron table, reading Dick Francis. Roger lies panting at his feet. Dad looks strong and brown. The years have fallen away from him. He reminds me a little of the flowers, battered by a life with stormy, wintry Miriam and now being nursed back to health by sunny late-summer Florrie.

He gets to his feet when he sees me coming, a huge grin splitting his craggy face from ear to ear. He reaches out to me, envelops me in a long-armed hug.

'Darling! How wonderful to see you.'

He smells comfortingly of childhood memories, of pipe tobacco and the distinctive smell of lamb's wool sweater.

'What do you think of my daughter then, Florrie?' he proclaims proudly, releasing me. 'Didn't I tell you she was beautiful?'

SARAH HARVEY

'He said the same thing to me about you,' I say shyly.

Florrie laughs. I can see her smiling at my father. Her eyes are coy, like a young girl in the first flush of love.

'He's an old flatterer,' she chides, her voice full of affection.

'I hope you don't mind, but I brought an extra guest with me,' I venture uncertainly.

'You did?' Dad is curious but unperturbed. 'A male guest perhaps?' he asks, voice full of innuendo.

'As a matter of fact, yes, he is,' I tease. 'He's waiting in the car. He's a little nervous, doesn't get out much, hasn't quite picked up the usual social skills . . .' I confide in a whisper.

Dad nods in understanding. 'Well, let's go and put the poor chap out of his misery then, shall we? The sooner introductions are over the better.'

We walk back round the house towards my car. Dad rests a hand on my shoulder. 'I must say,' he smiles happily, 'I'm rather glad you've found yourself another chap . . .' He stops as we reach the car.

Eric is leaning in friendly fashion out of the window.

Dad starts laughing. 'Well, hopefully he'll be easier to train than a new man.'

'And more loyal,' I add.

Florrie treads softly up the path and joins us.

'What a lovely little chap,' she murmurs, stroking his head.

'I'd hardly call him little.' Dad wipes his eyes with his handkerchief. 'What is it, Fliss?'

'A dog,' I say defensively.

'Are you sure? He looks more like a pot-bellied pig to me,' Dad guffaws, then looks apologetically at my uptight protective expression.

'I don't know,' I mutter. 'Heinz probably.'

'Well, I think he's wonderful.' Florrie smiles reassuringly at me. 'Lovely nature obviously.'

I decide that Florrie has a lovely nature, too, as Eric rewards her with a curling kiss on the inside of her wrist.

'You don't mind me bringing him, do you?' I ask uncertainly.

'We certainly don't, do we, darling?' Dad squeezes Florrie's arm. 'But what Roger will make of him, I do not know!'

We return to the back garden. Eric immediately introduces his nose to Roger's backside. Roger delicately removes himself from Eric's nasal intrusion, circling him, thumping his tail slowly and warily.

'We'll take them for a stroll together,' Dad suggests. 'Are you coming with us?' He turns to Florrie, who shakes her head.

'You go, I have dinner to see to.'

324

Dad and I go through a gate at the rear of the garden into the wood that surrounds it. We follow a twisting path strewn with leaves turning crisp as toast in the unusual warmth, and then walk through the beautiful parkland of the Hall.

Stately lawns, statuesque oak trees, sweeping vistas. It's all so beautiful. Dad proudly points out the local landmarks. He takes me to see the crumbling grey Bishop's Cross itself, erected in memory of an historical event.

He doesn't press me for information or news from home, simply chats about our surroundings, about his new garden, about how happy Roger is to be living in the countryside. We need to talk, but I'm grateful that he knows that now is not quite the right time.

We walk arm in arm back to the house as the sun is slowly sinking behind the trees, casting a soft warm orange glow over the green and russet leaves.

Outside Bluebell Cottage, Dad pauses and takes my hand.

'This place is more of a home to me than The Beeches ever was,' he says. 'Always remember, it's not the bricks and mortar, it's the people that make a place welcoming. Florrie and I want you to think of the cottage as a second home, Fliss.'

She is waiting with a welcoming smile. I'm still shy of her. We tread around each other, smiling, polite, unsure.

After dinner we sit drinking coffee round the open fire. Mozart is playing on the old gramophone. Roger is stretched out on the hearthrug. I am seated on the floor with my back against the floral chintz sofa, Eric stretched heavily across my legs, snoring quietly. Dad and Florrie are sitting together, discreetly holding hands. When the small German clock atop the Adam fireplace finally strikes midnight, I suddenly realise how very weary I am.

I think of where I was this time four nights ago, and sigh heavily. If only I could jump through time at will I'd just keep going back to the same moment when I was lying naked in the arms of Alexander Christian.

Dad is watching me intently. 'Are you all right, Fliss? There's something wrong, isn't there?' he probes gently.

'No, of course not,' I lie, scratching Eric behind his ears. 'I'm fine, just a bit tired, that's all.'

Dad shakes his head. 'You can't pull the wool over my eyes. I've known you far too well for far too long not to know when you're upset about something. You've been so quiet all evening.'

'It's a man, isn't it?' says Florrie intuitively. 'It has to be a man, they seem to be the main source of misery.'

Dad raises his bushy eyebrows at her. 'Oh, yes?'

'Oh, and of course a source of infinite happiness,' she laughs. 'If one's lucky. Which I am.'

She squeezes my father's hand and they both smile indulgently at each other.

'Well, Fliss?' he asks in concern.

'Nothing's wrong, honestly, I'm just a little tired like I said. It's been a long day. Actually, I think I might go up to bed.'

'Of course.' Florrie gets quickly to her feet. 'I'll help you take the rest of your things up.'

My room is a quaint little place tucked away under the eaves. Its sloping ceiling is too low for Dad to stand up straight, even at the highest point. It's painted a delicate rose pink, and the throw on the bed and curtains at the little paned window are tiny rose print. A huge cream earthenware bowl full of meadow flowers sits on the tallboy. The floor is of bare boards with a raffia rug of palest pistachio green thrown across.

'I hope you like it?' Florrie says anxiously. 'That's Elliot.' She indicates a huge shaggy brown bear seated on a Lloyd Loom chair in the corner. 'Drew thinks I'm daft, but I thought you might like the company.'

'Well, good night, dear.' Dad leans over, kisses my cheek and ruffles my hair like I'm a ten-year-old again. 'Sleep tight.'

A door at the other end leads into a tiny shower room.

All I want to do is fall into bed and sleep, but I feel dusty and dirty and horrible so I drag my weary body under the shower. I wish I hadn't had to wash for the past three days. Not because I'm a disgusting tramp who likes to be stinky, but I hated washing away the smell and the touch of Alex from my body.

I haven't washed the pillow that his head lay against, though. It's faded, but I can still distinguish his scent on it.

I have a sad confession to make. I head for my overnight bag and pull back the main compartment zip. Sitting inside is that pillow. Carefully pulling it out, I press my face into the soft cotton, and breathe in heavily. I feel like a sad perverted knicker sniffer.

To my chagrin, the smile that this thought induces begins to wobble pathetically, and the next thing I know the tears begin to fall again.

I wake at ten the next morning, still hugging the pillow as though my life depends on it. I must have cried myself to sleep. I feel stupid and pathetic, but a whole lot better for being so stupid and pathetic.

I shower again, then make my way downstairs. I can see Dad in the garden kneeling arthritically by a border deadheading delphiniums. I've never seen him look so happy and contented, especially not while gardening. Back at The Beeches he used the garden as a means of escape from Mother; now his objective is pure pleasure.

Roger is lying loyally and lazily by Dad's side. Eric is chasing Roger's tail, which is wagging slowly from side to side like a pendulum. Backwards and forwards he goes, never seeming to tire of his fruitless monotonous chase. I wish I had his energy.

Another beautiful day has dawned. The sun is streaming through the gauzy curtains, lighting on the old dark oak furniture. On top of the baby grand piano, taking pride of place at the end of the room like a queen holding court, are numerous framed photographs.

I wander over and pick up an old print of a handsome, laughing young man leaning against the bonnet of a vintage Morgan.

'That's my husband Alan. He died a long time ago.'

I turn. Florrie is standing behind me.

'He was very handsome,' I say.

'Oh, the cream of the crop.' She smiles.

She picks up another photograph, holding it out to me. 'That's my lovely daughter, Helen. Her husband Peter behind her, well, he's American. They live in Florida so I don't see them very often.' Her voice is wistful, and then full of pride as she picks up another photograph of a very pretty child. 'And this is my granddaughter, Abbie. She's four now.'

'You must miss them.'

'Oh, yes, very much. I haven't seen them since this photograph was taken, but Helen writes to me often. We have quite a correspondence going!'

I pick up another photograph of a brown-eyed little girl with golden skin and hair. It takes a moment for me to realise that I'm looking at a picture of myself. Next to this is a picture of Dad, Sally-Anne and me. I think it was taken one summer in France. I was seventeen, with wild hair and long lanky legs in cut-off jeans. Wow, was I ever that slim? Sally was just ten, small, slim and dark, huge eyes in a small pale face, but still as pretty and serene. Dad has his arms round our shoulders and is grinning broadly. Beyond that is a photograph of me at my graduation, and one of a young Sally as an angel in a Christmas nativity play. Then the three of us perched on a lion at the foot of Nelson's Column.

'You see, I know you all by proxy.' Florrie smiles affectionately, hesitantly, and I suddenly realise that she is as desperate for me to like her as I was nervous about her liking me. 'You've been rather like an extended family to me,' she says almost apologetically.

Florrie has photographs of Sally's wedding, too. There's even one of me, as I predicted, all hat, lips and legs, but fortunately no face.

'Your father got them for me,' she says wistfully. 'I would really have loved to have been there.'

'I wish you had been.' I turn and smile broadly at her. 'I could have done with a friend.'

'The sun's past the yardarm,' announces Dad, hauling his long frame from one of the low chintz sofas. 'Anyone for a jar?'

'Goodness!' Florrie looks up at the pretty grandmother clock ticking quietly in the corner. 'Is it that time already? You two go, I must start lunch.'

'Are you sure?' I ask. 'I'd like you to come.'

She looks pleased, but still refuses. 'Of course I'm sure. You two have some catching up to do.' She and Dad exchange a glance. In other words he is to have some time alone with me in order to attempt to worm out whatever terrible secret is making his elder daughter such a misery guts.

'We should stay and help you with lunch,' I say, not at all sure I'm ready for the third degree.

'Nonsense, you're a guest.'

'Well, why don't you come and join us when you're ready?' I reach out and touch her hand. 'Honestly, I'd really like you to.'

The White Horse is small and low, made of crumbling white lime with black beams, holding it together like the whale bones in a corset pinioning a genteel old lady. As we enter the cosy, smoky gloom, Dad is hailed from all sides. He's obviously a regular. It's really odd to think that these people have known my father for over six years, even though this part of his life is totally new to me.

'Hello, Evan.' Dad hails a short, swarthy man behind the bar.

'Afternoon, Drew, the usual?' He reaches for a bottle of whisky perched upon the top shelf. 'No Roger?' he queries.

'I've got better company today.' Dad smiles and squeezes my hand. 'This is my elder daughter, Fliss.'

'Daughter? No! I don't believe it. How did a hoary old sod like you produce a beautiful young girl like this then?'

We take our drinks outside, and sit on one of the beer-stained benches overlooking the village green.

'Your health.' Dad raises his glass. 'Well, what do you think of my Florrie then?' There's obvious pride in his voice.

'She's lovely,' I reply, pleased that I can answer truthfully.

'I knew you'd like her.' He smiles in relief. 'She likes you too, you know, a lot, I can tell. I've been so happy since moving down here, my darling, it makes me wonder how I managed to stay with your mother for so long.'

I've often wondered that too.

'You know, it's such a relief to get everything out in the open. I was ashamed of myself, Fliss. I mean, no matter what the circumstances, it's still wrong, isn't it? Having an affair? No matter how badly I got on with your mother she was . . . is still . . . my wife. It entails an awful lot of guilt.'

He's telling me! Guilt still flies in ever-decreasing circles around my head, the old ever-present vulture on the wing.

'I still feel guilty about what's happened,' Dad continues, 'but at least I'm not creeping around making excuses and lying to people about where I've been or where I'm going.'

I stay silent.

He sips his whisky and then, opening a packet of plain crisps, he begins to feed some ducks that have wandered over from the pond on the green in search of sustenance.

'How's your mother?' he asks, crumbling crisps on to the ground, not looking at me.

'Oh, busy making Sally's life a misery as usual.'

'Oh dear.' Dad sighs.

'She won't leave them alone. Richard probably thinks he's married Sal and Mother, not just Sal. The way things are going they don't stand a chance. I mean, things are ropy enough with this other business, they don't need Mother on their backs the whole time as well.'

'Other business? What other business?' He looks worried.

It's my turn to say, 'Oh dear.' I put my hand over my mouth, like a schoolgirl who's just let slip a secret.

'Fliss, if there's a problem, you never know, I may be able to help.'

'OK,' I say reluctantly. 'I'll tell you. The problem is, where do I start?'

'You see, if Alex and I . . . well, if he left Kat then there'd be nothing to stop her from running straight to Richard,' I finish lamely, and look from Dad to Florrie who has walked up to join us.

'Oh, Fliss,' Dad sighs, 'what a mess. I should have stayed and made sure you were all right.'

'Don't be silly, Dad. Besides, what could you have done?'

'I could have kept your stupid mother from interfering in Sally and Richard's marriage for a start,' he says angrily. 'I might have known she wouldn't leave them alone. I feel so guilty.'

'You're telling me,' I groan. 'If it's anybody's fault then it's mine. When I left Richard I never even dreamt the consequences would be so awful.'

'You weren't to know what would happen,' Dad defends me quickly.

'Yes, but I knew about Kat and Richard's relationship before I . . . well, before Alex and I . . .' I trail off, then try again. 'I mean, it's bad enough that Alex is *married*, let alone the fact that he's married to her! "Thou shalt not covet another man's wife", and all that. I could be really literal here and say that there is absolutely no mention of not coveting another woman's husband, but we all know the truth, don't we?' I sigh, resting my chin in my hands.

Florrie looks embarrassed.

'I'm sorry,' I gasp as I realise what she may think I was implying, 'I'm not getting at you, honestly I'm not. I haven't offended you, have I?'

'Of course not, Fliss,' she says quickly, 'I know you didn't mean it like that. Tell me about Alex. Do you love him?'

'Yes . . . no . . . I don't know. Yes, I do. I really think I do, but maybe it's best if I try not to think about that one at the moment.'

'So you sacrificed the man you love for the sake of Sally-Anne and Richard's relationship?' Florrie says quietly. 'It's a shame Richard isn't worthy of such magnanimity.'

'Oh, I didn't do it for him,' I say hastily. 'No way! As far as I'm concerned, he and Kat deserve each other. I did it for Sally, because she loves him and I don't want to see her get hurt.'

At least, I hope Sally loves him. She says she does. I've always found it very difficult to believe that somebody as infinitely sensible as she could love someone like him.

'Do you believe in love at first sight?' I ask Florrie, remembering Sally's words.

'Oh, I believe in love at first sight, though your father keeps telling me I'm the last of the true romantics. But I have to believe in happy endings. It's that belief that kept me going all these years waiting for Drew.'

'Why did you wait for him, do you mind my asking? I mean, you knew he was . . . I'm sorry, but it would really help if I knew, if I could truly understand.'

Florrie reaches out and touches my hand. It's an intimate gesture, carrying genuine affection, and I appreciate it.

'I knew your mother didn't love him. If I'd ever thought she did I could never have taken him away from her. It's not a role I wanted to play, Fliss, the "Other Woman", it just happened, I'm afraid. I fell in love with Drew. It's very hard to fight such strong feelings. I just knew I had to be with him, no matter what.'

'But . . . why wait so long?' I turn to Dad. 'Like I said to you when you first told me about Florrie, I don't understand why you stayed with Mother for so long.'

'Duty, misplaced loyalty, sheer stupidity . . .' Dad smiles ruefully.

'And he had you and Sally,' says Florrie softly. 'I know you had left home but, when I first met your father, Sally-Anne was still only fourteen. If Drew had left then it would have torn her apart.'

'Florrie was my salvation,' Dad says, gazing lovingly at her. 'My light at the end of a very dark tunnel.' He puts one arm round her waist and squeezes gently. 'I don't know what I would have done without her.'

Florrie rests her other hand on his knee and smiles up at him.

'I may never have met your mother, Fliss,' she says to me, 'but I think that I understand her. That may sound like an awfully arrogant statement, but I know Drew inside out, and through him I know your mother. I know she caused you all so much unhappiness, but sadly I think that only came about as an extension of her own discontent. I really do feel sorry for her.'

I nod my head in agreement. 'So do I, but she's taught me a valuable lesson. I don't want to make the same mistakes as she did.'

'So what do you intend to do, Fliss?'

'I haven't the faintest idea. All I know is that I'm trying to do the right thing. If I just stay out of everybody's way, Sally and Richard, Alex and Kat, well, they might all be able to sort themselves out. I'm just an added complication in an already disastrous situation. I know I'm not exactly whiter than white in this whole thing but, as far as I can see, Kat's playing a dangerous game that's messing up a lot of people's lives. I think it would help if I knew what she wanted—Kat that is. If it's just one big ego boost or if she actually really loves Richard . . . look, I think I'm going to go for a walk. Clear my head.' I stand up. 'I just need to be on my own, to think . . .'

'OK, darling.' Dad nods. 'We'll see you back at home then. Just remember one thing, Fliss. As you grow older your perspective on life changes. You learn that sometimes trying to do something for the right reasons means you end up doing the wrong thing for everybody.'

The Wakeley Estate is a very good place for indulging in a little heartache. An hour later, an hour of wandering through lonely groves, of pressing my forehead against tree trunks, of sobbing dramatically against the statues that are dotted throughout the estate, I realise that I am lost.

My father managed to disappear down here for years without ever being found out. Perhaps I should bring Kat here and set her free amid the shrubbery, hopefully never to be seen again. Could bumping off Kat Christian be the answer perhaps? Then Sally and Richard will be left alone, to get on with their marriage, and it would have the added advantage of a certain person being minus a wife.

Where the hell am I?

I'm trying very hard not to cry again, I've really done far too much of that just lately. If I keep it up at the current rate my cheeks will begin to corrode from all the salt water running down them.

I swivel round like a satellite searching for radio waves, and sigh with relief as I finally spot the church spire through a golden canopy of trees, guiding me like a beacon.

The interior of the church is cool and dark. It smells of incense and old damp hymn books. I'm drawn inside by the magnetism of some higher perfect force that can forgive even when we can't forgive ourselves, that will love even when we don't love ourselves.

I walk up the aisle, running a cold hand along the smooth wood of each pew end.

The last time I was in a church, Sally was marrying Richard. I never thought I could be more unhappy, but here I am, misery personified.

Dear God, I pray, give me the strength to do the right thing, to resist temptation. P.S. Could I have a lot of strength, please, because my particular temptation is pretty bloody irresistible?

You know, I always thought that love was God-given, but I realise it's wrong for me to love a married man. It's very confusing. My only consolation is that I've done the right thing.

The right thing for who? whimpers my heart dejectedly.

I nearly jump out of my skin as the sombre silence of the old church is broken by the sound of my mobile phone, finally receiving a signal and trilling the arrival of a voice message. I relax a little when the first voice I hear is Sash.

'Hello, flower, it's Tuesday, it's midnight, and I just wanted to let you know that I'm sitting in bed in a torn naughty night-nurse outfit, covered in half-consumed edible body lotion. The kids are at my mother's, so as soon as Niall has woken up from the best night's sleep he's ever had, we're going to do it all again! Hope you're OK. Tatty 'bye.'

Good old Sash. I feel a huge sense of relief that she is happy. Let's just hope Niall can keep it up, in more ways than one!

I'm still giggling as the next message gets under way, but the smile's wiped straight off my face.

It's Sally-Anne. She doesn't say much, just hello really, asks if I'm OK and then asks me to call her as soon as possible. But it's not what she says, it's how she says it. She's normally such an upbeat person. Today she sounds like she's just discovered her first grey hair, her first cellulite dimple, and her first major wrinkle all at the same time.

Worried, I phone Sally-Anne's work only to be told that she's off sick. Sal is *never* sick. She's far too healthy.

I can't sit down here, hiding away from everything, hoping it will all blow over and everybody will end up living happily ever after. It's not going to work like that. I thought if I handled it the way I have been then I could limit that hurt just to me, but I see now that I can't. All I've done is left Sally-Anne to face everything alone.

I've got to go back.

Back at Bluebell Cottage, lunch is a quiet affair. I announce my intention of going home, and Dad and Florrie are united in their attempts to persuade me to stay. They're so keen in fact that I end up agreeing to stay until the following morning, instead of leaving this afternoon.

Once lunch is over, I volunteer for the washing-up. Eric and Roger, the twin waste-disposal units, sit at my feet, clearing scraps. They have hit it off extremely well, best friends in less than twenty-four hours. Life is so much easier for a dog. Eat, sleep, walk, sniff, scratch, far more sensible and less complicated than human emotions.

The last plate dried and put away, I go out into the garden. The Indian summer is fading away like a false promise. The last rays of sun are only weakly warming, and the sky is turning the palest dove grey.

Protected by the house, the south-facing garden is still relatively warm. I sit down on the bench at the far end. Through the French doors into the lounge I can see Dad and Florrie curled up on the sofa, idyllically happy together. While the sight of them makes me incredibly happy, I can't suppress a slight pang of jealousy. Still, Florrie had to wait nearly six years for her man. I really don't know how she managed to do it. It's only been four *days* since I last saw Alex and look what a sorry state I've been getting myself into.

A bee is droning in a lavender bush next to me, a quiet consistent buzz like the noise of Mother manically hoovering every Saturday morning. I'm enveloped in the soft heat, fanned by the slightest of breezes that whispers across my face, the birdsong a lullaby to my tired mind.

I close my eyes, the wine we consumed with lunch helping me surrender to sleep. I can feel my mind slipping away. Hazy, fragmented images flit and dart across my vision like the swifts.

A shadow falls across my face. I look up and smile sleepily at Alex, who smiles tenderly back at me, his aquamarine eyes sparkling like the sun upon the sea. This is a lovely dream. It's so wonderfully vivid I can even smell the glorious heady tang of his aftershave.

'Hello, Fliss.' His voice is tender.

'Hello, gorgeous,' I murmur.

'Fliss?' He touches my face, pushes the hair out of my eyes. His hand feels warm and solid. Blinking hazily, I realise with a jolt that I'm no longer dreaming.

'Alex?' I sit bolt upright, rub the back of my hand across my eyes. 'What are you doing here?'

'Well, that's a nice welcome. Aren't you pleased to see me?'

A dying man is pleased to see an oasis until he realises it's only a mirage.

Alex sits down next to me and starts to stroke Eric who is resting on the grass at my feet.

Alex looks tired. His beautiful eyes are shadowed, his hair is tousled, but as usual he is breathtakingly desirable. I move away from him, breathing in so hard I think I might pass out.

'What are you doing here?' I repeat blankly.

Distractedly Alex starts to scratch the rough hair on Eric's head.

'I told her,' he finally ventures.

'You told her what?' My voice is less than a whisper.

'That our marriage was a farce. That I'd fallen in love with someone else.'

He loves me.

A surge of hope, a fresh renewal of guilt. Joy and pain.

'But that I was prepared to make a go of things if she was.'

Joy departs, pain remains and doubles. He's come to tell me that he and Kat are going to work at their marriage, that I should just forget about him.

'Oh.' I sigh heavily, all the air released from my lungs like a punctured balloon. 'I'm really pleased it's all worked out OK for you both.'

'Honestly?'

'Honestly. I just want you to be happy, Alex.'

Well, that's true enough. Although it would be quite nice if I could be happy too. However, if you love someone, set them free. I used to think they were stupid lyrics, but Sting was spot-on, unfortunately. The best thing I can do is put on a smiley face and wish him well. The right thing to do is often the hardest thing to do.

'You *are* happy?' I have to ask.

'Oh, I think I will be, amazingly so.'

'Then I'm happy too,' I mumble, crossing the fingers of the hand furthest away from him. I force myself to look up at him. Look into those laughing eyes, at the person I've grown to love so deeply my gut twists with longing every time I think of him.

He certainly looks happy. His eyes are shining so brightly he could do for Optrex what a dazzling smile does for toothpaste. A smile is playing about his lips, almost as though he could burst into laughter at any minute.

'You don't *look* very happy, Fliss.' His voice is teasing.

What does he expect? Fireworks? Tap dancing? For him to make a go of his marriage really is laudable, but for me it's not a cause for major celebration.

It's all too much. I'm fighting, but I can't hold back the tears.

He stops smiling.

'Fliss.' His voice is low and uncertain. He reaches out and gently wipes away a tear with his thumb. 'Do you love me?'

'You know I do.' I'm almost whispering.

'Oh, Fliss, I'm so sorry.'

'Don't be, I'll get over it.' I'm lying now as well.

'Fliss, look at me.'

I look. He's smiling again, grinning in fact. I'm rather confused. He's not the sort of person to take pleasure in hurting others.

'I don't want you to get over it. I love you, Fliss.'

'But I thought . . . what about you and Kat?'

'Kat and I are finished. I'm sorry, I shouldn't have teased you. I did offer to make a go of things with her, but only because you wanted me to. But thank God it never came to that. Kat left.'

'What happened, Alex?' I'm trembling.

'Richard finally got what he wanted: Kat made a decision. It seems that his marrying your sister was the right move in their interminable game.'

'Oh, no. Poor, poor Sally-Anne!'

'It's OK, Fliss, Sally's all right. She's upset, of course, but she's OK.'

'You've seen her?'

'Not exactly.' He shakes his head. 'You're not going to believe who came to see me this morning—your mother.'

'My mother?' I query incredulously.

He nods. 'Yes. You know, she actually wanted to apologise. She feels as if everything is her fault. She was the one who told me where I could find you. Apparently your father phoned her this afternoon to let her know you were here.'

'But surely she must have told him what had happened? Why didn't he tell me! He didn't say a word.'

'Because he knew I was on my way down here to see you. Miriam told him to try to keep you here until I arrived, thought it would be best if you heard it all from me. She gave me this to give to you.'

He hands me an envelope. My hands are shaking so much I tear the letter as I rip it open. Mother's small, neat handwriting is familiar and strangely reassuring.

Dear Fliss,

Well, what can I say? You were right and I was wrong. Richard has left Sally-Anne for another woman. I can't quite believe that they've been married for less than two months and are already heading for the divorce courts. Poor Sally is strangely calm about it, I really don't think it's sunk in yet. Please don't worry about her, though. I'll make sure that she's all right, I promise. It's the least I can do considering I am the major cause of this whole mess.

I'm sure that Sally really did love Richard, but I have to admit now that I shouldn't have pushed them into getting married so quickly. What makes me feel worse is that I think I wanted her to marry him for all the wrong reasons. For me, and not for herself. I think it was I who wanted the big white wedding, the successful husband, the golden future. Well, I've certainly found out that all that glitters isn't gold, and Richard is a . . . well, you know what he is. I just hope that in time Sally realises she's probably far better off without him too.

I'm taking her away for a week to try to help her get over the past few months. We both need a break.

Alex told me what you did to try and help them stay together, and I want you to know how proud I am of you for that. I really have no right to say this, but Alex is a good man. But I'm sure as usual you've worked this out for yourself, and don't need me interfering in your life yet again.

With love,

Mother

Alex waits for me to finish reading and then hands me another envelope. 'One last thing,' he smiles encouragingly at me, 'Sally asked if you could return the favour for her. She said you'd know what she meant.'

I open the envelope and tip the contents into the palm of my hand. Sally's wedding and engagement rings.

'Oh, poor, poor Sally,' I mutter again.

'Don't worry, I have a feeling it will all turn out OK in the end, Fliss,' Alex says softly.

'You really think so? She must be devastated.'

'Well, she's certainly better off without him, and although that's probably the last thing she wants to hear right now, I'm sure given time . . . James was last seen harassing Erica for the name of Sally-Anne's hotel.'

'James? Well, he swore to always defend and honour her. I always said he'd be better for her than Richard.'

'He's in love with her, Fliss,' Alex murmurs. 'I always think that's a good start to any relationship, don't you?'

Reaching out, he puts his hand under my chin and tilts my face upwards, forcing me to look at him.

'Now there are no more obstacles, do you think we might get to have a happy ending?'

Forbidden fruits taste sweet, but leave a lingering bitter taste of guilt. Alex's lips taste sweet, a lingering, delicious kiss, no longer spoilt by guilt.

Everyone in life is looking for something. The main problem is that half the time we're never quite sure what that something is. It's taken me a long time to find the right path. Along the way I've detoured and almost broken down completely, but, as Alex and I breathlessly, reluctantly, break apart, I know that I've finally found what *I* was searching for.

It feels very strange letting myself into Richard's apartment. The place is silent, cold and very empty. Even the ever-present, irrepressible Eric shudders. Sally brought a warmth to Richard's life that he was a fool to give up, and one he'll be lucky to find again with a cold fish like Kat.

I head straight for the bedroom, intending to leave Sally's rings in the same place I left my note and keys the night *I* walked out on Richard Trevelyan. But it's with a great sense of sadness at the way it's happened that I finally dismiss Richard the Turd from both our lives for good.

The wardrobes where Sally's clothes were kept are standing open. Where once was row upon row of neatly pressed, perfectly coordinated outfits, there is absolutely nothing. There are still some clothes in Richard's wardrobe, but on the other side of the bed I find a large open suitcase on the floor, filled with the contents of Richard's drawers: silk underwear, socks, sweaters. Richard is in the process of moving out and moving on as well, a For Sale sign prominent in the window.

I think back to the fateful dinner party and Ethelred the Unready-cooked. Poor old lobster. Richard deserves Ethelred's end far more than

Ethelred did. I have a lovely vision of holding Richard's head in an unlit gas oven, until his short stumpy legs stop kicking.

I shake my head and the picture clears. It would be nice to see him suffer, but after spending the whole of the past week with Alex Christian, Holloway is no longer a tempting option as the place to spend the rest of my life. Besides, I have a feeling Kat will make Richard suffer far more than I ever could.

I decide it's time for me to make my final exit. Alex is waiting outside for me in the car. Unfortunately, though, it seems I have lost Eric. I head back to where I last saw him. In Richard's bedroom.

I knew Eric was the right dog for me from the first moment I spotted him.

I find him squatting happily in Richard's open suitcase, his cute face a picture of strained concentration. I could almost swear he winks at me as he parks the remains of his lunch in a neat and stinking curl on Richard's favourite cashmere sweater.

SARAH HARVEY

Like most authors, Sarah Harvey has always enjoyed writing. She laughingly refers to her school leavers' report as all the encouragement she needed to become a fiction writer. 'The report said that if I could only stop myself writing a novel every time I was asked to write an essay, then I would do very well. As I so obviously turned everything I wrote into a story, I thought, Why not make the most of it?'

While writing her first novel in her spare time, Sarah worked full-time for the business planning department of Northampton General Hospital. It was a job she enjoyed but would never go back to now. 'I just couldn't stand the nine to five,' she says. 'I am so lucky because I absolutely love what I do. Writing gives you such freedom from routine.' Sarah's early success came when her short stories were published in *Just Seventeen* magazine; then followed the publication of her first novel, *Misbehaving*.

'Each novel takes me about ten months to write,' she tells me, having just finished her fifth. 'I have the main plot in my head, but sometimes I write the end and the beginning first and then jump around in the middle to see where it goes. I know it sounds a weird way of writing a novel, but it works for me.' she smiles.

Sarah spends a lot of her time with her partner Terry on the Cornish

riviera in Newquay, where Terry owns a hotel. 'It is so beautiful down there,' she continues, her face lighting up, 'that at some point we hope to buy a house and live there permanently.' Her love of Cornwall has led Sarah to set her fifth book there. 'A good excuse to drive around for research! But this book is going to be a new departure for me,' she says with a smile. 'A friend of mine kept joking that he really liked my novels but he thought that they were too light-hearted and wanted someone to die in them. Well, I have taken him at his word and *Postcard from Wit's End* should keep him happy, even though it made me cry while I was writing it.'

As I sit chatting with Sarah Harvey, what strikes me most strongly is her wonderful, natural sense of humour, and the fact that she just loves to gossip. 'I can't put sex in my novels,' she says, drily, 'my mum reads them'; and, 'Of course, I love to gossip! How else do you think I get the ideas for my stories? As I chat to friends and listen to all their problems and escapades, something just clicks in my mind for later use. I can't tell you anything specific, though,' she laughs, 'or else I'll lose all my friends and find myself in court!'

Jane Eastgate

Checking Out

Stevie Morgan

One fateful day was all it took to turn a young girl's life
upside-down. A day when tragic events conspired to ruin
every dream she held for the future. Now, ten years on,
that young girl has reinvented herself: she is Angie
Cassinari; wife to Dale, mother to Joe and Tony; honorary
Italian daughter-in-law and Stayfleurs supermarket's most
efficient worker. Only she knows that she is acting a part
and, as every actor is aware, the curtain has to come down
some time for real life to begin.

ONE

JUST ROUND THE CORNER from Deacon Road Primary School, between 'Shorthouse and Shepherd' (suppliers of wheelchairs, bath lifts and motor-aided Zimmer frames) and Firth's newsagents (suppliers of time-warp stationery such as Animal Friends Calendars 1981), Samantha should be enjoying a private Sisyphean moment.

The other mothers are enjoying theirs, as they disperse from the school gates, as separate and urgent as the splashes from a dropped pebble. It's not the demands of nine o'clock bosses or the breakfast washing-up that makes them hurry so, nor is it the weather, because even though it is the first Tuesday of Wimbledon fortnight, the weather is dry and warm. They rush away to savour the only time in their day when there is nothing that can be expected of them, there is nothing that they have to do. For the next few minutes, before they reach home or their workplace, they are free. They move quickly, walking fast or changing gear smartly at the green light, so that no one will guess that, inside, they are slacking; that inside their heads, nothing is going on but a blissful blankness of white noise, or perhaps, at the very most, a little light fantasy of the silken sand and fluffy cloud variety.

But Samantha, Mrs Dale Cassinari, does not enjoy having nothing to do. She finds her own peculiar variety of freedom in the all-absorbing effort of pushing the rock up the mountain. When there is nothing that she has to do 'now', she thinks what it is she has to do 'next'. When there is no one to expect things from her, she tries to expect things from herself. So, as she crosses the road, leaving the alarming displays of

343

chrome commodes and yellowing kittens behind her, she concentrates hard on improving the sound her new heels make as they hit the tarmac. She snaps her upper spine straight, pulling everything inwards as if gathering her whole physical being inside a fortress of control, and adjusts the way her shoes impact on the ground. Now, each time her heels come down, they do so with a satisfyingly self-possessed 'click'. Looking at her watch she is pleased to find that she is about to arrive at work a whole minute earlier than is usual.

Dressed in his brown stock-man's coat George is already out front, mustering the wire trolleys like a squad of unruly recruits. Hearing the sound of Samantha's heels he looks up. His whole face lifts, and becomes as bright and flat as smoothed tinfoil. 'Tad early today, Mrs Cassinari.'

'Just a bit, George. Must be my new shoes.'

'Ah yes!' he exclaims. 'Yes! That'll be it.'

Samantha smiles back, acknowledging that only she and George could find the correlation between walking speed and new shoe leather logical and satisfying. 'Well, better get on, George.'

Smiling still, she walks on, leaving George to scold his trolleys and ponder the influence of new footwear on the world at large. The moment George began their customary morning exchange, Samantha lost the need to concentrate on the interaction of sole and concrete. The day of providing for people's expectations has begun again; the barricades in her mind can be left less heavily defended as she puts her shoulder back to pushing the rock.

Round this side of the building there are no windows, only the little red security door in the huge metal wall, like a hole cut into a giant tin can. Samantha keys in the code and enters Stayfleurs' little warren of staff facilities and managers' offices. The atmosphere, reminiscent of the changing rooms of an old-fashioned girls' public school, is comforting, and the perfect antidote for the public part of the shop. After a few minutes in here she will be ready for 'out there', perched at a check-out surrounded by white melamine and saturated in light.

Samantha pushes open the door marked 'Female Changing'. Inside, three of her usual co-workers are already preparing for the day's work. They are not what you'd expect to find at a supermarket check-out but then Stayfleurs is a *better class* of supermarket. It flatters its clientele with a choice of three flavours of couscous, a selection of unpronounceable breakfast cereals and two sorts of air-dried reindeer meat. This kind of thing attracts a *better class* of customer and a *better class* of staff. There are no fat and feckless seventeen-year-old girls. Stayfleurs employs 'ladies' on its tills, women who would find the term 'woman' vulgar.

Stayfleurs ladies typically date from an age when middle-class marriage was a profession, but like miners and steelworkers, they have outlived the industry in which they began their careers. They work here to escape their houses—big and empty—and their husbands' egos—ditto.

They turn and smile at her as she comes in, then continue to slip the navy uniform housecoats over their Jaeger skirts and blouses.

'Oh. I think I must be electronic,' laughs Claudia, an Amazon of a woman in her late fifties, as the material crackles over her arm and her newly coloured purple-brown hair stands on end.

'You mustn't let a uniform put you off, Claudia. My mother refused to join the Salvation Army, all because she didn't like the hats. And she always regretted it.' Mary can afford to say this, because she is small and neat, and the navy coat with its cream piping rather suits her.

'I had an uncle in the Sally Army,' says Claudia, patting her static hair. 'But of course the men didn't have to wear those frightful bows.'

'Oh, well, perhaps they *do*, you know, *nowadays*.' Mary droops her right hand suggestively at the wrist, but Claudia stares blankly.

'Oh, for Christ's sake, Mary!' Liz shuts her gold compact with a snap. 'Nobody makes jokes like that these days. Don't you have any gay friends?' Liz, glamorously, brassily blonde, was an actress before Trevor swept her off her feet with his dentist's charm.

'Oh! Oh God! Silly me!' Claudia is laughing nervously now. 'Gay, of course. Queer. Oh, I'm such a chump!'

Quietly tying back her fine brown hair, Samantha has been waiting for five to nine, the moment when she needs to steal between their words and squabbles, to get them out to work. She knows what they need is a little distraction, a shared sense of mild outrage. It's easy to provide it.

'I think that Philippa, you know the under-manager from head office we had last Christmas, she was gay.' This is a fat worm none of the ladies can resist; there are appreciative gasps all round.

'Anyway, ladies. As usual I think you look lovely in your uniforms. Shall we get ready to do battle?' United by a common sense of delicious scandal and a little frisson of genuine shock, Claudia, Liz and Mary walk to their work stations smoothed and content, like fed hens.

So far, thankfully, it has been a difficult morning. Samantha has hardly drawn a breath in two hours or put more than three customers' goods through her till without interruption. It began with twin toddlers running amok on aisle B and engulfing the freezer in a tsunami of mayonnaise. Their mother hyperventilated with shock and had to be sat in the staff cloakroom with a paper bag over her head while Samantha rang her grumpy husband at the BBC. 'I'm calling from Stayfleurs, Mr Hannan. Your wife would like you to come and pick her up. Yes, I'm afraid it is quite urgent.'

Then there was a run on the Norwegian dried reindeer meat. Half of this morning's elderly customers have put at least one packet in their baskets (the Classic FM morning DJ announced casually between 'Gymnopodie' and the 'Moonlight Sonata' that Lapps don't get Alzheimer's). When its bar code was scanned the computerised tills buzzed bad-temperedly and flashed 'item not found'. Pensioners do not react rationally to computer glitches of this sort. Seven times this morning Samantha has had to leave her own till to calm an almost self-combusting punter at someone else's.

'I perfectly understand your concerns about the future of society, sir, but really this is just a small temporary fault and if you could bear with us for a few moments you can complete your purchasing.'

But not even Samantha's most professional charm can pacify two of Liz's customers. A pair of old gents of military bearing vow to write to their MP and demand to see the manager.

'Oh God. Mafeking all over again,' Liz breathes, rolling her eyes.

Luckily Mr Geoffrey is exactly the right figure to deal with the Sandhurst graduates of '41. He is the result of some strange crinkle in the time–space continuum. He exists apparently as the thirty-eight-year-old manager of a modern supermarket, dealing effortlessly with computer stock control and business projection graphics. Yet he has clearly been lifted from a genteel department store somewhere in the 1930s. Samantha always thinks of him as wearing collar studs, and formal navy three-piece pinstripes. He obviously makes the same impression on Colonel (Rtd) and Lieutenant Colonel Smyth Parker (DSO); although Mr Geoffrey says almost nothing—personal communication not being his strong point—his general demeanour does the trick. The Smyth Parker brothers soften in a mist of remembrance of buying school uniform at Dickins and Jones with Mother.

'I'm going to get on to head office about this reindeer meat,' Mr Geoffrey says to Samantha, as the brothers leave with a complimentary packet of shrink-wrapped Rudolph. 'Could you hold the fort down here? You are so marvellously diplomatic, Mrs Cassinari,' and he disappears through the doors behind the deli counter, nervously readjusting his collar, his fingertips searching for the studs he left behind in a former life.

The tense atmosphere has got into the ladies' fingertips, making them jitter inaccurately over the till keys, so that Samantha finally has to devote herself full-time to trouble-shooting with her master key for everyone else. Claudia is particularly disaster-prone this morning. 'I don't know how you stay so cool,' she says tremulously.

Samantha smiles professionally. 'Don't forget the "f" code on that alcohol, Claudia,' she says.

'Oops. Silly me.'

'And the "Delicat" is a special this week, it should come through on two for one, code four three nine.'

'Oh. Oh. Right. I don't know how you do it. Really I . . .'

'Code four three nine, Claudia!'

What no one understands is how relaxing stress really can be.

The offending reindeer meat has been withdrawn 'On Orders' and a lunchtime calm has set in. The only punters pushing George's trolleys are passing sales reps looking in vain for a simple cheese butty, husbands who have promised to cook dinner, and Women with Lists, shopping efficiently in their lunch hours. The Reps and Husbands wander the aisles with the same air of lost expectancy, hoping that some product will jump off the shelves and ask to be bought. The List Women cruise at speed, their heads full of the next six things they are going to do. None of them wants to talk as they come through the check-out.

Samantha feels as if all the people have turned their backs on her. The demands of the external world become faint, they don't hold her attention. Inside she tightens control, reining in her thoughts, but it's like being in the basket of a balloon and looking down to see that the ropes holding you to earth and home are being cut, one by one. She hopes for a customer with a problem, a query, a complaint, but the pale blue eyes of List Woman look clean through her and out to the world. As the basketload of olive oil, wholemeal pasta, Quorn mince and mackerel pâté pass under her scanner, Samantha feels the familiar unease of an unauthorised Imagination Leak occurring.

At first it's confined to the back of the shop, where the aisles begin to fade into the dimness of artificial light. Out of the corner of her eye Samantha can see that the shadows there are acquiring a kind of greenness; leaf shapes seem to be suggesting themselves, poking between the stacks of packets and tins. Then, a flash of movement catches her eye and a bright green gecko scuttles up the shelves, which themselves become taller somehow and then grow upwards quite unashamedly. Soon they are disappearing into a forest canopy that has spread high above all the aisles.

The next List Woman to bring her purchases to Samantha's check-out is quite unaware of the slim green vine snake twining itself luxuriously through her thick red hair. It is a particularly beautiful specimen; recently moulted, its lime-coloured skin has a little iridescent lustre. The woman puts her hand up to her hair, self-consciously checking that nothing real is drawing Samantha's gaze, and knocks the snake to the floor. It takes some self-control not to leap up and see where it went: Samantha concentrates harder on the parade of objects filing past her on the conveyor.

'Did you know that these ciabatta rolls were two for the price of one?' she says, without looking up. But her voice seems ineffectual and the woman with the red hair doesn't reply. Which is just as well as the vine snake has reappeared, popping asp-like from her cleavage.

Imagination started as 'her secret weapon' against little Dennis Williams. At eight he was at the peak of his career with an empire that stretched over all three tarmac playgrounds. Life for Dennis would never be this good again and he was making the most of it. Kids just did what he told them to do. Enslaved by his elfin charisma, they brought him sweets, toys, money and weaker children to torment. Samantha, tall for her age, too clever by half and stick-thin, was a favourite pastime. Smart enough to know that words were Samantha's currency, Dennis never spoke. Just made her stand in the middle of a silent ring of fascinated supporters and walked around her, slowly at first, then dancing and making kung fu kicks and karate chops, only some of which made painful contact with her shins and arms and head. The game was to make Samantha wince and cower. It became a regular feature of her day.

Then one day her imagination just kicked in, unasked, like adrenaline. She looked at Dennis's face and saw the most extraordinary thing. 'You've got spiders coming out of your eyes. Big ones.'

His eyelashes flickered, but otherwise he gave no clue that he had heard her. 'Ha! Ha!' he exclaimed chopping first the air, then her side.

'You have. Are you listening to me? You've got great big spiders just crawling out of your eyes and down your face.' Samantha could see clearly that first a hairy leg, five times the thickness of his eyelashes, would poke out, feeling around like a hand groping for a bedside-light switch. Then, the lump of the body would show under the lid, stretching the skin so that the fine veins showed like web. Finally, struggling to gain a purchase on the smooth eyeball, the whole arachnid wriggled out, only to be followed immediately by another, just the same. By now Dennis's face was almost obscured by them.

'They're all over your face now.' Her tone was completely flat, but informative. Dennis stopped his circling, and looked up at her. A particularly fat spider squirmed its way grossly from under the lower lid of his left eye. Involuntarily Samantha's nose wrinkled and, in reply, a ripple of revulsion shivered round the ring of Dennis's supporters. They turned questioningly to Dennis, leaning in to scrutinise his face.

Samantha waited in the corner of the playground at the start of break the next day, but no one came for her. A week later Dennis was running errands for a big boy with red hair. He turned his head from her as he ran past, and she felt suddenly that she must sit down under the weight of the revelation that had just landed in her lap.

Now, Samantha feels she has no one but herself to blame for the fact that there is a snake between the breasts of the woman who wants twenty pounds cashback, please. Imagination may have come to her unasked in the beginning, but then she trained it to be strong. Used it at first just at school, but later at home, too, when escape seemed the only option. It's her own fault that she never learned to control it better.

But luckily at Stayfleurs something always happens that throws her runaway balloon a nice anchoring rope. And today it's George. Liz, genuinely agitated, comes to Samantha's till. 'Mr Geoffrey says he needs you in the office. It's that poor creature George. He's practically foaming at the mouth.'

By the time Samantha pushes through the doors marked 'Staff Only' there isn't a leaf or a lizard left in the place.

George is sitting on the settee in Mr Geoffrey's office, rocking slightly to and fro. His face is a million creases. Mr Geoffrey comes towards her, sweating with relief. 'Oh, Mrs Cassinari. Thank goodness this happened while you were here . . .'

'I will still have to leave at three twenty-five, Mr Geoffrey . . .'

'Oh, yes. But . . . let me fill you in. A boy returned his mother's trolley to the wrong place. The front of a line rather than the back. George moved the trolley to the back, and the boy returned and took it to the front. I believe this procedure was repeated several times. The boy became abusive. Erm . . .' Mr Geoffrey shifts his weight uncomfortably. This is testing his ability to relate to humans, rather than figures or computers, to the limit.

'And George got upset?'

'Well, yes.'

'Would you give us just a few moments, Mr Geoffrey?'

He is out of his own office almost before she's finished speaking, relieved to escape. Samantha sits beside George on the sofa.

'D'you think they'll make me early every day?' she says, stretching her feet out in front of her. 'I mean they won't be new tomorrow will they?'

George stops rocking. 'Well. Not new as such. Not new *per se*. As it were.' His voice is shaky but his diction is as distinct and tight as ever.

'It could be the style of course. So different from my old pair. It could be the style that's making me walk faster.'

'Well. That is certainly a reasonable and valid theory.' For the first time since she entered the room George looks at her, blinking as if he has just woken.

'Would you like a lift home now, George? I'm sure it could be arranged. You have had a difficult day after all.'

'Ah. In that instance there would be no one to attend to the trolleys.'

'Mr Mullen from the deli counter would help out just this once.'

'Well. Yes. I am reluctant. It may endanger my position here.'

'I'm sure that won't be the case.'

'No. No. Well. Home then. I think. A trying day!' George smiles.

'You just wait here, George.'

Mr Geoffrey took a little convincing that a taxi for George courtesy of Stayfleurs was 'appropriate', so Samantha has had to run all the way to school. Her ponytail has worked loose and one bra strap is halfway down her arm. She feels hot and uncontrolled, but when she sees her boys there's no room in her for anything but the relief of being their mum again. She fills up with her children and all she must be for them.

Joe is holding his thick brassy hair off his forehead with splayed awkward fingers. He looks sticky and crumpled. Samantha can feel his hot little palm in hers even at a distance of twenty feet. Tony is standing beside him, quite still. As usual Tony has come through the day clean and unrumpled. One hand rests lightly on Joe's shoulder.

The boys notice Samantha and launch themselves towards her at full pelt. She holds them in her arms, her eyes closed as if they had been apart for a year not just a few hours. She is their mother again; defined by the food she will give them, the shorts she will iron for them, the way she will stand in their room and listen to their sleeping breath.

'Mummy!'

Yes, that's right. With four little hands to rope her firmly to Earth she is Mummy. At this moment Samantha can imagine that she was never anything else. Certainly never a child. Certainly never a person with a mother of her own.

She retrieves her bra strap and ties her straying hair, then taking Tony's hand in her right and Joe's in her left hand, they cross the road, and start to walk home.

TWO

AT FIRST DALE'S MOTHER, Maria, disliked their house in Lancaster Road, for the same reason that Samantha loved it. She came to inspect their purchase just before they moved in, clicking her smart shoes on the bare floors, swinging her small hips testily. 'Nnnah,' she said through her nose, her customary signal of deepest disapproval. 'Why you not get deetat-shed house? Make a good impression for Dale business. Eh? Why this house? Pushed in corner. Nnnnah.'

She was right, it was 'pushed in corner'. It was part of an Edwardian terrace built in a long L-shape to fit the hilly curves of the Bristol suburbs. Number eleven fitted the crook of the L by being wedge-shaped, narrow at the front, wide at the back. All its rooms were irregular, with no two walls of the same dimensions. This gave Samantha the distinct and rather delicious impression of being inside a giant china cheese keeper. Samantha felt a kinship with number eleven, almost a kind of compassion for it, from that first day.

But she didn't say that to Maria. Samantha could just see what her mother-in-law would make of that. 'You feel sorry for a house?' Maria would exclaim, stretching her eyes wide, her painted eyebrows diving under her fringe. 'Eh, Dale. I'm worried. That wife of yours, she is going loopy with baby, yes?'

Samantha liked to have Maria's approval, and knew exactly how to get it. 'It's a good house for us, Maria. It has a secure garden, and it's near a good school.' She stroked her round stomach, drawing Maria's attention to the approaching birth of her first grandchild. 'It's big, four bedrooms. It'll have five or even six when Dale converts the loft.'

Maria looked away quickly. 'Nnnah,' she said again.

But the vision of a brood of grandchildren to scold in Italian was too strong for Maria to resist. She opened and closed a few of the cupboards in the empty kitchen. Then shrugged. 'Maybe. Maybe. The kitchen is good. OK. Yes. I know it's not you choose this house. It's my Dale. He choose this house to spite me,' and then she grinned and chucked Samantha's cheek, and leaned down to address her bump. 'The little bugger. Hey, you in there, your daddy he still a little bugger.'

It wasn't spite that motivated Dale. There was no malice in the way he constantly contradicted his mother's wishes. It was simply a matter of survival against the virtually irresistible force that was Maria. To remain himself Dale had learned from birth to become an immovable object. They were like a tree and a prevailing wind; the tree always turned the wind aside, but the wind shaped the way the tree grew.

He opposed her encroachment onto the territory of his personality with determination, but also with a kind of understated delight. At ten months he'd done with his cot so climbed out every night until Maria got him a bed. At a year, he took all his clothes off whenever she turned her back until she gave up trying to make him wear a coat. As he got older he savoured confounding Maria's expectations over everything— from refusing to wear a collar and tie, to calmly announcing that he would not enter the family business. He would put money into it but that was all. Just as she had tried to 'educate' him to fit her model, he began to look on his guerrilla resistance as a learning curve for Maria. 'It's good for her,' he'd say calmly when Maria had been shouting down the phone over something he hadn't done, 'one day she'll get the message that her way isn't the only way.'

Nothing was too large or too small to be made into a contradiction for Maria to rage over. Number eleven was just another opportunity.

'Mum's got a thing about terraced houses,' he said the day they put in the offer. 'She thinks they're common. Outside bog, coal in the bath, whippet in the kitchen. This'll show her how lovely these old places really are. Mind you, we could get a whippet, you know . . .' he grinned.

Samantha kicked him slightly in the shin. 'She's getting old, why can't you just be nice?'

'What? And break the habit of a lifetime?'

He was doing some small-scale confounding and contradiction the day Samantha met him in the cake shop where she worked. She'd seen him before. He often came in to buy pies or doughnuts. Samantha was alone in the shop when Dale pulled his builder's van onto the double yellows outside and ran in to order a cake for the next day. Under two centimetres of masonry dust he still looked good to her. She'd noticed his looks on other days: not tall, not short, but well proportioned; very square shoulders, very straight posture, serious eyes. He moved with a kind of inexorable slow energy that made Samantha want to step back as he approached the counter out of a concern that he might simply step through it. His smile was total—eyes, mouth, cheeks, even his encrusted hair seemed to participate. So Samantha was disappointed when he ordered a huge cake with white marzipan covering and a tasteless message in pink icing.

'To Mum, 21 Today', he told her to write on the order. His voice was lower than she expected. Measured and slow, but rhythmic like someone playing a double bass.

'That's nice,' Samantha said, dutifully.

'I don't know about "nice"!' He smiled and raised an eyebrow in an expression that might have been disapproving or teasing, she wasn't sure. 'Pink icing? And that greeting? She'll hate it, it'll drive her wild!'

'Oh,' she said, 'I see.' But she didn't. Getting a birthday cake that the recipient would hate was intriguing. Samantha could only imagine it as some act of vindictiveness. The way he'd said, 'It'll drive her wild', had a definite heat in it. 'What name is it?' she asked.

'Cassinari, Dale.' He spelt his surname to her. 'It's Italian,' he told her, 'my mum, she's Italian. I'll pick it up tomorrow, yeah?'

Was this a clue? Did his mother make him take her name and not his father's? Was he too carrying some load of anger against his mother? For a moment her aloneness seemed less permanent, but she put the thought aside with the broken Eccles cake she'd take home for her tea.

The next day, as she packed the huge white cake in its box, she couldn't stop thinking about Dale and Mrs Cassinari. Why would pink icing make anyone quite 'wild' and why would 'wild' be a good thing? Julie, the cake-shop manager, thought it was easy to explain. 'He's thirty if he's a day. Nice looking. No wedding ring. Right then, he's gay. That's what. All fixated on their Mas those boys.'

'But he said she'd hate the cake!'

'Don't have to be a good fixation. Could be a bad one.'

Late that afternoon Samantha was wiping down the cabinets, and wondering if a person could survive on Eccles cakes, when he appeared. He was still dusty but his hair colour and skin tone were discernible: not at all the olive complexion you'd expect from someone with an Italian mum. Not an Italian *dad* then, she guessed.

Back then, Samantha was always wary of any conversation that went beyond the price of a Mr Blobby novelty cake. So, in spite of her curiosity, Dale was almost out of the shop before she found the voice to blurt out, 'Why are you getting your mum a cake she won't like?'

He looked at her closely for a moment before replying, assessing if she would grasp the answer. 'I'm teaching her,' he said, 'that her way isn't the only way of doing things. And it's a life's work, I can tell you. She's bloody stubborn,' and he looked down at his feet, smiling.

Samantha understood the heat she'd heard in his voice the day before was a variety of love. She shivered with envy at the thought of such fierce affection, and with the renewed sensation of her own isolation. Then he looked up. 'Can you come to a party tomorrow? You can see the effect of the cake! Early. After work. I'll pick you up here?'

He was gone before she could say no, I'm not like you after all, I'm not who you think I am. What, she wondered, would her identity be without the width of a counter and a box of eclairs to define it?

Dale picked her up bang on time and was gallantly attentive and complimentary about her rather plain outfit. 'Navy suits you. Nice cardigan,' he said as he walked round the car to open the passenger door for her, as if she were a small child. They set off, in silence. Then Dale began to talk and almost immediately she realised she shouldn't have worried about her identity, Dale had one ready-made for her: 'My-date-that-you-won't-approve-of, Mum.'

The party he was taking her to was the tea dance for his mother's birthday and also the celebration of the thirtieth anniversary of the opening of 'La Tavolino Verde', Maria's Italian deli.

'She started it on her own,' Dale told her as he drove his neat little hatchback over the Downs. 'I spent all my life there as a kid. My mum still runs it, but she's got people working for her now.'

'Do you ever work there?'

'No. I've cut enough salami for my lifetime. I'm a sleeping partner.'

Samantha understood now why a British bakery sponge covered in cheap pink icing would drive Maria 'wild'.

'My mother is a fine woman. She's tough. She brought me up and made a business all on her own,' he explained. 'But she thinks the whole world is like traffic lights where the colours always mean the same things. So all men without a tie are unemployed, all motorbikes are ridden by criminals, all doctors are saints. It's good for her to be contradicted. Surprised.'

What would make Maria crosser—the pink icing or Dale's new 'friend' turning up unannounced to her birthday celebrations in a navy twin set and a skirt someone's gran took to the Oxfam shop? Samantha considered getting out at the next red light and leaving Dale without a two-dimensional walk-on in his ongoing drama with his mother. But Dale seemed so warm and steady, if he had a part for her to play so much the better. She sat back in the seat and relaxed. She understood absolutely about playing a part: she could do two-dimensional. Easy. Hadn't she been living as a cardboard cut-out for almost a year?

Maria was a bit of a contradiction in herself, the proprietress of an

Italian deli who was thin as a stick, and dressed in a very English tailored suit. She looked very pleased to see Dale. She was also very surprised, which Samantha could only attribute to the presence of an unannounced girlfriend. 'You are very late, Dale. Hopeless boy.'

'Happy Birthday, Mum. Hope you liked your cake.'

'Nnnah. Dale! Hopeless!' she said. 'Now introduce me your friend!'

After ten minutes with Maria, Samantha could understand why Dale was so keen to contradict her expectations. She had so many of them. And once one set was displaced, a whole new phalanx of them sprang up in Maria's mind. Samantha had only to react to Maria's questions and watch a whole personality for herself forming behind the crows' feet. They sat together on the plastic chairs that lined the community hall, while seventy or so people waltzed in oddly matched couples.

'You meet my Dale in some disco techni yes?' Maria spoke without taking her eyes off the dancers. 'Dale tells me he meets girls there.'

'No, Mrs Cassinari. I met him in the cake shop where I work. I asked him about the message on the cake.'

'Oh. Very funny. Big joke. Nnnnaah.'

'I thought it was tasteless actually.'

'Yes?' Maria looked away from the dancers for the first time.

'Yes I did.'

'So. You live at home? Big snobby family in Sneyd Park, eh?'

'No. I don't.'

'You live with, students? Other unmarried girls, going out to pubs. Doing, I don't know.' Maria's shrug expressed a world of ills from drunkenness to illicit sex.

'No. I've got a bedsit off the Gloucester road. It's all I can afford. I don't go out much.'

'Where are your parents? You have run away from home yes?'

'No. They're—not around any more.'

'No! Terrible. Poor girl.' Samantha now had all Maria's attention. The disapproval had gone and was replaced with concern. 'Does Dale know this? You come and visit me any time you like. OK?'

'OK.'

She stood up and called over the dance floor, 'Hey, Dale, Dale! Come here. You know this little girl here is an orphan?'

Maria spent most of the evening asking a series of questions so specific and tightly constructed that Samantha had only to choose yes or no to see a profile of her life springing up before her. Female, employed,

355

under 25, no surviving relatives. A series of polite 'nos' let Maria see that she wanted to forget about her past. At least that bit was true enough. Dale had left them together between dances and had hardly spoken to Samantha all evening, until he drove her home. 'Thanks for coming. At such short notice.' He seemed sorry, a little shamefaced even. 'It was a bit of cheek to ask you. You didn't know me from Adam really. I'm very grateful that you came.'

'That's OK. I had a nice time.'

'Did you? Good.' He seemed genuinely relieved. 'My mother liked you, very much,' he said.

'And I liked your mother.' It was the safe response. Neutral but also true. Samantha had felt quite safe with Maria, because Maria would never see anything she hadn't constructed inside her own head first. Dale's teaching efforts would always go to waste. And Maria's general belligerence and constantly inflamed righteous anger were entertaining.

Dale parked the car at the kerb outside Samantha's house at the very downtrodden end of a pretty downtrodden street. The glass of one of the ground-floor windows was missing and there was rubbish strewn around the front door. Next door was a derelict building, roof half off and a litter of needles and broken syringes spilling onto the pavement. Dale was pointedly quiet, then he cleared his throat for a moment and asked, 'Which is your window?'

'First floor on the right.'

'Oh. I see . . . have you been here long?'

'About a year.'

'Is it . . .' Dale searched for a word, 'comfortable?'

'It's. You know. Not too bad.'

Of course it was vile. Dale knew that. She knew that. But the most important thing about her room was that the landlord was like Julie who kept the cake shop, he didn't ask any questions. She had endured the squalor of it all pretty well, protected by a blanket of inexperience of city life bestowed by her country childhood: she had wondered for ages why the hospital was evidently dumping its waste needles in a ruin off the A38. But now the cold and damp bit into her. The feeling that this was what she deserved was wearing off. Sitting in Dale's warm clean car, she was filled with a dread of going inside to her clammy bedsit.

'I'd like to see you again,' he said. 'I really would.'

She smiled a tight smile, Maria's questions had been so easy, Dale's might be too hard. 'But if your mother likes me, that rather defeats the object, doesn't it?'

'No!' He drew back a little, smiling the total hair-involving smile. 'No,

I like you, that's what matters to me. Anyway, getting up my mum's nose isn't all I do with my life.'

Samantha relaxed a little: that seemed to be a cue! He wanted *her* to ask *him* questions. 'So what do you do with your life then?'

'I work. I go out to the pub, I go to films. I read. Books about architecture, buildings, engineering. But mostly I work really.'

Another cue! Samantha was warming to this. It was as easy as yes or no. 'What's your work? You're a builder or something, aren't you?'

'That's me! One of those wide boys who whacks up a breeze-block wall and charges ten grand for it.' Dale had turned suddenly sad and fierce. He sat up and looked out of the window. Samantha didn't know what to say; she began to gather herself to leave the car.

'Don't go. I'm sorry. I just hate that word "builder". It's what people call those prats on construction sites. That's not what I do. I restore houses. I can make ruins come back to life. I can see the beauty through all the crap. I can see right through to what they're meant to be.'

There wasn't a trace of his mother's Italian accent in Dale's voice. He had the slightest Bristol burr, not the sort of voice that says things like 'beauty'. The words seemed almost embarrassingly revealing in his mouth. Samantha knew that Dale had told her something he perhaps never told anyone else. She could imagine Dale, the last to leave a site at night, conjuring his vision of period loveliness in the face of twenty years of dry rot, damp and DIY. Patting a piece of stonework before leaving it behind, imagining the life of a building springing up inside its rejuvenated walls.

She knew that feeling of holding onto an idea, a dream; it wasn't like relying on something solid like a person. It was lonely and required constant effort: forget your dream for a second, and like Tinkerbell it would stop existing. She wished she could explain how she knew and understood the tone in his voice, but she had to stick to her cues.

'I'd like to see one of the houses you've done up,' she said.

'You would? The house I'm working on is just up on Cotham Brow. It's empty. I've got the key. It's not ten yet. After, we could go for drink?'

Samantha looked at Dale's face, full of the quiet energy that had rolled up to the cake-shop counter. The evening had changed her into more than another part of the Maria education programme, more than the orphaned girl his mother had invented. Dale leant and kissed her, like a cousin, on the cheek. Samantha felt, just at that moment, that a person could not survive on Eccles cakes for ever, nor sleep next to a wall with black damp growing over it. Whatever they might have done. 'Let's go then,' she said.

Dale got her a dehumidifier that fixed the damp. He re-wired the kitchenette and got her a kettle—'So you can make me a cup of tea when I come round.' He redecorated. He'd pop in with a takeaway, or they'd go to the cinema and come back to the bedsit afterwards. Dale told her about his childhood, the deli, his mum.

'She just wanted me to fit in. To be some sort of pillar of society. She sent me to school with the kids of doctors and lawyers. But school never did it for me somehow. I got bored. All I wanted to do was mend buildings. I did the tiles on our house when I was twelve. I left school at sixteen. Went to learn how to cut stone.'

Once she asked him about his father. He shrugged. 'It was a holiday romance for him. She got pregnant. Her dad chucked her out so she came to England to find him, and never did. That's all I know. She would never even tell me his name. I used to wonder a bit about who he was. Not now. He's not interested in me so I'm not interested in him.'

He spoke of what he wanted and planned, but never what he really felt. And it suited Samantha to keep that space between them; it kept her secrets. She could love him just as easily from a safe distance.

Dale was building their relationship one room at a time, like a house. After a few weeks all that was left to build was the bedroom.

Samantha knew that Dale wanted to have sex with her. She imagined that he had slept with his previous girlfriends, although he never talked about them and she never asked directly. But Samantha knew that sex was what couples did, when they were alone together.

She told him that she was twenty-two, nearly twenty-three. Dale would expect her to know about sex. But all she really knew about was kissing, so she and Dale kissed. She liked kissing. She'd done kissing with boys from school. But the other cues Dale offered, the hand on her breast, the fingertips slipping up her skirt, she couldn't take. She didn't know what came next when she could choose what to do, when she was a consenting partner. When Dale began to hold her too tight, to pull her leg between his thighs, it reminded her of too much. How could anything loving be that hard? How could something so like a cosh do anything good? She pushed him away, her heart racing, her stomach turning. He never made any comment but every time he grew more sad, and left more promptly.

So Samantha made a practical decision. Like the decision she'd made to move to a city and work in a shop. As Dale's girlfriend, she felt safe. She wanted to go on being Dale's girlfriend. But real girlfriends had sex with their boyfriends, so she had to find a way to have sex with Dale. She booked a Monday off work to give herself two whole days and nights for research. On the Saturday lunchtime after work, she rang Dale's mobile to say she was ill and was going to bed. At least that part was true: she curled up with a pocket edition of *The Joy of Sex* and a pile of broken Eccles cakes.

It didn't take that long to read, once she'd got over the desire to giggle at the amount of hair there seemed to be in all the pictures. Samantha read it four times, as if she were studying for an exam. By Monday night she had found a way she could have sex with Dale. She had understood she could be in control, make Dale feel all the things he was supposed to feel, and yet give nothing of herself away. If hers were the wandering fingers and straying hands, she could remain completely hidden. She was going to be the one to build the bedroom of their relationship.

On Tuesday she drank alone for the first time in her life: a miniature bottle of gin in a glass of squash, before Dale came round. She put on the long strappy nightie she'd bought in her break, and spent half an hour changing her mind about wearing knickers underneath. It was Dale's good luck that he arrived at a moment when she had resolved 'off' for the fourth time. She kissed him awkwardly but with determination as he walked through the door. When she slid her hand inside his flies he was too busy seeing stars to feel her shaking.

'What happened?' Dale asked, incredulously, afterwards.

'I just needed to trust you.'

'I thought that you were scared. That you were a virgin.'

'Oh no! I definitely wasn't one of those!' said Samantha. It felt odd telling the truth.

Two months later, Dale took her to Bali for a week and told her about the girl of his dreams, the girl he wanted to spend all his life with, the girl he wanted to have his children. He described 'Dream Girl' with great conviction and in some detail. He explained that *she* was that girl. Samantha was glad to be told, as she would never have recognised herself from Dale's description. She was pleased that she had concealed herself quite safely inside Dale's expectations. She only wished there was a way to show him the tenderness and compassion she felt for the Dale who patted old stone and talked to houses, who smiled so totally, who seemed so grateful to be kissed. But it was too risky. So she looked out at him from deep cover, and wondered if he'd ever know that he was loved in a way he didn't expect.

They got married in a little makeshift temple on a beach. They had bare feet and each wore a white sarong. Dale smiled so much she thought he might break. They needed no form of identification for the ceremony. Dale laughed and teased her because he knew how sensitive she was about her passport photo; even he'd never seen it.

So just like number eleven Samantha has come to fill the space provided. And now every time she sees the house appear as they come round the corner from school, she gets a pang of affection for the place. As if the house, seven years on, knows what they have in common.

Maeve, from number thirteen, rushes out as she sees Samantha pass with the boys. Her greyish knickers are showing above the waistband of her long crumpled skirt; she has bare, dirty feet and her roots are showing. 'Oh, I'm *so* glad I caught you.'

'Hello, Maeve!' says Tony. 'Look what I made in school!'

Samantha is always slightly worried by how much Tony seems to like Maeve. How can a child so fastidious find someone whose breakfast crumbs are often to be seen in their hair, so attractive?

'Lovely. Lovely, Tony my sweet,' Maeve croons rapidly.

At least Joe is always suitably reserved in the presence of Maeve's rambling, unkempt body and loud plummy voice. He snuggles in to Samantha's legs and puts a thumb in his mouth.

'I've got a batch of carrot cake in the oven and the trip's gone again!' Maeve is almost wailing with distress. 'Would you be a *dear*? Pop in and do the switching thingy for me?'

'Yes, of course, Maeve.' Samantha is gracious, even though it is the third time in ten days that she has had to do this service for Maeve. 'Come on, boys, we're popping into Maeve's house for a mo.'

'Weeeeee.' Tony zooms ahead, and in through the purple front door.

Maeve is doing her usual apologetic twitterings, and Samantha is patiently (and ever so slightly patronisingly) explaining (again) that the trip switch is HERE, and ALL you have to DO . . . is . . . THIS. The light in the hall comes on, and the fridge in the kitchen shudders awake.

'Oh, you're so *brave*!' Maeve exclaims in wonder and gratitude.

Samantha smiles. She's given up telling Maeve she could do this for herself. Now she just enjoys feeling that she—supermarket assistant without an A level to bless herself with—is more capable than Maeve, who has two degrees and a part-time solicitor's job.

Tony emerges from the kitchen with Maeve's black cat, Archimedes, looped over his arms like a vast fluffy beanbag. Tony hugs the formless animal bundle to his face and wheedles, 'Can I stay?'

Before Maeve can invite him to sample the carrot cake, Samantha cuts in firmly. 'No, Tony, Daddy's coming home tonight.'

The door of number eleven closes. It's solid and heavily draught-proofed, so it makes a sound like a bank vault shutting. Once inside, the boys click into routine. They struggle out of their shoes and race up the stairs ahead of Samantha.

'Bring your clothes into my room, boys,' she calls, but she doesn't need to tell them. They do it every day. Still racing, they wheel into Samantha and Dale's white bedroom both making racing-car noises. They brake abruptly and screech to a noisy halt by the high double bed, grinning and squirming. They are both clutching a neat square of folded garments, the play clothes that Samantha puts on their beds every morning before they leave for school. They each put their clothes on the bed and step back theatrically.

'Where's your clothes, Mummy?' says Joe.

'I'm just getting them.' She piles a pair of beige shorts and a lemon T-shirt on the bed opposite the boys' clothes, then steps back. They all look at each other and smile.

'Tony's turn to say today,' Samantha announces. Joe squirms some more and claps his hand to his mouth.

'On your marks,' says Tony, 'get set . . . GO!'

They all begin to undo buttons, wriggle out of tops and socks, the boys panting with effort. Joe is giving this race his all. At five, dressing and undressing is a trial. Arms don't come out of sleeves reliably, and getting terminally stuck inside one of his own garments seems like a definite risk. 'Oh no!' he breathes as he finds that his little Thomas the Tank Engine underpants have come off with the elasticated waist shorts.

Tony's strategy is different now that he can handle almost any button. He's working on technique. Slyly he watches the economical way Mummy, a grown-up, takes her arms out of her blouse without rumpling the fabric. Doing it that way saves time at the end, because you can't say you've finished until you fold the clothes you took off.

Samantha is proud of her invention of this race. She paces the unzipping and hanging of her skirt, the unbuttoning of her work blouse, so as not to be first today. She has to be first sometimes to keep Joe interested in the unpredictability of winning.

'Done!' Joe shouts triumphantly. He's got his T-shirt on the right way round for the first time in a fortnight, and he's managed to approximate folding his school shirt pretty well.

'You beat me, Joe,' says Tony untruthfully. He doesn't smile. Letting Joe win is right but doesn't yet feel good.

'Me too!' says Samantha.

'I'm the winner!' Joe is delighted with this evidence of his maturity and dances round the room. There is something generous about Joe, his victory somehow includes his brother, so Tony feels that he can't say that Joe didn't fold his shirt really properly. But Samantha knows he needs her to notice that. So while Joe is still dancing about, she catches Tony's attention and rolls her eyes as she pointedly refolds Joe's crumpled top and shorts. Now, Tony smiles.

Samantha sees how much they are learning, from T-shirts the right way round, to elementary human relationships. She pushes down the tiny ripple of sick panic that runs across her heart from their every step toward autonomy; she knows it's foolish, they'll be making demands on her for the rest of her life, they'll always need her, she tells herself.

It's still warm at five thirty and the boys are happy getting their cars clogged and buried in the sandpit. Samantha decides to allow herself another few minutes' intensive snipping, cutting back the invading forces of next door's garden. Keith and Felicity in number nine have taken to rowing as a full-time occupation—they are at it now, near an open window upstairs somewhere—so their garden is completely out of control. Shoots of all sorts are continually scaling the wall and poking into Samantha's territory. They should know better; the moment any plant strays to her side of the wall, it's chopped. She cannot endure unchecked plant growth, it's too stimulating for her imagination. Dale wanted space to grow things when they bought the house, and went on about all the plants that could grow in Bristol's mild climate.

'Exotics,' he said, 'that's what we could have. You know, tropical palms, like the ones they have in Torquay. They look great in small town gardens like this.' She didn't tell him that *Cordyline australis*, the Torbay palm, wasn't a palm at all but a member of the *Liliaceae*. He wouldn't expect her to know things like that. But when he started going on about climbers and arches and making a 'jungle' for children to play in, Samantha had to do something. She showed him the leaflet about the parasites in cat faeces. Unless they paved the garden, she said, it would not be so much a jungle as a giant cat toilet. Archimedes and some of his down-market buddies were yowling on the wall at the time, for which Samantha was grateful. The thought of his little baby boy being blinded by such a thing so affected Dale that he brought a concrete mixer and a lorryload of stone paving over the very next morning.

So now Samantha's garden is concrete with four little square islands of compost. She grows flowers in these, lobelias, petunias, things that look limp-wristed and unthreatening, in neat geometric patterns. When they die down in autumn she rips them out, and savours the blank earth all winter. When the boys want to run about on grass, she takes them to the park. Its keeper is rather old-fashioned and still grows a succession of bedding plants in straight lines. Samantha has never noticed a weed there or even a French marigold out of alignment. It is very restful.

'Cooo-eeee, cooo-eeeee.' Samantha is distracted from dislodging a sow thistle from between two paving stones by the sound of Maeve calling over the low   part of the wall that separates their gardens.

'Oh, Mother! For God's sake. Can you be like, less *sad*?' That's Callendula, Maeve's highly pierced fourteen-year-old daughter. 'I mean "cooo-eee". For God's sake!'

Maeve and Callendula haven't noticed Samantha crouched by the wall, and the boys are too engrossed to hear anything. Samantha stands up. 'Hello,' she says tentatively.

'Oh there you are!' Maeve is leaning over the top of the wall, but Callendula elbows her out of the way. Callendula has on a purple velvet top, too hot for a summer day, and is in her usual full 'alternative' regalia—scarlet dreadlocks, eyebrow, nose and lip rings. She smiles angelically at Samantha.

'Hi, Mrs Cassinari! Mum and I were wondering if the boys would like to come and see Archimedes. We didn't even know he was pregnant, but he's having kittens in my bedroom.'

The word 'kitten' has some consciousness-piercing quality that 'Cooooo-eeee' clearly doesn't, for the boys now both leave the sandpit and come racing to the wall. 'Kittens!' they say together. 'KITTENS!'

'Mmm, little tiny ones. Newborn and he's still having them.'

'WOW!' Tony is speechless, but Joe is sceptical. Even kittens may not be enough to make him brave the terrors of number thirteen.

'I thought boys didn't have babies,' he says suspiciously.

'They don't,' Callendula announces eagerly, 'Archimedes is a girl!'

Joe makes no comment but sticks his thumb in his mouth and turns into a leg limpet: kittens might have been believable but Archimedes, a girl? No. That's too much impossibility for Joe to cope with. But Tony would go in search of kittens born to a plastic dog at this moment.

'Can I go and see them, pleeeeeeese.'

'Go on then. Run round to the front door,' Samantha says. She turns back to Callendula. 'Please make sure he's back by six! I'm expecting Dale home, and he's been away all weekend. C'mon, Joe. Let's get Daddy's tea!'

Having Mummy all to himself is better than fictional kittens any day. Joe is standing on a chair with a bowl of dried beans in front of him on the worktop. He stirs vigorously with a huge wooden spoon.

'I'm making boff-hoffie pie, Mummy. What are you making?'

'Smoked haddock soufflé, darling. Daddy's favourite.'

Samantha is enjoying herself again. She is a very convincing cook. She can picture herself at this moment, the woman smiling at her son and folding egg white expertly into a sauce. But Joe doesn't smile back. She can see he's about to ask one of his big questions.

'What would you eat if you could have anything in the world?' says Joe. His question is so direct, so full of desire for a real answer, that Samantha finds it unsettling. She feels a blush rising up her throat.

'Oh. I don't know. What would you eat?'

'I'd have Granny's *tartufo nero*.' Joe is already a likely successor to the Tavolino deli empire, a gourmand at five. The only Italian he knows refers to food—*prosciutto, bresaola, scallopini, gelati*—he savours the words, rolling them round his mouth. He says *tartufo nero* again as if he could taste the chocolate and ice cream.

'But what *would* you eat, Mummy, really?' Joe is looking up at Samantha as if his life depended on the answer.

'Oh um. Smoked haddock soufflé!'

'No! That's Daddy's favourite. What's *your* favourite?'

Samantha is flustered. 'Chocolate cake!'

'No, Mummy, that's Tony's favourite.' Joe's mouth is very straight now and his eyes could cut a hole in a pane of glass. Samantha can't meet his gaze. She turns away to put the soufflé in the oven, prematurely. It'll be ready too early now, will go leathery and fall.

'I don't know what my favourite is,' she says, but Joe's gone. She can hear him tipping Lego aggressively onto the playroom floor.

It was all downhill after that. Dale rang from his mobile just as Joe trapped his finger in the playroom door. Between technological inadequacy and full-volume screaming all she heard was something about 'body plasterers' and 'fate worriers'. He wouldn't be home until after 'hen flirty' or even 'larf never'. Then, when she went to retrieve Tony, she found the number thirteen household in crisis: one of Archimedes' miraculous kittens had apparently been stillborn. Maeve sat on the floor whimpering. Malcolm, Maeve's tall and uncoordinated husband, was stepping back and forth over the cat and kittens, his huge feet threatening death by crushing with their every move. Tony crouched between Archimedes and Callendula looking from the live kittens to the apparently dead one, his face caught between tears and smiling. Only Callendula was doing something sensible: she wiped the pinprick nostrils clean then gently blew into them through pursed lips. The tiny

364

mouth opened and the smallest mew in feline history came out of the shell-pink space. Maeve and Tony burst into tears.

The kitten was christened—Lazarus of course—and Maeve invited the boys to breakfast the following morning to see him again. Tony said goodbye twice to all the other kittens and Archimedes. By that time, the soufflé was more of a sort of rubbery Spanish omelette. The boys wolfed Tavolino's ciabatta moistened with olive oil and pushed the yellowish lumps of eggy fish round their plates.

'D'you think Lazarus would like to eat mine?' asked Tony hopefully.

'Lazarus can only eat his Mummy's milk, darling.'

'But he hasn't got a Mummy!' said Joe.

Tony rolled his eyes. 'Archimedes is his Mummy, Joe.'

'*Archimedes is a boy.*' Joe spoke with laser-like intensity, his anger building behind his eyes. 'Just having kittens doesn't make him a Mummy.'

'Of course it does!' As usual Tony's response to anger was mannered calm, affected rationality. As usual it only made Joe more passionate.

'No, it doesn't!' Tears welled up in his eyes. 'He wasn't a Mummy to start. You can't just *make* yourself be something.' He looked at Samantha. 'And you can't just *pretend* about favourites!'

It's gone 'hen flirty' now. Probably beyond 'larf never'. Samantha has exhausted nearly all the tasks her house and children can provide. She has bathed her boys—singly tonight—read them stories and kissed them to sleep. She has washed up, ironed, hoovered and darned two pairs of socks in front of an hour's worth of TV. She is tired enough to sleep, but she stays up, waiting to be Dale's wife when he comes home. She likes to be his wife, and he likes her wifeness. She sees herself sometimes as a happy portrait looking out at Dale through holes cut in the canvas of the eyes. Occasionally she wonders if they are both standing behind portraits—a picture of a husband and a picture of a wife facing each other over the heads of real children.

She wanders around downstairs plumping cushions and picking specks from the carpets. She turns on lamps and admires the vistas over sofa arms and table tops, the pearly half-reflections in the paintwork. These rooms are her creations, cleverly concocted by Samantha, the Taste Magpie. Each object, every square foot of wall or floor has its own history: the Knole sofa, now the colour of a lightly mouldered strawberry, she found brown and sagging in the corner of an auction room in Portishead. She got it reupholstered in material that she noticed tumbled in a crate outside a junk shop in Montpellier, that turned out to have been the ex-curtains of a castle in Monmouth.

These still-life stories have helped to construct Samantha's world. Her rooms reassure her tonight, after Joe's unsettling outburst. You *can*, they tell her, *make* yourself into something, aren't they themselves the proof of the self that she has made? Calmer, she goes upstairs with an armful of clean towels and stares blankly through the spare-room window as she folds them.

Out there the falling dusk is drawing the streetlights into the air, bleeding brightness above the rooftops and gardens. When they first moved in, she didn't like to be alone with this view. Ten minutes of staring idly was enough for her to see the whole of downtown Bristol clothed in Central American lowland rainforest. It was worse at dusk. The trees could creep in subtly from Temple Meads, the blue-green canopy blending at first with the urban haze. Only when the crown of some rainforest giant—a kapok tree perhaps—appeared two hundred feet above City Road, would she notice that howler monkeys were chorusing above the traffic. The huge trunks dwarfing the Victorian façades, the inscrutable continent of leaves taunting her, showing again what she could never have.

But worse than what she imagined, was what the view from the window made her remember. Those successive curves of roof lines reminded her of the ploughed furrows at home in Suffolk. She remembered how, in autumn, stubble fields surrounded her parents' house, falling away in slow arcs and crescents from the end of the garden to the horizon. Then, the ploughing tractors would come, turning the gold and green of the cropped fields under the clay. As each bright field was crossed out with lines of dead earth, a lifeless chill seemed to crowd closer. Then the frost came and set the furrows like bars, shutting out the softness of living things. Always before the landscape had been her friend. Even in winter. It shared its secrets then: the hidden nests, the mouths of burrows, the bones and withered flesh of kills made under the cover of summer leaves.

But that December, the fields, lanes and hedges had no heart. Their faces set against her, with mouths shut in a hard line. They drove her back into the house, where it was always some Godforsaken Sunday night. Granny Pearl would be waiting to be served her tea, shifting her false teeth rhythmically over her gums. Dad would be making sandwiches, with tinned ham and lumps of butter too cold to spread, whispering 'Samantha', over and over under his breath. In the sitting room, Mum would be on the sofa, very flat and still. The dismal emptiness of Sunday night religious programming would project onto her sick mother's face, like an ineffectual treatment ray. Upstairs, doing homework alone, Samantha would feel all the fear and silence seeping up like damp.

She'd come to a city to escape those winter furrows and that longing. And she had done it, finally, by adding time to the distance between her and the past. Now Samantha has memories of her husband and her children, and her suburban life, to keep her from the landscape of her girlhood. Looking over the rooftops as she folds the last few towels, she remembers the last time she looked over the rooftops and folded towels. Or Dale dozing on the patio. Or the boys on their climbing frame. Or the fairy lights strung all round the garden walls at Christmas. Nearly a decade filled with Tony and Joe and Dale has pushed the imaginary rainforest and the memories of East Anglian winters far under the surface of her life.

She is not the girl who left the frost-bound Suffolk landscape. The proof of that is all around her and in her and now, too, walking through the front door. Dale comes straight upstairs. 'I'm home!' he calls.

She meets him on the landing. He doesn't reach out to her or embrace her. He never does, never has. Instead he kisses her on the cheek, lightly, and for a moment holds her face in one hand. This is Dale's habitual expression of affection, understated but infinitely precious.

'I'm so late! Sorry. Bloody plasterer didn't turn up and then the lorry with the slate on it got stuck in the lane. I spent four hours digging him out of the hedge. I'm so knackered.'

'Come on, get to bed then!' Samantha says.

'Bath first. I'm filthy. I'll go and run it.'

'Cup of tea?' She knows he wants one.

'Phoor. I'd kill for one. Thanks for waiting up.' Then he smiles his total smile. 'Angie. My Angie.'

THREE

'WHAT D'YOU THINK about taramasalata?' Louise is sitting with her skinny legs very crossed. She is hunched over them, leaning on her elbows. Her pointy folded-ness reminds Samantha of a pair of dividers. 'I mean, taramasalata could be a kind of cross-over thingy. You know, like Geography?' The inside of Louise's head is like a tornado in a library, pages from Dickens fly past next to headlines from the *Daily Star*. Louise's connections are hard to follow: most people don't pay enough attention ever to understand what she's talking about. But Samantha likes having to concentrate.

'At school,' Louise explains, 'they used to say it could be a science or an art. So if you couldn't cope with *e* equals *m c* whatever, or remember the future tense of *venir*, then you did Geography and it did for both. See?' She smiles hopefully.

Louise and Samantha constitute the Catering Subcommittee of the Deacon Road Primary School PTA. This afternoon, a Wednesday, Samantha's day off from Stayfleurs, they are sitting in Samantha's kitchen and discussing the menu for the next PTA event, the annual Staff versus Parents' Cricket Match and Tea.

'I understand the Geography part, Louise, but what's that got to do with taramasalata?'

'Well, it could do for vegetarians *and* meat eaters, couldn't it?'

'It's fish eggs, Louise. I think that's meat.'

'Well, I don't know. I mean some vegetarians eat eggs, don't they? *And* fish. So taramasalata is the best of both worlds. It's a cross-over in two ways really.' Louise suddenly looks very happy—she enjoys the way her tornado mind blows things around. Samantha decides that the vegetarians could eat both cheese options so taramasalata is neither here nor there. Which is kind of Louise's point anyway. 'All right. We'll do ham and salad, cheese and pickle, cheese and tomato *and* taramasalata.'

'Great.' Louise scribbles in her notebook. 'Mixture of granary and farmhouse white, sixty more rounds than last year. Settled.'

'And I'll do the cakes as usual, shall I?'

'Oh. Well, yes. Of course.' Louise looks up, momentarily scandalised: even her brain couldn't come up with the idea that *someone else* might 'Do The Cakes'. 'Your cakes are half the reason people come to the Cricket Tea. They're a sort of tradition now.'

'Hardly that, Louise.' Samantha turns away to refill the kettle and to hide the pleasure that Louise's compliment gives her. But she knows it's true. Her lemon sandwich, her chocolate gâteau, her coffee and walnut cake—they compensate for rain, they celebrate sunshine, her cakes are the very soul of the whole event.

'More tea, Louise?'

'I'd love to, but it's Barney's swimming lesson and I didn't bring the "you-know-whats".' Barney is Louise's six-year-old son. He is charming and bright, a friend to both Tony and Joe, but he rules Louise's life like a fascist dictator. The 'you-know-whats' are the only brand of biscuit that

Barney will eat. Without them to fuel his stroke he might as well puncture his own arm bands. And with Barney's obsession with success in general, and swimming in particular, Louise might as well slit her own throat. This is why she refuses tea. She must drive across the centre of town to buy 'you-know-whats' before picking Barney up from school. But before Louise can pick up her handbag, Samantha is up on her little kitchen steps, reaching for a yellow tin, stored on top of the units.

'I've got some "you-know-whats". I got them when Barney came here after school. There's a whole lot here unopened.' Samantha hands the flat purple and white packet to Louise.

'Angie! You are a saint! There's only one place you can get them!'

'Mmm. I know. The Post Office Stores on Coronation Road.'

Louise is speechless with gratitude and admiration; she can only beam and wrap her legs into a reef knot again.

Wednesdays for Samantha can be difficult. No matter how tightly she plans to pack her day, there is often some unexpected hole in her schedule. She tries to keep some chores in reserve, something meaty like a cupboard to tidy, but it's not always possible. So sometimes she's reduced to re-ironing sheets, or changing the labels on the frozen food.

Today it looked as if everything was conspiring against her. First Tony persuaded Joe to come with him to check on Lazarus, and have breakfast at number thirteen. They got themselves dressed and disappeared *with Dale's blessing* while she was in the shower. She did Dale a cooked breakfast to make up for some of the loss of tasks, but then he began to dismantle her day too!

'I'll drop the boys at school,' he said over his fried egg. 'It's on my way. I've got to go to a couple of reclamation places the other side of Stroud. I'll be finished there by twelve so I can do the shopping, pick them up after school and take them to swimming too.'

Dale had just emptied most of her day. She'd done so much housework waiting for him last night that there was nothing to fill it with. Samantha was irritated, but she smiled calmly and refilled his teacup. 'That's OK. I'm all set to do it. You just get straight on with what you need to do.'

'No, I want to do it. I'll be away again for the next three nights. I want to see them. And it's your day off. Relax!'

He patted her bottom gently but she snatched herself away. 'That's not the point of my day off.' She pulled his breakfast plate away from him knowing she'd lost. Her only chance of restoring her itinerary lay in trying to get Dale to storm off without the boys. But he'd grown so placid that it was almost impossible to manipulate him in that way any more. Worth a try all the same. She tutted as she piled up the plates. 'You've left your fried bread again. I don't know why I bother!'

'Neither do I really.' Dale sipped his tea unruffled. 'I've never liked fried bread, but you always cook it. It's a mystery. Some kind of ritual?' This was where Tony got his ice-cold response to Joe's temper.

Samantha found herself getting hot-faced in spite of her plan. 'No. It's just not a Full English Breakfast without the bread!'

'So what?' Dale shrugged. 'What does that matter?'

It wasn't working. 'It's like pizza without anchovies!' She was almost shouting now.

Dale was just getting more logical. 'But suppose I didn't like anchovies? I'd just leave them.'

Samantha could feel tears wanting to form behind her eyes. What did Dale know about the dangers of dead time? Did he ever wonder why they had a colour-coded label system for everything in the freezer? For a chip of a second Samantha felt she would tell him about encroaching rainforest and the remembrance of winter fields. She stomped to the sink and yelled instead. 'Yes, but the pizza's still *made* with them.'

Dale followed her as far as the kitchen door. 'Ah! There you are!' he said. 'It *is* a ritual. You don't care if I don't *eat* the fried bread as long as you *cook* it!' He smiled in triumph, reminding Samantha of the confounding birthday cake. It wasn't his fault that he didn't understand her world. She'd made it that way. So she smiled through the holes in the canvas and wondered how to fill the spare hours of the day.

Dale turned to leave. 'Post's come!' he called from the hall. 'I'll take it—looks like work stuff. I'm getting the boys. Have a nice day off.'

So it could have been a very tricky Wednesday. Louise wasn't due to arrive until ten, but by nine all the breakfast things were cleared. Then, miraculously, the phone went.

'Oh, thank God you there!' It was her mother-in-law.

'What's the matter, Maria?'

'Marcella phoned a sickie.' Marcella was Maria's newest assistant. 'She says that *no way* she gonna make it in 'ere today. I have a big delivery coming, also big *big* lunch party, antipasto order to get out . . .' Maria trailed off, she wasn't good at asking for things. Dale would never collude with Maria's inability to admit any sort of defeat. If Maria had complained of Marcella's absence to him, he would simply have said, 'Bad luck, Ma. I can't think how you'll manage alone.' But Samantha could always see Maria young, a foreigner with a bastard child in mealy-mouthed 1960s Bristol: only her stubborn self-reliance had kept her alive. So Samantha was happy to press her assistance on Maria, especially when the alternative was ironing tea cloths.

'Would you like me to help?'

'Oh! But it's your day off! No, no, no.'

'I'm not doing anything, Maria. Really.'

'Well. Well.' Maria sighed hugely. 'OK. I guess, if you sure.'

'Yes I'm sure. But I'll have to go about two.'

'Nnnah. Oh. That's not so good. But OK. I can manage around that.'

By the time Samantha had phoned Louise to move their meeting to the afternoon, a cab was waiting to take her to Tavs. Maria must have ordered it before she rang.

Tavolino Verde has become an institution for the middle-class community that surrounds it. If you know about 'Tavs', then you are one of the club. Your preferences in newspapers, books, films, clothes, children, furnishings and partners can be predicted to be within a certain range of liberal acceptability. Tavs is part of the social landscape, and 'having a Tav' has a meaning for all age groups. On a hot summer day, Mummies, home from the office, promise their kids 'a Tav' on the way home. They pull up in their Volvo estates and while the children eat *tartufo nero*, *gelato grosso*, or little pots of *tiramisu*, their mothers chat to Maria, and buy a 'Tav' dinner: *canaroli*, saffron, Parmesan. On Saturday mornings Dads are dispatched for 'a Tav' for lunch: they shuffle in, blurred and uncombed, to buy *ciabatta* and *focaccia*, Ascolane olives, *soppressata*, *mortadella*, *prosciutto*. Children buy 'Tavs' with their pocket money—a *gelato* in summer, a slice of *panettone* or a Florentine in winter.

Tavs has been there for so long that it has spun its own special myths: *ratafias* bought from Tavs are reputed to be especially accurate at predicting the sex of babies. A lighted wrapper floating to touch the ceiling means the birth of a boy, one that turns to a tissue of carbon and flutters down before it's over the candlesticks, a girl. So, for as long as most people can remember, Tavs' ratafias have been the present to give a newly pregnant woman. Tavs' chocolate *gelato* is said to be a sure-fire aphrodisiac, so synonymous with sex that 'chocky Tav' has become local slang replacing other nastier words like 'shag' or 'fuck'.

More generally, Tavs has come to be associated with all things pleasant, celebratory and romantic. A perfect holiday, a romantic day out, a well-struck deal, a successful examination paper would all be described by local residents as 'good as a Tav' or even 'better than a Tav sandwich'. Tavs is the living embodiment of the axiom that the way to any human being's heart is through their stomach. Which is very good for business.

For an establishment with such a big place in the local psyche, Tavolino's is tiny, squeezed between an estate agent's and an ironmonger's. But Maria makes the most of the small available space. The whole of the shop front is plate glass; the interior is cream, and lit so that no corner escapes a bright pearly glow. From outside you can see everything: both sides of the counter, and all the goods. It looks like a particularly enticing theatre set, a world of homely magic which you can join just by stepping through the almost invisible door.———

As she steps out of the cab Samantha can see Finnian wrestling with a large wicker basket full of anchovy jars. Finnian has been Maria's manager for years. He is tall, soft and white like dough, without being fat. He has dark red hair, as thick and curly now in his thirties as it was when he came to Maria, a forlorn university drop-out. He has the lilting remnants of a Cork accent, in spite of the fact that since he left at sixteen he's never been back: it wasn't, he says, 'a good place to be queer in'.

Maria, in an orange shirtwaister and matching shoes, is arranging the morning's bread delivery at the far end of the shop. Samantha can see that they've already had a row this morning.

Maria calls, 'I do the bread. I be there, just minute, OK?'

'Hi,' says Finnian, unfolding over the anchovies to lean and kiss her on both cheeks. 'Glad you could come.' He rolls his eyes and pinches in his nostrils. 'You know what she's like when she gets in a paddy.'

'Shall I help with this basket?'

'No, I'll manage. Could you finish the display cabinet for me?'

Samantha knows the routine in Tavs quite well. Over the years she has always been happy to fill in. And of course she came to Tavs as soon as she began going out with Dale.

'In that cake shoppe,' Maria insisted, 'you will learn nothing. With me, you learn all Italian food. Ev-er-ee-thing. *And* I will pay you more.'

It was Finnian, in fact, who taught her 'ev-er-ree-thing'. He had all the fervour of the convert. 'I was raised on the chips and the vinegar from the shop next door,' he told her early on in her apprenticeship, 'so I thought the Saints had taken me the day I ate my first proper antipasto. Jeezus. First communion or what?'

His enthusiasm was infectious and his desire to share it unstoppable. He required her total concentration. Soon, learning the difference between '*cotto*' and '*prosciutto*', between '*toscano*' and '*sardo*', began to make her feel safe again. Cheeses, hams, salamis, chocolates, pastas and breads encrusted her new persona along with Dale and his visions in stone and brick. The more she accumulated the more protected she felt.

Yet with customers, she noticed, Finnian was different. He chatted in the same engaging way, but the chat was padded with empty enquiries. What was the forecast for tomorrow? How did they plan to use the *farfalle*? It was weeks before she realised how Finnian too was protecting himself. It was the most valuable thing she learned from him—that the best camouflage is to reflect the image of the observer. Pretty soon she'd got the trick too.

'Such a brilliant jacket!' she'd chirp. 'How do you plan to use the buffalo mozzarella?' She could look any customer in the eye and know that they'd never really see her.

Samantha had always been a good pupil. By the time she and Dale were married there were only a few times a week when Finnian could show her something new. But with no need to cram Samantha with more knowledge, Finnian found a new sort of question to ask.

'So, where were you born then?' he said one sleepy Tuesday morning. Samantha woke up fast. 'Suffolk.'

'Ah! A country girl, then. Are your family farmers?'

'No. They're dead.'

'Oh, I'm sorry, I had no idea.' That was as far as eighty per cent of people ever got—gagged by their own embarrassment at uncovering two dead bodies in an ordinary conversation. Even Dale hadn't got a lot further. But Finnian had survived being called an abomination by his own mother, so death was a breeze.

'No, actually, I tell a lie there. I did know, because I remember Maria saying you were an orphan. When did they pass on?'

'When I was little. I grew up in care.'

'I bet that's a bloody euphemism and no mistake. What was it like?'

Finnian was now part of a tiny minority prepared to brave the possibility of being confronted with another person's pain. People only went beyond this point to find a convenient place to turn round; all she had to do was provide it. 'Just like you'd imagine, really.'

'I don't have that kind of imagination. Were you in a home or what? Foster parents?' Finnian wasn't going to turn round.

'Look, I don't want to be rude or unkind, but I don't talk about it. Not to anyone. Not Dale even.' She'd never used such a tone with him before. It was like a hamster snarling.

'Well, I respect that of course.' He paused for a moment then spoke again. 'But you know it's not a good thing to keep anything locked in the closet. Believe me, I know!'

Samantha watched him sadly as he turned to serve a customer, and knew that Tavs was just too risky a place to work any more. Morning sickness gave her the escape she needed, and she never went back permanently because, with two of Maria's grandsons to raise, she couldn't commit herself to working for Dale's family business. 'I don't mind letting a supermarket down,' she told Maria, 'but if one of the boys is ill, I'd hate to leave *Family* in the lurch.'

'So nice you come. On your day off too!' Maria is on tip-toe to embrace Samantha. 'You make Finnian better temper. He is getting to be a grumpy old queen!' She sends her most Italian film-star smile down the counter to him.

Turning away in mock outrage he calls back, 'You are a dried-up old has-been, Maria, so it's a blessing I'm here to look after you.' The air thaws, a Technicolor cartoon spring rushes its tendrils all over the shop just as the first customers of the day come in.

With Louise's assertion that she should once again provide the cakes for the cricketers' tea, Samantha's next three Dale-less evenings are to be filled with baking and icing. At four o'clock, with Dale and the boys not due back for an hour, a whole sixty minutes of empty space had opened up in front of her. But even that got filled. Felicity from number nine turned up not two minutes after Louise's departure. She was as usual perfect—a tailored suit, a smooth chignon, quietly expensive jewellery. Hard to imagine that this was the woman whose domestic party trick was throwing TVs through closed bedroom windows.

'Could I possibly just come in for a minute?' she said in a very small voice. She'd appeared like this before to borrow sugar, tea, coffee, staying for a minute of empty pleasantries then going back. 'I don't suppose you've got any dried sheets of lasagne have you? I think I'd like to make Keith his favourite meal.' She burst into tears. Samantha led her into the sitting room and made her drink some sweet tea. Felicity stopped crying. 'I'm all right. Just a silly minute.'

It was clear she wasn't going to offer any sort of explanation. 'Thank you, Angela,' she said. 'I'm sure I can trust you not to mention this to anyone. I don't want everyone in the street knowing my private life.' It was touching the way Felicity failed to realise that arguments at eighty decibels with open windows tend to render the private somewhat public. But Samantha reassured her and gave her a whole homemade lasagne from the freezer to take next door.

So now it is ten to five. Still quite hot and gold outside. A chicken casserole is in Samantha's oven and she decides she'll walk to the corner of the street to meet Dale and the boys. But as she steps out through the front door, Dale's car draws up to the kerb. He turns to speak to the boys and for a moment the three of them don't see Samantha. They are so alike now with their hair all wet, she is filled with a rush of passion for them. This, *this* is her true life. This is the flowering fruiting apple tree, spreading into the light, the root stock to which it was once grafted, far below, buried safe under the brown earth.

The boys tumble out of the back seat and chase up the path.

'Am I forgiven for not eating fried bread?' says Dale.

'Yes, Dale. I won't even make it any more.'

They smile at each other as close to setting aside their portraits as they have been for quite a while. Then Dale reaches into the back pocket of his baggy jeans. 'There was this among the mail I took this morning. I thought it might be a PTA thing. I know they give your address for all the committee members sometimes, yeah?'

He gives her a stiff brown envelope. The address has been typed but the name written by hand. The good formal copperplate is as easy to read as any printed typeface, but Angela Cassinari stares at it for a long time while her blood screams round her head.

'Samantha Powell' it reads.

'Samantha Powell' it still reads.

'Coming in, love?' says Dale from the doorstep.

'Yeah. Yeah.'

'You OK?'

'Yeah. Just wondering who she might be.'

FOUR

AT 2.00AM consciousness is a fish out of water, flapping on the surface of the great wild continent of the unconscious. Elephantine shapes of long-lost fears and unexpressed desires lumber down the shadows, and multicoloured fogs of memory roll in from the deep ocean of a zillion brain cells. At 2.00am time goes anything but forward, the past and the future sit down like lambs and lions. At 2.00am we have nothing to protect us from the universe. It is the hour of least resistance, to birth, to death, to ourselves.

So at two twenty this morning Samantha is lowering herself down the stairs, leaning her weight heavily on the smooth banister to avoid the creaky treads. A blade of orange streetlight is slicing between the imperfectly drawn curtains in the living room. Falling into the black, it cuts a thin sector of the room from the huge darkness. At one edge of this pool of brightness a pair of china paws shows, apparently preparing to paddle. At the other is the long thin envelope.

All evening and half the night Samantha has resisted the call of that envelope, pushing it down with tasks and busyness. She even managed a sort of sleep, with her eyes wrenched shut and her mind burrowing down out of the way. But at two she woke to find all the lurid possibilities that the envelope and its copperplate name had conjured, free, dancing round the bed like Dervish bears.

So now she is sitting on her Castle-clothed Knole sofa staring at the envelope's indistinct outline and trying to be calm. She tells herself that after so long she is safe. That whatever it contains can't matter. She switches on the brass lamp, reaches for the envelope and rips it open, flinching only a little at the loud tearing sound.

Like the envelope, the writing paper and the words are oddly archaic. Samantha reads them several times before they settle into a meaning. The letter is not from any relative, nor the police, so the very worst has not happened. It is a solicitor's letter from the executors of the 'late Lawrence Spence'. The *late* Lawrence.

'The *late* Lawrence Spence desired that the house, gardens and glasshouse of Lime House be made over into your name.'

So much information in so few words. Samantha looks around the room searching for something to steady herself—the china dog, the patterned rug. But her lips are whispering on their own, 'The late Lawrence Spence. Lawrence. Lawrence is dead.' It is after all still the hour of least resistance, and Lawrence always was hard to resist.

Sam had met Lawrence on a Sunday in April. As usual on a Sunday she had spent most of the day shut in her room doing homework. That Sunday it had been mostly chemistry. She always felt that there was really only just so much organic chemistry that a person could be expected to absorb in one sitting without having a sense-of-humour bypass. By five or six that day she'd had enough.

'Going for walk. Taking the dog,' she called as she went out.

Bracken bounced up the hill ahead of her, pushing his flat nose into the banks of new grass as he tried to sniff out baby rabbits. At the village sign she stopped and peered over the edge of the verge. Yep. There they were, the first cowslips of the year. Up to Lords Wood then. With this mild weather the first oxslips could be out. She knew that other people went to Lords to look at their botanical celebrity, but the oxys, as she called them to herself, still felt like hers. A bit like having the Koh-i-noor diamond stashed away for your own private gloating session.

She and the dog set off down the unmade cart track between the wide fields of winter wheat and barley. Late on this bright spring Sunday the fields were empty. They made Sam think of huge faces turned up to the sky, calm and open. The ground was still wet enough to hold clear puddles in the ruts, tiny crystal worlds with silken mud at the bottom. Bracken's feet made a strange rapid plopping sound as he streaked past her, full of the joy of speed, disturbing everything. Only the skylarks were unperturbed, tens of them. Twenties. Hundreds. Thousands perhaps, suspended fluttering, falling, climbing, and singing, singing, singing. The light burned their tiny dots of bodies into the blue, so that it seemed that the sky itself was singing.

Sam turned left towards the wood, calling to the dog and looking back over the field for him. He wasn't in sight. Instead, out in the shimmering sea of green, four hares were boxing. First one pair then another rose from the wheat and battered with their front paws, heads thrown back. They moved with a quickness and abandon that made Sam's throat catch.

Suddenly the dog burst between them. One in a panic took off across the field with the over-excited boxer in pursuit, and both were across the next field before Sam could call Bracken to heel. Turning her back on the wood and its oxslips she stomped after them, swearing.

She crossed three fields and from the top of the last watched Bracken's rear end disappearing into a thicket of trees surrounding a large house. The thicket enclosed a high brick wall, crumbled in one place where Bracken must have gone through. Sam followed, making for the house. The dog would no doubt be following his nose to the kitchen having lost the hare. From what she'd seen from the hilltop, she'd expected the dense thicket of overgrowth to go almost to the front door. But as she walked, the tangled wilderness changed quietly to garden. The scrubby saplings were replaced by large trees, perfectly spaced in a simulation of natural colonisation. Spring flowers scattered across the grass. A special stillness drew her on as she forgot all about the missing dog.

She came to a band of whitebeams coming into first leaf, with their pale buds lifted up like church candles. And glowing in the dusk below them were oxslips, fifty or more all in full bloom. The harmony of the whitebeam shoots and the oxslips was flawless, artifice made into a perfected version of the natural. Beyond was the velvety emerald of a lawn, surrounded by tree ferns. Tree ferns! The soul and symbol of the tropics, of jungles and steamy heat. Tree ferns were a shorthand for all the places Sam wanted to go to and everything she wanted to do. She walked out onto the lawn towards them. The trunks were still partially swathed in jackets of straw and last year's fronds dangled sadly from the top of the trunk, but nestling at the base of the old fronds were the vulnerable silky heads of the new, curled croziers covered in silvery hairs. Sam reached out to touch with featherlight gentleness.

'So, another fan of *Dicksonia antarctica*?' A voice straight out of her mum's favourite TV dramas about nineteenth-century toffs spoke behind her. Sam snatched her extended hand back to her side and almost screamed. Lost in the admiration of the garden, she had forgotten entirely about its owner. And here he was, walking towards her over the velvet grass. It was too late to run or think of excuses.

'I'm sorry,' was all she could manage to say.

'Why? What have you done?' He was right next to her now. Smiling, apparently relaxed in the presence of this intruder on his property. He didn't look much like anything she was used to. He wasn't a young man, like stringy Mr Volta the trainee PE teacher, nor middle-aged in the way dads were middle-aged, with the look of a bag where everything had dropped to the bottom like her own father. His body had a tightness about it that reminded Sam of a whippy stick. He certainly wasn't old, but then he did have a lot of grey in his dark hair. His clothes were a puzzle too. Faded blue jeans but worn with a crisp formal-looking shirt, white, with a button-down collar. He was, she decided, exotic, like the tree ferns, a non-native species.

'Um, nothing. I mean, I'm sorry I came into your garden.'

'Are you?' He had raised an eyebrow. 'You didn't *look* sorry a minute ago. You looked quite pleased with my *Dicksonias*.' His tone suggested some sort of joke, but it was hard to read his languid upper-class pronunciation. Sam smiled anyway, seeing that he wasn't really angry.

'I *love* tree ferns.' Her enthusiasm usually charmed adults, especially as she almost invariably knew more about her subject than they did. 'My dad only grows ordinary things like roses in our garden. Tree ferns are so *tropical* . . .' she gushed.

But the performance hadn't impressed him. 'Well, no actually not all *so tropical*,' he said rather irritably. 'These are *Dicksonia antarctica* from a perfectly temperate region.'

Sam could feel the blush rising up her throat. 'Oh,' she said.

There was a small silence. He looked at her with his peat black eyes. 'I'm being ungracious. You're quite right, of course, they are synonymous with tropical habitats. So tell me, why are you so keen on the tropics?'

'I'm going to be a biologist *when I grow up——*' She blushed again. Damn. At seventeen she had to get out of that phrase! 'I mean, when I leave school and university.'

'Really? What sort of biologist? That's a bit general.'

Brave again she trotted out her little party piece, her potted plan for the future. 'I'm going to study rainforest. Tropical rainforest. Probably Central America, Costa Rica perhaps. The plants, mainly, but the ecological interaction between plants and animals I find interesting too.'

He threw back his head and laughed. The straight dark hair fell away from his head a little, making him look for a moment very young. But Sam was insulted, hot with anger all over again. She wasn't used to this response to her earnest expression of her life's dreams.

'It's not funny. It's very important. We're losing species faster than we can catalogue them!'

'No, no.' He recovered himself and held up his palms in a gesture of apology. 'I'm not laughing at you at all. I think it's wonderful. It's just that most young women are more interested in silk underwear and lipstick than in tropical rainforest. Forgive me, I didn't mean to be disrespectful.' He stretched out his right hand and Samantha stared at it stupidly. No one she knew shook hands. Awkwardly she stretched out and grasped his hand firmly, determined not to seem like the limp sort of 'girl' who would trade a wild kapok tree for a pair of French knickers. 'I'm Samantha Powell,' she said, taking care to look straight into the black hole eyes.

'Pleased to meet you, Miss Powell. I'm Lawrence Spence, a fellow enthusiast. Plants are my passion. I have quite a selection of truly tropical species that I grow under glass. Would you like to see my conservatory?' Lawrence's hand, light as a leaf, held on to her as he waited for her reply. Samantha hesitated, feeling herself on the edge of something, then the dog started up an unmistakable barrage of loud barking somewhere close by, and she drew her hand away.

'That's my dog,' she said. 'He ran in here and I followed him.'

'Sounds as if he has cornered a squirrel.'

Lawrence walked her to his gate with Bracken restrained on a lead he had provided. He stopped between the two stone pillars, as if there were some invisible barrier that barred his way. 'I won't come further than this if you don't mind, I've business to attend to,' he said. 'But do come back some time. I'd really love you to see the conservatory.' He marched away, and Sam was reminded of something robotic and non-human. She wasn't sure she'd take up the invitation. Then she remembered the fine leather lead, too good not to return to its owner. Lawrence always found a way to make you come back.

There is pale grey showing through the slit in the curtains and seeping around their edge. Now tomorrow and yesterday are restored to their usual setting. If Lawrence was really dead, then she was safer than she'd ever been. She didn't want his house or the hothouse or the garden. It could all rot, forgotten. She didn't need to give him a thought ever again. All she had to do was push the letter down in the dark along with everything else. Easy.

Samantha flicks off the light and shoves the letter deep into the heart of the settee.

In spite of the drizzle Jack Mullen is leaning against Stayfleurs' security door. His small, pale frame has its habitual limp, greasy look. How does someone so young manage to look quite so used? Samantha wonders. He is sucking a roll-up and exhaling slowly through his nostrils. As usual the smoke has a suspiciously spicy smell. As usual Jack is reluctant to step aside without some attempt at an exchange of words.

'Good morning, Mr Mullen,' Samantha says in her brightest and most businesslike tone. Everyone else except George of course calls him Jack. He is possibly the youngest staff member Stayfleurs has ever employed. 'I play golf with his grandfather occasionally,' Mr Geoffrey said on the day he was taken on, 'Jack was at Cambridge you know, before his, er, illness.'

Liz, rather closer to the family than Mr Geoffrey, as they share a cleaning lady, had a different perspective: 'Illness!' she said. 'Smoking pot during lectures on the romantic poets more like.'

'Well! Good morning,' Jack drawls at her but doesn't move, 'and how is the Ice Maiden of Bishopston this morning? Impervious to my charms as always?' Normally Samantha would just smile sweetly and ignore him, and after ten seconds he would stand aside, his eyes on her like chewing gum stuck to a pane of glass. But this morning, before she has the chance to be surprised at her own irritation, she has spoken.

'*Mr* Mullen, I don't know if it's escaped your attention, but it is actually drizzling. And I am getting wet.'

'Really?' He cannot quite conceal his delight in having, after so long, got a rise out of her. 'I'm flattered by that remark, Angela.' He throws his stub into the bin by the door and stands aside at last.

'After you, *Mrs* Cassinari. I always like to get behind a woman.'

In the changing room Samantha tries to tighten all her psychological sphincters. She concentrates hard on the day ahead and what will be required of her, but all she can hear this morning is the detail of her work force's conversation grating under her attention like sand in the eyes.

'Well, I told him at least now we know what it is.' Claudia is tucking her pearls inside the neckline of her blouse. 'One has to be positive.'

'Forgive me, but giving something utterly spurious a name *isn't* positive,' says Mary in her 'my-husband-was-a-GP-you-know' voice.

'What *do* you mean, Mary?'

'Well, my husband says that there is really no such thing as ME. It's just depression. Or laziness of course.'

'Are you suggesting that my Richard is depressed or malingering?'

'No. Of *course* not, Claudia. I'm just giving you my perspective on ME. Perhaps Richard has something else instead.'

'Or perhaps all he needs is sex.'

'I beg your pardon, Liz!'

'Sex. Has your son had sex recently, Claudia? It's a simple enough question. I've never heard you mention a girlfriend.'

'Ohh! *No girlfriend eh?* Mary is off. 'Well perhaps it's another sort of treatment he needs. You and Richard *are* very close, Claudia, and that's supposed to be one of the things that turns them queer.'

'Oh, for God's sake! Will you three shut up!'

Only a dousing from a bucket of ice water could be more shocking. The three women are struck utterly dumb. Samantha has her hand over her mouth and looks like the bridesmaid who broke wind during the exchange of rings. 'I'm sorry, ladies,' she says, 'I think it's nearly time.'

They walk to their check-outs silent, and smarting like burnt fingers.

For the first time in her retail career Samantha is not savouring this difficult morning. The Hannan boys have been back with their mother and have clearly got a taste for Drama. This time it was two giant jars of organic pasta sauce that they launched across an aisle. Samantha rings their father while their mother pats her eyes with wet tissues.

'Mr Hannan, why don't you just wallop your boys a bit more?' Samantha has never walloped her own boys, and has never suggested such a thing to anyone before. She has shocked herself again.

No sooner has the pasta sauce been cleared up, than the over-seventies with ambitions to become the over-nineties turn out in force. They have finished Rudolph and are back to get Donner and Blitzen. What's more they have told their friends of the power of Stayfleurs' reindeer meat.

Obviously it works or how else could they have remembered what they bought for supper over thirty-six hours ago?

Although the reindeer was selling well, there seem to be endless problems with other lines. Everyone has been directing queries to Samantha who has had to abandon her till for long periods to pacify disgruntled customers and find replacement products. All of which has made the other tills busier and created an atmosphere of tension.

Samantha is helping a mother of four to pack her purchases. The twin babies are sitting in the trolley like a pair of pink sugar pigs, hungry and grizzling. The smallest toddler is holding onto its mother's leg and hampering her movements, so that the transfer of every item from trolley to check-out is a twenty-second job. Meanwhile, the eldest toddler is running from till to till like a demon, leaving a trail of sweets and chocolate bars that he grabs, then drops. Just as Samantha is about to field him, a small, elderly woman marches up to her, encased in tweed, pearls and the several cords of her archaic hearing aids.

'I can't find tapioca pudding. Where is it?' she demands, addressing a point somewhere past Samantha's left shoulder. Samantha attempts to look her in the face, to give her the best chance of lip-reading, but the woman is not used to direct contact with the lower orders. She averts her eyes. 'Tapioca, girl. Don't just stand there gawping at me!'

'Aisle four, madam. Next to the tinned soups and condensed milk.'

'What? What?'

'Aisle four. Next to condensed milk and tinned soup.' Samantha leans down a little, attempting to make communication possible.

'Speak up, you stupid girl!'

Demon toddler fixes on Sam's hand for some reason and begins to pull at her as if her whole body were a maypole string. The child's pulling and the woman's shouting are as sharp as a needle to Sam's perceptions. She snatches one of the woman's hearing aids and speaks into it at close range, like a football commentator.

'Aisle. Four. Next. To. The. Tinned. Soup. You. Rude. Old. Bag!'

She snaps the hearing aid back into position and grabs the toddler's ear. She drags him to the trolley and presents him to his mother. 'The next time you bring this dysfunctional little brat in here, can you make sure he isn't shit-faced on sugar?'

Under the circumstances Mr Geoffrey was very good about it. White and whispering with shock, he suggested that Samantha take some time off. She agreed without a word. As she left, Jack Mullen opened his mouth to wisecrack but she beat him to it.

'Don't you dare say anything, you pathetic little dope head. I could pick up one of your roaches out of that bin and even your granddad being on the square couldn't save your skinny arse.'

And now it's two o'clock, a whole one and half hours before her duties as Mother begin again. For once, such a gap in the day's schedule seems a good idea. She has ninety minutes to work out what is happening to her today and try to resume normal service. She felt nothing out of the ordinary as she left the house with the boys. Everything that had flown out of the long brown envelope along with Lawrence's name had been stuffed back in. Yet somehow she had shouted at 'the ladies', insulted a customer and given Jack Mullen the satisfaction of a reply. She feels distinctly odd. And the oddest thing about the odd feeling is the absence of the usual panic about any loss of internal control. Inside she feels a kind of comfortable blankness that is focused—in a blurred sort of a way—on a snippet from a natural history film that she must have seen on TV as a child. It shows the smooth white caps of mushrooms bursting with inexorable force through the hard crust of a concrete surface. It plays and replays, soothing, like a mantra.

Without a thought of a plan Samantha wanders into the large shabby shop that sells secondhand clothes for charity and busies herself with a rack of unseasonably heavy garments. A stained sheepskin coat, a dogs-tooth skirt in Crimplene, several puffy anoraks. And then, between two navy nylon blazers, a little jacket that stands out like Audrey Hepburn in a crowd of New Jersey fish packers. Samantha caresses the material. Cashmere. *Cashmere*. She whispers it to herself. It's a word she hasn't said in a decade. It is a word that belonged to Bea. Her mother. When her mother said 'cashmere' it filled the air with perfume, with stories. Samantha leaves the shop and walks fast down the road. But the mushrooms have pushed through the pavement, and the cashmere, soft as mascarpone on the tongue, has done its work.

Nothing particularly shocking or exciting ever happened in Bea's stories, but still Sam loved to hear them. They made her feel close to who Bea was, before she was ill, before she was old, when she could have been Sam's best friend and not her mother.

All Bea's stories began in the same way, with an outfit. Clothes were the set, the stage, the lighting, the atmosphere.

Bea would begin: 'It was the most gorgeous material, dove-grey *cashmere* with a little mauve check. In *mohair*. Very fine.' Her voice would have that special lisping, confidential tone, the words *cashmere* and *mohair* taking on a sacred, spell-like quality that could transport you to the fairy-tale world of luxury and idleness. Sam and Bea would be sitting together almost cheek to cheek; on the sofa downstairs with the telly off, or on Bea's bed, sometimes with Bea in it, everything but her voice as limp as a popped balloon in the wet. Never in Sam's room, because there was never anywhere to sit amid the litter of books, files, paper, house plants and discarded clothes. Today they were sitting in deck chairs on the lawn, Bea wrapped in a nest of blankets even though the late spring sun was warm. Sam snuggled close to her mother, savouring the first time for weeks that they'd been together like this.

'Mauve,' Bea said, 'mmm. No, not really *mauve*. More a deep lavender. Look! That wallflower, next to the lemon yellow and before the crimson. There. *That* was the colour.'

'Anyway,' she continued, 'I made a skirt and jacket from a Vogue pattern of Auntie Dilys'. I used to tailor things properly in those days, lined it and everything. And I cut it very close fitting.' She put a wiggle in her voice so that Sam would imagine her wriggling into the suit and coaxing the zip to close. 'Classic style,' she said patting Sam's cheek, then turned away, looking into the air as if seeing herself in all her youthful glory, hardly believing that she had once been so lovely. 'I had to starve for a week before I wore it the first time. And I stood up all the way to Gloucester station so the skirt wouldn't seat.'

Sam tried to see her mother as the slender immaculate figure, teetering off the train in her too-high heels.

'Roy was at the station to meet me. Imagine, I had this beautiful suit, little sealskin handbag; I'd dyed an old silk hanky of Dad's the *exact* same shade of lavender as the check, for a little scarf at my throat. And grey suede shoes. Can you *imagine*? Grey suede shoes in *those* times? We hadn't long come off the ration. And all *he* said was, "Oh, Bea, you'll catch your death without an overcoat." I can laugh now, but then! Oh! I made him take me to the station two hours early and told him I never wanted to see him again.'

This of course was supposed to be the real point of the story because, freezing in her close-cut classic suit on Gloucester station was how Ralph, Sam's father, first found her. 'At least *your father* appreciated it,' Bea said. '"It's a shame to cover you up, but you *are* shivering," he said, and he gave me his coat. It was a very good coat, black, pure wool with a raglan sleeve and satin lining. Soft as butter, warm as toast.'

This point was the end of the ritual part of the story. Now came the interactive section. When Sam had been little, this was the bit that had told her about steam trains, roads almost free of cars, milk from pails not bottles, and houses without electric light. But now her questions were different. 'Was it love at first sight then, Mum?'

'No. I'd known him for years, but he'd been away doing National Service then College. I suppose you could say that day was the first time I'd noticed him.'

'All right then, was it love at first notice?'

'Yes, Sam. Yes I think it was.' Bea sighed and looked away. When Sam had first asked these questions Bea had talked fondly about their court-ing, of long walks, and posies of wildflowers. But the contrast with their current state of siege was too painful now.

Sam changed tack, back onto the safe ground of clothes. 'Did you wear that posh suit after?'

Bea smirked. 'Lots of times. Your father loved me in it. In fact the skirt got ripped on a hedge one night when I was out with him. We just nipped into a gateway for a little cuddle, you know.'

Yes, Sam did know about 'cuddling'. She'd been kissed first at four-teen, on a school trip to the Lake District. She and her friend Christine got off with two scouts from the campsite next door. But regular boyfriends seemed to Sam a bit of a drag. They kept you away from homework and expected a lot more than just a twenty-minute snog and a little grope. By the time they started sixth form Christine was on the pill and Sam a contented virgin, tipped for an Oxbridge place. What use was a boyfriend to a woman who was going to spend her life in the rainforest?

'Did you mend the skirt after that?' Sam asked.

'The material was just too fine to be mended.' Bea sighed. 'You know, I've never seen any like it since. I never knew where Mummy got it.'

Another reason Sam loved the stories was because they featured her dead granny, Agnes, whom she had never met. Dead Granny Agnes sounded a lot more jolly than the live Granny Pearl who they lived with.

'She was such fun,' Bea always used to say, 'I'd put my feet in her bath and we'd talk for hours.'

Pearl would never have run a bath generous enough for anyone to even put a little toe in. She was always going on about how you could keep clean with just a teacupful of tepid water.

'Daddy would bang on the bathroom door sometimes. "How long are you girls going to go on giggling in there." Oh, how we used to laugh!'

'Just like us, Mum!' Sam said. 'Just like we laugh!'

And it had been true once. Sam and Bea used to laugh a lot. And Ralph, like his father-in-law before him, had loved to hear his wife and daughter 'getting the giggles'. But now, in the summer when Sam was seventeen, there wasn't much to laugh at any more.

It wasn't as if Bea had ever been really well. By the time Sam was ten, 'Mum in hospital' was like an annual festival. Ralph took time off work to care for Sam; it felt odd yet thrilling to be alone with Daddy. He burnt chips almost every night for tea, and ironed things that didn't need it, so that all the towels went from fluffy to flat.

Sam never worried that her mother would die, because her illnesses seemed an ordinary part of things: there were lots of other mummies in the hospital so they couldn't all be dying. Ralph worried though, she could tell because he constantly reassured Sam.

'Now don't be surprised if your mother's a bit groggy. She's fine.' 'She's doing very well.' 'The doctor says she'll be home in a week.' And he'd try to hug her resisting body, which only wanted her mother's touch.

Yet, when Bea came 'out' he seemed angry with her. He'd snap at her if she tried to come downstairs for a meal, or tell her to get dressed if she'd just popped down to see half an hour of telly. In a month or so it would wear off. They'd be back to normal. Bea cooking and cleaning. Ralph coming home from work and mowing the lawn. But gradually there were fewer patches of calm between the snarling, as the gaps between Bea's spells 'in' got shorter.

That, Sam supposed, is why they ended up having Granny Pearl as a permanent resident. 'She can take care of you while Mum's "in",' Ralph said, 'and be here for Mum when I can't be.' But really what Ralph wanted was a buffer between him and Bea, between him and his anger about her chronic ill health. The moment Granny Pearl moved in she forgot that seventy-one really wasn't that old and that she'd just been wallpapering ceilings in her own house. A week out of hospital Bea was running up and downstairs getting Pearl's morning coffee and malted milk biscuits, salad sandwich lunch and cake and tea at four.

Afterwards, Sam thought of Granny Pearl's arrival as the event that marked the beginning of the end. Pearl made the house feel like shoes that no longer fitted, cold, tight and chafing. She grumbled about every-thing, and turned personal criticism into a kind of art form.

'Those trousers would be lovely on a young woman with nice legs, Bea.' 'Intelligence is all very well in a girl but I think grooming goes a long way, Samantha.'

Pearl could rival any RADA-trained actor in her rendition of the tear-ful retreat in the face of any retaliation. Even after months of its repeti-tion it still worked well enough to leave behind it a pall of guilt. Ralph and Bea spent so much time and energy in their conflicts with Pearl that they barely spoke to each other.

But there were still times when Bea and Sam could laugh.

'Sorry, Sam, no cornflakes left. She ate the last of them.'

'Oh! There was half a packet left yesterday!'

'I don't know where she puts it. She's so skinny.'

'She's probably shoving them up her jersey, so she can sell them back to us on Sunday when we've run out and the shops are closed.'

'Sam!' Bea tried to sound censorious but she was laughing too much.

Pearl came to live with them at Christmas, and after New Year Bea seemed to get weaker. Then, one morning in the Easter holidays, a single word extinguished the last flickers of fun in Sam's home. It escaped whole and intelligible from a muffled phone conversation. *Cancer*. Sam was transfixed. She tiptoed downstairs to the sitting room. One look at her mother's face, still held to the phone, was enough. Bea kicked the door shut. But they both knew what she'd heard.

Sam didn't dare ask about this new invasion in her mother's body and Bea offered nothing. There were just the usual platitudes: 'Doctor says I'm doing well.' 'Not feeling too bright. But a little rest and I'll be fine.' Silence encased the cocktail of broken glass that had become home. Nobody spoke and nobody listened to her. She felt she had been handed this deadly information and then shut out. It was like being on the outside of a soundproof screen. Sam had never felt so alone. She sat on her bed at night stroking the leaves of her cheeseplant in the dark and asking out loud for her mother not to die.

On weekdays there were distractions: giggling on the bus with Christine and taking the piss out of her taste in music; standing up to spotty Mr Brett's sexist banter in physics lessons; battling with Mrs Farz's low horizons: 'All I'm saying is, don't set your heart on Oxbridge. It's just very difficult to get in.'

'Look. Can I take the entrance exam in school or not? Yes or no?'

'Well. Yes, but . . .'

'Thanks, Mrs Farz. Bye.'

But at home the deafening quiet of the unsaid had only one antidote: another kind of unreality, dreams and fantasies of her future world as it would be when somehow the awfulness of 'now' was done with. So Sam imagined herself in the rainforest. No, not the rainforest, not that flat, academic word but 'Jungle'. She saw herself walking on the forest floor, in the dim, sage-coloured light, as if she were at the bottom of a great sea. Far, far above her the breeze blew the canopy into billows of green, saturated in sunlight and alive with birds and monkeys; but down here among the boles of the trees, as big and archaic as dinosaurs, there was a profound stillness. Sam could close her eyes and put her hand on the warm, rough skin of a trunk and sense the sap singing under her palm;

electric, alive, potent with tangible magic. But even in her green world that solitude had been turning into the same loneliness she experienced in the real world. Until the day Lawrence had stepped so lightly from behind a tree fern.

FIVE

'YOU LOOK AS IF you've seen a whole fleet of ghosts. Or whatever the collective noun for them is. A wobble perhaps or a scream.' The hand on her arm is for a moment incomprehensible, in the way ordinary furnishings are on waking in a hotel bedroom. It is the first thing in the external world that Samantha has been sensible to since the moment she blundered out of the charity shop. 'You're white as a sheet, are you OK?' The face looking anxiously up at her is at last recognisable.

'Oh, Louise!' says Samantha, suddenly flushed with relief that she can put a word to something in the scene around her. 'How lovely to see you!' She kisses Louise on the cheek. Louise blushes with surprise at this unprecedented display of affection from her usually unemotional friend.

'Are you *sure* you're OK?'

'Mmm. Oh. Fine. Just feeling a bit, you know, under the weather that's all.' Samantha looks around. She is in the school playground. She is here because of her children. But whether to drop them off or pick them up seems to have slipped her mind for a moment. Tentatively she searches for clues: 'What time is it?'

'It's gone twenty-five to. They're always late out on a Thursday.'

Samantha is just about to ask who are, when the big double doors open and a horde of children tumble out, like sweets from a spilled box. And the two foremost little morsels look to Samantha and cry 'Mummy' simultaneously and run towards her. Two lovely little boys; the taller one with dark obedient hair, keeping his tartan satchel on his shoulder as he runs; the other more solid, hair a little bleached, approaching with the abandon of a small whirlwind. They are completely beautiful, and of course utterly familiar. And yet today, Samantha finds her eyes filling with tears because somehow this is the first time in her life that she has seen her own children. She kneels to hug them.

Joe puts his sticky hand on her face. 'Are you sad, Mummy?'
'No, darling. I'm not sad.'
'But you're crying.'
Tony pulls her arm. 'Get up, Mummy, everybody's looking.'
As Samantha gathers herself, Louise hovers closer nervously. 'Um, Angela, I wonder. Um, is it still OK for Saturday? You know, the cricketing tea? Cakes. Taramasalata. All that?'
'Oh . . . yes. Cakes, of course. I'd forgotten.'
Louise titters nervously. 'That's not like you! Will you still do them?'
'Of course. We'll start tonight. You can help, can't you, boys?'
There is a moment of disbelieving uncertainty.
'What, and do *real* mixing?' says Joe.
'And put things in the *oven*?' says Tony.
'Yes! Why not?'
'Wow!'

The interior of number eleven is not looking its customary immaculate self for this time on a Thursday night. The playroom floor is still invisible under a layer of plastic bricks, toy cars and felt-tip pens *without their lids*. In the front room, all the cushions are on the floor and piled under a canopy made of two pink sheets held in place by safety pins and pegs. Among the cushions are plates with crumbs and crusts, peel and apple cores. The air in the kitchen is still warmed with the sweet homely scent of baking, but all the work surfaces are as jumbled as scrapyards. Bags of flour and sugar lean at odd angles, losing their contents through open mouths. Squalid as dirty knickers, margarine wrappers lie scrunched beside soiled wooden spoons. Splodges of cake mixture spot the walls and the floor. But some order has come out of this chaos: on the kitchen table under a sheet of muslin are a line of cakes, baked but not yet iced. Not one is round or square or any sort of normal cake shape: two teddies, a pyramid, an amoeba, and a hand. Their colours are unusual too—blue, purple and bright pink except for the one brown chocolate bear. It seems odd that now the house is quiet, after so much has obviously been going on. But it is completely still, breathing out gently in the twilight, like someone who can finally undo the waistband that has been too tight all day.

Tony and Joe have had a wonderful evening. You can see it on their faces. Each wears a little moustache of chocolate cake mixture, and a delicate spotting of lurid food colour. They have fallen asleep on their parents' bed. Tenderly Samantha peels off their socks and shorts, covers them with the sheet and stands in the twilight at the end of the bed looking at them. Her heart squeezes as she thinks how much they enjoyed this evening's release from routine. 'What do you want to do?' she'd asked them.

They knew immediately. 'Make an indoor tent!'

'Have all the cushions *on the floor!*'

They wanted things that Samantha's little rules didn't allow: spontaneity and mess. Most of all they wanted her participation. So she sat on the floor and played car crashes, ate toasted sandwiches in the 'tent' and showed them how to make cakes in the most un-cake like colours.

She whispers 'thank you' to her sleeping boys—because she too has had a wonderful evening—and wanders into the spare room to look out over the rolling landscape of gardens and rooftops. Great trees are gathering on the skyline, but she doesn't flinch. There is something comforting tonight in the inevitability of their spread. At last the orange lights in the next street are extinguished by lianas, and she lies down on the smooth, cool bed. The expanding blank white of a huge mushroom cap fills her mental frame. There is almost no room left to wonder where this might lead her tomorrow.

'Phooooo!' Max from the garden centre sticks out his bottom lip and blows his blond fringe from underneath. 'I dunno how we're gonna do this.' His square shoulders are straining and his biceps are damp under the tight cap-sleeved T-shirt. They are on the path outside number eleven, with a native of subtropical China, *Trachycarpus fortunei*, a Chusan palm, in a pot the size of a hip bath. It has a just-caught, untamed look about it with its five spikey fronds spread in alarm like the giant hands of a drowning witch. After two hours of manoeuvring large pots through Samantha's house and out onto her patio, Max's customer care is wilting. 'It's not going through that door. No way!'

Samantha looks from palm to door and back again. How can they have spent forty minutes wrestling this plant out of the van and up eight feet of path, without noticing that it is three feet bigger in almost every direction than number eleven's front door?

'Wow. Cool. What is it?' Samantha peers round the palm to see Callendula, out early from school.

'The Chewing palm,' she replies. 'But it won't go through the front door.'

'It'd go through ours though, Mrs Cassinari,' Callendula says. 'And there's that old fence panel at the bottom of the wall. We could move it and get it in that way. Dad's in too, he can help lift.'

Normally Samantha finds offers of help unsettling; they necessitate a doubling of the internal guard. But 'normally' she's not filling her garden with a selection of plants that look as if they could have been flown in from the Amazon. 'Well, that's very kind, Callendula, if you're sure your parents won't mind?'

By the time *Trachycarpus* has been navigated through number thirteen's hall, down the garden, through the gap in the wall, and up to Samantha's patio, everyone concerned is much better acquainted. They have, by that time, been through so much together: setbacks and solutions, improvisations and discoveries. It's taken two banana loaves, twenty-three cups of tea, a roll of old carpet and some pram wheels to get this far. Plus the contribution of everyone at numbers nine to thirteen and Louise and Barney.

It is now after six. Tony, Joe and Barney are chasing round the pots dodging leaves and tendrils. Eight adults, counting Callendula, are in Samantha's garden toasting her palm, and reminiscing about their roles in its journey, like mountaineers after an ascent of Mont Blanc.

'I'd completely forgotten about the wall behind the fence panel,' Malcolm is saying to Max.

'Yeah, if Keith hadn't stepped in there we'd have been well stuffed.'

Keith beams and reaches a long arm out to engulf Felicity's shoulder. 'Yes, but Flick remembered about the railway sleepers . . .'

'I'm just sorry I couldn't help lift that's all,' Felicity simpers.

'Oh yes,' Maeve pulls up next to Felicity and Keith like a suddenly braking bus, 'have you done something to your back?'

Keith and Felicity exchange a look of powerful delight.

'Well,' Keith says slowly, 'it is pretty safe to tell you now . . .'

'I'm having a baby in October. We've been trying for a long time.'

'A very long time.' The shouting, the rampant garden, the flying tellies and the tearful lasagne are all explained.

'Oh, how lovely. I'm very happy for you both.' Maeve is crying again. How she manages to be a solicitor is quite beyond Samantha's comprehension. Everyone crowds round Felicity and Keith. Samantha refills glasses and says thank you to them all, for about the twentieth time. She had no idea that feeling grateful could be so nice.

Eventually the children brought the impromptu party to an end. Exhausted, they had to be fed and put to bed.

'What'll you do with all those plants, Mum?' Tony asked sleepily.

'I'm going to make a jungle in our garden.'

'Ooooh, can we have parrots?' said Joe.

'We'll see. Sleep now, boys. Daddy's home tomorrow.'

Outside now in the light cast from the kitchen window, Samantha is wrenching up paving stones and revealing the good earth beneath. Here the huge purple spikes of giant *Echium* will reach for the bedroom windows, here the spiny pineapple leaves of *Fascicularia* will coat the soil like a pangolin's scales. She's planting canna lillies and Himalayan ginger. By August this selection of plants from all over the world will be a little counterfeit of jungle. Dale was right all along, this south-facing plot is a perfect place for an exotic garden. She shudders at the memory of the four little holes in the paving.

Later, nails broken, sweaty and soil encrusted, she sits on the patio steps and looks at her new planting. The half-light doesn't hide the starkness of the bare soil, or the rather shocked appearance of the plants, not yet settled in their new home. But this new clearing calls the rainforest closer. Soon there is a whispering wave of a million leaves blocking out the streetlight. In the darkness under the fence panel something growls, then steps from the shadows. Samantha holds her breath as a jaguar sniffs delicately at the newly turned earth, then clears the wall in a bound.

Louise and her Catering Subcommittee helpers are in the pavilion kitchen buttering bread as if their lives depended on it.

'I'm so glad the weather's nice!'

'Oh, doesn't it make a difference?'

'D'you remember last year?'

Samantha stands in the main hall, listening. She should be hurrying to lay out her cakes: the table is waiting to receive them, draped in white cloth like an altar. But Samantha is not at all sure what people are going to say about the cakes this year: the thought of a purple amoeba with green icing and silver sugar balls in the middle of that virginal expanse of table cloth is too shocking—like the Pope giving his Christmas blessing in drag. The pink hand has lost its hand shape somewhat, in the process of being iced, and the pyramid seems to have doubled in size since it was mortared together with layers of cream. The two teddies are still convincingly bear-shaped inside their rough furry buttercream. But the ordinary lemon sponges and chocolate and walnut cakes only serve to make the rest look even more bizarre.

'Goodness!' Louise exclaims, arriving by her side. She puts her hand over her mouth.

What, Samantha thinks, *have I been doing? These cakes are like an insult.* 'Shall I just take them home again? It won't look too sparse if I just put out the normal ones . . .'

'What!' Louise takes her hand from her mouth to reveal the widest smile Samantha has ever seen on her face. 'Oh no! They're lovely. I'm terribly impressed. They're very sort of Barcelona-ish. Like that sculpture park with the multicoloured monsters. Oh, *you know*.'

Samantha doesn't, but is reassured. She scuttles to the table with the cakes that Gaudí, apparently, would have been proud to call his own.

Taramasalata *and* purple blob cake? Mummy's a revolutionary, boys.' Dale is laughing, but only with his mouth. He arrived late at the cricket match having driven from the site that morning, his eyes dull and shadowed. All afternoon they have been sinking further into their sockets. But Samantha has resolutely ignored whatever is cooking behind Dale's face; like the boys, she is full of the surprise that Dale will get when he walks out into their new back garden.

Outside the front door the boys pop like over-shaken lemonade.

'Mum, Mum, can we show him now?'

'Shut your eyes, Daddy,' commands Joe.

Samantha notices how pale and worn he seems, how relieved to give his hands to his two little sons and let them lead him. Samantha is struck by the thought that perhaps, of all four of them, it is only Joe and Tony who really understand where this family is going.

'OK,' says Tony, 'open them!'

It is an astounding transformation. Dale wanders down the central path, all that is left of the paved garden. An intermittent carpet of stiff pointed leaves like green icicles replaces the flagstones. Springing up from among it are big bold plants, like a series of living sculptures: long tongues of green; tiered layers of dancers' skirts on stalks of green bone; purple spikes, straight as metal. He looks back towards Samantha, his face a frozen traffic jam of questions.

'I got it all out of Stayfleurs money. Money I've been saving. The garden centre recommended everything. They're all pretty hardy. It'll all fill out a bit. The boys like it, don't you, boys? And we can go to the park if they want to run about or play football.'

There is a little silence. 'D'you like it, Daddy?' Tony asks.

'Oh, yes, I think it's fantastic.'

'Mummy said we might have parrots,' says Joe.

'Oh, did she? Run inside a minute, boys . . . turn the telly on and see what the Test score is.'

Joe opens his mouth to dispute the dismissal but Tony, wise to the stillness in the air between his parents, grabs his brother, 'C'mon, Joe.'

Dale stares about him. Sam wants so much to tell him not to be afraid, to beg him to accept the surface of things as they are. There have always been questions neither of them asked each other. They have always acknowledged the safety of their positions behind their respective portraits. But making a jungle of the garden has somehow broken the rules, so that the questions stand in the air between them shouting.

'What made you do it? What about the cat poo?' he asks.

'I did it as a surprise for you. Because it's what you wanted when we moved in.' She squeezes his hand and looks out at him, willing him to feel the love he's never been told about. But all he can see is something he doesn't understand.

'But why now? What's changed?'

How can she begin to explain? If she gives him even the smallest thread to pull, her whole life will unravel. She shrugs. Turns away and goes inside. 'Shall I make tea?' she calls from the kitchen. 'Cannelloni?'

They ate in the garden. Dale busied himself with the boys' jungle fantasies, imagining all sorts of animals peeking from behind the plants: lions, hyenas, giraffes, wildebeest. Samantha smiled and bit her tongue so as not to point out that none of the animals Dale suggested would be found in a rainforest. Dale stayed downstairs in front of the TV while she bathed the boys alone. They wanted to find animals in the bath so she risked revealing a little knowledge.

'The bath is freshwater, Tony . . . we can't have sharks in it. But you can have river dolphins, and sturgeons and anacondas.'

The thought of giant snakes under the suds got them far too excited so she sat with them until they fell asleep. Then the bathroom was dirty, and the linen cupboard needed a little tidy; it seemed silly to go downstairs and have to come up later to do a few little chores. But now it's ten o'clock and there's nothing left to do. Dale has been alone with the TV since seven. She should go down and coax him back into faith in the solidity of the surface of things. She steps across the landing, resolved, but at the top of the stairs she turns back. A bath would be nice. She locks the bathroom door, turns on the taps and peels her clothes off anyhow, careless as a snake sloughing.

There is a gentle knock. Dale whispers, 'Angie? Are you OK?'

'Oh, yes. I'm fine. Just having a bath.'

'Can I come in? Please?'

Dale has never asked for this before. Their only physical intimacy happens in bed; at all other times they are as chaste as siblings.

'Oh, all right. Just a second.' She wraps herself securely in a towel and lets him in.

'Thank you. Can I sit down while you take your bath?'

'Well, I suppose so.'

'What's the matter?'

'Nothing. Nothing. It's just that you've never done this before. Seen me in the bath.'

'You've never made a jungle in the garden before!'

'Don't you like it?'

'Yes, I like it. But I don't understand why you did it now.' He looks at her unflinchingly, almost angry. 'You know, with the purple cakes and everything. What's happening to you?'

'Nothing's happening to me. What d'you mean?'

Dale slumps on his seat. 'Oh, I don't know. I've had a horrible week.' He rubs a hand over his eyes. 'Are you getting in this bath?'

'Yes, I suppose so.'

'I'll wash your back for you.' Dale is aroused, she knows by that tone. But he never makes the first move, that's her role. She starts it, she sets the pace, and she gives Dale all he wants. Her control gives her safety.

The bathroom is the only place where she is truly naked. She feels it now under her towel, vulnerable, exposed and real. Dale's desire feels threatening here, out of its usual context. Reluctantly she steps towards the bath, holding the towel in place with both hands.

'Better take your towel off then.' In a single step he is beside her, unfolding first her arms, then the towel. He notices her shiver. 'I'll warm you, Angie love.' His hot hard fingers are all over her, strong and insistent, taking the initiative that is usually hers, being in control. But her flesh is as dead as plasticine, and her heart gallops. She feels so frightened that she knows she will be sick. She ducks violently over the bath and retches. Gobbets of chewed cannelloni, like broken internal organs float in the hot water. Dale picks up the towel and drapes it roughly round her shoulders. She could make up some story about having felt ill all day, but she knows it won't be convincing.

'I'm sorry, Dale. I'm really sorry,' she says. And she is more sorry than he can know that she can't explain any of this to him.

'S'right,' he says in a flat voice, unfamiliar in its lifelessness. 'Can't help how you feel. I'm done in. I'm going to bed.'

By the time she's scrubbed the bath free of dirt and probably two layers of enamel, Dale is just a dark hump on the far side of the mattress. She creeps into bed. Sleep seems unlikely. But she spent most of last night taking up paving stones and planting the garden. Soon she is struggling over a frozen plain, a mixture of sand and snow whipping her legs, Dale always just ahead of her somewhere in the twilight.

'Cup of tea?' Samantha opened her eyes. The daylight in the window had a reproachful mid-morning sort of look to it. She took the mug that was offered and gulped. Dale's face swam from the brightness, paler and more shadowed even than the night before.

'What's the time?' she asked.

'Half ten. You've been asleep for eleven hours.'

On a normal morning that would have been shocking; Samantha is always up early. But all she said was, 'Oh. Where are the boys?'

'Number thirteen. Looking at kittens with Callendula. She said she'd keep them for an hour.' He took her wrist. 'I'm taking the boys to Mum's for a bit,' he said. 'She can pick them up from school and take them home. I can be there by six.'

'What?' It was as if Dale was speaking backwards, his words didn't seem to mean anything. She looked around the room bewildered: the smaller of their suitcases was packed. Three pairs of underpants identical, except in size, sat on top waiting for it to be shut.

'I think you need some time alone. Some rest. Time to think. And I do too. So me and the boys are going to Mum's for a while.'

'Why? I don't understand? Is it the garden?'

Dale couldn't look at her any more. 'The garden's part of it. It's been a bad week. Disastrous. The business is in trouble, Angie. Really big. Too many people owe me money. I've got thirty grand of outstanding invoices, I need to get ten grand's worth of materials to finish the Bath job and the money's just not there. I came back from the site yesterday to tell you we might have to sell the house. And you'd done that to the garden but I don't know who for. And now we'll have to sell.' He wiped his palm over his head, pushing some weight aside. 'Oh, it's all knotted up in my head.' Huge fat tears began to roll down his face. 'I can't cope with it now. Not with the business and all, it's just too much.'

He stood up and crossed the room to shut the case. Samantha sat very still. Nothing was making any sense. All she could grasp was that he was leaving and taking the boys. She opened her mouth to speak several times but couldn't fix on what to say.

'I'll ring you,' Dale said, now almost choking. 'Or you can ring me. Or something.' He didn't kiss her or say goodbye. Just took the suitcase and stumbled out, down the stairs and through the front door. She heard the boys bounce out of number thirteen and into the car.

'Where's Mummy?' Joe's voice was clingy and plaintive.

'Mummy needs a rest.' Dale had regained that steady double bass.

The car doors slammed and her husband and her children disappeared out of her life. Who was she now?

396

Rest. That's what Dale said. She's had that all right. All day in bed with her arms around a pile of pillows. It's afternoon. Lawn mowers hum and children's voices chink across garden boundaries with a sound like morning milk bottles. Dale's words knock around the room as if they were coins left in a washing machine. They have formed themselves into many permutations over the course of the day, losing meaning rather than gaining it. Even the bedroom is growing unfamiliar.

What she needs are the old remedies: tasks. She gets up and goes downstairs. The living room still bears the traces of Thursday night's encampment. She will, she says to herself, just tidy the cushions a little. But she knows where her hand will reach, deep into the settee.

The moment she touches the stiff, slender envelope something shakes out of the last few hours; some of Dale's words at last have a meaning:

'The business is in trouble. I came back from the site yesterday to tell you we might have to sell the house.'

The washing machine stops in mid-cycle and all the words and images fall in a heap to the bottom of the drum. She looks around at the unequal walls of number eleven. At this moment the old cheese-crock house is the only thing that is solid and real. It is the container for her children, her nest with golden eggs. Half of Dale's tears suddenly make some sense: he too needs this house, it's the proof that he provides for his family in the way his lost father never did. She can pull the solution from the envelope: Lawrence's house will buy a terrace of number elevens. But the house can't be pulled out alone. Like Hope in Pandora's box it keeps bad company.

SIX

THE OFFICES OF TUCKER, Fryer and Woodward, Lawrence's lawyers, stood on a recently built estate apparently made from the plastic bricks in Tony and Joe's toy box. The little ticky-tack houses gathered round a square of green, so synthetic-looking that she expected to see a blue plastic cow grazing there. Immediately she could imagine police cars pulling onto the neat little brick forecourt and thought she caught sight of her father's green estate parked round the back. It was a struggle not to run, but she held back the thoughts of parental saloons and panda cars by imagining them like matchbox vehicles with model people inside. It was effective enough to let her walk calmly into the bright anodyne consulting room and sit opposite the young woman lawyer, Miss Taylor, as if the whole scene was happening to someone else.

Samantha watched her own white fingers pulling documents from the bag on her lap. She heard her own voice explaining the link between Samantha Powell and Angela Cassinari. The lawyer's red-lipsticked mouth moved to make words but they arrived at Samantha's brain some time later, in the way that the sky roars after the fighter plane has passed.

'There's no problem, Mrs Cassinari, you have all the documentation here,' the words announced from the now still mouth. 'In any case Mr Spence included reference to the use of your middle name as your Christian name and your married surname in his will.'

Lawrence *knew* she was Angela Cassinari? Had *known*, all along, where she was? Samantha shuddered as the room become coldly real.

'Did Mr Spence give you any idea how he knew my address? We haven't been in contact for ten years. I just wondered . . .' Miss Taylor was clearly surprised.

'Forgive me, Mrs Cassinari. I assumed in the light of the bequest and the details Mr Spence gave us that you were . . . *close*.'

'What details?'

Miss Taylor blushed, caught out in professional indiscretion. 'I wasn't personally acquainted with Mr Spence, but I understand that he spoke warmly of you and your husband and children. As he was something of a recluse, I assumed that you had perhaps visited regularly . . . I apologise if I have offended you.' The shutters went down on the lawyer's eyes. 'Your signature here and here . . .?'

Samantha's fingers took a pen, and moved it to make a signature: 'Samantha Angela Cassinari née Samantha Angela Powell.' The two names for the first time together on the same page. And then she was outside in the dry East Anglian noon, the deeds for Lime House in her bag and its keys in her hand.

Inside the old café on North Street it was comfortingly dim and familiar. Weren't those brown splashes on the wall the ones Christine's spilt Coke made a decade and more ago? Samantha sat over a coffee trying to stop the ringing in her head. She had imagined Lawrence contained in the past, with the clock on the study mantelpiece stopped at the moment when a seventeen-year-old girl had walked from his front door. But that had never been the truth. Although Lawrence may never have left Lime

House, he'd been watching and following. Running his sinewy hands over her life. She felt him now, pressing the breath out of her body.

How many times in ten years had a camera clicked on her life? On her bedsit curtains, on the baby in her arms, on Dale as he kissed her on the doorstep. She imagined Lawrence's desk strewn with photos of the life she had begun to feel safe in. As she watched, a dark stain drew across each one, like blood seeping through a bandage.

Delivering the keys to an estate agent and taking the next train home just wasn't possible. She had to *know* that Lawrence was dead, and without a body to bury, an empty house would be the next best thing.

She asked the taxi driver to be back in an hour, then got out of the car and stood in the time-travel landscape. It hadn't changed a bit. The barley still stretched from skyline to skyline, the green already gilding under the sun. Down among the stems the grasshoppers still shushed and chipped, their bodies desiccated as paper. The sounds measured out the silence and the heat, like the equidistant poles on a fence line. Lead-heavy, she turned and walked towards the avenue of lime trees that marked the approach to Lawrence's home.

Time folded. Angela Cassinari and Samantha Powell were side by side on the same page, on this lane on the same hot afternoon . . .

It is four but still too hot to cycle. She must have done five miles already. She knows she'll have to get used to temperatures much higher than this over the next few years. She sees herself looking sinewy and intrepid, walking along a jungle path with last night's rain rising as steam from the soil around her. People don't get cancer in the rainforest. If Bea would only live long enough Sam could find her a cure, some plant distillate or extract of frog.

She leans the bike against the bank and sits down. She thinks about the day, trying to flatten the creases out of it and lay it down. There had been the usual start: the sound of her father's electric razor buzzing in the bathroom and him singing some out-of-tune snatch of something, it always made her smile.

'O sole mio!' it had been this morning. Then she heard him walking about on the landing doing up his tie, and saying 'Samantha' out loud to himself in various different ways. 'Sam*antha*. *Samantha*. Samantha.'

He'd always done it but she'd only just started noticing and now it was far too late to ask why, or explain that she didn't like it. What did he think when he said it? Of some little girl in a pair of flowery shorts and a sun hat, she was pretty sure. *His* little girl Samantha, who was nothing to do with her any more.

Samantha stayed in bed until Ralph had gone this morning because today had been another of Bea's hospital days. Sam had taken a day off school to go with her. That's what always happened now. Ralph didn't even mention taking his wife to Addenbrookes as he had two months ago. She took herself on the bus, and Sam went with her.

It's double biology now, Sam thought as they stood at the bus stop. She'd be missing a chemistry practical today too. How could she prepare for the Oxbridge entrance exams like this? What did Ralph care? She felt a hot wave of panic and resentment rise from her stomach.

They sat at the back of the bus. Bea leaned against the window and dozed a bit. 'You don't mind do you, Sam?' she said. 'It's just this radiotherapy makes me so tired. Still, halfway through now. Another two weeks. They say you feel better after it stops.' Bea used those giveaway words 'radiotherapy' and 'chemotherapy' all the time. Today they walked through the plastic corridors to find 'Oncology' again. But they never talked about Bea's *cancer* and the fact that she might die. They sat waiting, Bea in her horrible hospital gown, and looked at the back copies of *Woman's Realm*.

They were surrounded by other poor victims, all women, similarly brought low and humiliated by sickness. From their whisperings Sam gathered that their cancers were indeed particularly 'feminine': wombs and breasts brought nothing but trouble it seemed—burdensome husbands, wailing babies, tumours, pain, and death.

'Mrs Powell?'

Smiling, Bea gathered her dressing gown and got up. 'Back soon, poppet. Watch my bag won't you?' and the nurse led her away. While she was gone Sam paced the squeaky tiles and swore silently. She was going as far as she could get from this, the designated 'Realm of Women'. She seethed that her mother should submit to it all so quietly. When Bea came back she wanted to shout at her, but she just walked meekly to the cubicles, to wait while Bea changed.

'Look,' Bea laughed, pointing to her chest: 'I'm the Golden Shot!'

Samantha looked: there were three concentric circles, black and ugly, with Bea's skinny breast bone at their centre, red and hot like a knuckle of roasting pork. They had drawn a target on her mummy's chest and burnt its bull's-eye red with their X-rays. Bea laughed again. Sam swallowed hard and stretched the corners of her mouth outwards, hoping her face would appear to smile. 'Bernie, the Bolt!' she said.

The bus seemed to take for ever. Bea dozed again, nodding like a toy dog on a parcel shelf. Sam wanted to smash her head against the window until the glass broke, but Bea was propped against her side, snoring very slightly, so Sam sat still and imagined a scream so loud it would cleave the road in two.

They had to wait half an hour for a taxi home from Haverhill. Bea sat on the town hall steps amid the crisp packets and last Saturday's confetti. She picked up a tiny blue fragment. 'Oh look!' Her drawn face was lit up with genuine delight. 'It's the exact same colour as blue sky and a *perfect little bell!'*

How could her mother take such pleasure in something so small? Sam was amazed and repelled. You're dying of cancer, she thought, and you care about a scrap of trodden tissue paper?

'Nothing like this when I married y'father,' Bea went on, still staring hard at it. 'People threw rice at us. Mummy collected it all up and made a pudding. Never got over rationing did your Granny Agnes.'

It was gone three when they got in. Granny Pearl's voice came thin and wavy, like an asp from her bedroom, 'Bea? Samantha? Is that you? Don't bother about my lunch. I've gone beyond hunger now.'

'You've got to hand it to her for performance,' Bea smiled, but Sam threw her mac across the hall, furious.

'I don't know how you can laugh. I want to kill her!'

'Oh, Sam, don't start. It doesn't help.'

'Why don't you get angry with *her*? Why are you snapping at *me*? I'm going out for a bike ride. Don't you *dare* make her *anything*.'

Sam slammed the back door and cycled fiercely up the hill, crying, sweating and swearing all at once, not aiming to go anywhere but away.

It's only now after resting in the sun that Sam knows that she's decided to seek out Lawrence again. She looks at the emptiness of the shallow valley and wheels her bike towards the lime-lined drive.

She rides her bike slowly down the cool, dappled passageway, closing her eyes to feel the stripes of light and shade fall on her skin, throwing back her head to catch the first sweet scent of lime flowers. Then she shoots out into the sunlight, the house rises up before her, and Lawrence is standing in the open front door, sudden as a conjuring trick.

'Well, well!' he says, smiling. 'That was fortunate timing!' There is that strange unreadable languor again, a private joke against the world in every word. 'I was about to inspect the conservatory. I seem to remember my last attempt to show you around was hampered by a dog! Do you have time now?' It is as if it were two minutes since she last came instead of two months.

'Um. Yes, please!'

Like a well-prepared tour guide he ushers her through a gate, telling her the names of plants as they go . . .

Inside Lawrence's conservatory, the atmosphere is hot and weighted. Sam feels she could wring out the richness from the air with her hands. Every surface is slick with fine moisture, and the floor is slippery. 'This was in ruins when I moved in. Plants didn't interest my father. They were my mother's domain,' says Lawrence. 'I had it restored but with a few more modern features, automated heating, watering and ventilation, that sort of thing.' Sam isn't listening. She is taking in full-sized palm trees, ferns, orchids, climbers. Everything twined and tangled, with no artifice of neatness.

Lawrence turns to see her standing like Saint Teresa before a vision of the divine; rooted, euphoric. He has never encountered anything like her before. At least not anything female.

'It's a cheat really,' he says, 'these plants are all things that will grow readily in an intermediate house like this, where they can take a little air in the summer and don't need a great deal of winter heating. Suppose you'd call it a pretend jungle.'

Sam's eyes snap open, her attention focuses on his face with such sudden intensity that Lawrence flinches. 'You said "jungle".' She sounds shocked. Then she smiles, 'I mean the word "rainforest", it doesn't sound *wild* enough.'

Her face is so open, so naked that Lawrence is almost embarrassed. His speech becomes less formal and more hesitant. 'I'd never thought about it that way. You know real jungle is much, much better than this!'

Sam gasps with the intense desire to hear first-hand reports. 'Have you been? What was it really like?' He is blinded by the expression in her eyes. What is it about this girl? Is it just that he meets no one these days in his house-prison? Or is there really a magnesium flame of intensity here, in her?

'Yes, I have,' he says, 'often. Belize, Venezuela, Brazil, twice to Malaya, several times to West Africa. At the end of business trips, you know. Some of these plants are things I brought back myself.'

He tries hard to regain his indifference and detachment, but he's drawn to her, the way you are to deep clear water; you lean over the still surface to wonder at the way you can see all the way to the bottom of another world.

''Did you see really big trees? Buttress roots and things?' Sam steps closer, almost touching his chest with her pointed little breasts. He doesn't remember standing so close to a girl like this. Her desire for his experience draws up the memory of the Malaysian dipterocarps. Closing his eyes for a moment, his heart, like hers, beats faster at the very thought of them.

'Yes. Yes, I did. Huge trees. They feel as if they're on another scale, as if one had stepped into some sort of land of giants!'

'Oh, that's what I want to see. Really, really big trees, with trunks the size of a house.' She spreads her arms wide. 'I want to walk around their roots, where it's almost dark, and then climb up two hundred feet to their crowns where it's all light.' She looks up as if she were already reaching for the highest branch in the canopy. And Lawrence finds himself looking up too, expecting to see that intense blue sky and feel the heaviness of tropical sunshine.

Lawrence brings drinks to have on the terrace beside the conservatory. They sit side by side on the weathered wooden benches, sipping their Pimms and talking mostly about plants. Lawrence asks about Sam's ambitions, and out they fly, natural as butterflies around her head. Lawrence could swat every one of them, because Sam is like every other idealist he's ever known, full of dreams and no concrete idea how to achieve them. His father, Fraser Spence, would have seen no reason not to strip her silly dreams to the bone. Fraser, who had climbed from a room over a wet fish shop to the gracious velvet lawns of Lime House, had taught his son that ideas and dreams were a waste of time, and the folk that harboured them foolish. Faced with such people Fraser was gripped with the same feeling a fox must get in a shed full of clucking chickens—the desire to rip and bite and see blood on the walls.

But, in spite of all his father's training, Lawrence retained a soft spot for dreamers. His mother had been one. Margaret had lived for her flowers. Lawrence learned to walk among his mother's herbaceous borders, in the canyons of *Cimicifuga* and *Phlox*, *Achillea* and *Kniphofias* where nothing existed but the flowers, the blue sky and Margaret's sweet lisping voice. Sometimes afterwards, dwarfed in some tropical forest, Lawrence would catch a brief chiffon touch of that old bliss. Always, it was gone before he could even name what he felt.

So Lawrence listens attentively as Sam chatters on about species destruction and the loss of biodiversity. Somehow she imagines she will combat it all with a few scientific papers read by a handful of academics. He can imagine his father's distaste for such talk, the curled lip, the coldness in the eye. He experienced it himself as a tiny child when he trotted round the garden after his mother. Fraser Spence had had no patience with her frivolous obsession. Flowers were for the soft, the weak, the self-indulgent and indolent. Lawrence's mother was barely cold in her grave when her flowers were removed and replaced with shrubs. Hard and undemanding plants that could be controlled with a pair of shears. The icy willpower of his father blew around Lawrence's heart, cauterising it, shrivelling its growth to nothing.

But now that Fraser is dead too, it is the pollen-light memory of his mother that has settled on him and drawn Lawrence back to wander in her garden. He replaced her flowers in the first year at Lime House. He feels protected here by Margaret's dreams; the bitter acidity of his father's long influence is neutralised a little. Lawrence feels that if he stays safe at Lime House, he may become a better person. In time he may wear away the patterns ingrained by his father's long training: the taste for blood, the old reflex to manipulate and control.

But only in time. Lawrence leans forward to replace his glass on the tray. It is a gesture so apparently natural, that Lawrence hardly recognises he is about to manipulate an idealist yet again.

'It sounds to me as if you've planned things out quite carefully. Oxford, a doctorate, then fieldwork.' He notices how she glows under his praise; it's the perfect moment to deliver the well-aimed blow. 'But I think your only possible problem could be funding for your doctorate, and beyond of course.'

Sam has always believed that academic excellence alone will get her to the rainforest: it has never occurred to her that money could stand in her way. In one sentence Lawrence has flicked the 'off' switch on the hologram of her ambitions.

'Please, Sam, don't look so worried. I don't mean to pour cold water on your plans. I just wanted to know if you have a sponsor, someone who can support your research in future.'

'No. I don't have anyone.' Sam is blank with dismay.

'Well, then. I think that's where I could come in. Given my interest in plants and my business contacts, I think I could find you sponsorship. Maybe even some funding for a gap year trip . . .' he trails off, tantalisingly vague. 'We could discuss it further next time?'

Sam nods. He understands her speechless silence. In the space of ten seconds Lawrence knows he has taken Sam from despair to wild hope. He's not even sure himself why.

In his study Lawrence watches her reflection bending over the maps, her neck so curved and delicate, her face completely absorbed. He points to the areas where he's travelled in the past.

'All this is above the tree line. Incredible landscape almost four thousand metres up. Are you familiar with the *Masdevallia*? No? Marvellous plants. South American genus of orchids. *Masdevallia veitchiana* is the most astounding orange with electric-blue hairs that glint in the sun. I collected some very good specimens from there!' Her intense attention is unsettling. It calls back the memory of the orange flowers and his lungs burning with the altitude so powerfully that he shivers.

'What did you do with them? The orchids you collected.'

He's caught off guard, still panting over the cowering plants on an Andean mountainside. He wants the answer he gives her to be the truth. He thinks of it as truth as he tells her, 'Donated to botanical gardens.' At that moment he wishes the smuggling of rare orchids hadn't proved to be such a lucrative sideline. But the truth is that it was. The truth is that the passion for plants seeded by his mother was nipped by his father's chill, infected with the impulse to use, and control. The truth is that Lawrence has ripped and plundered and possessed what his mother and this gangling girl hold to be almost sacred. Lawrence hasn't blushed for thirty years as he blushes now. He's grateful that the clock on the mantelpiece strikes loudly enough to be a distraction.

Samantha looks up, startled he guesses at the time, but then attracted by the clock itself. A perfect box of glass holds a little golden tree, in whose branches a white clockface sits amid rows of perfect miniature white blossoms, its hands are tiny rows of enamelled leaves.

'It's so beautiful. I've never seen a clock like that before!'

'It's seventeenth century. Quite unique. It has two different faces, Summer,' he turns the glass case through a hundred and eighty degrees, 'and Winter.' The tree is gnarled with broken branches, bare of any leaf or blossom. The clockface is black and its hands two chains of withered leaves. Involuntarily Samantha shudders at the obvious symbolism of the passage of time leading only to death and decay.

'I can see why you have the green tree side showing. Not the other.'

'Oh, I turn it round sometimes. In memory of my father. He and my mother had a sort of silent battle over it. Each time Mother passed, she would turn the Summer face outwards. And when he passed Father turned it the other way.'

She gazes for moment, transported. 'Who won?' But she doesn't wait for an answer. 'I've got to go,' she says.

'Do come again, whenever you like.'

She cycles away, with those long white legs, that wispy hair, catching the patches of light then shade under the limes. As he puts away the maps and books in the study he tells himself he will take responsibility for realising her dreams. He will be her friend and mentor. Perhaps he could fund her studentship and research himself, why not? It would be penance for all the logging concessions, the hydro-electric dams, the open-cast mines to which he has been midwife. Her idealism will absolve him.

'I *hope* she comes back!' he says aloud and turns the Winter face of the clock to the wall, hiding the knowledge, that he *knows* she'll be back. Her dreams are in his pocket.

Samantha stood just inside the shade of the lime trees looking down the drive to the house. Nothing but the breeze had moved in half an hour or more. The gravel was waist high in weeds and she could see that the front door was boarded over. He really was gone. She didn't need to go any closer to feel the lack of him. The taxi horn bleated and she fled down the road towards the sound.

But the past wasn't finished with her for the day because the taxi driver, being one of the last true locals in that part of the world, was taking a nice quiet short cut. A route down a lane where only one house stood, almost invisible now behind an overgrown hedge. Years ago he remembered that the people who lived there had lost a daughter, though whether dead or simply run off he couldn't recall. So when the apparently exhausted young woman passenger yelled 'stop' at the top of her voice as they passed its gate he began to wonder who she was and why she wanted to stop here.

SEVEN

SAMANTHA IGNORES the taxi driver's surprise. She leaps out of the car and runs towards her old home without thinking what she is doing, like a pigeon homing by instinct. She puts her hand on top of the gate—the old wooden gate that Ralph made—ready to push it open and walk round the hedge as if this were just the end of another school day long ago. Everything looks much the same, just a little softer at the edges, blurred by vegetation growth. She hears a young child's voice come through an open window, and wonders if she'd find her baby-self sitting on Daddy's lap in sunshine by the living-room window, pushing her bare toes into his hands and laughing.

She stops stock still to listen.

'Go on! Harder!'

The whole length of Sam's foot fitted easily into Ralph's palm. She braced her back against his chest and pushed his hand away using all the strength of one leg. 'Keep pushing! Go on, nearly done it! There!'

She could feel the warmth and roughness of his calluses under her pink sole. He took both feet crammed side by side into his hand. 'Right. Two legs against one hand. One, two, three, GO!'

She shut her eyes and pushed with all her might. He never let her win easily, she had to try right to the end, when her legs were stretched straight and her toes pointed between his fingers. Fully extended her legs didn't reach the end of his lap. She must have been less than two.

That was just before Bea's first operation, when she was in hospital for the first time. But Sam never remembered that, because in those first years she was her daddy's girl. They were always together, out in the garden. Sam wheeled tiny barrowfuls of topsoil to make a vegetable patch. She held strings straight so Daddy could plant long rows of carrots and peas, and wrote labels with her tongue sticking out of the corner of her mouth. They had a greenhouse then, and Sam would stand on a box and watch Ralph pricking out seedlings.

Every spring, until she didn't need to stand on a box any more, Sam spent Saturday afternoons in the greenhouse with Ralph. They had the radio on in the corner and they worked side by side without speaking, comfortably silent as dogs in the same basket by the fire. They shared the excitement when the first tiny green shoots showed that seed had germinated and it never seemed less than magical.

Bea came into the garden like a visiting Royal. Sam would show her all the things that she and Ralph had been doing: as she talked, Bea would smile at Ralph over her head, and he would smile back. Sam loved those moments; she felt that by being their words she held their hands in each of hers.

Those times trickled gradually away to nothing. The sweetness of a shared family life took years to drip, drip, drip away. Only the last dregs were left after the summer of 'The Scottish Holiday' when Sam was fourteen. Afterwards that's how Bea and Sam referred to it; like actors refusing to say Macbeth, it was always darkly 'The Scottish Holiday'.

Bea had been ill, but insisted they should still take their holiday as planned in a tiny caravan on a lochside, an hour's drive from the nearest loaf of bread. It was wild and beautiful with red deer passing the windows every evening and naive little brown trout jumping onto Ralph's hooks every morning. But fifty-yard clambers over rocks and heather to an earth closet and standing in a stream in the rain for hours, wore Bea to greyness in two days. After four she was getting incoherent with pain and cold, and Ralph panicked. Sam had never seen her quiet father flustered before. Never even heard him say 'Damn'. So when, outside the caravan, he hissed, 'We've got to get her home tonight, or she's going to fucking die on us!' she felt as if she had been punched in the face.

They loaded the car in silence. By the time they set off Bea was groaning and semiconscious on the back seat, Sam rigid and terrified in the front. They got home in a dawn drained of any colour or warmth and put Bea to bed. Ralph dug out the flower beds the same day. He demolished the greenhouse too, smashed it in ten minutes with an axe. Sam crouched behind her bedroom door and cried.

'No time for this nonsense any more,' he said when he came in, 'not with your mother the way she is.'

There were no days to spend with Ralph in the garden after that. If Sam tried to help with the vegetable patch at weekends, he snapped at her if she made the slightest mistake. Yet he still seemed to harbour a longing for those sweet Saturday afternoons. She heard it in his voice every morning, when he said her name aloud over and over again to his reflection as he shaved. At first it made her sad, and then it made her angry. How could he go on saying her name like that, as if he hadn't pulled down the greenhouse and become an old cuss overnight? How could he pretend he loved her when he'd pushed her away?

Later that same summer, when Bea had seemed to be sinking fast, Ralph took time off from work to care for her.

'Sam,' he told her, 'Mummy's very ill.'

'I know that!'

'I mean, she's iller than we thought.' He reached forwards and took Sam's hand. 'We'll be all right, Sam, just the two of us. Won't we?'

She snatched her hand away with such ferocity she scratched his palm, and ran out without looking back at his face. It was no excuse that he didn't understand what he'd done.

But Bea rallied. In the years after 'The Scottish Holiday' her health was like a yo-yo, and Ralph's strategy for coping became avoidance. It became easier and easier for him to ignore Bea's relapses as Sam grew old enough to take on the burden of nursing her and running the house. By the winter of what they believed might really be her mother's final illness, Ralph was coming in late every night. And he'd perfected a relentless plastic cheeriness that gave the house an atmosphere of unpleasant surrealism whenever he was in it.

He beamed as he came through the kitchen door when Samantha was cooking their meal. 'Ah! Samantha, Samantha!' he sang. 'How was school today, my little chickadee?'

'Fine. Why don't you go and say hello to Mum?'

'And the bus, that was on time was it?'

'Yes, Dad. It always is. Go and see Mummy.'

'How's your Gran? I'll just take her up a little sherry.' And out he drifted, humming.

He bought another telly and took to watching it upstairs in his bedroom in the evenings. 'So I don't disturb your mother,' he told Sam conspiratorially. So Sam sat downstairs with Bea while she watched the TV in the old sitting room where she now had a bed. Just before he went to bed himself, Ralph would pop his head around the sitting-room door and smile impishly at Bea and Sam, before producing two mugs of cocoa and a mound of cheese sandwiches. 'You have to keep your strength up, Bea. Night night, love,' he'd say and leave, humming, without waiting to hear her speak or even looking at her properly.

'You should put all these in the freezer,' said Bea. 'You've never liked cheese sandwiches, and I'm not going to be around to eat them.' Her tone was blankly commonplace. Sam packaged up the sandwiches and stuck them on the bottom shelf with last year's frozen gooseberries that no one really wanted. She felt as if she was shutting her heart in with the ice and the dark too.

Bea got weaker every day. Day and night lost their division and she drifted in and out of the same twilight twenty-four hours a day. At night in her room Sam could sense Bea awake and suffering downstairs. Sleep was impossible so in the weeks before her entrance exam Sam studied until three. Sometimes she'd hear a suppressed groan and go down to find Bea wide-eyed, in agony, biting her lips so as not to cry out.

'Get me my pills,' Bea would say. Sam had taken to hiding them, leaving Bea just a few within reach during the day. 'Sam, just give me all of them. I can't stand this pain.'

'The dose is two every six hours.'

'Sam, please. Please. Let me have all of them.'

'Mummy, don't ask me that.'

Granny Pearl had hit on a new attention-seeking role: The Self-Sacrificing Matriarch, Suffering in her Final Years for the Benefit of her Family. She began to insist on doing everything for herself, wedging herself in the kitchen alongside Sam, making a single portion of cheese on toast while Sam made an evening meal for everyone else.

'Sure you don't want spaghetti Bolognese, Gran?'

'No, no. I can't have you cooking for me while you're catering for your poor mother. I'll just have a little snack.'

While Sam was at school in the day she started to 'take care' of Bea.

'She flutters around when the nurse is here,' Bea complained, 'stands and watches while I have my injection. It's humiliating enough without having her as an audience. Then if I try to sleep in the afternoon she comes in and rattles the curtains until I wake up and pay her some mind. She's driving me mad, Sam.' The humour and resilience had gone from her mother's voice, she now simply sounded desperate.

'I'll stay home tomorrow, Mum, and keep you company.'

'Oh, Sam. It's your entrance exam soon . . .'

At weekends the only oasis of brightness was the supermarket on Saturday mornings. Sam had taken to going with Ralph to supervise the weekly shop after two weeks of having nothing in the house but cheese and cocoa. She found the rows of products cheered her up, and deciding what they needed made her feel grown-up and responsible. Away from home Ralph's gossamer-light hold on reality beefed up a little, and he would sometimes walk beside her as she pushed the trolley, and suggest something sensible like a chicken that they could roast, or frozen fish. But most of the time he would go on little forays of his own, returning with endless products that Sam quietly put back.

'How about some nice cream horns? That might tempt your mother. Half the problem is that she doesn't eat enough, you know. Look! Disposable cutlery! Now that's what we need. Scented drawer liners. Marvellous!'

One Saturday, after Bea had begged to be given the whole bottle of pills, Sam tried to talk to Ralph on the way home from the supermarket.

'Daddy, at night when I get up for Mummy, she asks me for more pills. You know, she asks for more than she should have.'

'She gets confused, Sam.'

'No, it's not that. She wants . . . she's asking me to give her all of them. Because of the pain. Could you talk to her? Could you get up for her?'

'There's no need, Sam. It's all right. I know you're coping brilliantly with her. I'm so grateful. I'm proud of you.'

She could smell his terror, through the false brightness, that she would say something really blunt, like, 'Mum wants me to kill her, Daddy'. It was like being faced with a rabbit pleading for its life. She could never bring herself to deliver the *coup de grâce*, but she was left with a sticky ooze of contempt on her heart so that when they unloaded the shopping and she noticed several bottles of sherry, she wanted to hit him as he said: 'For your Gran. Her little treat.'

Sam didn't argue. She knew who it was getting through a bottle of Harvey's Bristol Cream every night.

In those snot-grey weeks of November leading up to her entrance exam, Sam swam in an internal tank of misery and exhaustion. As her careful revision plans unravelled, she saw the single foundation of all her dreams—an Oxbridge place—slipping away. It was like standing back in the playground, waiting helplessly for Dennis Williams to do something awful to her. The night before the first paper Bea had been sick until 3.00am. It had taken Sam an hour or more to change the sheets and get her back to bed. Bea had looked so ill when she left that Sam feared to find her still and cold at the end of the day. As she walked into the freezing examination room, Sam could think only of her mother's corpse, alone with Pearl rattling the curtains fit to raise the dead.

She sat on the bus at the end of the week of exams, cold through with weariness. Each paper had felt more like a dream than the last. She could scarcely remember what she had been asked to write. She was glad no one at home remembered to ask her how it all went, and on Saturday afternoon, when the house was quiet, she escaped. 'Going for a bike ride!' she'd yelled as she slammed the back door. And in fifteen minutes she was freewheeling down the drive of Lime House.

It wasn't that she and Lawrence had become confidants. He told her nothing of himself beyond the fact that 'a nervous complaint' meant that it was virtually impossible for him to leave his house and garden. It sounded romantic, almost like something out of Hardy, and fitted with the hints and insinuations he slipped her about his globe-trotting past and his business empire maintained from the study at Lime House. And she didn't tell him about having to hide her mother's painkillers, or her father's mounting pile of empty sherry bottles. When she visited Lawrence, Sam played the part of the person she wanted to be, and over the months she had got better and better at it. Being with Lawrence was like being able to visit her future, her adulthood, far away in the remote rainforests of tomorrow.

When Lawrence answered the door, Sam always got the brief impression that he had been standing behind it waiting for her. She knew it couldn't be true. Although his 'condition' made him a prisoner of his own grounds he still must lead a busy life. The world must come to him when she wasn't there, old friends, business associates. Surely? His study was full of machines and telephones to allow him to keep up with his business interests even in the middle of the countryside. Yet there was that moment as she arrived when the house seemed too still, as if everything had simply been switched off since her last visit.

'Sam! My dear girl! How lovely to see you! Can I get you a hot drink after your freezing journey?'

'No, I'm fine really.'

'In that case . . . The *Phalaenopsis* is flowering!'

Samantha's enthusiasm for his captive jungle made Lawrence smile. She invariably wanted to rush straight to the glasshouse and see whatever had come into bloom, seeded, or leafed or ailed since her last visit.

'It is rather wonderful, isn't it!' Lawrence was proud of this specimen.

Sam walked underneath the arching spikes of moon-white flowers, each one as big as her palm. 'It makes me think of a wedding dress. Or new snow. That white is so pure. What pollinates it?'

'Samantha! I'm simply a *gardener*. Biology is your department.'

'I wish I knew.' And feeling her frustration, her passionate desire to acquire knowledge, Lawrence too wished he knew. That was the effect she had on him, infecting him with good desires, worthy ambitions.

'I've a surprise. Somebody else in bloom. Look . . .' He led her to the opposite corner of the glasshouse where an epiphytic orchid had put out a spike four feet long and covered with frilly yellow and brown flowers. It was magnificent, mad, almost ridiculous in its extravagance.

'What is it?'

'*Oncidium papilio*. I thought I'd lost it. They can flower so vigorously they kill themselves. It put out five six-foot inflorescences two years ago. This is the first time it's flowered since.'

'Wow!' Samantha said. 'I wonder why it does this suicide flowering?'

'Suicide flowering. Very good, Sam. I like that. Well . . . this plant lives in a habitat where the right conditions for setting seed are very unusual. So when those conditions . . . whatever they might be . . . occur, then the right strategy is to go for bust.'

They looked up at the plant in silence. It was often like this. An exchange of information followed by silent contemplation.

But on this dull winter afternoon the silence went on, the tiredness of the week settling on Sam like dust. She wasn't sure how long it took her to notice that Lawrence's arm was just millimetres from her own. She could feel the faint touch from elbow to wrist where their shirt sleeves were rolled up. Lawrence's little finger crooked over hers and clinched it in a miniature embrace, a touch that was witty and light, but unmistakably sensual, intimate, the touch from an equal: testing the ground. But she didn't need to panic, this was just another scene from her future, something that happened between grown-ups. She didn't need to fear, or offend Lawrence, just gently step away. She drew her hand from his and stood up, making an effort to smile.

'It's like visiting Summer coming here,' she said.

'It's like Summer visiting me actually, Sam.' He took back her hand and touched the fingertips with his lips. His eyes looking at her over her knuckles were hard, as dark and unreadable as deep space.

'Perhaps you'd better come to the jungle with me, then you'd have a double Summer.' She pulled her hand away more purposefully.

Reluctantly he let it go and said, 'Or perhaps you'd better stay here and then Summer would never go away.' Lawrence's expression had an intensity that Sam didn't understand. She felt an emptiness open up beneath her, into which she could imagine herself falling.

'Can we have tea now, Lawrence?'

'Yes. Yes, of course, I've been neglecting my duties as host.'

She got in after six. Ralph was making sandwiches and Pearl was stirring a packet of soup into a saucepan of water and making a huge clattering noise with the spoon. 'Samantha, Samantha.' Ralph took her hands and waltzed her around the room singing.

'How's Mummy?'

'One round or two?' Ralph said.

'You could share my soup, cockaleekie!' chirped Pearl.

No one asked where she'd been.

A splinter from the gate pricks Sam's hand. Looking more carefully she can see it isn't the one Ralph made. She closes her eyes again for a moment remembering her reluctance as Ralph waltzed her round the kitchen. How she loathed him at that moment! But looking at his face in memory, from the perspective that time and experience have given her, she can see the terrible fear and grief etched there. He was trying to make things better somehow, to bring some light into their dark tight little world.

The child's voice is coming closer, its little feet crunch the path beyond the hedge.

'Max! Max, come here!' Another second and Max's mother will catch sight of the strange white-faced young woman standing transfixed at her gate. If Max and his parents are in residence here, then Ralph certainly isn't. For the time being that's as much information as Sam wants. She takes her hand from the gate and runs back to the taxi.

EIGHT

BRISTOL WELCOMES SAMANTHA home at one in the morning with a warm greasy mizzle that shines on the empty tarmac of the roads and smudges the streetlights. She closes the vault-like front door behind her, kicks off her shoes and is about to go upstairs when she hears the unmistakable sound of a sob coming through the closed door of the front room.

Dale is sitting on the sofa crying, completely unaware that she is in the room. Samantha has never seen Dale cry. He looks stripped bare, even more vulnerable than the day when the boys led him by the hand into the new garden. Samantha feels the terrible responsibility of her long deception. What can she say to him now? Tenderness and fear rush through her. There is no time to plan, she must just step into the unpredictable reality of the night. 'Dale. I'm home.'

He looks up slowly, groggily, as if he might be dreaming her. He's been caught unawares, just as she has. Both of them here in the dark room, without their portraits to stand behind. They feel shy, almost as if meeting for the first time.

'Oh, Angie. I didn't hear you come in.'

She sits down beside him. 'How are you?'

'Oh. You know. OK.'

'How are the boys?'

'Fine. Mum's been great. Where have you been?'

'Oh, Dale. I don't know where to start.'

'Just tell me who he is. That would be a start.'

'So you know about the will then?'

'What will?'

'Lawrence's will. That's who *he* is. Was. Lawrence Spence.'

'Was? So he's died?'

'Yeah. That's why I've got the house.'

'What house? When did he die? Were you upset?'

'Dale, we're not talking about the same thing, are we?'

'I don't know. I'm talking about your——' He came to a dead stop, his voice clogged so that the next words were squeezed out of a tight throat, 'Your affair. Your lover.'

414

'What affair? I'm not having an affair.'

'Then why were you sick when I tried to make love to you?'

'Dale, I'm going to put the light on. I want to see you properly and I want to show you something.'

Samantha swishes the curtain closed and puts the smallest lamp on. She feels much braver, now that the partial reality she will give Dale is better than the fiction he's been constructing for himself.

'So you aren't having an affair? I'd sooner know what's going on . . .'

'Dale, I'm not having an affair. I'm not in love with anyone else.'

He stands up white and unsteady and holds her so tightly she's ready for a rib or two to pop. 'I can't stand the thought of losing you.'

'Dale?' she says into his shoulder. 'Dale? I do have a lot to say.'

He releases her. 'So do I.' He looks guilty, worried. 'There's a lot I need to tell you about the business. About the house.'

'Well, what I've got to tell may help with all that. I've inherited a house that's probably worth twice what this is worth at the very least. A lot more maybe.'

'Oh my God!'

'So that should sort out the business and let us keep the house?'

'Yeah. I should say so. God. Angie. You don't know the weight you've just lifted . . .'

Samantha has that sensation of white mushrooms filling her brain. After so long keeping the facts on a lead, it's going to be a relief to let them go. The tricky part is the few she must still keep quiet.

'Wait, Dale. You haven't had the bad news yet. My name wasn't Angie Dawes when you met me. It was Samantha Powell. Angela was my middle name. I was younger than I told you, just eighteen. My parents didn't die when I was a baby. I've never been in care or a foster home. I left home at seventeen and I didn't want to go back. The man who left me the house—Lawrence—was a friend, without children of his own to leave it to.'

There is silence. Dale lets out a long breath, lets go of her hand and rakes his fingers through his hair. 'Well, that explains how you look so young. I was beginning to wonder if I was just ageing extra fast.'

'I'll be twenty-eight in two months.'

'Jeesus. And this bloke knew where you were and your parents didn't know?' Dale's face is struggling to understand so much so fast.

'I didn't know that he'd found me until I got the letter from his executors telling me he'd left me the house. It was a shock. All that purple-blob cake and the garden, it was all sort of shock. And that was more what I used to be like, before I left home.'

'A purple blob?'

'No! A bit wild. I was going to be a botanist, and ecologist. Whatever. I was going to study rainforest, jungle, all that stuff.'

'If you'd changed your name and age, how did Lawrence find you?'

'I don't know how he found me. I don't know if he told my parents. I don't think so.'

'Because they would have come looking?'

'Yeah. Maybe. Maybe my dad wouldn't want to see me any more.'

'Why?'

'Because I ran away.'

'What about your mum?'

'She's dead. I think. No, I'm sure. She was dying when I left.'

'But you don't know?'

The pace of Dale's questions is getting out of hand. Inside Samantha can feel a dangerous abandon. She reins it in, takes a deep breath and answers slowly, 'Yes, I do know. She had weeks to live, the doctor said.'

'But she was alive when you left?'

'Yes.' It's not so hard to say this with conviction. It's not quite a lie.

'What happened? Why did you leave?' Dale takes her hand again. She can see the marks of the tears on his face and the dark shadows left by the nights of worry he's had. She wants to tell the whole truth. But the best she can do is some of the truth, enough truth to take away the shadows and the tears, and keep herself safe.

'It was my mum's illness really. And the way my dad was about it and about me. All that and my gran, and failing my entrance exams. I think I was nearly going mad.' That, at least, is nothing but the truth . . .

The weather in the run-up to Christmas that year was particularly dismal. It never got properly light after the first week in December. The only colour in the landscape was the red of the tractors labouring up, and down, carving the fields into straight lines. Christmas loomed closer, inviting as a torture chamber. She couldn't see how she was going to manage Christmas Day with Bea glassy-eyed on the camp bed and Pearl and Ralph swigging sherry in front of *The Review of the Year*.

When Sam got home at the end of the last day of term, there was no sound in the house. Not even a welcoming 'wuff': Bracken had been sent to live with a work colleague of Ralph's. Samantha put her bag on the kitchen table and tiptoed into the sitting room. 'Mum? You awake?'

'Hello, love. How was school?' Bea's words were faint, but distinct. A good sign. When the pain was bad it blurred her voice and thinking.

'Oh. Like school. You know, teachers, lessons.'

'That bloody health visitor's been again today. She told me about the meek inheriting the earth.'

'She shouldn't be allowed to thrust her beliefs down your throat.'

'No, she shouldn't. Especially with a haircut like that. If that's the standard of coiffure Jesus accepts in his followers then I'm glad I'm not one of them.'

'You'll go to hell saying things like that!'

'I'm going there anyway. Always liked a good bonfire.'

'Cuppa?'

'Go and check on your gran first?'

Pearl was asleep in her armchair by the window, peaceful and apparently as blameless as a baby. Sam closed the door and hoped she'd go through to morning. Or the next century. There was a sudden cry and Sam threw herself down the stairs. Bea was crumpled beside her bed, panting and blue around the lips.

'Put me on my back,' she managed to say. Awkwardly, like moving a piece of furniture with no handholds, Sam turned her. Bea pursed her lips and tried not to cry out but a little scream of pain managed to force its way between her teeth. At last her colour returned a little and she spoke. 'I was feeling a lot better. So I thought I'd try and get to the loo alone without the chair. Stupid. Stupid.'

'Yes, Mum. Stupid stupid *stupid*, I'd say. Shall I get you back into bed?'

'Oh, Sam,' Bea began to cry, 'I need to change my nightie. Can you help me? I'm so sorry.'

Sam didn't mind Bea being soaked and filthy, she didn't mind the smell, or having to scrub the carpet. What bothered her was Bea's silence and the way the tears emptied onto her cheeks.

When Bea was finally back in a clean bed she said, 'If it's going to be like this, I don't want to go on. Sam, just give me all my pills.'

Sam had no idea how to answer. 'Don't be silly, Mum,' she said, 'don't be silly,' but she felt that Bea's request was a long way from being silly, and that some last line that heralded only the finish had just been crossed.

Pearl didn't sleep through until the next century. Early the next morning, Sam heard her take Bea a cup of tea and make toast for Ralph. Sam hurried out of bed to witness the unprecedented phenomenon.

'Good morning, dear, cup of tea?'

Sam could barely speak with the shock of seeing Pearl smiling and voluntarily doing something for someone else instead of for effect. She had her best travelling clothes on too.

Ralph cleared his throat and took a swallow of tea ready to make an announcement. 'Your gran's not going to be with us for Christmas, Sam,' he said. Sam was so surprised she managed by accident not to look delighted.

'Oh. Where are you going, Gran?'

'My sister-in-law Lydia in Brighton. I won't disturb your mother, just to say goodbye. I'm sure she's resting,' and Sam realised that Pearl too had noted that crossing of a 'last line'.

Sam remembered the injured mole she'd picked up last summer; all its fleas and ticks had jumped off onto Sam's bare arm. Pearl was just doing what any good, sensible parasite would do—she was quitting while her host was still warm.

The macabre significance of Pearl's departure went right over Bea's head. She was delighted. 'If I'm having Christmas alone with my husband and my daughter I'd better start looking more respectable. Give my hair a wash, Sam, there's a love?'

Sam wheeled her into the shower room downstairs and improvised a salon from the tiny sink and a large measuring jug.

'We need to get you some smart trousers and new shoes,' Bea said, 'and a good coat. We'll go in the January sales. We'll have a girls' outing.' Bea sounded so bright that Sam could have believed it would happen. But Sam could see the parched skin, the sparse coarseness of the grey hair. The cancer had sucked the last beauty out of Bea's pale luminous complexion and her dense silky hair. Sam massaged the lather into her mother's scalp tenderly, as if somehow she could draw the loveliness into the visible world once again, then curled the little tufts of hair round her fingers, trying to get them to hold a pretty shape as she blew them with the hair dryer. But the hair fell sad and flat. 'Oh, it's so nice to feel a bit smarter!' sighed Bea. 'Let's have a look then, Sam, like they do in a real hairdressers.'

'I can't get the mirror off the wall, Mummy,' Sam lied.

'Oh, come on, Sam. Just unhook it. It's not attached or anything.'

Reluctantly Sam did as she was told and Bea peered in. 'Oh God!' she said. 'Oh God. What's happened to me, Sam?'

There was nothing Sam could say.

The final retail frenzy of Christmas had set in. Already at 10.00am on Christmas Eve the streets of Cambridge were filled with a collective hysteria of acquisitiveness. Sam wandered miserably through malls and precincts. All she could think of to buy her parents was sherry glasses for Ralph, so that at least he wouldn't swig it from the bottle, and for Bea a set of children's glow-in-the-dark stars and moons so she would have something to look at in the deep nights. After an hour she settled for those and rushed to meet Ralph at the car park.

He was staring into space with the radio on and a huge expensive-looking carrier-bag on the back seat. He looked lost. For the first time in months, years almost, Sam remembered the Saturdays in the greenhouse, his smile over the top of the sea of tiny seedlings as he'd said, 'We need Mummy to come and inspect, don't we, Sam?'

She leaned over to squeeze his arm. 'Hello, Dad.'

'Hello, my little flower. Want to see what I bought?'

He lifted the carrier onto her lap. Inside, in a swathe of white tissue paper, were two hats. One was felt, with a big soft brim. The other was a stiff boater, covered in a cloud of lemon chiffon. They were hats for big occasions, for a social life Bea might once have dreamed of, but had never had, and now never would. Sam felt the blood go from her cheeks almost before she knew she was angry. The hats symbolised all of it: all the cheese sandwiches in the freezer, all the sherry bottles, all the avoided conversations. Every last bit of Ralph's head-in-the-sand behaviour rolled out of the hat bag in a white-hot mass and ignited, burning off the tenderness and pity she'd felt a moment before.

'And when the bloody hell do you think your wife is ever going to wear those? What planet are you on, Daddy? She's dying. She'll be dead by Easter. She's in so much pain she can't move most of the time, or even talk, or think. She keeps begging me to give her all her painkillers.'

Ralph sat so still and quiet that the ticking of the dashboard clock was suddenly audible.

'And all you can do is ignore it all and buy her posh hats!' Sam shoved the carrier onto Ralph's lap. She had never spoken to her father like that, never raised her voice to him. She stared ahead of her, shaking.

'Let's get home,' Ralph said, and he nosed the car out through the streets where the messy cocktail of 'Winter Wonderland' and 'Silent Night' was coming down over the town like rain.

Sam hadn't noticed when she fell asleep. She had screamed into her mattress with a pillow over her head for a long time, then lain, too tired to cry, listening to the tiny popping sounds coming from her bedroom radiator. When she woke it was dark outside and Ralph was at the door knocking. The sound was so insistent that Sam was afraid. She leapt to open it. 'Is Mum all right?'

'She's sleeping. Sam, St Hilda's rang, the admissions tutor wants you to ring before six, tonight or any time after Christmas, she said.' Ralph was completely detached from the importance of his message.

'Oh God. What did she say?'

'Just to ring.' He shrugged.

'And she didn't say anything about a place? About passing?'

'Nothing. She didn't sound like there was a rush or anything. Why don't you just ring? I'm popping out to get the turkey from Hundon. Mr Berry said he'd hang on to one till five.'

Samantha felt as if she'd been plucked out of a dream and placed into a new dimension of absolute sharpness and clarity. It was obvious to her that she had failed her exams. If she'd passed, St Hilda's would have said. It was only ever bad news that people were reluctant to impart. She'd failed. It was all over. The whole jungle dream. Her life felt over before it had begun.

Dale has his hand on her back, warm and strong and steady. There is a greyness round the edge of the curtains and the sound of a milk float passing the top of the street. Samantha is holding her own temples as if stopping her mind from spurting out onto Dale's lap.

'I'd failed my entrance exam, otherwise the admissions tutor would have told my dad I'd got a place. I couldn't bear to ring and hear her say it. I sat in my room. I thought about the rainforest. About how it would smell with the heat and wetness drawing the scents out of the leaves and flowers. How it would feel to know it, to be able to name and recognise everything I found there. And I felt it all peeling away from me, the way that Sellotape does on a wet surface. I couldn't get my dreams to stick to me any more. I'd lost it all.'

'But you couldn't be sure you had failed. And anyway, you could have tried again. Or just saved the money and gone there!'

'I was seventeen. I was three-quarters of the way round the bend with my mum and all. It didn't occur to me to try another way. It was like I'd been set some test, a trial of my worthiness. And I'd failed. I went downstairs to see my mum; she was in a lot of pain. And all I could feel was angry at her for being ill, and angry with Dad for being hopeless. She started asking for me to give her all the pills in the bottle again. Really begging. Then I knew I just couldn't stick it any more without my dream to keep me going. I left her crying out and I went upstairs. I took my passport, my birth certificate, my building society book and my warm coat and I walked out of the door.'

'You didn't say goodbye to her?'

'No. No, I didn't.' Sam sobbed. She had never told anyone even that much. Gently Dale gathered her up to his chest.

'Oh, my love. My love,' he said.

She lay against him with an ocean of tears flowing down her face.

Inside her, the story ran on through its real ending. She closed her eyes and saw Bea's face grey on the pillow.

'I can't stand this, Sam. Please just give me all the pills. Please.'

Sam had felt so cold, so empty. She looked at Bea's paper-folded face and she shivered with a chill of revulsion. This almost dead creature had snatched a whole green world of jungle from between her fingers. Her heart cracked like a glacier in a dry frost; inside she reached absolute zero. 'All right. All *right*. If that's what you really want.'

She fetched the tablets from the hiding place inside a cereal packet and tipped them slowly into her palm. 'One, two, three, four, five . . .' She'd counted them out, pressing each one into her flesh, imprinting it with the winter in her soul before submitting it to Bea's greedy mouth. Bea had taken them all, gobbling them like a starving peasant. Perhaps she had believed in her daughter's compassion. Perhaps she didn't see the murder in Sam's heart. Perhaps she just didn't care any more.

As Dale held her, Sam remembered the terrible long moments as Bea slipped from consciousness and her breathing seemed to fade. Her panic and desperation to quit the house before Bea's last breath could be drawn. She saw in her mind her own hysterical flight to Lime House, weeping and staggering in the tomb-cold darkness. She remembered Lawrence's sudden strength, sinewy as a strangler fig, wringing her out. She had walked away under the naked frost-glittered lime trees, a different person, metamorphosed into something that was no longer herself.

NINE

'MRS CASSINARI, MRS CASSINARI!' George hails Samantha as she stands at Stayfleurs' security door. 'Our theory concerning shoe design, vis-à-vis walking speed. I fear it may have been a little hastily constructed.' It has been more than a week, a lifetime in some respects, since Samantha has been to work. She stares at George blankly for a moment, and his features begin to pucker, pulled together by a drawstring of disappointment. Just in time she remembers their odd conversation.

'Yes, you're right. On reflection, I think the key factor is newness rather than design: quality of sole-grip, heel traction; that sort of thing?'

'Yes! Yes! Of course. Blindingly obvious when one engages wholly with the knotty problem!' Beaming with delight, George nods respectfully at her and goes to retrieve escapee trolleys.

Behind the red door nothing has changed, of course, yet today Samantha finds the atmosphere is not comforting, but dull and claustrophobic. It is hard to focus her attention on the hours ahead. Seeing her co-workers helps a little. They are pleased that she's back, but tentative, wary of another outburst.

'How are you, Angela?' Mary asks. 'Are you recovered?'

'Yes,' says Claudia, 'you didn't seem to be quite yourself the other week.'

Looking at the three women as they put on their navy uniforms, Samantha is struck by how attractive and intelligent they look. 'What did you all do before you worked here?' The women exchange nervous glances, but they are rather flattered that Angela, with her odd new atmosphere trailing about her, wants to know.

'Wives and mothers, darling!' says Liz. 'The world's most demanding role apparently. Certainly used my RADA training.'

'I was a fully qualified SRN.' Mary drew herself up to seem taller than her five feet, 'but I was more useful as John's receptionist when he set up his practice. Then the boys came along . . .'

'Tony always told me I was too dim to work, so I never got a job. Married him straight after Oxford,' said Claudia. 'But I got a better degree than he did, a two one in English.'

'What the hell are you all doing working here with qualifications like those?'

There is no time to answer as Mr Geoffrey's voice alerts them to the fact that it's almost nine, something which has for once escaped Samantha's attention.

All morning it's been busy with customers queuing five deep. Normally, it's the sort of morning that Samantha relishes. But loosening some of the bonds around her past has allowed the home guard of her mind to stand at a permanent 'at ease', so in spite of the tasks demanding her attention, great trunks have sprung up behind the rows of waiting customers. The back of the shop is in deep shade, the floor covered in fallen leaves and patrolled by skeins of ants. An agouti grabs a mango from the fruit and veg counter. Samantha's old ambitions, tattered, a little musty but still trailing clouds of glory, stir at the sight and smell of even this imagined forest. Once again she can see herself measuring, collecting, observing, learning. Samantha's heart turns and turns like a leaf in the wind. When it comes to the time for her break she almost runs outside, dodging past the lianas that threaten to cover the 'Staff Only' notice on the door.

Outside it's an ordinary summer day. Jack Mullen joins her to finish his fag. For the first time she notices his wrists, thin as bird bones, tiny, vulnerable and adrift.

'Well,' he begins his habitual leer, 'Mrs Cassi—' but she cuts him short.

'Samantha.' She holds out a hand to shake. 'Sam if you like.'

'Weeell,' he makes one last attempt at maintaining his lust-lizard persona and then gives up. He takes her offered hand, 'Jack, well no, John actually. Pleased to meet you, Sam.' His real smile is quite sweet.

'John, why don't you go back and get your degree?'

'I was, well, you know. They all know in there.'

'Go somewhere else, do another course.'

'Can't face it.'

'Can you face being here when you're forty?'

'What can I do? I messed up, Sam. Big time,' he says quietly. 'I can't go back. I'll just mess up again. I'll be OK here. I can cope.' He throws his cigarette down and watches his own foot crush it to dust.

John is twenty-two. He doesn't know how long life lasts. Samantha herself is only beginning to know how things don't last, how even the past changes once you're not in it any more. Quite suddenly she decides that she's had more than enough of Stayfleurs. A supermarket was OK for Angela Cassinari but for Samantha Powell it is never going to be enough, even if it does sell two sorts of reindeer meat.

Within fifteen minutes she has resigned with immediate effect, leaving Mr Geoffrey mouthing like a landed goldfish. She leaves through the front of the shop, waving to the three 'girls', neck-deep in customers.

The garden of number eleven is a sun trap, and all Samantha's exotics are looking very happy indeed. On the kitchen table is a fat white envelope with Angie written in Dale's hand. She squeezes the letter and smiles. After the weekend they've had together this could be the first love letter he's ever sent her. Sam feels a longing for him, his closeness, his body, that she's never felt before. She shuts her eyes and the memory of Friday's dawn comes like hot dew settling on her skin.

She'd clung to Dale long after the last parts of her story had run their course again in her mind. Neither of them moved, but a subtle awareness of the change that had come about seeped through them both as the light grew stronger in the world outside. Sam was completely relaxed, not holding herself as she usually did, just a fraction of a millimetre away from Dale, guarding herself against intimacy and the risk of discovery. And he in turn held her, rather than letting himself be held. In that simple shift of emphasis they could both feel that all the usual customs of their embraces were reversed. There was a vital pulse of new possibility waking inside them.

Sam took her head from Dale's shoulder, and raised her face waiting for him to kiss her. His mouth had a passion, a gentle insistence that was entirely new. Always before she controlled, never letting go of herself for a moment. Now, Sam let herself be soft, fluid under Dale's touch. His hands caressed her, smoothing her, opening her. She felt she was being unfolded, and with infinite care, so that the sweet slow burning sun of sensuality reached every part.

Afterwards they had lain on the floor incredulous, holding each other in a kind of wondrous shock. At last Sam said in a voice straight from her seventeen-year-old self, 'Wow! Can we do that again?'

Dale was no longer part of the outside world to her. He was inside her, a part of her. Finally, she felt, they had both stepped from behind their portraits, and she shivered to find that Dale wasn't quite as she expected him to be. She unfolded the letter.

Dear Angie,

Do you mind still being called that? I could get used to Sam. What can I say about the last three days? When you came home the other night, Thursday?, everything looked so bad to me. I thought I'd lost you, that you were just going to leave me. I thought the business was gone. And I found that everything was OK. Not just OK, but wonderful. Better than I ever imagined. It's like finding you again in the cake shop, except that now I really understand what I found that day. A beautiful, multi-faceted diamond.

I'm all over the place. I don't know what order to say things in.

I'll go and look at Lime House today. We can get the loan secured against its value now to tide the business over. By the sounds of things it's probably in our best interest for me to do the work on it, then sell it ready done up. I'll be back as soon as I can, Friday. Thursday maybe.

There's still so much to talk about. You've got to do your rainforest stuff, Angie. I loved the way you talked about it. And think about your parents. It's really hard but maybe you should find them.

Angie, there've always been times with you that I've felt there was something more behind your eyes. I never asked what. I told myself that you didn't want to talk about your past. But the real reason I never asked is that your secrets gave me the excuse to keep mine. And now I don't want there to be secrets between us any more.

All my love,

Dale

PS: If anybody calls for me, no matter what they say, just tell them I'll be home in a few days and to call at the weekend.

Sam had always thought that she knew the secrets Dale kept about himself. She'd always seen the person who patted houses as if they were old pets, and kept the boys' first shoes in the bottom of his toolbox. Were there other secrets? Supposing he still had as much to tell as she did?

Sam folded the letter and held it tight against her body, willing him to be as good and true as she'd always seen him to be. She leaned back and looked at the blue sky through the pointed frond fingers of the palm. High above her a little flock of parakeets flew south towards the Mendips. Imagination again? Or escapees from a cage with real bars?

'Why can't we sleep outside, Mummy?' Joe is dangerously petulant. He and Tony love their new garden and have taken to playing complex imaginary games about being explorers. Joe with his love of foreign-sounding words has even learned the Latin names of some of the plants.

'Because it gets cold in the middle of the night, Joe.'

'But we'll be under the duvet, Mummy.'

'We promise to come inside if it gets too cold,' Tony chips in.

Samantha sighs. A month ago they wouldn't have dreamed of requesting something so outrageous, but they've adapted to the new spirit of liberalism surrounding their mother. 'OK.'

They can hardly believe their luck. They run in to gather cushions, pillows and teddies. 'Can we have choklit bissskits in bed?' Joe calls.

'No!' Sam says. She has to keep some sort of hold on the reins!

Samantha has resisted the temptation to sleep on the playroom sofa to keep watch over the children. She lies awake in the middle of her own bed staring at the ceiling. She has spent an hour wondering with no conclusion and no particular focus what she will do now when the phone rings: Dale ringing from a hotel room.

'Hello, sweetie!' Samantha breathes sleepily into the phone. A small black beat of intense silence meets her voice, a slither of a moment but enough to make her sit up, awake, alert.

'Thank you, Mrs Cassinari. I didn't expect such a warm reception.' It is an old voice but the accent is cultured, the tone is velvet with a mannered politeness which only serves to emphasise an underlying desperation. It's not a voice Samantha knows. She runs to the window of the boys' room with the phone, and cranes her neck out of the open window.

'Who is this?' Looking down she can see Joe and Tony curled together in the moonlight. The voice is at least not that of a kidnapper. It continues slow and a little faltering.

'I don't think we've met.'

Calmer now she knows the boys are safe, she tries to regain control with a little righteous anger, 'Do you know what time it is?'

But the Voice is still unhurried, 'Oh yes, I know the time but I wanted to be certain to catch you in. Could you perhaps pass a message to your husband? Just tell him I called?' Before she can draw breath to say more, he's gone.

Samantha runs out to the boys. 'I've just heard a weather warning. There's a storm coming, you'd better get inside.'

She tucks her sleepy sons into her own bed to keep them safe and close. She lies between them, still hearing the Voice. The voice of a person at some sort of edge, ready to lose control. Inside her a nasty little trapdoor of doubt opens, and she wonders what secrets Dale really needed an excuse to keep.

'I can't believe we're planning the end of term barbie already. I have absolutely no idea where the time has gone! Just whooshed away like lemons!' Louise smiles beatifically and looks to the end of the garden where Barney has taken over as head of the Tropical Exploration Team of Joe and Tony.

'D'you mean lemmings, Louise?'

'Lemmings?'

'I thought because they whoosh over cliffs.'

'No. Lemons. Whoosh. As in lemon sorbet. You know! Hey, I adore what you've done to this garden! What prompted it, Angie?' Louise is having one of her moments of clarity, rare but utterly piercing. Samantha is pinned by the blue eyes, which say quite clearly that they know the garden signifies far more than a design decision.

'Oh, I don't know. I've just got more time now the boys are bigger.'

'Oh, yeah! Sure!' say the eyes. But they look away. They can see it's the only explanation they're going to get. 'Well, I suppose we ought to get down to business,' says Louise.

The Tropical Expedition is enjoying a supply stop. Tony and Joe are showing Barney how to make peanut butter and Marmite sandwiches, a skill they have recently been allowed to hone unsupervised. Outside, the Deacon Road Primary School PTA Catering Subcommittee have moved on from a discussion of per capita sausage consumption and age-specific pizza toppings, to the misdeeds of Louise's recently ex-husband.

'I've got a new accountant, Louise, he said, very creative, he said. You won't get anything!' Louise has no idea where her next, or any other, mortgage payment might come from: she has no job, because her CV goes straight on the reject pile when employers note that the last time she worked was just before Barney was born. Understandably she's getting a little tearful. Sam is about to make some unfavourable comparisons between the ex-Mr Louise and various forms of pond life when the phone rings.

'It'll be Dale. I'll tell him to call back. Here, take these tissues.'

She takes the call in the kitchen where a second round of peanut butter is being distributed over bread, hands, arms and the table top.

'Hi, Dale?'

There! That fragment of silence again. Speaking as eloquently as it did the first time. Then the Voice speaks with a wasp-trapping sweetness, 'Mrs Cassinari. Mr Cassinari—Dale—isn't home?'

'No.'

There is a hiss almost like a suppressed curse. 'Could you then kindly pass on my message? That I'm very, very anxious to speak with him. Soon.'

With the last syllable the phone is dead in her hand. It feels clammy and her heart is racing. She wipes her palms on her jeans and then calls Dale's mobile. 'This is the Vodafone recall service for . . .'

'Phone me, Dale. Soon as you can.'

She settles the boys in front of the TV and cleans up some of the peanut butter before she's calm enough to return to Louise, who has a pink nose and has used up all the tissues.

'Sorry I was so long. Crisis with the expedition team. Look, why don't you stay tonight? The kids will love it and you can drown your sorrows?'

The phone hasn't rung again, except with Louise's call to say that she'd got over her hangover. Samantha takes the boys to school and picks them up at the end of the day, but inside her things are getting out of proportion. The voice of the nameless caller is wandering around in her brain leaving doors open everywhere. One minute she can convince herself that he is just a disgruntled customer with a leaky down-pipe, and the next he's a Mafioso with a deadly hold over Dale and his business. When she finds herself standing beside the phone for the fifth time in a single morning, wondering if it will vibrate visibly before it rings, Samantha decides it's time for more effective distractions. She takes nothing but her door key and almost runs all the way to Tavs.

When she arrives, Maria runs the length of the shop, embraces her, and bursts into tears. She hasn't seen or spoken to Sam since the day Dale turned up on her doorstep with two boys and a suitcase.

'Finn, Finn, Angie and I, we have a little coffee.'

'No problem, Maria.'

With all the upheavals Samantha has forgotten to ask Dale what his mother knows. The way Maria has taken her arm and is so solicitously offering her a coffee in their tiny office, Samantha wonders if Maria suspects her son of being banished for wife-beating. Samantha takes a restorative gulp of coffee, but before she can speak Maria takes her hand again. 'Angela. You are like my daughter. Yes?'

'Maria, thank you!'

'Dale, when he come to my house with the boys—I think "what has that little bugger of mine done now?" He didn't say anything then. But after, he phone me. Told me everything.'

'I feel I lied to you, Maria. When we first met. I told you . . .'

'Don't matter. Everybody has some lies, yes? I have big lies I don't tell nobody. But I am still like your mum, OK?'

'OK.'

'Good. I worry about Dale's business. He say it's bad. I don't want you to waste your money on Dale's business if it's goin' bust.'

'It won't go bust. It's just a bad patch. Cashflow.'

'You and Dale OK?'

'Fine. He's gone to Suffolk to sort out the house I've been left.'

'OK. Then what are you doin' here?'

'I've given up my job in the supermarket. I don't know what I'm going to do in the long run. I just don't want that dead-end job any more. Can I work at Tavs for a while?'

'Music of the saints and angels! You know who call this morning? That Marcella tha's who! Say she's going to live in Cornwall with 'er boyfriend. Ppfff! Can you work here? You wanna start now?'

The boys love it when Samantha works in Granny Maria's shop, so they endure sitting quietly while Sam stays on and helps with the rush of business between four and closing at five thirty.

'Hey, boys, Granny going to invite herself for tea,' Maria says, pulling down the blinds, 'so you pick what you want to eat, eh?'

Maria and Samantha walk along the wide pavement towards

Lancaster Road, with the boys running ahead of them. Maria slips her arm through Samantha's. 'Hey, Angie, Dale told me Angie is not your name. Is Samantha. Very pretty. I wished I change my name too, when I come to England.'

'Why?'

'I didn't want Papa's name after the way he treat me. Nnah. So bad. He throw me down the stairs when he found I am pregnant.'

'But you didn't change your name?'

'No. I came here. Bristol. Big, wet, grey. People who don't smiles. I start my business and Cassinari is a good name for business.' Maria shrugged.

'And an easy name to trace if Dale's daddy wanted to find you?'

'Hah! No. I *know* Dale's daddy don't want to find me.' Maria's face is suddenly closed and dark, the dancing eyebrows low and straight. Then, like a passing cloud the darkness is gone, and Maria is laughing at the boys climbing on the wall of number eleven. 'Dale don't know about me and his daddy,' Maria says. 'What he don't know won't hurt him.' And she smiles her dazzling smile, so that Sam feels this secret is somehow a present, a silver charm, a symbol of trust.

Maria has added her own expert selections—wild boar ham, bean salad, stuffed peppers, rich cheese bread and a bottle of Frascati—to the boys' standard favourites of *bresaola*, *caponata* and *provolone*. 'Is a new one for you to try, boys: *fagioli con gamberetti e bottarga*.' Maria puts a spoonful of the salad into each of the boys' waiting mouths.

'Lovely, Granny,' says Joe through his chewing.

'I like the bean part and prawn part but not the other part,' says Tony.

'*Bottarga* . . . oh, but that is the best, the eggs of the tuna, *tonno*.'

As they eat, Maria tells the story behind each dish, polishing the bare facts to brightness with her passion and experience. '*Prosciutto di cinghiale*, this is the ham of the wild boar. Is very fierce. Is the beast that attacked Odysseus when he was a young hunter. This is made by my friend who has boar in the woods near his house. Now, Tony, you try this olive. Good? You know when Adam lay dead, there were three trees sprouted from the seeds in his mouth. The cypress, the cedar and the olive tree. Imagine that, three big trees with their roots in a skull.'

The boys run out to eat their chocolate bars in the garden, leaving Maria and Sam to savour figs and mascarpone. Maria's been waiting to talk. 'You know Mr Belling next door is giving up? He's got a bad heart, he can't work no more.' Maria has never got on very well with the proprietor of the ironmonger's next door to Tavs. In all his fifty-seven years the most adventurous thing to pass Mr Belling's lips has been a pork sausage. He still regards Tavs as a temporary fad and a hotbed of subversion. But Samantha can tell there's more point to Maria's observation than mere *schadenfreude*. 'So he won't need his shop, and the lease will be up to grabs.'

'Are you going to take it?'

'Maybe. I need new challenge. I'd like to do something bit different. A real Italian bakery. I'm fed up with chasing that Guy. You know, last week I ring him, "Where is my *focaccia*, Guy, I have a big order here." He says, "Oh Maria, you can have it tomorrow, I forgot to start the dough . . ." Blah blah excuses. Nnah! In the autumn I go home to Italy and I find a good baker. A young person who wants a big start.'

'I think you'll make a fortune, Maria.'

'Maybe. It's big money I need. Got to rip out all that Belling crap. Put in special oven. Twenty-thousand pound, maybe more.' Maria pauses. 'You know, Angie, I'm no good to ask things. But this is good idea. I think you're right, it will make a fortune. But I need money to do it.'

'And you'd like me to invest some of my inheritance?'

'That's it. Invest. I do it all proper so you get profit share and all. Maybe you could take over Tavs with Finnian while I do the bakery?'

'The money's yours, Maria, as soon as I get it. And I'll work in Tavs for a while, but I've got a lot to decide.'

'That's good enough answer for me. Now, another glass . . .'

Samantha stands at the sink with her rubber-gloved hands idle in the suds. Why hasn't Dale rung back? Maybe his mobile isn't working. But the whole of West Suffolk can't be a dead zone. She wants to hear that the voice that escaped the phone and is scratching at her peace of mind is not important, just some bloke with problem stonework or a kink in his flashing. She wants to be sure she already knows all Dale's secrets.

'Maria, has Dale rung you this week, while he's been away?'

'Dale ring me? Are you crazy? He didn't ring you? How long?'

'Three days.'

'Three days. Nnnah.' She takes a plate from the draining board and walks, with her testy hips swinging, to the cupboard. 'He's a bugger that boy. Don't worry. Maybe his phone is bust.'

'Maria, what was Dale like, before he met me?'

It takes no more than a second for Maria to master her reaction yet still she nearly drops the plate. 'What you mean? He was a little bugger. Same as now.' She shuts the cupboard and turns to take Sam's face in her hands, smoothing her cheeks with both thumbs. 'That Dale. He is a little bugger. But he is a good man. A real good man.'

'Thanks, Maria. I know. I know.'

The two women, suddenly close to tears, hug.

'D'you want to stay the night, Maria?'

'No. I like my bed. Call me a taxi?'

Samantha seeks the blankness of the spare room after Maria has gone. She watches the few late traffic lights track over the ceiling. She and Dale had made love in this room just a few days ago and the lights had moved over the pale paint work in the same way. Then they'd made her feel peaceful, lulled—she felt she'd beaten Pandora, and kept the worst things from the box of her past under the lid. Now the lights make her anxious, and the lid of her box, and of Dale's too, seem menacingly ajar. Dale's 'secrets' cast grotesque shadows on the wall; how could his healthy business have foundered so fast if not through some corruption? Outside of this house, away from her and the boys, Dale could be anybody, involved in anything; a victim or a predator. The lights race unpredictably down the wall. Soon the shadows of her own secrets are dancing on the bedroom wallpaper. She gets up at last, draws the curtains and falls asleep with the bedside lamp on.

TEN

EIGHT PEOPLE ARE SITTING ROUND Samantha's kitchen table with mugs of hot tea to ward off the chill of the rain. It's another committee meeting, not the PTA this time but the annual Lancaster Road Street Party Committee. All the residents who helped to get the giant palm tree into the back garden of number eleven are there, plus three of the students from the big tatty house on the corner.

'So then, in conclusion,' says Keith, 'although we've got away with closing off the road this year, next year's going to be really tricky.'

'Thank you, Keith.' One of the students is a business and tourism graduate called Julie. She sees running meetings as something she can put on her CV. 'I think we should run through what needs to be done tomorrow and on the day itself, yeah?'

'Josh at number thirty-eight'll help me put the crash barriers up at noon on Sunday,' says Keith.

'Right,' says Julie. 'That takes care of security issues. Now, the barbecue? I think that's your department, Spider.'

The large sprawling politics student, Spider, is caught with a mouthful of cake; all he can do is shake his head vigorously.

'What d'you mean, no!'

Spider swallows fast. 'I said I'd help run the barbecue. Not set it up.'

'Fine,' says Julie with a definite subtext of 'I'll-see-you-later-Spider-you-useless-div'.

'Um,' says Malcolm, fiddling with the bridge of his glasses, 'we usually use our barbie. It's big enough. I'll set it up, if Spider could lend a hand. Just outside our place, Spider?'

'Yeah, cool.'

Beside Spider, the other student, Jon (who's doing Women's Studies as it might offer him the only chance he's likely to get to pull), clears his throat. 'Umm,' he says as if trying out a new sound system, 'I'll like take care of the sounds. You know, put my system outside. Or in the window. People can just bring me, like, tapes of what they want to hear? OK?'

'Good! Now, drinks?'

'Two trestle tables outside our front door?' Felicity pipes up sweetly. 'And I've got lots of paper cups left over from a do at work.' Keith smiles at her adoringly.

Samantha offers to go and get the meat for the barbecue. Maeve says that there are very good Quorn patties available these days and so, the ritual contest of carnivores versus vegetarians begins.

'I personally had to throw away sixty-three unsold veggie burgers last year,' says Keith. 'It just doesn't make economic sense to buy half a ton of *Quorn patties!*'

'Well, the real solution,' retorts Maeve, showing some sign that she might really be a lawyer, 'is to give people no choice. Meat eaters can after all eat vegetarian food, while the converse is not the case!'

The phone rings. Gratefully Samantha tears upstairs to take the call. It's Dale, brimming with excitement. All he wants to tell her is bank managers, roof repairs, authentic leading and Victorian tiles. All she really wants is to know when he's coming home.

'Where are you?'

'Bury St Edmunds. I'm in a payphone, the mobile's bust. Angie, listen, the house looks fabulous from the outside. I could do wonders with it, I really could.'

'When are you coming home?'

'Not yet. After the weekend.'

'What's taking so long?'

'Oh. There's just a lot to do.' It's a vague answer and Samantha hears the tiny silence which is the sound of Dale coming up with something more specific and convincing. 'I'm trying to get as many quotes done for the work on Lime House as I can. I've had a couple of estate agents look at it, and as it stands it'll fetch six hundred thousand, at least.' Dale is back on truthful ground now, she can tell by the enthusiasm in his voice. 'So it's up to you to decide, you know sell now, or do the work and then sell for more.' He's ready to expand on this but Samantha isn't interested just now.

'Dale,' she says, with a tightness in her voice that makes him pay attention, 'this man keeps calling. Just says to tell you he called. Won't say his name. He really scares me.'

Dale goes quite still at the end of the line. 'Posh voice? Old?'

'Yeah.'

'Bugger. *Bugger.*' Dale pauses and sighs. This is not reassuring to Samantha. 'I'm sorry. I'm so sorry. Look. Don't worry about it. He's harmless. Just put the phone down whenever he rings. I'll be back soon. I'll explain then.'

Harmless is how her biology teacher once described a hornet the size of a Cuban cigar with a sting like a Mossad stiletto.

Downstairs the meeting is breaking up. In the hall Callendula is chatting to Jon and Spider. 'Wicked!' she says, and they smile shiftily.

'Bye, Angela,' they say in their best Addressing-Grown-Ups voices as they slope out, with the same bony, loose-limbed sway that Friesians have on their way to the milking parlour.

Keith and Felicity are holding hands like the Start-rite kids and being subjected to Maeve's opinions on birthing pools. They don't seem to mind, as they revel in anything to do with babies and pregnancy.

Julie is telling Malcolm about her job prospects in 'the business sector'. Malcolm is looking at the clipboard clutched to her chest and the way her cleavage peeps enticingly over the top. As she leaves Julie briefly squeezes his forearm, telling him she valued his contribution to the meeting. Immediately Malcolm plunges into panicky but rather exciting fantasies of telling Julie's heaving bosom that they can only be friends, that a physical relationship is impossible. Julie sails out, internally quoting from the 'Get To The Top' manual: 'Eye contact and arm touching can be among the most valuable of management tools'.

The cheese-wedge house has been host to many scenes like this in the past. Samantha has always been happy to host meetings, while staying safely untouched and unengaged by it all. And at the end of the evening she always refuses the offers of help or company, preferring to maintain

433

her safe separateness. So she's only herself to blame for the fact that tonight everyone leaves without offering to help wash up or stay and chat. But tonight she wanted them all to stay, to drink more tea, maybe move on to the whisky. She wanted to hear them talk about their kids, their jobs and their worries, to gather clues about how other people collect up the pieces of their lives—rows and loving, business sectors and sticky bean cans, burgers and Quorn patties, murky past and uncertain future—and make a whole. Alone in the kitchen with carroty crumbs and dirty mugs, she settles for a practical solution to her present anxieties: she unplugs the phone and sets the burglar alarm.

Sunday morning rain gets Maeve twittering with anxiety, but as the residents of Lancaster Road emerge after their first cup of coffee, the clouds disperse. Sunshine dries the pavements and slants through the trees. A band called Urban Tarmac Suckers are playing their hearts out through Jon's 'system'. Impromptu stalls of all sorts are springing up in people's front gardens as the residents of Lancaster Road begin to have confidence in the weather.

Eric Donaldson, the widowed French teacher at number seventeen, has covered a picnic table with shoe boxes filled with gooseberries with the sign 'Help Yourself' pencilled on the back of an empty cornflakes packet. Callendula has draped a sheet over the brick wall of number thirteen and is laying out her homemade bead and wire jewellery for sale. Margaret and Edith, the retired anthropologists at number six, have baked cakes and scones and have them neatly arrayed on starched cloths and china plates with little jars to receive 'contributions to charity'. Everyone is bringing chairs and tables, cushions and rugs out into the street, and the under-tens have formed a single collective entity which tears up and down the road beside itself with excitement.

Perhaps it was just the level of participation, every door in the street open, everyone outside talking, eating, drinking. Perhaps the sun and the steamy heat made people feel a little less British, but from the very start the Lancaster Road Street Party had a certain chemistry to it. Spontaneity is normally difficult for the English; it might involve interaction with people one hasn't been introduced to, or a course of events one cannot predict. Yet sometimes, when the sun shines, they can be different from their ordinary rainy-day selves and the repressed spirit of play, fun and mayhem can suddenly burst out. It's a chain reaction too—gathered in a group above a certain critical mass it can give rise to a collective ability to party quite outside the bounds of the National Character. The Sunday of the party was one of those times.

It really started with Spider getting the gang of under-tens to follow him round in a roving conga of outrageous movement and mime to 'Baggy Trousers'. Then, kids grabbed their parents, or any other adult who was close, to learn the routine and join in. Samantha was pulled into the circle of manically dancing children by both Joe and Tony.

'Pull your trousers out like this, Mummy . . .'

'Then flap your shirt . . .'

'And grab your hair . . .'

'Oh, Mummy, pleeeeese . . .'

Samantha was reluctant to join in, because 'Angie' didn't dance. Dancing was dangerous, like sex: potentially too revealing. But with so much already revealed, Samantha felt liberated. She let the boys coax her at first, then she was leading them, making up new moves and new steps, that they copied with laughter and delight. And it felt so good! She threw her head back, shaking her hair like a mane, and noticed flocks of macaws bending the TV aerials with their weight. 'Hey, boys! Can you do this? See how far down you can twist without falling over!'

The street filled up, the music got louder and the joint jumped. People from other streets came and joined in. Cars passing the top of the closed-off road pulled over. At five o'clock a salsa band on their way home after a competition in Birmingham leapt out of their van and set up in the tatty garden of the student house. They played until the surrounding roads were blocked with cars and everyone had danced holes into their shoes and kinks into their spines. Just as the fever of spontaneous pleasure looked as if it might spread across the whole city, the clouds cracked open, spilling cold water onto the revellers' heads and the police arrived to restore everyone to their normal wet-day selves.

Samantha and the boys had danced for what she realised now had been nearly six hours, solidly. The boys collapsed, whimpering with exhaustion, almost the moment that the rain and the sirens came to break the spell. Now the kitchen clock shows nine and outside darkness is just beginning to cover up the remaining litter lying limp on the wet tarmac. Samantha pads around her kitchen in two pairs of Dale's biggest fluffiest socks, wincing slightly with every step. She opens cupboard doors, foraging for some indulgence to eat—broken Eccles cakes would fit the bill perfectly. She settles at last for chocolate biscuits dipped in tea, and curls her legs up onto the chair, reflecting on how exactly like 3.00am it feels. There's a sudden shuffling outside the door: Maeve has probably tripped her circuits again cooking supper. Samantha smiles: that's OK. Having danced cheek to cheek with her to 'No woman no cry',

Samantha feels a bond of solidarity that will carry her through at least five more trip-switch incidents without irritation.

A key turns in the lock and Samantha knows it's not Maeve but Dale home early! The voices on the doorstep are suddenly quite clear as they move into the hall: Dale's and two others, a man and a woman.

'Thank you, Dale, I can manage really,' says the woman.

'Shall I take that from you, dear,' the man says to her.

Shaking, incredulous, rigid with shock, Samantha hobbles into the hall. The visitors are instantly recognisable, in the same heart-stopping thunder-flash way that God's face would be, peeping at you in your coffin. Samantha stares and they stare back. Standing there with her skinny brown legs stuck into a bulbous mass of sock, Samantha, the grown woman, looks just like the gangly kid they remember. The three of them are caught in a swell of time that builds over the moments to a wave, it crests and breaks, washing the daughter across the carefully chosen pile of her hall carpet into the arms of her father and her strangely, incomprehensibly, miraculously alive mother.

ELEVEN

IT IS MORE THAN AN HOUR before anyone can speak properly. There are many different sorts of tears to be cried. Ralph seems to suffer most, his sobs pulled out from deep inside. But at last the three of them can sit calmly, taking in each other's faces and sipping sweet tea.

Samantha can't stop staring at Bea. Bea is not simply alive, but is pink-cheeked and blooming, even a little round. Her hair—now completely white—is cut in a short straight bob, with a wispy fringe to just above the dark and striking eyes. She wears a short-sleeved cotton safari suit the colour of cornflowers, and neat brown sandals revealing a row of toenails painted bright pink. She sits erect and elegant with her legs folded together to one side. Even her teeth look better than ten years ago. Initially all Sam's attention is focused on the simple fact that Bea is alive. It is so huge a fact and yet so simple. The fear, guilt and grief, which have made her emotional life into a fortress for ten years, collapse. It is an almost physical sensation, as if Sam has a sandcastle in her stomach that the tide is washing flat. The word *murderer* that has branded her soul loses its power like a retreating thunder cloud.

Bea is simply a healthy version of herself, the self that Sam always talked and laughed with. But Ralph is transformed. A healthy leanness has replaced the old paunch. He is wearing jeans and sandals with no socks. There is even a copper arthritis bracelet round his right wrist which gives him a slightly bohemian air. He stands straight, and when he sits his posture is open and relaxed. His speech is slower and more flowing. He's come alive.

Gradually, something more than their obvious health and good grooming strikes Samantha. Bea and Ralph look like *people*, not simply her parents. They had, of course, always looked like people, but at seventeen, she had been too young to notice. She hadn't understood what her leaving could do or mean. Now she can't think where she will begin to explain and apologise.

Bea is the first to brave the hard task of starting to speak. Leaving the deep-water questions for later, when they might be ready to be asked and answered, Bea begins with a little paddle in the shallows. 'You know, Sam, you've grown a little bit. I'm sure you're taller.'

'Still a skinny ribs though!' says Ralph.

'You both look so well.'

'We've just been to Portugal for a week, staying with a friend of your mother's.' What friend? Bea and Ralph didn't have friends!

'Dale rang us the night we got back,' says Bea, 'then he came round and spoke to us. He had a very hard job convincing us you'd want to see us.' Bea tries to keep her tone light, but her voice is shaking already.

'We accepted that you wanted to be left in peace,' Ralph says.

'We understood how you felt. That you'd had such a bad time at home . . .' Bea looks forlornly at Ralph, pursing her lips. Samantha wants them to shout and be angry, to call her selfish, cruel, and what she's called herself all this time, a killer. But there isn't a scrap of anger to be found. They look at her with such gratitude that Samantha has to look away out of shame. Far from coming to her with retribution, they've come for forgiveness, and are afraid that she will reject them again.

Bea is crying anew. 'We're so sorry, Sam. When I was ill and Ralph couldn't cope, it was awful for you. I never blamed you for leaving.'

'I've felt all this time that I failed you.' Ralph is sobbing.

Samantha is dazed, how can they be apologising to her after what *she* did? All she can do is blurt her apology and hope they will listen. 'No, no, I'm sorry I ran off. Now I've got the boys I know how frantic you must have been. But in all this time I never tried to contact you.'

'Oh, Sam, don't. That's not even true. You did keep in touch.'

'We always knew you were all right. Because of your Christmas cards.' Ralph's words make no sense at all to Samantha. She stares at him stupidly. 'It meant the world that you sent those. Every Christmas. Even that first Christmas. We knew you were all right.'

'When you wrote to tell us about the boys being born . . .' Bea is crying too much to go on, she simply rummages in her bag and pulls out a weathered envelope. 'I've kept them with me every day.'

Sam takes two cards from the single envelope and opens each in turn. The first has a glitter-strewn robin on the front. Inside a typed message is pasted: 'Happy Christmas, Mum and Dad. Hope you're well. Dale and I had our first baby this year, a boy called Tony. Best wishes, Sam.'

The second card bears a reindeer with mistletoe woven through its antlers, the same style of typed message inside: 'A brother for Tony, little Joe born without a hitch this year. I'm well. Hope you are. Sam.'

'I don't know what we would have done without those cards,' says Ralph, 'I really don't. They made us able to go on.'

How can she tell them that she didn't offer them even this tiny scrap of compassion? That if she had known Bea was alive, she would have come home? That guilt, fear and cowardice kept her away? It will only make the pain of their separation worse, through having been unnecessary. Sam sees immediately that bearing that knowledge in her heart, privately, is her new penance. All she can do is hug her parents and tell them how glad she is that they got the cards, and how glad she is that Dale came to find them and bring them to her.

They are too exhausted for much more talk. The bare facts of Bea's recovery and Ralph's return to reality, their move from the family home, Ralph's early retirement and Bea's new career as owner of a vintage clothing shop, are run through like a news bulletin. Granny Pearl's death two years ago in a car accident is only slightly elaborated. Dale takes their bags to the spare room and everyone cries again as they kiss good night on the landing.

'What time do the boys go to school?' asks Bea.

'Oh. Day off tomorrow,' says Dale. 'Day off all round.'

Sam flops onto the bed as soon as the door is closed. Dale comes to sit beside her. He is not the same as he was a week or a month ago. He has produced the unexpected from the personality she always viewed as simply dependable. She reaches up and touches his face.

'Why did you do this?'

'It seemed wrong not to, for you and for them. Aren't you happy?'

There's still so much to lie about, she wants to give Dale as much truth as she can, so Sam thinks carefully before answering. 'I'm *glad*. I've got my mum back from the dead. But it's all too painful to be happy about. I am more at peace, but it feels weird. Not real yet. I feel better because Mum's alive and worse because I never contacted them.'

'But you did. Why didn't you tell me about the cards, Sam?'

'I don't know, Dale. Why didn't I tell you the whole story anyway? I'm sorry.' Sam is crying now, sorry that still she has to lie to Dale.

'You were just a kid. It's OK, Angie.'

'How did you find them anyway?'

'Determination. Just like tracking down an authentic Georgian door. Would have been easier with their address. *Why* didn't you tell me about the cards? Oh, I'm sorry, love. I mustn't keep asking.'

'I dunno,' she says, which seems close enough to her real feelings. 'You didn't tell me all your secrets, did you? Who was that man, Dale? Who kept ringing up?'

'He's nobody. It's nothing.' He scoops her up, holding her close.

She is not convinced, but she lets Dale persuade her into a languid lovemaking that drops her, soft as a leaf, into sleep.

It's going to be hot again today. Shorts weather. Samantha pulls out a pair of slightly frayed white denim shorts and a blue vest.

'You haven't worn those in ages!' Dale has woken up.

'No, but I can be officially twenty-seven now, so I'm entitled.'

'You look gorgeous. You make an old man very happy.'

Sam runs downstairs feeling light, and efficient, equal to the emotional day ahead. Bea and Ralph are up already, sitting on the patio. She calls good morning and they rush to kiss her good morning, the way they did when she was little. The memory is so sharp that Samantha's eyes prickle. Bea grins through tears and Ralph coughs a lot and takes a turn round the echiums, clearly resolved not to cry like a woman today.

'He'll be all right in a minute. Really he will. And I'm fine. So lovely to see my gorgeous girl.' Bea steers Sam back into the kitchen. 'What can I do, Sam, to help make breakfast?'

Together the two women lay the table, make a pot of tea, and manage to burn three lots of toast out of nervousness and crying by the time Dale comes down with Joe and Tony clinging to his hands.

Ralph's turn in the garden restores his composure and all through breakfast he has chatted, asking Samantha about her garden and Dale about his work. 'All I do in the way of work these days is Bea's business accounts,' he says. 'Apart from that I'm completely idle.'

'That's nonsense. He's busier than I am. He works in the over-sixties drop-in centre, he's got choir, and helps me out in the shop, and feeds us on wonderful veg from the garden.' She squeezes his hand. 'I've forgotten to mention the yoga. Go on, Ralph, you tell it.'

'All right. I started yoga to help me relax. Your mother was having all sorts of alternative this and that to help her. Acupuncture, Chinese herbs,' he rolls his eyes dramatically. 'I thought it was a load of nonsense. But whatever it was, she did get better. Back on her feet by that spring. So I thought I'd try something for my, well, depression—can't beat about the bush, that's what it was. I went to a yoga class. It did wonders. You remember what a wreck I was, Sam. Had been for years. Look, I'll give you a little demonstration.'

All through breakfast the boys have sat silently spooning cereal into their mouths without taking their eyes off Bea and Ralph. The trainee grandparents have contained their excitement wonderfully, and let the boys find the right time to make contact, saying nothing to them but a polite good morning. As Ralph kneels down in the middle of the kitchen floor, Joe stands up on his chair to get a better view of whatever is about to happen. Slowly, elegantly, Ralph's lean old frame is tilted upside-down until he forms a perfect line balanced on his head.

'Wow!' says Tony seriously impressed. 'Wicked!'

Joe starts to clap, then sits down suddenly, embarrassed by his own spontaneity. 'Dad,' he says in the sort of audible-at-two-hundred-metres' whisper that only five-year-olds can do, 'what's his name?'

'Ralph, but you could call him Granddad.'

'Oh. Granddad Ralph? Can you teach me and Tony to do that?'

'I expect so. Shall we try after your breakfast has gone down?'

The demanding day, full of difficult conversations and more crying, doesn't materialise. By noon the boys have learned, after a fashion, to do headstands, and have taken Ralph to the park with the promise of ice creams on the way home. Bea and Samantha are side by side in deck chairs as if they had never been anywhere else in their lives.

'That Knole sofa is gorgeous!' says Bea. 'The colour of the covers!'

'That material was once curtains in Monmouth Castle!'

'No!' Bea laughed. 'You've got a real eye for colour. Funny, I never thought you cared a fig for all that when you were at home. Full of your rainforest then you were. You could have gone to Oxford.'

'Not really. I failed the entrance exam. Found out the night I left.'

'You didn't, Sam. They wrote to us offering you a place. We had to write back and tell them we didn't know where you were.'

'Oh, my God! All this time I was sure I'd failed.'

'Is that why you went?'

Sam just looks at her; is it possible that Bea has forgotten the night she left and what happened? 'Maybe,' Sam says, 'maybe.'

Tired out by their first day as grandparents, Bea and Ralph are dozing in front of a video with the boys. Samantha is trying to think about supper, but her brain is running away with a stream of what-ifs. What if she had never left? What if she had known that Bea was alive? What if she'd known about her Oxford place? And, most of all, what if the Christmas cards had never been sent and Bea and Ralph had come to find her?

'Shall I get it?' Bea is calling. The phone is ringing.

'No, 's all right.'

'Mrs Cassinari. How nice to speak with you again.'

'I'm not going to "speak with you" if you don't tell me your name.'

'Then perhaps I could speak with Mr Cassinari.'

'He's not here. Now why don't you just go away?'

'Mr Cassinari wouldn't want that. Tell him to call me.'

Beaten to the hang-up again, Samantha almost throws the receiver back onto the hook. She is standing in the kitchen, shaking. What was she afraid of? Violence? Blackmail? Or the unseen, unguessed-at side of her own husband?

Irritation makes the decision about what to eat easy. Shepherd's pie, from the freezer. Next door in the playroom the killer whale has leapt to freedom and the kids are stirring Bea and Ralph back into action. They'll be tired now, unused to the demands of two small boys. But Sam doesn't rescue them. The phone call has left her sour and resentful, all the 'what ifs' that she's been dwelling on magnified. She takes her parents a sherry and resolutely ignores the weariness in their faces: they can damn well soldier on for a bit longer, it only serves them right for not spotting a fake card when they saw it!

'No bath tonight,' Sam announces to the children. 'You can make peanut butter sandwiches for your tea, and then go to bed.'

'Can Granddad Ralph and Granny Bea help us?'

'We'd love to!' Bea says, in a 'spirit willing, flesh weak' sort of tone.

'Right. Our dinner's in the oven so I'll go and have a bath.'

Sam shuts the bathroom door behind her and leans against it. There's lavender oil in a little phial on the side of the tub, its label promising to 'relax tension, remove aches'. Sam drips the oil into the running water. Never mind tension and aches, she thinks, what about unreasonable anger and unjustified resentment?

The lavender oil never really had the chance to show its capabilities. Within seconds of getting into the bath, Sam was out of it. There had been a crash, a scream that could have cracked diamonds, and, before Bea had the chance to call her name, Sam was rushing downstairs. Joe had fallen off his chair and hit his jaw on the table en route to the floor.

She'd have to get him to hospital as his lip was bitten right through. A three-stitches job at least, she guessed.

The population of Bristol has had a busy afternoon driving into each other's cars, falling off scaffolding and getting into fights. While ambulance after ambulance pulls up to the big swing-door entrance of the casualty department, the more domesticated of the accident-prone Bristolians wait quietly on the plastic chairs. They, too, have had a busy time chopping fingers instead of carrots, trimming toes instead of grass, and cooking skin instead of sausages. One little boy with a split lip is pretty small beer. Samantha wishes she'd taken Joe to the surgery, but having waited an hour and a half already, that option is long gone.

Joe dozes. She cuddles him half on her lap and half on the seat beside her, noticing wistfully how long his legs are getting; her own legs are going to sleep under his weight. She's beginning to notice little tendrils of green snaking their way over the filing cabinets in the reception area. Another ten minutes of this sort of inactivity and the whole of casualty is going to be knee-deep in leaf litter, and there will be spider monkeys experimenting with the ultrasound machines. Then, out of the corner of her eye, she sees Dale. She frees a hand from under Joe's shoulder, ready to call and wave to him. But Dale isn't Dale. Twenty years too old and two inches too short for that. He's holding a large dressing to the side of his face, but even without a clear close view of his features, there is something unmistakably Dale-ish about this man: when he moves there is that same atmosphere of unstoppable energy that is so distinctively Dale's.

Not-Dale sits two rows away. He is dressed in a neat navy boiler suit and shiny black safety boots. Samantha looks at his shoulders, the back of his neck, and is disturbed to notice that they too are like Dale's: the strange intangible feeling of recognition only grows. She burns her gaze into Not-Dale's hairline like Superman's X-ray glance, trying to see if this is the man who left his Italian girlfriend pregnant or simply a genetic fluke who reminds her vaguely of her husband.

A nurse leans out of the swing doors. 'Joseph Cassinari?'

At the sound of the surname Samantha scrutinises Not-Dale's seated figure, searching for some clue of reaction to the name.

'Joseph Cassinari? Are you here?' Not-Dale is very still, but he doesn't turn. The nurse calls again, 'Joseph Cassinari?'

'Over here,' Samantha calls, 'just coming.' Samantha gets up and Joe wakes in her arms and begins to wail and struggle. She shifts his weight and walks around the end of the row of seats to pass just inches from Not-Dale. She glimpses the turned-away bandage-covered face once more and can't decide if she is imagining the familiarity of the jawline. A moment later she and Joe are on the busy side of the swing doors.

Samantha checks on the boys one last time before going to bed. Dale is waiting for her. She strokes his close-cropped scalp and, somewhere in her mind, the iron-grey hair of the man in the hospital flickers. She sits beside the real Dale and he caresses the nape of her neck.

'Is he OK, Ange?'

'Fine. Flat out.'

'You OK?'

'Whacked.'

'How whacked?' His hand runs under her T-shirt up her bare spine.

Gently she wriggles away. 'Dale, who's that bloke who kept ringing up while you were away? He rang again today.'

'He's just some bloke I did some work for, hassling.'

'But *who* is he?'

'Nobody who matters.' Dale buries his mouth in her throat so his voice is muffled by her flesh. 'I'll finish the work with him pretty soon. Once we've got Lime House sold.'

'Why d'you need the money from Lime House?'

'You know why, Ange.' He sucks the words out of her mouth, and she feels her will slackening under the heat of his lips.

'Yeah, I know, for the business,' Samantha sighs. Gently, with that relentless steady energy, Dale pushes her backwards onto the mattress. She knows what he's doing, didn't she hide behind sex this way herself for so long? But being out of control is still unfamiliar, a deliciousness she can't resist. She lets herself go into his hands, like a swimmer slipping into a sea of sweet oblivion.

Around 5.00am, Samantha's dream life suffers a processing overload. In an attempt to assimilate all her anxieties past and present her subconscious reverts to a particularly terrifying version of the standard chasing dream, from which Samantha wakes soaked in sweat and crying. Immediately wide awake she goes downstairs to dispel the misery with a cup of cocoa and a piece of toast. Framed in the kitchen window, and lit by a pink-light-bulb dawn, she finds a pair of skinny legs in grey sweat pants. Ralph is out on the patio doing a headstand.

From what she can see of him, he seems utterly peaceful. She remembers this tranquillity from long ago, something he had when she was very tiny, pitting the tiny push of her legs against his broad hands. But it got lost. He'd grown uncomfortable in himself, as if his clothes always itched, or his head always ached. Even at their most peaceful times, silently pricking out seedlings in the greenhouse, he had a tension about him, his smile wearing a tight, bone corset. By the time she was an adolescent, she saw him as a cartoon cut-out, two dimensional, inadequate. For ten years he'd existed in her memory like that—a silhouette, something almost devoid of real human form. But from her new perspective she sees a man miserable to the point of madness. With a mother like Granny Pearl, how could anyone grow up with the emotional tools required for life's trickier DIY projects? He had become a haunted ruin by the time she was seventeen, barely inhabiting his life at all. How, she wonders, did he rescue this warm and peaceful man from that shell of a person?

The legs move, and with a shockingly youthful spring Ralph is on his feet. He turns, smiles, and joins her at the table. In the dawn-quiet house, fresh respectively from meditation and from dreams, Ralph and his daughter are in the same special space outside the normal constraints of the waking world. They sit and look at each other without embarrassment, each searching the other's face for clues.

'How did you get to be like this, Daddy?'

'I could ask you the same, Sam. My fierce little girl has grown into a mother, and a very good one too.'

Sam is filled with an unexpected sense of relief. The boys *are* her rock. If he can see that too, it makes it truer. She reaches for his hand. 'Was I fierce?'

'Well, perhaps not fierce. Determined. Frighteningly determined.'

'D'you remember pushing my feet with your hand, Daddy?' she asks.

'I remember, Sam. Yes.'

'You were like this then. Calm. Some time long ago.'

'That was before your mother got ill. I grew into an ostrich when she did. Ignored everything that mattered: her illness. You caring for her. My failure to help. I was too afraid to feel anything.'

'I didn't understand you then. I hated you for that. I'm sorry.'

'Don't be sorry. I hated myself. But when you left there wasn't anyone else to care for Bea. I had to stop being an ostrich and start feeling. It felt like being sliced open. Terrible pain. Terrible. I had to look at how I feared losing Bea, at what I'd done to you, how I'd failed as a father. When you've looked at what you fear most, you've nothing left to be afraid of.'

'I'm sorry I ran away.'

'Don't be. I'd have my head in the sand to this day if you hadn't gone. We had the cards, Sam. We knew you were safe. That was all we felt we deserved, to be honest. I think not knowing where you were or what had happened to you would have killed us both. But we knew.'

Sam drops her forehead onto his hand. The guilty secret she's lost has been replaced with another, even more precious, a secret she must keep to protect her parents, not herself.

'But none of that matters now, Sam. Bea and I have got you back.' Gently he holds her head upright, pushing his palm against her heavy forehead. 'There now,' he says. 'Don't cry, Sam. That's my strong girl.'

TWELVE

FINNIAN HAS HELD ONTO HIS CURIOSITY all morning, but at each lull between jobs his unasked questions have hung in the air between them. There is no Maria to offer refuge or distraction; she has taken a day out to wrangle over her bakery project. Sam wishes Finnian would just get on with it, as she knows she has to satisfy his curiosity about her parents and her past, because of what Maria said as she was leaving after dinner, on Bea and Ralph's last night in Bristol. 'They are lovely, your mummy and daddy. Hey! You know what Finny say when I tell him about them? I tell him your mum not dead. He said, "I knew it." Funny, hah?'

By now he is quite recovered from his sense of being somehow slighted by Sam's lack of honesty. Their banter is restored to normal and has even managed to incorporate some of the details of Samantha's newly revealed history. Finnian has told her several times during the course of the day that she is far too young to be slicing salami. 'You don't get the necessary wrist maturity until you're thirty.'

As they lean on the counter sipping juice, the man in the boiler suit floats back into Sam's mind.

'Has Maria ever talked to you about Dale's father, Finny?'

'It's a funny thing, but she never has. And she talks about everything else. She only ever tells the bare bones of the drama . . . she was young and foolish, she was deceived, he left her, she followed him here . . .'

'Yeah. That's as much as she told Dale. Or at least that's as much as Dale tells me.'

'Ah! You think they both know more than they say?' Finnian wriggles into a more comfortable position, ready for the exchange of some choice sweetmeat of information, or stuffed olive of theory. 'I'd say there was a lot more to it than that.' His eyes fix Samantha with an antenna-twitching stare. 'Just like I feel there's a lot more to your story of the guy who left you his house. When are you going to tell it all to me?'

'Some day, Finn. But not now. I'm dropping in on Maria on my way home.'

'Are you not picking up the boys?'

'I am . . . can I just give Louise a call to say I'll be late?'

'Don't know why you're asking me, you're the boss's daughter.'

Maria's voice floats from the open bedroom window, instructing Sam to let herself in. Upstairs, in Maria's ruby-red bedroom, Sam is amazed to find her in bed. It is three years since she even had a cold. Her lively olive colouring has faded to a dirty green and she looks small and broken, like a crushed bird. Maria seems too worn out for serious conversation. Sam's spirits sink. Until this moment she hadn't admitted to herself how much she wanted to share with Maria her nebulous misgivings about Dale's unnamed secrets, and fish for information about his mysterious father. She sits on the bed beside Maria, amidst papers covered in scribbled Italian, and Maria's pencilled plans for the bakery.

'Oh, Maria! Why didn't you phone to say you were ill?'

'I'm not ill. I'm OK. Little too tired I think.'

'What's the matter?'

'Nothing. Really. Thank you for coming. Nice to see my girl!'

'Are these the plans for the bakery?'

'Oh yes,' Maria brightens a little, 'just ideas. But you know when you think about the future so much you think about the past too.'

'Were you thinking of home? Of Italy?'

'Not so much.'

'Of Dale's father then?' In the open the question seems intrusive.

'Is no business of yours!' The colour flares back into Maria's skin.

But Sam goes on, quiet and gentle. 'Whoever he is, he's my children's grandfather. It is *my* business, Maria.'

'Why do you think of this now?'

'Because of my parents. Because, like you say, you think of the future and it makes you wonder about the past.'

'Angie. This the God's truth. I don't know him any more. I don't know where he is. OK?' and Maria's face is so full of sadness and of regret that Sam accepts that at least for now this is all the truth there is to be had.

'OK.'

'But you got more questions, yes?'

'Yes. Why won't you talk about what Dale was like, before me?'

This is not a question Maria expected or was prepared for. She is speechless, guiltily frozen for a tiny moment. Then all Maria's forces mobilise, the film star smile, the dolce vita laugh. 'You know that! I told you. You know what he was like. A 'opeless little bugger who give his mamma a lot of trouble. Now. Enough. Go to your boys.' Turning on her smile seems to have cost Maria an enormous effort, so now Sam feels sorry that she's pressed for answers.

'All right, Maria. I'm sorry. I shouldn't have asked when you were feeling ill. Can I call Dale before I go?'

'You know where the phone is.'

'Call me if you need me. If there's anything . . .'

Behind Dale's voice she can hear the swoosh of passing cars and footsteps on a pavement. He's outside a pizza takeaway place in Bury St Edmunds, he says. She tries not to think that cars and footsteps could be the backdrop anywhere.

'But how is she?' Dale is trying to reach down the phone for some tangible proof of his mother's well-being.

'I can't talk much. She's upstairs.'

'Is she ill?'

'No. She says she's OK. But I think she looks pretty awful. Says she's thinking about the past.'

'Oh. Right.' There, in the familiar glow of Dale's voice, is that little space where the thread is missing. She listens to it for a moment, then he speaks again, 'Look. If you're worried, why don't you get her to stay with us for few days?'

Everything is what Dale isn't saying. Everything is what Maria didn't say. Everything is not going to get said down a phone.

Sam sighs. 'When are you coming home?'

'In the morning.'

'See you then.'

'Bye, love.'

A little touch of Louise's maelstrom mind will be a good distraction from the half-formed uncertainties and shadows knocking around her own brain. Down the three streets Sam walks to Louise's, she tries to rid herself of the swirling suspicions, but when she reaches her hand to grasp them they run through her fingers like water.

Louise smiles, and welcomes Sam inside.

'Hello. Come in, come in. I wasn't expecting you.' She leads Sam into the little kitchen. 'Or rather I was really, but not now. Would you like a drink? Nail varnish?'

Sam is accustomed enough to Louise to understand that acetone cocktail is not what she's being offered; Louise is carrying a pot of clear varnish and has been doing her toenails.

'No, thanks, Louise. I can't stay. Are the boys OK?'

'Oh yes. I got the tap fixed so I could chase them round the garden with the hose pipe. They got tired pretty fast! They're all asleep in a heap like a litter of wombats or something. Except I don't think wombats have litters. Anyway. I'll take them to school in the morning.'

'Thanks, Louise. That would be great.' Sam feels tired to her bones.

'Do let me get you something. You look, well. Actually you look terrible. Have some toast and honey. Frightfully restorative. Just sit down.'

Louise is right about the toast. Sam munches gratefully and Louise pours them each a glass of some exotic fruit juice, then sits quite still watching her friend. She is having another of her moments of crystal-clear perception.

'You don't believe him, do you? That's what's the matter, isn't it?' Louise speaks slowly, dreamily. 'You don't believe Dale, because you hadn't told him about your past. So now you wonder what he hasn't told you! Right?'

'Right. Yes, I suppose.'

'But you love him.'

'Yes.'

'And he still loves you so?' Louise shrugs eloquently, as if to say after love everything else is just icing. 'Dale's up in Suffolk sorting out your inheritance. End of story. Yes?'

'Yes. Yes. OK.' Suddenly the heavy tangle that Sam has made of her present life seems ridiculous. She has been shying at shadows. Dale is as steady as a rock. Maria is just tired. The phone calls come from a crabby punter. The man in the boiler suit was just that and nothing else. 'No. You're right. I do believe him. End of story. I'm tired. Just tired.'

Number eleven feels very empty. It's more than the extra space left behind by Bea and Ralph. Number eleven was fashioned to fit Angie and Dale inside their portraits and now that they are both out of their frames, the old house feels changed too.

CHECKING OUT

In the sitting room Sam sees not the fabric from Monmouth Castle or the way the rug picks up the shades in the curtains, but Bea's stockinged feet curled on the sofa while reading a story to Tony, Ralph kneeling on the rug holding Joe's legs in the air, Dale asleep over the Sunday paper. She flicks on the light in the kitchen and the twilight garden disappears into a dusty blueness. This kitchen was made for Angie, obsessively neat, tidying for her life, for ever finding tasks to hold back the past and keep the present in its place. Now, the worktops are a little cluttered and the children's drawings have escaped the confines of the notice board and spread their exuberance all over the unit doors. Her home has learned to relax, it has learned to smile. That's why now it feels so empty, because at last it has been able to be so full.

Walking out onto the patio Sam can feel the big exotic plants breathing into the evening air. She takes a long lungful of their green scents and lets it out like a stream of corn pouring steadily from a split sack. She kicks off her shoes and feels the residual warmth in the paving stones. A large iguana is doing the same, lying belly flat on the warmest stones. It looks at her appraisingly and slithers away. This is the form her 'leaks' are taking these days, small scale, subtle, intimate almost, finding their way into the new habitat of her garden. She no longer finds her visions distasteful or unwelcome; she accommodates them, welcomes them almost. She is comforted by the way her home can host them and contain the changes that she is finding so hard and so confusing. If only Dale were here, her rock, her anchor. She could be really at peace and quell all uneasiness and suspicion.

The doorbell rings and Sam leaps towards it: Dale! She flings open the door and finds an unnerving version of Dale. Older and smaller, with nicotine-tanned skin. He has a nasty burn healing on his cheek.

'Mrs Cassinari?' The voice too is a variant of Dale's. 'I know it's a bit late. I called earlier but I didn't catch you in. We met, well, saw each other I think in the hospital last week?'

'Yes. You had a dressing on your face.'

'Yes. You were there with your little lad. Nasty chin injury. I noticed you when they said the surname. Quite unusual.'

'Oh.'

'I was worried about the boy. Because. Well. He's my grandson.'

It's not such a shock really. In fact all Sam can think of to say is 'Yes I know' because in her heart she'd guessed from the first moment she saw him behind the pad of cotton wool.

Dale's dad is called Gordon, Gordon Armstrong. He's a builder!

She can't help staring at him. This is Dale's father who should have cuddled his grandchildren, who should feel as familiar to her as Maria. Yet here she is politely offering him tea and calling him Mr Armstrong.

He stands in the middle of the kitchen looking slightly confused. 'It's a lovely home! Not quite what I expected,' he says.

Samantha sits at the table, her legs a little too wobbly to support her. 'Is Mr Cassinari expected home?'

'Dale?'

'Dale. Yes.'

'No. He's coming home tomorrow.'

'Your little boy, how's his chin?'

'Healing beautifully. He's staying at a friend's house tonight.'

'I see.' But Not-Dale—Gordon—doesn't seem to see at all. In fact he seems almost dazed.

'Are you sure I can't get you a cup of tea?'

'No. No. Thank you.'

'Maria, my mother-in-law, she's never mentioned you.'

'No. No, she wouldn't do.'

Samantha is getting over her wobbly legs and beginning to wonder what sort of lunatic she might have admitted freely to her house.

Gordon shifts uncomfortably from foot to foot. 'Perhaps I should go, I was clearly mistaken,' he says. 'Yes, I'll go,' and he turns as if decided, but doesn't move. Samantha decides that really Gordon looks pretty harmless and quite lost.

'Look, Mr Armstrong, Gordon. You're my boys' grandfather. I'd like to get to know you a little.'

'Would you mind if I smoked?' Gordon sits at the table and rolls a cigarette and is clearly comforted and calmed by the ritual. He talks as he rolls, without looking up. 'At the hospital, when I heard that name, I knew you had to be Maria's daughter-in-law. And that the little boy was . . . well, my flesh and blood. Dale's son. I don't want to offend you, but you looked worn out. The little one looked like someone had punched him. And I worried. I thought you might be in some trouble. That's why I came. I thought it was about time I helped.'

'Joe fell and caught his chin on the table. Just an accident.'

Gordon looks at her out of blue smoke. 'Yeah?'

She nods emphatically in reply.

Gordon takes the last toke of his roly. 'You don't smoke?'

'No. Nor does Dale.'

'Doesn't he?' Gordon seems surprised. 'He used to. How much do you know about Dale? You'd be too young to have known him when he was a teenager, I guess?'

'Yes, that's right. He was gone thirty when we met.'

Gordon fixes her in his sights, leaning closer to her face. 'And he's always been good to you? Never laid a hand on you? Never hurt the kids? Never been in any kind of trouble?'

'Never. He's so kind. Always gentle. He adores the boys.' Samantha is speaking without knowing what her mouth is doing. What Gordon *hasn't* said is disturbing and the flood of fears begins to wash towards her. She throws words towards it like sandbags. 'We've been together for almost ten years and he's never been anything but a wonderful husband and father. He was with me when both the boys were born; he nurses them when they're ill; he takes them swimming; he brings me tea in bed; he built sandcastles with them in Ilfracombe last summer; he built me a shelf for my cookery books; he would never . . . I've never felt . . .' The frenzy of words calls up images of Dale that melt and coalesce into a single impression of her husband, warm and true as a handprint on her heart. The wail goes out of her voice, she takes a deep, deep breath and slows down. 'He's my *Dale*. He'd never never do anything to harm us.'

Gordon's face is pulled into a thousand tight little ropes, his whole self focused on Sam and her words. 'You swear to me that's true?'

'Yes,' she says. Because no matter what this long-lost father knows about Dale's past, nothing he can say will change her answer.

'Then it's all right. Thank God.'

'But why *wouldn't* it be all right?'

Gordon gets up. 'It's not for me to say.' He moves into the hall.

She wants to hold onto him at the door. 'You haven't told me anything about yourself. You've met Dale before, haven't you? He always said he never knew his dad.'

He shakes her hand warmly but doesn't reply to that. 'I need to be getting home. I'm glad things are OK. That Dale's making a good job of his life. I was just worried. But now I know things are OK. I'd love to meet the boys. Here's my card. Just give me a call some time. You know. If you need me.' He's already halfway down the path and out into the dusk, slipping and slipping out of her grasp.

'What about Maria?' Sam says a little desperately. 'What shall I tell her about you?'

His shrug is youthful, a little shadow of the wildness he might once have had, perhaps. 'If you mention me use my middle name.'

Sam stares stupidly at the card: Gordon A. Armstrong.

'That's how she knew me. It's what my mates all called me when I was young, A for Alan. Alan a'Dale, you know, Robin Hood's mate? It was my nickname.'

THIRTEEN

SAMANTHA WOKE to find that someone had taken a blender to her brain overnight. Everything was in a tangle. When she finally made it downstairs she found that the bedside clock had been wrong and she was already late for work.

The morning at Tavs took its cue from Sam's flurried arrival. Things spilled, fell over and leapt spontaneously from shelves. Customers were rude, indecisive, mumbling. Some made a point of combining ignorance with arrogance. A grey-rinsed, pinched-looking woman at the front of a large queue asked for eight ounces of mortadella and, as Sam was slicing it, leaned over the top of the counter and said, 'You stupid girl! Mortadella is a cheese. I don't want that nasty cheap luncheon meat!'

The lunchtime sandwich rush was just as accident prone. Normally calmest when the shop was busy, today Sam was like a beginner who didn't know her *provolone* from a round of Dairylea.

'You didn't put the tomatoes in this roll!'

'I asked for *soppressata*, but this is *salami calabrese*.'

With Maria beside her, all Sam could think about was how to tell her about Gordon. Time after time she managed to put the wrong filling in the wrong sandwich, or served the right sandwich to the wrong person. For the third time Finnian was stepping in to calm an irate punter and remake the sandwich she had ordered, when Dale strode into the shop.

'Hello,' Sam said over the heads of the customers, 'can you hang on, I'm busy.'

'I can't, love.'

'Please! I've got something terribly important to tell you.'

'I just popped in to say I'm back is all. I've got to go, Ange.'

'Dale! I need to talk to you . . .'

'See you later.'

'Dale, you little bugger. Your wife call you. Come back 'ere,' Maria yelled at him over a huge carton of salad. 'Go get him,' she said.

Sam squeezed past Finnian and round the end of the counter. 'Dale! Wait!' she shouted as he went to his car. 'Where are you going?'

'Got to sort out that punter you've been so bothered about.'

There was something alarming in the way that Dale said 'sort out' that made Sam think of fists, tight wads of cash and the way that Gordon had asked if Dale had ever 'laid a finger on her'. The thicket of confusion that had been blocking her mind all day cleared instantly as if it had been defoliated and she knew that Dale must be told about his father and right now. 'Dale!!'

Sam ran to Dale's car. Rashly she leapt for the passenger door and wrenched it open as it was pulling away. The door swung wide, combining its momentum with the moving car, and Sam swung forward and smashed into the bonnet on top of her left arm. There was a nasty little crunching sound and a pain like hot wires shot up from her wrist.

Dale's car stopped and he rushed from the driver's seat. 'What the bloody hell did you do that for?' He peeled her off the car and she felt in his touch that he was frightened not angry. 'God, Angie! You could have really hurt yourself!'

It didn't hurt, but her hand looked odd, as if the glue that held it to her wrist had melted a bit and allowed a little sideways slippage.

She looked at it in surprise. 'I *have* really hurt myself.'

'Oh bugger. I'll take you to Casualty. What the hell's got into you!'

Injuring her wrist was the most help Sam had been to Tavs all day; the queue of customers had forgotten its sandwich orders and had been standing on the pavement enjoying the little drama that she had provided. Meanwhile Maria and Finnian filled rolls, sliced salami and sighed sighs of relief and utter mystification.

And now Dale has done some very out-of-character parking. His car is slanted across two spaces in the hospital car park and he is holding his father's business card as if it were a sacred relic.

'Gordon A. Armstrong. General builder.'

'He knew you, Dale.'

Dale looks at her blankly at first as if her words are in another language. Then their meaning solidifies. 'He knew you when you were a teenager. He asked me things about you, as if, I dunno. As if you'd done something bad, in the past when you were young.' Sam watches a kind of greyness spread through Dale's face. When he speaks his voice has shrunk to a dry whisper.

'Your wrist. We should go into Casualty. I'll tell you later. Let's get you strapped up before it starts to hurt more.'

He's right. In moments all she can think about is the pain of her wrist. Dale holds her good hand while the nurse puts on the plaster. He was like this when she was in labour, quiet and solid. But now his face is slack and sad. His eyes have the same lost look they had the day she first showed him the new garden. She wants to comfort him but she can't think what to say.

'I've made you late for sorting out your punter. I'm sorry.'

'It doesn't matter now, Ange. I'll tell you about it later.'

She feels once more that there is nothing she could know about him that could stop her loving him. She knows that he is true and good to the core, sweet like a honey pot, right to the very, very bottom.

Tony and Joe used every colouring pen in the box to convert Sam's plaster to an explosion of wiggles and faces and odd-shaped creatures. Sleepily Joe traces them now with one finger as Sam leans over his bed to kiss him good night.

'This is Archimedes and his kittens,' he explains.

'*Her* kittens!' says Tony, butting out of his cuddle with Dale.

But Joe is above being irritated by Tony's correction. He knows Archimedes is the only tomcat ever to have given birth. In Joe's view, it's Tony's problem if he can't spot magic when he sees it.

'Night, Joe.'

'Night, Mummy.'

'Will Mummy's arm get better?' Joe asks Dale.

Tony rolls his eyes conspiratorially at his mum, then looks suddenly concerned. 'Your arm will be better, won't it?' he whispers.

'Yes, lovely, it will. It's not even broken. In a couple of weeks it'll be fine. Nighty night.'

'Sleep tight, boys.'

Downstairs, Sam rests her arm while Dale potters around the kitchen in companionable silence getting cocoa and biscuits.

'So, what was it that you were going to "tell me later"?'

'I don't want to tell you, Sam. I want you to go on loving me.'

'Then tell me how your dad knew you and why he asked me if you've ever hurt me.'

Dale swallows hard, eyes glittering. 'Jeesus. I've cried more this month than I did when I was five.'

Sam squeezes his hand with her one good one, and Dale takes a deep breath. 'I spent all my childhood imagining what he was like, my dad. Inventing excuses for why he'd left her. Why he never came to find Mum. I invented a sort of Steve McQueen-type bloke who'd been killed in a terrible crash trying to get to Mum. I invented an English Lord who'd got amnesia and forgotten where to find her. Then, when I was older . . .' Dale shrugs, 'I settled for a heartless bastard who'd shagged a girl and left her in the lurch. I dreamed about who my dad might be almost every night of my life, nightmares about axe murderers. Nightmares about what might be in me.'

Sam can't believe how stupid she'd been to believe Dale's bravado: 'He's not interested in me so I'm not interested in him.'

Dale touches the end of the fingers that stick out of the plaster. Sam tries not to even breathe, this access to Dale's insides is so rare and precious she doesn't want to do anything to disturb it.

'I always saw there was something behind you that you never told. I let it go because I had something behind me I didn't tell.'

Sam doesn't speak; she is hearing the shredding of canvas and the scraping of layers of oil paint faintly but distinctly in her head.

'When I was at school, I used to get into fights. But I'd get so angry sometimes that I'd sort of black out, and I'd be hitting some kid without even knowing it. The second time I put a kid into hospital I was expelled. I was almost sixteen anyway. I had the whole psychiatrist do, the police, the social workers, the lot. Mum nearly went mad with it all, I think. It was her idea to get me a job with a stonemason. I think she thought that beating seven shades of shit out of a bit of sandstone might help. But it was the working on my own that did it. He was a nice bloke, old Kevin, just let me get on with things at my own pace. I felt calm for the first time in about five years. I didn't get into fights any more. I thought I was over it. Things went pretty well with the job. I did more on the building and restoration side. Then Kev was ill and he asked me to be foreman on a job he was doing in Bath.

'I was eighteen and I had two blokes working for me. One of them was nicking stuff from the client. I caught him. I don't even remember what happened but I fractured his skull. I got five years.'

It isn't really a revelation to Sam. Although she's never dreamed of Dale being violent, never feared his anger, the feel of him, his atmosphere is suddenly explicable, the way that a picture emerges when you join up the dots. His focused irresistible energy has a tinge of wildness to it, storm power driving a sensible turbine. Sam realises that Dale is waiting for her to make some sort of judgment. She can't think what to say. 'Oh' just isn't enough.

'Did you do the whole five years?'

'No. Two and half. That's where I met my dad.'

Of course. She can see it, that slow way Gordon rolled his cigarettes, the way you'd roll them if that was all there was in your day.

'He just walked up to me in the yard one morning. "Cassinari?" he said. "I used to know your mother." He was what they call a domestic lifer. He'd killed his wife's lover with a piece of copper plumbing pipe. He did twenty-two years for it. Got out the year I met you.'

'Did he help you, you know, get you through your time?'

'No. Not meaning to anyway. I only spoke to him a couple of times. He told me how he'd brought Mum from Italy. Sounded to me like they made a deal. He got her pregnant so he married her so she could get away from her dad. She divorced him after two years but he'd left by that time anyway. He said he hit her once. That would've been enough for Ma to want to put him six foot under. He married his childhood sweetheart, started a building business. He knew about his temper, his rages. He actually called them blackouts. He never did anything about them and he ended up killing the bloke he found in bed with his wife.

'He talked about it all as if it had happened to somebody else. Just smoking all the time. And then he got transferred I heard and I never saw him again. Not ever. Not once. I never told Maria.' He's been talking to their hands, and now he looks up for reassurance.

'Go on, Dale,' she says.

'He scared me. I could see my life going the same way. I'd thought I'd learned to cope with my demons, but I hadn't. I'd nearly killed someone. I went to the prison shrink the day after he was transferred and signed up for every kind of bloody therapy. They loved me. I wanted to be cured. All it did was make me give up smoking. Then I got this prison visitor. Befriender they called them. He'd been a heroin addict then taken up marathon running. He said, run. When you feel the anger coming on, get a pair of trainers and run. So I used to run round the yard every day. And when I got out Kevin took me back. Couldn't believe it. I kept a pair of trainers in my bag and whenever I felt that hot-behind-the-eyes feeling, I ran.'

'D'you still run?'

'Yeah. Sometimes. I keep the kit in the back of the truck. But I need it less for my head these days. More for my body.'

'It explains those nice legs. I never knew.'

'Course you didn't. I was terrified you'd start to be afraid.'

'Do I look scared to you?'

'No. Beautiful. Not scared.' He squeezes her hand and fingers so tight it hurts. 'I ran miles after I met you. Even when I didn't feel I needed it. I wanted to be sure you'd never ever see that side of me. I wanted to be *all* good, for you.'

Sam can't speak. She knows that feeling so well. She knows its cost. And she knows about the fear it makes. The purpose behind the anonymous voice is apparent now, clear as sunrise, clear as a light switch.

'That man, who kept ringing. He knows about you being in prison. He's been blackmailing you!'

'Yeah. He's called Maurice Stennar. He got out three years after me, saw me in the supermarket with you and the boys in April. He came up to me. "Bet your little wife doesn't know where we met," he said. I should have shrugged him off. But I was so scared of you knowing. I told him I'd kill him if he told you. So he knew just how much money he could bleed me for, right from that moment.'

'How much?'

'Twelve grand. Borrowed off the business. Then I had a couple of late-paying customers . . . and, well, it doesn't take much to wreck a one-man-band. But Lime House saved my neck.'

'Would you have gone on paying him?'

'For a while. But once I knew about, well, you and your parents I thought I can tell her. I can. It'll be all right. Just not yet.'

'Will you go and see your father?'

Dale shrugs. 'I dunno. Yeah. I will. At least he deserves to see I didn't make the same mistakes.'

'Should we tell Maria?'

'Probably. Maybe. Yes. Yes. I'll talk to her.' He downs his cocoa. 'Let's go to bed. I don't care how early it is. I've had it.' The porthole into Dale's inner life is closing. He smiles, takes her hand. 'Thank you.'

'What for?'

'For still loving me.'

Maria and Sam are walking up the road on Maria's afternoon off, carry-ing a bag of shopping between them.

'Angie?' Maria says suddenly. 'Dale told me about Gordon.'

Sam is not at all ready for this. 'When?'

'This morning. He come for coffee. He took me out of the shop. So now I guess you know my bugger son is a jail bird.'

'Not any more he isn't, Maria. I don't care about it anyway.'

'No. No. I know. You love my Dale.'

'Yes. I do.'

'I feel bad about this Gordon. He had big problem. Like Dale . . . explosion when he get angry. But I didn't help. I just kicked him out.'

'You were very young. You had a baby. And maybe you couldn't have helped anyway.'

'Dale says I should see him. What do you think?'

'It's up to you, Maria. It was good for Dale to meet his dad again. Laid ghosts, you know? Maybe it could do that for you?'

Maria nods. 'Maybe. Old crock like me these days? Lay ghosts before we *are* ghosts!'

They smile and walk on.

'What are you goin' to do, Angie? Your mum told me about the University, about your Tropical Rainforest.'

Hearing those words—Tropical Rainforest—from Maria's mouth is astonishing to Sam. She has always seen Maria's world as confined to a single square mile of Bristol, beginning with *antipasto*, ending with *zuccotto*, with Tony and Joe sandwiched in between.

'I know a bit about Tropical Rainforest you know,' Maria says. 'It's all bein' cut down, and it's full of animals and all. Nnnah. I don't like to think of that bein' gone, ppphtt.'

This is what Sam always used to tell people when she was a girl, that jungle was important to everyone, and here is the proof; Maria of all people caring about the wanton destruction of biodiversity.

'You're very clever girl. You could be a Tropical Rainforest *Professore*. Yes? Yes, I think so.'

Sam loses the rhythm of their carrying and walking for a moment, then pushes down the old passions. Be satisfied with an exotic garden, she tells them. 'I don't know, Maria. I've got the boys now . . .'

'You don't have to go and live in the bloody place to study it.'

'There's a lot of dust that needs to settle first. Bea and Ralph. Dale's dad. Lime House to sort out. Your new bakery even! We'll see.'

They turn into Lancaster Road. Dale is getting out of the car with the boys outside number eleven, full of inexorable energy, and beaming.

'You haven't been shopping for tonight's dinner, have you?' he says, taking the bag. 'Needn't have bothered. I'm taking both of you out!'

'What's the party?'

'Well. One: I signed off on the Bath job this afternoon. The money's all sorted at last, thank God. Two: a large wadge of cash courtesy of our friend Maurice who really doesn't want a conviction for blackmail. And three: we've had a very good offer on Lime House as it stands, before any work is done on it. So, heiress-Angela, you could be about to come into a lot of dosh!'

Sam has expected to feel relieved or even excited when the news of the sale of Lime House finally came. But all she can feel is uneasy; she senses some awful catch to this bargain that Lawrence has left her with.

'For a girl with money, you don't look so happy. You can be my investor now!' prompted Maria.

'Oh. I am happy. I mean I'm just shocked. I think tonight should be on me then!'

'No, no, Angie, after Lime House is sold, I'll never be able to treat you to anything ever again. Let me make the most of my last chance.'

'All right. Have you got a baby sitter?'

'Ah!' Dale has forgotten the essential component!

'Then I will baby-sit,' insisted Maria. 'You go, you two!'

Dale and Sam take their seats at a little round table in the pearly interior of the poshest restaurant in town. Dale is in a black suit and a plain white shirt. It isn't a style statement, simply his dislike of fuss and his distrust of flamboyance. All the same, he looks handsome, intense, even a little fierce. Sam has scraped her hair back into a clip, exposing her long neck and the line of her shoulders disappearing into the boat neck of a plain, dark red dress. Her thinness has lost its usual gangly quality and acquired an elegance that Dale has only glimpsed in passing moments before. They each take a sidelong look in the mirror behind them. There they are, Dale and Angie, looking handsome and interesting. They carry with them a kind of dangerous unpredictability that couples with potential have on their first date.

They study their menus in absolute silence. They drink half their bottle of wine before the food even arrives and are eating their starters before either speaks.

'Well. This a is bit daft,' Dale says, spreading his pâté as if he were mortaring a particularly precious piece of stonework. 'Our first meal out in I don't even remember how long, and we don't talk!'

'You look too handsome. I don't know what to say!'

'All right, then. Here's what we can talk about. The offer on Lime House. Airline pilot and barrister wife want country seat for four kids, nanny and ponies. Cash buyers. Want to move in before the winter.'

'We could pay off the mortgage on Lancaster Road and still put a pile in the bank and I could give Maria her money to invest in the bakery.'

'Or I could do it up for thirty grand more and sell it for another hundred and fifty thousand. It's such a lovely project, Ange . . . It could be a great showcase for my work, get me more of the really creative restoration stuff. I want you to come and see it.'

The thought makes the taste of the wine curdle in her throat. Lawrence is still tapping at her mind and she wants him gone, at least for the duration of the evening.

'Dale, let's not talk about this now. Let's just pretend this is a date.'

Dale is ready to argue, but he looks at Sam's glistening skin, her long mouth, then he picks up his glass. 'I think I was saying how very young you are, wasn't I? Barely legal when I married you.'

'I was eighteen, Dale!'

'Well, you seemed younger. It was only your experience that convinced me that you were as old as you said you were.'

Sam knows the kind of 'experience' he means. Dale has never asked about boyfriends, about a sex life before he met her. It was all part of the forbidden territory of the past she didn't talk about. For a moment Sam feels a little knock of the old panic, the fear of being found out. Then she remembers that this truth, or part of it, is what she *can* tell him.

'What d'you mean, experience.'

'When I came round that time. That first time we, you know.'

'And you think I was experienced.' Suddenly Sam knows that this isn't just about finding out for Dale, he's playing. Stroking her skin with his eyes, already in bed with her in his mind. Playing with sex the way they never have before. And she can play too. She lets one leg slip between his under the starched cloth, and speaks quietly, slowly. 'I was terrified you'd guess about me being a runaway. So that weekend I said I was ill? Do you remember? I went to bed all weekend, and I read.' Briefly Sam glances round, then whispers, '*The Joy of Sex*, from cover to cover. Four times. And I decided what I was going to do.'

Dale swallows a mouthful of pâté, and breathes out very slowly. 'OK. My turn for confessions. But for a bloke what I've got to say isn't much to boast about.' Dale's tone starts as a purr, part of the game. He drops a hand and caresses her knee. But in two sentences he's not playing any more but telling her secrets more serious than games. 'I was pretty awful-looking when I was a teenager. Acne. Greasy hair. Difficult personality. That part you know about. Busy acting the tough. I knew girls would reject me. So I just kept away. After I came out of prison I just worked. And ran. I went to the pub once a week. I read books, I learned things . . . But I kept keeping away from women. It was just easier, less painful, less risky. Girls would come onto me sometimes and I acted cool, told them to go away because I didn't dare show I had no idea what to do. I told myself that one day I'd have a girlfriend, but I wasn't really sure how. I was thirty-one and I'd begun to lose hope. Then I met you. Now or never I said to myself.'

'But. That first time. In my bedsit. You knew what to do . . .'

'No. All I'd ever done was read books, just like you did. Angie, Sam. I've never told anybody this. You were my first. You're the only woman I've ever made love to in my whole life.'

They kiss awkwardly across the table, causing cutlery to fall and other diners to smile indulgently.

'Dale. I love you so much.'

The main course arrives and they eat only half of it. They leave without pudding and totter out into the street to find a taxi to take them, by the fastest route, home, to bed. They leave Maria asleep in front of a flickering TV and climb the stairs by Sam's patented route which avoids the creakiest treads.

Still without speaking, they undress, efficiently, without frenzy. Then they hold each other, skin to skin, with a sense of freedom that feels like the first step on an empty tide-washed beach. Every touch brings them closer. They have climbed inside the word intimate. They are cuddled and twined within its counterpoint of consonants. It is a second and profound loss of some deep virginity. Feeling for her forehead, Dale straightens her hair.

'We've taught each other all we know, eh?'

She nods. 'I'll go to Lime House with you, Dale. Let's go tomorrow.'

She wants to lose the last lies, to be as open to Dale as he is to her.

FOURTEEN

THE SUFFOLK AIR is dry as a stick and hot. It feels to Sam as though it could ignite all on its own. In her childhood, when they burnt the stubbles in late summer, it always felt as if the fire came out of the air and ate the ground. Even the cold feels hot. The glass she's holding burns with it and the ice inside clinks with the tiny tremor of her hand.

She's grateful that Bea and Ralph were in the garden to greet them. It's anonymous out here. The neat square of lawn stretches to the picket fence beyond which is Ralph's vegetable plot. She can see Dale and the boys moving up and down the rows being guided around runner beans and peas, lettuces and radishes by the tall figure in the battered Panama.

Bea comes to sit beside her on the bench, touching her arm with the lightest of fingertips. 'Would you like to lie down, Sam?'

'No, really, Mum. I'm OK. I just felt wobbly after the car journey.'

'More to drink?'

'No. I'm OK. Don't fuss.' Bea draws back her hand and presses her lips anxiously together. 'I'm sorry, Mum. I didn't mean to be snappy. I'm really wound up about seeing Lawrence's house.'

461

'Love, Sam, I don't want to pry. I don't know anything about your friend Lawrence. But I can't help wondering if he had anything to do with you . . . going away?'

'No. No, Mum. You know why I went away. You *know*.'

Tony and Joe come running barefoot over the grass, recovered from their car sickness. Bea leaps up. 'Oh, here come the men. Better get the biscuits out.' She bustles back into the house.

'Better now, my Sam-sam?'

'Yes, Dad. I'm fine.'

'You sit on the bench, Ralph. I'll grab one of those deck chairs.'

'No, Dale, don't bother.' Sam gets up, knocking her drink off the arm of the seat. 'I'd like to go to Lime House now.'

'Oh, Sam, surely you'll have a spot of lunch first? It's all ready.'

'I'm sorry, Dad. We'll be back. I just want to get it over with.'

Dale and Ralph glance at one another and say no more.

The car door clunks shut and Dale pulls out into the lane. 'So what was that all about? Your poor parents, ready to have lunch with us and you walk out!'

'I'd never been to their house before. It'll be full of stuff from . . . From when I was little. I didn't feel ready. And it's awful going to Lawrence's house. You just don't understand.'

'Right. Bloody right, I don't. I've never understood why inheriting half a million is a bad thing.'

'Shut up, Dale. This is awful, and I'm doing it for you.'

'What's awful about it? From what you've said you hardly knew him. But he's left you a fortune. What did you do for this guy anyway?'

'What d'you mean? "What did I do?" Are you saying I was his tart? Didn't you listen to anything I said last night? Is that what you were asking when you asked about my being "experienced"?'

Dale pulls the car into the hedgerow. Turns off the engine and winds a window down. Slowly he lets go of the tension and irritation that have grown over the long tight journey from Bristol and the awkward half-hour at his in-laws.

'I'm sorry. I wasn't suggesting that. I can't say I haven't wondered. But not any more. I just don't get why you're so screwed up about all this.'

Sam swallows. She'd like to scream. But it's true there isn't a way Dale can understand just yet. 'You will get it. You will understand. Just remember what last night felt like. What it meant.'

Dale nods and they drive on in silence, the air conditioning singeing Sam's skin with its cool hotness. When they get to the gates, Sam shuts her eyes. Dale opens the passenger door and takes her arm. 'Watch your plaster, love,' he says kindly. 'OK, let's look inside. I suppose you don't want to hear the architectural stuff now.'

'No, that's OK. It might help. Make it easier.'

The interior is almost unrecognisable. The high arched hallway with its plaster cornices is gone: there is a false ceiling of dirty polystyrene tiles. The floorboards are bare but for dirt and old newspapers. The shining banisters are broken and stand sadly either side of the staircase like rotten teeth. There is a smell of damp and rat poison.

'He must have moved out about the time you left I think,' says Dale, 'this looks like a house that hasn't been lived in for a long time.'

'No. He was here to the end. Let's look in the study first.'

The study door is missing. The bookshelves are empty, the big mirror over the fireplace is like a giant web, with cracks radiating from a central impact. A clock and its glass case lie under the mantel, in several hundred pieces.

'Vandals got in at some point I think.'

Dale tries one last time to be practical, but Sam replies in a whisper. 'No. No, they didn't.' Sam can see, surely as if the mirror could replay what it once reflected. 'No. Lawrence threw the clock at it. It was very special. It had two faces, dark and light. I didn't like the dark one. We used to look at maps and books on a table in here.' The desk has gone, dragged out over the parquet floor judging by the ruts and scratches left behind. Sam is beginning to sense the trail that she is meant to follow.

'I want to look in the glasshouse.' She doesn't wait for Dale's reply.

Through the dead hallway and scullery, she's running now the way she used to run when the *Odontoglossums* came into bloom. She slams the door behind her and it loses the last of its tiny leaded panes, crashing under Dale's hurrying feet. Across the little covered courtyard, green with mould and slime. At last the door of the glasshouse, solid and intricate still, every pane perfect. Without waiting for a breath or to gather her wits and strength Sam steps in.

She has expected more ruin. A crumbled mass of glass and iron littering plants, dead from cold then drought. But Lawrence's glasshouse is just as it might have been if he had stepped out to make a cup of tea. The vents are open wide on this hot day, the watering system has recently been working. The plants are thriving—unkempt and uncontrolled they're taking over. The *Gloriosa speciosa* is now as tall as the roof and there are tangles of bougainvillea and hibiscus. The smell is the same, a slow thickening of the air that holds your limbs and stops your mouth. Only the orchids have suffered from neglect. Shrivelled and brown, they've become insignificant encrustations hanging among the rampant green.

'I could go away for a fortnight in winter and they'd cope,' Lawrence used to say, 'but in summer, even with the misting system I have to water some two or three times a day.' She can see him in her mind's eye, on a hot day like this, trickling water into a basket, bursting with shoots of one of his favourites. 'You should definitely see this in the wild, Sam. *Stanhopea.* Extraordinary epiphyte. Its flower spike only grows downwards. You can be the one to find out why!'

She pushes her way through the leaves and tendrils that catch and hold her hair and skin, following the old brick paths around to the far end of the glasshouse. There she finds where Lawrence has spent his time. Clustered untidily under the foliage are the essentials of his life: the desk from the study, its inlays and veneers dulled and splitting with neglect; his favourite books, mouldering in the damp; a camp bed, with a filthy quilt and pillow. And beneath the whole pathetic encampment, stacked against the glass of the walls, strewn like an understorey of fallen leaves, are empty whisky bottles. Wherever she looks they reveal themselves, camouflaged by layers of mould, twined in stems, too old to show their glassy shine or swanky label. There must be thousands, numbering the days since last Sam stood here, plainly recounting the last, long, bleak chapter of Lawrence's life.

She pulls the desk drawers out, wrenching free files, envelopes, pens, and crumpled papers, a thousand letters that began, 'My Dearest Samantha', and said no more. The last deep drawer is the only one in any order. Almost empty and properly closed, it's free of mould and dryer than the others, quite recently attended to, Sam concludes. Slowly now, less frenzied, she takes out its contents: a small portable typewriter in a neat grey case and a single box file, with a black door that makes Sam think of the dark interior of the confessional box. She opens the file and her own face looks out from a plastic wallet, fearfully locking up Julie's cake shop, hunted and big eyed. There are perhaps a hundred photographs snatched from ten years of her life. Here she draws the grubby curtains of her bedsit, her face indistinct and empty. Here she is with Dale, kissing in the front of his car. Each photo is dated. Beneath are invoices from a firm of private detectives—Marshall and Musgrove Limited of Yate—and a sheaf of flimsy carbons, held by a small black clip. They are copies of badly typed letters, each detailing the wording for a communication to be sent to Bea and Ralph Powell . . .

'Dale is self-employed. He's doing well. I have a part-time job.'

'Tony will be one this year.'

'Both boys are now in school, and doing well. We're all fine. Please don't attempt to contact me. Sam.'

A sample of the cards chosen by Marshall and Musgrove Limited—glitter-strewn robins, fat Santas and dancing holly leaves—are stapled together under the flimsy carbons.

The bottom of the file, its deepest layer, is a single sheet of paper protected inside a deep blue plastic wallet. This, Sam senses, is some last clue, a message left here by Lawrence, a piece of the jigsaw she didn't have before. It is a letter, on good paper with the logo of an oil company based in Caracas, Venezuela, dated November 19, just a month before Sam ran out of her parents' house and didn't go back. Below the printed header are spidery rows of handwritten Spanish. Clearly the writer was used to being understood without having to resort to English, yet Sam finds a translation on the back in green Biro. It's written in laboured capitals, the way Lawrence wrote addresses on envelopes or labels on plants.

DEAR FRIEND,

I WAS THRILLED TO HEAR FROM YOU AGAIN AFTER SO LONG AND TO HEAR THAT YOU'RE THINKING OF PAYING US A VISIT. THAT BUSINESS WITH AMOCO BURNED US BOTH SO BADLY I THOUGHT YOU'D NEVER WANT TO COME BACK TO VENEZUELA!

I CAN ARRANGE WHAT YOU ASK. IN FACT I'VE ALREADY MADE A FEW PRELIMINARY ENQUIRIES. MY FRIEND PROFESSOR VILLARS IS DOING ECOLOGICAL SURVEYS IN AMAZONAS NEAR PLANTANAL. HE IS ALWAYS LOOKING FOR KEEN AND KNOWLEDGEABLE PEOPLE TO HELP. YOUR YOUNG BOTANIST WOULD BE VERY WELCOME. AS FOR FUNDING, I THINK I CAN PULL A FEW STRINGS THERE. THE COMPANY WOULD BE WILLING TO COVER SOME EXPENSES FOR A VISITING STUDENT OF SUCH A PRESTIGIOUS INSTITUTION AS OXFORD UNIVERSITY (ESPECIALLY IF THERE WAS A LITTLE GOOD PRESS TO BE HAD), ALTHOUGH THEY MIGHT NEED SOME FORMAL ENDORSEMENTS FROM THE INSTITUTION ITSELF.

I CAN'T BELIEVE THAT SUCH AN OLD DOG AS YOURSELF IS AT LAST CONTEMPLATING THE BONDAGE OF MARRIAGE IN WHICH I HAVE BEEN SO BLISSFULLY BOUND NOW FOR TWENTY YEARS. BUT PERHAPS YOU HAD TO FIND A WOMAN WHO COULD UNDERSTAND AT LEAST SOME OF YOUR PASSIONS. IT SOUNDS AS IF YOUR YOUNG FIANCÉE SEEMS TO SHARE YOUR LOVE FOR PLANTS. THOUGH WHY A LOVELY YOUNG GIRL WOULD BOTHER WITH A BIT OF OLD LEATHER LIKE YOU, I CAN'T IMAGINE! HIDDEN TALENTS, EH?

LET ME KNOW WHAT YOU DECIDE. I CAN HELP ARRANGE MOST THINGS HERE. AS I'M SURE YOU REMEMBER,

WITH BEST WISHES

At the bottom, written with the same pen, is another date, in May. Three months ago. A month before the solicitors' letter arrived on her doorstep. How close to Lawrence's death? She doesn't want to think.

The photographs and the sheaf of papers lie on the desk, like the exhibits in a court case laid up for the Beak to inspect. The photos she had already imagined, and the cards too; who else could have sent them to her parents? But the green ink spells a reality she never guessed, that Lawrence too had been escaping into a world of his own dreams. A little fragment of conversation floats into her memory.

'Perhaps you'd better come to the jungle with me.'

'Or perhaps you'd better stay here and then Summer would never go away.'

Was it then he'd decided that she was his possession? That all he had to do was wait and she'd fall off a branch like ripe fruit into his hand?

'Sam?'

It's strange to hear Dale use that name so naturally, as if he always has. She looks up from the exhibits to his face. How long he's been standing next to the desk she doesn't know.

'Why did you call me that?'

'I don't know. It just came out. Angie, what's going on? Why are these photos here?'

'Lawrence had them taken by a private detective firm.'

'Bloody hell. He had you watched? Did you know this?'

'Not until I went to the solicitors, to hear about his will. I didn't know but I guessed then he'd been doing this . . .' She pushed the carbons and the cheap Christmas cards towards Dale. 'Look. Lawrence had the cards sent to my parents.'

'So you never did get in touch with them?'

'No.'

'Why?'

'I told you. I thought Mummy was dead. I knew she was dead.'

'How did you know she was dead?'

'I just knew . . .'

'But what about your father? And why did Lawrence send the cards?'

Dale is trying to pull answers from her too fast. She feels attacked and frightened. 'I didn't even know about the cards,' she snaps back.

'Why didn't you say?'

'Because they were so grateful for those cards. I couldn't tell them I'd never bothered.' Her voice is almost a squeal. Convulsively she pushes the letter covered with Lawrence's green capitals over the desk to Dale.

'Fiancée? Lawrence's fiancée? This is you, isn't it? You were engaged to this guy. That's why he left you the house!'

'No I wasn't. I wasn't. There was nothing like that. He just imagined there was. He was obsessed, and I never saw it, not then.'

Dale steps back from the desk and takes a deep breath. 'Angie,' he speaks quietly, 'Angie, why did you come here with me?'

'To tell you all the truth,' she almost wails.

'OK. OK. Then tell me. All you have to do is tell me.'

'It's so hard. I don't want to remember.'

'I think whatever it is you remember it all the time. You might stop remembering after today. That's what you came for, Ange, isn't it?'

She breathes in the green thick smell of growth and lets the past in.

Looking back at her teenage self Sam feels like a parent watching a toddler ambling to the edge of a cliff. At this distance of years she can see the danger, the rotten intensity at the core of Lawrence's life, quite clearly. Lawrence's hand that looked to the seventeen-year-old Sam as if it was pulling her into the light, was reaching to her as the last anchor to hold him back from the absolute darkness in his soul.

When Tony was a baby he couldn't play peek-a-boo. Once Sam hid, he forgot about her, so there was no joke in disappearance, no irony. Out of sight was out of existence for him, the only things in the world were what he experienced. At seventeen, Sam remembers, she was just the same as her baby son. What was out of her mind, didn't exist. And what was in, did, no matter how unlikely or outlandish. Out of her sight Lawrence walked in the rainforest of her imagination. Her mentor. Her provider. Her means to an end. He had no separate existence, he was a rung on her ladder. She didn't conceive of the real Lawrence and what he was when she wasn't looking. She never questioned why he was never busy when she called. She didn't see the layers of soft dust lying on the fax machine and the telephones. If she had, she might have guessed that Lawrence was a ghost in his own life.

He had told her just enough of his past for her imagination to invent the biography she wanted: a life that was glittering and adventurous, wild and bohemian, but somehow romantic and even noble. Building from the same elements now, Sam can see the dead tawdriness of it all. He was a broker without moral scruple, negotiating bastard deals outside of the marital bed of trade agreements. The 'major players' Lawrence had described to her were the shadowy representatives of multinational companies wanting cheap toeholds, and corrupt government officials with 'off the record' development opportunities to offer for personal gain. When business was good, he lived in the best hotels, had company cars, government permits. When it was bad he had to cross borders at night, bribe pilots to fly him from distant airstrips. He must have lost as many fortunes as he boasted of gaining.

Fraser Spence had hated Lawrence's adventures. He hated the way his son had perverted his stern upbringing. Lawrence often mentioned it. 'He couldn't stand it when I made money. Disgusting displays, that's what he called all my deals.' Lawrence spoke too of how Fraser hated his botanising trips. '"Wasteful extravagance," he told me. This man who regularly kept a suite at Browns Hotel. Indicative, he told me, of a weak mind and diseased will-power. *Just like your dead mother.*"

'I tried once to win him over,' Lawrence had told her. 'You know, the olive branch and all that. I had ten exquisite *Oncidiums* delivered direct to his hotel room in London. The most beautiful plants you could imagine, in full bloom. They were like wild animals, as if I had taken ten beautiful Bengal tigers and had them purring at his feet like tabbies.'

'What happened?'

'He sent them back to me chopped up in a plastic dustbin bag. I never saw him again.'

Sam's love of the tales of the countless botanising journeys must have been wonderful for Lawrence. The joy with which he described the landscapes and the delight of the search, the tension of the hunt for a plant electrified her. There was no doubt of his skill, his determination and his endurance. It was clear that he had bludgeoned his way through his own physical and financial limits to find the rarest, the loveliest, the biggest. But the 'kill', the actual taking of the plant that sickened Sam, was all to Lawrence. In the end, Lawrence was Fraser's own true son. Experience was always too flimsy, dreamlike. Possession, no matter how brief, was the only solid satisfaction. What happened to those plants that Lawrence took Sam can only guess now: hundreds withered in hotel bathrooms from Lima to Kinshasa she suspects. Hundreds traded, illegally mostly, to fund his trips.

Hunting plants became his talisman, a symbol for all his father abhorred and the deformed embodiment of the only affection he'd ever known. When his father died, he came home 'to bury the old bastard, dance on his grave and run away again'. But he stayed. Tended his mother's garden, brought some of his surviving trophy plants into the sanctuary of the restored glasshouse. Took a year out. Then another and another after that. He found he didn't want to leave. Found he couldn't. The day Samantha arrived, what she stumbled on was a man too frightened of the world outside to go back to it.

How had he seen her that first day, she wondered? A miracle. A Madonna with a worshipping face turned up to his *Dicksonias*. From that first moment he must have always been waiting for her visits. Inventing her to conform to his fantasies of some sensual redeemer, as she invented him to conform to her visions of herself.

She must have seemed to Lawrence to be leading him on. Her long legs in the shorts she wore on summer days, the worn T-shirts. It must have been 'obvious' to him how she 'chose' to display her figure for him; and her control, her intellectualism, was so artlessly arch. Incomprehensible to Lawrence that she was unaware of her attractiveness. To Lawrence her naiveté was just another hook in his flesh. He would touch her arm, or stroke her neck and she would tense, confused, waiting for it to stop. What had that tension felt like to Lawrence? Experience? An invitation? A half-written contract perhaps? Somehow he had felt in it a reason to write to his friend in Venezuela that he was going to marry at last. A young botanist . . . It was always going to be Summer now, for the rest of his life. Finally he'd felt that his life could be healed, made right through loving Sam. She would cut him loose from the claustrophobia of his mother's garden and the repression of his father's coldness. She would recast his tainted passions into purity. Her youth was the gift to wash him clean, his experience was the key to give her her dreams. He didn't mean it to turn out the way it had.

The night she gave Bea the pills was the first and only time she called on Lawrence after dark. She landed on his doorstep, desperate and hysterical. Shivering, crying, distraught. Transformed. Every shred of the intense, intellectual shell stripped away. For the first time she must have looked to Lawrence like a woman, not a girl. Out of control. Vulnerable.

He had helped her up the steps and into the hall and she had clung to him, hardly able to see or move.

'Whatever's the matter, Samantha?' he said, and all she could do was cry over and over again.

'I've killed her, I've killed her.' She felt cold. So cold. He had led her into the study, and sat her on the sofa by the fire. Made her drink a large glass of something burning, and alcoholic. And then another.

At last she was calm enough to take off her coat. Underneath was her old blue dress, too small for her by a year, its fabric worn and its tied front straining. Her white skin had showed at the collar bone, and the top of her spine. He sat beside her on the old leather chesterfield as she wept. Her skin was irresistibly lovely, bloomed like a pearl. Impossible not to touch. Impossible that she didn't want to be touched.

'Now. Tell me calmly what's happened.' He took her hand.

'Oh, Lawrence!' She began to sob again . . . So trusting in him. It made him feel strong.

'It's all right. Just tell me . . .'

'My mum. She's dying of cancer. She's in so much pain.' Her words came in gasps and fits. 'She keeps begging for more painkillers.' Once again she broke down. He slipped his arm round her shoulder, the ends of his fingers under the edge of her dress.

'Go on . . .' he said.

'Tonight. She was in such pain. And . . .' her voice dropped to a whisper, 'and I gave her all the pills. She lost consciousness . . . And I came here . . .' She collapsed sideways against him and, awkwardly, he drew her into his arms. 'I killed her. I killed her.'

He buried his face, then his fingers, in her hair, warm and damp. He wanted to be engulfed by her hair. 'No, no, Samantha. You didn't. You made a mistake. Just a little mistake. You didn't mean to kill her. I'll protect you, Samantha. You're safe with me,' he said, and how he believed it, how hard he believed he could be that person, the protector, the lover. The saviour and the saved.

Falling into semi-consciousness Sam had felt the gentleness of his touch as he pulled her into his arms. But quite suddenly the tenderness snapped. As if in pulling her towards him, slipping over the polished leather, he'd found he didn't want to be gentle now.

Right up to that moment he'd believed in his vision. That she could transform him, free him from the past. But all the time, hiding inside the sweetness of protection and covert desire, was the same sour old wanting to consume, to use, to *have*. Deep and ingrained as thirst in a desert, the irresistible craving to *take*, *take*, *take*, because no one had ever shown him how to give. And here was the ultimate in taking. *Taking* the very *body* of another human being, possessing it by force here on the hearth where the old bastard had stood and lectured his son so many times.

Sam is still standing, leaning over the desk and propped by her straight arms, as if shoring up the last of her strength. She exudes a force field of separateness that keeps Dale from reaching out to hold and comfort her, as he longs to do.

'I felt so safe and warm at first. It was the end of everything, but it was all right. I felt him hold me in his arms very carefully. Then he just switched, flipped. Smashed me onto the floor. I don't know what happened. I was face down on the carpet, and he was holding my legs, so my back hurt. And . . . my dress was over my head, and . . . Anyway, I screamed and I screamed. And he didn't stop. And then he turned me on my back. He was so strong. You'd never have guessed it to look at him, quite slight, wiry. And he wrapped my dress over my face so I could hardly breathe. Then. Then . . .'

Sam stops to wipe her face. Dale has never looked so terrible. He's aged ten years in as many minutes and is sucking in his mouth to stop himself from losing control. 'Then he did it all again. It seemed like days. Then he got up. He said "pull your dress down" as if it were my fault. I was shaking and bleeding. I was in so much pain I couldn't see straight. *He made me a cup of tea!* Jasmine tea. I sat and drank it. I kept smoothing my dress over my legs. I said, I said: "You raped me." And he said, "Who would believe you? You're a murderer. A mother murderer. I think we'd both better keep each other's secrets. Don't you?"'

'Oh God. Oh, Angie. My love.' Dale reaches out to her, but she swallows hard and holds up a hand like a traffic policeman.

'No. Not yet. I'm not at the end yet. I picked up my coat and told him I was going. I didn't know where. I couldn't go home, and face my dad and see what I'd done. He was right, I was a murderer. I couldn't tell my dad, not *that* dad, not the way he was then. Imagine it. "I've murdered your wife and I've been raped, Dad." But I didn't say that to Lawrence. I just said, "I'm going." And he said, "You'll be back. You can't do anything without me. All you've got is a few Latin names on your tongue." Then he rubbed my blood into the carpet with his foot, as if it was just a bit of fag ash or something. I left him there, and walked off up the drive and hitched to the bus station.' Sam's voice now is less than a croak. It's just a wheeze crushed out of her chest.

'That bastard. I wish he was alive so I could kill him again. He called you a murderer to protect himself. And then he kept track of you to be sure you wouldn't shop him. Kept your parents away with the postcards. He used all three of you, to keep himself safe.' The utter revulsion in Dale's voice makes the words sound as if he's thrown them up.

Sam pushes the green-inked translation towards Dale. 'He didn't mean to do what he did. He didn't plan it.' She's barely whispering now, but the silence is so blank around her that the words stand out. 'He did teach me a lot. As much as he could. He did mean to help. And he did want to be able to love me. But he couldn't. He didn't understand how. He didn't even understand how to be sorry. All this . . . letters, stuff, the house . . . is as near as he could manage. It's all to tell me what happened. All his life I think everything ate him up, his dad, his mum, his money, his plants. Then me. As soon as things took root in him, they grew out of control. He was swallowed by his own insides. I can see how that happens. Can't you?'

She stretches her hand to Dale and he takes it. Their touch is full of the raw force of their two lives, unpredictable in its power, dangerous to release without love.

'Yes. Yes, I can see,' Dale says. They stand arms extended and hands clasped for a long moment, then Dale says, 'Let's go now.'

Dale and Sam walk out through the glasshouse doors. The sunlight floods their faces and the sweet scent of the last lime flowers of the summer washes them clean.

FIFTEEN

DALE HELPS HIS MOTHER up onto the chair. She keeps one gloved hand resting lightly on his shoulder, and with the other pats the bursting curls of Giorgio, her young baker from Palermo. Once balanced, Maria starts to speak to her audience of fifty or more people assembled on the frosty pavement outside Tavs. Her words smoke into the air, catching the sunlight, and her voice carries, clear as the Angelus bell, to the farthest members of her audience.

'Dear Friends,' she begins, looking about her at all the familiar faces and smiling, 'today is a great day for me and my family. I always try to bring you the best Italian gourmet tastes. I want for so long to give good fresh bread, baked the way I remember when I was a little girl in Italy. Today with help of my family and Giorgio who come to me from his family bakery in Palermo, I can do that. Bread is simple. No?' Maria shrugs as her customers and friends have seen her do a hundred times, and a little murmur of affectionate laughter ripples through the crowd. 'Bread is flour and water. That's all. But bread is a big, big thing. Important. We break our bread with our family. With our lovers. Even with our God. Bread means home, and warm and happiness. So I want you, my friends, to have the best of bread. This is what I try to do here.'

The applause is rapturous. In one defining moment Maria's new venture embodies the community as it would like to be. Once again Tavs has touched the fickle heart of the Bristol middle class.

'God, how she loves it!' Finny is trying to be cynical but too late. Sam saw him wiping the corners of his eyes on his coat sleeve. There's no time to tease him as they are swept forward behind Maria, beaming like a beacon and trailing a film crew, towards the smell and warmth emanating from the doors of Tavs Bakery.

'We want to open in time to make special *panettone*, nice for Christmas presents,' Maria sweetly tells the camera, getting herself a few grands' worth of free advertising. Tomorrow there will be 200 orders for boxed gifts of Tavs' special Christmas *panettone*.

It takes two hours for the razzmatazz to die down. People finish their bucks fizz and bread and totter off unsteadily to work. True to form Maria has already rolled up her sleeves and joined Louise and Giorgio behind the counter of the bakery, leaving Finnian to field the extra custom next door, alone.

'Where were you?' Dale comes up to her smiling. 'You should have been down at the front toasting your investment.'

'All I did was shove in a spot of Larry's dosh. You and Maria, and Giorgio, Gordon and Louise too, you all did the work. Not me.'

He puts a hand on her shoulder, and turns her to look at the bakery, the new shop front, the repainted and repointed façade and brickwork, the new colour scheme that links Tavs and its new partner.

'So what do you think?'

'It's miraculous what you've done in such a short time. You and Gordon have worked like slaves! I love the way you've done it.'

'He can work, I'll give him that, my old dad. Did a great job.'

'Look, I've got to go, sweetheart. Lecture in ten minutes and I've an essay to give in.'

'Was that the one about rotting leaves?'

'Sort of. Nutrient recycling in tropical forest ecosystems.' She says it all in one breath, like a spell, or a good-luck charm. The words seem to give her such pleasure that Dale can't help beaming at her.

'OK. Right. Who's picking the boys up?'

'I am. I'll be finished at four and they're booked into after-school club until five. I'll shop on the way home. And we've got Barney tonight. Louise has a hot date.'

Sam kisses Dale, leaps on her bike and cycles off to the University. He stands for a moment grinning after her stupidly, bathing in one of those total smiles she gives these days. He turns to the bakery and goes inside. A bit more work on the stockroom and then the job's done. He'll be free to do a little bit of shopping himself later on.

'**W**hat did you learn about today, Mum?' says Tony. He and Joe have been delighted by the fact that since Sam began her botany degree course, they are all in the same educational boat.

'Active transport across the cell wall, Tony.'

'I know what that is,' says Joe proudly, 'transport's like buses.'

'Or bikes.' Tony is sitting on the seat of Sam's bike as she wheels it.

'I thought it was all about flowers, Mummy, what you're learning.'

'Well, even flowers are made of cells.'

'So why are they telling you about buses?' Joe is mystified.

'Look! Joe,' Tony says offering a distraction, 'I'm getting down early. You can have a long turn.'

'Wow. Thanks!' As Joe climbs up Sam and Tony exchange a smile.

They emerge from the alley and cross the road, where two big trees lean over from adjacent gardens and embrace above the pavement. Even in winter, Sam has seen all manner of plants and animals in their branches. Strangler figs and rattans, orchid species like the ones that Lawrence used to grow. One day when she'd lost concentration on Tony's story about the horrors of school dinners, a tamandua had pushed its sleepy, silky-furred little face out of the leaves and looked right at her. But since she started her botany course she's been on the real path to the jungle; now the two trees contain nothing but the odd crow or a shabby squirrel. Today their bare branches are empty, just a beautiful tangle against the blue sky. Overhead a little party of six para-keets flies high, making for the park. Odd, exotic and out of place, they are quite a famous little troupe and reports of their escape from the zoo's new aviary have been all over the local press.

'They asleep?' Dale turns from the drying-up.

'Yeah!' Sam yawns. 'Wanted to climb in with them tonight. It's freez-ing and I'm so tired.'

'Have you *got* to work tonight?'

'Only a bit. I'm sorry, Dale. Just an hour is all.'

Dale turns back to the washing-up, his shoulders showing his disap-pointment and irritation. 'Oh, *go on* then. Get it done.'

Sam slinks up the stairs to the bedroom-turned-study, feeling at once guilty and resentful. He was so keen for her to start this degree. Why is he being mean this evening?

She pushes open the door of the little book-lined room and flicks the light switch. Instead of the usual flat white illumination from the ceiling light, the room is spangled with little green fairy lights that flash and twinkle. They are draped around the shelves and desk space in a rough spiral that tightens to a nest of leaf-coloured glow. In the centre of the glow are two big white envelopes with her name on the front, and big numbers, one and two. She opens the first, and pulls out a card. On the front is a palmate leaf, a simple hand-drawn shape with the veins care-fully traced in pencil. Underneath in Dale's best printing is the Latin name *Cecropia*. Inside more Latin words in Dale's print march round the edge of the card as a decorative border, each one in a different coloured ink. The names of giant forest trees, of epiphytic orchids, of ferns and aroids, climbers and stranglers. The whole structure of a rainforest springs up between the letters reflected in their Latin meanings . . .

Dale must have spent hours, days, collecting these from library books. Cleverly, all the plants are South or Central American; he's picked not one from the Old World. Knowing Dale, that must be deliberate. In the centre of the card in neat black handwriting is this message: *It's not Christmas, or even nearly Christmas, but this is one present you have to know about six weeks early because of all the jabs you have to have. (Your bottom is going to be a pincushion, I'm afraid.) You deserve a reward for the hard work of the first term of your course, for all you've been through this year and before. I want you to have your heart's desire. Next time, we'll all go, but this trip is yours. Open the other envelope.*

The second envelope is fatter. It contains an airline ticket and a little brochure about the Green Mountain reserve and research centre. It's in Belize. You can have a holiday in the rainforest there, just laze about and look at things, or you can choose to help with any one of the scientific research projects always on the go. There is a picture of one of the little cabins under the trees over which Dale has written: '*This one is yours, you'll be "mapping tree species and studying height distribution".*'

There's a creak of floorboards outside the door. Sam turns to see Dale peering anxiously into the green light. 'Is it OK? You've been so long . . .'

Dale hangs at the door, his face a little crumpled with concern, afraid that his great surprise present is worse than a flop. Looking at him, she is paralysed, she can only stare and feel that nothing she can ever say could be enough. She walks to him slowly. Slowly puts her arms as far round him as she can reach and holds him tight. Tight and long. At last she holds his face between her hands and looks hard into his eyes.

'Thank you. Thank you so much.'

'You will come back?'

'It's a return ticket!'

'You know what I mean.'

'Yes, I do. I'll come back. But I'll take part of you with me and leave some of myself behind.'

January 28th

   My darling Sam,

     I was clearing out cupboards today and I thought of you. I found those glow-in-the-dark stars you left for me the Christmas you went to Bristol. Dad found them after you were gone. He put them up in the telly room where I was sleeping back then, in proper constellations over the ceiling. It was the first sign I had that there was still life in him! The second sign was his Christmas present to me that year. He gave me two fabulous hats. Utterly ridiculous considering the state I was in. I put those on the wall in that room too. They helped me have hope that I could survive. I wore one to the opening of the shop two years later; I'll show you the photos some time!

But there was something else that made me survive too. I should have talked to you about it before. It's that business with the pills on the night you left. I'm so ashamed of what I asked you to do, but I was in so much pain I just wanted it to stop. I didn't care how. I was so grateful to you for giving me all there were left in the bottle.

I was out for more than twenty-four hours. By the time I came round you were gone. I always wondered if you'd gone because you were frightened of what might have happened to me. I worried that you felt it was your fault. It made me determined to live, so you couldn't ever wonder, so that I could tell you that I'm sorry. Sam, you were a child, seventeen. I asked you for something I shouldn't have asked for. And you gave it just because I asked. I've always felt that you missed your chances because of me. I'm so sorry, from the bottom of my heart.

It was a terrible, terrible time for us all, but I have learned to see the good that came from it. My guilt about you made me determined to survive (and the stars and hats of course!); your father turned his life around because he'd failed you and he didn't want to fail me too. And you found Dale and had those boys. And now you've got to go to your jungle. It helps to heal everything for me because of that. I can't begin to tell you how much pleasure it gives me to think that at last you are there, in your rainforest. It feels like a final sort of resolution, you being there, living out your ambitions at last.

Perhaps it was only your friend Lawrence who lost out so completely, because you must have meant a lot to him, and you went away. But I'm only guessing, dear. Although I never knew Lawrence, I thank him with all my heart that his legacy has helped to realise your ambitions. I'm sure he'll rest more peacefully if somehow he knows.

This trip is just a beginning, Sam. There's no reason why you can't fulfill all your ambitions to study rainforest. I know Dale will support you all the way, and so will your dad and I. (He's blowing an upside-down kiss to you as I write!)

It's very cold here, snowing in fact. You know what East Anglia can be like with that lazy wind that goes through you not round you. It's so funny to think that on this same little planet, such a tiny distance away really, it is hot and steamy with huge trees growing while ours look so small and lifeless. I like to think about that, you being in the Summer as it were and us being in Winter, both at the same time. It's like having a complete set of something, matching gloves, hat, handbag and shoes. Listen to me rambling. Your father will tell me I'm going senile.

Ring me the moment you get back. I want to hear every last detail.

Your Old Ma

January 28th

Dear Mum,

The post is erratic to say the least! Although I feel I've been away for years, three weeks is so short a time. I bet as I'm writing this you're writing to me and our letters will cross! Never mind.

It's half an hour after dawn. I've climbed the ropes and pulleys that lift me up to where the birds fly in the tallest of the trees. They're called emergents in the jargon, 'cos they emerge from above the other trees. Technical, eh! A thread of mist is caught in the canopy this morning. It reminds me of that pale blue chiffon scarf you had years ago. You used to keep it in your dressing-room drawer with Granny's locket.

The canopy is below me up here. It stretches like a green sea as far as the horizon. Actually, green isn't a good description. There are a thousand colours in it, all of them woven into the mass of what I call 'green'. Sea is a good description, though, because things jump out into the air sometimes like leaping dolphins, then dive down below the surface. All you see is a flash of colour and then the parrot, or whatever it was, is gone, swimming down among the leaves again. It's peaceful and mysterious like the sea, but frustrating like the sea too, because you want to get a better look at the creatures that leap out and dive back. I'm glad I'm a botanist . . . at least plants never move much.

The weeks here have seemed so long. I've done so much. Don, my boss, is great, he's taught me loads. We spend all day tramping the forest mapping trees, measuring heights and trying to get samples from the canopy. I'm getting very fit. He's amazing, sixty-eight and he can still outwalk me every day.

Dale wrote with pictures that the boys had done of me in the trees. I can hardly look at them without wanting to cry. I miss them so much. But somehow that makes this better. Perhaps the best part of all will be telling Tony and Joe and Dale all about it.

*It's a noisy quiet up here. The sounds of birds and monkeys—
howlers—spurt up from where all the animal activity is, underneath
the shelter of leaves among the high branches. I'm above all that here.
This space belongs to the big trees. It's their world, their kingdom.
I feel their long slow years and the way they hold all the life that
depends on them, quietly without any sort of fuss. Up here it's their
pace, the pace of light and of the sky and of the air. I come up here
every morning at this time to feel the peace of the trees and to pretend
that the world is still all like this, with trees clothing all the planet like
a hug. It's funny, but up here I feel closer to everyone I've left back
home, as if everyone I love, everything I've done or will do is under
the same forest canopy, joined by intertwining roots and touching
branches, all together in one big, green, beautiful jungle.*

I'll ring as soon as I get home.

Love,

Sam

STEVIE MORGAN

I met Nicola Davies—she uses the pseudonym of Stevie Morgan when writing fiction—at the Tate Modern in London. She had been taking part in 'Young Cultural Creators', a scheme to bring art and literature together and to encourage schoolchildren to come into the Tate Modern. 'It's important that children are not intimidated by art,' she said with great passion, 'and it's just wonderful when they look at a painting and say, "I could do better than that" or "I like that bit, but not that."'

Literature, art and natural history are the backbone of the author's working life. At King's College, Cambridge, she read zoology, followed by a PhD on bats at Bristol University. 'In between times I studied humpbacked whales in Newfoundland and blue and sperm whales in the Indian Ocean.' Sadly, she had to abandon her PhD when her mother died. 'I guess that event is one that links me with Angie/Samantha in the novel, because my mother had cancer and was ill, on and off, for twenty-five years and so I had experienced many of the feelings I put into Angie.'

Nicola went on to work at the BBC Natural History unit in Bristol as a researcher and then auditioned for *The Really Wild Show*, which she presented for five years. 'Working on the show was pure pleasure for a person like me, who always has been and always will be obsessed by animals.' When I asked her which had been her favourite animal on the

live show, she replied without hesitation, 'The African crested porcu-pines. We had a female in with three tiny babies. They're about the size of potbellied pigs, with spines all over and cute little guinea-pig faces. The sweet thing about the babies is the fact that they are exact replicas of Ma, and do replica stamping and shaking . . . only teeny!'

Now a full-time author, writing fiction as Stevie Morgan and natural history books as Nicola Davies, she lives in Devon with her two children and a bevy of chickens. 'I love chickens because they are so easily made happy. I can be slightly depressive, as I think a lot of writers are, and to have creatures wandering around the garden purring with delight (chickens do purr, you know!) in a patch of sunlight, puts life into true perspective—and you get great eggs!'

When I asked her where the idea for *Checking Out* came from, she pulled a face and was silent for a few moments. 'I really don't know where the initial thought came from,' she told me. 'With writing, it's as if your life is like a whole great pile of discarded clothes and what you are doing, as a writer, is making patchwork quilts. Sometimes you might take big chunks out of your clothes, and sometimes you might take teeny, tiny bits, and then you sew it all together and hopefully make it into an original pat-tern.' *Checking Out* is certainly an original and, luckily for her many fans, Stevie Morgan is currently working on her next 'quilt'.

Jane Eastgate

479

THE MARRYING GAME. Original full-length edition © 2002 by Kate Saunders. British condensed edition © The Reader's Digest Association Limited, 2002.

LONG DIVISION. Original full-length edition © 2001 by Sarah Harvey. British condensed edition © The Reader's Digest Association Limited, 2002.

CHECKING OUT. Original full-length edition © 2002 by Nicola Davies. British condensed edition © The Reader's Digest Association Limited, 2002.

The right to be identified as authors has been asserted by the following in accordance with sections 77 and 78 of the Copyright, Designs and Patents Act, 1988: Kate Saunders, Sarah Harvey and Nicola Davies.

PICTURE CREDITS: COVER: © Scott Wohrman/Corbis. Kate Saunders photograph, and page 179: © Jerry Bauer. Sarah Harvey photograph, and page 339 © Stu Williamson. Stevie Morgan photograph, and page 479: © Clive Boursnell. THE MARRYING GAME: pages 6 & 7: illustration by Claire Rankin; bride & groom: Image Bank; man on chessboard: FPG. LONG DIVISION: pages 180 & 181: illustration by Annie Boberg @ The Organisation. CHECKING OUT: pages 340 & 341: illustration by Alex Green.

©The Reader's Digest Association Limited, 2002
All rights reserved. No part of this publication may be reproduced, stored in
a retrieval system, or transmitted in any form or by any means, electronic
mechanical, photocopying, recording or otherwise, without the
prior permission of the copyright holders.

Reader's Digest, The Digest and the Pegasus logo
are registered trademarks of The Reader's Digest Association, Inc.

Printed and bound by Maury Imprimeur SA, Malesherbes, France

601-017-1